Island of the Gods

Island of the Gods

John McLean

Winter Productions Limited

Published by Winter Productions Limited.

Grateful acknowledgement is made for permission to quote from the following works:

DELILAH, (Les Reed / Barry Mason) © 1967, Reproduced by permission of Donna Music Ltd., London WC2H 0EA.

YESTERDAY, (John Lennon / Paul McCartney) © 1965, Reproduced by permission of Northern Songs, London WC2H 0EA

ISBN 1 – 872970 – 00 – 1

Cover — Design: Nigel Hillier.
          Photography: Stuart Spence.

Printed and bound in Singapore for Winter Productions Limited, Oak Walk, Saint Peter, Jersey, Channel Islands, by C.W. Printing, 83 Genting Lane, Singapore 1334.

About the Author

John McLean, who lives in London, first went to Bali in 1974 as a young law student. Since then he has returned regularly and has developed a deep affection for the island, its waves and its people. Struck by the lack of light fictional reading about such a unique place he set out to fill the gap and "Island of the Gods" is the result. A graduate in both Law and History and a former Naval Reserve officer, he is a keen and active sportsman who has a special love of the sea.

For my Parents —
With Love and Thanks.

Glossary of Indonesian words

arak   locally distilled rice brandy

bagus   good

bale   an open-sided, thatch roofed area inside a temple courtyard where pilgrims may rest

balian   medicine man with spiritual powers.

banjar   the ruling organisation within a village

barong   mask worn at certain temple ceremonies

bemo   mini-bus or canopied truck with an open back used for transporting paying passengers

berhenti   stop!

brem   locally made rice wine

cukup   enough

dokar   pony cart for hire

gado gado   steamed bean sprouts and vegetables covered with a spicy peanut sauce

gamelan   percussion orchestra that plays music at temple ceremonies.

hati hati   be careful!

Jerone   Your Highness

kain   long sarong

kaja   towards the mountainous interior of Bali where the gods are believed to live

kelod   towards the sea; home of the demons and evil spirits

klian   village headman

kretek   clove cigarette

kris	straight bladed Balinese dagger
kulkul	alarm drum situated at the top of the signal tower in each village. It is beaten in various rhythms to inform the villagers of temple ceremonies or to warn them of approaching danger
lamaks	ornate strips of palm leaf that hang in the temple
legong	traditional Balinese dance
lewat sini	Come this way!
leyak	a spirit that assumes the form of a physical creature, e.g. monkey, pig, bat
lingaa	shrine of a stone phallus to symbolise fertility.
lontong	steamed rice wrapped in a banana leaf
losmens	small cottages or rooms that are rented out to travellers
mantra	prayer
mie goreng	fried noodles with meat and vegetables
mie rebus	boiled noodles and vegetables
nasi campur	steamed rice topped with vegetables, meat, fish and prawn crackers
nasi goreng	fried rice and vegetables
pantai	beach
pasih	the sea
pedanda	high priest
pelan	slowly
permangku	keeper of the temple, a minor priest
pisang goreng	banana fritters
prau	outrigger fishing boat with triangular sails

puputan	the conquest of Bali by the Dutch between 1906 and 1908 and particularly the battle between the Balinese and the Dutch that took place outside the palace of the Raja of Badung
puri	type of palace
pura dalem	temple for the demons and evil spirits
pura puseh	temple for the gods
rupiah	Indonesian currency
sakti	the magical qualities of certain sacred items that are kept in the temple
Selamat datang	Welcome
Selamat jalan	Good-bye
Selamat pagi	Good morning
Selamat sore	Good afternoon
Selamat tidur	Have a good sleep!
Siapa namamu	What is your name?
subak	a type of co-operative organisation that administers the rice fields
sungghu	priest for the demons
Terima kasih	Thank you
topeng	mask worn at certain temple ceremonies
warung	small restaurant or shop or both

List of Chapters

Chapter One

The West

Easter, 1978. The ancient city of Jerusalem. Pilgrims from every land were walking up the small hill of Calvary just as a young carpenter once did with a heavy wooden cross digging into his aching shoulder.

Easter, 1978. Rome. Hundreds of thousands of the faithful had gathered in Saint Peter's Square to receive the Pope's Easter blessing.

Easter, 1978. New York. The annual parade passed along Fifth Avenue to the cheers of a million people.

Easter, 1978. Bell's Beach on the south coast of Victoria. The top surfers of the world were competing against each other in the huge waves that roll in from the southern ocean and throw themselves against the Australian coast.

Like the pilgrims filing up Calvary, like the believers in Saint Peter's Square and the spectators on Fifth Avenue, the rubber clad surfers had come to Bell's Beach from all over the world. From Hawaii and California, from England and France, from South Africa and Brazil and, of course, from all parts of Australia. The contest was rich in prizes and prestige and, like Wimbledon in June, it had a special and magnetic pulling power all of its own. From Good Friday to Easter Monday the champions of the waves entertained the thousands of onlookers with their fast take-offs, spectacular bottom turns, radical re-entries and awesome wave riding.

On the first morning of the contest Warren Hartgood,

1

the chief organiser, found himself with a gap in the draw. The previous night one of the Brazilian entrants had broken his leg in a motor bike crash and Hartgood was frantically looking round for a replacement. Just as he was about to despair of finding a first class local surfer at short notice he saw Adrian Drake walk on to the beach with his arm around a slim, vivacious looking girl with long, auburn hair. Adrian, a well-built six footer with a deeply tanned face, infectious smile and fair, wavy hair, had just had his twenty-third birthday.

The short, nuggety Hartgood had often seen Adrian, a natural footer, riding the local waves and had been greatly impressed by his speed, style and apparent fearlessness in big surf no matter what its size. "Hey, Adrian," he called out, "have you brought your board?"

"Yes, it's in the van. Why?"

"Look man, some crazy Brazil nut rode down the wrong side of the street last night and wrote himself off. He forgot that we drive on the left. Anyway it leaves a gap in the draw and you're the first one I thought of," he said with convincing flattery.

Adrian's first instinct was to decline. Although he was a good surfer he had always eschewed the sport's competitive aspect. He liked to surf one on one. Just himself and the wave. That was far better than being in constant competition with others in style, technique, power, sponsorship and even the colour of one's wetsuit. He knew that he would never be good enough to make a living out of surfing and the constant hassles, controversies, jealousies and selective contest judging of the circuit turned him off. That was his first reaction to Hartgood's invitation. But then he looked out at the near perfect eight foot waves that were rolling into the bay. They were big, glassy and off-shore. He found them irresistible. And the free tickets to the *après surf* rages in the evenings were an added incentive. "Why not?" he thought as he made his way up to where his van was parked at the top of the dunes.

"I thought you always preferred watching surf contests to taking part in them," laughed his girl-friend, Alex, as she handed him a well-used slab of wax that she had prised from the top of the dashboard.

"Yes, but look at the way those waves are peeling," he replied as he pulled his six foot six, custom made surfboard out of its cover.

Adrian was in the second to last heat of the day. As he walked down to the water he was joined by a young Balinese surfer of slim build and with jet black hair who introduced himself as "Nyoman". It was the first time that he had competed in a contest outside Bali. Adrian shook hands with him and they wished each other luck.

But all the luck that day was with Adrian. On the first wave he found himself in the perfect take-off position and did some powerful high speed manoeuvres as he rode it shoreward for about fifty yards. On his other rides he got inside some nicely formed tubes and, besides competing and showing off, he was thoroughly enjoying himself. He ripped and tore the ocean apart as if he owned it. Bells was one of his local breaks and he was more or less claiming it as his own. When the hooter sounded for the end of the heat Adrian was given first place.

The next day the waves were bigger, stronger and wilder. Adrian surfed as well as he could but was eliminated by a seeded Hawaiian who had loads of experience in riding the greatest waves in the world — the ones that pound the north shore of the island of Oahu.

The dance that night at the surf club was quite as bizarre and bestial as any primitive tribal gathering in the jungle. Nyoman was trying to talk to Adrian and his girl friend, Alex, above the din of breaking glass, blaring music and smashing chairs. The Balinese boy thought what a strange creature was

3

the Australian surfer. Graceful sportsman by day and wild beast by night. When conversation became completely impossible Adrian invited Nyoman and a couple of the South African competitors back to his cottage to listen to some music and talk about the day's waves.

It was far more civilised at the cottage. They lay back on the big, floppy cushions in the lounge, drank some tequila, swapped surfing stories and listened to a range of tapes from Velvet Underground to The Beach Boys. When Adrian and Alex went to bed the others were too whacked to move on so they just fell sleep where they were lying. On the big, floppy cushions. By the time that the last tape had stopped everyone was fast asleep. Dreaming of the waves.

During the next few days Adrian took Nyoman surfing with him to some of the better and less crowded spots away from Bell's Beach. Nyoman told him all about Bali and its legendary waves. They became good friends and exchanged addresses before they parted. Nyoman was going back to Bali and he invited Adrian and Alex to visit him some time so that he could return their hospitality. "For sure", said Adrian. "So many people have told me what a great place it is. Some day we'll get there. Perhaps on our honeymoon."

This was no idle talk as he and Alex were just at the point in their relationship where they were making plans for a wedding and a permanent life together. After a courtship of a little over two years they reckoned that they had more or less adjusted to each other's foibles and faults. Alex knew that she was only one of two loves in Adrian's life; the other was surfing. "My two mistresses," he used to call them.

She realised from long experience that, when her lover was ecstatic after a really good surf session, she was able to pick up his happy vibes and share them. Adrian without his surfing would not be the Adrian that she knew and loved.

She realised that his surfing was a healthy and positive factor in their relationship and besides, she loved the beach

4

and happily spent many hours lying on the sand and soaking up the sun while her other half attacked the waves and carved his way through the ocean like a god walking on water. Their happiest times together revolved around the beach and surfing — from the long sunny days on the sand to the crazy and wild parties at the surf club in the evenings. They both enjoyed the natural, healthy life of the beach and the cheerful, straight shooting, "no bullshit" types who were found in the surfing fraternity. Some of the younger ones, Alex thought, were a little pseudo but, with an air of resignation, she decided that at twenty-three she must have some tolerance for the ones who had just come out of high school.

Adrian was a product of the century old, ivy covered Prince of Wales school in Melbourne which still followed the English traditions — boater hats, the house system, cricket and rotten food. Over the years it had turned out a host of soldiers, sailors, statesmen, sculptors, farmers, Test cricketers and drunks. And even a few surfers.

After leaving school he did a degree in Art History at Melbourne University followed by a year of creative art at the Royal Melbourne Institute of Technology. And now he was working as a commercial artist at a studio in Fitzroy. He was both smart and intelligent. Quite unlike some surfers whose conversation is limited to waves, wax and wetsuits. He had managed to get through his exams with the minimum amount of work. On days when there was a good surf he was more likely than not to be found on his board rather than in the lecture hall. "A man must get his priorities right," he used to say to anyone who commented on his frequent absences.

Almost every week-end he and Alex used to drive down to Torquay to the cottage that had belonged to Adrian's parents for as long as he could remember. The rest of his family only ever went there at Christmas and so he had more or less fashioned the place to his own taste. Around the walls were large action shot surf posters and the living room had

5

been turned into a cosy den with big, brightly coloured cushions on the floor and loads of stereo equipment around the walls. "We live at Torquay and spend the weeks in Melbourne," he used to joke. And it was true. There were very few reasons that ever compelled them to stay in the city. Only a really special party, a first class rock concert, an Ashes Test at the Melbourne Cricket Ground or, perhaps, the outbreak of war. Nothing else.

However, the second week-end after Easter was one of those rare occasions. Alex's sister had her engagement party on the Saturday night at her parents' place in South Yarra. Adrian and Alex had happily foregone their usual Torquay week-end for a bit of city mixing. He was pleased that they stayed in Melbourne as not only had the party been a smasher but the Sunday morning surf report on the radio stated that Torquay and most of the south coast was as flat as a pancake but there was a swell of three to five feet on the west coast beaches of the Mornington Peninsula.

"Let's go down the peninsula for the day," he said to Alex as he switched off the radio. "Besides, it fits in with that barbecue to which your friends invited us at the party last night. Don't they live at Rye?"

"Yes, it sounds like a good idea," she said sleepily as she opened the curtains to let in the bright sunlight.

They packed a picnic lunch and drove half way down the peninsula to a spot that Adrian used to frequent during his student days — a left point that, on a good day, could produce some nice, rideable tubes. They pulled into the gravel car park on the other side of the Nepean Highway and then had to wait a few minutes for a gap in the south bound traffic before they could cross the busy road.

"You'd think that they would have put the car park on the beach side of the road," said Alex.

"The town planners probably never go to the beach. Too busy re-siting and re-zoning everything," scoffed Adrian.

There was eventually a pause in the traffic and they ran across the road carrying the surfboard, towels, picnic hamper and an "esky" containing half a dozen chilled cans of Fosters. As they made their way across the sandhills they could hear the gentle crash of the waves which were in fact only about four feet high. They swam, they surfed and they lay in the hot sun and listened to the stereo. It was nearly dark before they thought about leaving. The barbecue was due to start at half past six and it was already 6.15.

"We haven't even bought any wine yet", said Alex, "and the wine shop is in the opposite direction to the party. Really, Adrian, talking to you is sometimes like talking to a brick wall."

"Eh, what's that?" he replied absentmindedly. His eyes were fixed on a set of waves — six feet and rising — that were rolling in and breaking cleanly in the light off-shore wind. As if in a trance his mind was far away from such mundane matters as barbecue arrangements. "I think I'll have a quick surf before we go," he said.

"But you've been surfing all day. Since eleven o'clock."

"Yeah, but that was just four foot slop. Like the wine at Cana the best has been kept until the end of the day."

He got up from the sand and snapped the velcro of the leg rope around his right ankle. Then he looked up at Alex who was putting a thin cotton blouse over her bikini top. He noticed how deeply tanned she was from the day's sun and he couldn't resist putting his arms round her and kissing her on the lips. Although there was no one else on the beach he whispered in her ear that, if she would go and fetch the wine and come back in twenty minutes, he would be up at the car park waiting for her. He then picked up his board and raced into the water.

Alex packed all their gear into the "esky" and made her way back over the sandhills. She stopped at the edge of the highway and looked through the fading light for any ap-

7

proaching vehicles. There was a large articulated truck roaring down the hill away from her. That was all. No other traffic. So she crossed. The noise of the truck had drowned out the quiet purr of the approaching Jaguar as it flew round the sharp bend well in excess of the speed limit. The driver was drunk and didn't see her before the impact.

■

Mr. Justice Hack was a stern, gaunt faced, unsmiling judge whose only interests, apart from his law books, were the golf club and the whisky bottle. He had acquired his judicial appointment by a combination of Masonic connections, political patronage, crude scheming and many years of time serving on the committee of the Law Society. He played golf every week-end in the same four: another judge, a millionaire brewer and a rich car dealer. The so-called stresses of his well paid job and the dark complexities of his personality had combined to make him drink quite a bit more than he should have on the nineteenth hole.

On the night in question he was well over the legal limit and far from sober. In the car-park of the golf club he fumbled around with his key-ring looking for one that would fit the door of his dark grey XJ6. He eventually found the key, the ignition and the accelerator and set off at a cracking pace along the Nepean Highway. He found the approaching bend a lot sharper than it looked through his alcohol hazed eyes. He took it wide and felt a heavy thump on the left front bumper of his car. He looked back and saw a young girl landing on the bitumen — head first. He slowed down for a moment, saw that there were no other cars in sight, and then decided to drive on and get away from the scene as quickly as possible.

The next car that came along was driven by an aborigine, Sonny Peters, who stopped to see what had happened. He got out and ran over to the side of the road where

Alex was lying. Her blood was starting to drop on to the dusty ground. Sonny Peters struck her on the cheeks but they were lifeless. Then he knelt down on the stony ground to give her mouth-to-mouth resuscitation. But it was no good as the body was already dead and cooling fast. The aborigine began to cry. Then some more cars stopped including a passing police patrol car. They picked up their two-way radio and called for more police and an ambulance. They later arrested Sonny Peters and, despite his protestations, accused him of dangerous driving causing death. Unfortunately for him he too was above the legal alcohol limit and he had the added disadvantage of having a couple of dents in his front bumper and grill from a recent encounter with a kangaroo out in the bush. He was taken into custody and formally charged with the crime of causing Alex's death.

■

Adrian gave himself another few minutes in the water to try and catch a nice, sizeable, well-shaped wave as his last for the day. He always liked to finish with a good one. About the middle of the next set he found himself in the perfect take-off position. He jumped up on his board and ducked his head so as to drive himself into a hollow tube that carried him for several magic seconds before throwing him into the swirling foam. "Thanks, Huey," he said to the god of surfing as he climbed back on his board and rode all the way into the beach on a gently dying ridge of water. He rubbed himself down with a towel and put on the clean shirt and pair of jeans that he had brought with him to wear to the barbecue. Then he picked up his board and made his way back over the mountains of sand to the highway.

The road being hidden by trees and sandhills, he was right upon it before he saw what had happened. He could see an ambulance, a police car and several other cars and people. In a state of shock he stared at Alex's bloody and battered shape as it was being put into the back of the ambulance on a stretcher. That beautiful, spunky, well-tanned body that he had last kissed only a few minutes before. "Is she dead? Is she dead?" he screamed as he pushed his way through the small group of onlookers.

"Afraid so," said the ambulance driver. One of the policemen came over and asked Adrian who he was. He told the officer how they had spent the day together at the beach and how he had arranged to meet her at the car-park. The young constable told him that, since he was in shock and in no condition to drive, he should let the police drive him back to Alex's parents' place at South Yarra.

The constable drove Adrian's car and, as they pulled out of the car-park, they caught sight of some other police snapping a set of handcuffs on the aborigine. "Bloody abbos," said the constable to Adrian. "They shouldn't be allowed to drive."

Adrian remained silent. He didn't really know what was happening and nor did he care. All he knew was that nothing could bring his loved one back to life. "If only I'd had time to say good-bye," he kept thinking to himself.

There were several people still clearing up after the party at South Yarra as Adrian's car drove up the oak lined driveway. Alex's father, a well-heeled architect, was on the lawn stacking some empty beer bottles into a couple of wooden crates. He looked up and saw Adrian and the uniformed officer of the law climbing out of the car. Alarm bells immediately rang inside his head. He knew that the policeman was not there on a social visit as neither his daughter nor Adrian had ever had any friends who were cops. Policemen just didn't live in nice, expensive suburbs like South Yarra. "Where's Alex?" he called out as he walked over to the car. Adrian was completely tongue-tied. The constable gave the terrible news as gently as he could. It was then that Adrian broke down. He began sobbing uncontrollably and was helped inside by Alex's father who remained cool and calm throughout. Inside the house the news spread like a bush fire and soon the whole place, which had seen such reckless hilarity the night before, was a shambles of screaming and sobbing people.

◼

When he reached his house Judge Hack drove into the double garage and locked the doors from the inside. Furtively he washed Alex's blood off his damaged bumper bar and blessed his luck that there was no one else at home who might see the dent. His wife was staying in the country for a week. She went away as often as possible as she had long since tired of her boring and impotent husband who always seemed to have the sour smell of whisky on his breath and who bossed her around terribly. The only reason why she kept up the pretence of the marriage was that she enjoyed the social standing and high income of her husband's position. But there was no affection between them and no children either; Hack had never been able to perform. However, to the outside world they were a stable and respectable couple who, because of the judge's status, were highly regarded by lesser beings.

The next morning the judge drove the car to the yard of his car dealer friend to be repaired. He claimed that he had banged into a steel stanchion outside his driveway in the dark. Two days later he collected the vehicle; it was as good as new.

When he read in the Melbourne Age that an aborigine had been arrested in respect of the accident the honourable judge managed to justify the events to himself by applying his cold, analytical legal mind to reach some rather self-serving conclusions. He decided that the most important thing was to protect the good name of the judiciary. After all, it would not reflect well on judges in general if it became known that one of their number had broken the drink driving laws and killed a pretty young girl. He reasoned that, since he was a highly qualified man who had given long service to community organisations, it would be less harmful for society to be deprived of the company of an aborigine than a highly respected pillar of church and state like himself. But the real reason for covering it up was the prospect of a knighthood.

For many years both Hack and his wife had craved for a title that would give them social importance and distinction over and above everyone else. To that end the judge had sought to ingratiate himself with the Government in a variety of ways. He even kept a running tally of how much he had secured for the Treasury over the years in the way of fines. Each year he set himself a target which he usually exceeded by always imposing the maximum fine whenever possible. And no one ever won a tax case in Hack's court. Only the Government. When, after twelve years of this acquisitive conduct, he reached the figure of a hundred million dollars, he duly let it be known to those in government who were in charge of recommending knighthoods. And he hinted that, in return for grabbing such a huge sum for the public purse, he should perhaps be rewarded in some way or another. Wink, wink, nod, nod. They understood.

Purely out of private interest he also kept a tally of all those whom he had imprisoned over the years. He marked them with a cross for the aborigines and a tick for the white Australians. And every year he was pleased to see that the aborigines far outnumbered the whites even though the natives constituted less than two per cent of the total population. Hack had always been prejudiced against aborigines and took great personal pleasure in sentencing them to long terms of imprisonment for trivial offences. Once he even had a bet with another judge to see which of them could slam the most aborigines into prison in the course of the next month. Of course, Hack won.

12

Although he knew that he was beyond suspicion Mr. Justice Hack nevertheless decided to make doubly certain of it by imposing the maximum penalty on the next drink driver who appeared in his court and giving him a stern lecture on the evils of alcohol on the road. This dressing down was reported in the newspaper along with an editorial expressing the public's gratitude that at long last a judge was taking a stand against the alcohol induced carnage on the roads. "That should get rid of any possible scent," thought Hack. And it did.

■

Alex's funeral was held in the local Church of England at South Yarra. More than three hundred mourners heard the vicar deliver a touching eulogy in which he described all of the deceased's fine qualities. He rued the ever rising death toll on the roads and said how pleased he was to read in the morning's paper that Judge Hack had taken such a strong stand against it. The congregation murmured its approval. The vicar ended with the old Greek saying that those who die young are loved by the gods. Adrian was moved by the fine words and the dignity of the service but, as he reflected, it still didn't bring back his precious love. "Please God make her happy in heaven," he prayed.

The afternoon before the funeral he had driven back down the peninsula to the spot on the beach where they had lain all day in the sun. He could still see the slight depression in the sand above the tide line where they had stretched out on their towels. He picked up a handful of sand and put it in a small plastic bag so that he could sprinkle it on her coffin as it was lowered into the ground. He knew how much she loved the beach and thought that the bag of sand would be an appropriate gesture.

At the grave he stood with her parents and other members of her family. As he pulled the small bag of sand out of his pocket he closed his eyes and could see for a moment her beautiful, tanned figure running over the sandhills — his last image of her.

He could not face going back to South Yarra for the wake so he drove down to the cottage at Torquay. He wanted to be alone so that he could collect his thoughts and try to think clearly about what had happened over the last few days. Besides, if he was going to break down and let all his sorrow out by crying, he didn't want anyone to see him.

The cottage felt so empty without Alex. He made some black coffee and went over to the boxes of cassette tapes. He rustled through them and finally pulled one out that he had often played when he was feeling down. It was the Beatles' Ballads and it even had a blue background — as if to reflect the sombre message of some of the songs. He clicked it into the tape deck and turned the volume on low. He lay down on the cushions and listened to the mellow music. "Norwegian Wood" followed by "Nowhere Man". Then came the slow and distinct sounds of "Yesterday". The words struck a chord.

> "Yesterday all my troubles seemed so far away
> Now it looks as though they're here to stay
> Oh I believe in yesterday."

He could feel the tears welling up in his eyes. "This is no good," he thought. So he got up and turned it off. He pulled out some papers and rolled a joint. The potent "Mullumbimby Magic" dulled his senses and gave him a pleasant, laid-back feeling. Then he reached for a copy of "Tracks" and another surfing magazine and started skimming the pages. He soon lost interest and got up to go outside. As he walked through the porch he saw his surfboard leaning against the wall. "Why not?" he thought. For a moment he wondered if it would be disrespectful to Alex's memory to spend the after-noon of her funeral enjoying himself in the waves. He remem-

14

bered how she had always encouraged him to surf knowing that it made him happy. He knew that she would prefer him to get it all out of his system by challenging the waves and drenching himself in their wash instead of moping around the cottage with his tail between his legs.

He picked up the board and walked down to the beach. The surf was pumping at about eight feet and there was no one else out. He left his troubles on the shore and paddled out past where the waves were breaking. They were wild and irregular and he was thrown around by their mighty thrusts. He always felt free and independent when he was out in the ocean. It was a different element. A different world. He also had a deep respect for its awesome power, its fickle moods and its strange currents. Like any big wave surfer he knew the power of Mother Ocean. But she was still a generous provider as she allowed him to carve tracks across her surface, lose himself inside her hollow barrels and give a greater range of thrills than could ever be found on land.

When Adrian came out of the water he felt much better. It had been like a cleansing experience. He knew that somehow he would have to get on with his life which was exactly what Alex would have wished. But the sense of loss was overwhelming.

The next few days were particularly difficult. He was unable to concentrate on his work and didn't feel like going out and mixing with others. After a couple of weeks of drifting without any set purpose he decided that the best thing to do would be to leave Melbourne and get away from all the people and places that were constant reminders of his life with Alex. "I think I'll write to Nyoman in Bali," he decided, "and tell him that I am going to take up his invitation."

The next day he wrote out his resignation from the art studio in Fitzroy and then visited a travel agency in Swanston Street to book a flight to Bali. He obtained a visa from the Indonesian Embassy that was valid for a month. "Don't

15

worry," said the well-groomed young lady in the travel agency. "You can always renew it over there if you want to stay longer." He did not widely advertise the fact that he was going away. Just a few friends and family.

A couple of nights before his departure he had dinner at his parents' place at Brighton, a bayside suburb a few miles south of the city of Melbourne. It was a large double storey villa just across the road from the beach. He had lived there all his life until he bought a small apartment of his own at South Yarra some two years earlier.

On this particular night his father, always a generous host, had uncorked a couple of bottles of Beaujolais. They sat down to a sumptuous seafood cocktail followed by a Beef Wellington. It was nice and tender and the pastry not too hard. Adrian's mother was a cordon bleu cook. She was a dark haired, well-groomed lady of fifty-five who always managed to look stylish — even at the end of a long day of pulling weeds out of her large and well-kept garden. His father was slightly older. A tall, thin man with a kindly, ruddy face and a well-clipped white moustache. He was a much respected professor of literature at Melbourne University and had an international reputation as an eminent Shakespearian scholar.

"How do you plan to spend your time over there?" asked his mother.

"Oh, a bit of surfing, eating some exotic food and meeting interesting people from other places, I guess. I won't really know until I get there."

"I think you'll like the East," said his father. "Of course, it's quite different to our way of life here. Very different in fact. You remember what Kipling wrote:

'East is East and West is West
And never the twain shall meet.'

It's still true to-day. At least it was when I was there and

I rather think that their customs and civilisation are so deeply entrenched that they would not have changed much in the last thirty years or so."

This was the first time that Adrian had ever heard his father refer to his time in the East. Of course, he had always known that he had spent nearly four years in Asia during the War. His mother had told him. So had his late grandfather. He had even seen the terrible scars from the Japanese lashings on his father's back and shoulders. But it was the one subject that was never discussed. Never.

As he looked at his only son across the fine mahogany dining table the older man could not help but recall some of the images of his own experiences in the East and the events that caused him to go there. He had been playing cards late one night at the surf life-saving club at Portsea with three mates when they heard the clipped and precise tones of Mr. Chamberlain's voice come over the big, home-made wireless set that one of them had recently built. "We are at war with Germany," said the failed peacemaker. They knew that, whatever else it meant — adventure, excitement, overseas travel — it would herald a complete change in their lives. He thought of those other three fellows — the best mates in the world — and of how he was the only one who made it back. The one who built the radio set became a wireless operator in the army and was killed by a shell in the North African desert. The two who joined the Royal Air Force were both shot down in the Battle of Britain. One was drowned in the Channel and the other was just a charred corpse when his burnt and blackened Spitfire crashed in a rose garden in Kent.

"Yes," he reflected, "I am indeed fortunate to have survived. I have had a good life apart from those dark and dreadful years."

He thought of his own enthusiasm and excitement at going to sea for the first time in a warship of the Royal Australian Navy. Indian Ocean sunsets, Mediterranean

17

ports, wardroom mess dinners and, of course, action. He got his first taste of it on a convoy to Malta. Then the Australian Government had to bring its forces back to defend the homeland as the treacherous Japanese advanced southwards.

His ship, the light cruiser H.M.A.S.Perth, was part of the doomed Allied fleet of British, Dutch and Australian warships that were sunk by the Japanese in the Battle of the Java Sea. It sank after four torpedoes ripped into its hull. He and some of the others managed to cling to a part of the superstructure that was floating free of the main wreckage. All around were dying men, floating corpses, leaking oil and jagged pieces of the warship. There were several survivors swimming around in the warm sea. They were calling out to each other, some were laughing, some were screaming and one or two were crying.

About ten minutes after the ship went down a flight of twenty-seven Japanese Zeros homed in and aimed concentrated and fairly accurate fire on the helpless and unarmed Australians who were floundering around in the ocean. They came and they came again. And again. Mercilessly. Like monsters from Hell. More screams. More blood trickling out and making purple puddles in the otherwise clear blue sea. Finally they left and returned to their aircraft carrier. "All killed. No survivors" was the message that was sent back to naval headquarters in Tokyo. But they were wrong.

Adrian's father had dived below the water every time that he saw the Zeros approaching. His years of surf lifesaving and competition swimming served him well as he held his breath for an incredibly long time before coming to the surface. Only two others of the Australian ship's company survived the strafing.

They swam over to a large piece of floating wood which had been part of the upper structure of the bridge. All three of them were thankful to be alive but had little hope of surviving. The Japanese were now in control of the whole area — the land, the sea and the skies. Bits and pieces were floating around in the ocean but the men took little notice of them. They saw some rope coming towards them. The ship's white ensign was tied to it. One of them reached out and grabbed it. They laughed for the first time.

A couple of hours later there appeared on the horizon a native fishing boat with brightly coloured triangular sails. As it came closer they waved. War or no war the islanders had been fishing these waters in their traditional way for hundreds of years. The fishermen took the men on board, gave them some food and laughed with them even though they couldn't speak a word of English.

Two days later they pulled into a crescent shaped bay, dropped anchor and swam in to the beach. They were taken to the village headman who could speak a little English. He told them that they were on the island of Bali and that all the Dutch administrators and colonials had left.

The three Australians were fed, given sarongs to wear and generally treated with the greatest respect and kindness. After three days the headman told them that the Japanese had landed and that, for their own safety, they should go up to the mountainous interior of the island where they would be well looked after by the villagers. They were provided with bicycles and an escort of four Balinese men to show them the way. They eventually reached the village of Semang where they were given refuge and hospitality by the headman, a thirty-eight year old man of noble birth whose real name was Gedé but who was always addressed as "Klian", the village headman. He was the hereditary leader of the village and the three sailors stayed with him for two and a half months. They lived among the villagers, ate with them, went with them to the temple and even worked in the paddy fields to help bring in the rice harvest.

Adrian's father exchanged gifts with Klian. He gave the Balinese the only thing that he had. The tattered white ensign from the sunken cruiser. They placed it in the village temple where it hung like a battle honour in a cathedral. It was brought out on special holy days and draped over a stone shrine. The villagers believed that it had magical powers and that its strange pattern, so different from their traditional batik, would attract the gods to come down and take part in the festivals. In exchange, Klian gave him a beautifully carved jade ring that was in the shape of a turtle. The stone was set in silver which had been handcrafted by the village silversmith. "The island of Bali rests on the back of a giant turtle," Klian had told him. "The ring will always remind you of our island." Adrian's father tried it on but it would fit only his smallest finger. Because it was so small he managed to keep it for the rest of the war, concealing it in his mouth every time that he went through a Japanese check-point.

Early one morning — on a holy day when there was no work in the rice fields — a Japanese patrol arrived to impose their brutal rule on the village. The advance guard came on bicycles — ever so silently — and there was no time for the Australians to hide in the cave up the mountain as they had planned. Adrian's father and his two friends put their hands up as the Japanese soldiers with fixed bayonets ran into the headman's house and pulled them out of their beds. They were roughly thrown to the floor and dragged outside into the already hot sun. There they were stripped naked and made to lie on the ground for two hours while the Japs searched and tore apart the rest of the village in the belief that there were further Allied servicemen in hiding. The three of them had to lie completely motionless. If they moved an arm to scratch their itchy mosquito bites they were kicked or struck with a rifle butt.

"You bad Australians. Now prisoner of Emperor. You now must obey Emperor," said the Japanese officer.

"That filthy shit," said Adrian's father under his breath as he thought of the hated Hirohito with the ridiculous looking glasses on the end of his little nose.

Their captors ordered them to stand up. They tied their hands and feet together, threw them into the back of a jeep and drove them down to the coast. Before the Japs left they set fire to Klian's house as a punishment for harbouring the men. Then they ransacked the village temple. First they desecrated the shrines by urinating on them and then they brought down the stone walls with sticks of gelignite.

When they reached the coast the three Australians were put on an old fishing boat that the Japs had commandeered from its unwilling owner and they were taken across the Bali Strait to Java. There they were put in a stifling hot cattle truck that still stank of cow dung and were pulled across Java for the next thirty hours. They were given a small ration of rice at the start of the journey and the only light in the covered cattle truck was a few shafts that peeked in through the cracks between the badly fitting boards. When they arrived in Jakarta they were told that they had to wait for a tramp steamer for Singapore. For eleven days they were kept in cages that were only three feet high. The Japs allowed them only one bowl of rice a day and a bottle of warm, cloudy, polluted water to quench their thirst in the tropical heat. When they finally reached Singapore they were put into the prison camp at Changi with all the other British and Australian servicemen who had been bagged by the Japanese when Singapore fell on 15th February, 1942.

The Japanese believed that Adrian's father knew where there were other pockets of Australians hiding in the mountains of Bali. He swore that he didn't and that the only survivors from his ship were the three who had been captured. The Japanese interrogators did not believe him and took him for long sessions to the Y.M.C.A. building in Singapore which the Kempetai had converted from a Christian haven

21

for travellers into a gigantic torture chamber. He was given the bamboo up the orifice treatment and on several occasions was taken down to the cellar and beaten mercilessly with whips of bamboo, leather and electric wire. When the horrid little sadists found that they could not extract any information at all out of him they let him go and moved on to other victims.

After several months in Changi he was selected to go up to Thailand with a work party of several hundred other prisoners-of-war. They were to provide slave labour on the "Death Railway" that the Japanese were frantically trying to construct between Thailand and Burma. It went for hundreds of miles and it was estimated that one prisoner-of-war or coolie labourer died for every sleeper that was laid. Adrian's father nearly died there. He got malaria, beri beri and yellow fever. The Japanese refused all requests for vaccines and medicines. However, unlike many others, he survived and at the end of the War returned to his studies at Melbourne University.

His scars of those years in the East were both physical and mental. The lash marks on his back and shoulders would be there until he died. So too would his resentment and hatred of the inhuman way that he had been treated. And, of course, his memories of all those in the camps who didn't survive.

He looked up from his reverie and saw his wife and son in animated conversation about the architectural merits of the Sydney Opera House. As he did so he realised that he was looking at the living proof of the good and happy side of his life. His real life. The here and now. Not the long past years of starvation and misery in the East. "Yes, I'm lucky," he reflected. "Happily married, doing work that I like and with a son who, for all his impulsiveness, recklessness, self-indulgence and lack of punctuality, is always a delight to be with."

He then thought of how Adrian had suffered in the days

since Alex's sudden death. "There is a bit of purgatory in everybody's life," he thought. "Mine was in the East and my poor boy is now going through his. But unless you suffer the bad times you will never be able to recognise the good ones." He could see the irony of Adrian trying to escape his suffering by going to the very place where he, the father, had to endure his own pain. "How times change," he thought. "And thank God they do."

Adrian's mother too had spent many years in the East. She had been born in Shanghai in China. Her parents were White Russians who fled the Soviet Revolution at the end of the First World War. Her father, a cavalry officer in the Tsar's army, had fought against the Bolsheviks and then fled with his family east to Vladivostok. When that city fell he and thousands of other White Russians crossed the border into China. He took a job as a clerk in the Hong Kong and Shanghai Bank in Shanghai and Adrian's mother's first memories were of that huge and bustling city. When the Japanese invaded China the family moved to Hong Kong. They found the British colony civilised and endlessly fascinating and were very happy there.

She and her sister, Olga, began training as nurses at the Jockey Club Hospital. But in the weeks before Pearl Harbour it became increasingly obvious that there was little hope of the beleagured British holding the colony against a Japanese attack. So the family decided to leave yet again. That is, all except Olga who could not tear herself away from the Royal Navy lieutenant from H.M.S.Tamar with whom she had fallen in love. The rest of the family jumped on a ship that was sailing to Australia. Olga promised to follow in a couple of months.

Less than six weeks after the ship sailed the Japanese invaded Hong Kong and it fell on Christmas Day, 1941. Olga and the other nurses went to church on Christmas morning to sing carols in honour of the Prince of Peace. Then, in the evening, as they were attending the hundreds of battle casualities, the Japanese soldiers rushed into the hospital and raped every single one of them. Then, to destroy the evidence, they finished them off with their bayonets. It wasn't until the end of the War that the facts of the outrage were revealed. Adrian's mother had wept for weeks. Tears of sorrow and tears of relief that she had left before it happened.

That too was all in the past. Her family had now been in Australia for nearly forty years. After fleeing Russia, fleeing China, fleeing Hong Kong they had finally found security. Australia had been good to them. Good years, prosperous years, happy years. Like to-night. Sitting around the dinner table *en famille*. Good food, good wine, good conversation.

At the end of the meal Professor Drake produced a bottle of Taylor's port and poured it into three small glasses. They toasted the coming trip and talked on for a while until his wife got up from the table and went out to the kitchen to stack the dishes. Adrian walked into the lounge and put a Rolling Stones LP on to the disc of the fine old radiogram that stood in the corner.

His father went upstairs to his study. He pulled out a volume from the well stocked bookshelf. It was Gibbon's "Decline and Fall of the Roman Empire". Behind it was a small key. He pulled it out and unlocked the bottom drawer of his teak desk. Inside was a tin box containing various personal papers and items — his will, his war medals, some old gold sovereigns and, right at the bottom, the jade ring that Klian had given him and which he had kept all through the years of war and peace. He picked it up, locked the drawer and replaced the key behind the Gibbon tome. When he walked into the lounge Adrian was sitting there alone listening to the Stones' record.

"Listen, son," he said. "This was given to me by a very kind and courageous village headman in Bali in 1942. He was a true friend. I kept it all through the war and always intended to give it to you some time. If I give you the name of the village you might like to go and see where your father spent a few difficult months of his life. You don't have to go there as it is way up in the mountains but you might find yourself in the area and be keen to have a look. As you know, I've never been back to the East myself and I never want to see it again." He pulled out one of his visiting cards and wrote on the back the name of the village, "Semang." And the man's name — "Gedé (Klian) — Village Headman."

Adrian looked at the card. "Thanks," he said. "I'll try to go there."

"I am sure that the fellow would be dead by now. He was about forty then and they don't live that long in Asia. But his sons and daughters probably still live in the same village. If you go there and by some strange chance he is still alive I would like you to give him a message." Adrian wondered what on earth it might be. "Tell him that two of us survived the war. The other man, Griff from Queensland, didn't make it."

"Why? What happened to him?" asked Adrian.

"Do you really want to know?"

"Well, only if you want to tell me."

"I have never told anyone since I got back to Australia. I just want to forget it but I can't." He paused for a moment. "But if you really want to know, I'll tell you."

"Okay, Dad," said Adrian with much understanding.

"He was eaten by those uncivilised barbarians. It happened up on the Burma railway. The perverted Japanese officers were having a cocktail party in the evening and one of them, the most brutal dog of all, decided that it would be fun to serve some human flesh. My friend, Griff, was the healthiest prisoner in our particular camp. He had miraculously avoided all the diseases that the rest of us had caught and had quite a bit of flesh on him. That, of course, was why he was picked out. He was in the same work gang as me and the guards just came and took him away one morning as we were chipping away at the rock to form an embankment. We never saw him again. Later we discovered that they had cut him up and boiled his thighs and arms and eaten him for a snack. That is the type of thing we were up against with the Japs. In the matter of cruelty and brutality they were in a class of their own." He paused and then returned to the matter in hand. "Tell Klian that we never forgot his kindness in taking us in. *Terima kasih* from the bottom of our hearts." There were tears in the old man's eyes as he walked back up the stairs to his study.

Two days later Adrian was at Melbourne's Tullamarine Airport checking in his two surfboards and blue nylon bag of clothes for the Qantas flight to Bali. As he went through the metal detector it made a small squeak. A rude, heavy-set man in a uniform grabbed him and spat out the words, "What have you got on you, sonny? Turn out your pockets." He reminded Adrian of a bouncer at some seedy Saint Kilda nightclub. Adrian emptied his pockets — a handkerchief, some American notes, a pen and the silver and jade ring that his father had given him. The big man in the uniform grabbed the ring and stared at it. He then gave Adrian a filthy look. He hated all these young people who could afford to travel overseas all the time while he, a lowly public servant who had never been further than Sydney, could barely afford to pay the monthly bills out of his meagre government wage.

"Go through again," he said to Adrian. This time there was no reaction from the machine. "Here's your ring, you bloody fairy," he said as he handed it back.

A few miles away in the city Sonny Peters was standing in the dock of the criminal court facing trial for causing Alex's death. He had been in custody since the accident. The prosecution was being conducted by an experienced Queen's Counsel while Peters was defended by a young legal aid lawyer who was in his second year of practice. It was quite a straightforward matter. Peters had had more than the legal amount to drink and there were incriminating dents on the front of his vehicle. Even though he strongly denied hitting the girl nobody on the jury believed him. He looked like a criminal and the court convicted him and sent him to jail for six years.

Chapter Two

The East

As the Boeing 747 flew across the vast emptiness of the brown Australian interior Adrian was able to look down on the rough surface of the desert as it corrugated its way across the continent. Sometimes there were huge caverns with steep sides but more often it was just endless and bare plains without any sign of habitation. After three hours the captain announced that they were beginning their descent into Darwin to pick up the rest of the passengers for Bali. Soon a patch of green trees and modern buildings appeared out of the limitless red, dusty plains. This was the new Darwin. The third attempt at building the town. The first Darwin had been wiped out by massive Japanese bombing raids in 1942. On these ashes rose the second city of Darwin which in turn was destroyed by Cyclone Tracy on Christmas Day, 1973. Now the persevering citizens had built their third town albeit with the persuasion and financial support of the Australian Government which decided that, for strategic purposes, it was necessary to have a settlement in this far northern outpost.

When the 'plane landed the passengers filed into the sterile transit lounge. It was stifling hot and the fans had broken down. The flight on to Bali passed over the sparkling waters of the Timor Sea. It was just after five in the evening when they approached the Ngurah Rai Airport in Bali. The 'plane landed towards the sea and into the most vivid sunset that Adrian had ever seen. His artist's eye was alert as he saw the huge expanse of red that stretched the whole length of the horizon. He had sometimes seen the great glow of bush fires on the Australian plains with fronts many miles long but the sunset that he was now looking at seemed to be a creation of the gods themselves.

As he looked down on the water he could see some small outrigger canoes and bodies on surfboards near some white water that was breaking over a reef. The golden hairs on his head stiffened as a surge of excitement passed through his body and a broad smile spread across his face.

He walked down the steps of the 'plane into the sticky tropical heat. The smiling immigration officer stamped his passport and handed it back with the words, "Thank-you for coming to our island, Sir, and I hope you will be happy here." The baggage area was completely chaotic with piles of cases, bags and surfboards chugging along ever so slowly on an antiquated black conveyor belt. Porters, trolleys and passengers packed around the bags in a state of general disorder. Adrian grabbed his surfboards off the belt and then saw his blue bag fall off a trolley on the other side. He headed towards the customs barrier.

"Welcome to Bali, Sir," said one of the two khaki clad officers who were standing there." You have come at the best time. End of April. One month after the end of our rainy season. From now on it will be warm and sunny."

"I have really come for the surf," said Adrian.

"Yes, I can see that," laughed the man as he cast his eyes down to the two surfboards. "There is always good surf on Bali. Make sure you surf at Uluwatu. Good waves there. Off you go and have a good time in Bali."

Once outside in the half light of the early evening Adrian was assailed by a cacophony of voices as a mob of taxi drivers and hotel touts vied with each other to attract his custom. Some of them tried to grab his luggage. He stood there and stared into the sea of dark faces that all looked very much the same. Suddenly he spotted Nyoman pushing his way through the colourful and noisy crowd. He was wearing a pale blue T-shirt, a grey sarong folded at the waist and some old leather sandals. "Welcome to Bali. It is so good to see you," he laughed as they gave each other the surfer's handshake. "I have brought my uncle's car. It is over there."

They walked across the car park to an ancient and rusted Mercedes that was parked in the furthest bay. When Nyoman started the engine a loud roar came through the exhaust pipe.

"No muffler?" laughed Adrian.

"Yes, muffler but not a very good one," was the reply.

Adrian thought back to some of the old bombs of cars that he had owned over the years. Most of them he had wrecked by forcing them over deeply rutted farm tracks that led to secret surfing spots. "But they were only Holdens," he thought. "This is a Mercedes. Sacrilege!"

Nyoman said how sorry he was about Alex. "I would have enjoyed showing her around too," he said. "She was very kind when I stayed with you at Torquay."

"Thanks," said Adrian, "but I'm sure that you and I will have lots of good sessions in the surf in the weeks to come."

"Unfortunately I am going away on Wednesday for four weeks to surf in contests."

"Where?" asked Adrian.

"Hawaii and California. But between now and Wednesday we will get some good waves together. And you can stay in my cottage at Legian while I am gone. Like the car it is owned by my uncle but he lets me stay there and he said that he would be happy for you to live there while I'm away."

"Gee, thanks. Are you sure that it's cool?"

"Very cool."

It was almost dark but Adrian was able to look out at all the bustling activity that was part of the Asian night — brightly dressed natives lighting their candles and kerosene lamps, women opening the tiny restaurants for the evening trade, old men pushing carts of hot food on wheels along the dusty road and small, slender women carrying all kinds of loads on their heads — perfectly balanced.

And the traffic: hundreds of bicycles being ridden by men wearing wide, conical, coolie type hats, motor bikes with as many as three or four people riding side saddle, and battered old *bemos* that sped along the narrow roads honking their horns continuously. Nyoman pulled up behind one of the *bemos*. It was an old truck covered by a canopy and completely open at the back. He shone his headlights inside. Under the canopy Adrian could see two benches on each side that were filled with laughing, waving tourists. They were sitting facing each other and falling into the laps of others every time that the ancient vehicle turned a corner.

"You like to have ride in *bemo*? Maybe to-morrow?" smiled Nyoman.

"Yes, looks like fun," replied Adrian.

Past the shops of Kuta — all throbbing with people and activity — and on down the road to Legian. Gradually the shops gave way to trees and the occasional candle lit restaurant. Then the old Mercedes turned into a side road on the left and crawled in and out of some really narrow lanes that were lined by walls of grey stone. There was only about two inches of space between the sides of the old car and the walls. Suddenly Nyoman turned it into a dusty cul-de-sac and brought it to a stop. Slowly. "Brakes not very good," he smiled as he helped Adrian pull the surfboards out of the back.

Nyoman led his guest along a dark, narrow path that was shaded from the moonlight by the overhanging fronds of a row of palms. One or two kerosene lamps flickered their weak glow from the branches where they hung. Out of the darkness appeared two boys who spoke quietly to Nyoman.

31

They were each carrying a small lantern. Nyoman introduced them as Wayan and Ketut. "They live at uncle's house too. Part of family," he said.

They reached an open lawn and Adrian could see a large thatched roof cottage rising up in the moonlight. The two boys hung their lanterns on its wide verandah to reveal a stucco and bamboo structure. On the dark, tiled floor of the verandah were a couple of faded and torn armchairs, a low table and a really old sofa. Inside was a large room with a narrow spiral staircase that led up to a small loft in the high part of the roof. They filed up the stairs and Nyoman placed a kerosene lamp on the top of the wooden railing that surrounded the loft. Adrian leaned against the rails and looked down at the room below.

A large mattress lay on the floor of the loft and there were some wooden shelves and a carved wardrobe on the side farthest from the stairs. Adrian lay down on the mattress and looked up at the dark thatch of the roof. He could see the moonlight and stars through the walls of spaced bamboo; sometimes the vertical pieces of bamboo were touching and in other places there were gaps a few inches wide. "You sleep up here?" smiled Nyoman. "I stay at uncle's house until I go to America next week. Like it?"

"It's pure magic," said Adrian as he walked outside the loft on to a tiny balcony that was set in the roof.

They walked back down the staircase to the big room below. By now the two boys had lit a few candles which were strategically placed in saucers around the room. Through the flickering candlelight Adrian could see another room through a partition that was part bamboo, part rattan blind and part a red sarong that was hanging down from the roof.

"That's another bedroom," said Nyoman. "Maybe you like to sleep there instead? It's bigger."

"No way," said Adrian. "I fell in love with that loft as soon as I saw it."

"What else you fall in love with in Bali? Maybe a very beautiful girl?"

"Hope so," he laughed.

At the back of the house was a door that led outside to two small huts: one was a shower and toilet and the other a kitchen with a bench, sink and running water.

They sat down on the verandah to drink some hot coffee which had mysteriously appeared on the small table. The thatch roof came down very low over the verandah so as to shade it from the heat of the sun. Outside in the moonlight the coconut fronds were rustling gently in the breeze and the big leaves of the banana trees cast their shadows on the ground. Somewhere on the roof could be heard the shrill croak of a gecko.

Nyoman spoke in Balinese to the other two boys and they slipped away in the darkness towards the uncle's house only to return half an hour later with a couple of large plates of chicken and fried rice and some bowls of fruit salad — sliced bananas, paw paw, mango and pineapple with some peanuts and coconut sprinkled over the top. Nyoman sent one of them off again and he returned with a large lemonade bottle that was filled with some colourless liquid that wasn't lemonade.

"What's that?" asked Adrian.

"Arak," he laughed as he began to pour the locally distilled rice brandy into four glasses. "Very good brew! Knocks you out like machine gun. Bang! Bang!"

"Why is it in a lemonade bottle?" asked a curious Adrian.

"Because it is stronger than the arak that you can buy in the shops. We get it from the *warung* across the road." Had Adrian seen the old lady at the *warung* pouring it out of a forty-four gallon drum into Nyoman's well-used and not too clean lemonade bottle he might not have been so keen to drink it. They touched glasses and drank to some good times

33

in the waves.

"How long are you going to be away?" asked Adrian.

"Two weeks in Hawaii and two weeks in California," he replied. "There are four contests altogether and my American friend, Brad, who was here last year, has arranged a small sponsorship for me. It will only cover the air fares and I get free entries to the contests. But he said that I can stay with him and his new wife at Newport Beach and he has arranged for me to stay with a friend of his in Hawaii. So I should manage all right. I probably won't win any money but the competition will be good for me and, of course, it will be interesting to ride different waves."

"You lucky sod," said Adrian with a twinge of envy as he began to think of Hawaii. Of Sunset Beach, Waimea and Pipeline. And the greatest waves in the world that come all the way down from the Aleutians and hurl themselves on to the north coast of Oahu. Sometimes thirty feet! And more! Of Hawaii. Where surfing began. Where Captain Cook saw members of the Alii — the Hawaiian nobility — riding their great planks of wood on the breaking waves.

The moment of envy passed when Nyoman offered to take him to Uluwatu the next morning. "I was surfing there to-day," said Nyoman, "before I came to the airport. If the wind stays off-shore then the waves should be as big as they were this morning."

"How big was that?"

"Ten feet."

"Classic. Then I'd better take my big board."

By now Adrian was beginning to feel the effects of the arak. Whether it was solely the arak or a combination of the alcohol, the jet-lag and the sheer exotic impact and culture shock of his new environment he neither knew nor cared. He was aware of a pleasant feeling of lightness in his head as he sat back in the big old armchair on the verandah. The night was warm, the laughing Balinese were such pleasant company and he soon forgot the problems of the last few weeks. Suddenly he heard a rustling sound in a big tree a few feet from where he was sitting.

"What's that?" he asked.

"Monkey," laughed one of the Balinese.

They walked over to have a closer look. In the moonlight Adrian could see a small monkey jumping between the branches and occasionally stopping to stare down at him and bare its teeth. Around its leg was a reasonably long chain that was tied to the tree. It gave the creature enough leeway to prance around in the branches without being able to run away to join its brothers in the forest.

"What's his name?" asked Adrian.

The Balinese all laughed. "Deadhead," they replied.

"Then maybe we should play some Grateful Dead music for him."

The Balinese laughed again and said, "Grateful Dead very nice. Very good band but Rolling Stones Number One."

"Yes, Rolling Stones Number One," laughed Adrian. He could hear the strum of a guitar coming from another cottage a few yards further along the path. "Who lives there?" he asked.

"Terri and Nicul from France," said Nyoman. "When you have finished drink I shall take you to meet them."

"How many cottages have you got here?"

"Three — plus my uncle's house. Besides this one we rent out two more to travellers. The French couple are in one and there's another at the far end of the lawn."

"Then maybe I should pay you some rent," said Adrian.

Nyoman wouldn't hear of it. "No, you're my friend. And anyway my uncle is very rich and doesn't need the money."

"Has he got a big business?" asked Adrian.

"He has several businesses but that is not why he is rich. The reason he has a lot of money is because he has a jim. Not many families have a jim but those who do always become "rich."

"What's a jim?" asked Adrian, a little puzzled.

"A little man. So small that he fits into your pocket and can't be seen. Because a jim is invisible he can do all sorts of things without being detected. He is very powerful and does many good things for the family that owns him. Makes them rich."

"How?" asked Adrian.

"He can pop into other people's pockets and take their money out and put it into his owner's pocket instead. When a cash register springs open a jim can jump in and pull out all the notes. The owner of the shop can't even see him. He only notices that his money has disappeared and there is nothing he can do about it. He does not tell the police because he knows that it is a jim. And the police can not find the thief because the jim is invisible. And jims are more powerful than the police anyway. That is how their owners become rich. The jim gives them everything."

"How do I go about getting one?" laughed Adrian. "It sure beats working for a living."

"Ah, I see that you have now finished your drink. How you feel? Good? Come, I'll take you to meet the French couple."

Thierry, who had black curly hair, was wearing a dark green sarong and a necklace of white puka shells. He stood up as Nyoman and Adrian approached. Nicole too was wearing a light blue sarong that fell from her breasts to her knees. She was slim and petite with long auburn hair. The light from the kerosene lamp outlined a side view of her face and Adrian was quick to detect her fine classical features.

"*Bonsoir. Je m'appelle Thierry et c'est Nicole,*" said the Frenchman. Nicole bowed and smiled.

"She is truly gorgeous," thought Adrian. "*Enchanté. Mon nom est Adrian. Je suis anglais et j'ai peur que je ne parle pas français très bien. Est-ce que vous pouvez parler en anglais?*

Les Français, vous parlez trop vite pour moi." He realised that he was speaking very slowly as he tried to remember words that he had not spoken since he left school.

"That is true," said Thierry in English. "We do speak fast and I am sure that we must sound very funny at times."

"No, not at all," said Adrian. "I love listening to French. I just wish that I could understand it better."

"Well, maybe we go out for dinner one evening and speak French all night? What do you say to that?"

"You'll regret it," laughed Adrian.

"We have been learning a lot more English since we arrived in Bali," continued Thierry. "Both Nicole and I learned English at school and I have been to England three times. Once I was there for six weeks for an English language course at the University of Kent in Canterbury. That was six years ago. Unfortunately I have forgotten many of the words. But I am starting to learn them again."

"Well your English is far better than my French," said Adrian, "so maybe we should speak in English. I am truly sorry."

"No problem," smiled Nicole.

"I learned French at school and I think it is a very beautiful language," continued Adrian. "And in my last year at school I went to New Caledonia as an exchange student."

"And that is where you learned to speak our beautiful language? Slowly!" joked Thierry.

"Yes, among other things."

"What other things?"

"How to appreciate good wine, how to scuba dive, how to surf reefs. And I must say that I learned a few things from the chicks also."

"Chicks? What chicks? The ones that lay eggs?" asked Thierry with a puzzled expression on his face.

Adrian laughed. "No, that's just Australian slang for 'girls'."

"But why do you call them chickens? They do not lay eggs; they have babies instead. And as far as I know they do not have any feathers. Well, not unless they are in the Folies Bergères."

"Yeah, I guess it's pretty crazy but it's better than calling them 'sheilas'."

"Girls are also called 'sheilas'?" exclaimed Thierry.

"Yes, and sometimes they're referred to as 'birds'."

"What kind of birds? Blackbird? Stork? Magpie? Or thrush?"

"I suppose it all depends on the girl," laughed Adrian.

"Does anyone ever call them 'girls' or 'ladies'?" asked Thierry.

"No."

"Why not?"

"Gee. I don't know. You ask such difficult questions."

"I do not think it is a difficult question at all," said Thierry as he puzzled over the oddities of the Anglo-Saxon world.

It was all too much for Nyoman; he announced that he was going to bed. "Too much arak," he kept saying as he pointed to his head. Then he turned to Adrian. "I shall wake you up in the morning and we go Uluwatu and crack some big waves, eh?"

"Great," replied Adrian. "And thanks so much for everything. It's been a super evening." Nyoman disappeared into the darkness.

"Has Nyoman been giving you an arak attack?" laughed Nicole.

"Yes, it's pretty wild stuff," replied Adrian. "But I feel happy for the first time for ages." They talked on for another hour and Adrian asked them all sorts of questions about Bali. They had already been there for three weeks and intended to stay another two months. Thierry had just finished a degree in architecture at the Sorbonne while Nicole was on long leave from the *perfumerie* where she worked on the Champs Elysées.

"Of course, the longer we stay here the less desire we have to go back to work," she said. "Everything is so easy here."

Thierry explained how he had taken up surfing since he had come to Bali. "I just love it even though I can ride only the small waves. Up to one and a half metres. I do all my surfing down here at Legian Beach. There is a good break about a hundred metres along from here. I will show it to you to-morrow. If you are from Australia you are probably a very good surfer."

"Oh, not as good as some," replied Adrian. He was beginning to feel a bit tired so he took his leave and walked back to his own cottage to go to bed. He felt relaxed, light headed and happy as he lay on the mattress in the loft. "I think I'm going to like this place," he said to himself as he fell asleep.

When he woke the next morning just before six the cicadas were already singing in the trees. Nyoman had borrowed from his rich uncle another motorbike and the two of them, with surfboards strapped over their shoulders, set off for Uluwatu.

Adrian was amazed at all the early morning street activity. It seemed that all the Balinese rose at first light so as to use the coolness of the early morning to do the physical tasks — carrying baskets of vegetables to market, scrubbing down the floors and walls of their shops and houses, feeding the pigs and digging the gardens. Even the children were hurrying to their classes at 6 a.m.

Nyoman and Adrian weaved their way in and out of all the cyclists, pedestrians, *bemos* and motor bikes. He could see the bare breasted women returning from the well with great buckets of water on their heads. And men were carrying on their bony shoulders long bamboo poles from which hung neatly tied bundles of rice. Big black pigs dragged their bulging stomachs along in the dust, hens squawked and strutted while ghastly looking mongrel dogs scavenged in the piles of rubbish that lay on the sides of the road. Adrian knew that he was in Asia with all its noise, activity, colour, craziness, bustle, squalor and disorder. Even the smells were different. Pungent. Exotic. The impact of the East. Strange, powerful and mysterious.

Soon they had to slow down because the road was being rebuilt. The way was blocked by some big open trucks that were loaded with rocks about eighteen inches in diameter. Adrian was surprised to see teams of delicate women workers − some quite old − carrying the great stones from the trucks to where they were being pressed into the ground to form the foundation of the new road. Men who were perched on the back of the trucks were lowering the rocks on to the women's heads. Each woman had wound an old towel into the shape of a turban and had placed it on her head to provide a soft base for the rocks. Then, with straight backs, a steady walk and one raised hand steadying the load, they carried them through the tropical heat for about fifty yards to where they were needed. "Great for the old posture!" thought Adrian. Further along the broken and deeply rutted road there was another truck that was filled with bags of cement. The scene was the same. Languid men on top placing the heavy bags on the towelled heads of the women porters.

By now Adrian and Nyoman had slowed to a complete stop while they waited for another truck to turn. Adrian looked along the road. In addition to those with loads on their heads there were two long lines of women kneeling and sitting on the roadside as they pushed the rocks into place with blows from metal hammers. They sang and chanted as they worked in unison. They banged on the rocks together to embed them further into the ground. There were several men standing around giving directions and supervising the women. None of the men were doing anything physical.

"Why do the women do so much hard work?" asked Adrian.

"It is always the way in Bali," replied his friend.

They soon left behind the teeming crowds of the coastal strip as they climbed about two hundred yards up the steep hill that led into the countryside. Cow fields, banana plantations and the occasional palm tree. There were still people walking along the road but they were fewer and farther between. And friendlier. They all smiled and waved and called out their greeting *"Selamat pagi."*

Nyoman and Adrian turned off the dusty road and went down the narrow trail to Uluwatu. On either side of the track were prickly cactus fences. Beyond lay barren looking fields with a few lean brown cows chewing clumps of dry grass and thorns. When they reached the end of the track they parked their bikes under an overhanging straw roof. They could hear the surf booming against the cliffs. Several native girls in bright sarongs and boys in boardshorts ran up and offered to carry their boards down to the sea. Adrian was assailed by a torrent of questions.

"What's your name?"

"You a friend of Nyoman?"

"First time here?

"How long you stay in Bali?"

Nyoman led the way and Adrian followed with a boy and a girl carrying their gear. They walked down the big, roughly formed steps that wound down the rocky hillside to the cave below. The sea was turquoise in the early morning light. A bright green *prau* with an outrigger on each side was lying out towards the horizon. It rose and dropped with the incoming swells. Adrian could see the dark shapes of the fishermen as they sat back in their boat and trawled.

When Nyoman reached the top of the cave he climbed down a roughly made bamboo ladder which descended through a great hole in the rocky roof of the chamber. Adrian followed. When he reached the bottom rung he jumped about four feet on to the soft sand below. As he looked up he could see the blue sky through the hole where they had climbed down the ladder. The rest of the great cavern was covered with a vast, roughly formed roof of brown rock. The only other opening was a natural archway at the far end where the waves were thundering in and flooding the sandy floor. The cave echoed with the tremendous noise of the surf.

A couple of Americans were sitting on the sand waxing their boards. They called out "Hi" above the deafening roar of the ocean. Nyoman, who knew the wave well, led them out through the swirling white water and into the Indian Ocean. They paddled past a big mushroom shaped rock until they came to Outside Corner, the hardest and most challenging section of Uluwatu. For Adrian it was a baptism of fire.

The waves were truly huge. At least ten feet. For a while he lay on his board which rose and dropped with the swell. He was awed by the extremes of nature that lay around him. Everything seemed to converge at this one point. The strength of the ocean swell and the violence with which it threw itself against the cliffs. The cliffs themselves. So high. So sheer. So forbidding. And, of course, the cave. "There's definitely something supernatural about this place," he thought. Just then he looked up and saw a tiny temple that was standing high up on the edge of the clifftop. "Even the gods are here — looking down on us," he said out loud.

He looked up and saw Nyoman paddling furiously to catch a wave. Then the dark, shiny figure of the Balinese stood up on his board and started manoeuvring it with skill and determination as he weaved his way shoreward on the great crest of water. Then one of the Americans caught one and rode it brilliantly to the left. Adrian knew that he was too far out so he paddled in a few yards. And waited. He looked up at the jagged rocks of the cliff face and could feel the power of the waves as they began to form underneath him. He knew that they could throw him to his death against the cliff. But that was part of the thrill of surfing. The danger. The adrenalin. "Sometimes you put your life on the line just by being in it," he thought. "Like now."

He felt nervous and not very confident as he made a few false starts. Then he looked behind and saw a massive ten foot plus rolling inexorably towards him. Head down and arms stroking madly he felt its tremendous motion pick up his board and drive it on. Up he jumped and pointed his board down its massive face and into the great tube of water that he could see forming on his left. In he went. It was long, fast and completely hollow. Like the cave. It lasted so long that he thought he must be nearing the cliffs. Then it collapsed over him and he fought his way through the swirling water. When it passed and he flicked the salt out of his eyes he looked across and saw Nyoman and one of the Americans trying to battle their way out again. They hooted at him. He waved back. When he caught up with them he called out to Nyoman, "My first ride in Bali. Fantastic!"

"You have been blessed by the gods," called back the Balinese. "It is their way of welcoming you to their island."

They rode several more of the great peeling tubes and still there were only the four of them out. They could see other surfers sitting up on the cliffs watching but no one else was brave enough to venture into the water with their boards. "That's what is so good about the really big stuff," said one of the Americans. "Most of the guys are too scared to come out. At five to six feet there's at least forty in the line-up and you may as well be at Malibu. But ten to twelve feet sorts out the men from the boys."

In the big surf Adrian took more risks than most. He always believed that there was another thrill awaiting him on the next wave. And the bigger the wave the greater the thrill. With his fast, fluid style he usually managed to take more out

43

of the wave than the wave took out of him. But his wipe-outs were big ones. And a constant reminder of the overwhelming power of the sea. He was daring, carefree and not always wise. And definitely a thrill seeker. It was really an insatiable thirst for adventure. The same impulse that drove Columbus to the New World, Livingstone to Africa and Hillary to the top of Mount Everest.

He watched one of the Americans catch the third wave of a set. He grabbed the next one himself and took off on a sharp angle and rode into another tunnel of water. And a bit later another one. They were all revelling in the feast of powerful, perfectly formed barrels that Uluwatu was serving up.

After a couple of hours the waves started to change and close out. Soon they became impossible to ride. All four of them were tired and hungry but at the same time drained and stoked from their long session in the water.

As soon as they were washed up on to the sand inside the cave Adrian looked up and saw the girl who had earlier carried his board down. She and Nyoman's porter had waited for them in the cave. She grabbed his towel from a ledge in the rocky wall and started to rub him dry. "Massage? Massage?" she kept asking.

"No, not now," he said, "I must have something to eat. And drink." She insisted on carrying his board up the ladder as they climbed out of the cave and up the hill to the big, open-sided warung with tables and chairs that overlooked the ocean. They all flopped down at a table and Nyoman spoke in Balinese to the girl who was serving the food and drinks. She came back with some hot coffee and fresh pineapple and, later, a dish of nasi goreng — fried rice and vegetables with an egg on top.

Several Balinese girls were leaning against the rail a few yards from the table. When the surfers finished the food the girls caught their eye and again asked if they would like a

44

massage. They were pointing to some old mattresses at the back that lay on some rough benches of split bamboo.

"You simply must have a Balinese massage after the surf. 'Tis so relaxing," said one of the Americans as he pulled some money out of his pocket to pay for the food. Then he handed one of the girls a thousand rupiah note for a massage and went and lay on one of the mattresses. The others followed. Soon all four were having tired muscles rejuvenated by the skilful and soothing touch of the massage girls. Adrian now felt completely relaxed after the exhaustion of the waves. As he lay there feeling the small but strong hands working their way over his back, shoulders and legs he closed his eyes and thought about the beautiful tubes that he had been riding that morning. "There's no other feeling as good as being inside a tube," he thought. "Matchless! And a massage afterwards is like the icing on the cake."

The price of Adrian's trip to Uluwatu was a couple of dings in his surfboard — caused by some jagged rocks that he touched on his second to last wave. So he spent the noonday hour at the cottage repairing them. He dug out of his bag the repair kit that he had brought from Australia — resin, hardener and sandpaper — and set to work on the shaded verandah.

Three small Balinese children watched him from a distance of about five yards. They were at first very shy. However, after he winked at them a couple of times, they began laughing and walked a few steps closer. Then they began playing games with him and he gave them some sweets that were lying on the table. They came and sat right next to the surfboard and watched his every movement with great interest. When the resin hardened and he began sanding it down, they grabbed a piece of sandpaper and imitated him by rubbing it lightly on another part of the board. Nyoman came across and started talking to him about their surfing arrangements for the morrow.

When Adrian finished the sanding he stood up and stretched his back. The Balinese tots immediately stopped rubbing their end of the board and stood up too and arched their little backs. They began laughing and hitting him lightly on the legs. Then one of them handed him a flower. "Maybe he thinks you're a god," laughed Nyoman, "and he is giving you an offering." They were all laughing and Adrian put his hand down and patted the little boy on the head and ruffled his short, fuzzy hair. Suddenly the atmosphere changed. Nyoman stopped laughing. "You mustn't do that," he said.

"What?" asked a mystified Adrian.

"Touch him on the head. You have insulted his soul. It is the worst thing you can do to a Balinese."

"How come?"

"The soul exists in every part of the body but especially in the head which is the most sacred part of all."

"Gosh, I didn't know," said Adrian. "I'm really sorry."

"Oh yes, it was a mistake but it is good for you to know these things."

"Of course," said a humbled Adrian. He looked around for the children but they had fled. The god to whom they had given the flower had turned into a devil who insulted their souls.

After Nyoman left him Adrian went out on to the lawn to feed the monkey whose sharp teeth looked even more fearsome in the daylight. From the tree he could see Thierry and a topless Nicole sitting on their verandah in the shade. "Her breasts are as beautiful as the rest of her," he thought.

The Frenchman called out to him, "Come on over. We are about to go down to lie on the beach. Why don't you join us? And we may as well take our boards. I was down there this morning; the waves were only about a metre. But maybe they will get bigger."

"Good idea," said Adrian as he grabbed his towel off the tree and walked across to their cottage.

They walked Indian file down a narrow path that was lined with bright tropical flowers. Then they crossed some low sandhills and walked on to the clean white sand of Legian Beach. It was unbearably hot on their bare feet. Adrian looked along the beach. It stretched for miles each side, disappearing into the distant haze. Far away on the left he could see a Garuda DC10 landing from the sea on to the runway which protruded into the sparkling ocean. It was an amazing sight as the great silver bird, glistening in the blinding sun, slowly glided off the sea and on to the tarmac. He watched until it disappeared behind a row of distant palm trees.

Thierry walked down the beach and stopped by an old grey log that had been washed up by the tide. He dug his heel into the sand and raised his arm in the air. "This is our spot," he laughed. "We always lie on the beach in the very same place. Right here."

"What would you do if you found someone else here?" asked Adrian with a grin.

"Oh, I would ask them to move. Very politely, of course."

They stretched their sarongs over the sand and lay down in the hot afternoon sun. There were other groups of deeply tanned, exotic looking creatures scattered here and there but the swathe of beach was so big that it could never be crowded. The waves were still only about three feet high but were breaking cleanly. Adrian and Thierry paddled out through the luke warm water for a "fun" session in the small waves. Thierry's determined and strongly accentuated movements on the board were in the same style as Gerry Lopez but, alas, without the same skills. He was a crazy surfer and laughed every time he fell off — which was often.

Back on the beach Balinese hawkers were going from group to group as they tried to sell all sorts of handcrafted items to the Westerners. The native women wore cotton sarongs that fell to their feet and colourful blouses with long sleeves. Balanced on their heads were wicker baskets that were overflowing with brightly coloured clothes. Adrian watched with interest as one of the women came over to him and bent her knees to the squat position. She then put her thin, wiry hands up to the basket and lifted it down on to the sand. She went into a sing song chant as she lay out her wares on the beach — boardshorts, thin scarves, sarongs, G-strings, bikinis and shirts. There were batik and floral designs and the whole array was a mass of colour. Adrian bought some shorts and a G-string — the latter so that he could dress like everyone else on the beach. When she had put the basket back on her head and walked away Nicole turned to him and said that he could have bought them for half the price if he had bargained.

"But they were only a couple of dollars each as it was," he said. "I would have paid eight times that price if I'd bought them in Australia."

"Yes," she continued, "but it is such fun to bargain with them and they expect it. In fact, they respect you for it. That old lady will go and tell all her colleagues that there is a brand new prospect just off the 'plane and you will be a ripe picking for every seller on the beach." No sooner had she spoken than vendors of all kinds of articles began homing in on them. Some had beautiful tropical shells, some paintings on canvas and others cheap watches and bangles.

After a spark of initial interest in what they had to show him Adrian soon tired of their constant requests to buy. "Special student price. Good price for you, my friend." He told them that he didn't want to buy anything but it wasn't until he rolled over on to his stomach and closed his eyes that they began to go away to hunt further prey.

As the sun dropped towards the end of the afternoon several Balinese families began to arrive on the beach. Their work finished for the day they liked to sit on the sand and watch the sunset. Some of them brought nets to catch fish, some went for a swim and others made up games of football.

Thierry and Adrian had one last surf just before the sun went down. They lay on their boards facing out to sea and watched the bright orange glow far out in the west. "I have been here for three weeks and I never get tired of watching the sunsets," said Thierry. "To me, they are Bali at its most magical." As the last speck of colour suddenly slipped below the horizon they turned their surfboards a hundred and eighty degrees and paddled in to the beach.

Back at the cottages the Balinese houseboys were full of smiles and questions — did Mister Adrian enjoy his day, how many pretty girls did he see, what did he buy and how big were the waves? Thierry and Nicole asked him to join them for a meal about nine o'clock. "We always have a sleep now for about three hours before we go out for dinner. Then we are not tired for later in the evening. Bali is dead between six and nine. Everyone is relaxing after a day on the beach and before they go out for the night. Why don't you have a sleep too and we shall waken you just before we leave," said Thierry.

"Good idea." But he found it harder to wake up than usual. Guided only by the moonlight they walked up a narrow lane as far as the main Kuta-Legian road with its intermittent night time traffic of *bemos*, motor bikes and open tourer cars that were rented out to the tourists.

They ate at a small *warung* called "Charlies". There were only four tables which were set below a very old poster of Charlie Chaplin on the wall. They washed down their fish meal with some cold beer.

"There are two types of beer in Bali," said Thierry, "Bir Bintang and San Miguel. We prefer the Bintang. It is similar to Heinekens. See here at the bottom of the can — 'Brewed in Indonesia under the technical supervision of Heinekens Brewery'. You can be sure that Heinekens would not let their name be used unless it was the real thing. I think that the beer is one of the best things that the Dutch left when they quit Indonesia."

"I'll drink to that," said Adrian.

Nicole suggested that they move on to the Mango Tree for coffee. She looked at her watch and said, "The rest of the crowd should be there by now and if we don't go soon they will have moved on to the disco."

The Mango Tree was always crowded with Europeans between nine and midnight. The music was not too loud, the cups and glasses were always clean and the friendly barmen managed to remember every name, every face and how everyone liked their drink. It was built around a big mango tree and, when they walked in, Adrian could see groups of young people sitting at tables and speaking a variety of European languages.

"Ah, Mister Terri and Miss Nikul, how are you to-night?" asked Ketut, the barman from whom they ordered some black Balinese coffee. One corner of the bar-cafe was surrounded by a bamboo wall about three feet high. Inside this area rattan mats were laid over the floor and everyone who was lying there on the big red cushions had taken off their sandals and left them in a pile at the entrance. The three of them kicked their leather sandals on to the pile and found an empty space next to some backgammon players. Thierry explained about all the long term itinerant travellers in Asia who make their living by playing backgammon for quite big stakes.

"They win enough money to move on to the next place," said Nicole.

They ordered some glasses of *arak madu* — the local brew mixed with honey and lemon juice — and soon merged into the *beau monde* that surrounded them. About quarter to eleven people began to move out of the bar and on to the Jolly Frog disco. Thierry paid the bill and they went outside and hailed a *bemo* which rattled along the narrow road in the direction of the disco. They sat on the long seat at the rear of the truck and could look out through its open back. A couple of motor bikes roared up behind them and the high spirited drivers began honking their horns. Thierry reached out and touched the front of the moving bike. The rider came closer until the front of his wheel was less than three inches from the back of the *bemo*. Just a gentle touch on the brakes by the *bemo* driver and the motor cyclist would have been a pile of bones. "That looks like fun," said Adrian. "Almost as much adrenalin as riding a ten foot wave." He immediately resolved to hire a motor bike the next day. After a bit more laughing and fooling around the bike riders began to pull back so that by the time they reached the courtyard outside the Jolly Frog they were able to glide easily to a stop.

The disco consisted of an open-sided dance floor beneath a high thatched roof which was supported by long wooden poles. On one side was the long counter of the bar where drinks were being served to the thirsty dancers and on the other was a large outdoor terrace with ornamental ponds and candlelit tables and chairs under the palm trees. At the far end of the terrace was a stone sea-wall which separated the disco from the beach. From the tables on the terrace one could hear the disco music out of one ear and the breaking of the waves through the other.

Everyone was talking, drinking, laughing, kissing, dancing and gyrating on the dance floor as a Dire Straits tape thumped out of the loud speakers. Thierry and Nicole introduced Adrian to all sorts of interesting looking characters from a German doctor in black leather and studs to a girl clad in only a gold bikini who was surrounded by at least a dozen hot-blooded admirers.

While Thierry and Nicole swanned on to the dance floor with true Gallic flair Adrian took a walk over to the sea-wall and looked out at the silvery tops of the waves as they glistened in the moonlight. There were some vehicles parked on the beach below. In the moonlight he could see others driving along the sand on their way to the Jolly Frog. Suddenly he thought of Alex. He sat down and put his head in his hands and closed his eyes. The music reminded him of the last time that he held her in his arms on a dance floor. It was at "Mojos" in Melbourne the week before she died. It was even the same song that was now playing. He thought of the blue dress she was wearing. His eyes moistened as he began talking to her under his breath. He must have sat there for nearly ten minutes in the dim light all on his own while the music and laughter went on around him. Suddenly he felt her soft fingers sensually caressing the nape of his neck. He looked up and through his tears and the faint light of the disco he could see Nicole looking down at him with a warm, inviting smile.

"Thierry is talking to some friends on the dance floor," she said. When she saw his wet eyes she was momentarily startled. She slipped her arm sympathetically round his waist and they walked for a few yards along the sea-wall. Her female intuition told her that inside his strong, muscular body there must lie a heavy heart. But she didn't ask him about it. "It is for him to mention it, not me," she thought as she reflected on all the people whom she had met in Bali who were trying to run away from some trouble or sadness.

Adrian perked up under the spell of her gentle touch and asked her for a dance. "*Certainement et avec plaisir,*" she replied.

The music was getting faster and wilder. Thierry was dancing with some dark haired Italian girl over on the other side of the floor. Adrian looked across at him and noticed that his extremely accentuated movements and broad grin were in the same style as he had shown on the surfboard earlier in the day. "I suppose he is practising for the next Rolling Stones' concert," thought Adrian mockingly, "in case Mick breaks a leg just before he goes on stage." Nicole swung round and Adrian changed direction to suit. Out of the corner of his eye he could see a small group of Balinese men standing under a tree in the dark. One of them had a long python wound around his body. They were laughing and drinking and talking. The music stopped. Then the disc jockey slipped on a Bob Marley tape — "No Woman, No Cry."

The faces of the Balinese men lit up as if they were mesmerised by the reggae. They all rushed on to the dance floor and began cavorting wildly in all directions. Like men possessed. The snake became agitated and began to move. Its owner kept on dancing. He was in a trance. The python began to unwind. "It must be at least fourteen feet," thought Adrian as he watched it stretch horizontally out from the man's shoulders, holding itself rigid by its powerful muscles. Momentarily stunned, he stopped dancing and just stood there — rooted to the spot. Everyone else on the floor was laughing, dancing, kissing. All in their own little worlds. He wondered if it was for real. Suddenly the python lurched forward and began to wind itself around the neck of a small Javanese "good time girl" whose lips were coated with at least two tubes of bright red lipstick. At first she thought it was her escort's arm. It felt nice, sensual and slippery. But no man had a grip that strong. Still the reggae blared out of the speakers.

The serpent was now completely free of its keeper as it tightened its grip on the girl's soft, tiny neck. Suddenly she let out a piercing cry. The vibrations of her voice caused the python to panic and so it squeezed her neck into an even tighter vice like grip. Crunch! All the muscles and bones of her neck were crushed together.

Adrian and some other chaps rushed over to try and pull it away. But its muscles were far too strong. In the darkness he couldn't see any change of colour in the girl's face. But the sight of her eyeballs was enough to convince him that she had had her last dance. The left one was hanging ghoulishly from the end of a membrane and was at least a full inch out of its socket. The other eyeball had popped out completely and was lying on the floor. The terrifying, contorted appearance of her face was made worse by the zany coloured lights that were flashing down on to the dance floor from above. Suddenly a deep blue light illuminated her ghastly face as she fell down on the shiny wooden floor. Dead.

Several girls in the immediate vicinity were screaming and running away. But on the edges of the dance floor stylish, well-tanned couples were still holding each other in warm embrace or just staring lovingly into their partner's eyes. And, like the band on the Titanic, the music played on. The disc jockeys were shut inside their own little room behind the bar drinking arak, laughing and tapping their fingers to the wild music.

The men in the middle of the dance floor formed a ring with their outstretched arms and started pushing people away from where the python was beginning to unwind itself from the Javanese girl's corpse. Adrian was surprised to see that the men linking arms were all Europeans. As soon as the Balinese saw what had happened they all disappeared into the darkness. Including the group who brought the wretched thing in in the first place. They were in a state of terror. They believed that a powerful evil spirit must have come up out of the sea and got inside the python and there was no knowing what further mayhem it might cause. They knew that the sea — pasih — was the home of all demons and evil spirits and it was the darkness that brought them out. It was all the fault of the stupid Javanese man who built the disco right next to the ocean. No Balinese would ever have dared the spirits thus.

Fortunately there were some Javanese men working behind the bar who, being followers of the Prophet, didn't share the powerful Balinese belief in bad spirits of the sea. As soon as they saw what was happening they rushed out to the kitchen and grabbed some big knives and meat cleavers.

54

Then they ran on to the dance floor and attacked the reptile which had just finished unwinding itself from the girl and was now heading towards the edge of the wooden floor. They fell on it from behind and chopped and hacked it to death. The screams of the dancers were now drowning out the sounds of The Wailers and even the disc jockeys realised that something was wrong. They pushed the "Stop" button. The music ceased; the screams got louder. The manager rushed out from behind the bar and began clapping his hands in the air in an effort to persuade everyone to leave. Some jumped over the sea-wall on to the sand. Others began to run towards the main entrance. A team of Perth footballers and their ladies were just coming in through the gate. They didn't relish everyone charging at them and knocking them down and so they showed their feelings in no uncertain terms. Fists were soon flying in all directions. Head locks, punches, head butts, karate chops — the lot. The escaping partygoers gave as good as they got. Soon there were injured and bleeding bodies lying all round the entrance.

"For Christ's sake, you guys, there's a crazed python in there that's already killed one girl," screamed a deep American voice. "Can't you let us get out of the way."

"Did you say 'python'?" asked one of the footballers in a quivering voice.

"Yes, P.Y.T.H.O.N." he spelt out.

That was enough for the footballers. They turned tail and fled in terror. Their wives and girl-friends could barely keep up with them.

The lights above the dance floor were turned on to full to reveal a pile of black dress which was the dead Javanese girl and bits and pieces of the python that had been chopped and thrown all over the floor.

Adrian and Thierry held Nicole's hand as she jumped from the sea-wall on to the soft sand. She was still shaking. So was Adrian. Thierry was calmer; he had seen only the aftermath. But that was bad enough. They walked along the moonlit beach past the flickering lamps of the beachfront bars and restaurants that were hidden in the trees at the top of the sand. When they arrived in front of their own cottages they sat down on the beach and looked up at the full moon.

"Well we won't be seeing a Balinese at that disco for a long time," said Nicole.

"Why not?" asked Adrian.

"Oh, once they believe that a place is inhabited by an evil spirit they avoid it like poison. And that is how they will interpret to-night's incident. It was all the doing of an invisible demon that just happened to get inside the snake."

"The only way I would interpret it," said Adrian, "is that it was all the fault of the silly fool who took his python there in the first place and then didn't look after it. I mean, what a stupid thing to do! There's a time and a place for everything and discos are not for pythons. I reckon that it was all the noise and the people and the flashing lights that sent the poor thing crazy. It started to panic and that's why it reached out and crushed the unfortunate little girl. I saw the owner dancing and he wasn't looking after it at all. In Australia he would be charged with manslaughter. I mean, if he hadn't been so irresponsible by taking it there in the first place then the girl would still be alive."

"Yes, but that's not how the Balinese see it," sighed Nicole. "Their explanation would be that its owner became possessed by an evil spirit which caused him to forget about the python and the spirit was so powerful that it was able to get inside the snake as well and cause it to kill the girl. So it wasn't the fault of the keeper at all. He was in the hands of the spirit. And besides, the snake is the reincarnation of a being that was once a man and the keeper might very well be a python in his next life."

"You have a very fertile imagination," laughed Adrian.

"It is not imagination," replied Thierry. "That is what

they believe. To us it might sound crazy but in Bali crazy is normal."

"Yeah, well I feel like a swim before I go to bed," said Adrian.

"You are not afraid of the demons of the deep?" asked Nicole with a smile.

"Certainly not," he replied. "The ocean is my friend. Anyway, Huey always looks after me."

"Who is Huey?" asked a mystified Thierry.

"The god of surfing."

"See, you also believe in strange gods and spirits. You should fit into Bali very well." They all laughed, stood up, took off their clothes and ran into the warm, moonlit sea.

Back at the Jolly Frog the only ones left were the few members of the staff who were Javanese. They loaded the dead girl into a *bemo* which rattled along the pot-holed roads to the hospital. The loose eye had been picked up off the floor, wrapped in a paper serviette and placed inside a whisky glass. The *bemo* driver handed it to the receptionist at the hospital along with the body.

The barmen scooped up the fleshy pieces of the python that were scattered all over the dance floor and put them into plastic buckets. They scrubbed all the congealed blood and other pieces off the polished floorboards and then took it all out to the kitchen. There they cut the pieces of python into small, thin slices and boiled them in a great black cauldron on the wood stove. The manager added various spices and tasted it every now and then to see if the small pieces of meat were soft enough. When he was satisfied that they were just right he got the others to help him lift the big pot off the fire and they all sat around and drank a bowl of the tasty brew. There was still heaps left in the cauldron and so the manager walked across to where the menus were stacked for the next night. He wrote a new entry on each card — "Snake soup — 2,000 rupiah." He smiled to himself and thought, "To-morrow's diners are very lucky. It's always tastier when it's fresh."

■

Nyoman's departure for the surf contest was preceded by a special ceremony at the local temple to ask the gods to enter into his body and give him the extra powers that were needed to win. Then he could bring back the prize money and all the villagers would share in the proceeds. That is, provided his crafty uncle didn't get his hands on it first.

Adrian went with Nyoman to the temple. He tied a bright orange sash around his waist and walked through an old gateway into the temple courtyard. Nyoman had a straight bladed knife slung over his shoulder. "What's that?" asked Adrian.

"A *kris*. It has been in my family for many generations and is used for ceremonial occasions. Like to-day." Adrian took a closer look at its ivory and gold handle that was sparkling in the afternoon sunlight. On the end of the handle was a figurine of a garuda bird. Nyoman explained how almost every family in Bali had a *kris* which they regarded as a treasured possession.

Almost the whole village seemed to be packed inside the courtyard. The men wore decorative silver headbands and some of them had a bright scarlet hibiscus tucked behind their right ear. They were carrying long handled gold and white umbrellas which they placed over the stone statues of the gods — to denote their divine status and protect them from the hot sun.

The women were dressed in long sarongs that fell from their tiny waists to the ground. Over their shoulders they wore brightly coloured blouses. Balanced finely on their heads were baskets of sweet smelling orchids, frangipani and gardenias which they had brought as offerings to the spirits. Nyoman explained how the strong scent of the flowers was intended to lure the gods down to the temple. "We do not see the gods because they are invisible," he said, "but we often feel their presence."

The old priest blessed the offerings and everyone began praying and chanting to the accompaniment of cymbals and an xylophone. Then Nyoman walked slowly up to the priest — the 'pedanda' — and placed an offering of rice and flowers at the old man's feet. The pedanda sprinkled some holy water over Nyoman in order to purify him for the journey across the perilous sea. Even though Nyoman was flying to America there would still be dangers from the spirits of the deep since the path of the aircraft would take it over the sea. And so, by coming to the temple and making their offerings, the villagers hoped to appease the spirits enough to enable their champion to be carried safely on his journey and to return with great riches for the village.

After the ceremony had finished everybody walked the short distance back to the house of Nyoman's uncle who turned on a great feast. Adrian reckoned that there must have been nearly two hundred people on the lawn of the compound. The garden boys had dug a deep pit where a sucking pig was roasted. It was cut up and served on banana leaves.

Some of the fishermen from the village had managed to snare a turtle that they had seen swimming a couple of hundred yards out from the shore. They tied it behind their outrigger and made for the beach. There they killed it by stabbing a long knife into its flesh, thus avoiding any damage to its valuable shell. They were pleased to see that it was a male turtle which was more highly prized for its meat than the female. Since the fishermen owed Nyoman's uncle some money they offered him the turtle as part payment. The men of the household cooked it, spiced it and served it up with the rest of the meat. The food was washed down with a native beer which had been made from black rice. There was also coconut wine and some *brem* — a locally made rice wine.

Adrian felt sorry for Nyoman who was the repository of so many hopes and expectations. "Hell, I'd hate to be under all that pressure," he thought. "They all expect him to go away, win the contests, return with the prize money and share it round with all the neighbours. He's only human and contests can be so fickle. Hopeless surf, unlucky waves, biassed judging and all the other imponderables. I don't know how he can stand it."

Later, when the people had left and the servants were clearing up the food, Nyoman walked across to the cottage to share with Adrian a bottle of arak. Adrian began talking about the coming contest in Hawaii. At the first mention of the contest Nyoman became serious again and Adrian began to wonder about all the pressure that he must be under as a result of the day's ceremonies.

"Surely you're not going to take any notice of them?" he said. "I mean, it's your ability that's taking you there and surely anything you win is for you and not for all those hangers-on. It's good to have a bit of backing but they're trying to prime you up like a racehorse and they expect a share of the dividend in return."

He was surprised by his friend's reply. "I do it for my village as much as for myself. If I win, it brings honour to all the families in Legian. It would mean that the gods were pleased with our offerings this afternoon. If I don't do well it means that the offerings were not enough and next time we will have to make a bigger effort."

"But what about your uncle?" Adrian had seen the ease with which he seemed able to accumulate riches and he was giving Nyoman a gentle warning against letting any of the prize money move in that direction.

"My uncle has been very kind to me. He paid for my trip to Australia. It was only because I got some good results there that I was given the free air fares for this trip. But my uncle is part of the village community and so will share the honour if I manage to succeed."

There was nothing more to be said. Nyoman's attitude reflected the communal nature of Balinese life — he surfed for his village. Adrian, loose in his ways, highly individualist and sometimes selfish, surfed for himself. Although they rode the same waves they came from different worlds. But the arak soon had the same effect on them both.

■

When Adrian woke up the next morning he felt drowsy. But the heat soon became so unbearable that he simply had to get up and go out on to the verandah. He poured a cup of hot Balinese coffee from the thermos that had been placed on the table by the servant girl. It was a dark, sweet brew. He sat and looked at the well kept garden that was filled with tropical shrubs and brightly coloured flowers. Some Balinese ladies were walking along the path. "*Selamat pagi*," they smiled.

"I must buy an Indonesian phrase book so that I can at least carry on a basic conversation with them in their own language," he decided.

Later in the morning Nicole and Thierry came over and sat on the verandah with him. Apart from the sea it was the only place to shelter from the burning noonday sun. Across the lawn they could see three women of the household sitting beneath a row of banana trees as they made up their offering baskets for the temple. Nicole watched them place flowers in the small dishes that had been woven out of palm leaves. Then she saw them pour in some rice. There were about twelve offering bowls altogether but two of them remained empty. Then Nyoman appeared with a large box of brightly coloured packets.

"What's Nyoman got in that box?" she wondered out loud. Thierry and Adrian looked over and saw him pulling out several small packets which the women placed carefully in the two empty baskets.

"They look like packets of food," said Adrian. "Maybe exotic spices from the Spice Islands. Let's go over and have a look. Anyway I have to ask him if he wants to come surfing with me later this afternoon. A last surf before he leaves."

"*Selemat pagi*," smiled Nyoman when they approached.

"*Selemat pagi*. Oh, look at all the fireworks. When are you going to let them off?" asked Nicole.

"We are not letting them off. They are an offering to the opium god. It is his holy day to-day."

The others looked disappointed. "You mean you give him these as an offering?" asked Adrian.

"Yes, but we give him other things as well." He pulled out some chopsticks from the bottom of his box and handed them to the women. They entwined them with the carefully laid out fireworks. Then Nyoman pulled two small rolls of silver paper out of his pocket. He handed them to the women who placed them on top of the two piles of offerings.

"What's that?" asked Adrian.

"Opium," replied Nyoman. "He is the god of opium and so we must keep him supplied with it."

"Does he smoke it?"

"We just place it in front of his shrine and the next day it is gone."

"I think I'll become a god," laughed Adrian.

"No, I would rather be Tintiya," said Thierry.

"Who is Tintiya?" asked Adrian.

"Tell him, Nyoman."

The Balinese boy smiled. "Tintiya is the supreme being of our cosmos. You might have seen his statue when you came to the temple. A tall figure with a three pronged penis."

Chapter Three

The Vet

The cottage at the far end of the lawn was taken by a tall, fair, curly haired American who kept very much to himself but who always gave Adrian a polite greeting when they passed on the track. Adrian had noticed that sometimes he was with a tall, slender Chinese girl but other times was on his own. Thierry had said that the man's name was "Matt" but, apart from that, they didn't know anything else about him. "He is not overly friendly but nor is he unfriendly," said Thierry. "His manner is correct."

It was dusk and the cicadas were buzzing in the trees. Adrian had just come back from the beach after watching the sunset. He walked out to the kitchen hut at the back of the cottage and pulled a bottle of Bintang out of the sink that he had earlier filled with big slabs of ice. He felt the bottle. It was cold enough. He poured himself a frothy glass and went out to the verandah where he lit an oil lamp to provide some extra light for reading. He also lit a mosquito coil to keep the little blighters at bay. Then he ensconced himself in the old armchair and picked up the book that he had been reading down on the sand — "Reach For The Sky." He had found it in a second hand bookshop at Kuta and had bought it for the equivalent of fifty cents. He had always known the legendary story of Douglas Bader and was becoming more and more fascinated as he read the details. He was just raising the cold, frothy glass to his lips when he saw the American walk past.

"Hello," said Adrian.

"Hi, how're you doin'?" replied the other.

"Would you like a beer? I've just poured a cold one for myself."

The man hesitated. "Well, thanks. Are you sure I'm not disturbing you?"

"No. I was just about to start reading but it can wait. And besides, in this light I guess that it's not very good for my eyes." The American sat down in the other chair and introduced himself.

"Super place, don't you think?" said Adrian.

"What? Bali?"

"Yes. The only things I don't like are the mosquitoes."

"I like it here too," said Matt. "It's pleasant and laid back. But unfortunately it's changing all the time. Too much in fact. The whole place is very different from when I first came here."

"When was that?"

"1970. Eight years ago. I came here on R and R. There was hardly any tourist development at all."

Matt Wilton was one of those rootless Western characters to whom the East has provided both fascination and refuge since the seventeenth century — traders of the East India Company, rubber planters in Malaya, opium dealers like Jardine and Matheson, the founders of Hong Kong, pirates, newspapermen, shipowners, rouseabouts, artists, drunkards, beachcombers and bludgers. Most came out originally to escape from something unpleasant — a failed marriage, creditors, the police or the drab routine of suburban life.

Matt was twenty-six. He had been raised in southern California and was thrown into combat in Vietnam before his eighteenth birthday. By the time that he was twenty he had hardly ever been out with a white girl. Just Asian ladies. Bar girls in Saigon. Shop girls in Singapore. Dancing girls in

Bangkok.

When his extended term in Vietnam ended he returned to the United States. It was like a foreign country and he felt very much an alien. No one wanted to employ him. No one invited him to parties. No one asked him about his time in Vietnam. No one was interested in him. They were all too busy making money. But the incident that acted as a catalyst happened one morning at the local shopping centre. Matt was sitting outside McDonalds eating a cheeseburger while he searched the classifieds of the Los Angeles Times for a job. Suddenly the local church minister walked up, spat in his face and accused him of being a sinner for going to Vietnam and killing innocent peasants. Matt just stood up, turned away from the crazed cleric, walked straight to the nearest travel agent and booked a flight to Bangkok. One way.

Since then he had been drifting round the East for nearly six years. Supporting himself with a bit of this and a bit of that. Smuggling gold into India, watches into Nepal, running a bar in Bangkok, acting in a porn movie in Hong Kong. He had been to Bali several times. It was cheap. And pleasant. And he felt very much at home. He spoke Indonesian fluently.

His latest bit of income had come from a rich Balinese businessman who had asked if he could procure for him a blond European girl for a couple of nights while his wife was away in the mountains visiting her ancestral village. The man had offered Matt a hundred and fifty American dollars with a further three hundred greenbacks for the girl. Matt knew just the lady for the task — a Scandinavian with long blond hair who was down to her last twenty dollars and was prepared to do anything to prolong her stay in Bali so as to avoid having to go back to the Nordic cold.

When he walked up the steps on to Adrian's verandah for a beer Matt was on his way back from collecting the hundred and fifty dollars from the Balinese man. The crumpled notes were stuffed in the back pocket of his shorts. Matt was happy with the money, the Balinese man was happy with the girl and the lady herself was happy to be able to extend her holiday.

Adrian asked him what it was like on the island back in 1970. "It was simply paradise," was the reply.

"But …," mumbled Adrian, "it's still paradise, isn't it?"

"Yes and no."

"What do you mean?"

"Well, of course, it has changed. Some of the change has been for the good but a lot has been for the worse. There is more to do now. Especially in the evenings. Back then there were no discos. Nothing. And the restaurants were just a few tables under the palm trees. And there were hardly any shops. If you wanted anything more than a cake of soap you had to ride into Denpasar. Of course, Denpasar is still the same dirty, noisy, crazy metropolis. Except that there are now many more vehicles for the same narrow streets and lanes."

"Anyway, Matt, if there was so little to do in those days how did you fill in your evenings?"

"Oh, we just sat around and played guitars and talked and laughed and smoked with the Balinese. There was more freedom then. It was even less organised than it is now and the police were much friendlier. Probably because there were less tourists. In those days Bali was for poets and surfers and artists and freaks. And a few off-duty soldiers like me. Some of them had to come across from Java on an old tramp steamer. The airport had only recently been built and there weren't many flights. Compared to Saigon Airport it was like a country airstrip. Mind you, it's still pretty disorganised. Just like everything else here – the 'phones, the hospital, the traffic, even the electricity can be spasmodic. But you get used to it. It's all part of Bali's charm – the thrill of the unknown. Nothing is predictable.

Now the authorities are trying to make Bali more accessible for everyone. But in the process it has become a little less special. But there is nothing that one can do about it. The Indonesian government has to pay its bills and they know that the high oil prices won't last so they'll have to fall back on the tourist dollar. And open the place to everyone. The masses. And that is already starting to happen. But I still like it and — you are right — it is still a paradise in many ways. I like to be able to go to the discos and pubs and meet all the crazies from the West.

The Balinese are very tolerant of Westerners even though they think we're nuts. Mind you, most of us are a bit. That's why we get on so well with them. It's a crazy place. They love jokes, card tricks, laughter and any kind of magic. The more outrageous and uninhibited you are the more they like you. Bali is a place for individualists. It is not a place for the average boring bureaucrat to come to for his annual holiday. He'd hate it. And the Balinese wouldn't like him either. The more crazy you are, the better you'll fit in.

Some folk who come here are never the same again. They go away with different values. Most people seem to have some special memory of Bali — something that lasts for the rest of their lives. Like a passing love affair. But a strong and passionate one.

You will find a real feeling of freedom here even though Indonesia is technically a dictatorship. But it's a very benign dictatorship. The people are free to do most things except have political campaigns. Fortunately it's still a primitive land and they don't suffer the shackles of technology that have enslaved the so-called sophisticated nations of the West. You know what I mean — computers, plastic credit cards, ID numbers and all the other insidious technological weapons by which Big Brother in the West is able to keep a complete check on every citizen — how much people earn, how and where they spend their money, credit ratings, traffic convictions, everything! But here you have thirteen and a half thousand islands with only primitive communications so the government can't control everybody down to the last petty detail. The villagers run their own affairs as indeed they have done for centuries. And they don't have to worry about building permits and licensing hours and parking metres and seat belts and speeding fines and all the other rubbish that people in 'advanced' countries are forced to put up with."

"But surely they must have some effective government?"

"Oh yes," replied Matt. "Each village has a *banjar* which is an organisation to which every householder belongs. It makes its own village laws and can punish people for infringing them. The worst punishment is to be banished from the *banjar* because then the man loses face and is ostracised by his neighbours. The *banjar* has jurisdiction over things like marriage, divorce, property transfers and keeping the streets tidy. The system works very well.

It's the same with the rice fields. They are run by a similar association called the *subak*. All the rice farmers belong to it and they decide things like how much water should be allocated to each field and when to plant and harvest. Although the members all own their own fields it's a sort of co-operative and they can punish people for disobeying the arrangements."

"What type of punishment?"

"They wrap a bamboo pole in palm leaves and place it in the middle of the errant man's field until he pays a fine to the *subak*. While the pole is there he can't get water for his field or even work it. So, as you can see, almost all the main decisions are made at village level by the people who all know each other. That way power is more diluted than it is in the West where the central government and its horde of bossy bureaucrats seek to rule every little aspect of the people's lives.

I am an individualist and I hate all forms of power.

Especially communism which is so brutal because it seeks power at any cost. You should have seen some of the atrocities that the Viet Cong inflicted on the Vietnamese villagers. I saw some of them with my own eyes and they don't bear repeating. But all power is brutal because it is diametrically opposed to individual freedom and a man's right to think for himself and make his own decisions. Freedom is the greatest thing that a man can possess. And these days one of the rarest. Just because a country has an election every four years doesn't mean that it's a haven of individual freedom. All it means is that you have the tyranny of the masses. And they can sometimes be just as intolerant of real personal freedom as the communists. The more organised a place is the less freedom you have. That is why I prefer countries like Indonesia, India and the Philippines. They are all so delightfully disorganised and if you ever have any trouble you can always buy your way out of it. After all, corruption is usually only an attack on government revenue. Nothing else. It doesn't hurt anyone or involve violence."

"Methinks you're a bit of an anarchist, Matt."

"No, not at all. I just like my freedom and I don't like being made use of by people in power. Many of us in Vietnam felt that we were being used and when you run a good chance of losing your life in the process you do tend to take a dim view of being a pawn in someone else's power game. I am not an anarchist at all. Just an individualist and I find that there's more scope for that out here than in the tightly structured rat race that masquerades as advanced civilisation. After you've been here a while I think you'll understand what I mean.

When I first came to Bali in 1970 I was with some buddies. We were in a pretty bad state. We'd been in combat for longer than we should have been and so, instead of going to one of the usual R and R places — Manila, Bangkok, Sydney — our C.O. arranged for a small group of us to come here. He was a wise and caring chap and we all respected him one hell of a lot. Poor man, he was later killed by a land mine. He booked us in at the Bali Beach Hotel and the first night everyone got drunk and started talking about 'Nam. I just wanted to forget about it — even though we were only away from it for a week. So the next morning I got up early and left a note for the others saying that I would see them at the airport on the day of departure.

I jumped on an old rattletrap of a *bemo* that chugged its way through Denpasar and then on to Kuta. It was hot, dusty and sticky and I felt as sick as a dog after all the beer that I'd drunk the night before. Every time the *bemo* jerked a whole gaggle of women in bright sarongs would fall on top of me. Soon we were all laughing.

When I got off at Bemo Corner in Kuta a boy who saw the bag over my shoulder came up and asked me if I was looking for somewhere to stay. He led me through a maze of narrow, dusty lanes to his family's compound which had four *losmens* that they rented out to guests. It looked clean and was certainly cheap. One dollar a night. There was a tall Swedish fellow lying on a deck chair and I asked him if the place was okay and he said that it was the best value on the whole island. So I paid the rent and settled down to one of the most beautiful weeks that I've ever had.

The Swede and his wife had one of the *losmens*, there was an Israeli girl in another and, shortly after I arrived, the same boy who had led me there arrived with another guest, an Egyptian student from the university in Cairo.

Stig, the Swede, was a doctor and was an active member of the anti-war movement which, as you would know, made all sorts of allegations against the troops in 'Nam; some of them were true but most of them were not. So there we were — the Egyptian student, the Israeli girl soldier, the Swedish pacifist and me, a machine gunner on leave from 'Nam. By rights we should have been scratching each other's eyes out but instead we all mixed together, swam together, smoked together, laughed together and had dinner together. By the time I left we had shared a wonderful week of pleasure and had many happy memories. I said at the start that I didn't want anyone to mention Vietnam and they were kind enough not to. Then, after a week, I had to leave this beautiful dream world and catch my 'plane back to Hell. But it was in Bali that I learned to see things in a different perspective. It opened my eyes to a simpler and more gentle world.

If two countries are ever thinking of going to war they should first of all send groups of their young people to Bali. When they see the peace and beauty of the island I'm sure they would soon change their minds about fighting. It is an island of gods. There are gods everywhere — in the mountains, in the temples, gods of nature, ancestral gods. And I think that the gods cast their own magic spell on all who come here."

"Hmmm," said Adrian with a smile. "I wonder what they'll do to me."

"It's all a matter of karma," replied Matt. "If you are basically a good person and do not harm others then nothing bad will happen to you. It means that you give out good karma and receive the same in return. It also works the other way. The power of karma is very strong in the East and especially in Bali."

"Do you believe in it yourself?" asked Adrian.

"Of course. It is the way that the East works. In my case I do many illegal things but I don't hurt anybody. I have smuggled gold from one country to another and there has always been a smiling, happy buyer at the other end. The only one that is hurt is the government revenue. And they deserve bad karma because they are always inflicting it on others. I learned a lot about that in Vietnam."

Adrian yawned. "Would you like another beer, Matt? I have one more left in the ice sink."

"No, I can see that you are tired. So am I even though it

is still early. My girlfriend left for Hong Kong this morning. She had to get back to do some commercials; they are starting shooting to-morrow."

"Is that the Chinese girl?"

"Yes," he replied. "She is my Hong Kong girlfriend. I have another one in Bangkok and another in Singapore."

"The East has many pleasures," smiled Adrian.

"Especially for those who embrace it. But it can also be cruel and treacherous."

"You speak from experience?"

"Yes. You have to be smart and streetwise to survive in Asia. And, of course, there is no welfare or charity to fall back on. But I prefer it that way. I have enough confidence in myself to get through life on my own wits and I don't need any help. I have always had enough money to get by and many Asian girls to please me. I am — as the saying goes — 'well into the bamboo'. I find Asian ladies so soft and gentle. And all their movements have a natural grace about them. They are also mysterious and ever so subtle. They make the man feel like a king. And that is always a nice feeling. In the East they are still feminine and sweet and they are unaffected by all the feminist nonsense. That is so silly and, of course, it is against the laws of nature for women to try to play the masculine role."

"It is also very unattractive," said Adrian.

"Yes, but in Bali the woman's role is strictly proscribed. They have very few rights. They have to help with the rice harvest and do all the hard work on the roads and construction sites — as you would have noticed. But they are not allowed to do the more pleasant things like painting, carving and playing music. Those are tasks for the man. And it is the man who makes all the decisions both in the household and in the management of the village.

Bali is very much a man's world. It is easy for a man to divorce his wife if he tires of her and he doesn't have to give her any property. Not like in the West where the laws are designed to encourage a gold digging wife to set up a divorce situation so as to get rid of her husband and fleece him of half his wealth."

"What about the wife? Is she able to leave her husband if she gets sick of him and wants to run off with another man?"

"No," replied Matt. "Even if she catches him in the act of adultery she cannot leave unless he wants her to go. A woman can get a divorce only if her husband is impotent or is extremely cruel to her."

"That's not very fair on the woman," commented Adrian.

"No, not by our standards. But I'm sure that if the Balinese looked at the way the Western system works they would be equally shocked. Callous, scheming women who, acting on the advice of their lawyers, pounce at the right moment and rob a man of most of his life's earnings. Perhaps the answer lies somewhere in between the two systems. But for the moment I prefer the Balinese way. But don't be deceived; in some ways the Asian girl acquires just as much hold over you. But in a far more subtle and pleasant way." He was staring into the darkness. Adrian could see his eyes in the glow of the oil lamp. They had a slightly vacant look about them.

"Well," said Matt, "I really must go now. I shall be going to Hong Kong in a couple of days. Please come over for a sundowner before I leave. I would like to return your hospitality. And besides, I like talking to Australians. They are direct and there is no bullshit about them. I had some good buddies among the Australian soldiers in 'Nam. And man, did they know how to enjoy themselves!" He said good-bye and walked across the lawn to his own cottage. Adrian watched him through the moonlight.

There was a clump of frangipani and banana trees along

73

one side of the grass. Squatted down between two of the bushes was Ketut, one of the gardeners, who had chosen a dark spot to smoke some ganja. He could hear Matt saying good-bye to Adrian and then watched him walk across the lawn. It was dark around the trees and Ketut waited until Matt passed directly in front of him before greeting him. "*Selamat malam*, Mister Matt," he said quietly. Adrian saw Matt jump about two feet in the air as he let out a sudden scream. His hand rushed to his side for the gun that wasn't there. When the startled vet saw Ketut's smiling eyes and white teeth through the darkness he calmed down. "Good night, Ketut," he said in as even a tone as possible.

"Poor bugger," thought Adrian. "He must have thought that Ketut was a Viet Cong. The nightmare lives on."

After a short nap Adrian jumped on the trail bike that he had hired and rode to the Australian bar at the far end of Kuta. It was noisy, boozy, smoky and crowded. As he looked around him he wondered if he was back in Australia. "The Asian barmen and barmaids are the only sign that I'm not in Carlton or Saint Kilda," he thought as he watched a Balinese bar girl with four cans of Bintang on her head walk across the room and deposit them on a table.

Adrian went over to talk to some other surfers whom he knew from Melbourne. They chatted for a while until the general noise became too loud for coherent conversation. At one end a rowdy beer drinking contest was taking place. Everyone watched as a macho looking Darwin truck driver won the men's section while a sixteen stone, fuzzy haired Melbourne policewoman guzzled down several pints to win the women's contest. Then the two slobs kissed each other and everyone roared like cattle.

At the other end of the bar he could see the football team from Perth who had fled from the disco when they heard that there was a python at large. But to-night they were braver. They were doing a "Ra-ra-ra" chant which involved them taking off an extra item of clothing at the end of each verse. Soon they were down to their underpants as everyone egged them on in the final chorus. With success. Adrian was talking to the barman. "We Balinese think that some of your Australian tribal customs are very strange and funny," said the little man.

"So do I," replied Adrian.

The barman hurried off to take some orders and Adrian stared into the clear, amber glass that he was holding in his right hand. "I now know what Matt meant when he said that Bali is changing," he thought as he looked outside and saw two more pubs across the road. All three were competing for customers with really loud music. Three different tapes — Lou Reed, the Doors and the Sex Pistols. And, of course, the constant revving of motor bikes as people came and went. The resulting cacophony sounded like a tank battle. Adrian sighed to himself. "I don't think I'll come here again," he decided. "It's not my idea of Bali."

The next afternoon he surfed the local beach break until it was almost dark. Salt water was still dripping out of his hair when he walked past Matt's cottage which was lit by several oil lamps. There was a crowd of Balinese boys sitting on the floor of the verandah sorting through a mass of exotic looking sea shells that were scattered across the tiles. Matt, in a brown sarong, was kneeling on the floor and giving instructions to them in Indonesian. He called out to Adrian, "I shall be finished here in about ten minutes. Then you must come for a drink as I am leaving on the 'plane to-morrow."

"Okay, I'll go and have a shower."

"Right. See you in ten minutes."

When Adrian returned a quarter of an hour later the scene was no less chaotic. Half a dozen Balinese were wrapping the shells inside brand new sarongs and packing them carefully into suitcases. Matt was supervising the operation and checking the shells with a handwritten list that he had made.

"Won't be long," he said. "I am taking all these to Hong Kong to sell. The profit will be more than enough to pay for the air trip."

Adrian lifted one of the cases that had been closed and strapped. It was heavy. "But what about the excess baggage charge? Won't that cancel out the profit?"

"No," replied Matt. "This is all it will cost me." He pulled a couple of ten dollar notes out of the pocket of his shorts that were lying under a chair. They were from the money that he had been given by the Balinese businessman for arranging the Scandinavian girl.

"What do you mean?" asked Adrian.

"I will just put these two notes inside my ticket when I present it at the counter and, with a nod and a wink, the clerk will turn a blind eye to the excess weight. I have done it many times before. It is the way that things are done in the East. I will be putting through more than a hundred kilos of luggage which is not bad considering that the limit is only twenty. Then, when I get to Hong Kong, I shall sell it all. The sarongs, the bikinis and the shells. This is how I have lived for the past five years. I take things from one country to another — always at a profit."

Adrian had never seen such beautiful shells. "Do you mind if I have a look at them?" he asked.

"Not at all," replied Matt. "They have all been pulled out of the sea by divers and polished. The colours are so vivid. And virginal. The ones that live in the deepest water are the most colourful of all. And the most valuable. See." He unwrapped a beautifully formed deep green shell which was about fourteen inches across. "This is a very good specimen of green snail," he explained. "The crust has been ground off and the shell has been polished so as to highlight its iridescent colours. I buy them very cheap from a Balinese man with whom I have done business for four years. They are brought

76

out of the sea by the fishermen at Madura. That is a small island off Java. Not far from here. It has a huge shell market but it is not as big as the one in Jakarta."

He pulled out some other shells and explained them. Adrian could see that, apart from the profit aspect, Matt had a genuine interest and pride in his wares. Each shell was beautiful, different and unique. There were cowries that had been polished by the waves and others that were richly spotted like a leopard. There were many specimens of the chambered nautilus with its rows of chestnut brown streaks.

"See these stripes," said Matt. "They show how the shell grew. The nautilus is built by an animal that makes a continual series of chambers, each one larger than the one before. And this is the result."

There were long tusk like shells and spider conches with white spikes jutting out in all directions. Red and white mitre shells and small, pointed cones with deep black spots. But the ones that Adrian liked the most were the beautiful polished pieces of mother-of-pearl. Matt laid a few of them on the table and pulled out a magnifying glass so that Adrian could look at the detail, purity and clarity of their surface.

"There is a very good market in Hong Kong for mother-of-pearl," said Matt. "Because it has such a hard surface it can be carved very precisely and polished to a rich sheen. They are used for the inlay of furniture. Each piece is cut up and embedded into the backs of those big Chinese wooden chairs. And Koreans snap it up for their furniture which is of a similar design. It is also used for the handles of cutlery and pistols. And for scabbards and sword hilts. And jewellery too. Even buttons. Because it is so hard you can drill holes in it and it doesn't crack."

"But," remarked Adrian, "the shape and colour range of a whole piece is so beautiful that it seems a crime to cut it up. Like when they cut big diamonds into smaller ones."

"I agree," said Matt, "but it's all a matter of economics.

We live in an age of greed and everything has its price. And so does everybody."

"What are these used for?" asked Adrian as he pointed to a large, solid looking helmet shell. It had a white crust on the outside and a shiny orange-brown interior.

"Lamps," replied Matt. "Although some people buy them just to place on their mantlepiece. They like to look at the natural and beautiful shape." He opened another case and pulled out a pair of giant clams with their great undulating lips. He closed them over to show how they could seal into each other. "These are used for all kinds of purposes", he said. "Bird baths, flower containers and some of them I have even sent to the States to be used as christening fonts in churches."

"How long will it take you to sell them all when you get to Hong Kong?" asked Adrian.

"No more than a week. I know the people who want to buy them and they are always pleased to see me. Or at least what I bring them. Already some of them regard me as an 'old friend'. The Chinese use those words as a term of trust and they don't invest you with them lightly. It is really a business expression which means that they have known you long enough to trust you. They trust me because they know that I select only the best shells. Ones without imperfections. Therefore, my customers get good value. And I also make a very good profit."

"And what about all the sarongs and bikinis?"

"I sell them too. To a big clothing emporium on Nathan Road. I take a smaller margin because I only really buy them as wrapping for the shells."

"What's Hong Kong like?" asked Adrian.

"It's endlessly fascinating but very hectic. And, of course, it's the best governed place in the world because it is the least governed. No trade or import duties, no currency restrictions and hardly any taxes. Everyone is prosperous.

And they have the best of both worlds: British liberty and government and Chinese industry and enterprise."

"Yes, I'd like to go there one day. My mother lived there before the War and she loved it."

"I shall give you my address. I am not often there but I use a secretarial office for my mail and 'phone calls." He reached across to his wallet and pulled out one of his business cards and handed it to Adrian. One side was written in English; on the reverse side were Chinese characters. "You see, I go to other places all the time – Manila, Bangkok, Singapore and Kathmandu. Especially Kathmandu as a lot of the contraband that reaches India goes from Hong Kong to Kathmandu by air and then into India on mules over the mountains. Watches, gold, cameras. It is so silly for the Indian government – or any government – to restrict these things because they still get through anyway. It's just that people have to pay more for them and middle men like me can make a good profit."

He pulled out a packet of hand rolled Gudang Garam clove cigarettes and passed them round. First to Adrian and then to the Balinese who were still wrapping up the shells. The cigarettes gave out a strong, pungent smell.

When the Balinese lads had packed the last of the shells Matt gave them all a glass of arak. They sat down on the dark tiles of the verandah and started drinking, talking and laughing. Matt pulled out a pack of cards and showed them some tricks. They laughed and watched keenly as he flicked the cards. Then the Balinese grabbed them and carefully and proudly demonstrated a trick or two of their own. Everybody was laughing. Matt opened another bottle and refilled their glasses. They gulped it down and then said with great politeness that they had to go. They made a few more jokes with their host and left. The air was thick with *"Terima kasih"* and *"Selamat malam."*

"Well, you sent them away happy," said Adrian. "They

are all smiling."

"Yes, but don't be deceived by that. They can smile even when they are angry with you. But you are right. They are happy to-night. They are only about eighteen and already three of them are married. With children."

"Eighteen is the best age," said Adrian without thinking. The arak had made him feel relaxed. "I remember when I was eighteen. I went to a party almost every night of the year. Can you remember some of the crazy things you did when you were eighteen?" There was a long silence. He looked up at Matt who was staring fixedly into the darkness with the same vacant look that Adrian had noticed the night before. The American was thinking of when he was eighteen. The M-60 machine guns, the hidden land mines, the search and destroy missions, the assault on Hill 714, the burnt out vehicles, his dead buddies, the napalm, the screams, the corpses, the blood, the body bags.

"Yeah, I remember," he said.

Chapter Four

The Village

"Bali blues" began to set in on the third consecutive day of dull, cloudy weather when even the ocean was flat and lifeless. When Adrian woke up and found that there was no surf and no sunshine, he had his usual breakfast of fruit salad and hot tea on the verandah and then went back to bed to catch up on some much needed sleep.

When it stopped raining in the early afternoon he made another inspection of the surf. No change. Just gentle little six inch waves lapping on to the beach. By now the sea had turned brown. The heavy rain had washed a lot of mud and debris down the streams and there were several branches, pieces of wood and plastic containers floating around in the muddy water. The sunbathers, the food carts, the singing massage ladies and the persistent jewellery sellers were all absent. It all looked very uninviting.

Adrian spent the rest of the afternoon browsing around the maze of shabby looking stalls in the day market. By now there was only light, intermittent rain and many of the stall owners had erected canvas overhangs in front of their "shops" so as not to deter the tourists. They knew from long experience that rainy days were the best one for business. They regarded the rain as a gift from the gods because it drove the tourists off the beaches and into the shops and markets. These rain sodden shoppers were always happy to part with large sums of money for clothes, hand drawn cotton batiks, paintings, carvings, rattan caneware and endless other items that were worth only a fraction of their asking price. But the gods could kill with kindness. Rain and clouds for two or three days were like a shower of money from the heavens but, if they should persist for weeks or months — as always occurred during the wet season from November to March — then it kept the tourists from coming to Bali altogether. Then the shop owners regarded the rain as a curse. The rice farmers saw it differently. They frequently invoked the help of Wisnu, the god of water, and his wife, Dewi Sri, the rice goddess, to fill their paddy fields with the sacred water.

The blaze of brightly coloured sarongs, board shorts, bikinis, jewellery, paintings and fearful looking wooden *topeng* masks staring from every direction were a vivid contrast to the dull, grey weather. There were hundreds of stalls selling more or less the same things.

"Hello, sir. Special student price for you." The female voice came from behind a mass of sarongs and cotton batik shirts that were hanging from the roof of a shop. Adrian had been drawn in by the bright colours and the fragrant smell of sandalwood that wafted through the small shop from the back. "Ba-teek sarongs for you. Special price for rainy day." She was pulling them off the hangers one by one and placing them against his legs.

"How much is this one?" he asked as he pointed to a deep green sarong.

"That one is very good quality. Only six thousand rupiah."

"Six thousand!" he exclaimed in mock horror. "Too much."

"For you, sir, a special price of five thousand rupiah."

"No. I pay four thousand and no more." A wounded look of victimisation came across the woman's face.

"No can do. I lose all my money at four thousand," she pleaded.

"Well, me no can do at five thousand. I'll leave it."

He walked out of the shop. The woman followed and tapped him on the shoulder. "All right, four thousand," she whispered. "But don't tell anyone. Secret between us. Me bankrupt if I sell any more at four thousand."

She put it in a cheap plastic bag and Adrian handed her the money. "*Terima kasih*" he heard her say as he walked out to the wet courtyard. A couple of stalls along he saw a sarong exactly the same hanging at the front. "How much is that?" he asked the stallholder.

"Two thousand rupiah," was the reply.

There was another stall selling fluorescent board shorts — pink, red, blue, luminous green. He tried on a few pairs. "Four thousand rupiah for each shorts," said the man. "But if you buy many shorts can do lower price."

Adrian chose three pairs and the man went out the back to fetch a wooden abacus. He flicked some of the round black counting beads along the wire and then wrote the price down on a piece of paper. It was ten thousand, five hundred rupiah. Adrian pulled out a ten thousand note and handed it to him with the words, "My last price."

"Okay," said the man who was secretly delighted at the profit he had made. The shorts had cost him a thousand rupiah each.

The yard outside was muddy and crowded with tourists who had become bored with staying indoors and had taken advantage of the pause in the rain to do some shopping. Everywhere people were haggling over prices. It seemed to take longer to settle on a price than to choose the item in the first place.

Adrian ambled slowly along the lane to the big square in the middle of the market. It was a hive of activity and noise. *Bemo* drivers were calling out and honking their horns for business; police in rather wet khaki uniforms with white leather holsters were blowing their whistles continuously in a futile attempt to control the *bemos* and motor bikes that were whizzing off in all directions and skidding in the mud. There were hungry looking pi dogs and a few stray hens that were flicking mud up on to their wet feathers as they strutted between the legs of the tourists and the touts.

Adrian bought a leather hat, some sunglasses and an exotically painted cane opium pipe complete with clay bowl and ivory mouthpiece. The loudest stall in the market was selling bootleg cassette tapes for a dollar each. Two different songs were blaring out from two tape decks at the same time. He stopped and bought some tapes of the Doors, the Stones, J.J. Cale and Lou Reed. Then he stopped at a jewellery stall and began trying on some bangles. Some were mother-of-pearl, some copper and bronze, and others beaten native silver. The man and the girls behind the stall began admiring the green turtle ring on his finger. It was the one that his father had given him. They asked him to swap it for a bangle.

"No can do," he said.

"Two bangles?"

"No."

"Three?"

"It's not for sale. Or barter."

"Listen, sir, I give you ten bangles and three pairs of beads for your ring."

"No, I don't want to sell it."

"How long have you had it?"

"It's been in my family for forty years."

"Then you must be tired of it by now. Don't you want to look at something different for a change?"

"No."

The man tried another tack. He pointed at the three young ladies who were helping him behind the counter. They all smiled sweetly. Then he leaned across to Adrian and spoke to him in a low and confidential tone. Adrian could see that he was going to up the bidding.

"You may have the bangles, the beads and any one of my girls for the night if you trade your beautiful ring."

Adrian smiled. "The ring is not for sale." The man knew that everything had a price and that Adrian was just being clever in order to raise the stakes to the highest possible level.

"Well, sir," said the man. "I shall now give you my last price. You may have all three girls for the night. Not 'short time' but all night."

Adrian paused for a moment. He remembered how his father had kept the ring all through the War. Through prison camp, hunger and despair.

"Ah," thought the man in eager anticipation. "He is going to accept."

"No," said Adrian. "I've got a better idea. You let me have the girls anyway and I keep the ring."

"What? Are you crazy?" said the man as Adrian walked away laughing.

He was approached by a boy of about fourteen who offered to carry his parcels for him.

"For how much?" asked Adrian.

"You decide, sir. I know that you will not cheat me."

His manner was irresistible so Adrian handed him two of his plastic shopping bags and the boy walked alongside him. He told Adrian that he had been to the school in his village and had now come down to Kuta to try to earn some money and learn English.

"That is why I like talking to people like you. I can practise my English and learn more words from what you say. To make good money it is necessary to speak English."

Not only did he carry the parcels but he also directed Adrian to stalls in the back alleys of the market where the prices were cheaper. Adrian was fascinated by a double stall that was piled high with carved wooden jewellery boxes and cassette containers. They were all beautifully sculpted out of teak. The dark wood was highly polished and glistened in the light of the three kerosene lamps that were hanging from the canvas roof. The insides of the boxes were divided into compartments; some were lined with fine silk and others with tortoise shell and mother-of-pearl. There were separate places for rings and earrings and brooches and necklaces. When their hinged lids were raised some of them played music.

Adrian immediately thought of his mother's sterling silver engraved jewel box which was one of the few heirlooms that her family had been able to sneak out of Russia when they fled the communists. It was quite a bit smaller than the ones that were now before his eyes. He knew that his mother had far more pieces of jewellery than could fit into the fine velvet lined casket on her dressing table so he decided to buy one from the stall and send it to her as a present. He chose a delicately carved oblong chest with mother-of-pearl inlay. It was lined with red silk and he could easily imagine it filled with his mother's silver and diamonds.

"For your girlfriend?" asked the lady behind the counter which was just a slab of wood on two trestles.

"No, for my mother," he replied.

"Ah, for your mother. Yes, I know. But what about your father? He very sad if he not get present too."

"That's a point," thought Adrian.

"Does father smoke cigars?"

"All the time."

"Well, maybe we have just the thing for him."

She went to a shelf at the back of the "shop" and pulled down the most beautifully carved object that Adrian had ever seen. It was a turtle carved out of teak. There was mother-of-pearl on its nose and two emeralds for its eyes. It stood an inch off the ground on its short, lightly sculpted legs. The exquisitely carved wooden shell lifted up on a hinge to reveal several compartments inside for laying out the cigars.

Adrian looked at it for a few moments and the woman

stared at him hoping for a positive reaction. "It's in the shape of a turtle," he said to himself. "Just like the ring that he gave me. So I can give him the box as a return gift." He then remembered that the desk in his father's study was made out of Burmese teak and he began to imagine the beautiful cigar case resting on the top of the big desk. And his father drawing a cigar from it as he sat there marking the papers of his students and dreaming of the Elizabethan stage.

Adrian looked up at the lady and smiled. "Yes, how much?" he asked enthusiastically.

"Not finished yet."

"What do you mean?"

"Cannot send box empty. Bad spirit might get inside and stay there. Must fill with cigars." She pulled out a couple of boxes of fine panatellas that were individually packed and began to lay them out inside the box. Adrian watched as her tiny fingers deftly stacked them without leaving any spare space for possible bad spirits.

"*Terima kasih*," he said. "Now how much is all that?"

The lady held up the palm of her hand like a traffic policeman at an intersection. "Not finished yet."

"Yes. Finished. That's all I want."

"Your girlfriend will be very angry that you spend all this money on others and nothing on her. What do you want for girlfriend?"

"No girlfriend at the moment," replied Adrian with a smile.

"Then I be your girlfriend," she giggled. "And then you can buy me a present."

"Not to-day," he smiled as he opened the bargaining process.

"It doesn't matter," thought the lady as she put the money in the drawer. "He has paid more than double the amount that I would have accepted. Eee! It is my lucky day."

When Adrian and his boy porter returned to the main

87

square they were accosted by a beggar woman. She was dressed in shabby cotton clothing and had a baby in a bag that was slung over her back. When she saw Adrian and his porter with all the bags she assumed that he must have plenty of money to have bought so many things and so would not be averse to handing a few more rupiah to a poor beggar. She shuffled up to him with a plaintive look on her face. One hand was out in front — palm upturned — to receive the money and the other was pointing to the baby who was sound asleep and looked as healthy and well fed as any other.

Adrian had never seen a beggar before and was more surprised than sympathetic. The boy carrying his parcels had ignored her and kept on walking. However, when he noticed that Adrian had stopped he looked round to see what was happening. He was standing behind the woman's back. He saw Adrian look at him as if for guidance. The boy slowly shook his head and mouthed the word "No". Adrian smiled at the woman and walked on. She then went over to accost the next passer-by. An elderly Englishman walked past the other way. "Quite right," he said to Adrian in a crisp tone. "It's different in Calcutta but there's no poverty on this island and certainly no one needs to go a-begging."

A few yards further on the boy spoke up. "That woman is bad. She is from the lowest caste on the island. She has plenty of money because she steals it from the tourists. If you give her money she will ask for more next time. You were right to say 'No'."

Over the next few weeks Adrian saw the same woman many times. Always in the same rags and with the decoy baby slung over her shoulder. She was the only beggar that he saw all the time he was in Bali.

Finally they returned to where his bike was parked. Adrian paid the boy a thousand rupiah. The lad smiled profusely, shook Adrian by the hand and said that he hoped to have the honour of carrying his parcels another day. "And, sir, thank-you for letting me learn my English from you."

"No trouble," said Adrian as he started the bike and roared off through the mud.

When he arrived back at the cottage he could hear a lot of noise and cheering coming from the wide verandah in front of the uncle's house. He looked over and saw a big group of Balinese sitting on the floor watching a portable television set. "No doubt another one of the worldly goods provided by the family jim," he thought with more than a little cynicism. One of them called out to him to come and join them.

He dumped his parcels in his own cottage and went across to see what all the noise and excitement was about. On the screen was a boxing match between the Indonesian champion and the leading boxer from Thailand. Every time the Indonesian scored a punch they all cheered. When things went the other way there were howls of disappointment. Some of them were praying and asking the spirits to enter into the body of the Indonesian so as to give him more power and strength. The gods must have heard because a few rounds later the Indonesian battered the Thai into a corner and pushed him down for a knock-out win. The Balinese were ecstatic. They laughed and jumped up and down and made a great din.

"The gods were powerful to-night. And very kind to our man," one of them beamed.

They passed around some coconut wine and poured a glass for Adrian. Then the women of the house began to serve some food. They brought out some big banana leaves and handed them to the men who were sitting on the verandah. Each leaf was filled with a meal of warm fried rice with chicken and the men all started eating it with their fingers. One of the ladies bent her knees gracefully and placed a banana leaf in front of Adrian. He picked the food up with his fingers and washed it down with another glass of coconut wine.

The next day was the same. Rain, no sun and no surf. Adrian spent most of the time playing backgammon with Thierry and listening to the stereo. That night they ate at Manoel's. "It is always spotlessly clean," said Nicole. "Manoel is an old Portuguese gentleman who always looks after us so well even though he asks everyone lots of questions." Adrian soon understood what she meant.

He looked up and saw a thin, gaunt, grey-haired gentleman walking across to their table with a bottle of Mateus and three glasses. He could detect both kindness and nobility in the man's face. "He always starts us off with some wine on the house," whispered Thierry.

"Ah, good evening," said Manoel. "I see that you have at last brought your Australian friend to meet me. He has already been here a week and yet this is the first time that you have seen fit to bring him into the finest restaurant in Legian."

"Who told you that he has been here a week?" asked Thierry in surprise.

"You did," laughed Manoel, "when you were here for lunch yesterday."

They introduced Adrian and Manoel immediately asked him how long he was staying, was it his first trip to the island, did he come on his own, what was his job in Australia and a host of other questions. "Please treat my restaurant as your home away from home," he said as he turned to go out to the kitchen and give their orders to the chef.

When the rice dishes were brought out the waiter lifted them high in the air before placing them gently on the table. Thierry explained how rice was regarded as a sacred plant and was revered as a god. "Therefore it must be presented from a higher position than those who are going to eat it. They believe that rice is a spirit that enters into the people who eat it."

"Well, it's certainly going to enter me — straight down

the throat," laughed Adrian as he picked up his fork and began eating.

Although he was patently Portuguese Manoel spoke perfect English with an accent that was somewhere between public school and BBC. It made Adrian feel humble. "He speaks better English than I do and yet it is my native language and not his."

"That is sometimes so," replied Thierry.

"I wonder where he learnt it," asked a curious Adrian.

"Why don't you ask him?" said Nicole.

"No, it might sound condescending, don't you think?"

"Oh, come on," said Thierry. "You want to know so we'll ask him. After all, he's always asking everyone else questions." He turned his head towards the proprietor. "Hey, Manoel. Adrian says that you speak better English than the Queen. Where did you learn it?"

Manoel came over and sat down at their table. "You embarrass me with such compliments. But I shall tell you. After I left the university in Lisbon I went to Cambridge to write my history thesis on the Duke of Wellington's campaigns in Spain and Portugal. It was his great victory at Torres Vedras that forced the French to evacuate Portugal in 1811. That was before Waterloo. Of course, I had been learning English since I was eight years old."

"How long were you at Cambridge?" asked Adrian.

"Two years. The two happiest years of my life. I was studying things that interested me. I was mixing with cultured and refined people and nearly every week-end I was invited into the country to stay with hospitable families with beautiful daughters. Ah yes, Cambridge in the 1930s was my idea of heaven."

"It must have been perfect," said Thierry.

"No, not perfect. There is always a dark side to these things. Poor England was going through a bad time. She had no leadership and when there is no leadership there is no energy and no morale. But at Cambridge we were insulated from the worst of it. My main memories are very happy ones – the magnificent May Balls and long summer evenings punting on the Cam or just cycling through the beautiful lanes of the Fen country. It all seemed so peaceful in those days before the outbreak of the Second World War." There was moisture in his eyes.

"What other languages do you speak?" asked Nicole.

"Spanish and French and, of course, Indonesian." He looked across the restaurant. "*Hati hati*," he called sharply to one of the waiters who looked as if he was about to drop a plate of hot soup on the coiffure of a large lady at Table Number Three. "Excuse me, I must attend to my customers. That boy is not concentrating and all these people who have just sat down are waiting for their meals."

"He's not very happy with Ketut, is he?" said Nicole.

"Why is everyone in Bali called Ketut or Wayan?" asked Adrian.

"They're not," replied Thierry. "Only about half of them."

"What do you mean?"

"It's true," said Nicole. "The first born child in a Sudra family – which constitutes about ninety per cent of the population – is always named 'Wayan' – regardless of its sex. The second child is called 'Madé', the third 'Nyoman' and the fourth 'Ketut'. Any children born after the first four are named in the same sequence – 'Wayan, Madé, Nyoman and Ketut.' Then for the ninth, tenth, eleventh and twelfth children the process is repeated and so on *ad infinitum*. Thus, apart from the high caste people, every Balinese has one of four names which he shares with about a million others on the island. Of course, their surnames are different."

"Well, I suppose it solves the problem of choosing a name," said Adrian.

"Yes, it is all pre-ordained. Like so many other aspects

of their lives."

Adrian looked across at the cane magazine rack that was overflowing with well thumbed magazines and newspapers. He reached across and pulled out a Straits Times from Singapore. He looked at the date. "Well, that's no good," he laughed. "April the fifteenth. A week before I came here."

"After you have been here a while you begin to feel that the rest of the world doesn't matter," said Thierry. "We started off buying a Jakarta Post each day but then we stopped. We lost interest in the news. Sometimes we pick up an old copy of the Herald Tribune or Straits Times when we are in here but it is only to fill in time while we wait for our meal. It is funny, you know, but things like elections, the Common Market and terrorism seem so far away as to be quite insignificant. You tend to see it all in a different perspective. So many self-important men in the West all running around with frowns on their faces and giving themselves heart attacks and yet here it is possible to live such a simple and relaxing life. But, of course, it doesn't last. Soon we must return to Paris and rejoin the 'rat race'. That is such a good word for it." He started laughing. "The Balinese feel the same way. They believe that Bali is the only place that matters in the whole world. To them all other nations are irrelevant. Bali is the peaceful centre of their universe. It stands out of the ocean like a beautiful and proud cock. And the mountain ridge across the middle of the island is the bird's backbone."

Nicole took up from where Thierry left off. "But although they are a bit chauvinist about their island they don't mind sharing it with tourists. It seems they know that they live in a paradise and are quite happy for others to come here and enjoy it too. They get along well with Europeans. Maybe it is because we come as holiday makers to have a good time and laugh with them and they know that we are not colonisers come to push them around. Sometimes they must think we're crazy. I think that is why they like us. I know they think that Thierry is crazy — like one of their strange spirits. But they like him because he makes them laugh."

"But what about all the tourist dollars?" asked Adrian. "Doesn't the influx of money have a corrupting influence on a simple society?"

"Yes, of course. But it's not too bad. They really are quite sensible. All the tourist development is confined to this one small corner of the island. That way they can preserve their traditional culture and also benefit from the tourist money. It gives them the best of both worlds. The Bali Beach Hotel over at Sanur is the only high rise structure on the whole island. All other buildings are no higher than a coconut tree — about ten metres."

They ran back through the mud and rain to Thierry's cottage where they towelled themselves down and had some coffee. As they sat on the verandah watching the big tropical raindrops Thierry began to tell Adrian what he knew about Manoel. "He is a bit of a mystery man. All that is known about him for certain is that he is civilised, intelligent and Portuguese. Some people are suspicious of him — jealous maybe — because he is more or less the only European who is allowed to live in Bali and operate a business. It is very hard to do that. The normal rule is that they will let a European lady live here if she is married to a Balinese. But it does not work the other way round. If a Balinese girl marries a non-Balinese — for example a European or a Moslem from Java — she loses face in her community. She no longer has the right to call herself Balinese. If she marries a European man he is not allowed to reside in Bali permanently. He can come here for a few months but then he must leave for a period. Two or three months. Maybe longer. Usually such a man will have a business here with his wife — a bar or a restaurant — which means that she would have to stay here and look after it on her own until he comes back. It is not at all satisfactory.

Of course, the man often just goes to Hong Kong and takes up with a Chinese girl for a few months or to Bangkok. So it is probably good for the man but not for his Balinese wife.

That is why people are so suspicious of Manoel. He does not have a Balinese wife or even a girlfriend and yet he is allowed to stay here all the time. Of course, he is friendly with the police and some say with the Governor of Bali himself. It is sometimes said that he is homosexual but I don't believe it. Although he has many Balinese boys working for him in the restaurant I have never seen or heard anything to suggest that he is that way inclined. Others say that he is a police informer and that he is allowed to stay here in return for giving the police information about drugs. But I do not believe that either. People are just envious of his idyllic life-style and wish that they too could stay in this paradise forever. They know they can't so they spread untrue rumours about those who can. People are just so jealous and the more fortunate a man is the more spiteful will be the comments. It has always been so. I am sure that Manoel would have a very good and no doubt interesting reason for being allowed to stay.

He is probably one of those many colonials who have been washed up on the beach after the dismemberment of the European empires. So used to the exotic style of a colonial life that they could not bear to return to the cold of Europe and be slotted into a semi-detached house and given a pension number, a tax number, an identity card number and all the other uninspiring indicia of our new social welfare states. Manoel is an individualist. He is slightly eccentric and set in his ways. Every day he carries out regular activities at a leisurely pace. That is the mark of a civilised man. He has breakfast, reads the Straits Times, goes for a swim, jogs along the beach, presides over the restaurant at lunch time, then a siesta, another swim, prepares the restaurant for dinner, has pre-prandial drinks with his regulars, dines and then goes to bed about midnight. How could he ever go back to a drab life in Portugal? Especially now that the Socialists have taken over."

The rain eased off for a moment so Adrian decided to dash back to his own cottage and go to bed. "Maybe it will be different to-morrow," was his last thought as he fell asleep.

But it wasn't. Although the rain had stopped in the early hours of the morning the muddy sea was still as calm and lifeless as a millpond. And the sun was still well covered by clouds. "I can't surf and I'm sick of hanging around Kuta and Legian looking at all the tourists trudging through the mud in their raincoats," he thought.

He asked Thierry and Nicole if they wanted to go for a ride up into the mountains on the trail bikes. "No way," said Thierry. "Not in this weather. It might rain again and I do not want to spend the night bogged down in some remote village with no electric light and no cold beer and having to eat just a tiny bowl of rice for dinner."

"These roads are not too bad," said Adrian. "I have often ridden through far softer tracks in Australia. Some of the secret spots where I surf at home can be reached only by motor bike and often the tracks disappear altogether."

"Oh yes, I know that in Australia you have dirt roads. So you would be at home on these muddy tracks. But I'm not. What will happen if I fall off? I do not wish to come back to Legian wearing a suit of mud."

"We could always hose you down. It would be like cleaning a statue," laughed Adrian.

"No, I am quite happy to stay here with Nicole and wait until the sun shines again."

"All right," said Adrian. "I'll go by myself. It'll be an adventure."

"Where will you go?"

"Don't know yet."

"Well, wherever it is the roads are going to be difficult

and you will probably fall off. I shall keep the hose ready for when you return."

Back at his own cottage Adrian pulled out a map of Bali and studied it. The only part of the island with which he was familiar was the Uluwatu peninsula. The rest was unknown territory. All he knew was that the Balinese gods lived up in the mountains which formed a ridge across the middle of the island. "I wonder if I'll meet any of them if I get high enough," he laughed to himself.

He didn't know where he was going to go when he pulled up outside Manoel's for some coffee and chocolate cake. He sat down by the magazine rack and picked up an ancient copy of "Rolling Stone". Manoel wasn't there but the waitress came over and put his cake and coffee down on the low cane table. As he reached over to pick up the coffee she noticed the impressive jade turtle shaped ring on his finger. She smiled demurely. A few minutes later the head boy came out and smiled broadly. "Excuse me, Mister Adrian, but the waitress girl would like to have a closer look at your beautiful ring. She says that it is most unusual but is too shy to ask you herself."

"Of course," smiled Adrian. The girl came over and knelt down on the floor beside him. He took it off and showed it to her. Knowing the universal fascination of women for jewellery he slipped it on her finger. She was wearing a green dress and she derived considerable pleasure from putting her hand over the dress and highlighting the similarity of colour.

"Where did you get it?" she asked.

"It was given to my father when he was here many years ago. He gave it to me just before I left Australia."

"It is from Bali?" she asked in surprise.

"Yes, but from a long time ago." She didn't understand English very well and the double meaning of the words "long time" momentarily confused her.

"You know," said Wayan, the head boy, "it is said that

the whole island of Bali rests on the back of a giant turtle and that when it groans we hear the thunder and when it moves we feel the earthquake. Some even say that when it cries we feel the rain."

"I think that your ring is very beautiful," said the girl as she dropped it back into the palm of his hand.

They left him to finish his cake. He put Rolling Stone back into the magazine rack with all the other out of date editions of Paris Match, Time, Vogue and Punch. He began to think of the ring and of the man who gave it to his father. "'Gedé' was his name," he remembered. He wondered if he would still be alive. His father had said that he would probably be dead by now. "Well, there is only one way to find out, I suppose. After all, I was trying to think of somewhere to go to-day to get rid of the old 'Bali blues'."

He rode back to the cottage to have a look at the address that his father had written on the back of his visiting card. He checked the name of the village — Semang — against his tourist map but couldn't locate it. He remembered his father saying only that it was up in the mountains. He went to the police station and showed them the card. They produced a much more detailed map with an index and they eventually found it. "Just a small village," they said. "Why you go there? Friends?"

"Yes", he replied, "I am going to visit the headman."

"Ah, you know the *klian*? Now we understand because it is not a place where tourists go. No disco," they laughed. One of the officers drew a map for him with roads and turnings and the names of villages. They told him that it would take about three hours to get there, taking into account the condition of the roads.

The journey was not nearly as bad as he expected. It had not rained all morning and, once he got above the low lying coastal plain, the road became drier and on a couple of occasions the sun even managed to peep through the thick clouds.

After he left behind the noisy and disorderly traffic of Kuta and Denpasar he had the road more or less to himself. Just a few old trucks, bicycles, horse carts and pedestrians who turned and waved as he sped past. He felt free and independent as he roared past the paddy fields with his hair flying in all directions. "Thank God I don't have to have my head imprisoned in one of those accursed crash helmets," he thought. "This is the only way to ride a trail bike!" With some fresh mud on his bare legs he was beginning to get the feel of the Balinese countryside which, he acknowledged, was a very different and more simple world than the noise, the hassle and the crowds around Kuta. "These people must think we're mad down there," he thought. "Kuta is like a half-way house between East and West but to the Balinese it must seem like New York City."

The countryside through which he was travelling seemed ancient and timeless. Slow moving men and women working knee deep in the flooded rice-fields were as much a part of the landscape as the rocks and the trees. Patient men plodded behind big, black buffaloes that were turning over the soft ground with primitive wooden ploughs. They had been tilling the same soil in the same way for thousands of years.

The first people of Bali — the descendants of whom live on in a few remote and isolated villages and are known as "Bali Aga" — came originally from the south of China some five thousand years ago. They brought with them their traditional rice culture, their water buffaloes, their animist beliefs and their worship of ancestors. They even used to eat the corpses of their dead relatives so as to absorb their magical powers. Then, about two thousand years ago, the Indians arrived from across the Bay of Bengal. They introduced the Hindu religion and established themselves as a ruling class over the original inhabitants.

Hinduism became the dominant creed and the island remained unaffected by the rise of Islam in the thirteenth century when it was spread through the rest of the Indonesian archipelago by Moslem traders from the Middle East. By the end of the fifteenth century the island of Java had converted to Islam and its Hindu ruling class fled across the water to Bali along with their priests, their art and their music.

As he turned round a sharp bend Adrian noticed that the clouds were parting to let the sun through. Raindrops were still fresh on the leaves and he could see small mountains of steam rising from the hot ground. Browns cows were grazing in the fields with big wooden bells around their necks. And he could see herons and bats and deep red dragon-flies. And a family of monkeys on the side of the road.

He wondered if his father had seen the same sights when he had travelled up to the village in 1942. Or on his way down again — as a prisoner in a Japanese jeep. "Poor chaps," he said to himself. He reflected on his own good fortune at being born into a generation that didn't have to go to war. "Thank God for the nuclear deterrent," he thought. "And our alliance with the good old U.S. of A. That frightens off the over-populated countries of Asia as they look with envy at Australia with all its mineral riches, its abundance of land and small population."

Other thoughts passed through his mind. Like how he was going to introduce himself to old Klian. That is, if he was still alive. "Maybe it is a mistake to come here and remind them of all those unpleasant things that happened so many years ago," he thought. "Perhaps I should let sleeping dogs lie."

He was considering whether to turn back and just put the day down to a pleasant and interesting ride through the countryside when he came to a signpost of a small town the name of which he recognised from the map that the police had drawn. He pulled up outside a *warung* and went in for a glass of mango juice. The map showed that he was one village away from his objective. He looked down at his legs and saw that they were covered with rapidly hardening mud.

He carried on. The road crossed a small stream where he stopped to wash his legs. The water was cool and pleasing so he stripped off and immersed himself in the water to wash all the sweat and dust out of his pores. Near the edge of the stream was a small shrine that was dedicated to the god of water. Adrian wiped himself down with his spare T-shirt and looked in the mirror of the motor bike and combed his hair.

The road became narrower. It was just wide enough for a small truck. There was a big coconut plantation on one side and flooded rice fields on the other. Small groups of people were working in the fields and some of them looked up and waved as he roared past. From the height of the road he could look down on their wide coolie hats. The dusty track led uphill to a small settlement that was surrounded by a six foot stone wall with thatch on top. He passed through an open wooden entrance gate and into the single street which bisected the village. He rode on a few hundred yards and then stopped beside a big open space in the middle of the settlement.

On one side of the green was a cockfighting ring and on the other a small market place with a couple of *warungs* and some stalls selling vegetables. Beyond the wide open space were seemingly endless stone walls broken here and there by narrow lanes. Behind the walls could be seen the thatched roofs of the houses with smoke rising from their cooking fires. In the farthest corner of the green he could see a huge banyan tree and, beyond it, a temple. A heavy and oppressive humidity seemed to hang over the place. A few old men were sitting in the shade of some gently swinging banana trees while they kept a careful eye on their valuable fighting cocks. Some of the birds were red, some brown and others pure white. Each was inside its own round, bell-shaped bamboo cage that stood about two and a half feet above the ground. A few yards further along a couple of black pigs with huge stomachs were having a feed out of a pile of rubbish.

At the sound of the motor bike several of the women and children ran out to see what was happening. The children laughed but most of the women just stared in surprise. Adrian realised that a visit by a white man on a motor bike must be a rare occurrence.

When he brought the machine to a halt outside the open front of one of the *warungs* about a dozen people formed a circle around the bike. Two of the apparently lifeless old men guarding their cocks made the effort to stand up and come over to see what all the commotion was about. So did several of the bare breasted women and some laughing naked toddlers. "*Selamat pagi,*" they began to shout. Adrian got off his bike and stood to his full six feet. "*Selamat pagi,*" he smiled. They all cheered. Then they began discussing among themselves in Balinese whether or not he was a god. He was at least a foot taller than anyone else they had ever seen. One of them asked very loudly, "*Siapa namamu?*"

"Adrian," he replied.

They attempted the three syllable word among themselves. "Ay - dree - un", they laughed. He read out Klian's name from the card. Several knowledgeable heads began to nod. One of the men extended his hand with the palm facing down and fingers pointing to the ground which was the Balinese way of beckoning. "*Lewat sini,*" he said.

He took Adrian along to a narrow lane which led into another but smaller open space. At the far end was a long grey stone wall which was broken in the middle by an ornamental arched gateway. On one side was a shrine for offerings. Inside the wall a long straight path led to a brick and stucco house with a heavily thatched roof. There were several outhouses dispersed at the sides and rear of the main house. The grounds consisted of closely clipped lawns with clumps of flowering hibiscus, white petalled frangipani and unusual looking mango trees covered in pink blossoms. There were two high fig trees at the rear of the property and a row of coconut palms down one side.

A couple of long tailed monkeys were playing on the lawn and huge colourful butterflies with bird like wings were fluttering around the mango blossoms. On one side of the path leading to the house was a large pond that was overflowing with water lilies. Bare breasted women were clipping the grass with hand cutters and sweeping the front verandah. They worked so silently and effortlessly and seemed to be as much a part of the environment as the flowers and the butterflies. The compound was surrounded on all sides by a long stone wall. It was about five feet high and was designed to keep out the evil spirits as well as the more tangible species like wild boars and pi dogs. Adrian was struck by the privacy that the house and grounds enjoyed inside the wall. "A whole world of its own," he thought.

He could see an old man reclining on a sofa on the shaded verandah. He was wearing a blood red sarong and old leather sandals. Adrian's guide went up and spoke to him. The man rose from the sofa and walked along the path to greet the visitor. He carried a cane walking stick but had a straight and dignified gait. "*Selamat sore,*" he said. And then in English, "Who is it that you wish to see?"

"Klian."

"I am he."

"My name is Adrian Drake. I am from Australia. My father, Austin, asked me to call on you and give you his greetings. He said that you were very kind to him and his friends when the Japanese came. They stayed with you until they were taken away in trucks as prisoners."

The old man spat on the ground in contempt when Adrian mentioned the word "Japanese". Then he extended his wrinkled right hand to greet the visitor.

"Mister Ostin is your father?" he asked. Adrian could see that he was trying to remember back nearly forty years.

"Yes, and he asked me to thank you for all your kindnesses to him and his friends."

"Where is Ostin?" he asked as he looked over Adrian's shoulder into the distance.

"Oh, I'm sorry. I did not make myself clear. Austin is in Australia. It is only me who is visiting Bali."

The man scarcely concealed his disappointment. "Ostin — good man. Also his friends. They were very funny. Many jokes. They made us laugh. Then Japanese come. Bang! Bang! Japanese — very bad people. They burned some buildings in our village." He pointed with his right hand in the direction of the temple and explained how that building and his own house were put to the torch by the invaders as a punishment for allowing the Australians to stay there. The temple, he said, was rebuilt after the War and fortunately the great banyan tree alongside it escaped the fire.

"Where you stay?" he asked.

"I am staying down at Legian near the sea." A slight expression of fear showed in the old man's face.

"*Kelod*," he said, pointing in the direction of the sea. "It is not good near the sea. Better up here in the mountains where the gods live. There are too many demons in the sea and too many bad things happen down there."

By now quite a few villagers had gathered in the *klian's* garden to view the newcomer and witness his conversation with the village headman. "You should stay up here with us for a while," he said. "Like your father did. He and the others were very happy here until the Japanese came and took them away. We always wondered if the Japanese soldiers killed them or did the gods protect them?"

"The gods looked after them for a while," said Adrian, "but then one of them was eaten by the Japanese soldiers. The others survived."

"That does not surprise me," said Klian. "The Japanese did many terrible things to our people also. Here in Bali we were occupied mainly by the Japanese Navy and, because they had so many other duties, they were not as cruel as their army was over in Java. But they forcibly took away many of our young girls and shipped them to Burma to work as prostitutes in their camp brothels. None of them ever returned. Thousands of our men were also sent to Burma to work as slave labourers and they died like flies. And the Japanese took all our gold and jewellery to help pay for the war. Very bad people."

He saw Klian looking at him — at his hand. Then he heard him say, "I see that you still have the turtle ring that we gave to Mister Ostin. That is good because we still have the flag that he gave us. When the Japanese set fire to the temple it was one of the few things that was saved. The *permangku* grabbed it, put it under his robes and ran off with it. When the new temple was built after the War the flag was returned and has hung there ever since. It has now acquired magical powers."

The old man pointed to the verandah. "Come now, we must have some tea," he said. He called out to a couple of the women in Balinese and they ran off to the cookhouse to prepare the tea.

Adrian followed him on to the wide verandah. The thatch roof fell down low to shade it from the hot sun. The thatch was held up by several deeply carved wooden pillars that were well faded on their outer sides. The carvings depicted flower and fruit designs as well as gods with strange heads and many limbs.

Klian called out a few more instructions and Adrian saw two other women putting a mattress into one of the huts at the side of the house. "You may sleep out in that building," he said to Adrian. "We are greatly honoured to have you just as we considered it a privilege to look after your father and the others."

"Oh, I didn't intend to stay the night. I only came to pay my respects and I plan to ride back to Legian later on."

"It is a great honour for the people of our village to have you. I hope that you can stay a long time."

Adrian came to realise that it would be singularly ungracious if he were to go back that night. He didn't want to stay out of the surf for too long but realised that there might not be any waves for several days. Besides, he had left his "Bali blues" mood down at the coast. His ride through the countryside had cheered him up. "If my poor old man and his mates could stick it out up here working in the rice fields all those months then I should be prepared to spend a bit more time up here than I anticipated," he thought. "These people seem very kind and I'm sure I'll find it interesting." He smiled at Klian and said that he would be greatly honoured to accept their hospitality only so long as it did not put them to any inconvenience.

"It is a very great honour for the village," replied the *klian* with moisture in his eyes.

One of the women came out to the verandah and placed the tea on a low table. She poured it into two china cups. Adrian was struck by the deference and politeness that they showed to the old man. They all addressed him as "Klian" — the highest form of respect in the village. Because he was a high caste Satria the other villagers, who were lower caste Sudras, spoke to him in a refined high Balinese language that was different from what they used in ordinary speech. Each caste group had its own code of behaviour and the whole society was as neatly structured as the class system of old England. In the matter of manners, praying, eating or even posture the upper caste Brahmanas, Satrias and Wesias could be distinguished from those of lesser rank. However, the Balinese caste system, although derived from that of India, was never so cruel and rigid.

106

Adrian knew from his father that he was speaking to a noble and honourable man who had willingly taken a great risk to shelter them and who had been punished by the Japanese for doing so. As he sat there listening to Klian he became more and more aware of his wisdom, his graciousness and his exquisite manners.

Klian had been born a couple of years before the great *puputan* of 1906. Every society has suffered some convulsive experience that has left a lasting impact on its soul. Just as France had its Revolution, America its Civil War, England the Reformation, Scotland its Highland Clearances and Ireland the potato famine, so too did Bali experience its *puputan* in the years between 1906 and 1908.

The origin of the *puputan* lay in the events of the previous century. The first European to discover Bali was the Dutch sea captain, Cornelius de Houtman, in 1597. While his sailors jumped ship and made off with the Balinese girls de Houtman struck up a friendship with the Raja of Klungklung, the leader of one of the island's nine kingdoms. The Raja enjoyed life with his two hundred wives, a chariot pulled by white buffaloes and a retinue that included fifty court dwarves whose bodies had been deliberately bent to resemble the arched handle of the *kris*.

However, in spite of this early contact, Bali was one of the last islands of the East Indies to be colonised by the seafaring Dutch. Without any deep water port and fortified by steep cliffs and coral reefs, the island was able to keep at bay the trading ships of the Dutch East India Company that penetrated all the other large islands and took their spices and textiles back to Europe.

Well ensconced in Java by the early nineteenth century, the Dutch sent their first permanent representative to Bali in 1826. He established himself at Kuta where he lived the magical life of an eastern prince. The island at that time was still divided into nine warring kingdoms which, like the clans in the Scottish Highlands, sometimes joined forces against a common foe but more often fought among themselves.

In the 1890s the Dutch managed to annex five of the nine kingdoms. Then, in 1906, came the *puputan* when the Dutch landed a large military force on the beach at Sanur. The ensuing fight was a classic colonial confrontation with the guns of the sophisticated Dutch conquering the spears and *krises* of the natives.

The battle took place in front of the main gate of the royal palace of Badung on the site of the present town of Denpasar. As the Dutch columns approached his palace the Raja, dressed in his white cremation clothes, led his people out of the palace in a long tragic procession. They all wore their best jewels and were each armed with two gold *krises* and a spear. At a distance of about a hundred yards from the Dutch lines the procession halted and a deathly silence prevailed. Then, at a given signal, a priest plunged a *kris* through the Raja's heart. The Balinese immediately went into a trance and began stabbing themselves and each other in a massive and spontaneous orgy of blood. Some *krises* and lances were thrown at the Dutch soldiers who responded with a barrage of rifle and artillery fire. At the end of the day there were three and a half thousand corpses piled on the dusty, blood spattered road in front of the palace gates.

It was another two years before the Dutch succeeded in capturing the island's remaining kingdoms. These tragic years saw the death of Bali as a separate and sovereign island. Henceforth its Hindu culture would be merely a small part of the East Indian colony of the Christian Dutch and, later, of an Islamic dominated Republic of Indonesia. In the Balinese story these terrible events were like the death of Christ — all things led up to them and all things led away from them. They were called the *"puputan"* — the release of all the forces of evil and destruction at one time.

Among those killed outside the gates of the Raja's

palace was Klian's father. And so, from an early age, Klian had been brought up by the rest of his family to be the head of the village of Semang — a position that had been held by the family for many generations.

Klian had fond memories of his early years and the tranquil and settled life of the village. Although the Balinese were no longer masters of their own destiny they were resilient enough to maintain their religion and culture within the context of the Dutch colonial empire.

The Dutch grew to be very fond of Bali and its people and it wasn't long before a posting to the island was regarded as the most desirable job in the colonial service of the Netherlands. Dutch administrators and traders began to spend their holidays in the small bamboo huts alongside the beaches at Kuta and Sanur. Larger and more comfortable cottages were built as more and more discriminating travellers came to savour the charm of the island and its people. The British came from Singapore and so too did the occasional artist, anthropologist, round-the-world sailor, beachcomber and well-heeled traveller — a Roosevelt here, a Guinness there and even Lady Clementine Churchill arrived in 1935 on Lord Moyne's yacht and took a pair of Bali doves back to Chartwell.

Klian had noticed how the orderly and pleasant life of Bali began to change during the rainy season of 1941-2. The tourists stopped coming and were replaced by soldiers — Dutch, British and Australian. Aeroplanes buzzed overhead while on the ground rifle carrying troops in camouflage uniforms cursed and swore as they tried to extract jeeps that had become stuck in the soft mud of the jungle tracks. The natives were forbidden to go to certain parts of the island — especially near the open coast where mines had been laid.

For some years Klian had been friendly with the local Dutch district officer as, being the *klian*, he often came into contact with him on a variety of matters. Pieter Crouzen was a big, red-faced man of about fifty with slightly balding hair. He had served as a colonial officer in Curacao, Java and Sumatra before he came to Bali. He had always been both friendly and fair to Klian and his family and the relationship between them was convivial and easygoing.

On the third Monday of February, 1942, Klian and two of the village elders made their way through the heavy rain to the district officer's house to ask him how long the road would be closed by the army as they wanted to use it to drive their cattle down to the lower fields. When they reached the house they found the Dutch officer packing his suitcase. The house itself was in a state of bedlam with the servants saying that there were many evil spirits around. Pieter took Klian into a room and informed him that he was leaving in a few minutes and going to Australia.

"When you come back?" asked Klian.

"Not for a long time. All the Dutch are leaving," he replied.

Klian thought back to the *puputan* and wondered at the strange ways of the white man who made such a great effort to capture Bali and who now seemed to be walking out of the most beautiful island in the world. "Why you all go? What's wrong with Bali?" asked Klian who felt that his island was being slighted.

Pieter leaned forward and lowered his voice. "Singapore has fallen. The Japanese are in the city killing the inhabitants. It won't be long before they are here."

The big Dutchman sat back in his chair and began to cry. All sorts of terrible things were tormenting his mind — his elderly parents back in Amsterdam who had been living under the Nazis for a year and a half, his favourite sister who was married to a Jewish tailor at The Hague, his wife whom he had sent to Australia a month earlier and whom he wondered if he would ever see again, and his only son who was serving on a Dutch warship that would soon be facing the sea and air forces of the apparently unstoppable Japanese. He thought of the friendly and smiling Balinese — like Klian standing in front of him — and their lovely, happy island and wondered what would come of it all. Would he ever see it again? "The whole bloody world is falling apart," he cried. "For us — for all of us — it is like the *puputan*."

Klian had never seen a white man weep before and he was amazed more than anything at the sight. "If Japanese so bad then I go to Australia too. And my family," said Klian.

"No can do, I'm afraid," replied Pieter with a terrible feeling of guilt. "We are meant to be here to protect these people," he thought, "and yet when real trouble comes along we run away and leave them to their fate." He could not look at Klian any longer. Overcome with both grief and guilt he said good-bye and stated that he would come back one day but it might not be for a long time.

As he drove off in his ancient Ford to the embarkation point at Singaraja he wondered how the Japanese would treat the natives. On the basis of their record with the Chinese and other peoples of Asia he could not be very hopeful. When all the Dutch civilians had departed there were only a few soldiers left to guard the island. After a couple of days they too climbed into some large motor boats and sailed off into the sunset.

Helpless and completely unarmed, the Balinese anxiously awaited their terrible and unknown fate. It was during this twilight period that Adrian's father and his two shipmates arrived on the island. For a few days an eerie atmosphere prevailed. On the surface everything appeared to be normal as the people went about their daily tasks of praying, catching fish and working in the rice fields. But underneath all this was a deep fear that permeated the air and disturbed their minds. The power of the demons could be felt everywhere. There were visible signs that the gods were angry. The rice farmers on the lower slopes of Mount Agung witnessed a terrible air battle in which twenty-seven Japanese Zeros destroyed with blazing fire half a dozen Dutch Air Force 'planes which fell into the jungle. From afar they heard the loud explosions of bombs and shells as the Battle of the Java Sea raged in all its fury. Pieter Crouzen's son went down with his ship, R.N.A. de Ruyter.

A few days later the arrogant and unpleasant Japanese sailors arrived and set themselves up as overlords of the island. The gentle and polite Balinese were horrified at their brutality and regarded them as the personification of the evil spirits of the nether world. Apart from their insensitivity and bad manners the invaders were not unduly cruel to the Balinese. They reserved their torture and worst atrocities for the small groups of Chinese traders and their families who had settled on the island over the years. Many of them were beheaded by the swords of sadistic Japanese officers and their heads were hung from trees and fence posts like *topeng* masks.

The Balinese came to believe that the Japs were demons who had to be appeased in much the same way that offerings had to be made to the evil spirits. The natives naturally did what they were told and they had to bow very low every time they passed a Japanese soldier or sailor. If they didn't they received a blow on the head from a rifle butt. While ostensibly obeying the Japanese they simultaneously prayed to the ancestors and gods to rid their island of its cruel and brutal invaders.

It was some years before the gods answered their prayers. Not until August, 1945, when the Japanese suffered their own "*puputan*" in the form of the atomic bombs that were dropped on Nagasaki and Hiroshima.

The Japanese surrendered to the British who duly handed Bali and the other islands back to the Dutch. In 1949 the Dutch eventually left and Bali found itself a part of the new Republic of Indonesia — a tiny Hindu island in a vast

Islamic sea.

Klian looked up at the setting sun and told Adrian that his grand-daughter would be returning just before dusk. "She has lived here with me since her father and mother were killed in the troubles in 1965." He was silent for a moment but there was no change of expression on his inscrutable face." I have been both father and mother to her and she has grown into a very beautiful young woman." He smiled with a kind of paternal pride. "She has been visiting the *klian* in another village. She will come back on the farm truck before dark."

He took Adrian inside his tidy and spacious house. There was a large living room with some fine woven mats on the wooden floorboards. Partitions of thin bamboo separated the sleeping rooms and rattan blinds substituted for doors. The high roof was held up by some sturdy wooden pillars.

Inside the big room Adrian noticed several cane chairs and tables. Klian explained how he owned a small plantation of rattan palms about a mile further up from the village. "When they are ready to be harvested the villagers go there and pull the vines off the trees. They are dragged down here by bullocks and we make them into things like walking sticks, baskets and tables and chairs. Sometimes the workers split them and weave them into seats." He lifted a bright red cushion off a chair and proudly showed the fine wicker surface that lay underneath. "You will see a lot of rattan tables and chairs in the houses of our village," he continued. "But the best pieces we make are put on the truck and sent down to an agent in Denpasar who exports them to Hong Kong. The money that he pays us is used for improvements in the village."

After showing him the main house the old man took Adrian outside. They looked into a mud hut where the women were cooking the evening meal. Another hut, elevated on stilts a couple of feet above the ground, served as a granary and storehouse and there were two guest huts; one

113

looked quite comfortable, the other less so. Klian pointed to the better one and told Adrian that he was to sleep there as the guest.

In the farthest corner of the compound in the direction of the mountains was the family shrine. Adrian could see the burning incense and fresh offerings of flowers and rice that had been placed in front of the stone figures of the various ancestral spirits. Ornate strips of palm leaf, which Klian referred to as *"lamaks"*, were hanging from the top and reached almost to the ground.

"That is the most important part of the house," he said as he pointed to the shrine with his rattan walking stick. "It is where we pray to the family gods and ancestors. It is situated closest to the mountains where the gods live. We call the direction of the mountains *'kaja'* as opposed to the sea where all the evil spirits are. That is *'kelod'*." A very slight look of fear and contempt was visible in his eyes. "We regard the whole compound like the body of a man. The shrine is the head, the rooms in the house where we sleep and live are the arms, the yard in front is the navel, the gate — the opening in the wall — represents the sexual organs and the kitchen and granary are the legs. The hole in the ground at the back where we burn the rubbish is the anus."

"Have you lived here all your life?" asked Adrian when they got back to the verandah.

"Yes," he replied. "As *klian* I am responsible for upholding the laws and customs of the village. Within the walls of the village we are more or less an independent community. Our main problem is asserting our traditional rights against the authorities. We would be very happy to be left alone. We do not like it when the police or army come here because we usually have to give them some money. However, because we are fairly isolated up here, they do not bother us very much."

"As the headman do you own all the surrounding land?"

asked Adrian who was beginning to see the *klian* in the role of a lord of the manor in medieval England.

"No," replied Klian as he astutely observed the usual Western interest in the ownership of material things. "I own some paddy fields, a small bit of the grazing land and the rattan plantation that I mentioned before. Most of the people of the village have their own pieces of land outside the walls. Some grow maize and sweet potatoes, some graze cattle but most of them have paddy fields. The few who don't have their own land work on the land of another and they share the crop between them. It is a good village. The gods look after us and the wall protects us from the evil spirits of the dark. At night we shut the big wooden gates that you would have seen when you rode into the village. That way we try to keep them out. Oh look, here comes Dayu."

Adrian looked up and saw a slim and very beautiful girl walking up the path to the house. When she stepped on to the verandah she bowed politely to her grandfather and then turned to Adrian. Klian spoke to her in Balinese explaining the circumstances of Adrian's arrival and the relationship between "Mister Ostin" and the village. She smiled and told Adrian in English how honoured they would be to have him to stay. He was beginning to think that it might not be such a bad idea after all.

As he looked at Dayu he guessed that she must be about twenty. She had a flawless complexion and fine silky hair that fell well below her shoulders. Her beautiful, moon-like face conveyed the impression of both mystery and innocence. What struck him the most were her deep brown eyes that seemed to possess some strange mystical power. Klian smiled to himself when he saw Adrian's ill-concealed interest in his grand-daughter.

After some polite conversation Dayu excused herself and went to wash and change her clothes. Adrian and Klian stayed on the verandah and drank some of the local rice wine as they watched the sun go down over the hills. The women lit some oil lamps which they hung from the roof of the verandah and from the branches of some of the trees. When darkness fell the lamps twinkled like fireflies and the whole garden looked like a vast glow-worm cave. The entrance gate at the front of the compound was closed to keep out the dangerous spirits.

Dayu plucked saucepans of water out of the big tub at the back of the house and threw them over herself to get rid of all the dust and sweat that had settled between her pores during the journey back in the truck. As she washed she reflected on the kindness of the gods in bringing a tall, good-looking man like Adrian all the way to her village in the mountains. "He is probably rich too. All Europeans are rich," she thought as she watched the water flow off her breasts and down her thighs and legs to the ground.

Dayu had been born in 1958 into the Satria ruling caste who believed that they were descended from the gods. When she began to make talking sounds she was treated with the greatest deference by all in the village who addressed her as *"Jerone"* — Your Highness. They believed that she was particularly close to the gods since she had just been reincarnated from some other form of life; therefore, her every utterance was a sacred message from the world of the spirits. Old people, being about to end one life and be reincarnated into another, were treated with similar deference; they too were close to the gods — albeit at the other end of the cycle.

One hundred and five days after her birth and in accordance with tradition her mother let her feet touch the ground for the first time and she was given the caste name of "Dayu". Her childhood had been a happy one and she was doted on by all the villagers. After the rest of her family were murdered during the communist uprising in 1965 she had come to live with Klian to whom she had always been a good and dutiful grand-daughter and for whom she had the

116

greatest love and respect. But she wanted to break out of the confining walls of the village which she had come to regard as a prison. She was tired of the village routine of temple, rice harvest and *legong* dancing.

Klian had been extremely protective of her and insisted that she not marry into a lower caste. This had narrowed her options considerably since her own caste constituted only five per cent of the population, the majority of the people being Sudras. A much lower caste.

Dayu had already had several lovers. They had been fairly short affairs as the young men — all Sudras — knew that, in spite of the recent relaxation of caste rules, old Klian would never consent to a union with a member of a lower caste no matter how good their prospects, how fine their character or how strong their love. Klian was old and getting close to the gods. He had led a good and honourable life and did not want to mar his record at this stage with a breach of the caste rules. It might anger the spirits and they would take revenge on him in his next life. By reincarnating him into a lower being. "Better to become a prince than a pi dog," he thought.

Caste rules were one thing but Dayu's feelings and aspirations were another. Although she had gone along with Klian so far she was beginning to crave for a new and more exciting life. For stimulation. For love. For children. "I want to be reincarnated in this life," she laughed to herself. "Same body, same person but a different lifestyle."

As she rubbed herself down with a towel she began to believe that Adrian had been sent to her by the gods. As a reward for all the offerings that she had been putting on the shrine at the back of the house. And for the filial piety that she had always shown to Klian. And for staying with him in the village all these years. She knew that she had had other lives in the past and that there were more to come but somehow the present one seemed supremely important. Standing naked as she dried off in the dimming light she decided that from now on she was going to follow her own instincts and desires. After all, why should Klian make all the choices for her? Like where she lived and whom she married. He would soon be dead and she would have to live with the consequences of his decisions.

She wrapped a sarong around her and walked into the room where she slept. She opened the carved teak wardrobe that stood in the corner. It was filled with clothes. Klian had always been most generous and had given her plenty of money to buy nice clothes, perfume, books and anything else that she wanted. She pulled out a dark blue brocaded cheong-sam with high slits up the sides. She had bought it at the Chinese store in Denpasar when she was last down there. She had never worn it before except when she tried it on in the shop. In fact, it was the first cheong-sam that she had ever bought. It was mainly the Chinese ladies who wore them. Not the Balinese. She slipped it over her lithe body and looked in the mirror. There was something wrong. "It's the hair," she thought. "It falls down and competes with the long, slender lines of the garment." She picked up a wide tortoise shell comb and brushed her hair up and tied it. "Much better," she said to herself. "Now I'm ready to go and join them."

Adrian and Klian were laughing and joking when she stepped on to the verandah. With natural grace she sat down on the sofa next to her grandfather. The tight fit of the cheong-sam accentuated the lines of her shapely figure. Even though it was not a Balinese style Klian could not help but reflect on how beautiful she looked in it. Adrian thought so too.

The conversation was polite and indirect. When they talked of the village and its customs and routines Adrian thought that he detected a faint look of sadness pass across her face. "But," he reminded himself, "one should not read too much into the Asian countenance. They have an amazing ability to mask their true feelings. That is, until they reach breaking point. Then they run amok and go into a trance and there is complete havoc."

"There is always potential for violence lying just beneath the placid surface," Klian had said earlier. "Our society is evenly balanced between the power of the gods and the destructive forces of the demons. They can be placated only by prayers and offerings. But when the balance is upset — as it was in 1965 — then the evil forces that are always hovering in the background assert themselves and there is a bloodletting until the balance is restored."

They sat on the verandah for about an hour and then moved inside to escape the increasing irritation of the mosquitoes. The meal consisted of chicken and rice that had been prepared by the old ladies out in the kitchen hut. Afterwards Klian announced that he was going to bed to rest his tired old bones. Adrian and Dayu stayed up to talk. On a small table was a portable stereo that she had bought in Denpasar. She had a small but well chosen collection of English tapes and asked Adrian to select one. He pulled out a Bob Dylan and snapped it in.

They talked as they listened to the music. Adrian asked her if she had ever been on a surfboard. Her smile waned a little. "No, I never go in the sea. Too many bad things," she replied.

"You mean the sharks?" he retorted.

But she was thinking of more than the sharks. In fact, the whole of the sea. *Pasih*.

"I have been in the sea every day for years," he continued, "and I have never seen a shark although I don't know what I would do if one of them decided to have me for dinner." He was talking flippantly but noticed that he had transmitted a bad vibe of fear. He quickly changed the subject and asked her where she had gone to school to learn such good English — albeit with a very slight American accent.

She said that she had spent several years boarding at a school near Denpasar that was staffed by members of the United States Peace Corps. "They are young American graduates who are prepared to live rough and impart their language and other skills to the people of Indonesia and other Asian countries," she explained.

Adrian's eyes were on her tight fitting cheong-sam. "Hmmm," he thought to himself, "a career in the Peace Corps could have many unexpected benefits."

"They taught us not only English but also a lot of Western habits and ideas. I liked it very much and I was not at all happy when I finished there and had to come back here to live with Klian."

"Yes, I can understand that," said Adrian.

"But, Klian has always been very good to me," she added.

"I can believe that too," he replied. "He was extremely kind to my father and his friends."

They talked until late and then decided that it was time to sleep. Dayu picked up the oil lamp and led Adrian out to his hut. "Thank-you, Dayu," he said, "and *Selamat tidur*." He took her hands into his and looked at her through the dim light of the oil lamp.

"*Selamat tidur*," she said, "and I hope that you will stay with us for many days."

"I will," he replied as she pulled her hands away and went inside the house to her own room.

Adrian put on a sarong and lay on the mattress in the dark. "She is so beautiful," he thought. "So soft and gentle. And always wanting to please. And so delightful to be with." On the one hand he wanted to stay at Klian's as long as possible. Or at least long enough to get to know Dayu a lot better. But on the other hand, he reflected, he had come to Bali to surf its matchless points and reefs and he wondered how long he could bear to be out of the water and inside a walled village that was more than two hours inland by motor bike. "I shall remain here for a few days and then try to persuade her to come down and stay with me at Legian. Then I can enjoy both her and the waves." He felt relaxed and happy. Soon he was sound asleep. Far up in the mountains and near the gods.

About twenty yards away inside the house Dayu was also lying on her mattress in the dark and covered by a sarong which she used as a top sheet. She too was thinking of the other. "He is handsome and strong," she thought. "And I enjoy being with him. He cracks good jokes which make me laugh and feel happy. But I know that he will not stay long as he has come to Bali to surf and he will soon get tired of being up here. It seems that there is only a short time for us to have together. What if he asks me to go down to Legian with him? Maybe Klian would let me go. After all, he is the son of Klian's old friend. Also, because he is not Balinese he can not be regarded as being of a lower caste. Therefore, Klian's objections to my mixing with Sudras would not apply. But, if Klian objects, I think I'll go anyway. It is time that I left the village and made a life of my own. I am not happy here like I was at the American school.

The villagers, although they are good people, are dull and boring. Most of them have never even been down to the bottom of the mountains let alone to a Peace Corps School to learn proper English. Which is quite different to 'bemo driver English'. If I stay in the village I shall probably never marry as there are hardly any Satrias in any of the neighbouring communities. And yet, if I run away, then maybe Klian will not have me back. But I don't think that I want to come back. And the gods might punish me for running away from my responsibilities.

But Adrian is so nice and I have been so happy to-night. Such a change from all the other nights when I just sit here with Klian and discuss the affairs of the village. To-night I have been laughing and happy and it was so nice to wear the cheong-sam for the first time. I felt good in it and I know that Adrian liked it. And so did Klian. I could see from the look in his eyes." By the time that she fell asleep she had decided that, if Adrian should ask her to go with him when he left, she would go. Preferably with Klian's blessing. If not, without it.

Adrian was woken the next morning by the sharp sounds of the palm leaf brooms with which the women were sweeping the yard outside. The last of the rainclouds had passed. The sacred mountain where the gods lived, Mount Agung, was now visible from the village. Adrian could see smoke rising out of its peak. At ten and a half thousand feet the mountain that the Balinese call "The Navel of the World" stood majestic and supreme. Klian explained that the dark area without any vegetation was where the lava poured down during its last eruption in 1963. "It rains a lot up there and it is not every day that the clouds let us see it," he said. "It is where the gods live. In fact, it was created by the gods."

"How did they do that?" asked Adrian.

"When the people of Java converted to Islam their gods moved across to our island. Bali then was a low, flat island and there was nowhere high enough for the gods to live. So they created Agung and the other mountains and have lived there ever since."

They ate breakfast on the verandah. Paw paw, pineapple and bananas. And some hot, sweet Balinese tea. Dayu went out and placed her first offering for the day on the steps of the shrine to the ancestral spirits.

She stated that she had to go to the temple to help them prepare for the monkey dance in the evening. "I'll come and help you too," said Adrian.

"It is women's work," replied Klian.

"Well let's pretend that I'm a woman for the morning." He got up and imitated some gentle and female movements in a most exaggerated fashion. They all laughed.

"All right," said Klian, "you may go to the temple with Dayu and she will explain it to you." He was a little confused. Since Adrian was completely outside the caste system the usual rules did not seem to apply. Anyway, there was no harm in him going to the temple and helping with the preparations. At least it would be a novelty for the other women.

Dayu led Adrian across the village to the temple which lay beneath the shade of a giant banyan fig tree. The masses of aerial roots that it sprouted gave it the appearance of being a whole grove rather than a single tree. She explained how the gods had directed that the temple be placed next to the banyan tree.

"Why?" asked Adrian.

"Because the banyan tree is like our beliefs. It never dies."

"Surely it must die some time?"

"No. See all the vines that drop down from its branches. They take root in the soil and form a new tree. The banyan lives on. So does our religion."

Adrian could see that the brick and plaster walls of the courtyard were — by Bali standards — quite new. They replaced the ones that had been razed to the ground by the Japanese in 1942 as a punishment for allowing Austin and the others to stay there. When he thought about it he felt a passing pang of guilt to think that his father had been the cause of the earlier temple being destroyed. "No, not him," he corrected himself, "but the bloody Japs."

Dayu explained that the main entrance to the old temple was along a tunnel through the aerial roots of the banyan. The new temple had been built in the same place. She handed him an orange sash to tie around his waist when he entered its sacred grounds.

They ducked their heads and made their way through the maze of vines and branches. Adrian could not think of a more exotic — or more difficult — way to enter a holy place.

The banyan was almost as sacred as the temple itself. There was even an altar in its branches.

The temple consisted of three courtyards which were all open to the sky. Inside the first yard was a small pavilion with open sides and a thatched roof that was held up by four deeply carved wooden pillars. There were some flowers growing along the edges — hibiscus, cream leafed frangipani, gardenias and marigolds. Their sweet and pungent scent permeated the whole temple. The earth floor of the courtyard was being swept out by the *permangku* whose sacred task it was to keep the temple tidy.

"This is the *pura puseh* temple for the gods," said Dayu "It is on the side of the village that is nearest to the mountains. Across on the other side — in the direction of *kelod* — is the *pura dalem* which is the temple for the devils and bad spirits. I do not like going there as it is inhabited by demons and monsters. Even its stone carvings are grotesque."

Adrian could hear some rustling in the banyan tree. He looked behind and saw some women crouching down and appearing through its great roots. They had baskets of fruit and flowers on their heads. Not one of them lost their balance as they slid through the entrance. All the movement and bending was done with their legs and trunks; the baskets remained evenly balanced throughout. They walked with great dignity and piety across the courtyard and through an elaborately carved archway at the other end. Adrian and Dayu followed the little procession and found themselves in a second courtyard with several altars and shrines. One was a high tower of thatched pagoda roofs which was the resting place for the gods and on another a replica of the god Wisnu was astride a great garuda bird, riding it like a jockey. Adrian's eyes caught sight of a small shrine in the far corner. Draped over it were the remains of the White Ensign of H.M.A.S. Perth that his father and the other men had salvaged from the wreckage of their ship in the Java Sea some thirty-six years before. He walked over to it. Dayu followed. "The gods enter into the bodies of all who touch it," she said. Adrian carefully held it up. The Union Jack was still intact in the upper left corner but much of the white background had been torn away.

An old priest in flowing white robes appeared through a gateway at the other end. The women moved forward and placed their offerings down in front of him. As they said prayers to the gods they put out their hands and the old priest poured sacred water over them.

"Why do they bring such grand offerings?" asked Adrian.

"It is to attract the gods. To lure them down to the temple," she replied.

The priest disappeared through the gate as quickly as he had come. "What's through there?" asked Adrian. "A third courtyard?"

"Come, I shall show you," she said. There was a big lotus throne that sat on a giant stone turtle that represented Bali. It was held down by snakes to prevent it moving and causing earthquakes. Adrian was fascinated by a great stone phallus which Dayu explained was a "*lingaa*" to symbolise the importance of fertility. They both began laughing. The atmosphere changed from that of guided tour to one of relaxed joviality.

Adrian helped Dayu and the other women to place colourful hibiscus flowers behind the ears of the stone figures. Then they wrapped sashes and black and white checked aprons around the stone legs so as to ward off any bad spirits that might be hovering around. And small oil lamps were placed on their stone heads. Finally, brightly coloured parasols were placed above them to denote their godly status.

By midday the work of dressing up the statues was finished and the women went and sat under the thatched roof of the pavilion and began plaiting strips of palm leaf into offering baskets. Adrian was thirsty and suggested to Dayu that they go and have some fruit juice at the *warung*. As they were tunnelling their way back through the banyan branches Adrian looked up at the huge, sprawling tree. He could see a big, hollowed out tree trunk hanging by ropes from a high branch. "Hey Dayu, what's that up there?"

She looked up and replied, "The *kulkul* drum. Every village has one. It is an alarm drum which is beaten to summon the people to the temple for festivals. Like the monkey dance to-night. It is also used as an alarm to warn against disasters."

"What disasters?"

"A storm or an earthquake or a fire. And in former times it warned us of the approach of an enemy."

"Just like the church bells of Merrie England," said Adrian.

"What? Are there *kulkul* drums in England?" asked Dayu.

"No, not quite," he replied. "In England every village has its church — just like your temple — and every church has a bell-tower. The bells are rung to summon people to church or to warn them of an approaching enemy — just like you said. In 1940 Churchill ordered that the bells remain silent and they were to be rung only if the Nazis actually landed. The bells — like your *kulkul* drum — were to be the warning signal to the villagers. Fortunately, they were never rung."

"It would be good if the *kulkul* drum was beaten only for festivals," she said. "But alas, that is not so. In the last two years it has been beaten for three fires, two floods and several storms."

At the *warung* they found a table in the shade of some banana trees and Dayu ordered some rice cakes and mango juice. A few children gathered at a polite distance to stare at Adrian but after a few moments the novelty wore off and they returned to their games. This time the old men watching over their cocks didn't even turn their heads.

The fruit juice was luke warm and so was the *brem* that followed. But it didn't matter as they scarcely noticed anything but each other. It was an attraction of opposites: the one tall, light featured, European and well versed in the ways of the world; the other short, dark, Asian and the product of a traditional Balinese upbringing in a remote village in the mountains. He found her exotic, refreshing and oozing with softness and femininity; it was her mystery and difference that formed such a large part of the attraction.

Dayu for her part felt comfortable with the big, strong Australian who laughed a lot and made jokes of everything. More importantly, she regarded him as her passport to get out of the village and away from all the restrictions that were placed on her. Caste. The village. The mountains.

When they returned to the house the brigade of bare breasted gardening ladies were still sitting on the ground clipping the grass. Klian later explained how the bare breasted women of Bali have survived in spite of several attempts to instil in them a sense of shame and make them cover up like Western women. First of all it was the Christian Dutch who tried to get them to wear tops in order to protect the morals of European sailors and to increase the demand for Dutch manufactured clothing. The same theme was thrashed by the dour and puritanical communists when they were active in the villages prior to their 1965 coup. "But Balinese women have dressed this way for centuries," said Klian. "The Dutch come and go, the communists come and go but the Balinese customs survive. Just like the banyan tree." Then with a laugh he mentioned the irony that the European women on the beach at Kuta were now emulating the Balinese and baring their breasts to the sun.

That night, as they were sitting on the verandah listening to the ci cas and the geckos, they heard the distant thud of the *kulkul* drum. It was being beaten in a certain rhythm to inform the villagers that the monkey dance was about to begin.

"Does it always send out the same message?" asked Adrian.

"No, it has different rhythms that are known only to the people of our village," replied Klian. "To have these secret codes is a symbol of the independence of our community. Only we know what the message is. Not other villages and certainly not the government or the police. To-night the signal is that the monkey dance will be starting soon. You had better be off if you don't want to miss it. I am too old to go."

Adrian and Dayu joined the throng of brightly clad villagers who were entering the temple. The banyan tree was even more exotic at night with oil lamps suspended from its branches to guide the people through the dark tunnel of roots. High in the tree young men were still beating the *kulkul*.

Inside the temple courtyard men and women were packing around the sides to watch the dance. The strong smell of clove cigarettes competed with the scent of the many flowers that had been brought in during the day as offerings. Many of the women had their hair tied in a bun that was held together by a clasp of frangipani or hibiscus. They wore long sarongs and their tops were covered by a plain stole that was bound tightly around their breasts. And the sarong clad men wore silver headbands that glistened in the candlelight.

The actors and dancers wore monkey masks over their faces. They re-enacted the tale of the Monkey Prince whose army came to help Rama rescue his wife who had been kidnapped. It reminded Adrian of those plays of Shakespeare that are based on some famous event in history involving love, elopement, poisoning and murder.

Afterwards there was a feast in the courtyard and much joviality. When he stood up straight after emerging out of the banyan tree Adrian felt full of energy and vitality. "Say Dayu, let's go for a walk around the village before we go back to Klian's. I don't feel like going inside just yet."

Thinking of the spirits of the night she hesitated for a moment and then said, "All right, if you so wish."

They walked past sleeping pi dogs and jumping frogs as they wended their way along narrow lanes that were bounded by stone walls and bamboo picket fences. They passed several other people who were on their way home from the monkey dance. "*Selamat malam*" they said. "*Selamat malam*" came the reply.

By the time they got back to the banyan tree the place was deserted. Just a few fading oil lamps. It was still hot and humid and Adrian was intoxicated by his magical and exotic surroundings, the warmth of the night and the alluring nearness of Dayu. "Let's sit under the banyan tree for a while and inhale the sweet aroma of all the temple flowers that I can smell from out here," he said.

"No, it's better to go home," she replied.

"Yes, later. It's so nice here and I just want to savour the moment and make it last as long as possible." In the light of one of the oil lamps he could see that her expression had changed to one of fear. He put his arm round her tiny shoulders and asked what the trouble was.

"The *leyaks* hang round here at this hour of night," she said. "When it is this late they have the whole place to themselves."

"Who are the *leyaks*?" he asked.

"They are dangerous spirits that are always around the banyan tree in the dark. If you fall asleep here at night you will wake up crazy. It is the power of the *leyaks*." She was shivering slightly. Adrian could see that she was frightened.

"All right then," he said, "we'll go back to the house and have some coffee."

When they were walking down the last lane towards the compound Adrian looked up at the stars. There were thousands of them. "I just love the tropical nights," he said. "In the East they seem so mysterious." Crash! Down he went. He didn't see the bicycle wheel sticking out from the broken down fence.

"Ooh, are you hurt?" asked Dayu as she bent down to help him up.

"No blood but I think I've dislocated my back. It's very sore and there's some pain in my groin." He tried to get up but found that the lower part of his back was rigid. He eventually raised himself and stood to his full height. He tried to arch his spine backwards but it hurt too much. "Damn," he muttered. "I should have been looking where I was going instead of gazing up at the stars."

He limped the few yards back to Klian's and lay down on a sofa in the living room. Dayu went out to the kitchen hut to boil some water on the still burning fire and they had some hot coffee.

"How is it now?" she asked.

"It's still sore," he said. When he stood up the pain intensified. "I think I'll go to bed," he said as he struggled over to the door.

"If the backbone has moved then it needs to be pushed back," she said. "Would you like me to massage it and push it back to where it should be?"

"Yes, if you think that you can do it."

"I shall heat some oil and rub it on so as to soften the back and make it more responsive to manipulation. Go out to the hut and lie down on the mattress until I come out." She went to the kitchen hut and warmed some oil on the fading fire.

Adrian lay down on his mattress and waited. If he lay on his stomach his groin hurt. If he lay on his back he could feel the pain in his lower spine. So he compromised and lay on his side.

Dayu appeared through the darkness with an oil lamp in

one hand and a towel and bowl of hot oil in the other. She reminded Adrian of Florence Nightingale in the hospital at Scutari. She closed the door of the hut to keep out the spirits.

Adrian turned over on to his stomach and she began rubbing the oil on to the lower part of his back. It felt hot to start with but the continuous movement of her tiny but strong hands soon had a powerful soothing effect. "Ah, that feels a bit better," he said.

"No, it won't be better until I click it. I just have to loosen the muscles first." After a while she turned him on his side and pulled him this way and that. Suddenly the back went "click".

"That is what we wanted," she murmured as she lay his big frame back down on the mattress.

"There's still a bit of pain," he said, "but not nearly as much as before."

"Yes, that is because — even in the short time that the back was displaced — the muscles around it have gone lazy and dead. They need to be moved around to get them back into circulation." She began rubbing and pressing them in several directions. Soon they were rejuvenated. So was Adrian as she rubbed her delicate hands from his shoulders down to his buttocks. Sometimes hard, sometimes soft, but with never a halt in the movement.

"How's that?" she asked.

"Much better," he said. "There's hardly any pain now. Except in the groin."

She turned him over on to his back and began pressing through the thick, soft flesh where the pain was. Sometimes she pressed with her whole hand. Other times with just the deft touch of her finger-tips.

"Ah, you are so strong," she said. She was pleased to see that Adrian did not have much hair on his body. She had seen some European men on the streets of Kuta and Denpasar with unbuttoned shirts that showed chests of hair so thick that they reminded her of brooms. What she found especially funny — and repulsive — was men who had no hair on their heads but great bushes of it all over their chests and even on their backs. "Ugh!" she thought. "But Adrian is just right. Lots of hair on his head and hardly any on his chest." Also, she liked his colour. Deeply tanned. The colour of coffee. Not like some Europeans whose skins were the colour of a white gardenia and who, when they went out in the sun, turned bright red and peeled like a banana.

By the time she finished massaging Adrian's rejuvenated body she had come to the conclusion that, the night being at its darkest, the evil spirits would be so concentrated in the small space between the hut and the main house that it would be dangerous — indeed pure madness — to step outside. So she smiled softly and lay down next to him, nestling her head in the crook of his arm.

Adrian was stimulated by her silk like skin and the soft warmth of her body — so close, so sensual, so enticing. He kissed her gently — first on the lips, then on her small, firm breasts. He unwound her sarong and dropped it on the floor. She slid down to his feet like a snake and massaged his toes with her tiny fingers. Then she climbed up his body — from the feet to the head — kissing him all the way. By the time she reached his lips their bodies were locked in tight embrace. The foreplay continued for several magical minutes until their passion exploded in one sheer burst of intense, simultaneous, uncontrolled pleasure.

The next morning they woke to the sound of a crowing cock. It was already hot and they could hear the noise of the women who were beginning the household chores. After breakfast they went for a walk together towards the village green. "*Selamat pagi*" they said as they passed several men who were tending their cocks. The birds were being washed and rubbed with fresh cow dung to make their feathers shine in the sun. Some of them were having a feed of snails and frogs and pieces of grass. When the men finished tending them they put them back in their cages and parked them in shady positions on the roadside so that the birds could get used to the noise and the people. Their owners believed that this was the best way to inure them to the noisy crowds at the fighting ring.

Adrian saw a young boy walk on to the green from one of the narrow lanes. He was carrying a long bamboo pole and was followed by a large flock of ducks that were walking in formation like Guardsmen at the Trooping of the Colour. They were advancing at a gentle pace.

"What's all that?" asked Adrian who, apart from some small muscular pain, had recovered from his accident.

"Duck boy," replied Dayu.

"What's he doing?"

"He is taking his ducks to the rice fields for a meal."

"What do they eat? The rice?"

"No, no. They wander around in the mud and eat frogs and eels."

Adrian was fascinated by the way that the ducks followed the boy's every turn and change of pace. There must have been fifty of them. "You mean they're on their way to the fields right now?" he asked.

"Yes, he will lead them through the big wooden gates at the entrance to the village and then into the paddy fields."

"Why don't we go with him? I'd love to see them running around in the mud capturing frogs."

"Well, we shall have to ask him. They are his ducks," said Dayu.

The boy was both surprised and delighted that the Westerner who was staying with the *klian* would take any interest in his routine and daily chore of taking the family ducks for a feed.

When they reached the rice field outside the village the boy drove the bamboo stick into the ground and tied a scarf

133

around it. The ducks sauntered off in all directions and began their search for food. Adrian later saw some of them with frogs and eels hanging out of their beaks.

The men and women in the paddy fields were wearing wide coolie hats to keep the hot sun from their faces. It was harvest time. The fields had just been drained of water and the farmers were cutting the golden rice with big, curved knives.

It was an impressive sight. The field where Adrian and Dayu were standing was not far from the village gates. At the top of the hill. From there they could look down on rows and rows of long rice terraces that were dammed in and held up by primitive dykes made of mud, wood, bamboo and rocks. Every part of the descending land was utilised. It spread out beneath them like a patchwork quilt. Men, women and children were working in every field all the way down the hill. At the bottom of the valley they looked like an army of ants as they cut the rice stalks that had been planted in neat rows with mathematical precision.

Scattered here and there among the fields were small shrines dedicated to the rice goddess, Dewi Sri. Tightly tied bundles of rice were being carried up the road where they were loaded on to the village farm truck and taken to the big rice shed inside the walls. There was no end of work to be done so Adrian borrowed a spare coolie hat and joined in. So did Dayu. They toiled through the heat of the day as they denuded the field — and the next one — of all the golden stalks.

Towards the end of the day the workers threw their knives over their shoulders and began to head back to the village. The ducks returned from all directions — like homing pigeons — to gather round the bamboo pole that the duck boy had planted in the ground. He pulled it out and put it over his shoulder and the army of ducks marched dutifully behind their little general who led them back to his home in the village. "It is such a well-ordered little society," thought Adrian as he trudged through the village gates with Dayu.

"So you spent the day helping with the harvest?" asked Klian with amusement. "You are the first European to work in the fields with us since Mister Ostin and the others. What do you think of that?"

"A very small world," laughed Adrian.

"It is the gods," remarked Klian.

After Adrian had had a wash from the tub of water at the back of the house and put on a clean green sarong he went and joined Klian on the verandah. "You like fighting?" asked the old man.

Adrian didn't know how to take it. "Well, I tend to avoid fights myself. Only if it's necessary," he replied.

"Cock fight," laughed the old man. "To-night I take you. We put money on the cocks and maybe come home with pockets full. What do you say?"

"Sounds great fun," answered Adrian. Just then Dayu appeared through the doorway. Fresh and clean after washing off the mud of the paddy fields. "Guess what, Dayu? Klian wants to take us to the cock fight to-night."

"No," corrected Klian. "Just you and me. Women do not go to cock fights."

"Oh," replied Adrian somewhat disappointed.

"I shall stay at home and make some rice cakes for supper," she said.

When Klian and Adrian reached the cockfighting ring it was alive with noise and activity. A crowd of men were cramming into the seats that had been set up around the fighting arena which was about twenty feet square. The whole place was brightly illuminated by large oil lamps. The two of them sat down next to a group of old men who were chewing betel nuts and studying the form of the various cocks that were being held by their owners around the edge of the ring.

Six judges were going around trying to match the birds

to ensure that the fighters in each round were as physically equal as possible. As soon as a pair was matched the spectators began calling out wagers to each other. Klian pulled out a fistful of notes and pointed to a red cock below him. He raised his hand in the air and began shouting in Balinese. A man over the other side raised his finger to accept the *klian's* bet. The atmosphere was tense and exciting as the judges began to tie five-inch razor edged spurs to the right legs of the birds that had been matched and selected for fighting.

Adrian recognised one of the cock owners who was squatting down in front of the ring stroking his white bird. It was the old man who had led him to Klian's house on the day that he arrived in the village. "I'll put some money on his bird," he said to Klian.

"Good bird," remarked Klian as he looked down and saw the spurs being snapped on its leg. Adrian pulled out some money and raised it in the air as he pointed to the cock. A man three rows in front began nodding vigorously. The bet was on.

One of the judges beat a gong and suddenly everyone was quiet. The first two cocks were taken out into the middle of the ring by their owners who smacked and rubbed them to fire them up. Then they let go and the fight began.

The cocks sparred and pecked to start with. Then one of them rushed in and simultaneously struck with its spurs and jabbed with its beak. The crowd roared. Klian was jumping up and down with excitement. It was like a country race meeting with the horses coming down the home straight. The other bird dropped down. Blood was dripping on to the ground from its slashed throat. It was all over in twenty seconds.

The men exchanged hundreds of dirty, crumpled rupiah notes as they settled their wagers. The man who had lifted his finger to Klian was now sending over — through several sets of hands — a bundle of red notes. They were pressed into

Adrian's hands and, when he passed them on to Klian, he noticed the childlike twinkle in the old man's eyes.

The white bird that Adrian had backed was in the next fight. "And they're away," he said to himself in mimic of the race commentators in Australia. This time the cocks began more cautiously. They strutted around for a few seconds as they assessed each other and then one withdrew a few paces. They took some perfunctory stabs at each other as if shadow boxing. However, nothing decisive had happened when the judges brought Round One to an end.

"What's happened? Have I lost my money?" asked Adrian.

"No, it's just the end of the first round. There are five rounds altogether. The length is determined by the time that it takes for the coconut to sink in the bowl of water that is on the judge's table." Adrian looked down and saw half a coconut with a hole through it floating in the water.

He could see his bird being rubbed and nursed by its owner who was spitting in its face and blowing into its beak to give it more air for the coming fight. And hot chilli was rubbed on the bird's backside to fire it up for the kill.

In the next round there was no restraint whatever. Adrian's bird rushed at the other with its spurs but the intended victim rose in the air. Then, with fully spread wings and legs extended, it zoomed down from above on its now helpless attacker on the ground. Like a vampire. Through the melee of flying feathers Adrian saw his bird stagger a couple of steps and then drop to the ground. Its blood was falling on to the floor of the ring. He stared at the bright red fluid pouring over its shining white feathers. "Oh, it looks like I've lost my money," he exclaimed.

"Ah, but look at all the blood that is flowing on to the floor," said Klian. "That will be pleasing to the gods and they will look after you. If the blood from a dead cock falls on to the ground it purifies the earth and ensures a good harvest."

At the end of the night the owners gathered up the cocks that had survived the slaughter and put them back into their cages. Some of them had broken or cut legs and many were bleeding. It was like putting the wounded into ambulances after an artillery battle.

The spectators all filed out of the ring — some richer, some poorer but all of them in good spirits after a night of watching their favourite sport.

When they arrived home Klian went to bed but he couldn't get to sleep. Cockfights always excited him and he was more than happy with the money he had won.

Adrian too was full of enthusiasm as he related to Dayu what he had seen. He reckoned that it was far more exciting than the horse races but he expressed concern at the razor sharp spurs that the birds used as their weapons. "But they are bred and trained to fight," she said. "That is why their owners spend so much time looking after them. It is their job. In every fight it is expected that one of them will die."

Their supper of coffee and rice cakes lasted until after midnight when Adrian began to yawn. Klian heard them tiptoe out of the house to Adrian's hut and he smiled knowingly to himself. "How strange are the ways of the gods," he thought as he fell into the world of dreams.

Adrian stayed on in the village until the following week. He was completely besotted with the grand-daughter of the house and he enjoyed talking to Klian and taking part in the life of the village. He spent most of the time with Dayu who never failed to please him and sometimes surprised him. He noticed that her upper teeth had been filed down to a uniform level and so decided to ask her about it. She said that they had been ground down by a Brahman priest who had then collected the filings and buried them beneath the ancestral shrine at the back of the compound. Adrian was horrified.

"Did it hurt?" he asked.

"Yes, very much. But it had to be done."

"Why? What was wrong with the teeth? Were they too long?"

"No, there was nothing wrong with them. It is just that when a Balinese girl reaches puberty she has to have her teeth filed so that her soul can pass into the spiritual world when she dies. Otherwise a soul can't be born again. Teeth filing is a condition of reincarnation."

"How far do they file? Right down to the nerve?"

"No, they just file the sharp points and edges of four upper teeth and two others. These are bad teeth. Each of them represents a bad quality and only by grinding them away can we lose these qualities."

"Well, I haven't had my teeth filed so I must have all the bad qualities that you don't have," he laughed.

"But maybe not forever."

"What do you mean?" he asked.

"If a man gets married in Bali he has his teeth filed during the ceremony."

"What?"

"But only if the bride's family insists," she laughed.

He told Dayu all about his cottage at Legian and asked her if she would like to come down and stay with him. She said that she would ask Klian and that he would probably consent. She had already decided to go anyway. Klian said that he would have to think about it during the night and that he would let her know on the morrow. The old man had shrewdly observed how fond they seemed to be of each other and, much as he wanted her to stay with him, he knew from long experience the folly of standing in the way of young love — so long as it was not with a wretched Sudra. "She will probably go anyway so it is better that I should give my blessing," he thought.

The next morning, while Dayu was placing the offerings on the shrine, the old man spoke to Adrian on the verandah.

"You know how fond of her I am," he said, "but she is a young woman with her own needs and her own desires. I must not be too selfish with her. As long as she does not marry a Sudra I will not stand in her way. But you must promise me that you will look after her — just as I looked after your father. Then, before you leave Bali, you must bring her safely back to me. I do not mind her going down to Legian for a while to enjoy herself. If I was a young man I would rather be down there making money and dancing with all those blond girls than up here working in the rice fields. So I understand why Dayu wants to go and it is better for her to go with you than with a Sudra.

It is just that she is so precious to this old man's heart. She was only seven when she came to live with me. And when they are that young they are very close to the gods. It is the very young and the very old — like me — who are closest to the spirits. People are most human when they are in the middle of their life — when they are furthest from the gods in time."

"Were her mother and father both killed at the same time?" asked Adrian.

"Yes," replied the *klian*. "It was during the troubles in 1965 when the whole island exploded into a frenzy of killing. The communists tried to stage a coup and overthrow the government. They infiltrated their agents and supporters into the police and army and the schools. Many communists became school teachers so that they could spread their poisonous ideas to the young people in their classes. They tried to undermine our religion and our traditional society. They promised to give free land to the peasants if they joined the party. Many joined but they never got any free land. The only thing that the communists gave was trouble. Then, when they killed the generals in Java and tried to take over the government, the people here decided that they had had enough. They were tired of the communists bringing discord and hatred to our peaceful and well-ordered society.

It was known which people were communist supporters and they were attacked by bands of villagers who killed them with whatever weapons they could find. *Krises*, swords, clubs. Even rice knives. Then the communists started killing each other. Some of them were deeply ashamed and went to the temple and asked the priest to purify them with holy water. Then they went outside and asked the mob to stab them to death. Which they did.

Once the killings started it was very hard to stop them. It was a chance for everyone to get rid of all the hatred that had been building up inside them. And that is how the trance killings began. People went into a trance and killed anyone who got in their way. Old enemies killed each other. Moslems in the west of the island were killed just because they were Moslems. Chinese were killed. Even children went into trance and cut people's throats and chopped their arms and legs off.

One night a group of people who had gone into a trance and were running amok smashed their way into the house where Dayu was sleeping with her parents. They slashed to death with their sharpened *krises* every one in the house except Dayu. She hid under her bed and in the dark the crazy killers didn't see her. She waited until the daylight and then ran outside to fetch some help. She was brought up here to live with me and she cried for many months. They were terrible and frightening times."

"How many were killed?" asked Adrian.

"Some say it was forty thousand. Some say fifty thousand and some say that it was even as many as a hundred thousand. Who knows? Eventually the army came over from Java and restored order and since then we have not had any political or revolutionary trouble of any kind. Thanks to General Soeharto. He has brought stability to Indonesia and we have all prospered. But it was terrifying to see the demons unleash so much evil power all at once." Adrian listened in horror to the old man's story; it made him realise how fortunate he was to live in such a peaceful land as Australia.

When they said good-bye to Klian the old man was both sad and confused. Although Adrian promised that they would come back in a few weeks the *klian* remained unconvinced. "Who knows what the spirits might do?" he thought. "It is dangerous to stay near the ocean for too long. All sorts of bad things happen there. Maybe I'll never see her again." He turned to go inside. His heart was so heavy that he didn't hear Adrian thanking him for his hospitality. The last thing he felt was Dayu kissing him on the cheek. Then they were gone. He heard the roar of the motor bike. Gradually it faded away. Then there was just the deadly silence of the village. Broken only by the occasional yelp of a pi dog or the croak of a frog.

Dayu held on tight to Adrian as they drove through the neat and cultivated countryside back to Legian. It became very hot towards the middle of the day and they stopped a couple of times for cold drinks. By the time they reached Legian they were drenched with perspiration. Adrian brought the bike to a screeching halt on the path outside his cottage. The door was open and the servant girl was sweeping it out — as she had done every day since he had been away. By the time they reached the verandah some of the garden boys had turned up and so had Nicole and Thierry.

"*Selamat pagi* and welcome back, Mister Adrian," said Ketut. "Did you have a nice time away?"

"*Bagus, bagus*," he replied with a laugh as he introduced Dayu to everyone.

"*Enchanté*," said " Turning to Adrian he said, "When you didn't come back from your bike ride on the day when it was raining I said that you must have found yourself a girlfriend. Then, when the surf picked up and you still weren't back, I said to Nicole that the girl must be a real 'smasher'. Now I understand."

142

"How big have the waves been?" asked Adrian.

"Big enough for me but maybe not for you. About two metres. I have been out in it this morning but I have missed surfing with you and that is why I am glad to see you back."

"Let's have some coffee and some fruit and then hit the beach," said Adrian. "We are so hot after the dusty ride that we need to cool off in the sea, don't we, Dayu?"

"Yes," she said. Her smile masked her true feelings about immersing herself in the dangerous waters of *pasih*.

"It is so good to see you back," said Thierry. Nicole playfully pinched Adrian on his rump as she walked past. "Listen," continued Thierry, "we shall go and get our things ready for the beach and we'll come back in ten minutes".

When they had gone Dayu squeezed Adrian's hand and whispered in his ear. "I don't want to go for a swim in the sea. For me it is too dangerous."

"You mean the bad spirits?"

"Yes," she said quietly. He took her in his arms and looked into her dark, mysterious eyes. "Listen, my sweet one, we are both hot and dirty after the bike ride. We can throw ourselves into the sea and cool off and come out clean and refreshed. Besides, it's fun. Nothing to worry about."

"But I've never been in the sea before."

"Never?"

"No, I have always been away from it up in the mountains and when I was at school down here we never went to the beach to swim. Only to watch the sunsets."

"Well, I've spent half my life in the water. The surf means more to me than almost anything else. It is part of me. It is one of the main reasons why I want to live. To surf. To ride a bigger and more scary wave than the one before. The ocean is as much my home as anywhere else. But that doesn't mean that I'm an evil spirit. At least I hope not. The sea is *not* the home of evil spirits. Apart from the sharks. And the chances of being attacked by a shark are so small as to be non-existent. You are more likely to be killed walking across the road. In the whole of Australia there is never more than about one shark death a year and yet there are hundreds of thousands of people who swim every day. I can honestly tell you from long experience that the only dangerous creatures are — as I've said — the big brutes with the fangs. Nothing else. And just to prove it you are going to come for a swim with me right now. And you'll enjoy it."

Just then Nicole and Thierry arrived back complete with surfboard, wax, Vuarnet sunglasses, Pierre Balmain towels and some Vogue magazines for Nicole to read while the boys surfed. Adrian picked up his board and they made their way down the shady track to the beach. Scattered groups of sunbathers, stretched out lethargically on the sand, were roasting in the hot sun like sausages on a barbecue.

A laughing Balinese lady walked past with a basket of bright sarongs and bikinis on her head. When Adrian called out to her she rushed up to them and carefully lowered her basket on to the sand. He told Dayu to choose a bikini. The lady began singing, "Bikini, bikini — very good price to-day," as she pulled out a pile of cheap cotton creations and spread them across the sand. Dayu eventually chose a pink one and Adrian felt so happy to be back at the beach that he paid the singing lady her first asking price without bothering to bargain.

"Why don't you two girls lie on the beach and work on your tans while Thierry and I go for a quick surf? Then we can all go for a fun swim afterwards." He challenged Thierry to a race to see who could get the first wave.

Nicole gave Dayu one of the magazines and they lay there looking at the pictures and chatting. Dayu was fascinated by Adrian's surfing. The speed with which he stood up on the board, the grace and determination of his style and the apparent ease with which he mastered the waves and directed his course. She began to think of the gods. Their power and their beauty.

When the two surfers returned the girls were asleep in the sun. Dayu had changed into her bikini and Adrian found her quite irresistible. He crept up and threw his dripping wet body on top of her and began smothering her with laughter and kisses. He picked her up and ran down into the warm, foamy waves. But he kept a protective eye on her. He didn't want her to get knocked over by a big breaker that would give her even more unrealistic fears of the ocean.

After conquering her initial apprehension of the sea Dayu actually began to enjoy it. She picked up the fun vibes of the others as they splashed and kicked and fell down in the water. She even came to like the feel of the sea swirling over her body and tossing her around. She felt free and independent. And natural. It was like being in a new dimension — limitless and mysterious.

When they ran back up the beach she appeared to be just like any other girl coming out of the water — cool, refreshed and happy. The sea was not nearly as dangerous as she had imagined. But deep down she knew that it was the home of some very powerful spirits that were capable of all sorts of unimaginable evils. "Maybe they live further out from where we swam," she thought. "Even further out from where Adrian and Thierry were surfing. I hope … " She felt a large slippery arm grab her round the waist and heard Adrian whisper in her ear, "To-morrow we'll get up early and come down here on our own and I'll teach you how to swim."

Dayu filled the cottage not only with her feminine fragrance but with a spiritual aspect as well. At various times during the day Adrian watched her place small offerings on the ground in front of the verandah and burn incense over them. These offerings of rice and flowers were put in a small flat tray about as big as a hand that she made from banana leaves. Before each meal she always put out an offering of some small pieces of food. After all, the spirits had to be fed

145

too. The offerings that she placed on the ground were to appease the evil spirits and keep them at bay. These demons — in the form of the mongrel dogs — were forever eating the scraps from the offering dish and in this way were assuaged and pacified for the time being. But the offerings had to be maintained at intervals throughout the day in order to prevent the demons from entering the cottage and bringing bad luck to its occupants.

At other times she put similar offerings on a small bamboo throne that sat on a high shelf outside the front of the cottage. These were for the sun god, Surya. It wasn't just the bad spirits that had to be appeased.

Inside the cottage she filled the loft with bowls of fresh and fragrant flowers. She called it "The Pleasure Room" and on its creaking floorboards the strength of their passion knew no bounds.

Chapter Five

The Party

Back in Paris Thierry had often come across the de Ratton brothers, Jerome and Pascal. Handsome, rich and well-connected they were the types who were just as much at home lunching at the Relais Plaza as they were romping around in designer jeans on the Rive Gauche in the evenings. The two brothers had a natural knack of knowing all the right people and going to all the best parties.

Jerome, the elder, was tall and thin with an aristocratic looking face and black, wavy hair. He was a gifted and original fashion designer who managed to put out some of the most stylish and exciting creations of the season for both men and women. He also owned a vineyard in the Loire valley which produced a fine Cabernet that was bottled in the de Ratton name and carried the family coat-of-arms on its label.

The younger brother, Pascal, was an up and coming Parisian lawyer who was forever being consulted by others in the smart set to help them through their various confrontations with the law. On some days he divorced them; on others he obtained damages for libel from the gutter press which picked on them and fabricated stories about their private lives. If a model had a car accident and damaged her nose or her breasts, then Pascal would invariably extract a large compensation payment from the insurance company. If a rock star or ballet dancer got nabbed for drugs it was usually Pascal who stood up in court and got them off with a caution.

In addition to his legal and social advantages the younger de Ratton was also a talented rugby player who played on the wing for France.

Thierry and Nicole were on the dance floor at the Jolly Frog when they unexpectedly bumped into Jerome and his partner, an Italian princess. They all burst out laughing, kissed, hugged and carried on dancing. Later they joined up at a table on the terrace outside and ordered some wine. Jerome explained how he and Pascal and their retinues were staying at the palatial home of a Spanish artist who was away for a couple of months painting portraits of rich and ugly motor magnates in Detroit, meat millionaires in Chicago and conceited congressmen in Washington. Jerome also told Thierry and Nicole that it was his birthday on the morrow and he was celebrating it with a massive party to which he warmly and enthusiastically invited them. The de Rattons celebrated most things with a party — except Bastille Day. For the simple reason that their forebears had been on the other side — royalists, aristocrats and supporters of *"l'ancien régime."*

The two brothers visited Bali regularly and knew all the beautiful people who hung out there for months at a time while on the run from irate wives, carping creditors and troublesome tax authorities. Most of life's pleasures could still be obtained there very cheaply and it was generally agreed that Bali was a better and cheaper place of escape than either Brazil or the Bahamas.

When Jerome invited Nicole and Thierry to his bash he told them to bring anyone else whom they found *"charmant et intéressant."* And so they invited Adrian and Dayu and told them that, if it was anything like the de Ratton affairs in Paris, it would be worth attending.

On the night Dayu looked truly stunning in a long, high-necked, deep green dress set off with a pair of small emerald earrings that Klian had given her for her last birthday. She again had her hair combed high.

As soon as they walked into the main room of the party Adrian was hailed by Amanda, the social climbing daughter of the tall, dark haired Lady Beaton-Flaunty-Hughes who had told several people at the previous year's Melbourne Cup that she didn't expect Amanda to marry any man with less than a million in the bank. "Pounds not dollars" had been her oft quoted remark. Amanda gave Adrian a peck on the cheek and then resumed her concentration on George Patras whose father was reputed to be one of the largest shipowners in Greece.

Thierry and Nicole began chatting in French to some of the others and Adrian moved over to the corner to talk to a bunch of Brazilian surfers whom he had met in the line-up at Uluwatu. They switched from Portuguese to broken English and began talking about the only thing that surfers ever talk about when they come together — the waves.

Jerome came over and introduced them to Maria, a beautiful, dark haired model from Rome, and two American girls, Susan and Louise, who were stopping over in Bali between films. "That could mean anything," thought Adrian cynically.

The two actresses were extremely friendly and voluble as they went about their task of being the centre of attention. Their loud voices could be heard above the cacophony of French, Spanish, German, Italian and Portuguese. And on the other side of the room their sounds were picked up by the antennae of Lord James Chelmsbury, a suave, confident looking, fair haired young man who was wearing red cotton trousers, a white lace shirt and a silver pendant around his neck. The heir to a thousand acres in Buckinghamshire and a seat in the House of Lords, he had decided to sow his wild oats first and worry about his inherited responsibilities later. He had spent the early part of the evening listening to the adventures of Jean-Paul Giraud, a graduate of Saint Cyr, who was commissioned in the Paratroop Regiment of the Foreign

Legion. Jean-Paul, a solidly built, clean cut looking chap of thirty-two, was already starting to lose some hair on the front of his head. He was currently on long leave from the Legion and had been getting some first hand experience of soldiering by helping Rhodesia's small but highly professional army in its jungle war against the communist terrorists. He was telling the Englishman all about it. "It's a super little country. You would like it. So very English. I just hoped it doesn't get screwed up like so many other places. Bloody terrorists." He spoke with the bitterness of first hand experience.

"Too right," said Lord James. "I've often thought of going down there myself and having a crack at the bastards but I never seem to be able to get away from all these wretched parties. If it's not London, it's Paris. And if it's not Paris, it's Bali." He looked at his watch and then at Jean-Paul and said, "Listen, old chap, I think it's high time that we found ourselves some ladies. There seem to be so many delightful creatures here to-night and opportunity is certainly knocking. I can hear it."

"Mais oui. Je consent," smiled Jean-Paul.

They made their way over to where Adrian and Dayu were talking to the American girls and Lord James introduced Jean-Paul and himself. "Say, it's jolly good to hear a bit of the old English spoken to-night," he said to Adrian. "From the colonies, are you?"

"Melbourne," replied Adrian.

"I've been to the Melbourne Cup. Quite as good as the Derby," said Lord James. The waiter refilled their drinks while they carried on their conversation – the surfer, the actresses, the legionnaire, the young peer and the Balinese village girl.

"I hope to go to England some time," said Adrian. "To see all the famous art galleries and museums. And to watch a Test at Lords – one in which Australia can beat the M.C.C. by at least an innings." He drew his finger across his throat like a dagger and smiled. "I hear that there's some really strong surf down in Cornwall."

"We are always happy to have our Australian cousins visit us," replied Lord James. "Even if you do sometimes beat us at cricket. Here's my card. London during the week; Bucks most week-ends. I could probably get you an invitation to the Long Room. My father's a member."

The room buzzed with the conversation, play-acting and intimacy of a very international young set whose common denominator was a hedonistic and reckless pursuit of pleasure at the expense of all else. Pascal came up and shook hands with Adrian. "You must be Thierry's surfing friend. Welcome. I'm Pascal."

"*Enchanté. Je m' appelle Adrian et c'est Dayu,*" was the reply. Pascal kissed the back of Dayu's right hand. The younger de Ratton brother was tall, lean and handsome and, at twelve stone, was the lightest man in the French rugby team. But he was a fast and elusive winger who had scored numerous tries by dodging in and out of the opposing players until the white goal line glared up at him. His mischievous grin and warm, open face won him friends and clients from an extremely wide circle. Adrian had difficulty imagining him as a lawyer; he seemed the eternal partygoer.

In the far corner of the room Adrian could see a fairly non-descript looking man sitting in an armchair drinking a glass of whisky. He was dressed in blue jeans and a white open neck shirt and had a small gold chain around his neck. With his short, military type haircut he seemed to stand out from everyone else. He was chatting quietly to a very beautiful woman who, judging from her accent, was obviously American.

Adrian thought at first sight that he looked like an undercover DEA agent but then doubted that even they would be so stupid as to plant someone who stood out so prominently from the rest of the guests. He had seen both

Jerome and Pascal making a great fuss of the man and so he decided to ask Pascal who he was.

"Ah," said the Frenchman, "I have promised not to tell anyone who he is. He does not want people to know. But I shall give you a clue. He is easily the bravest man at the party. And certainly the most interesting. There is no one more *intéressant* in the whole of Bali. Not in the whole world. What he has done is more *intéressant* than if you surfed a forty foot wave. More *intéressant* than the weirdest acid trip. In a hundred years' time he will be more famous than the Beatles. In a thousand years he will be as famous as Caesar, Columbus and Churchill."

"Oh, come off it, Pascal. How could such a boring and normal looking man be so famous? I can not even recognise him," said Adrian.

"That is good," said Pascal, "because he does not want to be recognised at parties. He is so tired of all the silly questions that people ask him."

"You have a good imagination, Pascal. You should write a novel."

"Ah, but it is not imagination or — how do you say in English? — exaggeration."

"Well then, tell me. I promise that I'll keep it to myself although I can not think for a moment why he is so special."

In melodramatic manner Pascal put his mouth to Adrian's ear and whispered, "That man is one of the American astronauts. He is the first man to walk on the moon." Adrian gasped in astonishment and took a closer look at the man. He tried to picture him in a space suit and helmet. But the man still looked terribly normal compared to all the other colourful and flamboyant characters in the room.

"Now you understand why he does not want people to know," said Pascal. "It is all the stupid questions that people ask. How much is a three bedroom house up there? On what side of the road do they drive? Did he meet anyone whom he knew? Is there a McDonalds on the moon and what are their cheeseburgers like? Will he come to the next moon dance? Everyone asks questions and that is why he does not want people to know who he is."

"Hmmm. That's fair enough," said Adrian. "But I just want to ask him one question."

"What question?" asked Pascal nervously.

"I want to know how big the waves are in the Sea of Tranquillity."

"That is just what I mean," screamed Pascal in exasperation. "Always a stupid question. Remember, you promised."

"Yes, I promised," said Adrian with a smile.

At that moment they were joined by the blond haired American tennis player, Danny Holland. He had his arm around the perfect body of the sensuous and exotic looking Yvonne Férier who was an up and coming model in Paris — part French and part Tahitian. She was wearing a tiny see-through dress of white muslin and was smoking a black cheroot.

"Say, Pascal, this is an even better party than the one that you took me to during the French Open," said Danny.

"Which one was that?" asked the Parisian.

"At the chateau. Just beyond Versailles. When you fell into the pond. Remember?"

"Oh yes. Do you know that that *comte* has never invited me back. Apparently the water lily that I broke had been in his family for generations."

Danny was taking a couple of weeks off before beginning his build-up for Wimbledon. Pascal smiled at the contrast between the two blond haired sportsmen and the dark features of their ladies. He called out to the Balinese disc jockey to put on "Ebony and Ivory" next. Adrian realised why and winked at Pascal but the point was lost on the others.

Adrian led Dayu outside and across the stone slabs towards the pool. The area around it was illuminated by the dim glow of lights that shone down from unobtrusive positions behind leafy tropical shrubs. Colourful peacocks strutted across the lawns and monkeys were running up and down the branches of some of the bigger trees.

There were many beautiful bodies standing and prancing around the pool. The dark haired Italian contessa, Maria Sophia d'Annunzio, was at the far end in a long black lamé dress with a neckline that plunged several fathoms below her navel. She was the centre of an admiring group of interesting young men — the wildly gesticulating Giovanni who was taking time off from running the most popular night club in Milan, the ever smiling Hannibal, a Bob Marley look-alike from Jamaica, the well-known Israeli novelist, David Isaacs, who had lost his left arm in the Six Day War, and the richest of them all, Pablo, the cocaine dealer from Colombia whose father was one of that country's leading judges.

By far the most interesting looking body around the pool belonged to a thin young man in red leather pants, a silver studded dog collar around his neck, and long spiked hair that was bright pink on one side and luminous green on the other. He introduced himself to Adrian and Dayu as "Crazy Dog".

"Yes," laughed Pascal, "that is his real name. He has shown me his passport. Before that his name was 'Bill Smith'." Crazy dog blushed pink — the same color as the left half of his hair. "He has his own punk band in London," continued Pascal.

Adrian had always disliked punk music and didn't have much time for punks either. The surfing crew regarded them as ugly, anaemic looking inner city thugs who were basically unenlightened because they never went to the beach or got on a surfboard. The dislike was mutual. The pale skinned punks viewed surfers as fancy poseurs with one track minds who, with their deep sun tans, would all die of skin cancer before they were forty.

Dayu stared at Crazy Dog in amazement and a little fear. "He must be a *leyak*," she decided as she contemplated those powerful witches in their various guises — monkeys, dwarves, pigs, even poisonous mushrooms. And now this! "He must have enormous magical powers," she thought.

Crazy Dog smiled at Adrian and Dayu as he introduced the German model who was clinging to his pale, spindly arm. Adrian was surprised to find that the punk was gentle, polite and friendly. He asked Adrian about surfing and what it was like to ride the waves.

"You can come out with me some time if you like," he replied.

"No, I never go in the surf."

Adrian could hardly believe his ears. "Not even to cool off during the day?" he asked.

"Oh, sometimes I go down and lie in the shallow water but I don't go in the waves because of my hair. It's too difficult to get it back together again."

They all laughed. But Dayu still felt uneasy. "Yes, he is definitely a *leyak*," she said to herself.

The party was genteel at first but, after a few crates of Dom Perignon had been emptied, some of the more flamboyant Latin characters began to lose whatever inhibitions they might have had at the start. Pascal put a long tailed monkey on a rubber mattress and tried to push it across to the other side of the pool. It got becalmed half way across and the monkey stood upright on its two feet and began waving its arms around. Everyone roared with laughter. Then it started to go crazy. The contessa kept calling out: "Clever monkey, clever monkey," as she tried to exhort it to greater achievements. Eventually Giovanni jumped in and rescued it.

Adrian and Dayu wandered through the tropical foliage and sat down beside a small stream that was flowing down the gently sloping lawn. They put their feet in the cold water and lay back on the soft grass. In each other's arms and in a world of their own.

When they rejoined the party Adrian walked over to the bar that had been set up by the pool. He asked Ketut, the sole barman, for a couple of glasses of champagne. The main bar inside was under the care of three other Balinese — all aged about eighteen. All the barmen had taken up Jerome's offer to help themselves to a drink whenever they felt thirsty. It was a hot night and Ketut had started off with a couple of chilled cans of San Miguel which he had drunk before any of the guests had arrived. He then had a few glasses of arak from the several dozen bottles that Jerome had provided. He began to feel light headed. He had always liked arak. Especially when it was free. Like to-night. By the time that Adrian asked him for two glasses of champagne Ketut was on to his third glass of the bubbling French liquid. His head felt even lighter. It was almost as good as going into a trance at the temple when all care and restraint were thrown to the winds.

"Bloody good party, eh?" Ketut said to Adrian with a smile. He began pouring the champagne into a glass. Through the sparsely lit night his eyes were fixed on Adrian's as he smiled and laughed. The glass overflowed. He kept pouring.

"Hey man. *Cukup, Cukup,*" said Adrian. The sharpness of his tone snapped Ketut out of his drunken trance. He was so startled that he dropped the bottle. Crash!

Pascal came running over and said, "Oh, not another one!"

"Afraid so," said Adrian. "How many bottles have you lost now?"

"I'm not talking about the bottles," said Pascal. "It's the barmen I'm losing."

"What do you mean?"

"Well, first the chief man inside fell down on the floor

156

because he had drunk too much arak. The other barmen took him outside to lie down under a tree but they also took some more arak with them. Now they are all lying under the tree and can not move. Then the disc jockey began playing the same song four times in a row. I know that 'Stairway to Heaven" is a very good number but I thought that just maybe we would like to hear something else. So I go up to him and tell him to put on another tape and he just smiles at me and does not move. I say it again and he just looks at me and then falls off his stool. He too has drunk too much arak. So Pablo has taken over the stereo but things are no better as he has played 'Cocaine' three times running. And the kitchen staff. They are all drunk too. They are sitting down on the floor laughing and giggling at each other. And so the contessa — can you believe it — is now in the kitchen getting the last of the food ready for supper. She has taken off her long black dress and is wearing just an apron. Nothing else. Oh, this is such a crazy party. Anyway, come and meet another sportsman, my good friend from South Africa."

He introduced them to a short, muscular fellow with sandy coloured hair whose name was Tommy Hopewell. He was the current captain of the Springbok rugby team. Pascal had often played against him in internationals and regarded him as the most talented fly half in the world. Tommy was on his way to Australia to play in an invitation match and was glad that he had taken up Pascal's invitation to stop over for a few days in Bali.

"Do you know," Pascal said to Adrian, "that when I went with the French team to South Africa this little man here stopped me from scoring the winning try in the last test match. I thought that I had a clear field to the goal line and I was almost there when — crash! — he came across the field like lightning and grabbed me around the legs. Down I went and the referee blew his whistle for the end of the match. I was crying when I walked off the field. It was our last chance to beat the Springboks and we got so close."

"And yet you're the best of friends?" asked Adrian.

"Of course," replied the Frenchman. "Rugby players are an international brotherhood. Just like surfers I suppose. Because it is not professional and we are not competing for huge transfer fees we are able to enjoy it and fraternise with the other team after the match. What happens on the field is one thing but off the field is quite another."

"Do you know that Pascal once punched me on the nose? And it bled," said Tommy.

"You're kidding," said Adrian.

"No," replied Pascal. "Unfortunately he speaks the truth. It was at Ellis Park in Johannesburg in front of sixty-four thousand people including two Prime Ministers. Oooh, I was so embarrassed. I did it in the heat of the moment and Tommy never lets me forget it. Every time he mentions it I feel guilty and so I have to get him another drink. Give me your glass, Tommy, and I'll go and fill it for you." Off he went to the bar.

It was to be Tommy's first visit to Australia and Adrian asked him what he expected it to be like. "Oh, probably not too different from South Africa. I have played rugby against quite a few Australians and we've always got along famously. I think that there are a lot of similarities between South Africans and Australians. We both come from the same stock and we are both nations of sports fanatics — cricket, rugby, tennis."

"I'm afraid that I'm a little ignorant about rugby," said Adrian. "Because in Victoria where I live everyone plays Australian Rules and it's quite different."

"Yes, I know," said Tommy. "I played it yesterday."

"Where?" asked Adrian in surprise.

"On the beach at Kuta. There are a couple of teams on holiday here from Perth and they were playing a game of Rules on the sand yesterday afternoon. I was fascinated at the way they moved around and especially all the jumping in the air. We only do that in the line-outs. So I asked if I could join in. They asked me if I had played before and I said, 'No, but I've played a little rugby'," said the world's finest fly-half. "It was great fun even though I found all the movements so different and of course the scoring too. I was just starting to enjoy it when the game ended suddenly."

"Why? What happened?"

"Some Indonesian boy came on to the beach with his pet python and they all fled. So quickly that they even left the football on the beach. I've still got it. Seems they're terrified of pythons."

"So I've noticed," remarked Adrian drily.

Pascal arrived back with some more glasses of bubbling champagne. "This is such a good party, Pascal," said Adrian.

"And why not?" replied the host. "We are on the most enchanted and romantic island in the whole world. It is a natural place for people to enjoy themselves. And I hope that that is what everybody is doing."

"For sure," replied Adrian as he handed a glass of the champagne to Dayu.

About two in the morning the contessa, still wearing the apron and nothing else, managed to lay out the supper on some long tables that were set on trestles. Fortunately most of the food had already been eaten when one of the trestles collapsed and sent all the plates smashing on to the paving stones.

After the food had gone a few of the jaded ones began to drift away. The party came to life again when "Twist and Shout" was played at full volume and everyone got up to dance. Even some of the monkeys danced wildly on the paving stones. Thierry and Nicole had long gone but Adrian and Dayu stayed on and danced and talked and kissed until dawn.

The last to leave the party was Pablo. Like the

bandsmen on the Titanic he stayed at his post as disc jockey until everyone else had either left or fallen asleep. When he went outside he saw that the sun was already high and assumed from its heat that it must be about nine in the morning. He walked over to where his motorbike was parked under some banana trees. He opened the carrier box on the back and pulled out his Rolex watch to check the time. "Holy mackerel!" he exclaimed. "Quarter past ten." He was just beginning to feel tired. "Hope I don't fall asleep on the way down," he thought as he kick started the machine and set off through the grounds of the palatial residence. Through his glazed eyes he could see the bright colours of the hibiscus and the yellow and white of the frangipani that lined the dirt driveway.

Fifteen minutes later he pulled up at his beachfront hotel and parked the bike under a roof of thatched palm. He was sweating like a pig after the hot ride so, in spite of his drowsiness, he decided to go for a swim. He went up to his room, changed into a pair of fluorescent orange and green boardshorts, picked up his towel and dragged himself down to the beach.

"Too much, too much," he said as he was confronted by the blinding sun, the sparkling sea and the white sand. He put on his sunglasses, rolled his towel into a ball and threw it down on the sand. Then, still wearing the sunglasses, he walked down to the sea and sat in it up to his neck. It was cool and soothing and the little waves that rippled in were no more than six inches high. He was too tired to swim or splash or do anything more strenuous than gently move his arms and legs through the water. He felt refreshed as he walked back up the beach to where he had left his towel. Too exhausted to go any further, he decided to rest on the sand for a few moments and then walk back to the hotel and go to bed.

He lay down on his stomach and two minutes later was sound asleep. Pablo dreamt that he was a pilot in the First

World War having dog fights above the blazing guns of the Western Front. The dream was so vivid and lasted for a long time until it turned into an even more realistic image of being chased by a U.S.Air Force Tomcat as he tried to fly a 'plane full of cocaine into Miami.

Two hours later he woke up. He could feel something touching his face. It was a horrible looking pi dog — dirty white with black and grey spots. "Oh, shove off," he said as he sat up and blinked his eyes at all the brightness, movement and colour of the beach. A young Balinese man in a green sarong and white shirt was walking towards him. Pablo saw him kick the dog which then ran along the beach to annoy someone else.

"Very bad dog," he said to Pablo. "If dog like that bite man then man get babies and hepitis."

"You mean rabies and hepatitis?"

"Yes," smiled the Balinese.

"Well, I'm glad it didn't bite me. It only touched me with its ugly snout. I'd better go and have a swim to clean it off." He stood up.

"I wait here and guard your towel, sir. My name is Madé. What is your's?"

"Pablo. Very well. And you can look after these as well." He handed Madé the sunglasses. The Balinese boy put them on and smiled.

When Pablo returned from his swim he saw Madé sitting by his towel and wearing the sunglasses in a cool dude pose.

"I like these sunglasses very much, sir," he said.

"Yes, you need them on the beach. It can be so bright at times," replied Pablo.

Madé wanted the sunglasses but he had nothing to offer in return. He sat there thinking. Then he looked at Pablo. "Yes," he thought, "I am sure he is the type who would like some magic mushrooms. Then he will better understand the

161

dog that touched his face. He will not see it as a dog but as a bad spirit. And he might even see what it was before it became a dog. A very bad man who stole things and hurt others and offended the gods."

Madé's plan was a simple one. His friend worked at the Green Orchid restaurant and had told him that they sometimes had magic mushrooms which they served with pineapple juice to eager young tourists who wanted to escape from reality for a few hours in a non-alcoholic manner. But not many people knew of the Green Orchid or its special menu. "Maybe," thought Madé, "I could give him the information and take him there and he will then give me the sunglasses in return for my service. That would make me very happy. And the owner of the restaurant will be happy because he charges five times more for the 'special' pineapple juice than for the ordinary stuff. And Pablo will be happy because he will be laughing at all the funny things that he will be able to see."

Madé decided to make the suggestion in an indirect way. "I like your shorts, sir. They are very colourful."

"Yes," said Pablo. "I bought them in New York."

"You must be like a Balinese."

"Why?"

"Because Balinese also like bright colours. And your skin is like the colour of coffee. Almost as dark as a Balinese. And do you like magic?"

"Oh yes," said Pablo, "but not the witches."

"No, no. Balinese not like witches either. You like to have some magic mushrooms?"

"Oh yeah. I didn't know that there were any. I mean, they don't serve them up at the hotel."

"No, not at the hotel. But I know special place where they serve magic mushrooms. If you want, I take you there. And, if mushrooms make you happy, then maybe you give me present." He pointed to the sunglasses.

"Oh, that's no problem," thought Pablo. "I've got

several other pairs in my room."

He led Pablo along the beach and up a narrow track. They passed some cottages and *warungs* and then came to a small restaurant that was tucked away behind a high wall. It's sign — "The Green Orchid" — hung crookedly over the split gate entrance.

They walked in, Pablo wearing just his shorts with the towel slung over his shoulder and Madé proudly sporting the sunglasses. Madé's friend came out and gave them a warm welcome. He ushered them to one of the four tables that constituted the restaurant. Madé spoke to him in Balinese and he went away to mash the fresh mushrooms into pulp and blend them into a large glass of pineapple juice. "We are lucky," said Madé. "They don't always have them but they have just received some that have been brought down from the mountains."

Madé's smiling friend walked across with a large glass of juice that was the colour of mud. Pablo thought that it also tasted like mud as he sucked the thick and foul smelling liquid through a wide straw. He drank half of it and pushed the rest across the table to Madé and told him to finish it.

Soon things started to become distorted. First it was the tall palm tree that Pablo thought was crashing down on his head. He ducked under the table to avoid it. But nothing happened. All he could hear was the laughter of the two Balinese. Then he swore that the other tables were moving towards each other. But they weren't.

"Let's go back to the beach," he said to Madé.

He went to pay for the drink. "Five thousand rupiah, sir."

Pablo pulled his wallet out of the pocket of his fluorescent shorts. There were four ten thousand rupiah notes inside. He grabbed all four and threw them into the air. "Who cares about money? It's only pieces of paper," he cried as he walked through the split gate on to the narrow dusty path.

Madé looked back and saw his friend picking up the notes. He crossed his fingers and gave him a secret sign. His friend understood and went to put two of the notes aside for Madé to collect later.

"Eeeee!" he thought. "It is a lucky day for both of us. That man is only an instrument of the spirits. It is really the gods who dropped the money to us out of the sky."

When they walked on to the beach Pablo started to laugh. He thought that he was in a game park in Africa and that everyone else on the beach was a chimpanzee. Then he picked up some grains of sand and said to Madé, "Look at all this gold."

"Yes," said the other as he took off his shirt and made it into a bag so that he could carry off as many grains of the new found wealth as possible.

They laughed at everyone who went past. So many funny looking chimpanzees! Especially the boy who came up to sell them some silver bangles. "Good afternoon, sir. How are you to-morrow?" were his opening words. Pablo fell into a fit of hysterics. He laughed until he was almost crying. The boy stood there smiling politely as he wondered what had made the Westerner and his friend so happy.

"You like silver bangles for girlfriend?" he asked hopefully.

"Yes, but I've got no money left," said Pablo as he looked at his empty wallet.

"No problem," said Madé. "We'll pay him in gold. One grain of gold for each bangle."

The hawker pricked up his ears at the sound of the word "gold". He could hardly believe what he was hearing. Pablo took some of the bangles and held them up to the sun. Their cheap silver coating sparkled in the bright light. He eventually chose half a dozen which he thought would look nice on the arm of his girlfriend in London. Madé counted out six grains of sand. "Give him some big ones," said Pablo. Madé started again and picked out six large grains that were really small pieces of broken shells.

"Here you are. It is your lucky day," said Madé as he handed the boy the six grains of sand.

"What? You crazy?" he said in annoyance as he picked up the bangles and walked off to find some other buyers who would have more money and hopefully more sense.

A dog came by and sat down on the sand only a few feet away. "What is that?" asked Madé.

"A dog. A horrible, flea bitten Balinese dog," replied Pablo.

"Yes, but it was once a man. A very bad man who robbed his neighbours and beat his wife and stole other men's rice. The gods were so angry with him that when he died they reincarnated him as a dog. That is his punishment for living an evil life. Let's throw sticks at him to punish him some more for his bad deeds." They picked up some pieces of driftwood and started hitting the dog. The animal squealed and ran down the beach.

"What the hell are you brutes doing?" called out a middle-aged tourist who was sitting a few yards away with his wife. "You shouldn't hit a dog like that."

"It's not a dog," said Pablo.

"What is it then?" asked the man in surprise.

"It's a man who has to be punished. That's why we hit it."

"And if it stays round here its evil spirit might harm us. And you," put in Madé.

"Yes," added Pablo. "You should be pleased that we chased it away."

"You know, Doris, sometimes I just feel that I don't understand the younger generation," the man said to his wife with a shrug.

Pablo sat there until sunset. When it started to get dark Madé decided to leave. He knew that the evil spirits emerged with the shadows that were thrown down by the dusk. And in his present state of mind he didn't want to have anything to do with bad spirits. So he shook hands with Pablo, told him that he hoped to see him on the beach the next day and walked off up the sand — still wearing his sunglasses. He went straight to the Green Orchid to collect his half of the money that had fallen out of the sky. And to have another glass of muddy pineapple juice.

Back at the hotel Pablo had a shower and ordered some *nasi goreng* and fruit salad to be sent across to his room. Then he lay on the bed and listened to a Pink Floyd tape on his Walkman. About eleven o'clock he felt like going out and socialising. So he drove to the Mango Tree. Most of the party guests were there — laughing, joking and talking about the night before.

"And here is our crazy disc jockey," said Pascal as Pablo walked through the door.

"I was the last one to leave the party," said Pablo. "When I left you were all asleep." Everyone laughed.

"I suppose that you've slept all day. Like the rest of us," said the contessa.

"I slept on the beach for a while and then this crazy Balinese guy came up and wanted to trade my sunglasses."

"For what?" asked Pascal.

"Who knows?" laughed Pablo as he walked up to the bar to order a cold beer.

When they moved on to The Jolly Frog Adrian was sweating profusely. It was one of the hottest and stickiest nights of the year; the air was thick with humidity. The only one who was really happy with it all was Gedé, the owner of the disco. He had never before sold so much beer in a single night. He told the DJs to put on slower music lest some of the dancers might faint on the floor. Many of the men had taken off their shirts and were dancing in their loose cotton trousers, boardshorts and even Speedos. But most people were just sitting at the tables fanning themselves and sipping ice-cold beer. Even the contessa — always the life and soul of a party — was sitting out the dances.

"It is just too hot," she gasped to Jean-Paul, her legionnaire escort for the night. "And I don't even have a fan."

Jean-Paul had learned the art of improvisation during his long anti-terrorist patrols in the Rhodesian jungle. He could see a banana tree over near the wall. He picked up a dirty knife from a plate of half eaten *gado gado* and went over and cut off a banana leaf. Then he walked back to the contessa and started waving it in front of her face. It produced a wind. Not a cool wind but a wind nevertheless. She lay back in her chair, closed her eyes and called out, "Faster, faster!"

When the music finally stopped for the night only a few people departed. Most didn't believe that they would have enough energy to walk as far as the exit let alone ride home through the oppressive night air. So they just sat around and ordered more cold beer. The Bintang had long run out and everyone was now drinking San Miguel. Gedé asked the barman how much of that was left. "Only eighteen more bottles," was the reply.

"I suppose you'll raise the price now that you're starting to run out," was the comment of one drunken patron. The manager fixed him with his eyes and said, "I don't know what your custom is in the West but in Bali it is considered bad karma to raise the price of something. And I don't want bad karma. We will not be raising the price."

When the last bottle was sold the barmen began to wipe down the tables and sweating couples made their way to the *bemos* and motor bikes that were parked on the road. Adrian and Dayu walked out through the stone gateway with the contessa and Jean-Paul and Pascal and Maria whose model like poise was beginning to wither in the humidity.

"Well, where shall we go now?" asked Pascal. "It is too hot to go to the Hamburger House. That place is far too small and they don't have any fans."

"Let's go for a walk on the beach," said Maria. "There is a very small breeze coming from the sea so maybe it will help."

Jean-Paul still had a glass of beer in his hand so he passed it round and they all had a sip. They walked down to the sea and Maria and the contessa took off their dancing shoes and walked in the shallow water. "Ah, that is better," said the contessa. The others remained on the beach talking and laughing. Then the contessa announced that she was going for a swim.

"What a good idea," said Pascal, "It is the only thing that will cool us down."

They put their clothes in small piles on the sand and ran naked into the warm sea. Dayu was torn between immersing herself in the dark and dangerous waters of *pasih* with the others or waiting on the beach on her own where all sorts of unimaginable misfortunes might befall her. She decided that it was safer to go into the sea provided that she stayed very close to Adrian. Which she did. He held her tightly in his arms as they floated in his favourite element. As soon as they were in a few feet of water it was refreshingly cool. "Ah, this is so perfect," Pascal kept saying.

In the moonlight they could see a pi dog running along the sand. When it saw the six piles of clothes it ran up to them and began to sniff around. Dayu believed it was a *leyak*. Sometimes they took the form of a dog. No one took much notice of it except Jean-Paul who, trained to detect all movement at night, kept his sharp eyes on the mongrel. Suddenly he began to laugh. "Oh look! He has taken somebody's clothes," he said.

Pascal and Jean-Paul leapt out of the sea and began chasing the dog. But it was too late. The mongrel had a head start. It disappeared into the casuarinas at the top of the sand with the contessa's bright green Pierre Cardin designer dress between its teeth. They soon lost it in the darkness. The others came out of the water and went to their piles of clothes. But there were only five of them. Where the contessa had left her dress there was only sand.

"But where are your other clothes?" asked Pascal.

"What other clothes?" she laughed.

"Your expensive lingerie."

"I didn't wear any. It was too hot. I only wore the dress." By now they were all laughing. None more so than the contessa. "Oh well, I shall just have to go home *au naturel*. At least I shall be cooler without it."

Jean-Paul was zipping up his black trousers. He bent down, picked up his red and black shirt and shook the sand out of it. It was a long, loose fitting style. He handed it to the contessa who tried it on. It fell almost to her knees. "But it is so hot to wear," she complained. "I am much cooler without it."

"I suggest that you wear it," said Pascal. "Otherwise you might cause a riot when we get back to the car-park. And it's too hot for a riot."

"Yes, I suppose it is," she said with a shrug.

They were all laughing but Dayu was starting to dislike the way that the contessa always managed to be the centre of attention. She seemed to have a constant bevy of good looking men fussing over her at all times. Dayu, with her petite figure and exotic looks, liked to be the centre of attention herself and had enjoyed all the complimentary glances that she had received on the dance floor. Another thing that irked her was that the contessa all but ignored her. It seemed that she talked only to men.

When they got back to the cottage Adrian started to say what fun it was to be with the contessa because she always did such crazy things and so made the night more interesting.

"I don't like her at all," said Dayu. "I think she is a silly lady. And that is why the *leyak* came and took away her clothes."

"You mean that yelping pi dog?"

"It was a *leyak*," said Dayu with finality. "It was in the shape of a dog but it was really a witch of the night that came especially to punish the contessa and steal her expensive dress."

"Well I thought she looked quite cute in Jean-Paul's shirt. It suited her more than the dress; made her look more spunky." He could see that Dayu was getting angry so he stopped.

"Well I think she's a tart," said Dayu.

"No, she is not a tart. She is in fact an aristocrat."

"What's an aristocrat?" asked Dayu.

"A high caste person. Like a Brahmin."

"She's no Brahmana," said Dayu. She almost spat out the words. "Brahmanas are *pedandas* — priests. You mean that contessa woman is a priest?"

"No," laughed Adrian. "She's anything but a priest. But she is still a high caste person." Dayu looked at him in confusion. Adrian was too tired to explain the matter any further. It was all getting too crazy. The heat of the night, the obvious female bitchiness, Dayu's amazing claim that the pi dog was not a dog at all but a witch dressed up as a dog and now the mind boggling suggestion that the contessa was some sort of priest. He struck a match and lit a mosquito coil. "Let's go to bed." he said.

Chapter Six

The Punk

The next morning when Adrian was on his way back from the beach after a mid morning surf he walked past the garden boy who was watering some shrubs in front of the cottage. "Ah, *Selamat pagi*, Mister Adrian. Did you have a good surf?"

"Fine, thank-you. Nice day, isn't it?"

"Yes, it is a holy day and to-night there is a Barong dance at the temple. Have you ever seen a Barong dance?"

"No, I've only been to a monkey dance."

"Yes. I know that one. Monkey dance very good but Barong is more exciting. It is a fight between Barong and Rangda but neither of them ever wins. It is the most famous dance of Bali. If you wish to see it then you should go along to the temple just before eight o'clock. It is quite all right for non-Balinese to attend. You would find it very interesting. Maybe I shall see you there."

"Yes, I'll talk to Dayu about it," he replied.

Dayu's eyes lit up at the suggestion. "Oh yes," she said, "it is always very exciting. I would like to go very much and I think that you would enjoy it too."

So they had an early dinner and rode along the Kuta-Legian road to join the throng of people who were pouring into the temple. They walked into the crowded courtyard and squatted down on their haunches like everyone else. There was a sea of dark faces and black hair that was broken a few feet along by a small group of Europeans the most prominent of whom was Crazy Dog with his shock of spiked pink and green hair. As Adrian caught his eye the punk winked and made a dagger sign across his throat to indicate that he didn't expect to get out of the place alive.

In one corner sat the members of a *gamelan* orchestra. Rice farmers and fishermen by day they came together in the evenings to play their percussion instruments with skill and dedication. They sat cross-legged as they blew their flutes and banged their gongs and flat, bronze discs. The core music was fairly repetitive but, when the gongs were thumped and the metal plates crashed together, a mighty crescendo of sounds rent the air. Many of the men wore *barong* masks over their faces.

Dayu explained that the Barong dance was a demonstration of the eternal struggle between good and evil. The forces of good were represented by Barong, the lord of the forest, who was regarded as the protector of mankind. It was his role to ward off the evil threat posed by Rangda, the queen of the witches and of all the evil spirits.

All eyes turned to the ornate gateway that led into the courtyard. Suddenly Barong appeared under a huge and fearsome looking mask in the shape of a boar's head. This monstrous creature was played by two men who huddled together under a cover and, using their combined total of four legs, pranced around in front of the crowd. A great flowing tail waved up and down from its rear end.

Next came Barong's adversary, Rangda, representing the powers of darkness. With her long, unkempt hair, evil looking fangs, great long tongue and a necklace of human entrails she looked every bit the personification of Evil. Her hands were in the shape of pointed animal claws and her huge, grotesque breasts swung horribly from side to side as she danced across the courtyard to face Barong.

"Why is Rangda made to look so evil?" asked Adrian.

"Because she drinks people's blood. And eats corpses and little children with those dreadful fangs," replied a slightly frightened Dayu. "She even tries to destroy the whole island. But Barong won't let her."

An air of tenseness and excitement gripped the crowed as all eyes concentrated on the two strange and unworldly creatures.

"Why is she carrying that long white cloth?" whispered Adrian.

"That is her secret weapon," replied Dayu.

"How can a cloth be a weapon?"

"It is a magic weapon. Wait and see."

The two mysterious looking characters rushed at each other and so began the mighty struggle between good and evil. After the first two jabs members of the crowd began to jump up and join in the tussle. They attacked Rangda with their *krises* and anything else that they could lay their hands on. Under no circumstances must she be allowed to win for then her black magic and evil powers would be a threat to the whole community.

Just when it appeared that Rangda was about to vanish under a mass of men and *krises* she lifted her white cloth and waved it over their heads. Immediately the men seemed to go into a trance as they began to turn their weapons against themselves. They jabbed their *krises* into their own flesh but they didn't bleed or feel any pain because Barong had made them invulnerable to wounds.

Then a strange thing happened. About half a dozen men, whose view of Rangda had been blocked by Barong's bulky form, rushed across to where Crazy Dog was sitting and began attacking him. With *krises* and sticks. His friends and the Balinese who were sitting nearby rushed to his aid and tried to ward off the attack. A general melee ensued. Adrian quickly realised that, with his spiked and colourful hair, Crazy Dog had been mistaken for Rangda. All he could see was a mass of flailing arms and legs. Crazy Dog could feel the weight of their hot, sweating bodies pressing down on him. Their stale breath smelt of betel nut. Suddenly the punk threw off his attackers and stood up. He pulled out a white handkerchief and flicked it up to his bleeding nose. At the sight of the piece of white cloth the attackers retreated and turned their weapons on to themselves.

Adrian and Dayu had watched in amazement. Adrian tried to rush across and help Crazy Dog but there were too many people in the way. Dayu was completely transfixed. When she saw Crazy Dog pull out the white handkerchief and wave it at the attackers and send them into a trance she knew that he was definitely a *leyak*. With magical powers. But his powers were those of Rangda. Of evil.

By now many of the people were in a state of deep trance — all those who had attacked Rangda — and Crazy Dog — as well as all the men who were wearing *barong* masks themselves; the masks were vested with magical powers which caused those who wore them to be entered by a spirit and go into trance. Adrian looked anxious as he wondered what would happen next. "Don't worry," said Dayu. "They will not go crazy."

"How do you know?"

"Because before the ceremony the masks would have been taken in procession to the river and purified with holy water."

"And what does that mean?"

"It means that their great magical powers won't get out of control."

After a while the activity and excitement began to wane. Dayu was right. Even though so many had been entered by the spirits and had gone into trance they were now withdrawing from the scene of combat. The outcome between Barong and Rangda was — as always — indecisive. Neither good nor evil had conquered. They would have to play out their eternal

174

struggle another night.

Adrian could feel the change in the atmosphere as normality began to return and the spirits passed out of the bodies of those who had been entered. He looked across at Crazy Dog who was laughing with his friends about what had happened. He wasn't hurt. More lanterns were lit and the crowd began to file out through the temple gate and congregate on the road outside. The food trolleys that were parked on the dusty footpath were doing a roaring trade in hot nuts, soup, rice and fruit juices.

Adrian and Dayu rode straight to the Three Monkeys and sat down on two of the high bamboo stools that surrounded the bar. "Two coffees please, Wayan," said Adrian. "And a couple of your special hamburgers. We've just come from the Barong dance at the temple." They chatted about the dance and laughed at the amazing masks that had been worn by the two characters. A few minutes later they heard some motor bikes pull up under the trees outside. Then Crazy Dog came in with three of his friends. Dayu froze. Wayan smiled and Adrian winked at him.

"You know what his name is, don't you?" asked Wayan.

"Yes," replied Adrian.

"Why does he have such a name? Did his parents know that he would turn into a crazy dog?" They both laughed.

In fact Crazy Dog was a lot smarter than either his name or his hair would suggest. An extremely talented musician he had dropped out of his London polytech to devote himself full time to music. He knew what the market wanted and adapted his music to suit its ever fickle and changing tastes. Where other bands had stuck with the music they liked and had been reluctant to move on, Crazy Dog knew that music and popularity were as evanescent as most other things in life. And so he and his band had always tried to anticipate what the public wanted and play to it.

They had started off with hard punk, dabbled in cross-over music using African bongo drums and Indian sitars, and were now looking for a new trend. The more he thought about what he had seen at the temple the more convinced he became that a brief descent into sorcery and black magic was just the thing to keep the fans enthralled for a few more weeks. He knew that they would all be expecting something new and different after the band's six week break.

Crazy Dog and his weird looking friends sat down at a table at the far end of the bar. Dayu was busy talking in Balinese to the barman and Adrian walked out to the men's room. As he passed Crazy Dog's table he asked the punk if he was all right.

"Oh yes, I wasn't hurt. In fact I rather enjoyed it. These idiots," he pointed to his friends, "now want me to change my name to Rangda but I'm not going to. It was only a few months ago that I changed it to 'Crazy Dog'. If I was to change it again the officials at Somerset House would think that I'm trying to dodge my creditors. By the way, Adrian, I want to have a private word with you."

"Certainly. Can you just wait a moment until I come back from the toilet."

"Of course."

When Adrian returned he found that Crazy Dog had wandered out to the terrace and was staring fixedly at a caged white mynah bird. "Yes, what can I do for you, Crazy Dog?" asked Adrian who laughed when he uttered the name.

"That dance to-night? What was it called?"

"Barong."

"Yes, Barong. When I was sitting there watching all those people go crazy a wonderful idea came into my fertile and imaginative mind. Maybe it was the spirits that put it there. But I need your help."

"Why?"

"Because you are in with the Balinese and I want to use you as a channel for a special request."

"What is it?"

"Those masks, and the claws, and the tail and those grotesque, thumping breasts and, of course, the necklace of human entrails. I want them for my punk band back in London. We have to be different and outrageous to survive. Otherwise our fans will get bored and will no longer pay to come and hear us. Fans are so fickle. They are not loyal like the Deadheads are in America. Now, how can I get my hands on all that magical gear? In four weeks' time we are playing at the Hammersmith Odeon. One of us could dress up as Barong and another as Rangda and we could have the fight all over again. Except that I would let the evil one win. She could be the Princess of Darkness and could cast a spell over the whole crowd. Just like she did to-night when she waved that white cloth and sent everyone into a trance. And we could have a *gamelan* gong on the stage and all those metal plates crashing together. And it would look so good on video. Punk has been so boring lately. People are getting tired of all the disgusting antics of the Pistols — the spitting on stage and the chundering. A new direction is needed and to-night I think I found it. Most of those who come to our concerts are gentle people who just want to be a little bit different. They don't want to conform to the ordinary norms of society which they see as drab, grey and downright boring. They want a bit of colour in their lives."

"And in their hair," laughed Adrian.

"Of course. On some days we are pink, on others bright green and sometimes orange. For the Queen's Jubilee last year we went red, white and blue. As punks we are totally apolitical but we do like the Queen. My problem is that I don't know the Balinese like you do. Could you please find out for me if I can buy all that paraphernalia. I don't mind how much it costs. What do you think?"

"It's a zany idea. Certainly has possibilities," replied Adrian.

"Well we can only ask. If you can get them, we'll wear them at Hammersmith and I shall dedicate the first number to you."

Adrian went back to the counter where Dayu was still talking to the barman about the Barong dance. He asked them if he could buy the masks that had been worn by the two characters.

"No," said Dayu, "because they are *sakti*."

"What's that?" asked Adrian.

"It means that they have magical powers," she replied.

"But they're not gods, are they?"

"No, but they are kept in a special place at the temple and are surrounded by offerings. They are kept there until the next time there is a struggle between Barong and Rangda." She didn't want Crazy Dog to have anything to do with the masks. His powers, she thought, were already strong enough. All those people whom he sent into trance! If he were to acquire the extra magic of the masks then he would be truly awesome and frightening.

"Oh well, it was just a suggestion," said Adrian off-handedly.

The barman had been listening with interest and could smell money in the air. He was working at The Three Monkeys on a very low wage which was meant to be supplemented by whatever extra money he could make from the contacts with tourists that the job provided. Sometimes he performed a service like arranging girls for lonely European men or selling a bit of hash to young and eager travellers at exorbitant prices. It was only this extra income which enabled him to provide for his wife and five children.

Dayu wandered outside to the terrace to feed some bread from her hamburger to the caged birds that were hanging from the branches of a huge fig tree. The barman told Adrian in a low voice that he could probably obtain the items that had been requested provided that the price was right.

"How much?" asked Adrian.

Wayan thought for a moment. He went away and wrote some figures down on a sheet of paper. Four amounts only. The first line was the fee that he would have to pay his friend, Rasul, to steal them; the second was his own commission and the third was the total of the two. Then he added an extra amount in case Adrian tried to bargain with him. Which he fully expected. On another sheet of paper he wrote the total amount of 1,800,000 rupiah and walked over and handed it to Adrian.

"Wait," said Adrian as he took it over to Crazy Dog. He showed him the figure and said that he was sure that he could beat Wayan down by about a third.

"Why?" asked Crazy Dog who had converted it in his head to about seven hundred pounds. "We pull in thousands every concert. Pounds not rupiah," he smiled. "Seven hundred pounds is cheap. Does he want the money up front?"

"Hold on. I'll ask him."

When Adrian asked Wayan if he wanted the money now or later the barman's heart jumped a couple of beats. "They have accepted my price without even trying to bargain. That is just unbelievable and ever so good for me and my family." He managed to conceal the ecstatic joy beneath his serene and unchanging smile. So as not to give the appearance of being too pleased or greedy he said in an even tone, "It will be all right if you give me half now and the other half when I deliver the goods."

"When will that be?" asked Adrian.

"In two days' time. Maybe three. But there is one condition. You must hide them and not tell anyone that you have them. Otherwise big trouble. Who should I give them to in two days' time? You or your friend with all the coloured hair?"

"Give them to him," said Adrian who now decided that

179

he wanted to have as little to do with the transaction as possible.

Wayan was puzzled. How could Adrian collect the commission if he were to take himself out of the deal when the final money was to change hands? "Ah, he will probably take his cut when he goes over and gets the deposit from Crazy Dog. I shall watch and see if he puts some of it into his pocket. Of course he will. He would be a fool if he didn't."

Adrian walked over and spoke to Crazy Dog who pulled out a roll of notes. He counted them out. Both pounds and rupiah. Then he handed them to Adrian. Wayan watched the latter walk up to the bar and hand the full amount across the counter. He could hardly believe his eyes. "He is not even taking anything for himself," he thought. "He must be the most stupid man in the world. He's the one who should be called 'Crazy' instead of the clever one with the pink hair. Oh yes, that one is smart all right. He has managed to do the deal without having to give any commission to Adrian who, after all, made the whole thing possible."

The next day Wayan spoke to his friend, Rasul, and put to him the scheme that he had worked out. Wayan had decided that he could not offend the gods directly for fear of what they might do to him in revenge. But, he reasoned, there would be no harm in telling Rasul where the masks and other items were kept in the temple and then casually mentioning that there was a buyer waiting to pay big money for them. The rest would be over to Rasul. After all, he was a Muslim from Java who believed in an all powerful God with Mohammed as his Prophet. To Rasul all the Balinese gods were just figments of rather fertile imaginations and temples were no different from other buildings. And, like Wayan, he too needed more money to feed and keep his young and growing family.

Wayan was very coy when he gave the information to Rasul. He didn't want to bring down the wrath of the gods. "It's not me who is stealing them," he kept rationalising to himself. "If Rasul takes them it is his act and not mine. And I need the money. I'm sure the gods understand that."

The next night Rasul and another of his Javanese friends crept silently into the temple. It was after midnight and the whole place was dark and deserted. They found their way to the shrine where Wayan had told them that the gear was stored. By the light of a couple of weak torches they took the masks, claws, breasts, fangs and tail out to their truck which was parked in a lane nearby. They had just climbed in to drive away when Rasul remembered the necklace of entrails. He jumped out and slipped back into the temple. There was something wrapped in a white cloth at the back of the shrine. He unwound it and saw the hideous object. He secreted it under his jacket and hurried back to the truck. His accomplice was waiting for him with the key in the ignition. They started the engine and drove along some back roads to Rasul's cottage where they unloaded their haul and placed it in a storehouse.

Wayan had told Crazy Dog that they would deliver it all to him the following night at his losmen. Crazy Dog knew that there was something suspicious about the whole business because of the barman's insistence that all the items be hidden so that they wouldn't be seen by the cleaning girls. The punk believed that the need for caution arose because they were all sacred items and therefore should not be sold to tourists. It didn't cross his mind that they had been stolen. He didn't understand all the ramifications of Balinese life and presumed that some priest was being paid off to allow them out of the temple.

In order to comply with Wayan's request he went out and bought two large, square shaped cases. Despite their size they were comparatively light in weight and, even with the masks tucked safely inside, would not be too heavy or expensive to send back to London by air.

When Rasul and Wayan delivered them at ten o'clock

the next night Crazy Dog's first instinct was to put them on and prance around the room like Rangda at the temple. But "No" said the two Indonesians. "Too dangerous. Must put them in the cases now. We will help you." They packed it all in carefully and put the necklace of entrails into a separate small box so that it wouldn't be crushed. Crazy Dog knew that it was illegal to import human parts into Britain without a permit and he more or less expected them to be seized as soon as the cases reached Heathrow. "However, nothing ventured nothing gained," he said out loud.

He realised that the first hurdle would be getting them out of Indonesia. If they were sacred or in the nature of antiquities then they might well be seized before they even left Bali Airport. He decided to have some bribe money ready just in case. However, in the event it wasn't needed. The two cases were checked in as unaccompanied baggage and he was told that they would be sent on a later flight than the one on which he was booked. He watched them pass along the slow and ancient conveyor belt and wondered if he would ever see them again.

When he arrived at Heathrow he had only one bag containing his clothes and a few things that he had bought in Bali — some wooden carvings, jewellery, pink leather pants and a black leather vest studded with silver turtles and snakes. It was nine in the morning and he was extremely tired after the long flight which, with refuelling stops, had taken twenty-one hours.

He joined the queue for Returning British Citizens and waited his turn as the line of weary travellers siphoned off to ten desks that were manned by a bunch of immigration clerks who all looked exactly the same in their drab uniforms and sad, expressionless faces. They reminded Crazy Dog of a row of corpses.

The immigration clerk winced when he read the name on the passport — "Crazy Dog". Underneath was a small notation to say that it had recently been changed to that by deed poll. The clerk smiled inwardly but still managed to maintain a deadly serious countenance as he stamped the blue and gold document and sent the passenger on his way. To Customs.

Crazy Dog was nabbed by a scruffily dressed customs officer who, by his dark face and alien features, looked as if he had just arrived in Britain on an earlier flight. He nearly dropped the punk's passport when he read the name. "Come dees way, sonny," he said as he led him across to a small room. Crazy Dog couldn't help but compare the man's rude and authoritarian attitude with the polite, friendly and disorganised officers at Bali Airport.

The customs man pulled each item out of the bag and examined them carefully. He deliberately broke a couple of delicate wooden carvings that the punk had bought for his mother. Then he found some of Crazy Dog's letters and started reading them although, having received only a primitive mission-school education, he couldn't understand any of the big words. But he found nothing in the nature of contraband. "Have you anything to declare?" he kept asking.

"No. Nothing. Just what is in the bag," replied Crazy Dog.

The officer remained suspicious and walked over and closed the door. "Now vee shall see if you are telling ze truth. Take off all your clothes."

"All of them?" asked Crazy Dog in surprise.

"Dat eez what I said. Take them all off. Even your underpants. Hurry up."

Crazy Dog did as he was told. But not willingly. He hated authority of any kind. Especially when he was subjected to it in his own country by an alien. He felt like telling the officer where to go. But he thought better of it as he didn't want to fall foul of the insidious Race Relations Act by which a bunch of know-all legislators at Westminster had deprived

Englishmen of some of their traditional right of free speech. "Filthy government," he thought to himself, "to let all these people into the country in the first place."

By now Crazy Dog had stripped off all his clothes. Even his dog collar. He was standing naked in the middle of the room and the customs officer was looking him up and down with a lustful leer. He was enjoying the sight of Crazy Dog's slim, lily white body. He usually chose handsome Latin boys to strip search but couldn't resist picking out the interesting looking punk as soon as he saw him. After a few more minutes he told the naked boy to bend over. Crazy Dog felt angry and humiliated but he knew that the officer was acting legally albeit disgustingly. Then he touched him. Crazy Dog screamed. The greasy little man pulled his hand away and told the punk to put his clothes back on. Crazy Dog felt like smashing him in the jaw but he knew that he would then be on a serious charge of assaulting an officer of the government and that it would just be his word against the customs man. He realised that, because of his punk hair style, it would be almost impossible for him to establish his credibility to a crusty old judge. So he stormed out of the room and into the terminal building where he was met by two other members of his band.

The next day he collected all the Barong gear from the Unaccompanied Baggage Section at Heathrow. The two big cases hadn't even been opened. "Just sign here," said the busy clerk. Crazy Dog did so and walked away with the cases.

He smiled at the stupidity of the Customs people. "Too busy staring up people's bums to find anything," he laughed to himself.

Chapter Seven

The Camera

Turtle Beach was a twenty minute drive from Kuta. It could be reached only by a long narrow track that zig-zagged down an almost sheer cliff face to the flat coastal strip below.

When Hilton Smee parked his hired jeep in the grove of banana trees just off the main road he noticed two motor bikes that were standing in the shade. "There must be some other hardy and adventurous souls around besides ourselves," he said to his short, dumpy wife as they unpacked a mass of underwater camera gear and diving equipment from the jeep.

"Or perhaps just as stupid," she replied sourly. "Really, Hilton, I don't know why you couldn't have made do with Airport Reef which is so much more accessible. It will be bad enough carrying all this gear down but what about coming up the hill afterwards?"

"You know why I can't film the coral at Airport Reef. All those bloody surfers get in the way and scare the fish off," replied her husband.

Hilton Smee was a free lance photographer from New York whose two main interests in life were photography and diving. He made his living by the former and spent as much of his leisure time as possible pursuing the latter. He had even combined the two to produce a couple of pictorial books about life under the sea. He was now working on an even more ambitious project: a tome of photographs of all the colourful fish that inhabit coral reefs. He produced these books for interest and pleasure and didn't care whether he made any money out of them or not. In fact he didn't. But they served their purpose as tax deductions for his real income which was substantial. As a free lance photographer his specialty was obtaining intimate shots of celebrities in embarrassing or compromising circumstances. There were no holds barred and it didn't matter whether they consented to be photographed or not. Not surprisingly, he was the darling of the tabloid editors and the bane of the rich and famous.

He had been sued many times for trespass, breach of privacy, deceit, misrepresentation, breach of contract and even breaking into people's houses. But in all cases he had cheerfully paid the fine or the paltry damages which were only ever a pittance compared to the huge sums that he was paid for the pictures when he syndicated them to American, British and European newspapers. In fact, he had taken to loading his prices by ten per cent just to cover possible court costs. He knew the maximum amount of the fines that could be imposed and was thankful that they were infinitesimal compared to what his pictures could fetch.

Unbeknown to the victims, he had snapped pop stars in the bath, topless princesses on motor boats far out in the Mediterranean, an archbishop sitting on the toilet and a Scottish earl allegedly chasing his half dressed countess around the castle grounds with an axe. There were no limits and no rules. Just big prices for the pictures. That was all that mattered. It meant that Smee and his wife could travel the world and photograph coral reefs to their hearts' content without having to worry about the cost.

Hilton Smee had just turned forty-eight. He was bald, had a brown moustache and was just starting to put on the middle-age spread. His wife, a small, non-descript looking woman, was one of those types who was never satisfied; there was always something to complain about. If they were at home in New York she wanted to be in London visiting the museums. After a day at the Victoria and Albert in London she was wishing that she was back in New York. But she did enjoy relaxing on the beach in Bali and doing nothing although she wasn't at all happy about having to help carry all the camera equipment and diving gear down the mile long track to Turtle Beach. She had very little interest in coral and often wondered why her husband had such an obsession about it. Although he never admitted it to himself one of the greatest attractions of swimming on his own amongst a reef was that it provided a complete escape from his loud and nagging wife. Fish don't complain and talk back.

When they finally emerged from the mangroves and nipa palms on to the virgin beach even the complaining Alice Smee had to admit that the long trek had been worth it. Beautiful white sand extended for about half a mile and, apart from a couple of native fishermen standing waist high in the water with their nets, there was not a soul in sight. Just some cormorants and seagulls and a few hermit crabs that were scampering across the sand.

The Smees established their base under a huge pandanus tree. They took some lemonade out of the ice box that was yet another piece of the impedimenta that they had carried down with them. Alice was drenched with perspiration after the long walk and decided to have a quick swim and then lie in the sun while her husband dived and swam around the reef photographing the coral fish. She rummaged through the bag for her swimsuit but it wasn't there. Then she remembered that she hadn't packed it.

"It's all your fault," she said to her husband. "If we hadn't had to worry about all your bloody cameras I wouldn't have been so rushed and disorganised. I mean, really, why on earth did you bring the telephoto lens? It's not even an underwater camera."

"I know," said her husband defensively, "but this place

isn't called 'Turtle Beach' for nothing. Apparently the green turtle sometimes clambers on to the rocks and basks in the sun. They hardly ever come on to a beach except when the mother lays her eggs. And that it always at night. So I might be lucky and get some rare shots of a green turtle sparkling in the sun. That's why I brought the zoom lens."

"Yes, but as usual we've got all your stupid gear and nothing of mine. I don't even have a swimsuit and it's as hot as hell," replied the disgruntled wife.

"Well, it doesn't matter. There's no one else on the beach apart from the fishermen and they're way down the other end. Surely you can swim in the raw."

"Yes, I suppose so," she sighed.

While her husband attended to his cameras and diving gear she took off her clothes and walked down to the sea. It was luke warm and she flopped around for several minutes in about three feet of water. Then she swam further out where the sea was cooler and lay on her back. Feeling refreshed she returned to the beach and stretched out on her towel to dry. Soon she was asleep.

Having loaded his camera and set it up for an under-water expedition Smee decided to eat a paw paw before pulling on his rubber suit and setting off. He sat down beside his sleeping wife and took a bite of the sweet, mushy fruit. There was a small group of rocks about eighty yards out from the beach and he wondered what — if any — marine life they might contain. He picked up the zoom lens and aimed it at the exposed rocks. It took him a few minutes to focus it clearly. He was fascinated by the colours on the rock — dark green, brown and various hues in between. He looked further and gradually saw the unusual but distinctive shapes of four huge turtles that were resting there in the sun. He identified them by their shape rather than by any movement.

He put the camera on them for several minutes and then walked along the beach to shoot them from a different angle.

He used up about half the film and then put the camera back in its case. "Who knows, there may be something even more interesting to film later in the day," he said to himself. "This beach seems to be the natural home of all kinds of exotic creatures."

He put on his rubber suit, grabbed his underwater camera and diving gear, and struggled down the beach. It was extremely hot. Especially inside the thick rubber suit. But he knew that he had to wear it. Coral can be very sharp and cutting. And some of the fish and sea snakes extremely venomous. Soon he was in the sea and swimming out to the reef which enclosed Turtle Beach. "Thank God the beach is totally surrounded by the reef," he thought. "No waves and therefore no bloody surfers to disturb the marine life and the photography."

When he reached the coral he felt that he was in another world. Different shapes, different colours, different creatures. The underwater reef with its maze of openings and crevasses was the home of all sorts of brightly coloured and exotic looking fish. They lived there in a thousand hiding places well away from the open sea where, because of their bright colours, they would be easily spotted and devoured by bigger fish and sharks.

Smee took phctos of flat fish, spotted fish, red and white striped lionfish and the rock like stonefish which were so hard to see. He watched them glide effortlessly through the warm, clear water, changing direction, turning on the spot and rising and falling vertically like a Harrier jump jet. Sometimes they brushed against the protruding branches of the coral. There were many crown of thorns starfish and spotted cowries and cone shells that were attached to the coral. In some of the larger hollows of the reef he could see giant clams four feet long with their undulating edges perfectly sealed.

The coral itself was an incredible living structure —

growing out of chalk in the warm tropical waters and held together by a mass of living organisms and algae. Some of it looked like ruined castles — with battlements and bridges. Some of the coral heads had broken off and fallen down into hollows or on to the seabed. Smee could already see the early stages of their regrowth. Some of the coral was round and some was spiky. He could see sponges and fans and giant mushrooms. There were branches and off-shoots that resembled stag horns and great hollow caverns with broken roofs and floors like stalactites and stalagmites.

Swimming among the infinity of pastel hues and psychedelic colours Smee imagined that he was floating through a vast subterranean flower garden. Schools of fish swam right past his face and he felt at one with the strange and exotic environment.

The two motor bikes that Smee and his wife had seen at the top of the track had been rented by Danny Holland who was having his last full day in Bali before winging his way back to Europe to start his build-up for Wimbledon. He was still enjoying the company of the beautiful, dark Yvonne who had cut such a spunky figure at Pascal's party. The two of them had heard about Turtle Beach and reasoned that, since it was blocked by a reef, it would be calm and sheltered and not crowded with surfers. They would have the beach to themselves and not have to worry about prying eyes and being recognised. "A day when we can be completely on our own," he had said when they parked their bikes. "Look! There's no one else here. It'll be just us and the turtles."

They found a secluded spot at the farthest end of the beach where they swam and sunbathed and laughed and played and ate wild mangoes to their hearts' content. Since it was the last day of his holiday Danny was determined to make the most of it. After that it was several weeks of hard grind. And pressure. First of all a tough indoor tournament in West Germany. Then the French Open. The Queen's Club tournament in London and then the toughest two weeks of the circuit — Wimbledon. The ultimate prize in tennis. He had reached the Final twice but his name was still not engraved on the Men's Singles Cup. "It's this year or not at all," he kept telling himself. But these thoughts were far from his mind as he lay on the beach beside Yvonne's warm and beautiful body and discussed the most ridiculous trivialities.

His usual girlfriend, Anthea, whom he had courted since high school days, was back in Virginia finishing her degree at the College of William and Mary. Danny had told her that he was taking a short break and doing some coaching in Bali as a necessary step in his preparation for Wimbledon. He knew that she could not even consider joining him because of her impending examinations. She for her part knew how vital it was for him — and for her since they planned to get married — to win Wimbledon. And naturally she would not dream of doing anything to undermine his programme of preparation. A Wimbledon crown meant money, prestige and a virtual top seeding for every tournament in the world for the next twelve months. Not to mention the product sponsorships which were more than enough to set one up for life. What Anthea didn't know was what had happened at the *après tennis* party at the end of the Biarritz tournament a couple of weeks earlier. Danny had won the title and the irresistible Yvonne had won the winner. "At least for a short time only," he kept telling himself. He wanted to have a quick and intense fling with her even though he knew that she would soon want to move on to other conquests.

Yvonne Férier had had affairs with all sorts of rock stars, ice skating champions, boxers and even a South American dictator who bought her several diamonds which he paid for out of his State Treasury. All these had been thoroughly documented in the gossip columns of the tabloids so Danny had bought her a ticket on a different flight to his and they had met up at Bali Airport within a couple of hours of each other. He intended to bring Anthea to England just before Wimbledon and by then he knew that Yvonne would be *passé*. In the meantime they could enjoy themselves and throw care to the winds. Away from the prying eyes of sports commentators and gossip columnists. Especially to-day. On this deserted beach.

As they ran along the water's edge kicking a rubber ball and splashing each other they saw the naked and slightly overweight figure of Alice Smee walking down the beach to cool off in the water. She had woken up from her sleep and was once again wet with perspiration. The sandflies and mosquitoes were annoying her so she decided that the best place of refuge would be the sea where she could cool off and wash away the sticky sweat and squashed insects. She passed within a couple of yards of Danny and Yvonne who were wearing no more than she was. They gave a cheery "hello" and passed on their way.

"She too must treasure her privacy to have come all the way down the track," said Danny as they kicked the ball along and then turned round and went back.

"It's him all right," Alice kept telling herself. "And I seem to recognise her face too. Something to do with Paris, I think. Hilton will know." Alice Smee played tennis at her country club on Long Island and always went to nearby Forest Hills to watch the U.S Open. She had often seen Danny Holland playing and had always been struck by his fine style and good looks.

When her husband came out of the water he was full of enthusiasm about his hours of camera work under the sea. "This will just about be enough to finish the book," he kept telling himself.

"You know, we're not the only ones on the beach," said Alice.

"You mean those two motor bikes we saw?"

"I presume so. There are two of them. One is Danny

Holland and I don't know who the girl is. I have seen her face in the papers but can't put a name to it."

"Where are they now?"

"They went back that way." She pointed to the far end of the beach.

Smee grabbed his telephoto lens and swept an arc of distant sand. He could see two bodies that were near the top of the beach. Close together. In fact on top of each other.

"Hmmm. It's our lucky day," he said. "The gods must be smiling on us."

"What do you mean?" asked his wife.

"We've just made sixty thousand dollars. I'll give you some of it seeing that you spotted them first." She could see the zoom lens working in overdrive as her husband recorded from a distance every movement and every position of the carefree young lovers further down the beach.

"You don't mean that you're going to sell them to the newspapers?" she asked.

"That is exactly what I mean. This is a real scoop. I can syndicate it across the States, Rome, Paris and, of course, those crummy London tabloids."

"But it's not fair. I feel guilty about it. After all, we're naked too. It just seems so natural down here."

"Yes, but not in the caverns of Manhattan or the slums of London. There it will be regarded as scandalous and obscene. There's nothing much else happening in the world at the moment — no wars or Watergates — so these pictures should be able to fill a double page spread."

"I don't think that they should be penalised for enjoying a nice day at the beach."

"It is the price he has to pay for being rich and famous. He'll get over it. Since it's an unexpected bonus I'm prepared to give you half of what I get for them. Now will you stop complaining?" She thought about it. About the diamond necklace that she had seen at Tiffany's. She didn't complain any more.

Smee got several shots of the girl's face. He too recognised it but couldn't match it with a name. "We'll wait until they come along here to go up the track," he said. "Then I might be able to work out who she is." He went and hid the cameras in the undergrowth. Out of sight.

About an hour later they saw Danny and the girl walking along the sand towards the track. He was wearing a pair of multi coloured beach shorts and she was wrapped in a bright pink sarong.

"Good afternoon," said Smee. "Lovely and quiet down here, isn't it?"

"Oh yes. We've had such a lovely day, thank-you," replied Danny. "Did you see the huge turtles out on the rocks? We swam out to them and they are truly amazing."

"Yes, I saw them from the beach," said Smee. "I wish I'd brought a camera down. They would have made a good photo."

"Oh well, we must be on our way. It's a long way back to the road." Danny put his arm around Yvonne and they set off up the hill. Smee watched them until they were out of sight.

"It's Yvonne Férier," he said. "You know, the one who was involved in that scandal at the race-track. I remember now; it was at Longchamp during the running of the Arc de Triomphe last year. She took off all her clothes in front of the Main Stand. Said that she was too hot but all the losing owners claimed that she distracted their horses and they had to have an official inquiry into it. The real problem was that all the television cameras missed the last few furlongs because they were firmly planted on her curves. Anyway, this gives the photos an even greater value. Perhaps up to ninety thousand dollars."

"Well I don't know why newspapers would pay ninety thousand for photos of a couple of young people on the beach. I still think it's unfair."

194

"Stop complaining. Life itself is unfair. It's just one mad scramble for gold. And you're in for half anyway. Half of the new and bigger amount."

They waited for half an hour before starting off up the track. Smee didn't want the other two to see the camera equipment and he reasoned — correctly as it turned out — that they would be gone by the time that he and his wife arrived at the jeep.

"Are you going to send the photos off immediately?" asked Alice.

"No, they can wait. There were no other photographers in the hunt. We'll hold off for a month or so. Until Wimbledon. Then they'll have the most impact. Especially if he reaches the final."

Chapter Eight

The Trance

Adrian rose at seven and went out to the verandah. He could see the women of the uncle's household reverently placing rings of red flowers around the bases of the coconut trees. He turned suddenly as Dayu appeared in the doorway. She was still wiping the sleep out of her moon-like eyes and was wearing a dark blue sarong that she had wound effortlessly around her waist. Her bare breasts hung loose in the Balinese way.

"What are those women doing?" he asked. "Is there going to be a party or something?"

She thought for a moment before she spoke. "No, no party. To-day is coconut festival day. Many coconut trees will be decorated with red flowers."

"Why?"

"Part of our religion is to worship nature. Also it is hoped that all those bright flowers will create a joyful atmosphere and attract the gods. Then some good things might happen to uncle's family. And to us."

"You mean he might get another jim?"

"No. One jim is enough and that uncle has one of the best." For a moment Adrian looked pensive. He was thinking how much easier life would be if he had his own jim.

They saw very little of Nyoman's uncle in spite of the fact that he lived only fifty yards away — behind the wall at the far end of the lawn. He was always out attending to his many and varied businesses and in some ways was as big a mystery as his invisible but highly effective jim. On the few occasions when he went past he always said "Hello" but that was all.

Nyoman had been away for four weeks. Adrian was expecting him back any day and assumed that he would want his cottage back. "We'll just have to find another one nearby," he said. "Shouldn't be too much of a problem but there's no point in worrying about it until he gets back. He'll let us stay on for a few days until we find something."

Four weeks became five and still there was no sign of the globe-trotting surfer. Then suddenly one morning, the uncle's daughter appeared on the verandah and very shyly handed Adrian a letter. "*Terima kasih*," he said as he sat down to read it. It was from Nyoman but it hadn't been written by him. Because of his poor command of written English he had asked one of his American friends to write it for him. He had signed at the bottom and drawn a small picture of a surfer riding into a tube.

"Dear Adrian — my good friend,

You are enjoying Bali? I know you will be. For you it is the right place to come. For me Hawaii was the right place to come. I won the Island Classic and came third in the Pipeline contest. Here the gods make the waves even bigger than at Uluwatu. And in California I reached the final heat in the Newport contest and won the Malibu one. So you can see that the gods have been very good to me and I have won much prize money. My uncle tells me that I must stay over here and make more money. I don't mind as I'm liking it and everybody is kind to me. But I think America is crazy! More crazy than Australia! Cars everywhere and no donkey-carts or pi dogs in the streets.

How is my little cottage? I hope you like it.

Please stay on there until I return. But that will not be for many months as I have entered more contests and am doing a sports sponsorship for a new line of board shorts. All this pleases my uncle very much.

Anyway, my friend, I wish you good surfing and next time you're at Uluwatu I want you to choose a wave and ride it for me. Although my body is over here in America my spirit is still in Bali.

From your good surfing friend,
Nyoman."

"Well," said Adrian, "that's both good news and bad news."

"What do you mean by that?" asked Dayu.

"The bad news is that Nyoman is not coming back for a long time. The good news is that we can stay on here a bit longer."

"Good," she said as she looked up from her task of preparing the offerings that were about to be placed on the shrine at the back of the house.

"Yes, but I'll have to go and talk to his uncle and see if it's cool for us to stay."

"But Nyoman says we can."

"Yes, but it seems that the place belongs to his uncle."

Dayu shrugged her shoulders. All she knew was that it was a nice house to live in and so far the bad spirits had been kept out. But only because she always kept the front door closed at night.

"I'll be back in a few minutes," he said. "I just want to go and check with the uncle that it's all okay."

Dayu began to worry; she felt that Adrian was looking for unnecessary trouble. The uncle might say "No". But only because Adrian went and asked him. "Better to let sleeping dogs lie," she thought. "To go and raise the matter is like daring the gods. Tempting them to say 'No'."

When he came back she looked up from the floor where she was still putting the rice and flowers into the tiny offering baskets. "What did he say?" she asked in trepidation.

"He wasn't there. He never is. They said that he'll be back in three days. He's gone to Java." The uncle was in fact in Jakarta with one of his business partners, a four star general. They were arranging a shipment of Javanese rhinoceros horn to Singapore where it would be used as an aphrodisiac by the Chinese who preferred it to the African rhino horn and accordingly paid a very good price for it.

When Adrian finally caught up with the uncle a week later he brushed the matter aside and said that if Nyoman said it was all right to stay then it was all right by him. "But please let me pay you some rent," said Adrian. "After all, I would have to pay if I stayed somewhere else."

"No rent," he said with a wave of the hand. "But I talk to you later." And he rushed off again to do some more business.

"Presumably," thought Adrian unkindly, "with his partner, the jim."

"Oh good," said Dayu when Adrian told her that they could keep the cottage, "I knew he would agree."

"But you seemed a bit worried a few days ago."

"Yes, but I have put lots of extra offerings out since then. Certainly enough for the gods to be pleased so as to let us keep the place. We have looked after it and not let the demons in the door."

"All I know is that we're having a bloody good time here," said Adrian.

"That's because I keep the front door closed at night."

Unfortunately Dayu's methodical ways were not always mirrored by Adrian. He had forgotten to fill the tank of the trail bike with the result that, despite several efforts, the thing just wouldn't start. "Oh well, it's a nice evening for a walk," he said as he took her tiny hand and led her up the road.

They went first to Happy Harry's for a meal. Harry's was a good place to eat so long as you didn't mind a long wait between placing the order and actually having it put on the table. Adrian never minded. He had become used to Eastern disorder and, besides, Harry had enough grace to entertain his diners while they waited. He had installed a screen high on the wall above the tables and had somehow acquired an old film projector and three surfing movies which he screened non-stop one after the other every night from six o'clock until closing time. Adrian had seen them many times but still found that he was drawn to Harry's slow service and sometimes indifferent food like a magnet. Dayu too had seen them several times and could even remember what shots were going to come next.

She was impressed by surfing — especially the really radical manoeuvres — and took a possessive pride in Adrian's fine style and achievements in the water. But she had no desire to get on a board herself. Like painting, carving and playing musical instruments she regarded it as men's work. Dayu had only ever seen one girl surfing — a buxom American off Legian Beach — and she thought that it all looked very undignified. Almost as bad as a woman painting a mural or tapping an xylophone!

When the waiter eventually brought their meals of *mie goreng* — fried noodles, meat and vegetables — Adrian didn't even notice him. Not until Dayu playfully jabbed him in the ribs. It wasn't until the film projector suffered one of its periodic breakdowns that they said good-bye to Harry and walked the few yards to the Mango Tree for some coffee. Soon Pascal arrived. He told them how he had just come from the airport where he had seen Jerome off on the Garuda flight to Paris. "He had to get back for a fashion showing. He was so unhappy at leaving. And you should have seen all the luggage. Four suitcases of leather designs that he had made here especially for his shop on the Boulevard Saint Michel. There were leather skirts, pants, jackets — everything. He says they will all be sold within two weeks."

"What about you, Pascal?" asked Adrian. "When do we have to say good-bye to you?"

"Oh, not for another couple of weeks. I have forgotten what day it is but the airline has promised to contact me two days before departure. Until then I just forget about it so that I can enjoy myself completely. Without any grey clouds on the horizon. Like returning to my office."

When Maria arrived Pascal kissed her warmly and suggested that they move on to the Jolly Frog for dancing. They all climbed into the Frenchman's big open VW Safari wagon. After a while the road began to narrow. When a big rubbish truck came the other way Pascal had to slow down and veer towards some trees at the side of the road to let it pass. Suddenly Maria screamed. Then they all began laughing. A monkey had dropped down from an overhanging branch and was jumping around in the back seat. It stood on the top of the headrest and began playing with Maria's long brown hair. It picked up some tresses and rubbed them against its face. Everyone was laughing and talking to the monkey. Except for Dayu. "It is a *leyak*," she thought. "The spirits must be very strong to-night. We had better be careful. Especially since we shall be so near the sea." But she kept her thoughts to herself. The monkey soon tired of his noisy human friends and jumped over the side of the car to return to the wild.

They resumed their journey and soon joined the crowd that was pouring into the Jolly Frog. The night was hot and humid, the music fast and the dancing wild. When "Take A Walk On The Wild Side" was played everyone got up on the floor and started dancing madly. Dayu was enjoying herself. She loved all kinds of dancing from the *legong* dances at the temple to rock and roll at the disco. She stared at all the

European dancers who were contorting their bodies into all sorts of weird shapes. "They are all in trance," she thought. "The spirits have entered their bodies. Just like at the temple. It is a communal trance."

When the music finally stopped Adrian looked at his watch. It was 3 a.m. The revellers were filing outside to the car park. It was the usual noisy, crazy Kuta night scene. Revving motor bikes, screaming *bemo* drivers, laughing partygoers, and people offering good time girls and younger sisters for those who had failed to make a pick-up on the dance floor. The night air was heavy with the fragrance of incense, clove cigarettes and smoke from the little fires of the roasted nut vendors.

The large open tourer vehicle that Pascal had hired was, he boasted, big enough to carry the whole French rugby team. He sat at the wheel while about a dozen people climbed in. "Come on," he said. "Everybody in. The more the merrier. I am going to drive along the beach."

Adrian was laughing at the crazy scene. He felt Dayu nudge him. "What's the matter?" he asked.

"Let's take a *bemo*. Pascal is too drunk to drive. Besides, he is going to drive on the beach."

"Not the bad spirits of *pasih* again?" said Adrian in exasperation. "Honestly Dayu, it will be quite all right. He is not drunk; he is just happy. And even if he does roll the car we'd only fall on the soft sand. Come on, let's get in. It'll be a bit of a thrill." She didn't say anything but took his hand as he lifted her over the side and into the crowded back seat.

"Are we ready?" Pascal called out. Most of the passengers were still holding on to their last drinks. Everyone was laughing. Except for Dayu. Zoom! Off they went.

"I am in a crazy mood," called the driver. "It must be the magical atmosphere of the Balinese night." He swung the car down the ramp to the beach and drove along the sand. Two motor bikes were having a race through the shallow water at the edge of the sea. Their wheels were throwing up a line of spray that glistened in the moonlight.

"Let's do the same," cried Pascal as he turned the car down to the water's edge. And into the sea. The rear wheels sent up a great spray that drenched the passengers in the back seat. Everyone was screaming and laughing. Dayu was smiling but Adrian could feel that she was tense. The car was starting to sway with the force of the water pushing against it. Pascal was loving it and the others were calling out and urging him on to even crazier heights.

Dayu saw it first. Then Adrian. Normally a four foot swell of water would have delighted him. But not this one. He leaned over to try and grab the steering wheel so as to turn the car shorewards. But there were too many sprawling bodies in between. The wave broke with a thunderous crash just as it reached the car. Its violent force picked the vehicle up and threw it. Everyone was holding their heads and cowering under the swirling water.

The engine was flooded. And dead. A couple of passengers had bumped their heads on the metal side when the car was momentarily thrown but no one was hurt. The mass of bodies provided protection for all. The undertow was now hurling its weight against the other side of the car as the aftermath of the wave returned to sea. There was no way that the car could be rescued. "Everybody out," called Adrian who knew the strength and moods of the ocean better than the others. When the tide receded they found that they were in about four feet of water and the car was sinking steadily in the soft sand. They all climbed over the sides and, somewhat shaken, began making their way to the beach.

The two motor cyclists saw the whole thing. They steered their own machines out of the water and pulled up on the sand. "What the hell are you crazy stuntmen doing?" one of them called out as they ran into the sea to help.

"Oh, it was just a little accident," said Pascal who had

been considerably chastened by the experience. Everyone felt safe again once they were on the beach. The driver was the butt of one or two jokes and soon they were all laughing. But Dayu was still frightened. It was just another manifestation of the terrible powers of *pasih*.

"Come on," she whispered to Adrian. "Let's get off the beach and up to the road." This time he didn't argue or make light of her fears.

"Sorry Pascal," he said, "we have to get going."

"Well, it looks like the party's over," replied the Frenchman. "Please accept my apologies. I went too far. It was all my fault."

"No, it was everybody's fault," said Adrian. "We all egged you on."

Dayu regarded such conversation as irrelevant. She knew whose fault it was. Not Pascal's. Not the passengers. But the demons. *Pasih*.

Adrian and Dayu did not have far to walk to the cottage for Pascal had ditched them only a few hundred yards along the beach from where they usually swam. Dayu didn't say much as they walked through the silent darkness. But she felt better with every step that took them further away from the beach. And the sea. "Maybe next time we take the *bemo*," she said.

"Perhaps, perhaps," replied Adrian. On the one hand he had rather enjoyed the spill. "It's not every surfer who can say that he's ridden a wave in a car," he laughed to himself. But deep down he too recognised the unknown and mysterious powers of the ocean.

The next morning they were woken by a lot of chatter that was coming from the coconut plantation on the other side of the six foot stone wall that surrounded the compound. The noise seemed to be coming from the sky rather than the ground. So Adrian jumped out of bed and walked out to the tiny balcony. When his sleepy head emerged through the narrow doorway he was assailed by a chorus of "*Selamat pagi*, sir."

He looked up and saw several boys at the top of the coconut trees — all laughing and chattering as easily as if their feet were place firmly on the ground. Some of the trees were as high as twelve metres and each boy's head was up in the bunch of coconuts at the top. With one hand gripping the tree's tall stem the other was holding a knife that was hacking off the ripe coconuts and dropping them to the ground. Thud! Thud! Thud! Then, having stripped the tree of all its ripe fruit, they put the knives in their mouths and, using both hands and legs, ran down the tree like a monkey. Then up another one. They climbed faster than they descended. Adrian was struck by the ease and non-chalance with which they went about their apparently dangerous task. They were the most cheerful and careless bunch of workers he'd ever seen.

As he stood there watching he felt some tiny, soft fingers run down his back. Dayu had come out to see what was going on. "It must be the time for them to cut off the coconuts," she said as she blinked her eyes in the sunlight. "It is good to see them drop to the ground. Otherwise they can be dangerous. If they are not picked they can blow down in a strong wind and hit you on the head. If the spirits don't like you they will throw a coconut at you from the sky. I have even seen one crash through the roof of a car. Like a bomb."

There were some women on the ground who, keeping a safe distance from the action, started to stack them into great square pyramids. Some of the outer shells split open when they hit the ground. "Look at all those neat pyramids!" exclaimed Adrian.

"Yes," replied Dayu, "but they won't remain like that for long. To-night the wild boars will be attracted by their smell and will come and break up the piles with their snouts. And they will crush some of the nuts with their jaws to drink the delicious milk."

Before he went in from the balcony Adrian was hailed by Thierry who called out that he had already been down to the beach and there was no rideable surf. So he turned to Dayu and suggested that they spend the day on the beach soaking up the sun. "Good idea," she said, "I'll have you for the whole day."

When they walked down to the water's edge they were able to look along the beach and see the car from the night before. It was sticking up out of the sea about two hundred yards away. Quite a crowd had gathered on the sand to have a look at it. Then a big group of Balinese started to file out from the trees and form a couple of lines on the sand.

"Let's go and see what's happening," said Adrian.

"No, I don't want to go near it," replied Dayu. "Too many bad things might happen."

"What? In the daytime?"

"Yes. The spirits are also present during the day. They are always around. It is just that they are stronger in the dark."

"Well I'm going to go and have a look. I wouldn't mind finding the money that I lost last night. It was in a bill folder so I might find it intact."

"The spirits would have taken it," she said.

"Maybe. But it's worth a try. Come on, let's go."

"No, I stay here."

"All right. I'll be back shortly."

As he got nearer the crowd a truly amazing scene met his eyes. Several Balinese men were out in the water tying a couple of very thick ropes to the car. These led on to the beach where they were being fed through the hands of two long lines of villagers — young men, old men, women and boys. Adrian estimated that there were at least a couple of hundred people on the ropes. They were laughing and smiling as they dug their feet into the sand to start pulling the car out of the sea. And there in the middle was Pascal in his Jean Patou beach shorts and designer shirt.

"One, two, three — pull. One, two, three — pull," he was calling out. The Balinese in the sea were now rocking the car out of the sand as those on the beach pulled for all they were worth. The car started to move. At first very slowly as it dragged a heap of wet sand with it. The men in the water managed, with the help of the current, to turn it round to face the beach. Things then began to improve.

"One, two, three — pull," cried Pascal. This time the progress was so rapid that the natives all fell down on the sand like two rows of skittles. They were all enjoying it immensely. It was another twenty minutes before the car was pulled above the tide line. By then the farthest ends of the two rows of tuggers were right up in the trees.

Pascal called out *"Terima kasih"* and picked up his black nylon bag. He pulled out several thick bundles of blue one thousand rupiah notes and started handing them out to the villagers as they filed past in line. Each one smiled and said *"Terima kasih"*. A couple of old fishermen who had been sitting with their nets a few feet away and who had treated the whole scene with studied disinterest now got up and joined the queue for the money. So did a group of massage ladies who happened to be passing.

There were several groups of Balinese on the sand. All with thousand rupiahs notes in their hands. After they took their wages from Pascal most of them got lost in the crowd and then rejoined the queue. Adrian saw one man go past five times. Each time Pascal handed him a crisp blue note and each time the man smiled and said *"Terima kasih"*.

Adrian overheard some of them talking. They said that Pascal had been sent by the gods to give them presents. Others said that he was an oversize jim who had taken money off the bad people and was now redistributing it to better and more worthy types. Like themselves. They were all wondering how the car ever got into the sea in the first place. They had only ever seen cars on the roads and they knew that, for a car to be in the sea, the gods must have been terribly powerful to have lured it all the way down from the road. Some of them regarded it as a punishment for some really bad deed that must have been committed by the car.

The news of Pascal's godly and generous qualities soon reached the nearby village of Seminyak and all the people who hadn't gone down to pull on the ropes were now making their way to the beach to collect the money. They even beat out a secret message on the *kulkul* drum which was in the signal tower by the temple. The drum beats ordered everybody to the beach to partake of the gods' largesse. But the latecomers missed out. After about half an hour Pascal ran out of money. A murmur of disappointment ran through the crowd and they began to point to those who had just arrived in the queue. But secretly they were all delighted with what they had received. Some families had made ten thousand rupiah.

Adrian could hardly believe what he had seen. It was like the loaves and the fishes. As the money was being handed out he had watched the crowd's rising excitement with concern. He feared that they might riot when the funds ran out. So he called out to Pascal in French and told him to back slowly up into the trees where he would join him and then they could both lose themselves in the maze of jungle tracks. Some of the people followed them. "No more, no more. *Terima kasih*," the two of them kept saying. Then Pascal held up his empty bag and turned it upside down above his head. Nothing fell out and most of the crowd turned away. Only about a dozen men kept following them through the mangroves and nipa palms. Pascal and Adrian kept walking and didn't look behind. Soon there were no more sounds of footsteps or the rustling of branches as the last of the villagers came to realise that Pascal's divine qualities had evaporated when he handed out the last banknote.

The two of them took a circuitous route that brought them back on to the beach where Dayu was lying. "What the hell did you do that for, Pascal?" asked Adrian. "It must have cost you a fortune."

"Oh no, not really. I cashed some traveller's cheques and the money-changer gave me his entire stock of thousand rupiah notes. The tow truck can not come until late this afternoon and I just had to get the car up on to the beach before the tide comes up high. Otherwise we might lose it altogether. Those devils that live in the ocean would take it and I'd never see it again. So I went and told them at the village that I would pay them to come and help me pull it out and ... well, you saw the rest."

Adrian began to laugh. "How much did it cost you?" he asked.

"I don't know. But it was cheaper than having to pay for a new vehicle. There is no insurance here, you know. Anyway, I got my money's worth. Not only did we retrieve the car but it was great fun as well. And I think the Balinese enjoyed it too."

"Dayu and I have decided that next time we're at the Jolly Frog we'll take a *bemo*."

"Ah, there is Dayu now," said Pascal. "And she looks so perfect in that pink bikini. There are always so many beautiful girls on this part of the beach. I think I'll stay here for the rest of the day."

They told Dayu all about the rescue. The more they told her about the money scramble the more she laughed. Pascal stayed with them for the rest of the day. They spent their time swimming, sunbathing, eating fresh slices of pineapple and having massages on the sand. "*C'est la vie, c'est la vie,*" he said as he closed his dark, Gallic eyes and fell asleep.

About half past three Adrian was woken by the loud noise of an ancient tow truck that was ploughing its way through the sand at about fifteen miles an hour. There were six men standing on the back and holding on to the hoist bars. They were laughing and joking and obviously enjoying the novelty of a beach tow instead of the usual calls to broken down and stranded vehicles on the roads and in the jungle.

"Hey Pascal! Wake up! There's your tow truck," said Adrian.

"Oh yes," he said as he blinked his eyes in the sunlight. Then he pulled on his shorts and ran down the beach waving his arms. The driver stopped and Pascal spoke to him. Then he jumped on the back and rode with the others to where the car was still sitting above the high water mark.

The men jumped off the truck and began attaching its chains to the stranded car. A small crowd began to gather in the hope of receiving further money but it took the men only a few minutes to complete the operation. Then the creaking truck dragged its cargo up the beach and on to the road. This time its speed was about ten miles an hour. Pascal walked back to where Adrian and Dayu were lying. "Well, thank God that's over," he said. "They are going to clean it with high pressure hoses and get it going again. I should have it back in a couple of days. In the meantime I shall have to use the motor bike. It was such a silly thing that I did last night. If it wasn't for that last freak wave it would have been all right."

"Yes," thought Adrian, "but if you were a surfer you would have had a better understanding of the ocean. It is always the master. Not even man's greatest invention, the motor car, can control it."

Dayu had similar thoughts. She too knew how dangerous it was to test the force of the sea. To dare the demons who lived in it.

When Adrian and Dayu walked back to the cottage they saw a huge, brightly coloured butterfuly resting on the leaf of a banana tree next to the verandah. Its wings were tucked together and folded edgeways to the sun so as to minimise its shadow and so make itself less conspicuous to predators.

"Look at that butterfly," said Dayu. "It is so lucky to have such a sunny day."

"What do you mean?"

"They only live for one day. If it is a windy or gloomy day then its whole life will be a disappointment. But that one is lucky. A life of sunshine and it is makimg the most of it. By resting!"

"We should all be like the butterfly," said Adrian. "I think it is so important to get the most out of every day. Just in case it's the last one. Like the butterfly's. That is why I live as I do. For whatever pleasure I can get out of the day — and the night. But pleasure doesn't always last."

Suddenly there was a great noise in the trees above. They both looked up to see a large brown bat with outstretched wings. It was flapping around at the top of the banana trees. It waved its wide wings and flew downwards. It seemed to hover for an instant. Then it dived. The two of them watched in amazement — then horror — as it caught the resting butterfly in its mouth and then winged its way back into the sky. Adrian could feel Dayu tighten her grip on his hand. "It is a *leyak*," she whispered.

They stood there craning their necks and watching the bat become smaller and smaller in the distance. Then Adrian spoke, "As I was saying, pleasure doesn't always last. Life can be very fragile. Just as it was for the poor butterfly."

"Do you think we'll all be destroyed like the butterfly?" asked Dayu. She was still getting over the shock of the *leyak* bat.

"Our bodies, yes; but not our souls," replied Adrian. "But while we're alive we just have to make sure that we have as much fun as we can." Which was what he had been doing ever since he arrived in Bali. Especially since meeting Dayu. She was so soft and gentle and pleasing in every way. She knew how to make him feel like a king — towelling him down

211

after a surf, unzipping his wetsuit and generally attending to his every need. But he was living only for the present — as if every day might be the last one to enjoy. That's how he had always surfed. He gave his all to every wave as if it was the last one that would ever break. Which was why he was such a good surfer. But he did tend to live for the moment. And in Bali that was very easy to do.

It had been different when he was with Alex. They had planned the future together and everything was moving nicely towards a wedding. He would have been happy with that. But all those dreams were shattered in one single terrible second. It suggested to him the futility of making plans when there was so clearly a higher force that could intervene and change everything.

Since he had been with Dayu he had never thought any further ahead than the next day and what sort of waves it was likely to bring. He didn't even think of *après* Bali although he knew that he would have to face it sooner or later. They wouldn't keep renewing his visa forever.

Dayu sometimes wondered at his attitude. She too knew that plans were always directed by the gods. As much as she was enjoying the western way of life with Adrian and all his friends she was starting to wonder where it would all lead. If Adrian would ask her to go and live in Australia with him she would say "yes" and try her utmost to keep him happy for the rest of time. After all, the only other alternative was to go back to Klian's and that was the last thing she wanted to do. Sometimes she carefully but gently alluded to the future but Adrian always brushed it aside and, of course, she wouldn't press the point. She knew from her upbringing that it was the man's job to make such decisions and her role was to go along with them and make a comfortable home that would be pleasing to the head of the household. She was often surprised at the way that some western women ordered their husbands and boyfriends around. She regarded such behaviour as very odd and determined that that was one Western habit that she would never adopt.

The death of the butterfly after only one day of life had made Adrian think of Alex and the way that she was taken after such a very short life span. Tears welled up in his eyes. Dayu pulled out his handkerchief and smiled gently as she wiped them away. She had never seen him cry before. In one way she was pleased because it showed his vulnerability. It meant that he needed her soft and soothing touch more than ever. But what was troubling him? He had never told her about Alex. Since he had come to Bali to escape the past and enjoy the present he felt no reason to inflict the tragedy of the one on to the joy of the other. He sometimes tried to kid himself that he had been reincarnated into another life. From Western to Balinese. But it didn't work. He had loved Alex too much to forget her so quickly. But Dayu didn't know any of this and regarded tears as evidence of the entry of some mysterious spirit into his body; one that she hadn't noticed before. What had got inside him that was so strong as to make him cry? A god or a demon? Then she remembered the *leyak* that destroyed the butterfly. Of course, it would have been the same spirit that entered Adrian and made him cry. Therefore, the tears must be ones of sorrow — inflicted by a very powerful evil spirit. She shivered in horror and wondered if it was still there.

"Let's go," she whispered. "It is not good to stay here. Many bad things happen. Let's go to Manoel's for afternoon coffee. Safer up there."

Adrian walked behind her up the track. "Ah," she thought, "the *leyak* has made him very weak. First he cries and now he just follows me without question. It is all due to the *leyak* for it is the spirits that determine everything we do."

Manoel's was almost empty. Only two tables were occupied. One by a group of laughing Americans and the other by two rather butch looking women in their mid-thirties with short haircuts, hairy legs and deep, authoritarian voices. Dayu led Adrian over to a table near the middle and they looked around for Manoel. Wayan, the head boy, came over and said that the master was having his siesta.

"Well, we'd like two coffees, please," said Adrian.

"Anything to eat?" asked Wayan.

"Not for me. Dayu?"

"Yes, fruit salad please."

The boy walked off to prepare the order and Adrian stared around the restaurant. He didn't feel much like talking or reading any of the well thumbed magazines. He looked across at the clock that stood on the cash register table. It was quarter past four. Somewhere on the thatched roof he could hear a gecko making loud intermittent croaks. The sounds coming from the other two tables were a study in contrast. The Americans were telling jokes and laughing loudly whereas the two butch women were engaged in a deadly serious conversation that ranged from pay rates for woman machinists to abortion. Adrian listened for a while and was able to deduce that one was a politician and the other some bossy and self-opinionated bureaucrat. It made him appreciate Dayu all the more. He looked at her across the table and wondered what was going on behind those dark, inscrutable eyes. "What are you thinking about?" he asked. "What was the last thought that passed through your mind?"

"I am counting the number of times that the gecko chirps before it stops. So far it has been six, five, five, four and six."

"Well, I guess it's as good as counting sheep. Are you trying to put yourself to sleep?"

"No."

"Then why worry about the gecko?"

"Because if it croaks seven times without stopping it is a sign of good luck. And we need some good luck after what happened this afternoon."

"Meaning?"

"The butterfly. And then I think that *leyak* got inside you. And it is still there."

"What *leyak*?"

"The bat."

Adrian began to flap his arms as if he were a bat. One of the butch women gave him a disapproving stare. Dayu started to laugh at his antics. She knew that the bad spirit must be on its way out. His tears of a few minutes ago had turned to laughter. But she wanted confirmation. She was still counting the gecko sounds. Six. Five. She knew that a lucky seven would mean that the *leyak* had gone altogether. There was no way that a gecko could croak seven times if a bad spirit was nearby. "We must hear seven of them in a row and then we know that the spirit has definitely gone," she said. Adrian was starting to enjoy it. They looked at each other as they counted. One, two, three, four, five, stop. Then one, two, three, four, stop. And again. One, two, three, four, five, six ... seven!

Adrian jumped up from the table and shouted with glee. "I'm free. I'm free of the evil spirit. No more bats inside me," he yelled.

Dayu was laughing at him and so were the Americans. One of them walked over to shake hands. "Congratulations," he said, "I saw it fly out the window." Everyone was joining in the joke. Even Wayan who was happy to see an evil spirit leave the restaurant. But not the two butch ones. Laughter was no part of their world.

"As I was saying," said the uglier of the two, "a woman should be allowed to abort whenever she feels like it. I mean, speaking hypothetically of course, if I was to get pregnant and a snap election was called then I would immediately have an abortion. I wouldn't want to campaign if I was pregnant. And my career must come first."

"Of course," said the other in an even deeper voice.

215

Then they picked up their masculine looking leather wallets and walked over to the cash register to pay their bill.

Dayu was happy to see Adrian back to his normal self and free of the *leyak*. She was still laughing about the way he jumped up from the table and screamed and made everyone laugh. All except the two women at Table Three. "Why did those two not laugh?" she asked.

"Oh, don't take any notice of them. They're just baby killers."

"You serious?"

"Yes," he said. She knew he wasn't joking. The very thought of it sent a shiver down her spine. Then she thought back to the gecko.

"Seven is always a lucky number," she said.

"Yes, I know."

"How do you know?"

"Because there are seven waves in a set."

After the Americans left there were no other customers in the restaurant. Wayan came over and sat down at their table. "What are your plans for the evening?" he asked. "Disco?"

"No," replied Adrian. "We've been invited to a farewell party for Eduardo. He's one of the Brazilians. Nice chap. We've surfed together a bit. But we're going to come here for a meal first. Anything special on the menu?"

"I don't know. I won't be here," replied Wayan. "I'm going to a fire dance in the Monkey Forest."

"I've yet to go to a fire dance," said Adrian. "I've only been to the monkey dance up at Semang and the Barong ceremony at the temple when they all attacked Crazy Dog. What will it be like to-night?"

"Dance and trance," replied Dayu. "But more trance than dance." Wayan looked at her as if she had spoken out of turn.

"May I come?" asked Adrian.

They both hesitated. "I suppose so," said Wayan without much enthusiasm.

"No," said Dayu. "I think you would have a better time at Eduardo's party."

"Sometimes I get tired of parties," he said. "To-night I would rather go to the fire dance."

Dayu then interrupted and said rather clumsily, "No, we go to the party. Too many bad things happen in the forest at night."

"Like what?"

"There are spirits and many monkey *leyaks* that jump down from the trees and harm you. That is why it is called the Monkey Forest."

The more that Wayan and Dayu hedged the more Adrian's curiosity was whetted. Finally he said, "I don't want to go to Eduardo's party. I want to visit the forest with you and watch the dancing." The other two just shrugged their shoulders.

Later that night they followed Wayan on his motor bike in the direction of the Monkey Forest. They drove through the loud and busy streets of Kuta and Denpasar and then into the country where the shimmering lamps of a dozen villages whizzed past in the hot, tropical night. Then all was dark. And silent. The road narrowed to a mere bike track as they drove deeper and deeper into the black forest. Dayu believed that she could see and hear the monkey *leyaks* and Adrian could feel the mounting tension inside her arms that were wound tightly around his waist. He too was beginning to sense that there were some strange and mysterious spirits in the air.

It was a new moon and everything was pitch dark. By his own headlight Adrian was able to follow the red reflector light on the back of Wayan's bike. He slowed down and then stopped. The darkness was broken by a group of lanterns that shone from the tops of bamboo staves that had been driven into the ground. When they dismounted Adrian and Dayu could see the crumbling and broken down walls of an old temple. And they could smell the burning incense wafting through the air.

They followed Wayan into the courtyard which was packed with people — including several children. A bonfire had been built out of grass, palm fronds and dried coconut husks; it was being lit by a weird and sinister looking priest. An invisible drum was beating out a slow rhythm and there was a great air of anticipation. Something was about to happen. The spirits were everywhere. Even Adrian could feel them.

The dark, silent crowd began chanting in unison. They became louder and more intense. Some girls got up to dance. But it was not like the wild dancing at the Jolly Frog. It seemed to be lethargic and lifeless. Their eyes were closed as if they were in some hypnotic trance.

At first Dayu held on tightly to Adrian's hand. But slowly her grip loosened. Adrian could see her eyes shutting and opening again. He noticed their vague, disoriented look. Then she yawned and closed them again. Adrian at first enjoyed the mellow music of the drum and the chanting crowd. But he could feel a definite tension all around him. Then Dayu's head dropped down as if her muscles had gone to sleep. He closed his arm around her which revived her somewhat. She then got up languidly and began ambling around the dancing area with the other girls. Adrian felt uneasy and looked across at Wayan who was sitting alongside him. His eyes were open and he too was staring trance like at something in the distant darkness which Adrian could not see.

The dancing went on for about half an hour and Adrian was beginning to get bored. "Why doesn't she come back and sit down for a moment?" he asked himself. "We never dance this long at the disco without a break. Besides, it's such pathetic dancing. No life in it at all."

The girls seemed to be responding unconsciously to commands that were being chanted by the crowd. Then they began to dance right across the burning fire in their bare feet. They didn't appear to feel the flames at all. Nor did they catch on fire as Adrian half expected. Indeed, each had been entered by a powerful spirit which made them impervious to physical things like fire and pain. Two more girls followed and walked slowly across the red hot embers. Then Dayu walked towards the flames. Adrian rushed up and grabbed her round the waist and drew her back. Then he pushed her over to where he was sitting. She didn't resist and when she sat down next to Wayan he didn't even look up. He was in his own trance. But for Dayu the spell had been broken. The powerful spirit that had entered her body had left the moment that Adrian grabbed her. She was now slowly adjusting to reality.

When she sat down she gripped Adrian's hand. He could tell that she was frightened. And so was he. He began to wonder what would happen next in this terrifying orgy of black magic and contact with demonic spirits. The chanting continued as more girls walked slowly and mindlessly through the fire. Then a few men got up and lifted the girls on to their shoulders. They danced to the same slow and — to Adrian — meaningless rhythm. Some of the men were quite small and skinny but they carried the girls with ease as the spirits had entered their bodies and given them superhuman powers of physical strength.

Some of the men were so dizzy and possessed by the spirits that they put their heads down into the fire and licked the flames. Adrian expected them to be burnt on the spot but nothing happened. Others were dancing strangely and bending their bodies into all sorts of amazing contortions. Soon all the restraints that regulated their normally strict code of behaviour were lifted. The whole crowd was in an extremely powerful communal trance and they began to run amok.

Some men committed the unspeakable sacrilege of pointing their sharp knives at the temple shrine. Others began eating live chickens that were running around in the courtyard. Adrian sat agape as he watched one man bite off and swallow the head of a squawking chicken and then devour the rest of it — feathers, legs and blood. Lots of blood. Some got down on their hands and knees and began eating plants and bushes. Wayan was crawling on his hands and feet and barking like a dog. Others were rolling around outside in a patch of mud and wallowing like pigs. Dayu saw one of the girl dancers take off her sarong and shake it so as to ward off the evil spirits. Then the sarong slid out of the girl's hands and started running wildly around the courtyard. Possessed by an extremely powerful spirit and in a trance of its own. All sorts of strange and bestial things were taking place and for anyone who was not part of the trance it was a terrifying and uncontrollable spectacle.

Adrian grabbed Dayu and literally carried her back to where the motor bike was parked. He sat her on the pillion seat, turned the ignition key and kick-started the machine. The last thing he saw was the priest running around wildly and trying to stem the madness by throwing sacred water over everybody in a desperate attempt to pacify them and drive out the evil spirits that had got inside their bodies.

Adrian was determined to ride away as fast as he could and put as much distance as possible between the bike and the horror he had witnessed. About a mile down the track they brushed the side of a low, overhanging branch. Dayu felt its touch as they rode past. She stiffened in terror at this physical contact by a monkey *leyak* which she knew had dropped down from the trees to stroke her. She now wished that they had never come to the Monkey Forest. Its spirits were far too powerful.

Adrian drove straight back to the cottage. He felt safe

and relieved when they reached the familiar noise and bustle of Kuta. He went inside the cottage and fetched some warm beer. Then he went out on to the verandah where Dayu was sitting on the big cane chair. She was quiet and subdued. "I now know why you and Wayan didn't want me to go into the forest," he said, "and it is my fault that we went. But why do the people carry on like that? I mean, the Balinese are so polite and well-ordered and disciplined and that is why it seems so out of character. How can such apparently well behaved people become like animals?"

"That's just it," she replied. "It is because we are so restrained by our customs and traditions that we have to have an outlet for all the demonic forces that build up inside us. When we go into trance we let them all out. It is better that way than to go around the streets committing acts of violence against each other. In each of us there are dark forces which should be allowed to express themselves under controlled conditions. Like during a trance when we are all together. Otherwise they build up so much pressure and suddenly explode. Like Mount Agung."

"And like the killings in 1965?" he asked.

"Yes," she replied with a look of sadness.

"I'm sorry, my sweet one," he said as he leaned over to kiss her. "Do you feel better after your little trance to-night?"

"Yes," she replied, "but I'm glad that you stopped me when you did. There's no knowing what that spirit might have made me do. At night when the spirits unleash their power all sorts of unimaginable things become possible. And to-night they were especially strong."

"Yes, I know," he said.

"Could you feel them too?" she asked.

"I believe that the spirits were there as I don't know how else all those people could have acted the way they did. I'm just glad that they didn't get inside me."

"You're not Balinese," she said.

221

Adrian lay awake in bed trying to make some sense out of what he had seen. He concluded that it was a temporary withdrawal from reality. "Just as we 'get out of it' with alcohol and drugs they achieve the same state by means of trance. I wonder why it is that people find reality so unbearable that they have to escape from it every now and then. I guess that surfing is the same. Just another escape from the real world. When you paddle out there it's like being in another space, another element, another time, another world. Far removed from all the problems and hassles that afflict the rest of mankind. It's in man's nature to be free and independent but there are some mighty powerful forces at work trying to prevent it. Like all the pressures to conform and perform. Like communism and socialism and their dangerous belief that the state is more important than the individual. Like the way that governments try to regulate every aspect of our lives and mould everyone into good, little, obedient citizens of a tightly controlled society that can be easily manipulated by the few who claw their way to the top. Yes, I reckon I'd go crazy if I couldn't get out there in Mother Ocean and away from all the pressures." He began thinking of Airport Reef and the waves that would be waiting to be ridden in the morning. He looked at his watch. "In six hours' time," he said to himself as he fell asleep.

Chapter Nine

The Lawyers

Back in Melbourne Judge Hack was opening his mail. There was a brochure from the Far East Law Association advising that their biennial convention would be held at the Bali Beach Hotel in June. He read it and put it aside. When he later found out that some of his colleagues were planning to attend he fished the leaflet out of his drawer and took another look at it. "Yes," he thought, "it would be a good chance for me to deliver my little lecture on the advantages of capital punishment." He looked up lovingly at the black cap that was hanging on the wall. Then, without consulting his wife, he rang up the local convenor and asked for two registrations at the conference in the names of the Honourable Mister Justice Hack and Mrs Hack.

The only times that he ever went on holiday with his wife were to law conferences where they both put duty before pleasure. The duty of being seen together as a respectable and happily married couple ahead of their pleasure which, in both cases, would have led them to take separate holidays out of each other's company.

Mrs Hack preferred shopping to law conferences. But, she had to admit, the conferences served their purpose in that they were the sole reason for the several overseas trips that she had enjoyed in recent years. And that was only because trips to conferences were tax deductible and so they didn't really cost her highly paid but penny pinching husband anything at all. He simply deducted all the expenses of the trips from his taxable income. Since he was on the highest tax rate he knew that he would be a fool if he didn't go to at least one overseas conference a year.

"We can go on to Singapore for a few days so that you can do your shopping," he said to his wife in the same cold and impersonal tone that he addressed counsel and defendants in his court. "So long as I look in for about ten minutes on a Singapore judge in the Supreme Court Building we can claim the Singapore part of the trip as a further tax deduction. I can say that I had to go there on business," said the man who only a week before had forced a sixty year old hardware shop proprietor to go out of business by imposing on him penal tax rates and the maximum fine of $60,000 for tax evasion.

The judge and his wife were shown to their room at the Bali Beach Hotel by the manager. It was on the second floor and overlooked the sea. Hack told the manager that it was not at all suitable and requested a room several floors higher.

"Why? What's wrong with it? I like it," said Mrs Hack.

"It's too far down. It'll be hard to sleep at night with all the screaming natives lying around the grounds," replied Hack.

The manager winced. Then slowly and politely he said, "We do not have anyone sleeping in the hotel grounds. But I shall give you a room on the seventh floor. It is no trouble."

The conference lasted for five days and several learned papers were read out on deep topics like the protection of intellectual copyright, the domicile for tax purposes of multinational companies and the limits of the doctrine of equitable estoppel.

Hack spent his days within the confines of the hotel. He went to all the lectures and social functions and cooled off in the hotel swimming pool where his black woollen neck-to-knee bathing outfit caused quite a few sniggers. He wouldn't bathe in the sea because he said that it was "too dirty." Mrs Hack ventured further afield and went shopping at Kuta with some of the other wives. Unlike her husband she swam in the warm tropical sea and loved it.

■

It was the contessa's birthday and, even though she refused to reveal her age, Pascal took her to dinner at the Bali Beach Hotel to celebrate. "It is the only place with anything like a reasonable selection of French wines," he said, "and afterwards we can have a swim in the pool. The waiters will serve us drinks in plastic glasses that float and we can just lie in the water and sip them. It is how the world should be."

The contessa wore a blue Christian Dior creation which was set off with some large earrings and a turquoise necklace that she had bought from a street seller at Kuta. They went into the red carpeted lounge and sat down at a table just inside the door.

The contessa began telling Pascal about the imminent financial collapse of her family due to her father's compulsive gambling. "That is why I came out here. To get away from the troubles and maybe find a rich American to marry and keep me in clothes."

"But when you are on the beach you never wear any clothes," said Pascal with a grin.

"That is true. I do not wear any clothes on the beach. But at night I need them to wear to all the parties. And I always feel better in expensive clothes and nice jewellery. What shall I do? I might be stranded here with no money to leave."

"Oh, I could think of worse fates than that," laughed Pascal.

"So could I but … "

"Excuse me, But aren't you Pascal de Ratton from Paris?" said the young Englishman who stopped at their table as soon as he recognised Pascal.

"Indeed I am and, if I am not mistaken, you are Howard Milton-Jones, barrister, from London," said Pascal as he rose out of his chair and extended his hand in greeting. He then introduced Howard to the contessa.

"*Enchanté*."

The two men had met a couple of years earlier on Whitsun week-end when Pascal had been a member of the Paris lawyers' lawn tennis team which had gone over to London to play some very social matches against members of the London Bar.

"I can't even remember which team won," said Howard. "It was you people, wasn't it?"

"No. no. It was the English barristers. But, like you, I don't remember much about the matches. Only the lunches and dinners!" laughed Pascal. "And I remember having lunch with you the next day in your lovely old Hall at Gray's Inn. It was all so *charmant*! Are you still practising in the same chambers there?"

"No, I have moved from London," said Howard. "I am now sitting as a magistrate in Hong Kong. I decided that I needed a change and I have been in Hong Kong now for almost a year. It is a well paid job and I like it."

"Ooh, it must be terribly exciting with all those triads and smugglers!" exclaimed the contessa.

"Oh, it's nothing like that," said Howard with unaffected modesty. "I sit in the New Territories and seem to spend most of the time imposing small fines on Chinese hawkers for selling things on the street without a licence. There's nothing exciting in that. I'm here for this law conference. I don't take it very seriously but it's a good excuse for a booze-up and a few peaceful days away from the noise and bustle of Hong Kong. We're going into a cocktail party shortly. Why don't you come too? After all, you're a man of the law."

"Not when I'm on holiday," replied Pascal.

"Oh, why not?" exclaimed the contessa. "Is it a party? I just love parties."

Howard led them into a big room where a large volume of alcohol was being consumed by a horde of hot and thirsty lawyers and their over-dressed wives. They came from every legal jurisdiction between Hong Kong and Australia. The atmosphere was congenial but restrained and the contessa soon came to the conclusion that it was not her type of party.

Pascal became an object of interest by virtue of the fact that he was the only French lawyer who was present. He politely answered all their questions about the differences between the French legal system and that of the Asian countries which follow the common law of England.

While Pascal was playing the diplomat and discussing legal matters the contessa went off with Howard and met some of the other delegates — Malayan judges, Australian lawyers and a Filipino law professor. Some of them asked her if she was a lawyer. "Good God, no," she replied at first. But to the next one she smiled and said, "Yes, I'm just stopping over on my way to The Hague for a sitting of the International Court." They took her at her word. She liked Howard. "He is full of fun," she thought, "and, apart from Pascal, is easily the most trivial soul in the room."

After about half an hour she caught sight of Pascal on his own as he was waiting for a drink. She ran over and threw her arms around his neck. This created something of a stir among the frumpish wives of the judges. "Oh Pascal," she whispered in his ear, "let's get out of this place. I can't stand it another minute."

"Why? What's happened?" he asked.

"It's like the Chamber of Horrors at Madame Tussaud's! I've just been talking to a judge from Singapore who sentences people to sixty lashes of a whip that cuts into their buttocks and makes them bleed, a Malayan judge who has hanged eight young men in the last six months, and some boring old fart from Australia who didn't smile until he started telling me about all the aborigines whom he has sent to prison. These people are all barbarians. It is not my type of party at all."

"Nor mine," said Pascal.

Just then Howard came over and Pascal explained that they had to leave as they were due in the dining room at eight o'clock.

"Well, it's been jolly nice to catch up with you again," said Howard.

"But surely you are coming with us to eat?" exclaimed the contessa. "It's my birthday, you know, and we are celebrating."

"Yes, I owe you one," said Pascal, remembering the fine lunch that he had had with Howard at Gray's Inn.

"Well, that's jolly kind of that. I'd love to come so long as it's no inconvenience. To tell you the truth I'm getting a little tired of this crowd. They're all so serious. Silly, isn't it, in a laid back place like Bali?"

They walked off together to the dining room. "A table in the name of de Ratton," said Pascal to the head waiter. "We booked it for only two people but I'm sure you can manage three."

"Of course, sir," said the little man as he led them across to the table by the big window. There was a birthday cake on it with one candle in the middle.

After dinner they went out to the terrace beside the floodlit swimming pool. It was still hot and sticky. The air was thick with mosquitoes and crickets and in the distance they could hear the noise of the waves breaking over Sanur Reef.

"I think we should have a swim to cool off," said the contessa. "We can have our drinks in the water."

They went over to a cabana to change. Howard and Pascal dived into the pool and waited for the contessa. She emerged from the bamboo cabana wearing nothing but a tiny blue G-string not much larger than a postage stamp. They sipped their iced drinks in the pool and lay on their backs and stared up at the heavenly stars. "Ah, this is so nice," said the contessa. "Maybe we sh..." She stopped in mid-sentence and swam a couple of strokes across to Pascal. "But there is he. Walking across the terrace," she said.

"Who?" asked Pascal.

"The barbarian from Australia who sends all the poor aborigines to prison. And look at what he is wearing!" Hack, who was on his own, was wearing his neck-to-knee woollen bathing costume. Pascal started to laugh. So did Howard. "He looks as if he has just emerged from one of those bathing machines that they had in Queen Victoria's time," said the contessa. "Someone should go and tell him that we are now in the year 1978."

In the semi-darkness Hack could not recognise the contessa's face as belonging to the woman whom he had met at the cocktail party and who had told him that she was on her way to the International Court at The Hague. But what he did see were her shapely breasts bobbing out of the pool. He went straight over to the pool manager to lodge a complaint.

"It is an outrage against public decency for a woman to flout her naked breasts in public and you should tell her to cover them up," fumed Hack.

"But Balinese women do not cover their breasts except when they go to the temple," replied the manager. "There is no problem, sir. She is not causing any trouble. She has had dinner here and so is entitled to use the pool. As far as I'm concerned she can stay in the water so long as she does not cause trouble. She has been here before and we all like her very much. In the past she has always been generous with her tips."

"Well, what about the other people? They should not have to look at an exhibitionist like that."

"They do not mind, sir. And besides, it is dark." For once the know-all Hack was stumped for words. He did not like to be beaten by an uneducated pool manager. He felt that he, the Honourable Mister Justice Hack, had lost face.

"Well, I'll call the police then," he spluttered.

"You may do that but I know that they would tell you the same as I have," replied the manager with an air of confidence. He smiled throughout even though his feeling towards Hack was one of utter contempt. Who was this elderly, badly shaped man in the ridiculous bathing costume to complain about someone as beautiful as the contessa?

Hack could stand it no longer. He turned around and stormed back to his hotel room.

"Oh look! He is going away again," exclaimed the contessa. "Thank God. He really gives me the creeps."

The next evening was the last one before the Hacks were to leave for Singapore. Mrs Hack finally persuaded her husband that there was more to Bali than the grounds of their hotel. During one of her shopping expeditions she had noticed an exotic looking restaurant called "The White Gardenia". It was down a narrow walled lane at Kuta and the tables were well spaced and set out under the trees. She described it as "tropical chic" and said that it was the only one that she had seen that was clearly "up market". It was on this basis that she persuaded the judge to forsake his legal cronies for a night and make the short journey across to Kuta.

They took a taxi from their hotel and Hack's worst fears were realised when they got caught in a traffic jam on the approach road to Kuta. All the cars and *bemos* were honking their horns and a couple of policemen were helplessly blowing their whistles and trying to look as if they were doing something. The taxi driver got out of the car to try and see what was causing the delay. When he got back in his seat he was laughing.

"What's the hold-up?" demanded Hack.

"Two dogs," laughed the driver. "Stuck together in the middle of the road. Making babies."

"What!" exclaimed Hack in horror. "This sort of thing would never happen in a civilised place. Like Melbourne!"

"Why not?" asked his wife. "After all, it's only an act of nature."

"In all my sixty-eight years in Australia I have never seen traffic held up by fornicating dogs. It would only happen in a place like this. Why don't the police pull them apart?"

Now it was the driver's turn to look horrified. "Can't do that," he said, "because of the bad spirits inside the dogs. They might escape and get inside the man who pulls them apart. Then all sorts of bad things would happen to the man."

"I suppose he too would start fornicating on the road," thought Hack in disgust.

By now the police were redirecting the traffic on to the mud at the side of the road. As they drove past Hack looked through the fading light at the disgusting act that was still taking place in full view of the public. "I think they are stuck together," laughed the driver. "Cannot separate."

"Imagine it happening in Collins Street!" sneered Hack to his wife. "It's all they do in the East is fornicate. That's why they've got so many bloody people."

"Oh, you can't blame the people for what the dogs do," she replied.

The driver overheard the conversation and decided to enlighten them. "But those dogs were once people. In a previous life."

It was all too much for the judge. "Just drive on to the restaurant," he ordered.

When they finally arrived at The White Gardenia Hack had to concede that his wife had made a good choice. Oil lamps shone down from strategic points in the trees and there were a couple of flaming candles on each table.

They were led across to their table by a well-trained,

smiling Balinese boy in a white shirt, black bow-tie and maroon cummerbund. Hack asked the waiter for a double whisky for himself and a gin and tonic for his wife. "No, make mine a treble," he said. He knew that he had to have something strong to get over the sight of those dreadful fornicating dogs. The waiter brought their drinks to the table and took their orders of turtle soup and *gado gado*.

The tables were crowded and there were even more people sitting on the high bamboo stools at the bar while they waited for tables to clear. More people arrived and the head waiter came over to Hack and asked him if he would mind if he brought another couple over to share the table. Hack was about to refuse when he heard the head waiter say that he would reduce the bill by fifty per cent if they would oblige. "It is such a problem to-night, sir. Everyone wants to eat at the same time," he pleaded.

"Oh all right then. As long as they're not riff raff," said Hack grumpily as he silently reflected on his good fortune at getting the meal for half the price.

■

When Adrian and Dayu looked in at Manoel's about seven o'clock there wasn't a single empty table. Manoel said that he didn't expect to have a free one for at least half an hour as there were others drinking at the bar who were there before them. "No problem," said Adrian, "we'll go somewhere else."

"As you wish. I'm so sorry," said Manoel.

When they were outside Adrian asked Dayu if she had ever been to The White Gardenia. "No," she replied. "What's it like?"

"Oh, I've only been there once. Shortly after I arrived. It was good. They have an excellent menu. Would you like to try it?"

"Why not?" she laughed.

232

They entered the restaurant through a gateway in the wall and saw that it was alive with crowds and chatter. "It's pumping — like the surf," said Adrian as he led Dayu up to the bar. It was hot so they bought a couple of cool Harvey Wallbangers to quench their thirst. Through the darkness they could see the white shirted waiters rushing hither and thither as they tried to cope with the unusually heavy numbers. There was lots of laughter and noise coming from the tables, a gecko croaking in the tree and an Alice Cooper tape blaring out of some hidden stereo.

"Well, Dayu, what do you think of this place? Good?"

"I don't know. It looks nice with all the pretty tables and lights and the well dressed waiters. But I can feel the presence of the spirits. As you know, they hover round at night and I just know that they're in here."

"Where are they then? Which ones are the evil spirits? The waiters? That one over there? Or maybe the man on the cash register who is fleecing everybody of their money?" It was Adrian's habit to laugh at some of the more extreme fears of the Balinese. On the one hand he recognised that they had a genuine awe and fear of the spirits but on the other he didn't want an otherwise enjoyable evening to be spoilt by Dayu imagining things that weren't there and consequently being tense and unresponsive.

"Well, do you want to go somewhere else?" he asked. "Maybe to a cheap warung? After all, there don't appear to be any free tables and we might have to wait for quite a while."

"Oh no, I don't want to spoil your evening. I mean our evening." She remembered how keen he was to come to The White Gardenia. How would she ever resolve the seemingly interminable conflict in her mind between the ancient beliefs of her upbringing and the apparently logical and non-mystical ways of the West? The matter was solved for the moment by the approach of the head waiter who told them that they could have a table if they didn't mind sharing it with two others. Adrian had shared many tables since he had been in Bali. Sometimes he had sat on and talked to complete strangers for an hour or so and, in a few cases, had later gone surfing with them. "No, we don't mind," he said. Then he whispered to Dayu that, if she was still unhappy about staying there, they would go elsewhere.

"No," she said bravely, "we stay here."

When Hack looked up and saw the head waiter leading Adrian and Dayu over to his table he nearly had an apoplexy. "I deliberately said 'no riff raff'," he hissed to his wife, "and they bring some character with long hair and his native tart."

"Well, they are nicely dressed," whispered Mrs. Hack in a vain attempt to appease him. "And besides, his hair's not that long. All the boys wear it like that these days."

"If he was ever in my court I'd give him an extra three months for his hair. I always judge people by their appearance."

Mrs. Hack smiled sweetly at Adrian and Dayu as they sat down. Hack grunted an acknowledgement. His main worry was that others from the law conference might also be at the restaurant and would see him at a table eating with a native girl. "Good God," he thought, "they could even think it's my son and daughter-in-law! I wish now that we had stayed at the hotel and not come to this accursed place." He looked around to see if he recognised any of the diners in the immediate vicinity. He didn't. However, in order to reduce the chances of being spotted at the same table as "riff raff" he decided to snuff out one of the two candles that were on the table.

"Say, it's awfully hot here, don't you think? You don't mind if I put out one of the candles?" were the first words that he offered to Adrian and Dayu.

"No, not at all," replied Adrian even though it meant that they could no longer see the words on the menu card. It

234

didn't matter as they had already decided to have a seafood cocktail followed by chop choy.

Mrs. Hack smiled and asked them where they were from. "I'm from Melbourne," said Adrian, "and Dayu lives in a village up in the mountains. My father knew her family when he was over here many years ago."

"Good God," thought Hack, "the father too. Well you can't expect much from the son if the old man is also into the native women. What a dreadful family they must be!"

"And where do you live in Melbourne?" asked Mrs. Hack in her sweet manner.

"I have an apartment in South Yarra," replied Adrian. Hack's fork dropped out of his hand and on to the concrete floor. Mrs. Hack bent down to pick it up. Adrian had watched the reaction with amusement and decided to press home the advantage. "But I spent most of my life in Brighton. That's where my folks live."

"Brighton?" spluttered Hack as he remembered that at least three of his judicial colleagues had expensive homes in that particular suburb.

"We live at Toorak," continued Mrs. Hack. "Next door to South Yarra. I always do my shopping at South Yarra."

Adrian decided to have a little more fun with the insecure husband so he added in the most off-hand manner, "Oh, that's interesting because when I go back with Dayu we shall be buying a place at Toorak. I'm tired of South Yarra. Too many retired people."

The judge was not liking it at all. He looked at his watch and then searched around for the waiter to speed up the arrival of the main course. His wife, however, was enjoying the opportunity of talking to two young people. Dayu was at first shy but soon began chatting easily to Mrs. Hack. But every time she looked through the dim light at the judge she felt a shiver travel down her spine. "He is so cold," she thought, "and has such cruel eyes. He must be the personification of some really evil spirit."

Hack kept complaining about how dirty the streets were and how disorganised the hotel was. He then criticised the restaurant, the service, the waiters. Even the weather. "Too bloody hot for my liking," he kept saying. Adrian began to wonder why on earth he had come to the island.

"And all these bloody dogs on the streets," said Hack.

Dayu shivered at his mention of dogs. She was sure that when Hack was reincarnated he would come back as a pi dog. "He is so horrible and he would deserve it," she thought.

"It's good to have the dogs," said Adrian. "They help to keep the streets clean by eating all the rubbish that lies around. And, of course, the people eat the dogs."

"What!" exclaimed Hack as he pushed his plate of food away. Even Mrs. Hack looked horrified.

"Oh, I wouldn't worry," continued Adrian. "They don't serve it at this restaurant. But the villagers up in the mountains sometimes eat dogs. They find them quite a delicacy." Despite this assurance neither Hack nor his wife ate any more of their main course.

"I think it's appalling the way that you have to give everyone here a bribe to get anything done," said Hack. "My God, we'd never stand for that sort of thing in Australia."

"Oh, I don't know. It's just that in the West it's a bit more subtle," said Adrian.

Hack could feel the blood rushing to his head. "What do you mean? This country is a dictatorship! A Third World dictatorship!"

"Yes, but that doesn't mean that the people are any worse off than if they had a democracy. They tried democracy and it didn't suit them. The communists took advantage of it and caused great trouble. Anyway, the Indonesians have just as much personal freedom as anyone else."

"But they don't have the right to vote," said Hack.

"So what?" replied Adrian. "Neither do the people of

Hong Kong and yet they enjoy far more personal freedom than the Malaysians who do have democracy and the right to vote. Democracy and personal freedom are not necessarily the same thing. A mob can be just as brutal and intolerant as a tyrant. Here in Indonesia the people have a few freedoms that we don't have in the West. The only thing that they can't do is engage in political activity. But that's not the be-all and end-all of existence. I've never bothered to vote and I probably never will. After all, it's really only preferring one bunch of liars to another."

"How dare you talk like that," snapped Hack. "I know several politicians and I can assure you that they're the finest body of men that you could ever hope to meet. They are all men of the highest integrity. And so truthful." Adrian's scathing criticism of politicians touched a raw nerve since Hack owed his appointment as a judge to political patronage. And, of course, he was counting on getting a knighthood from the same politicians. And a whopping great pension from the public purse when he retired.

"Anyway, young man, name me one freedom that these natives have that we don't have in Australia," continued the judge.

"Oh, they can build a house without having some creepy building inspector breathing down their necks, they can light a garden fire without having to get a wretched permit, they can work in a job without being forced to join a trade union and pay hundreds of dollars a year to keep fat union officials in luxuries, they can drive their cars without being forced to wear a seat belt, most of them don't have to pay taxes, they can start a shop or restaurant without having to pay some councillor a backhander to push through a zoning change ..."

"That is slanderous," fumed Hack. "How dare you cast untrue aspersions on worthy councillors who give so much of their time to serving the ungrateful public."

"Many councillors get rich on their kickbacks," continued Adrian. "After all, if a developer is prepared to spend a few million on a project it makes good business sense to slip a few thousand to a councillor or two to obtain the right zoning changes and make sure that the project goes ahead. No wonder the councillors are so keen to get on the council planning committee; far more remunerative than the stray dogs and floral clock committee."

"You can be taken to court for speaking like that," said Hack.

"Is that another freedom we don't have in the West? To speak the truth about crooked councillors and their developer friends?"

"This impertinent young whipper-snapper should be made to do two years in the army," thought Hack. "That would straighten out his dangerous ideas. A bit of discipline and a haircut is what he needs." Hack himself had been in the army during the War but he never saw any action; he had been far too busy behind the lines with court martial work — prosecuting battle weary young soldiers for drunkenness and hooliganism while on leave. Nevertheless, he had returned to Australia with a chestful of medals that he wore at every opportunity.

By now the judge had had enough of the undesirable company at his table. He didn't like being out in the real world. What with fornicating dogs, riff raff surfers, impertinent conversation and native tarts he had had quite enough for one night. All he wanted to do was to get back to his own narrow little world — Toorak, the gold club and the macabre conversation and gallows humour of the judges' common room. Although Mister Justice Hack judged the public and fined them and sent them to prison he had no wish to mix with them or get to know them. He turned to his wife and announced that they must go if they were to get back to their hotel before all the roads were closed. "They don't close the roads at night," said Adrian in surprise.

238

"You never know what they might do in places like this," said Hack, "and I don't want to be stranded over here for the night with all these Moslems. Anything could happen."

"The Balinese are not Moslems. They're Hindus," said Adrian. "It's the Javanese who are Moslems."

Hack hated to be proved wrong. "Well in my book they're all bloody pagans," he said.

"I don't want to go until after we've had some coffee," interjected Mrs. Hack. To her Adrian and Dayu were like a breath of fresh air. In fact, it was the brightest and most cheerful night that she had had in Bali. All the others had been spent in the company of her husband's cronies who, for all their brilliant legal knowledge, were boring and pedantic company.

"Oh, all right," said Hack, "but we mustn't stay too long. Don't forget, we have to fly to Singapore to-morrow."

"Yes," said Mrs. Hack as she turned to Adrian, "and then we return to Melbourne at the week-end. Vernon has to get back for *court* on Monday."

Adrian noticed the stress that she put on the word "court" and realised that it had been said to impress him with the importance of her husband's position. So he turned to Hack and said, "You work at the courts, do you?"

"I am a judge," said Hack pompously. He had been bursting to say it all evening. Adrian was hardly surprised since both Hack and his wife had let out several hints which suggested that they were somehow over and above everyone else. What did surprise him was that such an ignorant and narrow-minded character should have much immense powers over the lives of others of whom he obviously had no understanding whatsoever — young people, poor people, coloured people. "Pompous ass," thought Adrian as he looked through the dim light at the man who, unbeknown to him, had killed his beloved Alex.

Dayu excused herself and went off to the toilet. She was

away for about ten minutes as the restaurant was so crowded that there was even a queue for the lavatory. While she was away Adrian continued to talk with Mrs. Hack who, apart from her occasional efforts to remind him of her husband's social importance, was an extremely nice and understanding lady.

"I think that Dayu is very sweet," she said. "She is a lucky girl to have a man like you." A look of sadness came over her face as she compared Adrian, who was oozing with strength and virility , with her own boring and impotent husband. "How I would like a young man like that," she thought as she looked at Adrian, "even if it was only for a night." She smiled warmly. "And what is it that brought you to Bali?" she asked. "Running away from a broken love affair?"

"Well, yes and no, I suppose," he replied. "We were going to get married but my girlfriend was run over and killed one evening on the Mornington Peninsula." Hack pricked up his ears.

"Oh dear," continued Mrs. Hack, "when did this happen? Recently?"

"Exactly two months ago. Just north of Rye."

"Did they find out who did it?" she asked.

"Yes, they arrested some aborigine. I don't know what happened to him. And I don't care either. It's in the past."

Mrs. Hack looked across to her husband in anticipation of the tirade against aborigines that he always embarked upon every time their name was mentioned. But he was silent. Nor could the slight change in his expression be detected through the darkness. His cold eyes turned to hatred. Hatred of Adrian for mentioning — albeit innocently — the matter which he, the Honourable Mr. Justice Hack, thought he would never hear of again.

Just then Dayu returned and before she sat down Hack stood up to leave. He marched over to the counter to settle his account — or at least half of it. The man at the cash register added up the items and asked for the full amount. "I only have to pay half of it," said Hack.

"Why half?" asked the cashier in surprise.

"Because your bloody head waiter said that I could have a fifty per cent discount if I would let two others sit at my table. I now wish the hell I hadn't."

The cashier did not like his aggressive tone. He looked around for the head waiter who was nowhere to be seen. "Sorry, sir, but I know nothing about any discount," said the young Balinese who knew that any shortfall in the takings would be deducted from his own already meagre wages.

"Listen, young man, I have a contract with your disorganised restaurant. I have fulfilled my part of the bargain by allowing two dreadful types to sit at my table. Now it is your turn to perform by giving me the discount that I was promised. If you don't, I shall call the police." As a fine, upstanding man of the law Hack was always reporting people to the police for all sorts of trivial reasons — noisy parties, double-parked cars and young kids smoking cigarettes in the street. The only exception was when he found himself on the wrong side of the law; no one ever drove away from an accident faster than Hack. But it was hardly surprising; after all, several of his forebears were convicts who had been transported in chains and leg-irons to Australia for a variety of offences. Mostly fraud and deceit. But with Hack's appointment to the judiciary the poacher had become the gamekeeper.

At the mention of the word "police" the frightened young Balinese on the cash register decided that it would be foolish to press the matter any further. He did not want to be the cause of the police being called as that would probably make the manager so angry that he would sack him. "Even if I have to pay the difference out of my wages I shall give him his precious discount as I don't want any trouble," decided the cashier who earned less income in a whole year than

Hack did in a week.

When Mrs. Hack saw her husband walk away from the cash desk she said good-bye to Adrian and Dayu and walked out to the door. As soon as she was out of earshot Dayu expressed the thoughts that had been building up inside her all evening. "I think that she is a very nice lady but he is a really bad man."

"Yes," said Adrian, "there is no nastier emotion than the envy of the old for the young. He is a bitter and frustrated old man and the only thing he'd ever get a kick out of is throwing his weight around on all the unfortunates who finish up in his court. He could never enjoy any of the nice things of life like surfing or sex or sunshine. But not all old people are like that." He was thinking of his own father — always so tolerant and wise — and of Klian and all the pleasant evenings he had spent with him on the verandah — the camaradie, the simple wisdom that poured from the old man's lips, his rich experience of life and its application to the gods.

When the Hacks arrived back at the Bali Beach Hotel there were still a few parties in progress to celebrate the end of the law conference. The Australians were all gathered in one bar, drinking and swapping addresses with their colleagues. Hack and his wife went in to join them for about half an hour. As they entered the room some of the lawyers — inebriated and momentarily star struck at finding themselves in the exalted presence of a judge — looked up and made comments.

"Aren't they a fine couple? So decent and respectable!"

"Isn't it wonderful how they always remember your name?"

"They are real bricks; you can always count on them to turn up at law conferences — even though he doesn't like the tropical heat."

"He must have been so brave in the War; I've often seen him wearing his medals."

242

"Such a fine judge! Never any messing around or time wasting in his court. I reckon that he'll be given a knighthood when he retires."

"Why wait until he retires? He deserves one now."

"For sure!"

Hack finally announced that, since he was no longer a young man and was facing a four hour flight to Singapore the next day, he and his good wife would have to leave and go upstairs to bed. Some of the others were in high spirits by this stage and they began singing "For they are jolly good fellows." Mrs. Hack slipped her arm into her husband's as they walked out of the room together. Smiling. She pulled it away as soon as they had rounded the corner to the lift. She was thinking of Adrian and of how lucky Dayu was to be going to bed with him. "But," she consoled herself, "they'll never be given a knighthood. It won't be long now."

The Hacks received their title in the next New Year's Honours List. The citation was reported on the front page of the Melbourne Age: "Judge Vernon Joseph Hack to be Knight Commander of the British Empire for his services to Justice." On Page Two of the same edition was a report of the death of Sonny Peters. "The sixty-seventh aborigine to die in custody this year has been found dead in his cell at Pentridge Prison. As usual the authorities said that he hanged himself. He was Sonny Peters who killed a girl on the Mornington Peninsula last April when he drove his car while in a state of intoxication."

While Hack and his wife wallowed in their new titles and had everyone bowing and scraping to them, life was not so good for the Peters family. Mrs. Peters could not understand why her husband had been taken away. Forever. She took a day job and a night job to provide the basic necessities for her three young children who were the only focus of hope left in her life. She gave them whatever she could in the way of love and tenderness but one night she cracked under the pressure. She had been working at her two jobs for thirteen hours and the kids were all fighting and screaming. So, for the first time in her life, she slapped one of them. The girl. Tina. Across the face. The little girl fell over and hit her cheek on the fire grate. It bled.

The next day at school the teacher asked her about the cut. "Did your mother hit you?" she asked imperiously.

"Yes," replied the little girl.

"Where?"

"On my face."

Then, with a tremendous sense of self-importance, the teacher reported the matter to the government welfare people who visited Mrs. Peters. The social worker assigned to the case was a forty year old lesbian with short brown hair and buck teeth who had never had any children of her own. But she had all sorts of degrees. She had been a case officer with the Welfare Department for eight years during which time she had broken up more families than all the rakes in Melbourne. Tearing little children away from their mothers was her profession; the government even paid her to do it. She quickly decided that Mrs. Peters was quite unfit to keep her children and so they were all removed from her and placed permanently in foster homes.

As the children were taken out the door by the police and social workers Mrs. Peters stood on the steps and wept. Her family was now totally destroyed. What had been left after the court did its damage had now been finished off by the interfering and self-righteous busybodies in the Welfare Department.

■

Adrian was lying awake listening to the early morning cicadas. Suddenly he heard a rustling noise on the path outside. He couldn't tell whether it was a dog, a boy or a man. Then there was a soft tap on the door below. Dayu was still asleep. He looked across at her serene countenance which was rising and falling gently in rhythm with her quiet breathing. He crept out of bed and went downstairs. When he saw Thierry he put his finger to his lips to indicate that they must be quiet so as not to waken Dayu.

"I have been down the beach and the waves are just so big," whispered the excited Frenchman. "And the tide is so high."

"Then Airport Reef will be working. It's only rideable in a high tide. Let's go there before it gets crowded," replied Adrian.

"Ooh, I never thought of that. *Quelle bonne idée!*"

"I'll leave a note for Dayu to say that I'll be back by mid-morning. Poor kitten. She needs the sleep. We never seem to get to bed much before dawn." They pushed the surfboards into their covers and slung them over their shoulders. Then off they went on their motor bikes. It was a little after six o'clock.

Fifteen minutes later they reached the small beach by the airport. There were half a dozen bikes parked there which belonged to the other early bird surfers whom they could already see in the line-up about three quarters of a mile out.

They hailed a waiting outrigger and jumped in. The boatman pulled the rope to start the small horsepower motor and they putt-putted their way across the water. When they got near the reef Adrian told him to pull up. "You can leave us here and come back in a couple of hours," he said.

"No, no, I'll wait," said the boatman whose entire working life had been spent ferrying boatloads of surfers between the beach and the reef. He pulled the boat up near some other outriggers that were also waiting to take back the surfers whom they had ferried out. After Thierry and Adrian had dived over the side and grabbed their boards the boatman put some bait on his fish hook and dropped a line over the side. He then lay back in the early morning sun and waited for a bite.

Through the clear water Adrian and Thierry could see the coral formations beneath them. Airport Reef was one of their favourite spots. Its long and powerful waves maintained their shape and momentum as they passed over the submerged coral that lay just beneath the surface. The waves were about seven feet and Adrian managed to get inside some of the beautiful spiralling tubes that were peeling across the reef. Thierry tried too but he kept getting thrown off his board by the tremendous power of the surf.

They could hear the deafening noise of the wide-bodied jets that were taking off and landing on the nearby runway. While sitting astride their sticks of fibreglass waiting for a wave they sometimes looked up to see one of the big silver birds as it gained height or came down to land on the tarmac. Their only interest in the matter was that, if the 'planes brought too may surfers to the island, then the choicest and most accessible surfing spots — like Airport Reef — would become terribly crowded with fierce competition for every wave and a consequent drop in the level of enjoyment.

As he watched his friend disappear into a tube Thierry was nearly deafened by the noise of a 'plane that was roaring along the runway to take off into the light wind. He looked up and saw that it was a Linford American Airways wide-bodied jet. At first sight it didn't seem any different from the others that he had been watching. "But isn't it taking a bit longer than usual to get airborne? Oh, it's off the ground now. Good! No, it's back down again. It's bouncing. Good God, it's going to hit the concrete wall that runs across the end of the runway. Crash! Flames! Bang! Now there's some smoke. *Mon Dieu!* It's smashed through the wall and is speeding across the sea. Look at all the spray! She's slowing down now. Will it sink? No, it seems to have stabilised. It has stopped completely. Nose and front part of the body well under the water.

Tail up."

Thierry and the other surfers stared in disbelief from a distance of about a hundred and fifty yards. It was like watching a movie. For a moment the 'plane looked to be so much out of control that they all feared it would flop over towards the reef and smother them.

Adrian was inside a tube when he heard a distant bang. When he emerged and flicked the water out of his eyes he saw the flaming, smoking giant spinning along the top of the sea like some gigantic silver disc. The spray flew higher than any wave he had ever seen. He could see another set of seven footers rolling in from the deep ocean. But they weren't nearly as big as the wall of water that was approaching from the side — the huge volume of sea that had been displaced by the 'plane. He called out to Thierry and told him to paddle away from the reef.

Thierry got away just before the side wall of water arrived. Adrian could see it coming. "It's a once in a lifetime opportunity," he decided. "I wonder what it'll be like." The third wave of a set was powering in from the deep. It was at least an eight footer. He jumped up on his board and took it as it broke. A split second later the side wave arrived at a ninety degree angle. "This is it," he thought. He was no longer in control of his board, himself or anything. The board was pulled one way; its rider the other. Miraculously the leg-rope held. Then the greatest mass of water that he had ever felt came crashing down on his head. Like a mountain falling to pieces. It came and came and came. He was thrown in all directions. Like a scrap of paper in a whirlwind.

"I must get to the top," he thought, "to get my breath. Otherwise I'll be in *pasih* forever." The downward pressure of the water held him under. He felt so tiny and helpless. Then it began to abate as the moving mountain of sea passed on its way.

When he eventually reached the top he hardly had any

air left inside him. But when he tried to inhale he swallowed a lot of salt and didn't feel that he drew in any air. "Oh hell," he thought, "it's like those monsters that break on the north coast of Oahu where there's a stretch of non-solid water but damn all oxygen before you really reach the top." He closed his mouth and stopped inhaling through the nostrils. He tried to hold his breath — or at least what was left of it. The minutes seemed endless. Finally the sea began to settle and he put his head up for some air. He couldn't have lasted a second longer.

When he got his bearings he saw Thierry and a couple of Balinese surfers retrieving their boards after the explosion of water. "Oh, you're alive," cried Thierry. "Thank God! I thought that it was the end for you. I have never seen anything so wild. First the 'plane and then its wave." The two Balinese surfers looked terrified.

Adrian looked over at the rising smoke from the 'plane. There were already a few bodies floating around it and he could see one or two more jumping out of an emergency exit that was about twenty feet above the sea.

They joined all the other surfers who, having survived the wall of water from the side, were paddling for all they were worth across to the 'plane to rescue the survivors. Thierry and Adrian were thrown off their boards a couple of times by an incoming set but they pressed on.

By the time they reached the 'plane there were already about thirty people in the sea — floating and treading water. And several floating corpses. There were frightened and deathly screams coming from inside the cabin and smoke was pouring out through the single emergency exit that was open on the starboard side. Inside the 'plane the passengers were crawling both up and down the steep sloping aisle to the exit and then jumping down twenty feet into the sea. Little children were being tossed down into waiting arms. Some of the surfers who had got there first were lifting survivors on to their surfboards and then pushing them through the water towards the man-made rocky shore which was the edge of the airport. It was a journey of about two hundred yards which was the distance that the 'plane had skidded across the top of the ocean before it sank.

Thierry saw a woman in the water who was screaming with pain. Her arm, fractured in the humerus, was hanging obscenely from its socket. He jumped into the sea and gently lifted her on to the deck of his surfboard. Then he began swimming and treading water as he pushed her through the ocean towards the airport.

Adrian saw an old man with a mop of white hair make a gallant jump from the emergency exit. He paddled over, half expecting the gentleman to be dead with the impact of hitting the water. Quite the contrary. He was chirpy, chatty and full of life. However, Adrian did not like his chances of surviving too long in the sea so he put him on his surfboard and began pushing it through the water. He told Adrian that he was a New Yorker and that this was the second time that he had finished up in the ocean. "Both times the wretched captain's name was 'Smith'," he panted. "Just before take-off they announced that we were in the charge of Captain Smith. When I heard the name I asked the hostess if I could get out but she said that all the doors had been locked and the aircraft sealed. So I was half expecting to finish up in the drink."

"Why? Is he a bum captain?" asked Adrian.

"I don't know about this one but after the last time I sailed with a Captain Smith I swore that I would never do it again. And I haven't. Until this morning."

"When was the last time?" asked Adrian in an effort to keep the old boy's spirits up with some banter.

"1912. I was on the Titanic. Coming back from England with my parents. I was only thirteen but I remember it as if it was yesterday. My mother and I climbed into the second to last lifeboat. My father stayed on the ship and drowned with all the other men. It was much colder that night. There were icebergs floating in the sea."

"We'll soon be on dry land," said Adrian as he pushed the board as fast as he could while still keeping it steady so that the man wouldn't fall off. He looked across towards the beach where he had left his bike. There was a convoy of outriggers on their way to the crash scene. The few that had been sitting just inside the reef waiting to take their surfers back had all been overturned by the great mass of water that the 'plane had displaced. He could see the boatmen swimming around trying to right their craft. Without success.

Sirens were blaring from the airport as police cars and airport vehicles sped the length of the tarmac to the seaward end where the crash had occurred. Adrian looked up at the runway and could see dozens of khaki clad policemen and airport staff running around in all directions. But there was little that they could do as they were separated from the 'plane by some two hundred yards of ocean. The surfers and the boatmen on the outriggers were the men of the moment. Only they could pull the survivors to safety. No one else.

The old man thanked Adrian profusely as he was helped off the board and on to the rocks. He was a little unsteady on his legs but a couple of policemen grabbed him under his arms and helped him up the rocks and on to the tarmac. Adrian turned around and paddled back to the 'plane.

Thierry too had delivered his fractured cargo into the outstretched hands of two Indonesian policemen. The sea was now a mass of surfboards, canoes, corpses and survivors floundering around in the water. A chief of police had jumped on to an outrigger and set it up as a command post only a few feet from where the passengers were still jumping out of the emergency exit.

Some of them were asphyxiated by the smoke inside the cabin and blinked madly when they arrived in the bright sunlight. The chief of police directed each surfboard and outrigger to particular victims and a reasonably ordered evacuation ensued. A few had drowned and others had sustained injuries when they hit the sea after their twenty foot jump. Some died of shock. Some from a combination of shock and asphyxiation. One poor woman hit her head on the edge of an outrigger when she made her jump. She was a horrible mess.

Adrian and Thierry and the other surfers made several trips to the shore with survivors. Some were crying, some were shaking, but all were thankful to be on the surfboards and out of the smoky chamber of death. It was exhausting work but the surfers attacked it with energy and selflessness.

Soon the procession of people through the emergency door slowed to a trickle and then finally ceased. Police divers arrived with huge oxygen masks, axes and diving gear. They threw up a rope ladder which, after half a dozen attempts, looped around a protruding hinge on the emergency exit. They clambered up and went inside. In the smoke filled cabin they pulled out any bodies that they could feel in the rows of seats. They unfastened seat belts where necessary and carried the bodies down the rope ladder and into the waiting boats. Some whom they thought were dead were thrown into the ocean. A couple of these revived with the shock of hitting the water. It was horrible and gruesome work. The steep slope of the cabin floor made conditions inside even more difficult. And then there were the passengers in the front part of the 'plane. All the first class passengers and some of the economy class ones. They were all dead in their seats. Drowned.

■

The only lawyer at the legal conference who was not from the South East Asia region was Buckwheat Seton, a smoothly spoken and extremely personable attorney from

New York. He was a junior partner in the firm of Vultan and Heist whose offices were in a fifth floor suite half way along Wall Street.

At the conference Seton was not interested in the papers that were presented or the discussion groups which followed. His brief was to establish personal contacts with as many lawyers as he could. His firm sent him to law conferences all over the world for the same purpose. It was a good investment as Vultan and Heist's business consisted entirely of obtaining damages actions from the victims of disasters. Thus, every time that there was a bush fire in Alaska, a ship's collision in the mouth of the River Plate, a chemical leak in Pittsburgh or a 'plane crash in the Caribbean the firm was always on hand — often as quickly as the rescue services — to sign up the victims to make multi million dollar claims against the person or authority who allegedly caused the accident. And that is where it stopped. Vultan and Heist never took a matter any further than filing the claim. They then sub-contracted the work out to other law firms but retained the right to receive a hefty percentage of the damages that were eventually awarded.

It was one of the most profitable law practices in New York and pulled in millions of dollars in fees every year. Their main competition was a firm in Los Angeles which conducted a similar operation on the West Coast. The question of which of these two firms reached the disaster site first to sign up the victims usually depended on the location of the crash. If it was in Europe, Africa or the Caribbean Vultan and Heist were normally the first to arrive on an immediate flight from New York whereas the Los Angeles firm invariably picked up most of the Pacific and Asian disasters.

Seton's task at the law conference was to establish close relations with the Asian lawyers so that they could act as the firm's agents in some future disaster and so beat the Los Angeles speedsters to the scene. For this reason Seton had taken a pile of pre-printed forms which he intended to distribute to some of the lawyers. The purpose of the forms was to give Vultan and Heist or its agents the exclusive right to act for the victim in any claim for damages arising out of the accident. All that the victim had to do was fill in his name and address and date of the disaster and sign it.

Seton had managed to make a few useful contacts at the conference but not nearly as many as he would have liked. The problem was that for four out of the five days he was confined to his room and toilet with an extremely uncomfortable attack of "Bali belly". So at the end of the conference he decided to stay on for a couple of days to recuperate in the sun. From the prone position on his reclining chair beside the pool at the Bali Beach Hotel he began to consider whether the long trip had been worthwhile. In view of the meagre contacts that he had made he reluctantly came to the conclusion that it hadn't. Still, he didn't discount the possibility that the 'plane on which he was travelling back to the States might crash — thereby leaving him, with all the pre-printed forms in his briefcase, in the perfect position to sign up the survivors on the spot.

Back in New York Havelock Vultan III was sitting in his office smoking a fat cigar as he held a late night conference with a lawyer from Washington to whom he was farming out all the claims arising out of the sinking of a ferry off the Florida Cays. It was just after 8 p.m. when he closed the meeting and walked over to his AAP connected teleprinter. He wanted to see if there was any last minutes news before he went home to his Fifth Avenue apartment. "Bush fires burn holiday homes on French Rivière, Family of Dwarves killed while crossing Berlin Wall, Breakdown of Geneva Disarmament Talks, British Government loses two bye-elections, Call girl scandal in Congress", and then " — Plane overruns airport in Bali, Many killed."

"Holy mackerel!" he exclaimed. "When did that conference of Seton's end?" He pulled out the brochure and looked at the dates. "To-day!" he yelled in ecstasy. Then he remembered that Bali was a day ahead of New York. "Damn, it ended yesterday. That bloody kid's probably left and gone to some whorehouse in Bangkok by now. I'll give it a try anyway." He rang the New York telephone exchange and asked them to place a call to Buck Seton at the Bali Beach Hotel.

"It usually takes a couple of hours to get through to Bali," said the operator.

"Listen, babe, this is important," said Vultan with an air of authority. "They're holding some American hostages out there and I have to ring through with the ransom money. You don't want to have the deaths of some good, clean American boys on your conscience, do you?" The operator certainly did not. Two minutes later Havelock Vultan was talking to the receptionist at the Bali Beach Hotel.

"Has that kid Seton checked out yet?" he asked.

"No, sir. He is due to leave to-morrow."

"Where is he now?"

"He is by the pool. I can see him from here."

"Well, just go and wake him up and tell him that Havelock Daddy is on the 'phone and it's bloody important."

"Just one moment, sir. I shall go and fetch him." She ran out to the pool. "Excuse me, sir. Havelock Daddy wants to talk to you on the 'phone." Seton jumped up like a bolt of lightning and rushed into the reception area to take the call.

"That you, Buck? Do you know about the 'plane crash?"

"No. Where?"

"It overran the runway at Bali. Now you just get over there with those forms and a few pens and don't waste any time. Stay on as long as you think it's necessary. Gee, how I'd love to see the faces of those L.A. cowboys when they arrive to-morrow and see that we've grabbed all the business. They'll probably accuse us of blowing it up. Like they did last

254

year in Venezuela. See ya, kid."

Seton dashed up to his room and put on a pair of trousers and a sports shirt. He grabbed his briefcase containing the printed forms and bought a stock of ball point pens from the hotel paper shop as he ran out to get a taxi.

The cab driver had already heard of the accident on the Asian grapevine — the Eastern version of the teleprinter. When he saw the American rush out of the hotel with a briefcase and ask to be taken immediately to the scene of the disaster, the taxi driver assumed that he was a doctor.

At the airport there was complete chaos. The police had mounted a road block to stop all but essential services from driving on to the tarmac. The taxi driver had never seen an air crash before and was curious to get a first hand view of this latest manifestation of *pasih's* anger. He spoke in Indonesian to the policeman at the road block and said that his passenger was a doctor on his way to help the victims.

"Good," said the policeman in English, "we are very short of doctors. Go as fast as you can."

They sped along to the end of the tarmac and parked with all the police cars and ambulances. Seton jumped out and assessed the scene. He looked out to sea and the first thing he saw was the tail of the 'plane sticking out of the water. It carried the red and green logo of Linford American Airways. "Thank God it's an American 'plane," he thought. "You can't always get the high damages in other countries."

On his left were gathered some of the survivors who had been pulled out of the water and who were not seriously injured. The police were taking some details from them and food carts were providing them with soup, fruit and coffee. He went over to this group and began talking to the survivors individually as the police finished with them.

"Howdy, sir. Buck Seton, attorney from New York. I just happened to be passing and thought you might like to know that you can sue the airline for millions of dollars for putting you in the sea like this."

"But I'm not hurt. Just a little shaken, that's all," said the man.

"Doesn't matter. Nervous shock, ruined holiday, emotional stress, panic, possible phobias, future difficulty in concentrating, bad memory in later life, possible bad dreams, flashbacks and all that. Our firm has its own doctors and psychiatrists in the States and they will certify that you have suffered permanent psychological damage from this incident and the courts always listen to doctors. You will get an award of at least a million bucks and it'll cost you nothing. We've never failed yet. Aircraft disasters are our specialty."

The man was smart enough to detect the charlatan that lay beneath the pleasant and persuasive exterior. "But hell, if this guy has got firms of doctors on his books — with kickbacks of course — and is able to defraud the court with bogus medical certificates that can get me a million bucks, then why not?" He thought for a moment and looked Seton squarely in the eye. "Okay bud, if you can deliver the goods I'm game to play."

Seton pulled one of the forms out of his briefcase and began filling in the man's name and address. "Just sign here and my firm will file the claim on your behalf and get back to you."

The man signed at the bottom of the page. He did not see the clause that entitled Vultan and Heist to a percentage of the damages. Nor did Seton point it out to him. But it didn't matter. "It's like backing an outsider in the Kentucky Derby," thought the man. "I've got virtually nothing to lose and perhaps much to gain. I love a gamble."

Seton's next target was a young woman from Boston. She was still getting over the horror of jumping into the sea and seeing all the dead bodies floating around. She could barely turn her attention to Seton when he introduced himself. But when he said that he could get her at least a million dollars in damages she immediately forgot about the suffering and death all around her and began thinking of mink furs, Jaguars and a week-end house at Martha's Vineyard. She signed within three minutes.

"How much will it cost me?" asked the next victim who was an Episcopalian minister on holiday with his wife from Pennsylvania.

"Nothing sir. If we don't get anything for you we don't charge you a fee. But if we do win — and we've never failed yet — then we take a small percentage of the award as our fee."

"How much?"

"Thirty per cent."

"That's outrageous!"

"Well, you won't find any other law firm that's cheaper. We never lose with these ones."

"But what about the airline? Where will they get all the money from to pay out all the claims? They might go bankrupt and then we'd get nothing," said the suspicious and money conscious clergyman.

"They are heavily insured for this type of accident and it is the insurance company that pays. The premiums are built into the cost of your ticket. You have paid the premium so why not collect on the claim?"

The clergyman was thinking of his coming retirement. It would be difficult to live comfortably on his meagre stipend. But he felt it was a bit immoral to make a claim when he hadn't been hurt. His wife nudged him in the ribs. "It's the chance we've been looking for," she whispered.

"Oh, all right then. We'll sign," he said. Seton passed them a couple of forms and they affixed their sacred signatures on the dotted line.

The man from the Titanic was sitting on a deck chair under a canopy that had been hastily erected. He was sipping a glass of pineapple juice as he watched the amazing rescue operation that was taking place in front of him.

"Excuse me, sir. Were you a passenger on the 'plane?" asked Seton.

"Indeed I was. And I'm very thankful to have got off safely."

"My name is Buck Seton and I'm an attorney from New York. My firm is prepared to act for you to recover a large sum of damages from the airline for causing this terrible accident."

"You didn't waste much time getting here, did you, Mr. Seton?"

"I happened to be in Bali attending a law conference. Now, if you are prepared to sign one of these forms we can virtually guarantee to get you a substantial amount of money. Certainly enough to take care of you for the rest of your life."

The old man resented the condescending tone. "You weren't around when the Titanic went down," he said sarcastically.

"Pardon?" replied Seton.

"I didn't see you in the water in the North Atlantic in 1912. Perhaps it was too cold for you."

"I wasn't alive then."

"No, and I don't suppose that your law firm was either. I have my own lawyers in New York. The firm's been in existence since 1824 and they're quite competent."

"There weren't any aircraft around then. Or aircraft disasters."

"Nor lawyers like you, Mr. Seton." He spoke with such disdain and finality that Seton decided not to waste any more valuable time talking to him.

He signed up several more passengers and used the growing bundle of signed forms to woo the others. If anybody showed any hesitation he just pulled out the pile and said, "Look, everyone else has signed. Surely you don't want to be the odd man out." It worked like a charm.

When he had collected signatures from all the un-wounded survivors — with the exception of the Titanic man — he moved over to where the injured were being placed in the ambulances. He spoke to them and held their hand as they lay on stretchers screaming with pain. Some thought that he was a doctor and that they were signing an authority for him to operate on them. To others he whispered, "I can get you a million dollars in damages for this. All you have to do is sign here." Many signed just to get rid of him.

He bribed the ambulance drivers not to drive off until he finished his sordid business with their shattered patients. When an Indonesian official walked past he pretended that he was a doctor. He even put his hand on a man's broken leg and moved it slightly so as to make it appear that he was a medic. The man screamed with pain.

There was a dying woman in the back of an ambulance who was waiting for a life saving injection from a doctor. Seton positioned himself in the door of the vehicle and refused to budge until she signed. The doctor asked him to move. He said that he couldn't because he was stuck in the doorway. Eventually the woman signed and he moved away to admit the waiting doctor. But by then the woman was dead. "Thank God I got her signature," he thought. "Just in the nick of time."

Eventually the doctors complained to the police who came over and ordered him to get away from the ambulance area. He told them that he was from the United States Embassy in Jakarta but they stuck to their guns and said that, if he was from the Embassy, then he would fully understand how to behave in an emergency and that did not include blocking the doors of ambulances.

Seton walked over to the rocks at the edge of the airport where survivors were still being ferried ashore by surfboard and outrigger. He got his feet wet and gave a hand to help some of them on to the rocks.

"Thanks ever so much," said the middle-aged woman who was the fifth and latest victim whom Adrian had transported on his board. Three minutes later she took the outstretched pen from Seton's hand and wrote her name on the bottom of yet another of his pre-printed forms.

He tried to bribe the surfers and boatmen to bring their human cargoes to where he was standing but they refused.

"I'll buy you a new surfboard," he said to Thierry, "if you bring your next victim to where I am standing."

"I'm sorry but I am too busy saving lives to waste time bargaining and making deals with strangers," said Thierry with more than a little *hauteur*.

"Arrogant bastard," muttered Seton.

Many of the bodies that were being brought ashore were dead. They were placed on stretchers and put into covered police vans which took them to the hospital in Denpasar pending further arrangements.

Seton stood and watched with macabre fascination the landing of the corpses. "They can still be turned into fees and money," he kept telling himself. He knew that, although dead people couldn't sign legal documents to institute a damages action, their heirs and attorneys could. "If only we can get to their next-of-kin within a day or two."

He could see some Indonesians with the logo of Linford American Airways on their shirt pockets. He assumed that they were the executive and administrative staff so he went over and spoke to the one who looked the most senior. Seton said that he was visiting Bali from the U.S.Embassy in Jakarta and asked if he could have a copy of the passenger list as soon as possible.

"The ambassador has received a special request from the White House to furnish a list of passengers as soon as it is available," he said. "If possible we would like their addresses and next-of-kin as the President would like to send personal messages of condolence to the relatives of the dead."

The local manager was greatly impressed. He had always been amazed at the wonders of American technology and here it was in its finest raiment before his very eyes. The Indonesian police and airport authorities could barely manage a proper rescue operation, he thought, and yet America already has a man from the embassy on the spot seeking details of the passengers for the President who is sitting at his desk ten thousand miles away in Washington waiting to write condolence letters to the relatives. "What a great country!" he thought. "And if I oblige this charming diplomat and please the President then all sorts of blessings from the gods might fall upon me. Perhaps a green card for my son who is studying architecture at the university in Jakarta. Then the whole family could go and live with him in a big house in California. Yes, the Americans are like the gods. They have great powers."

He realised that it would be in his interests to assist the man from the embassy and give him whatever he requested. The death and destruction all around was soon forgotten as the little manager could think of nothing but the possibility of a green card to enter and work in the United States. "Of course, sir, I have a passenger list here but I need it. There is a duplicate in my car which you may have. Unfortunately it gives only the passengers' names and not their home addresses."

He sent one of the others over to his car to fetch the list. "Here it is, sir. Now if you'll excuse me I must attend to many things. I shall see you later and please give my compliments to your great President."

Seton went through the list and crossed out the names of those who had already affixed their signatures to his precious forms. He looked around for an immigration officer. Preferably middle management level. Senior enough to get him the information that he wanted but sufficiently lowly paid to take the bribe that he was going to offer. He spotted a short man of about fifty-five with the words "Immigrasi" on his cap.

Seton went over and said that he was from the U.S. Department of Civil Aviation and that he needed the home addresses of those names on the passenger list that he had not crossed out. Seton's computerised list was on two thin sheets of paper and the immigration officer could feel the crisp American banknote between the two pages. All that he looked for was the number in its bottom corner. He was ecstatic when he saw the figures "100".

"It will take a little time, sir, as I will have to go through all the departure cards that they filled out. But I shall go to the terminal building right away and get started."

To make sure that the man returned and didn't make off with the money Seton promised him another hundred dollar note when he handed over the details. They arranged to meet outside the terminal building an hour later.

The Indonesian quit his duties of helping with the rescue and hitched a ride in an ambulance to the terminal building which was almost deserted. The airport had been closed to further flights and all the action was taking place at the other end of the runway.

Seton continued to watch the procession of dead bodies being delivered by outrigger to the rocky edge of the reclaimed airport. The sea was now thick with small boats of every description – *praus*, fizzboats, a kayak and hundreds of surfboards. It was the corpses on the surfboards that fascinated him the most. Over the years he had descended like a vulture on quite a few crash sites where bodies were still being pulled out of the wreckage but he had never before seen a Dunkirk of surfboards bearing the injured and the dead. Some of them carried a body writhing in pain or with an arm or leg missing. The sea was now so thick with boats that some of them could barely move. It was like Aberdeen Harbour in Hong Kong. Some survivors were being lifted from boat to boat until they were eventually passed on to the rocks.

There were briefcases and cameras and watches and items of clothing floating around in the water and, of course, treasure hunters galore — both Balinese and European. The Balinese regarded the floating cameras and other goodies as presents from the gods. They plucked them out of the water and thanked the spirits for floating them their way.

The immigration officer was waiting for Seton near the entrance to the terminal. "I have managed to get all the information that you requested. I finished only five minutes ago. You will see that almost all the passengers are from America."

Seton took the list from the officer's outstretched hand and replaced it with a folded hundred dollar note. "*Terima kasih*, sir", said the officer as he thanked the gods for the 'plane crash which had made him richer by two hundred dollars — almost six months' salary.

Seton ran his eye down the column of addresses. "Couldn't be better, couldn't be better," he said out loud. "Most from New York, some from Massachusetts and none from the West Coast. We can get to most of them by to-morrow."

Now that there were no more survivors and only a few corpses were being landed from the boats and surfboards Seton decided to return to his hotel. There was nothing more that he could achieve amidst the chaos of the rescue operation and he wanted to 'phone Havelock before it was too late in New York. He found a taxi that had just driven some officials to the steps of the terminal building so he asked the driver to take him back to the hotel. As they drove through the road block at the entrance to the airport Seton was recognised by the same policeman who had waved him through. "Thank-you very much, doctor, for coming to help us."

"No trouble," he replied with a cheery smile.

When he placed his call to Havelock Vultan's apartment it was just after midnight in New York. "Well Buck, my boy, what percentage of them did you get? Is it as good as the last one in the Bahamas?"

"I signed up all the survivors except for a couple of pig-headed sons of bitches and I managed to get all the addresses of the dead ones. They are mostly from New York."

"You little beauty, Buck. Just telex them through to the office and we'll be on to the relations first thing to-morrow. Any whom we can't find straight away we'll hand over to the private investigators." He was already seeing the dollar signs in front of his eyes. With lots of noughts on the end. "Say Buck, this looks as if it'll be one of our most profitable crashes this year. How full was the 'plane?"

"It was almost completely full."

"The more people the better. Dead or alive it doesn't matter. Either way they make us heaps of good legal money." He blew a kiss through the air.

When Seton flew out of Bali a couple of days later he put the signed forms into a briefcase which he carried with him as hand luggage. He never let it out of his sight until he walked into his office in New York and deposited its contents in the safe. Those few pieces of paper — some of them bloodstained and soiled by salt and sand and sweat — were worth about ten million dollars in fees to the worthy and respected partners of Vultan and Heist.

━━━■━━━

It was the middle of the afternoon before Thierry and Adrian returned to Legian. Nicole and Dayu were sitting on the verandah waiting for them.

"Well, I know that we girls have to take second place to the waves," said Nicole, "but isn't it a bit much to stay away all day when you wrote that you would be back by mid-morning?" Dayu held up the incriminating piece of paper with

Adrian's message on it.

The two girls listened in horror as Thierry and Adrian related the events of the morning. Nicole was appalled at the tales of the dead and the injured and Dayu too was frightened at the apparently never ending expressions of anger by the spirits of the sea. When they decided to go down to the beach for a swim Dayu said that she didn't want to go.

"Why not?" asked Adrian.

"The spirits are too angry. Something else bad might happen. They must be very powerful to-day if they can destroy a big aeroplane. I prefer to stay here and wait until you come back."

Adrian thought that if he let her stay back this time it might be many days before she would agree to go near the beach. "No way," he said. "Nothing else will happen. They have no more anger left after what they did this morning." It took another ten minutes to persuade her. And only after she went and placed an offering on the shrine to appease the spirits.

Thierry and Adrian were absolutely exhausted after their frantic morning and were still fairly shaken after what they had seen. They both flopped down on the sand and went to sleep.

They later went for a swim and then watched the sunset. In the distance they could see the protruding red and green tail of the 'plane. "I wonder how many shattered dreams lie in that watery grave," said Adrian. "You just never know what's going to happen, do you? All those happy people who took off this morning and not one of them reached their destination. Man proposes, God disposes."

"It's the power of the spirits," thought Dayu. Whatever it was, they all felt very small and humble in the face of such an awesome power that could destroy a huge aircraft.

The next day a contingent of American air inspectors flew into Bali to ascertain the cause of the crash. They determined that the 'plane had not gathered enough speed along the runway to get it airborne. But it was going too fast to pull up. "Pilot error," they said. The pilot couldn't answer. His was the last body to be recovered by the divers.

The Indonesian authorities did not like the look of the crashed 'plane sticking up out of the sea at the end of the runway. It was too potent and obvious a reminder of the terrible powers of the demons as well as a very bad portent and advertisement for arriving holidaymakers. So, after a few days, they decided to get rid of it. When no one was around.

It was nearly dawn when Adrian and Dayu walked along the beach after a particularly lively night at the Jolly Frog. They could hear and, in the improving light, see the crashing waves. Adrian estimated that they were about five feet. "I'll go out later in the morning," he thought, "after a bit of sleep." They saw Thierry and Nicole sitting outside their cottage under the light of an oil lamp.

"We are just having some coffee before we turn in," said Nicole.

"I don't even feel tired," said Thierry. "All that wild dancing and lively music. It's still going round inside my head."

"Mine too," said Adrian. He saw Dayu yawn. Then Nicole. "Hey, Thierry, do you feel like a surf? At least we'll have the sea to ourselves." It was said more or less as a joke.

"But why not? By the time we get down to the beach it'll be daylight."

"I'm going to bed," yawned Nicole.

"Me too," added Dayu.

"Okay, Thierry, maybe a short energetic surf is just what we need to make us sleepy." They grabbed their boards and made their way through the half light to the beach.

"There's some special kind of feeling about being the first ones into the waves, don't you think?" said Thierry.

"Yes, it's only a new day but it feels like the beginning of

266

creation." They looked along the beach in both directions. Not a soul in sight. And not a sound either. Just the crashing of the waves.

"Isn't it peaceful?" said Adrian.

"Oh, we are so lucky," replied Thierry. "At the moment the beach belongs to us, the waves belong to us — in fact, the whole sea belongs to us."

"What about the whole world?" laughed Adrian.

"No, we don't want that. There are too many problems. Just this little bit of it will be enough."

Boom! Boom! Boom!

"God, what was that?" They looked in the direction of the noise and saw smoke rising from where the crashed aircraft had been lying in the sea just off the airport.

"Oh, not another 'plane crash," exclaimed Thierry. "This place really is crazy."

"No," said Adrian, "they must be blowing up the wreckage. You know how superstitious they are and how much they believe in spirits. Maybe they don't want to be reminded of the demons' anger."

"They are probably destroying it completely to appease the spirits even more," replied Thierry.

When the light improved they looked across and could no longer see any part of the wreckage jutting out of the sea.

"Let's go and have a look at what they've done," said Adrian.

"But there'll be nothing to see," replied Thierry. "It'll all be under the water."

"Maybe. But I'm curious to have a look. Let's put our boards on the bikes and ride down there and finish our surf out on the reef."

When they pulled up at the beach beside the airport there was no one else in sight.

"Look, the reef seems to have moved," exclaimed Thierry. "The waves out there never used to break so close to the airport."

"The reef hasn't moved," said Adrian. "It's a new reef. The 'plane must be sitting just a few feet below the surface of the water thereby forcing the waves to break over it."

They went to find a boatman but there was no one in sight. Finally they saw one who had been sleeping in his boat on the sand. He had been awakened by the noise of the explosion and was sitting by his craft on the beach contemplating this latest sign of *pasih's* power. Nothing less than the total destruction of the aircraft and the creation of a new reef.

"Will you take us out to the reef?" asked Thierry.

"Very dangerous out there now. Many bad things happening. I don't want to go." Thierry pulled out the normal fare and handed it to him. The man waved it away and said that it wasn't nearly enough. Adrian offered the same amount again. It was still not enough. Finally they settled on a price that was five times the normal fare.

"It doesn't matter," said Thierry. "If we are the first ones to ride the new reef then I don't care how much we have to pay."

The boatman would only take them to the normal location — just inside the coral reef. No further.

"It doesn't matter," said Adrian. "We'll just have a bit further to paddle." They jumped out and stroked their way across to the new creation with eyes as wide and starry as Columbus must have had when he first sighted the New World.

"Isn't it weird to think that, as a result of all the death and destruction of the crash, we finish up with a wonderful new reef," said Thierry.

"That's Bali," replied Adrian.

"What do you mean?"

"Out of death comes another life. The reef. It is the reincarnation of the 'plane."

"Who will be the first to ride it?" Thierry called out, fearing that his fast paddling friend would take the honours.

"It will be like when Hillary and Tensing climbed Everest," replied Adrian. "They both reached the peak at the same time."

"Oh, that is such a nice way to do it. The way of gentlemen. The way of aristocrats. The way of surfers."

The body of the huge 'plane resting on the seabed formed a giant submarine obstacle that created some of the cleanest six foot waves that Adrian had ever seen. The lines were near perfect. "It is going to be an excellent reef," he said, "and it will relieve crowd pressure on the old one."

"Well, what are we going to call it? I mean, we're the first ones to discover it and ride it so we should have the honour of naming it," said Thierry.

Adrian suddenly thought of Alex and remembered how much she loved being in the sea. "Much more than Dayu does," he thought. "Do you mind if we call it Alex's Reef?" he asked.

"Of course," said Thierry. "I should have suggested it myself. Now, let's ride it. Yahoo!"

They both took off together on a six footer that carried them forward on a dream ride. Adrian threw his hands up into the air and Thierry copied him. And then promptly fell off. Adrian managed some truly magic tubes but no matter how hard Thierry tried he could never get everything right at the same time.

A few more surfers arrived. The boatmen took them as far as the old reef and from there they paddled across to the new one. "It is called 'Alex's Reef'," Thierry told everyone. There was no need to put up a signpost as the word spread along all the guys in the line-up. Then to the boatmen. Then to the beach. And to the losmens. And right along the Asian grapevine.

"Have you surfed Alex yet?"

"Yes, I was there this morning."

"Alex is a classic. She's neat and clean and beautiful. And has real shape."

Adrian smiled to himself. "It sums her up perfectly," he thought. "That's just what she was like."

Chapter Ten

The Restaurant

The friendliest of the waiters at Manoel's was called Sugar. His real name was Edi Harbani but the similarity of his thick lips to those of a certain Rolling Stone had led him to adopt "Brown Sugar" as his theme song. Hence his name. He was seventeen and had been working at the restaurant for a couple of months, dividing his time between washing dishes and waiting on tables.

When he first approached Manoel for a job he was told ever so politely by the Portuguese that he didn't need an extra hand. However, the boy persisted and said that he had come all the way from his village in Java and had nowhere else to go. Manoel eventually agreed to let him work there for a few hours during the day in return for providing him with meals and letting him sleep in a bamboo hut at the back of the restaurant compound. He was told that any money that he earned would have to come from tips from the customers. Manoel had said that, although it was not the type of arrangement that he would normally make, he really didn't need an extra man and that Sugar could take it or leave it. He took it.

He started off by sleeping in the hut but had recently been spending the nights with Maybelle, an American girl from Minnesota, in her bungalow at Kuta. After a while Sugar found the lack of money more than a little inconvenient. Especially after he met Maybelle and wanted to impress her by buying drinks when they were out together in the evenings. He had begun to supplement his income by taking small amounts of hashish on credit from his friend, Bong Bong, who worked at the notorious Haight-Ashbury bar. Sugar then resold them at a considerable profit to a few grateful tourists.

The young waiter came to like the feel of the high denomination banknotes in his pocket as well as all the expensive drinks and new clothes that he could now afford to buy. He was not averse to making even more money when he met Bong Bong outside the Haight-Ashbury at midnight. Bong Bong took him into his confidence and put to him a scheme that had the potential to bring untold riches to both of them.

Bong Bong's younger brother, Nyoman, spent his days hawking oil paintings to tourists on the beach. The Balinese sunset scenes — some pink, some vivid orange — were particularly popular as were the more traditional depictions of Hindu gods. The landscapes were painted by several families up in his village in the mountains. They were entrusted to Nyoman on credit to sell to tourists for whatever price he could obtain. He had become an expert at bargaining and always managed to convey an impression that he was doing the customer a great favour by parting with such a priceless work of art for such a ridiculously low price.

He had found from experience that the best paying tourists were those who spent all day lying on the beach. Such people had plenty of time to look at the various canvasses that were unrolled in front of them and they usually made a purchase just to get rid of the pest who had interrupted their doze in the sun. He had worked out that those who had the most money to spend were busy people from distant lands who had only a few days to spend in the gentle and seductive world of Bali. Such jetsetters tended to spend all their time on the sand acquiring a quick tan and so were happy to buy paintings, carvings and shells on the beach instead of wasting time looking for them in the shops. Sometimes they didn't even have to move their limbs. Just the arm action of reaching out to their wallet for some money. They didn't mind paying a good price either. For them bargaining was a formality and entertainment rather then a serious effort to force the price down. Time was their scarce commodity. Not money.

Before quoting his starting price Nyoman would always ask them how long they had been in Bali. He would then tailor his price to suit their answer. If it was their first or second day he would pitch his price very high on the assumption that they were still quite green and would have no idea of the real value. They usually accepted and sometimes even told him how cheap they were.

He could only wonder at the strange ways of the West. "If they think that my over-priced paintings are cheap," he thought, "then the prices of things in their countries must be ridiculously high." Then he remembered that he had once heard the fantastic suggestion that people in the West did not have to pay for goods with money. Just a little plastic card which was said to have magical powers like the gods. One man had even told him that you didn't even need to have any money to obtain one of these plastic cards. And then you could buy a car with it! Or push it into a machine in the wall of a bank and bundles of cash would start falling out of the machines. As good as having a jim. "No wonder they all appear to be so rich!" he mused. "I wish that I lived in the West with a plastic card. Think how rich I would be!"

If the tourists said that they had been in Bali for a week or more then he had to bid a more competitive price. He knew they would have been approached many times and — horror of horrors — might even have been shopping and seen the same paintings in the shops for a fraction of his usual asking price.

"Why can't they all come here for just a couple of days and then go home again?" he asked himself. "It would make my business so much easier."

Even when they refused his high prices and said, "No thank-you. No paintings to-day," he was always polite. After all, the man who refuses to-day might think better of it to-morrow. Besides, Nyoman had a reputation to uphold. With a bundle of rolled up canvasses under his arm and an American baseball cap on his head he was a familiar sight to the regular sunseekers who took up their positions on the beach at Legian each day — often on the very same patch of sand as the day before.

Nyoman had sold seven paintings by the middle of the day. All at good prices. He decided to ease off during the noonday heat and pitch his wares again about four o'clock.

Pleased with the morning's results he wandered up to a food cart at the top of the beach and bought a plate of noodles and some sweet black Balinese coffee. He then walked along the track that meandered between the trees at the top of the sand. A mad dog began to follow him and he looked at it with contempt. It had a big head and vacant looking eyes. He wondered what sort of evil the creature must have perpetrated in its previous life to have been rein-carnated in to such a dreadful looking hound. They came to an open drain and the dog stopped to sniff at all the foul smelling refuse that had collected there. Nyoman jumped across the trench and walked on aimlessly. He felt like a sleep in the shade but wanted to walk as far along the beach as possible. Away from the people. He had quite a bit of money in his pocket from the morning's selling and he didn't want to be robbed of it while he slept.

He kept walking until he had the whole beach to him-self. He turned up into the mangroves and scrub at the top of the sand and looked around. There was not a soul in sight. He found a small clearing that was shaded by a large pandanus tree. It was a few yards off a narrow track that threaded its way through the mangroves. There was just enough space for

274

him to stretch out. The foliage was quite thick and he believed that he would be safe from prying eyes. So he took off his baseball cap and T-shirt and lay down on the soft, sandy ground. Soon he was asleep.

About half an hour later he woke up with a start. He lay completely still and listened. He could hear a rustling noise in some nearby bushes. Then it stopped. He heard something drop to the ground and click. Something quite heavy. It sounded like a pistol. He moved himself very carefully and in complete silence until he could see through a hole in the trees. He could see movement. He concentrated his eyes and saw the uniform of a policeman. He froze for a moment as he always did when he saw a member of the Indonesian police.

A new law had been introduced which prohibited hawkers from selling their wares on the beach. If caught, the hapless hawker had to hand over to the police all the goods that he was selling as well as any money that was in his possession. When goods and money were confiscated the police sometimes kept them. Other hawkers would follow the cops off the beach and behind some trees where they would start bargaining to buy back all the stock at a reduced price. This was good for everybody except the original culprit. The police received money instead of a pile of useless paintings and carvings, the hawkers who bid for them got a supply of stock at a greatly reduced price and could resell them to tourists at a good profit, the tourists were not deprived of the items and nor did the Indonesian economy do without the tourist dollars that were later used to buy them. Everyone benefitted except the silly hawker who allowed himself to get nabbed in the first place.

Nyoman had never been caught but he was still highly suspicious of the police whom he knew could swoop on the beach at any time and strip him of his paintings and money. He watched in amazement as the cop took off his khaki shirt and dropped his trousers to the ground. He was standing there in his black underpants. Carefully the policeman looked around him. Then, sure that no one had seen him, he walked through the trees and on to the beach. Nyoman watched him walk down to the water for a swim.

Hasan Subandra was a Javanese from the city of Jogjakarta. He had been in the police for three years and had only recently been posted to Bali. He had been doing patrol work during the morning in the village of Seminyak and, like Nyoman, was taking a long break during the midday heat. He had already had his lunch of soup and fried noodles at a *warung* in the main street of Seminyak. Normally he would have stayed there for an hour or so reading the newspaper but he felt uncomfortable at all the ugly stares that he was receiving from the villagers. He didn't know whether the barely concealed hostility was directed at him because he was a policeman or because he was Javanese. "Probably a bit of both," he thought. He felt uneasy so he got up from his table and walked out. It was hot and humid and he felt like a swim. He wandered down a track towards the beach and began to feel refreshed by the cool sea breeze. He stood and looked at the sparkling blue ocean with its gentle waves. It looked so inviting and there wasn't a soul in sight. He decided to hide his uniform and pistol in the trees and go for a swim. He knew that it was against police regulations to do so but reasoned that, if no one saw him, there would be no problem.

He walked back a few yards and turned off the track and into a small clearing. He could neither hear nor see any movement. Convinced that there was no one around and that it would be quite safe to leave his clothes and pistol, he pushed them under the thick and prolific roots of a mangrove tree and took his bearings. Then, wearing only his underpants, he walked down the hot sand and into the sea.

Nyoman waited until he was right out in the waves splashing and swimming like a dolphin. The young boy picked up his bundle of paintings and crept through the undergrowth to the tree where Officer Subandra had left his gear. He pulled the items out and packed them into a large plastic shopping bag that he had for his paintings. The haul included a full police uniform, belt and white leather holster, pistol and ammunition. With the paintings under one arm and the bulging plastic bag in the other, he darted back through the maze of jungle tracks that he knew so well.

After several detours which kept him off the main road Nyoman eventually reached his brother's place — a small hut where Bong Bong lived on his own. Breathless and excited, he roused Bong Bong who was lying on a mattress on the floor having a sleep before starting his night shift at the Haight-Ashbury bar.

"Oh, Elder Brother, look what I've got for you." Bong Bong was dumbfounded as the younger boy pulled the unusual haul out of the bag. With an air of suspense Nyoman left the pistol until last. "Now we'll be rich," panted Nyoman.

"Holy ancestors!" exclaimed Bong Bong as his brother narrated how he had come by the treasure. They decided to wait until dark and then bury it under the hut for a few days. By then the heat of any search should have passed and they could hide it back in the scrub until they decided where and when to use it.

They agreed that, since Nyoman looked too young to impersonate a policeman, Bong Bong would wear the uniform and Nyoman would be the bait to snare the tourists. It would be dangerous but the pickings would be rich. The trick would be not to do it too often. They knew that the best time would be between midday and one o'clock when the real police were mostly off duty. There was always a hiatus between the morning police who quit duty at noon and the afternoon police who took about an hour to get organised and who were rarely on the road before one.

Their first victim was a Dutchman with long blond hair and a pair of John Lennon glasses on the end of his long, thin nose. Shortly after midday on a fairly remote track through the mangroves he was approached by Nyoman who offered him a small block of dark green hash at a very cheap price.

Hank from Amsterdam was more than willing. After all, he could buy it in every café at home; they even advertised it with neon lighting. But he knew he had to be careful. Bali wasn't Amsterdam. He looked over his shoulder, saw that no one was watching and then pulled some notes out of his money belt. Nyoman observed with satisfaction the bundle of notes that the man put back in his belt. The Balinese boy unwrapped the hash from its silver paper and Hank took it, sniffed it and handed over the money. He had just begun to walk away when Bong Bong emerged from behind a bush. He was wearing the uniform of an Indonesian police officer complete with cap, white leather holster, pistol and badge of rank. He told Hank to stand still while he searched him. The Dutchman, a pale face at the best of times, went completely white. Bong Bong, the bogus cop, put his hand into Hank's pocket and pulled out the hash.

"Ooh, this is very bad. I can arrest you and send you to jail for seven years," he said in his best English. He paused for a moment to let the true import of his words sink in. Then he said, "But I know that it is very hard for tourists who do not know our laws. I want you to enjoy yourself here in Bali and not to have big problems. I want to be your friend. Maybe I can help you."

He motioned to Hank to step off the path and behind a thick bush for a full search. The frightened young man did as he was told. He didn't like the look of the pistol. Bong Bong searched his pockets and took off the money belt. He counted several thousand rupiah and six hundred and forty American dollars in cash. "You bring much money to Bali," he said in delight. Hank had been listening to a Pink Floyd tape on his Walkman when he was stopped. Bong Bong had always wanted a Walkman and decided to include it in the ransom. It was all over in a couple of minutes. Hank was too frightened to bargain. Bong Bong undertook not to take the Dutchman back to the police station and charge him in return for the Walkman, his watch and all his money.

Bong Bong was happy as he put the money in the pocket of his police jacket; he walked along another track towards a grove of fig trees where he took off the uniform and hid it in the undergrowth. Hank was happy beyond measure . He believed that he had just purchased his freedom for the next seven years for a cheap watch, a Walkman and a measly few hundred dollars. Even though he had just cashed all his traveller's cheques he knew that he could borrow his needs for the next few days from his travelling companion and telephone his father back in Amsterdam to send out some more money by telex. Young Nyoman was happy too as he watched Bong Bong count the money and then split it between them. They even recovered the block of hash so that they could use it again.

They repeated the performance a few more times. Always on a remote path and always during the police change-over time in the middle of the day.

The two brothers began to enjoy their new affluence. A couple of weeks after their first encounter with the Dutchman Nyoman was able to buy a motor bike. He was like a child with a new toy. He had never driven one before and revelled in its speed and power. When he pressed his hand on the accelerator and roared past the slow bicycles and motor scooters he felt like a god. However, lack of experience with such lethal toys has its price and Nyoman's was rung up one afternoon above five o'clock when he was riding across to Sanur.

He did not see the intersection with the right turn that led to Sanur until he was almost upon it. Instead of riding straight on and then turning round to come back to the junction, Nyoman spun the machine to the right in such a

279

sudden and violent movement that he lost all control of it. It skidded and spun and the next thing he knew was that the stone shrine in the middle of the intersection was rushing at him at great speed. The inexperienced driver did not try to eject from the wildly swerving machine. Nor was he wearing a crash helmet. He kept his hands glued to the handlebars. He didn't even move them to cover his head from the impact which was so great that the stones and concrete of the shrine crumbled under the shattering impact of the speeding piece of machinery.

The noise of the crash was heard over a great distance. People ran out of their houses, shops and *warungs* to see what had happened. When they saw that their local shrine had been reduced to a pile of rubble they automatically assumed that the unfortunate rider had been punished by the gods for destroying their shrine. He deserved his fate; it was a terrible thing to destroy a shrine. They attended to the functional matters like tying rags around his bleeding wounds and informing the police and ambulance but without any feeling for the victim.

When the ambulance arrived at the hospital in Denpasar Nyoman was taken into the emergency care section. It was found that he had two broken ribs, a fractured femur bone in his right leg and severe head and brain damage that would be permanent.

Later that night the police called round to Bong Bong's hut to inform him of his brother's accident. He was terrified when he opened the door and found three real policemen standing there. He thanked the gods that the stolen uniform and side arms were buried more than a mile away under the fig tree.

After they left he jumped on his own motor bike and went to visit his brother at the hospital. He was horrified at what he saw. Nyoman's battered body was roughly bandaged together and he was screaming in agony. Bong Bong asked the doctor if he had administered morphine to dull the pain. "No," replied the white-coated middle-aged man. "At present we do not have enough funds to purchase morphine. But I have given him omnopom."

"What! Only omnopom?" exclaimed Bong Bong who knew that omnopom was such an inadequate pain killer as to be almost ineffective.

After the doctor went out of the room Bong Bong asked the nurse if she knew how to administer morphine. "But, of course," she replied. "We used to provide it in really bad cases until a couple of months ago. Then we ran out of it and we haven't received any new supplies."

"I'll see what I can do," said Bong Bong as he walked out the door. He rode straight to the house of his friend who supplied him with the hash. He told him what he wanted and handed over some money. His friend rode off on his motor bike and was back in twenty minutes. He handed Bong Bong a small packet of powder. "*Terima kasih*," said Bong Bong as he bid good-bye.

Back at the hospital he handed the morphine to the nurse. She was secretly impressed by Bong Bong's command of the situation. "He must be close to the gods to have such magical powers," she thought. "Or, more likely, friends in high places. And the money to pay for it. I would like to marry a man like that. None of the doctors in the hospital can get their hands on the stuff and yet this young man can produce it in half an hour."

She injected the morphine into Nyoman's left arm and his screaming soon stopped. As Bong Bong was leaving the nurse told him that the injured man would probably never be able to speak another coherent sentence.

The next day Bong Bong rode up to his village and told his father about the accident. The old man with the weathered face and wrinkled hands kept muttering that he didn't know how his youngest son could afford to buy a motor bike which he repeatedly referred to as a "death machine."

Deep down Bong Bong thought that it was probably a warning from the gods that their recent money making activities would result in bad karma. However, he too had developed some expensive tastes and had formed a liaison with a very beautiful Chinese girl who was on holiday from Surabaya where she was a radio announcer and fashion model. She would soon be going back to Java and he had promised to go with her and stay for a while at her apartment on the sea front. He had showered her with presents and champagne and bacardi but now found himself without enough money to pay for the night's drinks let alone the air fare to Surabaya.

Since Younger Brother was now lying in a coma and would never be anything more than a jabbering vegetable, Bong Bong had to find a new partner in crime whom he could trust. The act was from first to last a duet and the drug selling decoy was just as necessary as the bogus cop.

His friend, Sugar, at Manoel's had always paid him promptly whenever he had advanced hash to him on credit and so he decided to offer him the chance of replacing Younger Brother. He knew that Sugar was streetwise and could be relied on to keep it a secret.

Sugar found the arrangement both timely and attractive. He had said good-bye to the girl from Minnesota and the next day had met another short, blond girl who talked the same way as the American but who came from a town that she called Toronto. Sugar assumed that it was also in the United States but he didn't really care as he set about yet another casual and exciting liaison. Whereas the Minnesotan girl had usually paid for every second round of drinks the Toronto girl expected Sugar to buy all the drinks in return for later favours. And, unlike her Minnesotan predecessor, she always drank doubles. So Sugar was also in need of money when Bong Bong put the scheme to him.

The next day Sugar was waiting on the tables at Manoel's when he overheard a group of Danes saying how they would like to smoke some hash but didn't know where to buy it. They had eaten regularly at the restaurant during the two weeks that they had been in Bali. They found the food good and wholesome, the service fast and friendly and, most important of all, it was always spotlessly clean.

Dagmar and Anne-Marie had both trained as nurses at the hospital in Copenhagen and their two boyfriends had recently graduated from the university there and were enjoying the last days of their freedom before flying back to Europe and joining the work force.

The taller one, Jens, who was engaged to Dagmar, had done a degree in public administration. He had already been accepted for a position in the Statistics Department and planned to make his career in the civil service. He was languid and lazy and certainly not over-endowed with ambition. He regarded the public service as a safe and secure way to enjoy a comfortable standard of living while doing the least possible amount of work to earn it. It was a good option for one who knew that he could never make it in the private sector.

His friend, Christian, was made of different and sterner stuff. With a first class degree in mathematics under his belt he had the world at his feet. He had been accepted by a leading American company for a good position in its computer division. He hoped that, after a short time, he would be transferred to the company's head office in New York. He knew that he could make it in the big city and anyone who knew him would not disagree. He was gifted, carefree and sometimes reckless. Properly harnessed, his gifts would be ideally suited to an aggressive international company.

They all had a leisurely lunch at Manoel's. *Gado gado* and green salad washed down with some glasses of Bintang. They paid their bill to the courtly Portuguese gentleman who was sitting over the cash register by the door.

When they left, Sugar followed them out to the street. He said that he had overheard their conversation about the hash and that, if they came again at the same time to-morrow, he would be able to provide them with some at a very good price. "Great," said Christian. "See you to-morrow." It was stifling hot and they headed off to the beach for a swim.

They arrived the next day full of anticipation and sat down at one of the front tables. Sugar was again the waiter as Manoel was out and Wayan, the head boy, was sitting at the cash register taking the money. Sugar whispered to them that he had the stuff in his pocket but naturally didn't want to be seen transacting the business in such a public place as a restaurant. He had already arranged with Bong Bong to lead them a short distance down a lane and behind a high stone wall. Accordingly he told them that he would follow them outside when they left. They gulped down their drinks and paid Wayan at the desk.

A few minutes later Sugar met them outside and, with an air of pretended innocence, told them that it was safer to walk off the road and away from any prying eyes. "Okay. You're the local chap. Guess that you know what is best," said Christian. Sugar led them down a lane that was lined with several pyramids of drying coconuts. They went behind the wall and he pulled out a small piece of silver paper from his hot, sweaty pocket.

■

At precisely fifteen minutes before the midday hour Bong Bong had gone to the thick bush beneath the fig tree where he had hidden the uniform. He was looking forward to the extra money that would be in his pocket within the hour. He was feeling carefree and confident as he pulled the bag out from under the bush. It was the sixth time that he had carried out the operation and he had already netted an amount that was many times greater than what he could earn at the Haight-Ashbury in a year.

What Bong Bong didn't know was that on the previous day old Guru, one of the village elders of Seminyak, had been walking his dog down to the beach when another pi dog appeared from nowhere and sauntered along in front of them. The white mongrel with mean looking eyes was a bitch in heat and soon Guru's dog was barking and chasing her in a high state of excitement. The white dog ran off to the left through the trees with Guru's dog in full chase.

The old man spat out his betel nut and started to shout and whistle but to no avail. The bush was not thick so he walked through it, pushing the vines out of the way as he went. His dog had settled down by the time he arrived at the fig tree and he could see it pulling at something underneath a thick, leafy bush.

Guru walked over and saw that it was a standard white plastic shopping bag and that it was stuffed full of what appeared to be clothing. He pulled out the shirt, tie, trousers and boots and then — by the great gift of the gods — a white belt and pistol. He knew that it must be red hot as policemen don't normally leave their clothes and weapons lying under trees. He decided to leave them there as he didn't want to carry such hot items on his person. Not even the short distance to the police station. He took his bearings and replaced the pack under the bush, covering it with some thick branches.

Guru continued his walk down to the beach where he sat for a couple of hours contemplating his discovery. He wondered why the gods had led him there and what great spiritual powers the dogs must possess to have known where it was. It was the white one, he believed, the female that knew where to go. She had the power and magnetism to lead his dog off the path and directly to the treasure. She must be the reincarnation of someone who was really powerful in the previous life but who had misused that power to cause untold evil and suffering.

Guru was a wise old thing and had seen many potent forces pass through Bali during his long life: the Dutch, the hated Japanese, and now the Indonesians who were represented at village level by the uniformed police with their many badges and shiny pistols.

"I could be policeman. Ha, ha!" he thought. "After all, there is everything there. The uniform, the belt and the gun." However, he knew better than to dare the mighty power of the police. It was like daring the spirits. The demons could instil one kind of fear but the fear of the police was something else altogether. They represented the here and now. They were police, army and tax collector all rolled into one. Their great power was backed by guns and bullets and Guru had always known that the safest course was to have nothing to do with them. He and his ancestors had lived in Bali quite happily for hundreds of years without any police and Guru had never understood why they had suddenly become so necessary. And they were damned expensive too. Like the gods you always had to make offerings to them for one thing or another. Not flower petals and grains of rice but real bank notes. "Yes," he thought, "the police should be avoided like the plague."

Then he considered that, if the items were stolen — as seemed almost certain, — then maybe there would be a big reward that he could collect. Now that he was in his declining years he did not need very much in the way of material things himself but he was thinking of all his sons and daughters and grandchildren. None of them were rich. He would like to go into the next life knowing that he had left them well off. Also, such generosity and thoughtfulness would surely help him to be an improved creature in his next life — perhaps a Brahmana. "Ah yes," he thought, "I must find out about the reward."

Early the next morning he made his way to the local police station. The cop on the counter looked up and cursed when he saw the old man, clad only in a sarong and sandals, come shuffling through the doorway and stare around the room in wonder. He hated having to deal with stupid old villagers and wished that he could be a cop in America — with his own patrol car in a high speed chase on the freeway and shooting at everything in sight with the most powerful guns that money can buy.

"What do you want, old man, that you come in here to waste my valuable time?"

Guru asked him if there was any reward for handing in a lost uniform and pistol. The cop dropped his pen on the floor and looked up in amazement. His whole attitude changed. The station had been in a terrible state ever since Officer Subandra had turned up in only his underpants. Even the lowest villager got round in more than that. Worse still, there were holes in the underpants. And as for Subrandra's claim that he had lost his kit under a tree! No one believed him with the result that he had been dismissed from the force and sent back to Jogjakarta.

Guru said that he would lead them to it but that it would take up much of his valuable time and that he would have to be properly recompensed for his troubles. The police mentioned a figure. Guru doubled it and after five minutes of intensive bargaining they settled on a fee that was exactly half way between their original positions. Guru was happy; he was getting a huge sum of money for very little work. The police were happy to recover the missing uniform and weapon without having to pay as much as they had anticipated. "Thank the gods that it was a stupid old villager who found it and not one of those hungry westernised young men who would have held out for much more," they thought.

The police considered the matter so serious that they wanted not only to recover the lost items but also to punish the man who stole them. If only they could find him ...

The chief of police felt humiliated to think that illiterate old villagers like Guru were able to go for a walk through the trees and find stolen police clothes and weapons lying in the undergrowth. "By the holy ancestors," thought the chief, "if certain paranoid senior officers ever came to hear of it I might even be accused of allowing secret arms to be stashed under trees in my district in preparation for an armed rebellion!" He would almost certainly lose his job. Therefore, the apprehension of the thief was just as important as the recovery of the items.

Intent on catching the offender, the chief decided to show as low a profile as possible. He ordered two of his best officers to walk with Guru along the road and told them to take off their uniforms. They did a quick change into shorts, T-shirts and sandals. But they had their pistols and a small radio set packed in a couple of bags that they threw over their shoulders.

When they reached the clearing and checked the items in the plastic bag they paid Guru the agreed amount plus a little extra "keep quiet" money. They threatened to arrest him and his sons if he told anyone about the find. He believed them. "Now run off, old man, and do not return here for many days." As Guru scampered off he thanked the gods for his good luck and for the nice fat bundle of notes that he tucked into the folds of his sarong.

The two cops replaced the bag of items exactly where they found it. They then withdrew several yards through the trees until they were completely hidden. One of them looked at his watch. It was half past ten and the sun was still rising. They made a small space in the scrub where they could sit and lie while they waited. They decided to stay until midday when one of them would go off for some refreshments and then return to relieve the other.

They rarely spoke. And even then only in whispers.

They did not have to wait long. They heard Bong Bong brushing against the branches before he even reached the clearing. At first they thought he might be a villager out for a walk but that possibility disappeared when they saw him look around and then, convinced that he had not been seen, walk straight over to the bag and pull away the covering branches.

They watched as Bong Bong took off his sarong and began putting on the uniform. First the shirt, then the trousers. It was then that they moved. Ever so quietly at first. One of them covered him with a pistol in case he should reach down for the stolen gun that was lying on the ground. The more junior and athletic of the two rushed out of the trees and pinned the imposter to the ground. Soon both cops were sitting on him, their hands around his neck nearly throttling him. Bong Bong screamed and they stuffed the end of his sarong into his mouth to stifle the cries. They threatened to beat him up and change the shape of his face forever.

From his helpless position on the ground with two strong cops on top of him Bong Bong's razor sharp and streetwise mind started to work in overdrive. He first told them that he had found the package the previous day and was going to hand it in at the police station. They didn't believe him and tightened their grip around his throat. Eventually, under extreme duress, he told them the reason why he had come to wear the uniform.

"You say at half an hour after midday?" one of the policemen asked.

"Yes," he stammered. "I promise you that I can deliver up one Balinese seller of hash and some Denmark tourists who are going to buy with much money." He knew that he was fighting for his life.

The cops loosened their grip and talked among themselves. They decided to test Bong Bong's word. If he could lead them on to uncover further offences then they might decline to charge him this time in return for performing useful undercover work for them in the future.

One of the officers looked at his watch. It was almost noon. He knew that he would not have enough time to go back to the police station to collect more men and put on his uniform. He picked up the pieces of stolen clothing and tried them for size. They fitted all right. Bong Bong led them to the rendezvous behind the stone wall. It was stifling hot. Nothing stirred. Just the occasional rustle of the coconut fronds.

They took up their position behind a pile of drying coconuts that had been stacked against a fence. They tied Bong Bong to one of the fence posts — well out of sight. They picked up an oily rag from the ground and stuffed it in his mouth. Just in case he might feel the urge to call out a warning! They needn't have worried. He had already decided that to drop Sugar and some unknown tourists into the mud was a small price to pay for getting out of the very serious trouble of impersonating a policeman and carrying a firearm without authority.

The two cops watched with mounting satisfaction as Sugar led the four young Europeans behind the wall. They saw him pull out a small block of hash and show it to the shorter of the two white men. "Yes," they heard him say as he pulled some notes out of his pocket and began counting them. He gave them to Sugar who rewrapped the hash and handed it over.

"*Berhenti*," yelled the uniformed policeman as Christian was putting the hash into his pocket.

"By the great god, Siva," thought Sugar, "why does Bong Bong have to pounce before I have got away?" He looked up and saw the uniformed man diving at his legs. But it was not Bong Bong. The other cop had the Danes covered with his pistol.

The police switched on their radio and sent a message back to the station asking for some more men. They arrived a few minutes later on three motor bikes and, to the amazed and angry stares of the passers-by, the police frog-marched Sugar and the Danes back to the police station.

Bong Bong was untied and told that he could go free in the meantime. The police accompanied him back to his hut and asked him many questions. He answered cunningly but convincingly. They told him that he would be required to perform various unspecified services for them at a later date. He didn't argue.

At the police station Christian quickly took the sole blame for buying the hash. Knowing that he had been caught red-handed he decided that it was better to accept responsibility in order to exonerate the others. Especially his gentle and beloved Anne-Marie whom he knew would never be able to stand the appalling rigours of an Asian jail.

The police took him at his word. Indeed they were happy to do so. One Dane could easily be charged and sent to jail for several years and quietly forgotten. But four Danes on the same charge of a single tiny block of hash might create an international scandal. And that was the last thing that the police wanted. If it had come to that they would have let all four of them go free. But Christian's honest willingness to own up precluded that result.

The other three left the police station after saying a tearful good-bye to Christian who had been put into handcuffs and heavy leg chains. He was led down to a small concrete cell the walls of which were covered with moss and mildew. It stank of urine and resounded to the incessant buzz of hundreds of mosquitoes. He could see mushrooms growing in the corner and enormous cockroaches all over the floor. He sat down on the damp ground and reflected on his sudden change in circumstances. A few hours ago Bali was for him a gentle paradise. Now it was a living hell.

Anne-Marie, Dagmar and Jens went to a small *warung* and ordered some beer while they discussed the terrible events of the afternoon. By now they should have been stoned and laughing. Instead they were stunned, distraught and very angry. They wanted to personalise their anger.

They went back over what had happened. Every detail. Sugar had trapped them even though he had been caught too. That part of it was confusing. Then Anne-Marie repeated the rumours that they had heard about Manoel. That he was allowed to live in Bali and operate a business in return for dobbing people in to the police for drugs. After all, it was Sugar who set up the deal the day before and he would have had plenty of time to inform Manoel and the police and have them lying in wait. They came to the conclusion that the only reason that Sugar had been arrested was for the sake of appearances. To confuse the situation so that it did not look like a classic entrapment. And who did Sugar work for? Manoel. And who is the only foreigner allowed to stay in Bali and operate a business? Manoel. And why should Manoel have these rights that no other European has? Obviously to help the police trap nice young men like Christian by using agents like Sugar.

By this stage Anne-Marie was nearly hysterical. Because of Manoel's treachery the man whom she loved — her charming, healthy, clean-cut Christian — would be locked up for the next few years in some festering hell hole of an Asian jail instead of joining the American company and making it big in New York.

They ordered another round of drinks and tried to change the subject. But it was impossible. They decided to contact the Danish ambassador on the morrow but they knew that it was a forlorn hope. Denmark was a small country and did not have much influence in the Far East. "If only he was an American citizen," said Anne-Marie. "I'm sure that the authorities here would take note of a complaint from the American ambassador."

"He'd be no better off if he was an American," said Jens. "Their ambassador wouldn't do a thing to help. The embassy would work in with those power crazy bastards in the DEA. Don't forget, the only reason they have these draconian laws in Indonesia is because of the pressure that is put on them by the DEA. The only way for an under-developed country to get the American and World Bank aid that it needs is for it to dance to every tune that the DEA sings. And that is why Christian is not with us now. They didn't have all these oppressive laws until a few years ago and they wouldn't have them now if it wasn't for the nefarious and imperialist activities of the DEA. The only reason why they lock up a few decent young people like us is to justify the billions that they suck out of the gullible American taxpayers to keep themselves in champagne and prostitutes as they go about their sordid undercover work — tricking and cheating nice people like ourselves into committing small offences and then destroying our lives by throwing us into jail for years. After all, they have to show a certain number of arrests each year to keep those funds pumping out of Congress and into their greedy little hands. And, of course, it wouldn't make sense for them to catch the big drug dealers because then they would risk putting a stop to the trade and they'd all be out of a job.

The best course for them is to let the volume of drugs keep getting bigger so that they can then justify building up their own organisation. Then all the little failed cops whom they now employ will become big executives lording it over more and more officers. Whatever they do they won't stop the drug trade; all they'll do is cost the stupid American Government a bottomless pit of money and they'll hurt a lot of small people along the way. But they won't stop the big boys. After all, they have an incentive to make the problem worse, don't they? To keep their jobs and increase their budgets. If you ask me, the DEA is the greatest fraud ever inflicted on the taxpaying public." They ranted and raved in a desperate need to find an outlet for their burning passions.

Anne-Marie kept thinking of poor Christian all alone in the grimy cell and she burst into tears. At last they decided to walk back to their *losmens*.

It was almost five o'clock and the streets were full of the day workers on their way home and the night people preparing the restaurants and bars for the evening trade. Their route took them past Manoel's. The elderly Portuguese was sitting at the cash register by the door. Adrian and Dayu were at a front table having some chocolate cake and pineapple juice. There was a portly looking chap with sunglasses and a baseball cap sitting on his own at another table.

As she caught sight of Manoel's gaunt, deeply lined face Anne-Marie lost control of herself and ran up to him shouting. She screamed in English that he was a drug informer who lured young people into his restaurant only to gain their confidence and then set them up with the police.

"My poor boyfriend is now in jail and I'll probably never see him again and it's all because of you," she yelled. Manoel looked up in surprise. Her angry words continued to flow. "That is why you are allowed to stay in Bali and live like a king, you dirty, dishonest narc. You use young men like Sugar as your agents. Give them a job in the restaurant in return for carrying out your dirty deeds. You exploit young Europeans like Christian and set them up for many years in jail just so that you can stay here and not be hassled by the immigration authorities. How many do you have to dob in each month to keep your residency status?" She finished her diatribe by slapping him across his left cheek. It stung. Even Jens, normally passive and rather timid, was fired up with anger and called out, "Let's get away from the dirty old man before he plants some more dope on us." With that, they turned tail and headed back to their *losmens*.

Manoel was stunned. He was also hurt. Not so much by the slap across his cheek as by the cruel and untrue allegations that had been hurled at him in front of his customers.

He had suffered a severe loss of face. The confrontation had come at the end of a very busy and trying day. He had missed his siesta as he had to stay on duty all the afternoon. His head boy had gone home after lunch with some strange stomach ailment and Sugar, who had been waiting on the tables, had disappeared at lunch time and had not been seen since. There had been a power cut for nearly two hours and all the ice had melted and the drinks had to be served in a far from chilled condition. And now this nasty and hurtful scene. As a civilised person Manoel did not like disorder. "Yes," he thought, "this has been one of the worst days since I came to Bali."

Those who were in the restaurant were shocked at the outburst which was so totally at odds with the usual civilised atmosphere of the place. They had stopped their trivial conversations and listened to every one of Anne-Marie's harsh words. When at last she stormed out she left behind her a deadly silence. It was soon broken by the old man's sobs.

Both Adrian and Dayu, sitting at the front table, felt instant compassion for him. To them he had only ever been polite and friendly and generous. He never charged them the full amount for a meal and on several occasions he put a glass of Mateus on their table as a gift from "the house". He appeared genuinely interested in both of them and asked Adrian many questions about surfing. "Although he is an old man," thought Adrian, "and is obviously very intelligent he always talks to us and others as equals."

He thought back to what Thierry and Nicole had told him about the rumours as to why Manoel, a European, was allowed to live permanently in Bali. Both Thierry and Nicole had said that they didn't believe the stories and nor did he. Even Anne-Marie's outburst did not move him to change his view of Manoel. Indeed, fair minded person that he was, he felt drawn more then ever to Manoel who, it seemed, was being wrongly blamed for the fate of the missing Dane.

Anne-Marie had given neither proof nor reason for her allegation. Just an emotional repetition of an unfounded rumour. Of course, Adrian felt sorry for the Dane with whom he was on nodding terms. He had often seen them eating in the restaurant but had never had much conversation with them. They seemed a fairly self-contained quartet who kept to themselves but who had always been pleasant and polite. Until to-day. "But," he reflected, "they are under great pressure. Still, that is no reason to come in and insult Manoel."

The old man stood up from his seat at the cash register and walked out to the kitchen. He pulled out a spotless white handkerchief and wiped his eyes. He was embarrassed and humiliated that Adrian and Dayu had heard such a tirade of untrue and jealous gossip and he wondered what they thought of him. He had got to know them well over the past few weeks and could see that they were both very fond of each other. He had always had a special place in his romantic Latin heart for those in love.

"I have never attempted to justify myself to anyone since I have been here as it is nobody's business but my own," he thought. "However, I would not like those two good people to have the wrong impression of me as a result of this unhappy incident. Maybe I should open my heart to them and tell them the real reason why I stay here. Just to show them the falseness of the allegations."

He felt a tiny soft hand on his shoulder and then it ran up to his face. The touch was ever so gentle. By now Dayu had her arm round his shoulders. She didn't say anything as she wiped away the remaining tears with the damp white handkerchief. He began to feel better and unlocked a cupboard to pull out a bottle of Johnnie Walker Black Label. He poured himself a dollop of whisky and added some soda. He then took a couple of sips and walked back into the restaurant.

Adrian was sitting on his own at his table. All the other

customers had left. He pulled up a chair for Manoel. "Thank-you," said the old man in a shaking voice. "It was so upsetting. And so untrue."

"Oh, don't let it get you down," said Adrian. "You know that it's all lies and so does everyone else who knows you well. Like us."

"Ah yes, I am sure that you do not believe these wicked rumours. But there are always silly people who do. I think that those three are so angry that they will spread some very bad stories about me and maybe people will no longer come to eat here. Perhaps they will think it is too dangerous. But it is all untrue. I have never informed on anyone and I never will. But not everyone will believe that. Maybe I should not have been so secretive about what I used to do before I came to Bali. But that is my own business and would probably be misrepresented by gossip-mongers just like this other rumour. Maybe I should tell you but it is such a long story." He looked at his watch.

"Don't tell us anything about yourself unless you want to," said Adrian. "And anything that you say will not go any further. I wouldn't even tell Thierry."

"Ah, Thierry and Nicole! They are very good people like yourselves. I like them very much but I do not feel like opening my heart to everybody. But I think that I want to tell you about my reasons for staying here. Unfortunately, it will take quite a long time. Maybe you don't have the time or the interest to hear it."

"Nonsense," smiled Adrian. "But don't tell us if you don't want to. We have to go now as we have to meet some people back at the cottage but we shall come back later this evening for a meal. That gives you plenty of time to think about it and, if you still want to open your heart to us, then we shall be delighted to hear your story which I'm sure will be both interesting and honourable." It was a white lie as there was no one for them to meet back at the cottage but he was tired after two long surf sessions and desperately wanted a short sleep before going out for the evening. If Manoel wanted to talk long and seriously Adrian preferred to be in the mood to listen and respond without nodding off to sleep.

As they got up from the table Dayu took Manoel by the hand and walked to the entrance with him. She kissed him good-bye and smiled warmly. As he walked back to the cash register his eyes were watery. But they were no longer the tears of sadness and humiliation. The old man was moved by the kindness and understanding that had just been shown to him by his two young friends.

When they returned at nine o'clock Adrian and Dayu were refreshed, rejuvenated and no longer tired.

"Hi, Manoel," said Adrian with a cheerful grin as they stepped into the candlelit restaurant. "Feeling better?"

"Yes, thank-you. And I always feel better when I see you and the beautiful Dayu. You bring joy and happiness to the heart of a lonely old man."

He led them across to a spare table in the far corner. "You are the best *Maître d'* in Bali," said Adrian. "Ritz service at Bali prices."

"Ah, you are too kind. Altogether too flattering. But I try to give good and efficient service and to create a friendly atmosphere. That is why I found to-day's incident so distressing. I have been thinking about you both while you were away and I have decided to tell you why I am allowed to live in Bali. But first you must eat. I have many customers to look after at the moment but most of them should be gone in about an hour. Then I shall come over and talk to you and bring some port for us to drink together. What would you like to eat? I have some turtle soup and it is fresh. Old Wayan, the fisherman from Pecatu, brought me in some fresh turtles this afternoon. He left just before that angry girl came in and caused all the trouble."

"No, thank-you, we don't like to eat turtle soup. If

people keep eating them then the fishermen will keep catching them and eventually there won't be any turtles left," said Adrian.

Slightly taken aback Manoel said, "I don't get them in very often. And then I offer them only to my special customers. Like you. But I understand how you feel. Maybe I shouldn't buy them at all. But, if I don't serve them, others will. Anyway, what would you like to order?"

"*Mie rebus*," replied Dayu. "I feel like noodles."

"May we have a plate of your nice hot chupattis to start with?" asked Adrian. "Then I would like some *gado gado* with lots of peanut sauce."

"We also have some fresh strawberries that were sent down from the mountains this morning," said Manoel. "There are only a few left. Would you like some for dessert? With cream?"

"Too much. But yes. Why not?" laughed Adrian. Dayu laughed too and said that she would be fat when she woke up the next morning. "Never," scoffed Adrian as he squeezed her tight.

"Cocktails? They're on the house," said Manoel.

"Yes, Dayu likes a margarita and so do I. Can we have them served inside the coconut husks?"

"Of course."

A few minutes later the waiter brought them two brown coconut husks that had had their tops sliced off and the juice drained out. The cocktail had been poured into the hollow of the husk and the top carefully replaced. A frangipani petal was stuck on top like a hat and a straw inserted though a small hole that had been drilled through the top of the husk.

By quarter past ten most of the diners had left and the cash register was full of rupiah, pounds and dollars. Manoel drew a bottle of port from the rack at the back of the kitchen and pulled up a chair at Adrian's table.

"I have not changed my view that I would like to tell you

the real reason why I am allowed to stay in Bali. Do you have the time to listen?"

"Of course," replied Dayu. "We have been away for a big sleep so that we are not tired to talk to you."

"I have been in Indonesia since 1975. Before that I was in Mozambique and Timor. I was working for the Portuguese government."

"What department?" asked Adrian.

There was a short silence. His eyes levelled with Adrian's. The words came slowly and distinctly. "I was in the Intelligence Section. Since 1938."

Adrian knew of the upheaval that occurred throughout Portugal and its large empire in 1974 and immediately assumed that Manoel, having been involved with the long established government that was overthrown, might not be welcome in the new order that had been established in that part of the Iberian Peninsula.

"That must have been interesting," said Adrian.

"Yes, and often dangerous," replied Manoel. "Even now."

"Why? Are you still actively engaged in the collection of information?"

"No, not since my beautiful country was betrayed in 1974. I was in Timor — the Portuguese half of the island — when I heard that our government in Lisbon had fallen. We believed that something bad was going to happen in Timor but not in Portugal. But we failed to take account of the treachery of the communists.

The communists who seized power in my homeland in 1974 were carrying out a plan that had been worked out by the KGB in Moscow some twenty years earlier. It was put into cold storage until the time was right and then it was carried out in their usual highly professional manner — brutally, ruthlessly and successfully."

"Why would they go for Portugal rather than Spain

which is so much bigger and more important?" asked a slightly sceptical Adrian.

Manoel flinched slightly at this unintentional belittling of his native land.

"Oh, it wasn't Portugal that was their objective. It was the Portuguese colonies that were so strategically placed. You will find that after a while the communists will lose interest in Portugal; it is not strategically important and nor does it have any important minerals. But they will keep control of our colonies in Mozambique and Angola as part of their scheme to control southern Africa.

Spain hasn't got any colonies left — apart from the Spanish Sahara which is only a small stretch of useless desert. But look at the Portuguese colonies: Mozambique, Angola, Guinea, Macao, Timor. All so useful to the Soviets. They had their own agents on the ground in every one of these vitally important places to seize power as soon as the government fell in Lisbon. They were so well prepared.

In Timor, where I was at the time, they had smuggled in arms which were hidden in the jungle. These were handed out to the TLF guerrillas. There was nothing that the authorities could do as there was so much confusion within our ranks. No government at the top and the soldiers reluctant to obey the orders of their local commanders for fear that they would later be held accountable to whatever left wing government eventually emerged at home.

TLF was a Marxist guerrilla movement and its leaders were guided by experienced KGB operatives who are active here in Asia. My brief in Timor was to report on the build-up of arms to the TLF leaders which we knew was going on even before the coup. Many of the TLF leaders were products of the Catholic college in Timor and others had been educated at good church schools in Portugal. They were quick to use their church connections to mask their true communist identity.

301

In the confusion that prevailed I spoke with the local commander of the Portuguese forces who said that he was powerless to keep control of the whole territory. From my intelligence sources I knew that the Soviets planned to install the TLF guerrillas as the government of a new and independent Marxist Timor so that it could lie like a dagger pointing at the heart of Australia. Just like Cuba does to the United States. Timor is only three hundred miles from the Australian coast and in the Second World War the Japanese used it as a base for bombing raids on Darwin. With to-day's technology the Soviets planned to establish a huge airbase there with inter-continental ballistic missiles that would threaten both Indonesia and Australia. Then they could neutralise both countries whenever it suited them.

The reason why I hate communism is because I am a traditional Roman Catholic and I do not like any government that denies its people their right to practise the religion of their choice. My elder brother is a Jesuit in Portugal. So, after speaking with the Portuguese military commander in Timor and learning that he had lost control of the situation, I flew to Jakarta to tell the Indonesian government what I knew. My own government, to which I had sworn loyalty, no longer existed. I was on the last 'plane that left Timor before the TLF guerrillas closed the airport.

I made two calls immediately after I landed at Jakarta Airport. First I called on Mister Jack Black, who was the Australian ambassador. I went to see him as a friend. After all, Britain is Portugal's oldest ally. Our friendship goes back to the fifteenth century. Continous.

The ambassador was a big man and, I thought, rather vulgar. I told him all I knew. He rang his government in Canberra and do you know what they said? I still can not believe it. They said that they would prefer Timor to be ruled by the 'nice, free, democratic' TLF movement than by the colonialist government of Portugal! I could not decide whether they were being treacherous or stupid. Probably the latter. I told him that I had seen TLF mobs murdering innocent Portuguese in the streets — even priests and nuns — and that I had firm intelligence information that the Russians planned to install missiles there that would be aimed at Sydney, Melbourne and Perth. And do you know what the ambassador said? 'Oh, well, I'm from Brisbane.' He didn't seem to care at all. Can you believe it?"

"Yes, I can," said Adrian.

"He then told me that his instructions were to welcome the TLF movement as the Australian government wanted to see an end to the 'colonial and racist' rule of the Portuguese. Ridiculous! The Portuguese in Timor had been good neighbours of Australia for two hundred years and yet now they wanted us out and the Marxists in!

I could not believe what I was hearing from the big mouth of this stupid man. I told him not to call my country racist as we have been administering our overseas colonies for more than four hundred years and we have always treated the natives fairly. Not like the Australians who exterminated a whole race of people — where are the Tasmanian aborigines now?"

"Only in the museum," replied Adrian.

"Yes, and yet this rude and ignorant man had the nerve to call my country 'racist'.

He was quite unbelievable. He was not remotely interested in what I was telling him. The only time he became serious was when he told me that he would shortly be retiring. He seemed more interested in his half million dollar pension and the retirement house that he had bought on the Gold Coast than in saving Timor from the communists.

So I left him and took a taxi to the Indonesian Foreign Ministry. I told them the same things that I had told the big oaf from Australia. They listened and arranged for me to see the military leaders. Their own intelligence supported what I said and so they sent in a military force to wipe out the guerrillas and so stop Timor from becoming a Soviet base in this part of the world.

The Indonesians lost many men as the TLF mob were well armed with AK 47s, Kalashnikov semi-automatics and other Soviet equipment. Unlike Australia, the Indonesians have already had first hand experience of communism and that is why they are more aware of the dangers than the nice but gullible Australians. In the 1960s the former President, Soekarno, allowed the communists too much influence in the government. They were trying to take over the whole country and it was a very difficult and bloody job to get rid of them. That is why the present Indonesian government, when they saw what was happening in Timor, decided to nip it in the bud at the earliest opportunity. Thank God they did and Timor is now part of the Indonesian Republic instead of a little patch of Marxist mischief in this beautiful and safe part of the world.

But I cannot understand the stupidity of the Australian government. They were too blind to see the danger right on their own doorstep. Really, it is sometimes so hard to understand your British character. You are so brave in wars and you have saved the world so many times — from Napoleon, from the Kaiser, from the Nazis. But you let yourselves down in times of peace by not safeguarding what you have won on the battlefield." Manoel reached over and poured some more port.

"So the Russians didn't get their own way in Timor after all," said Adrian.

"No, but that was due to the Indonesians and not to the silly Australians."

Adrian was thinking about what Manoel had said. He looked hard at the old Portuguese gentleman. At his distinguished and well-lined face. "Yes," he thought, "there is real character and strength behind all those wrinkles." He smiled at Dayu who had not understood all that had been said but who flinched at the mention of the communists who had killed all her family.

"Well," said Adrian, "your own role in the matter was certainly a piece of honour and bravery. You must be very pleased that it turned out the way it did. Checkmate the Russians."

"Yes, but their designs were frustrated only in Timor. Not in Mozambique and Angola. There they were also well prepared on the ground and were able to install Marxist governments. And those two territories are very important to the Soviet aim of dominating the world."

"Why?"

"They are an important step to the biggest prize of all: South Africa. That would give them control of the vitally important Cape sea route. The Suez Canal can easily be put out of action and then all trade between Asia and the Middle East and Europe would have to go around the Cape. All of Western Europe's oil from the Persian Gulf.

South Africa has most of the world's gold, diamonds, chrome, platinum, manganese, titanium, uranium and other minerals. The second biggest producer is Russia. Many of these are important in defence and space technology. If the communists could get South Africa they would have complete control over all these vital supplies. Yes, it is indeed the biggest prize of all. That is why they encourage revolution and opposition to the present South African government. The communists are not interested in helping the black man. They only want to seize the rich resources.

Nor is the Australian government interested in helping the black man. All their sanctimonious criticism of my country and South Africa is — pardon the expression — bullshit. If the Australians genuinely wanted to help the black man they would do so in their own country. But they don't. I have been to Australia and in Alice Springs I saw the most tragic sight that my poor old eyes have ever seen. Drunk aborigines lying on the river bed drinking turpentine and methylated spirits out of filthy bottles and rusty cans. And their women and children were rolling around in the mud. Some of them were crying. I have never seen such bad conditions anywhere else in the world. Not in the Portuguese colonies and not in South Africa either.

Before I went to Timor I was in Mozambique for many years. I was involved in counter-insurgency intelligence against the Frelimo terrorists. That is why I am interested in Africa. It will not be long before Rhodesia also falls to the terrorists who are committing such terrible atrocities in the jungle. I know, because when I was stationed at Vila Pery on the border between Mozambique and Rhodesia, I saw some of the victims of terrorism. White farmers who had been chopped up with meat knives, nuns who had been raped, black villagers who had been set on fire and little babies whose heads had been crushed by the big hob nailed boots that the guerrillas wore. The terrorists were well provided with AK 47s, grenades and missiles by the Russians.

For me Rhodesia has very special memories. Some of them good and one of them tragic. The greatest tragedy that I have ever suffered." Dayu noticed that his eyes began to moisten. "It was there that my beautiful wife, Maria, was taken from me. We had only fourteen years together but every day was precious. And her death was not only untimely but so unnecessary. She died the most horrible death at the hands of the terrorist murderers.

We were on holiday from my work in Mozambique and we decided to visit the Victoria Falls. They are truly amazing. Especially the train journey. Do you know that the bridge is built just close enough to the Falls for the spray to fall on the windows of the train? It was Cecil Rhodes himself who insisted that the bridge be built in that spot. We were staying at the Golden Elephant Hotel and everything seemed so perfect. The hotel was on the edge of the jungle and the elephants used to walk through the trees less than a hundred yards from our room. It was the first real holiday that we had had in three years.

Because I was involved in security intelligence in nearby Mozambique I was asked to go down to Salisbury to talk with their security chaps. We were just beginning to co-ordinate our respective counter-insurgency activities so that we could put pressure on the Frelimo guerrillas in Mozambique and Mugabe's murderers in Rhodesia at the same time.

I flew down on the morning flight from the Falls to Salisbury and returned in the evening. So that my wife would not be bored while I was away I arranged for her to go on a tour of the game reserve in the hotel minibus. When they were returning in the late afternoon the bus was ambushed by black terrorists and all the passengers were either shot or cut up with panga knives. When the army arrived they found that the men's private parts had been cut off and stuffed into their mouths and the women had also been desecrated. The army sent in helicopters and ground troops and they eventually found two of the killers. They were being hidden at the local mission school by the white missionary! Can you believe it?"

"What happened to them?" asked Adrian.

"They were tried for murder and later hanged. Thank God. Otherwise they would have done it again. Once an animal gets the taste of blood it is hard to stop him. Some wealthy bishop paid for a barrister to go down from London to defend them in court. He tried to say that they were engaged in fighting a just cause and should not be punished. But fortunately the judge found them guilty and ordered them to be hanged."

"And what happened to the missionary?" asked Adrian.

"Not much. He was given seven days to leave the country. They put him on a 'plane and sent him back to Ireland where he came from. But they just sent another one out from Ireland to take his place. You would think that there is enough trouble in Ireland for them to deal with instead of sending their men out to Africa to spread hatred and poison among simple minds."

"Have you got any children," asked Dayu.

"No, we married fairly late in life. That is a very great sadness. I have only a brother. The Jesuit whom I mentioned before. But I am happy here. Bali is one of the crossroads of the East. It is more primitive than Hong Kong or Singapore but I like it better. And Kuta is full of young people. All in the prime of life and full of hope and laughter. People come into my restaurant from all over the world. Although they speak different languages they are in many ways the same. They all want to have a good time and I can't say that I blame them. It is easy to enjoy yourself in Bali.

But I feel very sorry for that poor Danish boy who is in the jail. He seemed a nice young man and was always polite. It is very unfortunate for him as he was not hurting anybody. I wish that I could do something to help him but I can't. The law is the law. I think that these laws against drugs are very foolish and that, like Prohibition in America, they will fail."

"Agreed," said Adrian who, like so many fair-minded and thinking men of his generation, had no time for either the drug laws or some of the crooked cops and hypocritical, alcohol swilling judges who enforced them.

"Ah, but I have been talking too much," continued Manoel. "And I have not yet told you why I am allowed to live in Bali and operate a business. While I was briefing the Indonesian government during the Timor troubles they put me up at the Forty Dragons Hotel in Jakarta. I stayed there for several months while I was advising them how to operate in Timor and at the end they asked me if I wanted to go back to Portugal. Of course I said 'No' as I would be a marked man there because of my involvement with the former government. They then asked me where I would go and I shrugged my shoulders and said that the only place where I could really go and be allowed to stay would be Brazil but I had no great desire to bury myself in South America. They told me that they were eternally grateful for my assistance in preventing a territory within the Indonesian archipelago from becoming communist and that I could have permanent residence in their country for the rest of my life if I so desired. I eagerly accepted their kind offer and have been here in Bali ever since. Of course, because of the revolution in Lisbon, I do not have a pension but I make enough from my restaurant to live well here. As you know, things are very cheap.

The life here is simple and enjoyable. The Balinese are not nearly so rich or materially well off as Europeans. But I think that they are happier. If you walk along Oxford Street in London or Fifth Avenue in New York you do not see many people with smiles on their faces. They are probably rich but they don't look very happy. In Bali, although everyone has enough food and clothes, they are not nearly so rich but they seem much happier. Yes, life is good here for an old man like me."

"Oh, come on Manoel, surely you're not that old! I saw you jogging along the beach yesterday and I commented to Dayu how fit you are."

"Thank you, you are so kind. I will be sixty-nine next birthday. And so, my friends, I think that you have heard enough from this old man to-night."

"I must say, you certainly haven't been boring," laughed Adrian. Dayu began to yawn. Then Adrian.

Manoel looked at his watch. "Good grief! It is nearly one o'clock." All the other diners had left more than two hours ago.

"We must be off," said Adrian. "How much do I owe you for dinner?"

"The pleasure is mine," replied Manoel. "It is not every day that I meet someone to whom I want to open my heart.

You are both very good people and deserve much happiness. God be with you."

"Thank you," said Adrian as Dayu gave the old man a kiss on his cheek. "We'll see you to-morrow, Manoel," said Adrian as they stepped out the door.

"Yes. *Deo volente*," replied the other.

As they walked along the darkened street Dayu gripped Adrian's hand and laughingly suggested that they stop in at the Hamburger House. "Why? Haven't you had enough food?" he asked.

"Yes, but I would like to go there and have coffee and laugh at all the short, ugly Javanese 'good time girls'. Balinese girls are not prostitutes and it is so funny to see Javanese girls try to sell themselves to ugly, drunk European men," she giggled.

"Really, Dayu, you never cease to surprise me. Don't you like the Javanese girls?"

"Of course not."

"Oh, all right, a quick coffee and then home to bed."

As they walked along the broken stones that were an apology for a footpath they could hear the blaring music from the Hamburger House nearly a block away. They found a couple of places at a table and ordered two coffees and a pineapple burger. Thierry and Nicole came over. "Where have you two been? Sleeping again, I suppose," said Thierry as he gave Dayu a kiss on the cheek.

"No, we've been having a long and interesting conversation with Manoel," replied Adrian.

"And what sort of personal information has he been extracting from you this time? How many times you make love each night? Really, he is always asking questions — sometimes very personal ones — and yet what do we know about him?"

"Not much," said Adrian suppressing a smile.

"Oh, you should have been at the 'Frog' to see Pascal's

310

new girl friend," said Thierry. "She is just ... oh, there are no words to describe her. She is from Norway. Perfect features. She must be descended from a Norse goddess. Unfortunately she is only here for three more days." There was a slight commotion at the entrance as two motor bikes braked loudly and people were pushing this way and that. Then Pascal appeared like a genie. And the beautiful Erika.

"Bonsoir, tout le monde. Ah, Nicole, ma chérie, et Dayu, Adrian, et Thierry. Je vous présente Erika." Adrian and Thierry stood up from the table and smiled at the beautiful Scandinavian girl. She was tall with long blond hair and very long legs. Her complexion was perfect and there was just the faintest touch of lipstick on her Chanel scented face. Around her neck hung a huge silver pendant that plunged almost as deep as the neckline of her green leather dress.

Pascal was in the highest of spirits and bought a couple of bottles of wine for everyone. He always felt more lively at two in the morning than at two in the afternoon.

The Hamburger House was like a railway station. People arriving. People leaving. Movement. Noise. Bustle. Couples kissing. People talking. Others laughing. Single men giving the eye to Javanese girls with excessive make-up on their faces. Javanese girls giving the eye to single men with lots of money in their pockets.

"But this place is so crazy," laughed Pascal as a Javanese man with a mohawk haircut walked through the door on his hands. The motor bikes outside were revving, the cash registers ringing and Arlo Guthrie was singing "Alice's Restaurant" on the stereo.

Adrian felt an elbow in his ribs. "Look at that one," Dayu whispered in his ear as a short, squat Javanese girl in a cumbersome brassiere and loose fitting dress walked past. They both laughed. "How much money would you pay for her if I wasn't here?" she giggled. He put his hand deep in his pocket and pulled out a one rupiah coin and slapped it on the

311

table. "No, too much," she said. She reached over for a knife and pretended to cut the coin in half. Then half again.

"Her worst feature," said Adrian, "is the bra. Why does she try to put such a big bust on such a little body?"

"Why are European men so pre-occupied with breasts?" asked Dayu.

"Because they are mysterious and spunky and can be very beautiful. Especially small ones like yours."

"Then you don't want me to build my breasts into big soccer balls like that silly Javanese girl?" she teased.

"If you ever imprison your breasts in a bra I'll rip it off you," he laughed.

"Don't worry, I would never want to look like her. She is just like a pi dog."

They watched as the girl with the bra sat down at a table and began talking earnestly with a large, grey haired man of about fifty.

An aged hippy was sitting in the corner plucking a sitar, the contessa was at a table feeding pieces of wholemeal bread to a pure white mynah bird that she had bought the previous day from a street seller, and two people in batman masks and robes were cruising the tables and touching certain selected souls with silver painted wands.

Dayu was laughing and enjoying herself and Adrian, although somewhat tired after listening to Manoel, managed to pick up some of Pascal's infectious energy. About quarter to three he looked at his watch. "Gee, it's nearly three o'clock, Dayu. We must go." They stood up to leave.

"Ah, I see that surfers are not as fit as playboys to last the evening out," said Pascal with a wink.

"Well, I've been in the waves for a total of about five of the last twenty hours," replied Adrian. "How have you spent your day?"

"I have been asleep on the beach all day. The only times that I woke up were to have a massage from the beach lady. I conserve my energy for the night time. I sleep by day and live by night. It is fun." He gave Erika a kiss.

Adrian and Dayu walked back to the cottage along the beach. They were laughing and acting the fool. The waves were pounding away in the darkness. Silence. Then a crash. Silence. Crash! Silence. Crash!

"The surf should be good to-morrow but I won't be getting up early. I want to sleep late," he said.

"Me too," she answered.

■

The Australian ambassador in Jakarta whom Manoel warned about the situation in Timor was very much a figurehead. The main impact that he had made in his three years as ambassador was on the social circuit where his bulky frame, ill fitting suit and dribble on his tie were familiar sights at the diplomatic cocktail parties. He was renowned for always being the first to arrive and the last to leave. Most of the real work at the embassy was done by the diligent and highly capable First Secretary, Titus O'Connell.

After Manoel had gone the ambassador had immediately called in O'Connell and acquainted him with the allegations and information that he had been given by the former chief of Military Intelligence for the Portuguese Territory of Timor.

O'Connell, the son of a dock worker and active trade unionist, had been raised in one of the toughest of the western suburbs of Sydney. He had an excellent brain and had won a scholarship to Sydney University where he graduated in political science with first class honours. The next step was the London School of Economics. It was the mid Sixties and London was the youth culture capital of the world. The Beatles. Mini skirts. Calypso bands. But it was not the glittering night clubs and coffee bars of the King's Road and Soho that claimed him but the dour and dedicated Marxist ideologues who, over the years, had quietly infiltrated the L.S.E. and other educational institutions.

The small student activist groups that he joined — like the C.N.D. and the British-U.S.S.R. Friendship society — were filled with single-minded partisans of the far left who preferred to discuss Marx and Lenin in dingy student bedrooms until three in the morning rather than indulge in the more common student pastimes of parties, alcohol and sex.

O'Connell and his little group discussed how the working proletariate could be indoctrinated and mobilised to destroy all the other classes and institutions that held together the existing structure of society. There were no limits to what they would do to achieve their grotty goals. Not even the three hour lunch that the spotty-faced O'Connell had in a quiet back street restaurant on the South Bank with Sergei Leontov, a highly skilled agent that the K.G.B. had placed in the offices of the Moscow Narodny Bank in the City of London.

Leontov was one of the most successful and deadly operatives that the Moscow Centre had ever sent to the West. After singing the praises of life in the Soviet Union and carefully concealing the mass poverty of its people, the food queues and the empty supermarket shelves, Sergei asked O'Connell if he was completely dedicated to the cause. The answer was in the affirmative. The Russian then told him that they were finding it easier to infiltrate the British Government — especially since the Labour Party came to office — but that they were not very far advanced in Australia.

"You see, my friend, it is not so much Australia that we are interested in but the Australia-United States connection. Because of your military alliance with America there are many pieces of valuable military information that are given to the Australian government. If we could obtain this information through reliable people like yourself we would not have to try so hard in America. I tell you, America is the hardest place for us to operate. They are all so damned patriotic. And paranoic. If, for instance, you could make your career in the Australian Foreign Office you would have access to a lot of information that would be extremely helpful to our mutual cause. And, of course, we would make it worth your while. We pay well for good information. If we are to dominate the world we know that we have to pay those who help us." O'Connell, young and naive and with a permanent chip on his shoulder, was only too willing to help.

He made his formal application to join the diplomatic service at the Australian High Commission in the Strand and only just scraped through the interview. The careers officer who interviewed him thought that he was a little too sour and charmless to make a good diplomat. "Not really the type of fellow whom I'd like to have in the mess. Far too serious," he thought. But O'Connell's academic achievements were quite outstanding and managed to pull him through.

His first posting had been to the Australian High Commission in Canada, then New Delhi and now Jakarta. In the chaos of New Delhi it was easy for him to pass occasional secrets to Dimitri, a "Third Secretary" at the Soviet Embassy who was in reality a highly ranked K.G.B. officer. They met from time to time and anything that O'Connell considered to be of military or other importance was handed over — including two very valuable pieces of information about joint American-Australian naval manoeuvres in the Indian Ocean. For this the Soviets credited a handsome sum into his numbered bank account in Switzerland. Although he believed that he was ideologically committed to their cause O'Connell was always happy to take their money as well.

Since India maintains diplomatic relations with almost every country of the world New Delhi is a very important diplomatic meeting place and the secret services of the major powers find it a fertile area in which to operate — MI6, the

CIA, Mossad, the French SDECE and, of course, the KGB.

The Australian security service, however, being a relatively new and unsophisticated organisation, was fairly thin on the ground in Asia and indeed in most other places. Including Australia. And so the movement of Australian diplomats in India went unobserved by their own security organisation and was given only cursory attention by the CIA and MI6. It was only the KGB that kept proper watch. Thus it was easy for Titus O'Connell, Second Secretary at the Australian High Commission, to have occasional meetings with his KGB contact.

Sometimes they met in the teeming chaos of Old Delhi, sometimes in a coffee shop in Connaught Circus and once in the Red Fort where they both posed as tourists. It was such an easy city for espionage that, after O'Connell was promoted to First Secretary at the Australian Embassy in Jakarta, they decided to continue to use New Delhi as the meeting place. For the very good reason that the Soviets found it almost impossible to infiltrate Jakarta because, unlike Western governments, the Indonesians would not let them establish a large embassy that could be used for spying.

In Jakarta O'Connell's new *modus operandi* was to keep the same KGB case officer in New Delhi and fly there from time to time whenever he had any important information to hand over. It was a neat arrangement and he would always tell the ambassador that he was going to Singapore for the week-end. There were many diplomats who did not find Jakarta very congenial and who grabbed any opportunity to take the short flight to Singapore for the week-end. Fly there Friday night. Stay at the Cockpit or the Goodwood Park. All day shopping in Orchard Road. Afternoon tiffin at Raffles. A gin sling in the Long Bar with expatriate friends, Sunday lunch at the American Club and fly back to Jakarta on Sunday night. The Singapore week-ends were one of the perks of a Jakarta posting.

The only difference between O'Connell's "Singapore" week-ends and those of others was that he never left Singapore Airport. He had an account with a travel agent in Bencoolen Street who used to leave the air tickets — Singapore-New Delhi-Singapore — in the transit lounge. O'Connell would collect them and, aided by the different time zones, would still manage to arrive in New Delhi on Friday night for a Saturday tryst with Dimitri. And, like those who had spent the week-end in Singapore, he always arrived back in Jakarta on the Sunday night.

After he heard from the gin sodden lips of the Australian ambassador to Indonesia the startling intelligence information that Manoel had provided, O'Connell promptly booked a flight to New Delhi for the following week-end. He met Dimitri in the coffee shop of Maiden's Hotel in Old Delhi.

"Good God," exclaimed Dimitri, "the Portuguese intelligence services must be better than we thought. What was the reaction of the Australian government to this premature disclosure of our intentions?"

"Fortunately they discounted it and I encouraged the ambassador to believe that it was nothing more than the disappointed and embittered ravings of an old man who had lost his job of serving a corrupt colonialist government. That was the message that we got from Canberra too. But I heard that this garrulous and interfering old man has gone and told the Indonesians the same story and you know how paranoic they are. They are likely to believe him!"

"Do you think they would invade?" asked Dimitri.

"Yes, if they really thought that their interests were threatened."

"Is the Portuguese agent still in Jakarta?"

"Yes, I believe that he is staying at the Forty Dragons Hotel."

"You have done the right thing by informing us so

317

promptly. Now you must leave the matter to us. We shall have to expedite our friends' takeover in Timor and send in a lot more weapons for them to assert themselves over the rest of the population. I just hope that it is not too late." It was already too late. The Indonesian army had started to act on Manoel's information.

Three years later O'Connell was on another of his trips to New Delhi to give Dimitri a copy of the battle plan for the annual military exercise on the Malayan Peninsula by the forces of Great Britain, Australia, Malaysia and Singapore.

"Oh, by the way," he asked Dimitri, "do you remember that Portuguese intelligence agent who betrayed all your plans in Timor three years ago?"

"Of course I do. That filthy colonialist swine caused us more trouble than almost anyone else in this part of the world. It is not often that one man can cause us to lose an important base. Why do you mention him?"

"Well, last month I had to accompany my ambassador to Bali for a meeting with the Australian foreign minister who was on holiday there with his wife and family. One night I dined alone at this restaurant and who should be welcoming all the customers with exaggerated Latin flair but the same blood-sucking Portuguese colonialist whom I last saw when he visited the ambassador and gave him all that information on Timor. The restaurant even carries his name on the front so he must be living there. It is on the main Kuta-Legian road."

Dimitri's attitude changed. From hostility to calculated indifference. "Oh well, he must be an old man by now and, of course, it is all in the past. But a leopard does not change its spots, eh? I would not patronise the place again if I were you." They both laughed and Dimitri cleverly changed the subject. But his photographic memory had taken particular note of the details that O'Connell had so off-handedly supplied.

Dimitri shrewdly calculated that the reason why Manoel would be allowed to operate a restaurant in Bali would be because of some favour that he had done for the Indonesian government. He knew what that would have been. None other than the wretched information that persuaded the Indonesian generals to mount their invasion and so checkmate the Soviet move towards Australia.

"Men like that should die," he thought. "I do not have the authority to mount an operation against him but I shall write a report to Department 13 in Moscow and recommend that he be taught a lesson."

The report was duly written in which were set out the present whereabouts of Manoel da Silva in Bali as related by the spy, O'Connell. That was the last that Dimitri heard of it. The case was entrusted to more senior — and more deadly — hands. None other than Department 13, the section of the KGB in Dzerzhinsky Square, Moscow, which organises the assassinations of people in the West.

■

Herman Hoffnung was called in to the Controller's office at the Special Operations Division of the Ministry for State Security in East Berlin. The Controller, a short, bald, bespectacled former officer in the Waffen SS, motioned him to sit down.

"Well, Herr Hoffnung, your little trip to London has brought much praise from our comrades at Department 13 in Moscow. You have already received their cheque, of course, and I have now been informed that they like to stick with a winner.

There has been a significant reduction in anti-communist propaganda on the BBC Bulgarian language service since our friend in London died of 'umbrella' sickness. Oh, comrade, it is such a good story. Please tell me again. Every detail. It is so much more sophisticated than anything we ever did in the SS. And yet in those days we always thought that we knew everything there was to know about killing."

"Well, to be honest with you, it was quite the easiest job I've ever done. I just followed the target from his office in Bush House and waited until he joined the crowds on The Strand. Then I brushed past him, jabbed the point of the umbrella into his thigh and then lost myself in the crowd again. I even said, 'Frightfully sorry, old chap' in an ever so English accent. He died in hospital four days later. The pellet containing the ricin was only one and a half millimetres wide but it was twice as powerful as cobra venom."

"And were you afraid that the hypodermic needle on the end of the umbrella might become dislodged?"

"No. It was attached with a special bonding adhesive. There was a wire lever reaching from the syringe up to the handle so that I could apply pressure to the plunger and push the chemical killing agent through the tube and into his thigh once the needle was in. It was all over in thirty seconds."

"Well, *mein Herr*, as I said, Centre likes to stick with a winner. How would you like a holiday in the tropics? You deserve it".

"Where?"

"Bali. The holiday island in Indonesia."

"And who is the target this time?"

"An elderly ex-Portuguese intelligence chief who has done great harm to our interests in the Far East. Apparently he was instrumental in preventing a communist takeover in Timor. Although he is now retired, Centre has decided that he must be taught a lesson mainly as a deterrent to others. We shall never achieve world domination unless we intimidate and frighten our opponents and show them that, if they frustrate our plans, they are likely to pay the ultimate price. Here is the report on him that Centre has compiled from their records. It runs to five pages." He handed Hoffnung a copy of the report together with a photograph of the target.

The younger man read it in silence. Then they discussed some of the details.

"It says here that his wife was murdered by the terrorists in Rhodesia," said the Controller as he stubbed out a cigarette. "And that in the same attack the men passengers were butchered and their private parts were stuffed in their mouths. It is a shame that the target was not on the bus at the time. It would have been a suitable death for him. Of course, I know that your methods are different from those of the African savages. But however you do it you will do it professionally."

"Is that a challenge?" asked Hoffnung in apparent jest.

"Unfortunately it is necessary to do this job in order to dissuade others. Every one of our acts is part of a very big whole. None of us can see the big picture; that is for our masters in Moscow. We don't manage to get all our enemies but every one that we kill is a deterrent to hundreds of others."

"When is the operation to begin?" asked Hoffnung.

"To-morrow. Here is your air ticket to Zurich. You will go to the same contact who met you last time. He will have all the air tickets and a West German passport for you in the name of Wolfgang Schmidt. You will fly from Zurich to Bali and spend a couple of weeks there. In that time you will be able to complete the job. I believe that there are some nice beaches there and many holidaymakers so you should enjoy yourself. But just remember that they are all filthy capitalists.

As with the Bulgarian in London, you are not to use a gun. It is too hard to get one through the airport in Indonesia and we do not have any decent agents there. For us it has been unknown territory since 1965. I suggest a big meat knife. Since he is an old man it should not be too difficult. The payment for a successful operation will be the same as for the London job. Of course, all your expenses will be paid by us. Since you will be leaving to-morrow you should take the rest of to-day off and go back to your apartment to make your preparations. Good day to you, Herr Hoffnung, and I shall be interested to hear of your success when you return. And so will Moscow." Hoffnung stood up and looked into the Controller's cold, dark eyes. They shook hands in silence.

Herman Hoffnung was of medium height and slightly obese for his thirty-eight years. His father had died in 1944. Somewhere in Normandy. He knew not where or how. Just that his killers were members of the Allied Expeditionary Force that was driving the Nazi invaders out of France. He had been brought up in a one room apartment by his mother and grandmother. In great poverty. Things only started to go right for him after he left school and joined the Communist Party of East Germany as one of its most dedicated workers. He knew that the only way to get ahead in a communist society was to join the Party elite which treated the rest of the population like dirt. Hoffnung's reward was a spacious apartment just off the Karl Marx Allee in the centre of East Berlin.

Among the passengers who walked down the steps of the Garuda DC 10 at Ngurah Rai Airport in Bali was the West German passport holder, Wolfgang Schmidt. The immigration officer stamped the green document and smiled. "Welcome to Bali, sir. I hope that you enjoy your stay. And what is the purpose of your visit? Holiday?" Hoffnung nodded and passed on to the chaotic baggage claim area. Already his finely tuned Teutonic instincts were repelled by the Eastern disorder.

Outside on the roadway he faced a barrage of screaming, importuning taxi drivers vying for his custom. One of them grabbed him by the arm and pushed him into a waiting car. He asked the driver to recommend a clean and respectable hotel in the middle price range that was near the Kuta-Legian road but not right on it.

He was taken to the Kuta Sands Bungalows which he found eminently suitable. The manager welcomed him gushingly and showed him a small bungalow with its own verandah and small garden. It was separated from its neighbours by a high wall and was very private. "Splendid. I'll take it," he said.

He booked the accommodation for two weeks but made a point of telling the manager that he had business to conduct in Singapore and might have to leave a few days earlier.

"No problem, sir," said the ever accommodating manager. "We are happy to have you for however long you wish to stay. We have several people from West Germany staying here at present. You must all come from a very rich country, Mister Schmidt." Hoffnung smiled politely. He made a silent vow to keep away from the other German guests. Indeed from all other guests.

Hoffnung spent his first two days relaxing on the beach after his long flight. He enjoyed swimming in the warm ocean and lying in the hot sun but otherwise took a fairly detached view of the island's pleasures. He marvelled at the hedonistic and frivolous ways that the Western tourists wasted their time. He concluded that their moral fibre to resist the creeping onslaught of world communism must be very low.

"The only thing that the young men seem to be interested in is surfing," he mused. "They even get up before six in the morning just to prance around in the waves on their silly pieces of fibreglass. Young men of the same age in East Germany and Russia are already in the army being turned into highly trained killing machines. Just waiting for the day when the silly Nato countries drop their shield. Then we shall see how these pretty young men of the decadent West stand up to our tanks. What will they fight us with? Their surfboards? I don't think so. We would crush them into powder. Just like we did in Hungary in 1956 and in Czechoslovakia in 1968. Oh yes," he laughed to himself, "Communist tanks against Western surfboards. That will be a new one for the military manuals."

He bought a pair of very dark sunglasses and tried to

blend himself in with the general run of Western tourists. He walked past Manoel's restaurant several times and kept a discreet eye on the proprietor's movements: his arrival at the restaurant in the morning, then a siesta after lunch followed by a swim and a jog along the beach, then a return to the restaurant in the late afternoon to prepare the evening meal. Hoffnung noticed that he stayed there all night until the last diners departed and then spent about fifteen minutes counting the money and locking up. Then he went out to his cottage which was set in a garden behind the restaurant. And he always left the stereo on in the restaurant until the last moment. Perhaps to attract a last late night customer.

His eyes well hidden behind the dark sunglasses, Hoffnung even went into the restaurant a couple of times for an iced drink. He made sure that on the first visit the place was fairly crowded. The second occasion was at the end of his first week when he called in about 5 p.m. on his way home from the beach.

He had only just taken the first sip of his orange juice when he heard a commotion outside. A young, blond Danish girl ran in and started screaming at Manoel. Although she spoke in fast English Hoffnung was able to pick up most of what she said. After she had stormed out and more abuse had been hurled at the old man by her male friend, Hoffnung rose from the table, paid for his drink and walked out. He had heard enough. At least enough to know that there was some very bad blood between Manoel and his accusers. The details did not concern him. Just the fact of the confrontation which he tossed around in his mind as he walked back to his bungalow, dodging between the bustling people, the food carts, the bicycles and the pi dogs. "It has to be to-night," he thought as he quickened his pace in excitement and anticipation. "Then it will look as if those angry young people did it in the heat of their passion. Thank God I have already bought the knife."

Back at the bungalow he lay down on the bed and, to the background noise of a croaking gecko, contemplated his plans for the night. He decided that the best time to surprise the old man would be at the end of the evening when he was on his own counting the money and locking up. There were trees on each side of the restaurant and the noise of the stereo would be enough to drown out any unpleasant sounds. He would secrete the knife in its leather sheath and carry it inside his trousers. His loose fitting shirt would hang down and conceal it further.

He went out for a meal about eight and then returned to the bungalow. About ten o'clock he stuffed a pair of thin rubber gloves into his pocket and poured a glass of neat whisky from his duty-free bottle of Highland Mist. Its warm, bitter taste put a bit of fire in his belly. He had killed in cold blood many times before and saw his approaching job as just another step on the long path of imposing communism on the rest of mankind.

He could see the lights of Manoel's from half a block away. Just a couple of strings of naked electric light bulbs that illuminated an otherwise dark thoroughfare. He looked up at the sky. It was a new moon. And hardly any stars. Very dark. Before he reached the restaurant he crossed the road and passed stealthily under the trees on the other side. He could see that there were a few tables still occupied. "I'll give him another half hour," he thought.

Hoffnung turned and walked down a narrow walled lane towards the beach. The pale moon was shining on the sea. Otherwise all was inky blackness. Near the beach he passed a small *warung* that was still open. It was dimly lit by a single oil lamp. Under its canvas overhang were shelves of bananas, coconuts, toothpaste, soap and assorted odds and ends. Hanging from the top on a piece of string was a cheap looking torch. He paid for it and the Balinese girl politely fitted it with a couple of used batteries which gave out a small, pale light. "At least I'll be able to find my way back," he thought.

As he sat on the beach looking at the dark sea he considered the incongruity of the situation. Here he was, a communist in an anti-communist land, sitting on a gentle and peaceful beach about to murder an elderly gentleman whom he had only ever seen across the counter in the restaurant and who had never done him any personal harm.

"But he must be killed like all the others who have ever posed a threat to communism. Like the Tsar and his children. Like the twenty million Russians who were murdered during Stalin's 'economic reforms'. Like Mister Markov who was stabbed with the umbrella in London. Oh yes," he thought, "the cause and the state are far more important than any individual. That's just the way it is. I do my job and for that I get well looked after by the Party. I have been told that, when the Controller retires at the end of the year, I shall take his place and then my days in the field will be over. I shall have to organise others to do these hit jobs. But, of course, you cannot ask others to do things that you have not done yourself. I enjoy the adrenalin of danger − like to-night − but I will not be sorry to move into the Controller's chair. In life there is a time for everything and for me it is now time to move on. I wonder if Moscow will ask me to do any more jobs between now and the end of the year. Perhaps this will be my last contract."

He then reflected on how much the notorious Department 13 in Moscow relied on his section in East Berlin to carry out its deadly missions in the West. "It is just because we are German and so do not arouse as much suspicion as a Russian would. There are now millions of West Germans travelling all over the world − businessmen, holidaymakers, students and criminals − and it is so easy for an East German to merge in with these large numbers. A Russian abroad would stand out like a sore thumb."

326

His wandering thoughts were interrupted by two rather friendly prostitutes who were walking along the beach. When they spotted the lone white man sitting at the top of the sand they immediately concluded that he was a prospective client who had come down to the beach to find a lady of the night. They giggled and talked among themselves as they approached.

"Hello Mister. You want to go jig-a-jig to-night? I make you very happy," said the shorter of the two.

"No thank you. I just want to sit on the beach on my own for a while and look at the stars."

They laughed and one of them pointed to the dark sky. "No stars to-night," she said. They assumed that it was just his clever way of leading them on. The whites of their eyes and teeth shone in the darkness as they laughed and teased him. One of them put her arm around his broad shoulders and began caressing him.

"Christ," he thought, "if she goes much further she'll feel the knife." He jumped up and walked away.

They laughed and followed him and said in Indonesian, "Gee, this one really is playing 'hard to get'."

Hoffnung knew that they would pester him until he paid them to go away so he pulled out a couple of ten thousand rupiah notes and gave them one each. Unfortunately for him it had quite the opposite effect. They grabbed his arms and motioned him to lie down in the soft sand. After all, they were honest girls. He had fulfilled his part of the bargain; now it was their turn to perform. Preferring the business of murder to the joys of sex, he screamed out, "Piss off!" which surprised them so much that they left him alone and made off down the beach.

They believed that they would never understand the strange ways of the white man. "He pays us money and doesn't even want jig-a-jig," they laughed.

Hoffnung walked further along the beach towards the

road. He gave the two prostitutes a wide berth as he didn't want them to follow and pester him on this of all nights. No sooner had he shaken them off than he was approached by an old Balinese man with a limp who tried to sell him some opium. "Very good stuff for very good price. I'll even let you try it for free before you buy. Free sample," he pleaded.

"Piss off," spat Hoffnung. He began to wonder if there was no end to the decadent ways of the West. The road was further away than he thought and it was after eleven when he reached it. Then he had to go up as far as the Kuta-Legian road and turn left to Manoel's. He wondered if the target would still be there.

As he sauntered past on the other side of the road and looked in he could see Manoel talking to a young man with fair hair and a Balinese girl both of whom Hoffnung had seen there during his afternoon visit. The old man was gesticulating wildly and seemed to be in a highly animated state. The others were listening passively and asking the occasional question. They didn't look like leaving so Hoffnung walked for a mile or so along the darkened road and then returned. They were still sitting there talking. More animated than before.

"Hell, if they don't leave soon, I might have to kill all three of them," he laughed to himself.

There were a few motor bikes speeding up and down and he could hear the clip clop and bells of an approaching *dokar* — a covered cart pulled by a pony with large brass bells around its neck. It was full of inebriated partygoers who had paid the smiling, toothless driver double the *bemo* fare for the thrill of travelling home in such exotic style.

Hoffnung walked a long distance the other way. Then back again. They were still talking. "Oh well, he obviously wants to have a nice long conversation on the last night of his life so I won't deprive him of it. I'm not that mean," he laughed. "It won't be long now."

The next time he passed he saw Manoel standing at the entrance saying good-bye to Adrian and Dayu. She stood on the tips of her toes and kissed him on the cheek. "Oh, how well things are arranged! One last kiss from the beautiful Asian girl. If she should come back in half an hour to give him another he won't be so warm and responsive. Just as well I can see the funny side of these things," he thought.

He waited until Manoel had gone back inside to begin the regular nightly ritual of locking up. He watched him go to the cash register, empty its contents into a canvas money bag and then take it out to the kitchen at the back.

Hoffnung crossed the road in the dark and darted down a narrow path that ran along the north side of the restaurant. He slipped the rubber gloves over his fingers and was in the side door of the kitchen before Manoel saw him. The knife was pulled out from its leather sheath and plunged straight into Manoel's heart in one sweeping movement. It was all too quick for the victim to put up any resistance. Hoffnung slapped the palm of his hand over the surprised looking mouth to stifle any possible cries. But it wasn't necessary. A dead man can't scream. The only sound now was Tom Jones' voice on the stereo singing "Delilah." Hoffnung could hear the eerie words:

"I felt the knife in my hand and he laughed no more ... "

Manoel fell against a pile of rice sacks that were stacked against the wall. Blood was flowing out of the wound and forming a puddle on the stone floor. Hoffnung pulled the knife out of the body and looked at the mess. He felt no remorse. Nothing.

His thoughts went back to East Berlin. How pleased the Controller would be at yet another successful and highly professional operation. And Department 13 too. Thinking of the Controller reminded him of his last meeting with him when he was told of this assignment. He suddenly thought of the report on Manoel that he had been shown. Then, for no apparent reason, something in that report came to mind. The description of his wife's death in Rhodesia when the terrorists had cut off the private parts of the men passengers and stuffed them in their mouths. And what had the Controller said? "It is a shame that the target was not on the bus as it would have been a suitable death for him." All these thoughts passed through Hoffnung's mind in a matter of seconds. He was still in a frenzied killing mood. He ripped the light cotton trousers off the corpse and then repeated the unspeakable act of the African savages.

Hoffnung walked across to the sink and put the knife under a tap to wash away the blood. Then he disappeared into the blackness of the night.

There was nobody on the street in that part of Legian. Just the occasional pi dog sniffing at the vegetable peelings and other scraps that littered the roadway. In the distance he could see a rubbish truck standing on the side of the road. Its parking lights were on. When he reached it he could see its driver and attendants sitting inside a small *warung* drinking some cans of coca cola.

The truck was temporarily deserted but Hoffnung could see and smell its rubbish through its open back as he passed. Without stopping or even changing his step he reached into his trousers and whisked out the knife — once again safely ensconced in its sheath — and nonchalantly tossed it into the rubbish truck. And the rubber gloves. "Final act, final scene," he said to himself as he strolled back to his bungalow.

The first thing that he did was to turn on the shower. It took a long time for the water to become warm. Even then it was only tepid. It didn't matter as the taking of a shower was more of a symbolic act than anything. To cleanse his hands. Indeed, his whole body. To wash the deeds of the night away forever. But he still couldn't get to sleep. He was too alert to be able to relax properly.

About four o'clock he heard the first of the crowing

cocks. Then a few more. Then the birds and the cicadas. When daylight came he put on a pair of yellow shorts and walked down to the beach. There was a naked European girl practising yoga at the water's edge. He watched her for a few moments. Her body was long and shapely. Just like the stars whom he had seen on the movies in London. And there were two boys paddling out on their boards for a surf.

He walked along the sand and noticed a young Balinese man asleep under a coconut tree. Hoffnung looked at him in disgust and concluded that this was yet another unhealthy symptom of the capitalist West. While rich tourists stayed at luxurious hotels only a few hundred yards away the poor exploited natives had to sleep under trees.

The sleeping Balinese lad was eighteen year old Ketut Negara. He lived in a comfortable cottage on the outskirts of Denpasar but worked at a late night bar at Kuta. The previous evening the bar owner had put on a special party to celebrate the opening of a new extension. Ketut and the other waiters had spent all night serving the thirsty customers all the while drinking copious amounts of liquor themselves. When it closed at 3 a.m. the owner had given his boys a couple of bottles of arak and they had gone down to the beach to drink them. When the others left Ketut was too exhausted to find his way back to Denpasar so he staggered to the nearest tree and flopped down to sleep.

Because he was near the sea Ketut was dreaming of the demons of the deep. The combination of the alcohol and his unfortunate proximity to *pasih* had the effect of creating some very vivid images. Out of the sea came a great monster — a killer with blood still dripping from his hands — who was walking up the beach in the form of a paunchy white man with short black hair and yellow shorts. Ketut opened his eyes in terror and looked up. He could see Hoffnung staring down at him. He screamed out. "Killer! Murderer! Look, the blood is still on your hands! I know what you have done. Go back to *pasih* where you belong." He began to quieten down when he got his bearings and adjusted to the morning light. He turned and faced away from Hoffnung and closed his eyes again. The bad dream had ended.

Hoffnung prided himself on being a rationalist and an atheist. No glimmer of spiritualism had ever penetrated his cold and clinical mind. He was completely stunned and could hardly believe what he had heard. He was also very frightened. He fully expected the Balinese man to lunge at him and try to drag him off to the police. When Ketut turned over and seemed to go back to sleep Hoffnung was momentarily relieved. As soon as he saw him settle down again he turned tail and walked back along the beach as briskly as he could. "What was it all about?" he asked himself. He pulled the sunglasses out of his pocket and put them on even though the sun was not yet up.

When he reached his bungalow Hoffnung locked the door and began packing his bag. Before his encounter with the sleeping man he had intended to go to the Garuda office in the lobby of the Kuta Beach Hotel and book a flight to Jakarta for the middle of the day. Now it all seemed more urgent.

"If a sleeping native can wake up on the beach and start screaming at me about last night's deed," he thought, "then who else on this cursed island must know about it? Perhaps they all have some amazing sixth sense! The sooner I get out of this crazy, mysterious place the better — where sleeping people know what goes on while they are asleep, where the women do the work of the men and carry everything on their heads, where all the dogs are former human beings, where boys walk along the beach on their hands instead of their feet, where naked white girls perform strange contortions on the beach at dawn and their boyfriends spend all their time trying to walk on the water on their surfboards like the mysterious Christ did on the sea of Galilee. Maybe there's something in

332

all this religious business after all. But I'm not hanging around to find out. All I want to do is to get back to East Germany where things are at least logical and predictable."

When he saw the manager walking through the grounds at seven o'clock he went over and told him that he had urgent business to attend to in Singapore and so had to go to the airport immediately. He handed in his key and gave the manager a substantial tip "for all your kindnesses while I have been here."

"Ah, *terima kasih* Mister Schmidt. It has been our very great pleasure to have you staying here. You have been no trouble. In fact, we have hardly seen anything of you. I hope that you will return some day and enjoy more of our hospitality."

"Thank you. Now could you please get me a taxi as I have to go straight to the airport."

"I shall get my boy to take you in the minibus. It is the one that we use to meet 'planes when our rooms are not very full. There are so many arriving passengers who do not pre-book their accommodation and we persuade them to climb into the minibus and come here. I tell you, it has paid for itself many times over."

He called out to one of his boys to draw the keys and drive Mr. Schmidt to the airport "as he has an important business appointment in Singapore."

When he arrived at the domestic terminal Hoffnung went straight up to the Garuda counter and asked if he could get a seat on the next flight to Jakarta.

"Yes, there are some seats on the DC 10 that is boarding now," said the demure young lady at the check-in counter. "What name?"

"Neumann."

"Initial please, Mr. Neumann."

"K," he replied. "K for Konrad."

"Very well, here is your ticket. Do you want to pay in

rupiah or American dollars?"

"American dollars," replied the Communist Party stalwart.

"That will be eighty dollars."

He pulled out four twenty dollar notes and handed them to her. She gave him his ticket and boarding pass. Twenty minutes later he was in the air on his way to Jakarta. Mr. Neumann got off in Jakarta and later boarded the flight to Zurich in the name of Mr. Schmidt. When he flew on the Interflug flight from Zurich to Johannisthal Airport in East Berlin he was Herr Hoffnung again.

———■———

At the time that Hoffnung was boarding his flight at Bali Airport Adrian and Dayu were roused by a sharp knock on the door below. Adrian opened his eyes and could feel the already hot sun beaming through the spaced bamboo slats that constituted the wall of the cottage. He wound his sarong around him and walked down the steep, narrow stairs. There were three khaki clad Indonesian policemen on the doorstep.

"*Selamat pagi*," he said.

"*Selamat pagi*," they replied without smiling.

One of them spoke in English. "Last night you were with Senhor Manoel?"

"Yes."

"What time did you leave him?"

"Just after one o'clock. Then we went to the Hamburger House for about an hour."

"Senhor Manoel has been murdered."

Adrian's face went white. "Oh my God," he cried out in disbelief.

"It seems that you and your girlfriend were the last persons to see him alive. His body was found by his head boy when he arrived at the restaurant this morning to prepare the breakfast. There is much blood. The boy said that when he

334

went home last night there was just you and your girlfriend and Senhor Manoel left in the restaurant. It is very grave."

Dayu appeared at the bottom of the stairs and they told her what had happened. She looked very frightened and was uncomfortable with three cops on the doorstep.

"Where is the body now?" asked Adrian.

"Still at the restaurant. We have put a sheet over it until the ambulance arrives."

All sorts of confusing thoughts were racing through Adrian's mind. "Do they suspect Dayu and me? After all, we were with him for a long time after Wayan left. And what about the Danes who accused him of informing? They would have a motive. But how can I point the finger at them when I have no evidence? I don't want to be like that hysterical girl yesterday. Making wild allegations that are probably not true." He had never been one to pimp on others and hated those who did. It went against the great Australian concept of mateship. "If I was to point a finger at them," he reasoned, "and they had a satisfactory alibi then might not the police think that I was making false allegations to save my own skin? Oh God, what should I do?"

"It is very bad," said the policeman. "A very nasty killing."

"Was he shot?" asked Adrian.

"No, stabbed with a knife. And … " The policeman's voice trailed off into nothing.

"Maybe I can help you if I can see the body," said Adrian. He didn't know why he said it but thought that, if the police saw him able to front up to the body, they might not be quite so willing to suspect him of any involvement.

"Not nice to see body. Maybe you will be sick," said the English speaking officer.

"I just want to see how he was killed." He still didn't know what gruesome force impelled him to insist on viewing the corpse. He had never played private detective before and had still not got over the horror of seeing Alex's emaciated shape being put into the ambulance only two months before.

"All right, come with us in the jeep," they said. Adrian told Dayu to stay in the cottage and make some coffee.

When they arrived the whole restaurant was in a state of panic and confusion. The police had cordoned off the small kitchen at the back and Adrian was led past the gaping staff to where the body was lying on the stone slabs of the kitchen floor. The policeman watched Adrian's face as he lifted the sheet off the corpse. Adrian looked down. He could feel the sickness rising in his stomach. He rushed over to a big empty pot and vomited into it. It came and came and came until there was no more. He retched a few times and then walked out into the restaurant. The policeman replaced the sheet and followed him.

"Just like Rhodesia. Just as Manoel described," he muttered to no one in particular. His mind cleared a little when he walked out into the bright sunlight of the street. "Well, at least I know that it is not the Danes," he said to himself. "They are not renowned for their savagery. Nor is it me. That only leaves … Oh, my God."

The chief police officer at the restaurant gave orders to his men to remain with the body until the ambulance arrived. Then he motioned to his driver, who was wiping the dust off the windscreen, to take Adrian back to the cottage.

Adrian was in a daze. A few minutes earlier he had been happily asleep in bed. Dreaming of surfing down the slopes of Mount Agung at the head of a huge avalanche of water. Now he was face to face with a nightmarish reality. Manoel, who had been so lively the night before as he poured out the story of his life, was now just as lifeless as the stone carving that he could see on the other side of the road.

When they arrived back at the cottage the bemedalled chief of police came in and had some of Dayu's coffee. He asked them several more questions about Manoel. What was he like? What were his habits? Did he have any friends? Enemies? Then he asked them about their movements the previous night. Adrian repeated that they had gone to the Hamburger House for about an hour after half past one. The police later went there and spoke with the owner who was able to confirm that Adrian and Dayu had indeed been in his establishment at that time.

Now that Manoel was dead Adrian decided to tell the chief much of what he had heard from the old man's lips in the hours before his death. He concluded by saying that he felt that the killing was probably done by an agent of the communists. After all, Manoel had caused them a lot of trouble.

"Very likely," replied the chief of police. "In this country we have had experience of them before. In 1965. Much trouble and many killings. I think that your theory is probably right. We shall continue to search for the murderer but if it is the communists they are very clever and probably won't let their man be found."

■

The previous evening after Anne-Marie had returned to her *losmen* following her outburst in the restaurant she began to calm down as she realised that her feelings against Manoel were based on mere circumstantial connections rather than hard and solid evidence. "What if I am wrong?" she kept asking herself. "After all, he did look very surprised." In the more rational state of afterthought she decided that she had been hasty in her judgement and regretted losing her temper. She was considering whether she should return to the restaurant the next day and make an apology when she fell asleep.

The next thing she knew was being woken at nine the following morning by the screeching brakes of a police jeep in the courtyard outside the *losmen*. She thought that they must be returning Christian; she went to the door in eager anticipation. She could see four cops with pistols but no Christian. "Oh hell," she thought, "what do they want now? Money?"

The Asian grapevine in the form of the staff at Manoel's had told the police about the previous afternoon's altercation between their late employer and the "Denmark people" who were staying at Coconut Cottages.

The police were brusque and officious as they marched into the two adjacent *losmens* and began searching them. Jens, who shared the bigger one with Dagmar, thought that it was a drug search and was slightly apprehensive. Not because he had anything to hide but because he realised how easy it would be for the police to plant a small block of hash and then claim that they had found it. In a toilet bag, inside a box, under the bed. Anywhere. "Such things have been known to happen before," he thought. "And not just in the East but in the West as well." He began to wish that he was back in Denmark where the police chase real criminals — robbers and murderers — instead of playing cat and mouse over a small block of hash.

It was certainly a strange drug search. First the cutlery in the kitchen drawer. Every knife was taken out and its blade closely examined. "They must be checking to see if we've been burning hash on our knives," he thought. Then the suitcases were emptied and the beds turned over. Jens and Dagmar looked on in wonder.

Anne-Marie was watching a similar scene in her *losmen*. As they rifled through Christian's clothes she nearly cried. "Poor love," she thought. "I wonder if they've given you any breakfast."

The cops' energy started to wane when they realised that they were not going to find what they were seeking. A bloodstained knife perhaps? Or a red splattered blouse? Some item of Manoel's?

The police then subjected the three young Danes to a lengthy and rigorous interrogation as to their whereabouts on the previous night. They answered slowly while a bespectacled officer wrote down everything they said.

They explained how they had arrived back at the *losmens* about six and had stayed in all night. They did not mention their little contretemps with Manoel. They described how they had spent the evening playing backgammon with a couple of Americans in an effort to take their minds off the traumatic events of the afternoon.

Another two policemen then questioned the Americans as well as Cookie, the proprietor of the *losmens*. All were able to confirm that Dagmar and Jens and Anne-Marie had indeed stayed in all night.

The questioning went on for more than an hour until Jens finally realised that there was something more to it than a routine drug search.

"What is this all about anyway?" he asked.

"You know Senhor Manoel?" asked the policeman.

"Yes," replied Jens hesitantly.

"We understand that you had a violent argument with him yesterday afternoon."

"It was only words. We were very upset about our friend being arrested. We believed that Manoel might have arranged for the police to arrest our friend."

"Senhor Manoel is not a police informer. He did not inform on your friend. We made the arrest as a result of other information. Senhor Manoel was murdered last night." He watched for the reaction on their faces. It was a mixture of confusion, guilt and horror.

"When did this happen?" asked Jens in as even a tone as he could muster.

"We don't know yet," replied the officer.

Anne-Marie began to cry. She had already begun to feel pangs of guilt about her tirade of accusations and had been considering an apology. Now it was too late. Through her misty eyes she could see the police staring at her, trying to gauge her reaction. She seemed genuinely upset but was certainly not panic stricken. Besides, after their conversation with Cookie and the Americans the police were more or less convinced that the three Danes had been engaged the previous night in backgammon rather than murder. Nevertheless, before they climbed back into their jeep they took the precaution of taking all three passports with them.

"We shall return these to you after we have made further enquiries. In about two days' time. Then you must leave Bali as you cause too much trouble." These were the last words that Jens heard before the jeep, with a hole in its muffler, took off along the dusty track.

■

Manoel's bloodied corpse was taken to the hospital where the doctors tried to establish the time of death. They concluded that he must have expired shortly after 1.00 a.m.

The police did not announce any details for fear of scaring away the much needed tourists and their money. The last thing that Bali needed was a reputation for violence. Nevertheless the story spread like a bushfire.

As soon as the excitement at the restaurant was over and the mangled body was taken away, Wayan and the rest of the staff departed. They believed that the demons had well and truly taken over the place and that more bad things would happen if they stayed. First of all there had been the screaming incident with the blond girl and now the mysterious and bloody killing. They didn't even bother to close the doors when they left. If the evil spirits had got in to the place then it was better to leave the doors open to let them out again. None of the staff bothered to return and the restaurant never reopened.

The Governor of Bali was informed and he had to

decide whether the body should be cremated in the Balinese way or be buried according to Christian rites. The governor was fully aware of how much the old man had loved Bali and its people but he also knew of his strong Christian beliefs. He therefore decided that Manoel should be returned to his own people but then found out that this might be easier said than done.

The nearest Portuguese territory was Macau but, as a result of the bad feeling over Timor, there were no diplomatic relations of any kind between Indonesia and the Portuguese government. The Governor contacted the British Ambassador in Jakarta who arranged for the body to be taken on the Cathay Pacific flight from Bali to Hong Kong and then on to Macau by ferry. The Governor was aware of the reason why Manoel was allowed to remain in Bali and so, as a mark of respect, he sent an officer of his guard to accompany the battered corpse on its long journey to the cathedral in Macau.

The wood carvers of Ubud joined forces to create a beautiful teak coffin in the shape of a turtle. They knew that roast turtle meat — preferably from a male turtle — had been his favourite food and that his greatest pleasure was to serve fresh turtle soup to his special customers. And, of course, Bali — the island that he loved — rests on the back of a giant mythical turtle.

As the men and boys chipped away at the wood with their sharp, hand forged chisels they discussed among themselves the problem of Manoel's soul leaving his body so as to be reincarnated into another form of life. If he was to be buried, they said, then the soul would stay in the body and never be liberated. Only the cremation fires could set a soul free. It all seemed a terrible fate for such a good man and such a waste to bring an abrupt stop to the otherwise endless process of reincarnation. They need not have worried since Manoel's Christian soul had already passed into the after life.

Chapter Eleven

The Mountain

Pascal's night with the beautiful Erika had been so eventful that he ricked his neck. He woke up the next morning in considerable pain and realised that the bone in the back of the neck would have to be manipulated back into place. Erika tried to press it with her thumbs but that only exacerbated the pain. Her knowledge of massage lay in the erotic rather than the therapeutic aspect.

When he got up and looked in the mirror he could see his dark, handsome face tilting distinctly to the right. "Oh well, at least it's like its owner and is not leaning to the left," he laughed.

"What do you mean?" asked Erika.

"I have always voted for the Gaullists and have never leaned towards the left," he smiled.

"Maybe you should go to the hospital and have it treated," she suggested.

"*Mon Dieu*! Never! The hospital here is not the place you should go when you are sick. Not unless you want to die."

"Why?"

"Its reputation is one of dirty needles, rats, cockroaches and complete chaos and disorder. I will not go there under any circumstances."

"Well, you will have to put up with the pain until you get back to Paris."

"No. There is a witchdoctor in the next village. Danny

Holland went to see him when he had a slight touch of tennis elbow. He came back completely cured. Maybe he can fix my neck the same way. And I shall get him to look at the skin rash I've had since I was stung by a sea urchin."

"Is that the red mark on your arm?"

"Yes," he replied. "I was swimming off a reef when this nasty little sea urchin pointed its sharp spike into me. I think the end of it might have snapped off and still be in my arm."

"Ooh, I hope it's not catching," she said.

Pascal drove his open tourer vehicle to the next village and pulled up outside a thatched *warung*. He asked where the *balian* lived and was led away by a young boy of about twelve. Down a long lane lined with piles of coconut husks drying in the sun and freshly brushed cocks standing in their bamboo cages. Pascal was taken into a yard that was inhabited by several strutting hens, a sleeping dog and some tots who were playing on the dusty ground. At one end was a row of rough earthenware pots that contained some rather sickly looking shrubs. The boy spoke in Balinese to a woman who went to fetch the old *balian*. He came out clad in a dark blue sarong and chanting a *mantra*.

The *balian* of the village of Tengan performed an important role in the community. He was a witchdoctor, medicine man and type of priest all rolled into one. He used his healing powers on the sick and applied his spiritual powers to find any lost or stolen goods. He was even able to tell inquiring parents just who their child was reincarnated from. Many of the villagers lived in fear of *leyaks*. They knew that these powerful spirits could transform themselves into vampires, monkeys, dogs and even balls of fire and it was to the *balian* that they went for advice. He and he alone had the knowledge to say who was a *leyak* and who wasn't.

When Pascal saw the old man look up at him he pointed to his neck which was still falling to the right on an almost forty-five degree angle. The *balian* led him up a few steps to a large raised platform; it was covered with a thatched roof held up by several wooden pillars. The open sided structure was decorated with several silken paintings of Hindu gods hanging from pieces of string. One corner was curtained off with a bright red drape. He motioned Pascal to lie on the bed in the middle; it was just an old charpoy with a mattress. A flower patterned sarong served as a bedcover.

Pascal lay on his stomach and watched the man out of the corner of his eye. He was making a mix of massage oil out of many tiny and exotic looking bottles all the while staring upwards into space as he worked himself into a trance. His humming increased in both tempo and volume and he never once cast his eyes towards the patient.

"I suppose he knows what he's doing," thought Pascal. "After all, most of the best masseurs are blind. It is what they feel with their hands that is important, not what they see."

The *balian*, now at the height of his trance, knew that his body had been entered by a powerful spirit that was strong enough to drive the demon out of the injured man's neck. So he came across to the bed and began rubbing the back of Pascal's neck with his nimble and oily hands. Then he touched behind the ears and then the whole head. This way, that way. Then suddenly, click! He continued rubbing for another ten minutes as he made sure that he had rid Pascal's body of the evil spirit that had got inside and caused all the trouble to the neck.

Pascal lay still the whole time, not daring to interrupt the old man's communication with the spirits. The neck was now back in its rightful position and the pain was lessening by the minute. He sat up on the bed and looked at the *balian* who gave no hint of recognising the patient's continuing presence. In vain did Pascal try to catch his eye so as to ask him to treat the skin rash on his arm. So he just pointed to his arm anyway. The *balian's* eyes were closed and he was facing the other way humming a *mantra*. But he immediately picked up Pascal's signal and motioned him to lie down again.

The healing man walked over to his colourful array of medicines and placed his hand on the lid of a tin that was sitting on the bottom shelf. He took off the top and brought out the penis of a freshly caught crocodile. He then took a selection of herbs from various containers and put them into a metal cooking pot with the penis and some fish liver.

Still in a trance he walked down the steps and put the pot on an old wood stove that was burning in the yard. He stood over it for about ten minutes, adding water and bringing it to the boil. Then he took if off and placed it on the dusty ground to cool. He went about some other chores and Pascal began to wonder whether he had forgotten all about him. A few minutes later he came up the steps and poured the warm mixture into a large glass and handed it to Pascal. The Frenchman looked at it in horror.

"Drink," said the old man. "*Bagus, bagus!*"

Pascal closed his eyes and drank it all at once. It tasted foul. He could feel the *balian* rubbing over the rash on his arm. Gently at first and then more vigorously. He pinched and squeezed it. Very hard. Pascal could feel the man's fingernails extracting the broken off end of the sea urchin's spike. Then the *balian* walked back to his table and resumed working with his little bottles.

Pascal remained lying there in the deepest silence. There wasn't a sound in the village. Just the faintest humming noise that was coming from the old man's lips. The woman had taken the little children out of the yard and told them to keep quiet while the *balian* went about his healing.

After a few more minutes the *balian*, without looking at Pascal, motioned him to rise. Pascal stood up and pulled a five thousand rupiah note out of the pocket of this brightly coloured beach shorts. He put it on the table and walked out into the bright sunlight of the yard. The *balian* did not look up. He was still in the latter stages of his trance.

The young boy, who had directed Pascal to the place, was waiting for him outside the gate. They walked back to the car through the oppressive heat of the mid morning.

When he reached his house Pascal bounced in and gave Erika a jovial slap on the thighs. "I am happy again," he laughed. "Look, my neck is all right and the arm is no longer stinging." She looked at his forearm; there was no longer any mark at all.

Two nights later Erika flew back to Norway and Pascal went straight from the airport to the Mango Tree. It was still early and the only others in the bar were Adrian and Dayu and Thierry and Nicole.

"We are just having a quick snack before we go to the temple to watch the *legong* dance," said Nicole. "Would you like to join us?"

"Oh no," said Pascal. "I only like dancing myself. Not watching others do it."

"You would be too big for a *legong* dance," laughed Dayu. "And the wrong sex."

"Well, in that case I must decline your very kind invitation. I'll just sit here and talk to the barman until more people arrive."

Dayu nudged Adrian. "Come on, we must go. Otherwise we'll be late." And so the four of them set off for the temple which was only half a block away.

They could hear the thumps of the *kulkul* drum as they walked along the broken footpath. The temple was alive with people and oil lamps. There was a throng outside on the street milling around the stalls that were selling roasted nuts, soup, sashes and incense sticks. Inside the temple walls people were congregating in the first courtyard. Some were standing, some were sitting on chairs but most of them were squatting on their haunches on the stone floor. Adrian and Dayu and the French couple took their places along the courtyard wall that was furthest from the street. The beautiful music of the *gamelan* orchestra was wafting through the night air which was already pungent with the smell of betel nut, burning incense, clove cigarettes and roasted peanuts.

Dayu explained that the *legong* was the most graceful and beautiful dance of the Balinese culture. It told the story of an ancient king who abducted a maiden and imprisoned her inside a house of stone. Her brother, the Prince of Daha, demanded that the king release her. When he refused the prince challenged him to a battle. On his way to the battlefield the king was warned by a passing bird that he would be killed and that was exactly what happened. The *legong* dance was a re-enactment of this story with the parts being played by three beautiful young girls of about nine years old. They were wrapped tightly in gold brocade from head to foot which accentuated their fine youthful features. On their heads they wore colourful blooms of fresh frangipani.

At the beginning of the performance the girls stood rooted to the spot as if they were possessed by the spirits. They then rushed forward and moved around the courtyard with their tiny arms stretched out in front of them. As if in a trance their nubile and nimble bodies swayed and danced to the rhythm of the *gamelan* orchestra.

Dayu, who used to perform in such dances herself in her pre-puberty years, declared it to be a particularly excellent performance. When they left the temple they were all feeling good for the first time since Manoel's murder. They ambled along to The Mango Tree where they had left the bikes and then rode to the Three Monkeys. The proprietor had just returned from a trip to Singapore and had brought back some bottles of French Sauvignon to sell to his special customers. Like Adrian and Dayu and Thierry and Nicole.

Thierry began to yawn and said that he was tired as he had been up since his early morning surf at six o'clock. When they went outside into the warm night air Adrian suddenly felt full of latent energy. He said that, instead of bed, he felt like some action. "Let's go to the Frog and dance," he said. But when he looked at his watch he realised that it was almost closing time. Then he turned to Dayu and said, "Do you know what I would like to do right now?"

"Go surfing," she giggled.

"Well, that would be nice but it's not what I have in mind."

"What then?"

"Let's go for a long bike ride out towards Uluwatu. It's so warm and there's enough light."

Dayu felt mellow and relaxed after the temple dancing and the wine that followed. She tightened her arm around his waist and whispered into his ear that she knew of the perfect place where they could sit and look at the surf from the cliff top. They said good-bye to Nicole and Thierry and walked over to where the bike was parked.

Adrian kicked started it and they roared off towards Kuta. The night was still warm and there weren't many people around — just a few late night revellers returning from the discos, Balinese clearing up at the temple and one or two "good time girls" on the lookout for customers.

They sped past the airport and through groves of coconut and banana trees until they reached the bottom of the steep hill before Pecatu. Adrian changed down to a lower gear and planted his foot hard on the accelerator to get up the rise. Dayu was sitting close behind with both her arms around his waist, holding on tightly and lovingly. Her long black hair was billowing in the light breeze while Adrian's locks were blowing back and hitting her in the face. Both of them felt free and happy. Adrian started to do a few crazy things with the bike; Dayu screamed — from both fear and exhilaration.

As they approached the Uluwatu turn-off she directed him down a narrow track that went off to the right. They drove through a coconut plantation and at one point narrowly missed colliding with a cow. The black beast had been lying down on the ground and suddenly stood up when it heard the roar of the approaching motor bike. Adrian saw it just in time and swerved to avoid it with only inches to spare. Eventually they came to a clearing near the edge of the cliff and Dayu told him to stop.

When he cut off the engine they could hear the distant roar of the waves far below. They walked through the open space and past the temple that was perched on the edge of the cliff. There was a flat rock with some grass on it and they sat down and looked out at the grey sea that was sparkling in the moonlight. It seemed as if a million glow-worms were dancing on its surface. Boom! Crash! The waves were breaking into the cave far below and were smashing against the vertical cliffs. At night they appeared so awesome and forbidding and Adrian realised that the whole place felt quite different in the dark.

For one thing it was deserted. He had never been there without seeing at least half a dozen surfers in the line-up and many more in the cave and at the *warung*. Now there were none. Just he and Dayu sitting like gods above the ocean contemplating its mysteries, its life, its patterns, its beauty and its power. They didn't say much. It was still very warm and she lay with her head against his shoulder while gently running her tiny hands over his chest. They were alone with just the elements and the gods and each other. A truly magical moment. Then suddenly and without warning the heavens opened up and raindrops as big as finger nails started to pour down from the sky.

They dashed back to the temple and dived for shelter under a thick thatched roof that was held up by a series of ornamental wooden pillars in the first courtyard. Its floor was raised about a foot above the ground so that pilgrims could rest there. And late night lovers caught in the rain! And monkeys. Like the Rock of Gibraltar the temple had its own colony of monkeys and they too were sheltering under the thatch from the downpour. Adrian flinched as one of them jumped on to his shoulder and nestled there. He noticed that Dayu was a little tense. She explained that this particular temple was dedicated to the spirits of the sea. Demons.

After half an hour the rain eased to a steady drizzle. They were dry so long as they stayed under the roof of the *bale*. Adrian realised that, if they rode all the way back to Legian in their thin cotton clothing, they would get saturated. He wouldn't be able to travel very fast since the tracks would be a sea of mud. It was nearly dawn so he suggested that they wait until daylight and then check the rain and the state of the road. It seemed the most sensible thing to do and, to his fertile imagination, a rather romantic way to spend the rest of the night.

There was a pile of straw at one end of the *bale* and three large floppy cushions. By now they were getting a little tired and so they made themselves as comfortable as possible. As they lay together — alone in the rain and miles from anywhere — Adrian began to feel that lying in an exotic Eastern temple directly above the legendary surf and magical cave of Uluwatu was the perfect setting for an act of love. He pulled Dayu closer to him but she seemed hesitant and afraid.

"What's the matter?" he asked.

"Can not make love in the temple," she replied.

"Why not? Surely this is the best place of all. Close to the gods. And near the magic cave."

"To make love on a temple ground is most forbidden. Terrible punishment by the gods."

"What punishment?" he asked.

"Man is castrated and girl is dragged to graveyard and suffers terrible fate." She paused. Through the darkness Adrian could see a look of real terror in her eyes.

"What sort of fate?" he asked. "A horsewhipping?"

"No. Hot poker is pushed inside the girl who makes love in the temple. Then they smash down the temple and throw all its stones into the sea."

"Well, they won't have far to carry these ones — just to the edge of the cliff," he laughed. "Have you seen these things happen?" She admitted that she hadn't but she had heard about them from others.

"You know," he said, "in our culture there are similar taboos but they are not ordained by the gods at all. They are put together by a bunch of politicians and priests for the sole purpose of keeping the people under their thumb and destroying their pleasure. And I rather think that your *pedanda* and other priests are up to the same trick. Anyway, who would know? We are the only ones here — apart from the monkeys — and if we don't tell anyone then nothing will happen."

"But what if the monkeys are *leyaks*?" she thought. "Then they would know. And the gods ... "She could feel Adrian holding her tightly and kissing her. Relaxed by the wine and enjoying the strong physical embrace of her lover she soon forgot about the spirits and the petty prohibitions of the priests. She even forgot where she was.

"To-night let us be gods ourselves and do what we like," whispered Adrian. "Throw care to the winds." And that is exactly what they did. A few minutes later the gods spoke with a tremendous roar.

For some time great amounts of gas had been building up inside the bowels of Mount Agung, the home of the gods in the centre of the island. Unable to escape the gas created such enormous pressure that suddenly it blew the whole top of the mountain hundreds of feet into the air. Thousands of tons of white hot rocks, ash and debris fell on the surrounding countryside and the noise of the explosion was heard as far away as Singapore and Australia.

Inside the temple at Uluwatu it was a case of coitus

interruptus as the earth shook and the flimsily built stone walls of the temple courtyard came crashing to the ground. The monkeys went crazy and started running round in all directions. Dayu knew what the explosion meant and that she had been the one responsible for it. She had angered the gods by fornicating on the sacred ground of the temple and the wrath of Agung was a punishment to her and her people for such an unspeakable transgression.

The villagers in Semang, like all others in the mountains, were roused from their sleep by the deafening sound. Their houses shook, ornaments crashed to the floor, dogs began to bark and children were crying.

In the villages closer to the mountain thousands were dying from the highly toxic gases that had been unleashed by the explosion — sulphur dioxide, chlorine and fluorine. Huge rocks were raining down like bombs and killing anyone who happened to be in their path. Great showers of hot pumice and ash smothered whole villages. Roofs were crushed like eggshells under the weight of the debris. The air was thick with falling black dust that darkened the island for the rest of the day.

Villagers in the vicinity of the mountain who fled their burning huts were coated with hot ash and burnt to death on the spot. Others were dehydrated in fire flashes. When the ash settled on the sides of the mountain the heavy rain turned it into thick black mud. Great streams of boiling lava — some up to half a mile wide — were rushing at more than a hundred miles an hour into the valleys and rivers below. Whole villages were buried under ten feet of hot mud. And huge rocks and trees were swept into the avalanches as they rolled across open country and down into the valleys.

It wasn't only mud flows that buried the villages and wiped them off the map; many settlements at the bottom of the valleys were inundated by flood waters. Before the eruption the holy mountain of Agung had a huge lake in its crater which was the result of a previous eruption in 1963. The force of the present explosion threw the water out of the crater and sent it pouring down the terraced ricefields to fill the valleys below.

Like everyone else in Semang Klian was woken by the great bang. He immediately realised what it was. He could remember the same thing happening in 1917, 1926 and 1963. As on previous occasions he knew that the gods were very angry and that the eruption was a sign of their wrath. He had had a premonition that something terrible was going to happen because for the past few days there had been a plague of blue tailed rats running through the paddy fields and destroying the rice that was still waiting to be harvested. No one knew where they came from. They had suddenly appeared and, in the course of only a few days, were fast devouring the last of the crops. That, thought Klian, had been the warning. And now Agung had once again shown its anger and reminded the villagers of the great powers of the gods.

The women who stayed in the house with him woke up in great fear and went out to the family shrine and loaded it with offerings. In such a state of anger the gods had to be placated quickly with substantial offerings. Obviously the normal offerings over the last few months had not been enough. Otherwise the spirits would have been satisfied and would not have sent down this terrible punishment. It was still pitch dark outside and the cloud of black ash was getting thicker.

Fortunately Semang was quite a long way from the mountain and so was not instantly wiped out as were many of the closer villages. The people of Semang made their way through the darkness to the temple to pray and to place communal offerings to the gods. They carried torches and oil lanterns to find their way through the terrifying blackness. The presence of the demons could be felt everywhere. Some even believed that they could feel the touch of the monkey *leyaks* as they filed through the branches of the banyan tree. On the way to the temple Klian and the old women passed burning huts that had been hit by white hot rocks the heat of which had set the thatch on fire.

The courtyards of the temple were packed with desperately praying people. Klian was able to see very little in the dark but he could hear the tinkling of prayer bells that accompanied the *pedanda's* prayers. There was also the sound of the conch shell and the double drum which signified the presence of the *sungghu*, the priest for the demons.

Rain and dust and ash were still falling from the sky and there was a general fear and apprehension among the drenched supplicants as they stood in the open courtyards chanting their prayers. They were afraid of both the present and the future. To them the eruption was a premonition of anarchy and disaster. The last time that Agung had exploded and killed thousands of people was in 1963. And then a short time later — in 1965 — came the terrible killings that resulted from the communist coup. More people were killed in the political anarchy that followed than in the eruption itself. They wondered what terrible disaster would follow this latest expression of Agung's anger.

Klian and some of the elders sheltered under the roof of the *bale* while the rest of the villagers stood outside getting dirtier and wetter in the continuing rain of black dust and water. Deep in a trance of prayer the people didn't quite know what the gods were going to do next. The noise of the bells and drums drowned out the creaking sound from the roof of the *bale*. Then, under the weight of the mounting ash on its thatch, the roof collapsed in one corner. Klian was knocked sideways and his arm hit the solid bark of a great wooden drum. He suffered a fracture and bled copiously. The women applied a tourniquet which managed to stop the blood but it was clear that he was in great pain. The other elders who were sitting with him decided that, since he was

354

the beloved *klian*, he should be taken to the hospital in Denpasar for treatment. Two of them went and fetched the village farm truck and Klian was led through the roots of the banyan tree and put in the cab of the truck. Fortunately it was a four wheel drive vehicle and high off the ground; so it was able to plough through the ash that had settled on the road and across the whole countryside to a depth of several inches.

Even though it should have been daylight long before they left the village, they drove in pitch darkness with the lights on high beam all the way to Denpasar. When they approached the hospital there was a traffic jam for several blocks. They were confronted with honking horns and flashing lights from hundreds of *bemos*, ambulances, police trucks and pony-carts that were bringing the injured to the tiny, ill-equipped hospital. Klian's truck pulled up in a side road and they walked him the remaining blocks to the hospital. His friends told the nurse that he was the village headman and so he was given priority. But he still didn't get treated until the next day.

Towards the end of the afternoon a great wind came up from the east and blew away a lot of the dust that was still in the air. It was scattered over Java and Sumatra and then into the Bay of Bengal. From there it spread across Asia and Africa leaving spectacular red sunsets in its wake. When the darkness of the ash cloud lifted it was replaced by an eerie red glow that filled the sky.

In the temple at Uluwatu Dayu had begun to cry as soon as she realised what she had done. She stood up from the floor of the *bale* and wound her sarong around her cold and shaking body. Even though it was still raining she indicated to Adrian that she wanted to leave and so remove herself from the cause of the disaster.

They climbed on the bike and rode slowly through the mud back to the main road. In the darkness they could hear some after rumblings from the bowels of the distant mountain. When they reached the cottage, Dayu wouldn't get off the bike. She seemed to be in a trance. Adrian lit an oil lamp and eventually coaxed her on to the verandah. She took off her sarong and began shaking it vigorously.

"What are you doing?" he asked. She whispered that when Balinese are really afraid they shake their sarongs to try to get rid of their fears and to drive out the bad spirits that cause them.

They went inside and Dayu explained what she believed had happened in the mountains. She had often heard Klian speak with awe of Agung's eruption in 1963 when thirty thousand people had been killed. She said that, although Legian was too far down to be affected, her own village, within sight of the holy mountain, might well have been devastated.

"Well, shall we go up and see if Klian is all right?" asked Adrian. Her mind was in a state of confusion. On the one hand she would like to know if her grandfather had come to any harm but how could she face him or any of the other villagers who might be suffering because of her wilful and selfish act in the temple? And if she went back to Semang at a time of such great uncertainty might not the gods inflict a further punishment on her and the village? The eruption might only be the prelude for an even greater disaster.

Adrian could see that she was in no fit state to make a decision so he applied his own values to the situation and concluded that their first obligation was to go up and check on Klian and maybe lend a hand to clean up in the village if there had been any damage. "Hell," he thought, "they were kind enough to me and this is the least I can do in return." He turned to Dayu and said, "Let's jump on the bike and we'll ride up there."

They drove through the darkened streets and then up the road that led to the mountains. Although it was the middle of the morning the daylight was still blotted out by the cloud of black ash. They had to wipe the grime off their faces as they sped through the dead forests of the dark and spooky countryside. Sometimes ambulances and police vehicles went screaming past with their sirens blaring and top lights flashing. There were many *bemos* and buses coming the other way filled with the dead and the dying. At one point an immense lava flow was pouring its steaming hot mud across the road and the police were directing traffic on to an alternative side track.

They reached the village about midday and used the headlight of the bike to find their way through the maze of narrow lanes to Klian's house. The oil lamps were still on in the garden from the night before.

They were concerned when they couldn't see Klian sitting in his usual chair on the darkened verandah and even more alarmed when they could not find him inside. Dayu believed that she had been responsible for killing him and that she would be punished in the next life by being reincarnated in a suitably humble form. Perhaps a pi dog. Or a cockroach. Or a poisonous mushroom. Then from such a lowly state she would have to begin all over again her progressive path to eventual perfection.

The old women of the house appeared out of the darkness with the fear of death on their faces. They explained in whispers that Klian had been injured and had been taken to the hospital to have his arm mended.

"Will he be all right?" asked Adrian.

"It was only the arm. It became possessed by an evil spirit," they replied in Balinese. Adrian then asked if anyone from the village had been killed but the women replied that they didn't know and withdrew back to the kitchen.

When the light improved towards the end of the day Adrian persuaded Dayu to walk with him to the ash covered village green to see what damage, if any, had been suffered.

Everything had been covered with ash and some of the

357

roofs had fallen in under its weight. They saw some crushed and burnt out huts and villagers were busy shovelling the muck off the roofs of those that had survived. They were working in fear and silence and there was none of the happy chatter that had so struck Adrian on his previous visit. From the gloomy, grey expanse of the village square they could see people milling around the banyan tree outside the temple. Adrian asked Dayu if she wanted to go inside to pray.

"No," she said and turned the other way.

They walked out through the village gates and into the paddy field where they had helped to bring in the fine golden harvest only a few weeks before. The fields were now just paddocks of grey mud. They held hands as they stood on the edge and looked down the steep valley. Adrian could remember on the previous occasion seeing an infinity of green rice terraces alive with thousands of workers plucking the plants out of the ground. Now, with its coating of mud, it was a valley of death. Water from the crater lake had found its way to the bottom of the valley and was flooding the lower settlements. Men and women were trudging up the valley carrying their belongings on their heads as they fled from the rising waters.

A dozen people in Semang had lost their lives and plans were being made for their cremation. Villagers closer to Agung had fared much worse. Many had lost their entire populations. Those who survived were short of food as all fresh fruit, trees, crops and livestock had been destroyed.

The next day Dayu waited for Klian to return and Adrian decided to go further up the hills to see if he could render any assistance to the victims. He knew that he couldn't ride his motor bike any further because the mud would be too deep. So he took one of the few horses that had survived the rain of hot ash and set out at dawn.

He travelled for about twelve miles through a dark and bare landscape. He then reached a village that was so disfigured and thickly covered with mud that it looked like a piece of moonscape. The old horse could plod no further through the ever deepening slush so Adrian dismounted and took a few steps himself. The mud came up to his thighs and was still warm.

He could see a strange shape sticking up a few inches so he dug with his hands to see what it was. A mud covered corpse in a crouching position. There was an eerie silence that shrouded the countryside. No croaking geckos, no yelping pi dogs, no crowing cocks, no laughing children. None of the noises of Bali. Nothing. Just the distant buzz of an Indonesian Air Force helicopter as it flew around looking for signs of life. He soon realised that there was nothing he could do to help the survivors as there weren't any. And most of the dead were already buried. Under the mud. So he climbed on the horse and rode slowly back to the village.

"Thank God it just missed Semang," he kept saying to himself.

When he reached the house he discovered that Klian still hadn't returned. He did not like the atmosphere at all; he missed sitting on the verandah talking to the old man. Dayu was quiet and uncommunicative and the old women were like walking death. The silence of the house and village was unsettling. Finally he could stand it no longer.

"Listen, Dayu, why don't we ride down to Denpasar and go and see Klian at the hospital. I can't stand it up here another minute. I keep thinking of all the bright and happy times we shared when we were last here and now it's like living in a morgue."

"Me too," she replied. "I want to leave and I shall never return. Never." She had a strange look in her eyes which he hadn't seen before.

"Well, maybe we'll come back and see Klian some time when the sun starts shining again and the village is back to normal," he said.

"No, I shall never come back," she said with finality. She

still believed that she was responsible for the eruption. It was all her fault; by seeking a selfish and indulgent life with Adrian which culminated in the fateful act in the temple, she knew that she had insulted the gods and brought down their wrath on all the people of the mountains.

They were both pleased to ride out of the eerie, silent village. A village of fear and death. The dust cloud had lifted and through the haze they could see the distant outline of Mount Agung. It still had steam rising out of its top but somehow it looked different.

"It has lost its top," said Dayu.

"And its shape," replied Adrian. In fact, the mountain was now more than a thousand feet lower than it had been the previous morning.

The trip through the mud was slow and difficult and on three occasions they were diverted on to back roads to avoid the flows of lava that were still spreading their creeping tentacles across the countryside. They could see helicopters and transport 'planes dropping food and medicine into isolated villages.

As soon as the black dust cloud had lifted and visibility was restored the Indonesian Air Force had begun to fly in supplies of food and medical equipment. So did the Royal Australian Air Force from Darwin and the Americans from Clark Air Base in the Philippines.

Three hundred feet below the surface of the Sunda Strait the officers and men of the nuclear submarine, H.M.S.Conqueror, were in the process of celebrating the Queen's Birthday. They had been scouring the ocean depths for several days — first the Straits of Malacca and now the Sunda Strait between Java and Sumatra. Both channels are vital seaways that link the Pacific with the Indian Ocean, Japan with its Gulf oil supplies, Great Britain with its colony of Hong Kong, and the fast developing Pacific Rim countries with the powerhouse of Western Europe. The straits are narrow and Western strategic planners had long been aware of the chaos that would ensue if they were ever denied the use of two such vital international sea lanes.

The blood red port was being passed around the table in the cramped wardroom when one of the ratings from the communications room knocked gently on the door and handed a piece of paper to the commanding officer. The big, red-faced man unfolded the Admiralty message and began to read it.

"Proceed immediately to Gilimanuk, Bali, and surface. Volcanic eruption has destroyed island's electricity supply. Provide emergency nuclear power where required."

Commander Bridgeman put the message inside the pocket of his white cotton shirt and waited while the remaining glasses were filled. Then the most junior officer present called for silence and they all sat back in their chairs. "Gentlemen, the Queen," said the young man whereupon they all reached for their glasses and took a loyal sip. Commander Bridgeman then leaned across the table and spoke to the First Lieutenant. They excused themselves and went to the operations room to change course and head for the stricken island.

H.M.S.Conqueror surfaced in the bay of Gilimanuk less than twelve hours after the eruption. The power supply to Bali from Java had been destroyed by the tremor and, apart from a few emergency generators, the island was completely without electricity. A Chinook helicopter from Singapore dropped a converter and H.M.S.Conqueror was able to connect her nuclear reactor to the converter and thence to the local substation to provide the island with unlimited electricity for several days until the normal lines were restored.

■

It was evening before Adrian and Dayu rode into Denpasar and there were still great traffic jams around the hospital. They darted in and out of the vehicles and along the footpath until they reached the hospital which was crowded with the sick, the dying, police, taxi drivers, relations, and hordes of porters, doctors, nurses and clerks. A temporary register had been set up in the front which contained several lists of names: those who had been admitted, those who had been treated and discharged and those who had died.

Dayu and Adrian had to wait several hours in the queue which was moving at the pace of the proverbial snail. They bought hot soup and coffee from a food cart that was doing good business as it plied its way from one queue to another. It was 10 p.m. before they reached the desk. The clerk thumbed his way through the list and informed them that Klian's arm had been treated and he had been discharged three hours earlier to the care of the same men who had brought him down the day before. Dayu didn't say anything; she seemed to be in a trance.

"Thank God we're away from the village. I really hated it up there," said Adrian when they returned to the cottage. "Everything had changed so much since the last time. Not only its appearance but also its mood."

"I shall never go there again," said Dayu.

The next morning Adrian woke up early and took his board down to the beach. The tide was right up to the sand dunes many of which had been washed away by the waves.

"It's wild, man," called a Californian surfer. "I just love tidal waves." In fact it wasn't quite a tidal wave. A lot of the water that was spewed out of the crater had found its way through streams and rivers down to the sea. The ocean was still dealing with all this extra water as well as trying to accommodate some new fissures that had developed on the seabed.

The result was some truly gigantic waves that were too

wild to have any form. Nevertheless Adrian battled his way out through the crashing foam. They were closing out and hard to ride but he persisted and managed to score a few short, crazy rides. But mostly he wiped out and fought his way back to the top of the swirling sea. Some of the lava had been swept down the rivers and he had to battle his way through several floating banks of pumice.

It was too wild for the other surfers who had paddled out; they were all safely back on the beach. No point in getting wiped out wave after wave without finding a decent ride. But Adrian was loving it. Being thrown round in the mighty ocean was like a cleansing experience after the horrors he had witnessed up in the mountains. He just wanted to get those ghastly mud covered corpses out of his mind. And the great noise of the wave as it opened its face and crashed down was so reassuring after the deathly silence of the mountains.

"I can't understand Dayu," he thought. "She thinks that all the goodness in the world comes from the mountains and all the bad things emanate from the sea. But, as I see it, it's the other way round. And Agung's explosion proves it." Crash! Crunch! Boom! Another wipe-out. "This is fun," he thought. "It's just so good to be back in the water even though I can't seem to catch a rideable wave." He looked up and saw another great wall of water about to smother him. It carried him right up the beach and threw him on the sand.

Thierry ran up and slapped him on the shoulder. "I was watching you and every time I saw you go down I thought that we'd never see you again. Why did you stay out there when you weren't getting any more rides?"

"Don't know really. But I was enjoying it. I guess I just love being in the sea even when there aren't any decent waves."

"You should have been born a fish," laughed Thierry.

"No, I'd rather be a surfer. The ocean is my favourite

element. I like the feeling of being thrown round by its mighty force. It shows us how small and insignificant we are when we come up against the forces of nature. Dayu thinks that the eruption was a punishment from the gods. I prefer to regard it as a reminder that man, for all his wonderful scientific and technological achievements, is not quite as clever and power- ful as he thinks he is. There is a spiritual aspect to life that is often ignored. The eruption helps us to see things in their proper perspective."

"You are starting to talk like a Balinese," said Thierry.

■

Having determined never to go back to the village and instead to throw in her lot with Adrian and try to please him, Dayu was surprisingly responsive to his suggestion that they go to the Jolly Frog in an effort to distance themselves from the trauma of the last few days. It seemed that everyone else had the same idea as they all headed to the disco to dance the night away and put out of their minds the death and destruc- tion that lay only a few miles away in the mountains.

The coastal strip had been relatively unaffected by the volcanic activity that had devastated the centre of the island. The people of the coast had heard the bang and seen the great dust cloud but otherwise their lives had gone on more or less as usual. There were still mouths to be fed, money to be made and, most important of all, offerings to be placed for the gods to keep them happy and dissuade them from inflict- ing their wrath on the coast like they had in the mountains. The coastal folk knew that somehow the villagers in the mountains had been remiss in their respect for the gods. It could have been that they had neglected their offerings or desecrated the lotus throne or perhaps someone might have committed the supreme sacriligeous act of fornicating in the temple.

The Jolly Frog was throbbing with loud music, flickering

364

lights and gyrating couples. In spite of eruptions, death and destruction the endless pursuit of pleasure must go on. Indeed, with greater frenzy than before. Everyone was trying to jolt themselves out of the fear and misery that had momentarily prevailed in the wake of the eruption. There was nothing more that anyone could do to help with the rescue. Hundreds of 'planes from several air forces had flown in supplies and police road blocks had now been set up on all roads leading to the mountains. Only military personnel were allowed to pass.

It was the first night that the disco had opened since the eruption and everyone was hell bent on making up for lost time. The dancing seemed wilder and more vigorous than usual, the drinks were flowing at double the normal rate and a general "devil may care" attitude prevailed.

Pascal was in the middle of the dance floor whizzing Amanda Dawson-Flaunty-Hughes around in a mad romp that was part tango and part waltz. When the music stopped Amanda walked over to the ladies' room and Pascal sauntered up to the counter with a couple of empty glasses in his hand.

"Hi, Pascal," said Adrian.

"Ah, Adrian and Dayu. Good evening. You were not caught in the explosion? Obviously not."

"Let's not talk about it," said Adrian.

"Of course not. Pardon me. Can I get you some drinks? To-night we can imbibe as much as we like without paying for them."

"How come?" asked Adrian.

With a conspiratorial look in his dark, Gallic eyes Pascal lowered his voice almost to a whisper and said, "Because to-night I have met some Englishmen who, within the confines of this disco, are men of power and influence. But more power than influence. If it wasn't for them we wouldn't be here to-night."

"Not another astronaut? Like the one at your party," laughed Adrian.

"No, but you're getting hot. These men have as much power as Mount Agung. Come and I'll introduce you so that you can also partake of the free drinks."

He led them over to a slim, fair haired young man who was talking to Maria. Pascal introduced them to Lieutenant David Aston, R.N. and explained that he was a submariner from H.M.S.Conqueror which was at that moment providing power from its nuclear reactor to the whole of Bali including the Jolly Frog.

"Now I understand why you stressed that he was a man of 'power'," laughed Adrian.

The officer, immaculately dressed in tan sports trousers, cream shirt and brown cravat, explained how delighted the owner of the Jolly Frog was that power had been restored after the disaster and that he could therefore open his disco again and pull in some money. He wanted to thank the naval gods who had made it all possible. So he had sent a minibus around the coast to Gilimanuk to bring some of the ship's company back to spend the evening at his disco. He told them that they could drink as much as they liked "on the house" and even provided them with accommodation for the night in the bungalows at the back.

"The C.O. decided that he could spare only six of us," said Lieutenant Aston, "so he jolly kindly chose me and five of the ratings. My orders are to keep an eye on them but I have said that, so long as they wake up in the morning with two arms and two legs and their bodies basically intact, I don't really mind what they do to-night. After all, we've been cruising under the sea for many days. They deserve a night out. That's them over them. They look af if they're enjoying themselves, don't you think?"

Adrian was fascinated. "What sort of missiles do you carry?" he asked.

Lieutenant Aston retained his pleasant smile as he replied. "I never talk shop when I'm on leave. Now what can I get you to drink? You must be thirsty in this heat. Order what you like as Gedé — he's the owner — said that I may order for myself and as many friends as I can make during the night."

Adrian ordered a cold beer and Dayu asked for a tequila. Maria's glass was empty and by the time that Pascal had added his orders the methodical lieutenant had produced a pencil and paper and was writing them all down. Maria walked up to the bar with him to help carry the glasses back.

"I saw you dancing with Amanda," Adrian said to Pascal. "What happened to the Greek shipowner whom she was with at your party?"

"Oh, she started to get serious with him so he went back to Greece. He was frightened of losing his ships to her. I know all about her reputation as a gold-digger but she is quite spunky all the same. I think that I could have a good time with her before she makes a lunge for my cheque book."

The lieutenant returned with their glasses and Amanda came over and slipped her arm around Pascal. When the next number began Adrian put down his glass, grabbed Dayu and headed for the dance floor. They gyrated and spun around and kissed and touched each other. It was almost as if Mount Agung had been a mere dream. But not quite.

The mood in Semang was still one of fear. The evil spirits had attained paramountcy and there was no knowing what might happened next. Several army trucks filled with emergency food had arrived but the villagers had been pleased to see them leave. They had an ingrained suspicion of the authorities and were in no mood to be communicative or grateful. They knew that the eruption was a punishment from the gods for their sins and therefore they were quite prepared to suffer and make amends. It was a private matter between them and the gods. Accordingly the authorities, even with gifts of emergency food and medicines, were regarded as an unwelcome intrusion.

Those who had died in the eruption were buried temporarily in the gardens of their houses to await cremation. It was the prerogative of the *pedanda* to set the date of the cremation ceremony at which time the bodies would be exhumed from their temporary graves and ceremonially burnt. The flames would release their souls and so enable them to be reincarnated into another life form.

The *pedanda*, who was the living link between the villagers and their gods, would normally have waited several weeks or months to conduct the cremation. That would give the families plenty of time to save up the considerable sums that were required to build the ornate cremation towers that, like the deceased, would be consumed by flames. Cremations were occasions of joy and happiness. The villagers knew that they were helping to purify the soul of the deceased for a return to a new — and hopefully better — life.

Klian, the secular head of the village, believed that only the joy of a cremation could transform the village out of its misery and fear. So he decided to make a suggestion to the *pedanda* — in the most indirect way possible — that the cremation date be brought forward as a means of lifting the pall of gloom from the village.

With his arm in a colourful sling the *klian* made his way to the temple where the white robed *pedanda*, his hair tied in a knot on the top of his head, was in a state of meditation. Klian waited for him to finish and the two of them withdrew to the outer courtyard. The *klian* discussed all sorts of matters with him without mentioning the real purpose of his visit. Then he just slipped it in as if it were an afterthought. The *pedanda* said that he would consult the spirits to ascertain the most propitious date. Later that day it was announced that there would be a communal cremation in four days' time for the twelve villagers who died in the eruption.

As soon as the people learned of the imminence of the ceremony they set about building the high bamboo towers in which they would carry the bodies to the cremation ground. The towers, forty feet high, consisted of platforms representing the mountains and forests which they adorned with brightly coloured streamers and flowers. Above these rose a platform for the corpse which was surmounted by a series of pagoda roofs that became smaller and smaller the higher they went. They represented the heavens. The craftsmen of the village were busy building wooden coffins in the shape of various animals — bullocks, turtles and birds.

The corpses were dug up the day before the cremation and placed in the family pavilions under a yellow and white canopy where they were watched over by family members.

The next day the heavy towers were carried by dozens of sweating men to the cremation ground outside the village walls. Everyone took part in the procession. It was led by an orchestra of bamboo instruments — drums, gongs, flutes and cymbals. Then came the women in long *kains* and the men in brightly coloured caps with their *krises* tied to their backs. Klian was carrying a beautiful *kris* with a gold figurine of Semara, the god of love, on its ivory handle. It had been in his family for many generations and over the years had accumulated more and more of the ancestors' spiritual powers.

The procession twisted and turned its way in as long and indirect a route as possible. This was to confuse the spirits of the deceased so that they would not find their way back to haunt their houses. The excited bearers kept shaking and revolving the corpses so as to create further confusion.

By the time the procession reached the cremation ground all the mourners were screaming and shrieking in a state of near hysteria. Members of the deceased's families began climbing up the bamboo towers. One of them reached under a pagoda roof and pulled out a bundle of crumpled rupiah notes and tossed them to the crowd below. They screamed and yelled as they dived for the money.

The *pedanda* blessed the white shrouded corpses and they were put inside the wooden, animal shaped coffins. The priest then set fire to the straw; the flames rose wildly to consume the tinder dry bamboo towers, the wooden coffins and the bodies that they contained. Klian and the other mourners put handkerchiefs to their faces as the stench of death permeated the air.

As the flames rose the people laughed and screamed and egged them on with long pokers. They had good cause to be joyous as they watched the liberation of the soul from the body which would ensure reincarnation. Out of the flames would come an eventual new life.

After the ceremony the ashes were put into urns and carried in procession to the river where they were scattered on the water. Thus was fulfilled the last condition for reincarnation. It wouldn't be in the next generation but probably the following one. The step by step advancement to higher forms through reincarnation was a lengthy process. It could take hundreds or even thousands of years.

At the end of the ceremonies the villagers filed back to the temple for a great feast. There was laughter, eating, drinking, dancing and cockfighting. Like those on the dance floor at the Jolly Frog the people of Semang were hell-bent on having a good time as they celebrated the purification of the deceased's souls.

Klian had been right. The mood of the village had been transformed from one of extreme fear and anxiety to one of great gaiety and cheer. Balance between these two extremes was the normality of their daily lives. The normality that had been shattered by the eruption. But when they woke up the morning after the cremation they felt that the balance had been restored. They got up and went about their tasks in the usual way. The men exercised and fed their fighting cocks, the women swept away the remaining ash from their yards and the duck boy led his docile flock into the muddy fields for their daily diet of eels and frogs.

Chapter Twelve

The Peer

Like the mood of the villagers the surf soon returned to normal and Adrian was able to enjoy some nice clean tubes at Airport Reef; some of them were so perfectly formed that he came out the other end without even getting wet. But by midday they were closing out so he decided to spend the afternoon on the beach at Legian with Dayu.

As they walked over the burning hot sand to their usual spot they could see the myriad of activities that constitute a hot Legian afternoon. Westerners trading their T-shirts and even their towels for teak carvings, a shaggy haired hippy in a green sarong strumming a guitar, laughing native ladies weaving the hair of tourists into tight plaits and tying colourful beads on the ends, a Balinese boy sitting squat-legged like a minstrel of old as he played a xylophone to a giggling tourist in an effort to make a sale, a group of g-string clad Europeans down at the water's edge throwing a frisbee, glistening bodies being rubbed down by singing massage ladies, an old fisherman with dark, leathery skin sitting beneath his wide, woven palm leaf hat pulling in his fishing line, richly tanned bodies performing tai chi exercises at the water's edge, a seemingly motionless fishing *prau* out on the horizon, food carts selling slices of fresh pineapple and mango and, of course, the ever present motor bikes and pi dogs. "It's crazy but I love it. It's Bali," laughed Adrian.

Dayu unrolled a sarong on the soft sand and they lay

down on their backs, closed their eyes and soaked up the warm, delicious sun. After a while Adrian could sense someone approaching. He opened his eyes and saw a massage lady coming towards him. When she saw the flicker of interest she squatted down, took the basket off her head and offered a massage for two thousand rupiah.

"Yes, two thousand for a massage for both of us," was Adrian's quick reply. The lady smiled and nodded. She took her oils and towel out of the basket and began rubbing Adrian's back and legs. It was soothing and he closed his eyes again. Then she gently turned him over on to his back and started moving her slippery hands over his chest, arms and legs. When she finished she turned to Dayu and began massaging her soft, tight flesh.

The hot sun made them thirsty. Adrian opened his eyes and saw another Balinese lady standing over him with an ice-bucket resting on her hand. "Deee-rink, deeee-rink," she was saying.

"Terima kasih," he smiled.

She dropped to her knees and placed the big ice-bucket on the sand. "Coca cola, Seven-Up, Bintang. Coca cola, Seven-Up, Bintang," she sang.

"Two Seven-Ups, please," said Adrian.

The lady pulled them out of the fast melting ice and opened them. Then she put a straw in each bottle and handed one to Adrian and the other to Dayu. Without moving from the prone position Adrian reached out for his wallet and handed her a thousand rupiah note.

"Terima kasih," she laughed as she placed the now lighter ice bucket back on her head and went off in search of some more business.

"This is the life," said Adrian. "It's pure paradise." He leant over and kissed Dayu and then fell asleep in the sun.

Dayu too was asleep when Thierry and Nicole arrived on the beach. They had spent all the morning and part of the afternoon waiting at the telephone exchange to place a call to Paris to ask for some more money to be sent out. Altogether they were there for six hours. "If we'd been on the moon we would have got through quicker," complained Thierry. "At least up there they have satellites." By the time they stepped on to the sand they were exhausted, sweating and not in the best of moods.

"I am sure that a swim will transform us," said Nicole as they looked around for Adrian and Dayu.

"There they are over there," said Thierry. "I think they are asleep. Let's go and leave our clothes there and have a swim. Then we can jump on them with our cold, wet bodies and give them a fright."

"*Quelle bonne idée*," said Nicole.

They crept up to where the others were lying fast asleep and put their towels down on the sand. Then Thierry noticed the two empty lemonade bottles so he picked them up and took them down to the sea.

"I have a better idea," he laughed. "We shall fill the bottles up with the sea and pour them on to the sleeping beauties. But first, let us have a swim. I am so hot." They ran into the small breakers and soon forgot the frustrations of the morning.

"Now, let's fill the bottles," said Nicole as they walked up to where they had left them on the wet sand.

"No, not here," said Thierry. "The shallow water will be too warm. I shall take them out deep to where the water is cold." Nicole lay in about two inches of warm sea and kicked her legs until he returned.

"One each. On to their faces," he laughed as he handed her one of the bottles. They crept up as if they were about to stalk a deer. "*Un, deux, trois*," whispered Thierry.

Dayu had been dreaming that she was lying on the beach — right on the edge of *pasih* — with a four legged monster in the shape of Rangda standing over her. It was a black, hairy beast with four prickly legs. Dayu could feel two of the legs pushing into her shoulders and the other two into her ankles. The creature was holding her in a vice like grip. Its giraffe like neck was horribly contorted and stretched right down to only a few inches above her face. "What if she wants to spit on me," she thought in terror.

Then it happened. She screamed as the cold liquid started pouring down on to her face. Then she heard what she thought was Rangda's evil laugh. When she opened her eyes she saw a laughing Thierry being tackled around the legs by Adrian who was also laughing. Then she saw Nicole holding an empty lemonade bottle. She too was laughing. With a great effort Dayu managed a small, polite smile and then sat up to get her bearings.

Soon they were all laughing and joking and drinking some more lemonade. A small boy came up to them to hawk some faded postcards. Nicole took one look at them and said that, no thank-you, she wasn't interested in paying good money for surplus postcards left over from the 1950s. Further along the beach some children were flying kites. Others were searching for shellfish in the low tide. In the distance coming from the Kuta end they could see a big brown horse being ridden by two people. Sometimes it cantered; sometimes it walked. Sometimes on the sand; sometimes in the shallow sea. When it got closer Nicole recognised its two riders as Lord Chelmsbury and one of the American girls who were at Pascal's party.

"Oh look," she cried, "it's that English lord and the American girl with the loud voice." They all waved. Lord Chelmsbury slowed the horse down and directed it up to where they were all sitting.

"Greetings," he called out. "We've hired this nag for a couple of hours and it's quite the strangest and most undisciplined horse I've ever ridden. Seems to have a mind of its own."

"Oh, it's great fun," said Louise. "You never know where it's going to take you. We've been in the sea, up in the mangroves; we walked over a family of five who were lying on their towels and we even got caught in a fishing net."

By now several Balinese had surrounded the horse and were patting it. A lady selling slices of pineapple was feeding it with the remains of her stock. Lord Chelmsbury and Louise jumped down and Dayu offered them some lemonade.

"What have you been doing since the party?" asked Nicole.

"We've been up to Ubud in the mountains," replied Louise, "but we got back before the eruption, thank God. You should have seen all the paintings and carvings up there! It seems that everyone in the place is a born artist or carver. Only the men, mind you. The women do all the physical work."

"Yes, they seem to keep the home fires burning," put in his lordship.

"Well, I couldn't stand it myself," said Louise. "Thank God it's not like that in the States."

"You mean you don't have any artists in America?" asked Thierry in surprise.

"No, I don't mean that. I mean women having to stay in the house and do all the menial chores while the man do all the nice tasks."

"I must say they're absolutely bursting with creative energy up there," said Lord Chelmsbury. "Reminds me of what Florence must have been like at the height of the Renaissance. Or England in the time of Shakespeare. They all work on the verandahs of their houses. They can carve birds out of stones, elephants out of teak — anything! We visited one *puri* — a type of palace — and there were these beautiful paintings that had been done on long drapes that hung from the ceiling. All the scenes were from Balinese mythology and I must say the artwork was quite exquisite."

They heard a motor bike pull up behind them. They all looked around and saw Pablo's handsome face smiling at them. "Hello," he said. "I want to say good-bye to you all before I leave. I am going to-morrow to Singapore. Just for a day and then to London."

"How long will you be in London?" asked Chelmsbury.

"One week. I have a girlfriend there. She is a photographer. And very beautiful." His eyes lit up.

"Oh, what a pity! I won't be back before you leave. Otherwise I would have taken you to lunch at my club."

"Don't worry. I'm sure to catch up with you again some time. I'm always travelling. I have asked Pascal to come and stay on our ranch in Colombia but he says it is too far and too dangerous." Nicole thought that she detected a slight look of sadness on his young face.

They sat and watched the sun drop behind the long line of cloud on the horizon. It seemed to get suddenly brighter just before it disappeared completely. There was then a feeling of anti-climax as people began to pack up, get dressed and leave the beach.

"Guess we'd better get going," said Lord Chelmsbury. "I have to return this nag at six o'clock and we want to ride a bit further along the beach before we turn around. What's the time now?"

Pablo looked at the gold Rolex on his right wrist. "Five twenty," he said. "I shall ride along with you for a little while. Just slowly. I will keep a safe distance from your horse so as not to upset it. When it runs I shall speed up and when it walks I shall slow down."

"Okay, let's go," said his lordship as he helped Louise up on to the bare back of the nag. They waved to the others as they set off. The horse ambled diagonally down to the sea and then up towards the black trunked casuarinas at the top of the sand. Eventually its exasperated riders got it to trot along the beach just a few yards down from the casuarinas. Pablo roared up on his motor bike and then slowed down to the pace of the horse. He was riding inside it and only a few feet down from the tree covered sandhills.

Pablo was looking to his left and calling out to the two riders. He didn't see the mangy grey dog with white spots until it was too late. It darted out of the trees and straight between the two wheels of his speeding bike. The beast miraculously survived a million to one chances and came out the other side alive. But the stunned driver was so shaken that he lost control of his machine which lurched wildly at the horse which was only a few feet away. Pablo ejected on to the sand where, still in a state of shock, he landed on his bottom with a jerk. He stood up, got his bearings and was thankful that he wasn't hurt.

The bike had cut into the horse's front right leg and the pain went straight to its nervous system. It jerked forward, swerved to the side, ran round in a frenzy, threw its riders into the air and then fell down in great agony.

Louise grazed her arm when she hit the fine sand but, apart from that and the ensuing shock, was still in one piece. Not so Lord Chelmsbury. He was hurled in a different direction and landed on his legs. They were both broken. The right ankle and the left femur bone. The latter was a compound fracture. "Oh hell! No more dancing for a while," he thought to himself.

Pablo rushed over to him. So did Louise. And Thierry and Nicole and Adrian and Dayu who had watched in horror the unfortunate chain of events — the dog, the bike and the horse. A large group of people began to gather and the horse was letting out the most fearful sounds as it lay in great pain on the sand. One of the Balinese ladies pulled a sarong out of her bundle and tied a bandage to stop the blood that was oozing out of the peer's left leg. Adrian noted cynically that the blood was red and not blue.

"You must get me to the hospital," screamed the injured man. The pain was excrutiating — especially if he moved.

"No," said Thierry. "You must not go to the hospital. You would not come out alive."

"Why? Is it run by terrorists?" cried Lord Chelmsbury.

"No, but dirty needles, botched anaesthetics, sewer rats, bed bugs and a complete lack of hygiene are just as deadly."

"Well, I can't stay in this pain much longer."

"Thierry is right," said Adrian. "You are likely to come out of the hospital in a worse state than when you go in. It would be good if we could get you to Singapore. Or Darwin."

"Listen," said Pablo, "it is partly my fault and I want to help. I lost control of the bike and that is what caused the horse to go crazy."

"No," said Lord Chelmsbury. "It was not your fault at all. I saw the whole thing. It was that bloody hound that came running out of the trees."

"Well, I think I can help you," said Pablo. "I am due to leave Bali to-morrow and I have a Lear jet coming to pick me up at the airport at ten in the morning. It is staying in Singapore to-night. I could ring up the pilot and ask him to come over right away and we could be in Singapore in a few hours' time."

"It'll take you longer than that to make the 'phone call," said Thierry in a cynical tone. "They'll probably have to send the message on the *kulkul* drum."

"Then I shall give the operator fifty dollars to speed things up." Pablo walked over to his bike but it wouldn't start; petrol was pouring out of the tank and there was sand in the carburettor. A Balinese man on a motor bike offered to drive him to the telephone exchange and the others looked round for a vehicle to carry the wounded man to Adrian's cottage which was not far away.

"We must get him off the beach and into a bed or something," said Louise. Dayu nodded her head in agreement. She knew that the dog which caused the accident must be possessed of enormous powers of evil. To be able to destroy a motor bike and a horse and break two legs all at the same time — only the spirits could do that! The dog was obviously inhabited by a demon and Dayu just wanted to get off the beach as quickly as possible in case it returned and caused more damage. Perhaps to her. Or to Adrian. More likely to all of them.

They hailed a jeep that was being driven along the sand by a couple of Australian surfers and they all helped to lift the injured peer into the back seat. Then the driver slowly and gently made his way to Adrian's cottage where they laid out Lord Chelmsbury on a bed until they heard back from Pablo.

Lord Chelmsbury had been staying at a hotel over at Sanur and it was too far to take him when he was in such pain. So Louise said that she would go across and collect his things if they could arrange the 'plane.

A few minutes later Pablo returned with the news that he had roused the pilot at the Sundowner Hotel in Singapore and he was already on his way to the airport. "He expects to be here about nine o'clock. Then it will be a quick refuel and straight back. The reception desk at the Sundowner will make a booking at the Singapore hospital and an ambulance will meet the 'plane on the tarmac."

"Gosh, that's frightfully kind of you," said Lord Chelmsbury who was starting to get used to the pain that racked both his legs.

"It is no trouble. It was going to come to-morrow for me anyway. Now I must go to my hotel and collect my things so that we can leave from here together and get to the airport well before nine o'clock." Adrian loaned him his motor bike and he roared off in the darkness.

Nicole and Dayu were fussing over the patient and attending to his every need. Nicole sat by his head and stroked his forehead which was sweating heavily. Dayu gave him some beer to drink and apologised for it being warm. She knew how Adrian always insisted that it be cold.

"No need to apologise," he said. "I never drink it cold at home. I'm used to it." He took a few sips and perked up a little. "Bloody horses," he said. "They've been the curse of our family since time immemorial. The whole problem is that we've got one on our coat-of-arms — in the upper dexter corner — and it's caused us nothing but trouble. My father broke his back when he was thrown from a horse on his way to hounds, my grandfather lost all our Scottish estates by gambling on the bloody things and his father was killed in the cavalry charge at Omdurman. We must get that horse off our coat-of-arms."

"And with what will you replace it?" asked Adrian.

"I don't know but it won't be a dog." He was still in great pain and wondered how on earth he would stand the 'plane trip with all the bumps and vibrations.

Nicole and Thierry were whispering over in the corner. Then Nicole winked across at Adrian and he joined them. They spoke for a few moments in low voices. "Well, I don't know but I'll ask her," said Adrian. He walked over to Dayu and asked her to go out to the verandah with him. Then they walked out to the trees and he put his arms round her and whispered in her ear.

"To-day?" she said. Then she thought for a moment. "It is the special day of three gods to-day?"

"Which ones?"

She told him.

"I thought it might be," he said. He then whispered what he wanted to do. Her first reaction was one of horror. "But he's in great pain," pleaded Adrian. "It's the only thing we can lay our hands on to dull the pain."

Dayu thought for a moment as she looked up at the sky. It was very dark and there was hardly any moonlight. She was starting to regard Lord Chelmsbury as a nuisance. He ob-

381

viously had an evil spirit inside his legs. Maybe two evil spirits: one for each leg. And, by coming into the cottage he had brought the spirit with him. It might never leave and who knows what harm it might cause? She had always kept the front door closed at night to stop the devils getting in and now this wretched man with the broken legs had brought a particularly bad one right into the bedroom. And to top things off Adrian had just made one of the most outrageous requests that she had ever heard.

Then she thought back to the restrictions of Klian's household and the boring village life. And how keen she was to come to Legian with Adrian and mix with all the Europeans — like Nicole and Thierry. Her new friends were exciting; they were crazy and life with them was never dull. She liked them all — except the man-chasing contessa who never spoke to her. Dayu knew that she was much happier now than she had been up in the mountains and there was no way that she ever wanted to go back to her previous life. If she kept carping and living according to her traditional beliefs then might not Adrian tire of her and find someone else who didn't give so much trouble? She knew that she must make an effort to please him. But it was not easy. Her Balinese ways pulled her in one direction while Adrian and his apparently faultless logic pointed in the other.

She was frightened of accidents and illnesses — especially Lord Chelmsbury's grossly deformed leg with the bone sticking out. Ugh! What sort of a man would have a leg like that? It was probably a punishment from the gods. For doing something dreadful to the American girl, perhaps. After all, she wasn't hurt, was she?

She turned to Adrian and said, "Very well, I shall walk with you to the temple but you must do it and not me. I don't want to upset that god; he's a funny one and you never know what he might do. And you mustn't take it all. That would make him angry."

"Be back in ten minutes," Adrian called through the door to the others.

"Is operation about to begin?" asked Thierry.

"Yes, but keep security lid on plans until operation complete," replied Adrian.

"What the hell's going on?" screamed the patient. "Are they going to operate on me here? Before I get to Singapore?"

"No, no," said Nicole. "It is just a little joke. We want to get you to Singapore without too much pain."

"I tell you, I'm not looking forward to that wretched journey. The slightest movement and I feel the pain terribly. I don't know how one can keep perfectly still on a moving 'plane for three hours."

Adrian and Dayu crept through the temple gate. Past the two god figures that were carved out of stone on each side of the entrance. Like divine sentries. Dayu was sure that she saw one of them move when she went past. The temple was deserted; there were no ceremonies to-night. There were sticks of incense still burning on the shrines and one or two small kerosene lamps. And the sweet scent of all the flowers that lay at the foot of the shrines.

Dayu led him through the darkness to where the offerings were still burning to the opium god. "But only if there are many offerings," she whispered as they walked across the courtyard. "If there is only one you must not take it. That god is different to the others. He sometimes does strange things. And if he is deprived of his opium who knows what crazy things he might do! Not just to us but to the whole village."

"All right, all right," said Adrian. "I promise that if there's only one lot of opium I'll leave it for your crazy friend but if there's more than one I want some for Lord Chelmsbury to relieve the pain while he's in the aeroplane." He pulled out a small pen torch as they approached the rows of offerings on the steps of the shrine. "Besides," he thought

to himself, "if I don't take it some other thief or addict will."
He was surprised to find not one offering but eight. But there
were only seven tiny balls of opium; one had already been
taken.

"Look," he whispered to Dayu, "there's plenty for the
god and I'm sure he won't mind us taking some for a good
cause. Anyway we're probably doing him a favour. If he took
all this at once he might overdose and die." Dayu didn't say
anything. She wasn't so sure that the god would be as willing
to share his goodies as Adrian suggested.

"Besides, he has already used one ball so by now he
must be asleep and he won't see us taking them," said Adrian.
"So everything will be all right."

"Gods see everything," she said in a shaking voice. She
backed into the shadows as Adrian swiped three of the
remaining seven balls of sticky black opium. He dutifully left
the remaining four for the apparently insatiable god-addict.
Then they walked briskly out of the temple, along the road
and back to the cottage.

When they stepped inside the house it was more like a
party than a sick man's room. The stereo was on softly and
people were sitting around and drinking beer and laughing.
Pablo had returned with his bag and had changed into a pair
of finely creased light grey trousers, an expensive Armani
shirt and a pair of Gresson shoes. Louise had arrived back
with the patient's gear and was busy packing it. The two
Australians who had driven Lord Chelmsbury to the cottage
had now returned to see if they could be of any further help
and had brought a couple of dozen cans of San Miguel and a
bottle of arak. Thierry and Nicole were with the patient who
was now looking very white indeed.

"Did you get it?" asked Nicole.

"Oh yes," said Adrian. "Someone else had already
whipped one, I took three and I imagine that by now the other
four have gone as well."

He went into the bedroom where Lord Chelmsbury was lying on the big double bed. Pablo followed them. They drew the rattan curtain to keep out the noise and the others.

"We've brought you something to relieve the pain," said Adrian as he fumbled in his suitcase for the exotic looking pipe that he had bought at the market.

"Oh, what a good one," exclaimed Pablo when he saw it. "Where did you get it?"

"At the market. When it was raining I spent a whole afternoon there so I had time to find all sorts of interesting things."

"I will do it for you but I need a long sewing needle," said Pablo as he started to take the cellophane wrapping off the dark, gum-like substance. He put it on the end of the needle and held it over a spirit lamp. Under the heat of the flame it soon turned pale and started to bubble. Then he placed it in the bowl and put the stem of the pipe to the patient's lips. Dayu had already turned his lordship's head and placed another pillow under it.

"Now, draw it deep into your lungs," said Pablo.

Lord Chelmsbury did as he was told. Soon he could feel the pain lessening. It was a nice feeling. He inhaled seven times and began to feel sleepy. When the pipe was finished Pablo lit another ball and gave it to the dozy patient. This time he managed to get nine puffs. The injured man was drifting into another world — a world of brilliant colours and soothing shapes, of weightlessness, of ease and relaxation, and of great clarity. All the pain and problems of his leg receded into a misty background. He was now the centre of his own universe and nothing else mattered.

"We shall keep the last ball until just before we leave for the 'plane," said Pablo. "Then it should last until he reaches the hospital in Singapore."

They pulled back the curtain and Louise came in and joined them. "Oh, what a shattering afternoon it's been," she said. "By now we should have been having a nice seafood meal at the White Gardenia. And then we were going to go on to the disco. He just loves parties and dancing, you know."

"Why don't you come to Singapore too?" suggested Pablo. "I mean, I'm no good with sick people. They need the soft touch of a woman. I am all right at administering pain killers but I am not good at — how do you say it in English? — compassion."

Louise thought about it. She was not due to leave Bali for another five days and would have liked to put a bit more colour into her suntan before returning to Hollywood. Then she thought of the accident and felt considerable sympathy for Lord Chelmsbury whom she called "Buster." They had had some good times together on the island and she had grown very fond of him.

"You can stay at the Sundowner with me," said Pablo, "and we'll see how he is to-morrow."

"Oh, all right then. Can we stop at my bungalow to collect my things? It's on the way to the airport."

"No problem," said Pablo. The two Australians offered to drive them to the airport at half past eight. They packed some cushions in the back seat to make it more comfortable for the patient who was now half asleep and could feel very little pain at all.

"You should leave before half past eight," said Nicole, "because you'll have to drive slowly to avoid all the holes in the road. Any sudden jerk is likely to damage the leg further and cause much pain."

"Okay then, we'll leave at eight fifteen."

"In that case I'd better give him his third lot of pain killer," said Pablo as he stuck the needle into the last of the opium and held it over the flame.

When they put the pipe to the patient's lips he pushed it away. "No more," he mumbled. "I'm already in Heaven."

"Well, it would be a crime to waste it," said Pablo as he

386

put his lips to the ivory mouthpiece and inhaled deeply. Then he passed it to Thierry. And then to Adrian. They managed three puffs each and soon began to feel its soothing and seductive effects.

They carried Lord Chelmsbury out to the jeep and lay him carefully across the back seat. Louise sat next to him. Pablo climbed in the front with the two Australians and the bags were scattered over the floor. "Here, mate, have some more beer," said the driver as he handed each passenger another can of San Miguel.

"What a rotten way to finish his holiday," said Adrian as he watched them drive off in the darkness. "And such a freak accident. It could have happened to anyone. I'm glad that we were able to do something to stop the pain." Dayu was sitting at the table on the verandah. She wasn't so sure. She had not been at all happy with the raid on the shrine. It was only Adrian's overwhelming persuasion and logic that had moved her.

"Yes," she thought, "but gods can be very strange. They are not like men and what is given to them in an offering should not be touched. Not even to help a sick man. Still, nothing can change things now. And anyway the god will probably be happy with what is left. Most people would be."

The seats in the jet were folded down to make a bed for Lord Chelmsbury. The flight was smooth and uneventful and they landed just after midnight Singapore time. The patient was put in an ambulance and driven straight to the Mount Elizabeth Hospital where he was operated on within an hour of arriving.

Pablo and Louise went to the Sundowner and checked in for three nights. "That is the longest I can stay," said Pablo. "I planned to be here for only one night. But I have come a night early and I can delay going to London for one more night. So that makes three altogether. By then I hope the doctors will let him travel so that he can come to London with me in the jet. It is far more comfortable than a crowded jumbo."

Louise rearranged her airline tickets at the local Pan Am office and booked to fly out the same day that Pablo was leaving. "I am sorry that I can't fly to London by way of Los Angeles," he laughed, "but it would make the journey too long."

They visited the hospital several times and the doctors eventually agreed to release him — in plaster — to enable him to go on the jet to England. "Jolly kind of you," he kept saying to Pablo.

When they arrived at Heathrow Pablo took Lord Chelmsbury to his ground floor apartment in South Eaton Place. His father, the Earl of Huntering, came round in his Rolls Royce to collect him. The old man felt greatly indebted to Pablo for looking after his son and heir and bringing him all the way back from the East in his own jet.

"And where are you from?" asked the earl.

"Colombia, sir."

"Yes, of course," thought the earl, "the capital of Ceylon. It's near Bali." He smiled at Pablo. "Well, young man, would you like me to take you to lunch at the House of Lords? It's the least I can do to thank you for all your trouble."

"Thank you, sir," said Pablo who felt that an invitation to the Upper House of Parliament was important enough for him to give up just one lunch date with his luscious girlfriend. He went and bought a dark pinstripe suit in Savile Row and duly met the earl at the Houses of Parliament.

"And what does your father do?" asked the earl.

"He's a judge," said Pablo. He didn't add that he was also the head of one of the biggest cocaine clans in Colombia.

"Ah," thought the earl, "they must be a fine family. Father a judge, private jet and such a polite, well-mannered lad."

He led Pablo out on to the terrace overlooking the Thames. "Down that river has flowed the history of England," said the earl with pride. To Pablo it all seemed so civilized compared with the turmoil of Colombia. "Ah, here comes the Foreign Secretary." He introduced Pablo to Lord Grantall, the most genial and popular member of the Cabinet. "He's over here from Ceylon," said the earl. "His father's a judge out there."

"I didn't know we had any of our judges left in Ceylon," exclaimed the Foreign Secretary. "I thought we lost it when we lost India. I must be wrong. Maybe it still belongs to us. I must look it up some time. So many places on the map to remember. My degree was in eighteenth century history. Things were much simpler then. Words like "Zambia" and "Tanzania" were the types of names that people gave to their garden gnomes."

"Can you come to dinner with me next week?" asked the earl. "I've got something to discuss with you. Frightfully important. It's about the Hunt Club Ball."

"No, I won't be here. I have to go to Warsaw and Moscow."

"Are you trying to find out who really butchered all the Polish officers at Katyn?" asked the earl.

"No, we've always known it was the Russians but we let everyone think that it was the Germans. It's Foreign Office policy to keep the people in the dark. Otherwise we wouldn't have been able to get away with half the things we've done over the years. No, the main purpose of my trip to Warsaw and Moscow is to bring back a whole lot of caviar for my annual Christmas party. Duty free. The Customs never search the Foreign Secretary.'

Lord Grantall made to leave. He smiled at Pablo. "Well, young man, I hope you enjoy your stay here and if there is anything I can ever do for you don't hesitate to contact me. A friend of the earl's is a friend of mine."

"Thank you, sir," said Pablo who was flying on to the Caribbean in three days' time to supervise the next 'plane load of cocaine that was going from Colombia to Miami. The score so far: Pablo — eight and a half million dollars, DEA — nil.

Chapter Thirteen

The Turtle

The dance floor at the Jolly Frog was crowded with a throng of sweating, gyrating bodies. Two 'plane loads of young Italians had arrived the day before and it seemed that they all decided to turn up at the disco *en masse*. Adrian and Thierry were sitting at a big table under a coconut tree talking with some German surfers about the respective merits of the seven different breaks at Uluwatu. Pascal walked up and kissed Dayu and Nicole on the cheek. Dayu noticed that, although his face was smiling, his eyes were sad. "Just like a Balinese," she thought as she reflected on how the people of her island have a smile for every mood and emotion — including sadness.

"Ah, Pascal, have you had a good day?" asked Nicole.

"Yes, a happy day in the sunshine. But when the sun dropped behind the horizon it took my happiness with it."

"What do you mean?" asked Adrian.

"Yesterday my travel agent sent his boy up to tell me that to-morrow is the day that I must fly to Paris. So to-day was my last day here. I enjoyed it but now I am sad because it will be many more months before I see another Bali sunset. But I have my law practice in Paris and it is important that I apply myself to it. I was away from my office for such a long time last year when I went to play rugby in South Africa. You people are so lucky because you do not have the commitments that I have and you can stay here for such a long time."

"No, no," said Thierry. "It is you who is the lucky one. You have a good position in society, a good income and you are one of the best rugby players in the world. Many people would like to change places with you — even though you do have to leave to-morrow."

"And on top of all that you are so nice and crazy," said Nicole.

"Yes," laughed Adrian, "you are the craziest lawyer I've ever met."

"Ah, but I am not crazy when I am in my office. I try to be serious but sometimes it is very difficult because I am a laughing man by nature. That is why I like Bali. So many people laughing and smiling. If you smile at someone in the street in a big city like Paris they will run off and fetch a gendarme. But here they are more interested in smiling and laughing than anything else. I shall miss it. If I get bored in my office I shall just think of Bali and of when I can come back here which will be in a few months. I have met so many good people here — *charmants et intéressants* — whom I would not have met if I had not come. Like you, Dayu, and you, Adrian."

"And what about me?" cried the contessa as she suddenly appeared out of the darkness of the path by the sea-wall.

"Ugh!" thought Dayu. "There she goes again! She would have to come from the direction of *kelod*. Just because Pascal makes a compliment to me that woman has to butt in and steal all the attention for herself."

"Oh you, *ma chérie*. You are totally unique and quite unforgettable," said Pascal.

The contessa threw both her arms around his neck and sobbed uncontrollably. "This place will never be the same without you," was all she could say.

Shortly after midnight Adrian bought some drinks and he and Dayu went over and sat on the sea-wall to sip them. It was a full moon and the tide was further in than usual. "There are too many people here and too much noise," he said. "Why don't we go for a walk along the beach and come back just before closing time?"

Dayu would have preferred to stay at the disco but she knew how pointless it was to argue with Adrian once he had set his mind on something. She was enjoying looking around the dance floor at all the stylish young Italian men in their designer shirts and their exotically dressed ladies who reminded her of painted dolls.

She looked out at the vast, forbidding sea. *Pasih*. She was thankful that there was a sea-wall between her and the dark beach. That meant the demons could not reach her. She looked along and could see that there was no gap in it for steps. "Good," she thought, "they can't get in." Then she remembered that there was a ramp from the beach up to the road at the side of the disco. And from there an open gateway where everyone was coming in and showing their tickets to the heavy-set, dopey looking guard. "Maybe the demons could get in through there," she thought. "But only if they had a ticket!" It was all getting very confusing. So she decided that, provided she stayed close to Adrian, she would probably be just as safe on the beach as in the disco. She therefore agreed to go for a short walk and then return for the last few dances.

They stepped off the ramp and on to the beach where a few motor bikes were screeching to a halt outside the "Frog". They walked along in silence. Soon the music faded and was replaced by the periodic crashing of the waves. They could see one or two small fires on the beach with groups of natives sitting around them. Then there was nothing. Just a swathe of empty sand with dark trees on one side and the sparkling ocean on the other.

In the distance they could see a dark shape that protruded down on to the beach further than the bush line.

As they got nearer they could see that it was a huge pile of dead trees. At least ten feet high. The night was becoming cooler and there was a gentle breeze blowing from behind them. They walked round to the far side of the pile and sat down on the sand. Out of the breeze. The only sound was the intermittent crashing of the sea.

"Think of it, Dayu, all those waves are being wasted. No one can ride them in the dark and they will never come again."

"No, but others will," she said.

"Yes, of course. But maybe to-morrow it will flatten out and there might not be any waves for a week. Then you realise how much these ones are being wasted. Maybe I should go surfing in the full moon some time. A midnight surf."

"No, don't do that," she said. "Something bad would happen and I would never see you again. The spirits are worse at night. If you dare them by surfing in the dark I'm sure they would get you. No one should go in the sea at night. During the day the spirits share their ocean with you but at night they like to have it to themselves. If you try to intrude into their world after dark they will be very angry and will do you great harm."

"You really believe that, don't you," he laughed.

"Of course. Many bad things have happened in the sea at night. That is why all the fishermen try to sail their *praus* back before sunset."

"Hmmmm!" he mused. They lay with their arms round each other. Above the rhythm of the waves they could hear a faint sighing sound. "Listen, what's that?" whispered Adrian. They lay still and listened. It was getting closer and clearer but was still not very loud. "What is it, Dayu? It sound like a man struggling with a heavy load."

"It's a green turtle," she said. "They live in the sea. It must be coming up the beach to lay its eggs."

"It sounds exhausted," he said.

"So would you be if you were carrying hundreds of eggs inside you," she laughed. "It nearly crushes their lungs. They much prefer the buoyancy of the sea."

"Where does she lay them?"

"She will drag herself up the beach to a dry spot that is well above the high water line."

They could still hear the panting in the intervals between the waves. Sometimes the sighs stopped for a moment while the labouring creature paused to fill her lungs with air. Eventually they became fainter and then stopped for good.

"Is she going away?" asked Adrian.

"No, I think that she has found her spot. She must be far enough up the beach."

By now they were both peering around the pile of branches to try to catch a glimpse of what was happening. In the moonlight they could see the dark mound of the massive five hundred pound creature. She appeared to be about three feet in diameter across the shell.

The turtle began digging a hole in the sand with her hind flippers. Adrian, aware that the poor old thing was about to give birth, was tempted to go down and help her burrow away the sand. "It is like asking a pregnant girl to build the maternity hospital just prior to going into labour," he thought. But he realised that he might frighten her which was the last thing that he wanted to do. So he just sat there with Dayu and stared with great interest at the amazing reproduction process that was taking place in front of them.

When the hole was big enough the turtle positioned herself over it and dropped the eggs — all one hundred and forty of them! As soon as she had finished she began covering them with sand. Then she carefully flattened out the surface so as to camouflage it. Satisfied with her work, she made off back towards the sea to join the male turtle that was waiting for her at the water's edge. This time she travelled faster; not only had she lightened her load but also the return journey was downhill.

The eggs that she had left in the sand had been conceived many thousands of miles away in the Bay of Bengal. But the beach where she had just laid them was well known to her. Indeed, she had come to the same beach in Bali to lay eggs at regular two yearly intervals for all of her fertile life. Like all of her species she had powers of memory and navigation that enabled her to swim through thousands of miles of ocean and yet always return to exactly the same beach to drop her eggs. After about seven weeks the baby turtles inside the eggs would break their soft shells with an egg tooth that is on the top of their upper jaws. They would then burrow their way out of the sand and scurry down the beach and into the sea.

Adrian couldn't take his eyes off the turtle as she clambered down the beach to join her mate. She was about half way there when two young men rushed out of the bushes with torches and began attacking both turtles with long, sharp knives. They were careful not to smash the shells; instead, they jabbed the knives into the flesh underneath the shell with rapid and vicious strokes. The poor old female came to a complete halt when they chopped off her flippers. A moment later she was dead. Then the male turtle collapsed on the sand.

Adrian could hardly believe what he was seeing. One minute he was the fascinated witness of the act of procreation by one of the sea world's most wonderful creatures. And now this terrible and brutal slaughter of a mother that had just given birth. His first instinct was to rush out and punch the attackers. But he thought better of it. After all, they had knives and if they were callous enough to kill a beautiful mother turtle they would think nothing of turning their knives on him. And he wondered how many more of the gang might be hiding in the trees. He could see Dayu's face in the moonlight. She did not look in the least bit surprised. In fact, it seemed that she had been half expecting it.

When they had finished off the two turtles the men went to the patch of sand where the eggs were buried. The mother had carefully replaced the sand over the eggs to protect them from predators like dogs and rats. But she hadn't taken account of humans.

The men shone their torches down and began scraping the sand away. One of them went up to the trees and returned with some cardboard trays. The two killers began placing the eggs carefully in the trays. They never spoke.

Adrian and Dayu remained hidden behind the big mountain of branches. Completely silent. Dayu was nervous. She knew that they should never have ventured on to the beach at night. She wished that she was back at the Jolly Frog looking at all the foreign princes and princesses prancing around the dance floor and strutting like peacocks.

When the two Balinese butchers had packed all the fragile eggs into the trays and had satisfied themselves that there were no more left in the sand, they turned their attention back to the two turtles. They tried to lift one of them but it was too heavy. So they sliced off the shell and began cutting away pieces of the flesh underneath. They loaded the big chunks of turtle meat into several sacks which they dragged up the beach to a vehicle. Adrian heard a door open and close. The whole exercise took nearly two hours as some of the meat was solid and tough and it took a long time to cut if off.

While one of them was putting a sack of flesh into the vehicle and the other was slashing at the male turtle down by the sea Adrian whispered in Dayu's ear: "What do they do with all the meat?"

"It is a favourite food here in Bali," she replied. "It is always served at marriage banquets. Also part of the turtle is used as the base of turtle soup but most of it is sent to Japan. That is where the shell goes and also the eggs. They use the eggs as aphrodisiacs. And the oil is used for making cosmetics and the skin is made into shoes. Japanese traders come here to buy them and they pay big money. Sometimes they organise the killing of the turtles."

"Yes, just like they kill the whales and the dolphins. Just like they kill the rain forests all over South East Asia for their wretched plywood factories. Just like they kill all the marine life with their bloody great driftnets. Just like they killed the prisoners-of-war," he spluttered. "I tell you, those bastards have no respect for any form of life — neither human nor animal." Dayu could feel him shaking with anger. It was the first and only time that she had ever seen him really upset.

"Shut up," she whispered. "The man is coming back."

They cautiously turned their heads and saw the light of the torch moving down the beach about forty yards away. The dawn was starting to break. The men filled one last sack and began dragging it up the beach. Just like the mother turtle had dragged herself up the sand only a couple of hours before. All that was left in the improving daylight were a couple of dark and emasculated carcases and a hole in the sand where the poachers had dug out the eggs.

Adrian and Dayu remained hidden. They watched the men disappear into the trees. Then they heard a couple of doors slam and an engine start. Adrian ran up the sand in a crouching position and threw himself into the bushes. He caught a glimpse of the back of the moving Daihatsu jeep and was able to see its number plate. He went back to where Dayu was sitting and started cursing and swearing about what they had seen.

They walked down to the hole where she had laid the eggs. There was a straight furrow running from there down to the tide. "Look! That's where the poor old girl dragged herself up," said Adrian. "She really needn't have bothered."

Dayu just shrugged her shoulders. "What else do you expect," she asked, "when we venture on the beach at night?"

Adrian, however, believed the opposite. "The poor turtles have probably lived happily in the sea for years. Then they come on to the beach for only a couple of hours to lay their eggs and they are attacked in the most brutal fashion by violent thugs who then sell them to the Japanese to use as aphrodisiacs! Really, Dayu, if I were a turtle I would feel far safer in the sea. Even with demons, *pasih* and all the rest. Come to think of it, I always feel safer myself when I am surfing a couple of hundred yards out from the beach. No one ever upsets me out there. I am free and independent. Far better then hanging about on land where all the bad things happen."

"What about the demons?"

"The only demons are the ones on land. The ones who kill turtles and pollute the environment, the drunken drivers, the racketeers, the child molesters, the terrorists and all the corrupt politicians who are milking the public. Those, my sweetheart, are the demons. Not your imagined and invisible spirits of the deep."

Two days later Adrian had to go to the police station to collect his local driver's licence. After it was stamped he asked to see the chief officer. He told him about the turtle massacre that he had witnessed and gave him the number plate of the jeep. The cop just shrugged his shoulders. He told Adrian that there was no law against taking turtles out of the sea and that he had bigger problems to worry about.

"But can't you do something about it?" pleaded Adrian. "Otherwise more and more turtles will be killed and they'll become an endangered species."

The cop didn't understand what "endangered species" meant and nor did he care. He had no interest in turtles although he had often enjoyed their meat at wedding feasts. He knew that the Japanese paid good money which provided the Balinese turtle hunters with an income that they would not otherwise receive. To him it made good sense and good business.

"One day there won't be any turtles left," muttered Adrian as he walked out the door. He couldn't understand the complete indifference of Asians to living creatures. The place was infested with street dogs and yet nobody had a dog as a pet. Then he thought of the contempt with which they regarded dogs. As reincarnations of people who had sinned in a previous life. "Maybe they think the same about turtles," he thought. "Especially since they live in the sea. *Pasih*."

Chapter Fourteen

The Finalist

When Hilton Smee arrived back in New York he developed the roll of film that he had shot of Danny Holland and Yvonne Férier on Turtle Beach. He chose a selection of the most saucy shots and had several copies taken. He sold them in advance to the American papers with an embargo until Wimbledon Finals week-end. Then he flew across to London and sold them for an even higher price to a London Sunday tabloid.

"This will be a six page spread," said the editor as he rubbed his hands with glee at the thought of the extra sales and profits that would result from such a scoop.

Smee and his wife stayed at the Hyde Park Hotel and bought some Centre Court tickets for the Men's Final from a street tout on the platform of Southfields Tube Station.

Danny and his girlfriend from America were staying at the Carlton Tower. He had finished with Yvonne after the Bali holiday and was truly happy to be back with Anthea, his high school sweetheart. He had decided to propose to her after the Final.

Danny won his early round matches and then had a five set tussle in the semi-finals against the relatively unknown Californian player, Jimmy Hargreaves, whom the press had dubbed "the dark horse of the tournament." Danny eventually won 7-5, 4-6, 2-6, 6-3, 15-13.

The last hurdle to getting his name on the most coveted

of trophies was Sven Magnusson, his Swedish opponent. The bookmakers were offering odds of six to four on for the Swede and only five to one against for Danny. But he was determined to prove them wrong. He knew he could win. That was why, on the afternoon before the Final, he handed Anthea £10,000 in notes and asked her to place them with William Hill at its kiosk inside the Wimbledon grounds. "Better that you do it than me," he said. "They won't recognise you so they won't change the odds." She paid over the money and received a betting slip in return with the quoted odds of five to one against.

On the night before the Final Danny and Anthea spent a quiet evening together in the hotel. They dined in the Rib Room and then watched television in their suite on the top floor. Just before midnight he rang the reception desk and told them of his schedule for the following day. "I shall sleep until eleven and then have breakfast in my room. Kippers, toast, fruit juice and coffee. For two, please. The Wimbledon courtesy car will be calling at twelve at the main entrance."

"Very well, sir. I'll inform the Head Porter and we'll send a bell-boy up at quarter to twelve to bring down your gear."

"Thank you. Oh, and no 'phone calls. None. I don't want to be bothered by the press. At the after match media conference I'll talk to them as much as they like."

"Understood, sir."

Danny woke about ten and picked up the newspapers that had been pushed under his door. Just the two that he had ordered: the Sunday Times and Sunday Telegraph. He always liked to read what Sir John Smyth and Lance Tingay had to say about the tournament and he usually agreed with their comments. Especially when they both said that the Final was wide open. "Too right it is," he laughed as he tried to visualise the beautiful silver cup sitting on the coffee table in the corner.

At 10.30 the 'phone rang. Anthea was still asleep. It was the hotel manager. "Good morning, Mr. Holland. There is a pack of newspaper reporters hanging round the lobby and they refuse to leave until they have a few words with you."

"Tell them that I have nothing to say until after the match."

The hotel manager knew that Danny was being picked up at midday and feared that there could be some unruly and violent scenes if the reporters and photographers tried to chase their prey for an interview.

"Sir, would you like me to contact Wimbledon and ask them to send your courtesy car to our service lane off Sloane Street? That way you wouldn't be seen from the front lobby."

"Yes, that's a good idea," replied Danny.

By now Anthea was awake. He turned to her and said, "There seems to be more press interest in the Final than in other years. Probably because this time it doesn't clash with the cricket Test."

At ten to twelve the manager knocked on the door and escorted Danny and Anthea down the service stairs to the narrow lane at the back of the hotel where a Rolls Royce was waiting — courtesy of the All England Lawn Tennis and Croquet Club. The manager had seen the scandalous photos that filled the first six pages of the morning's tabloid but he didn't mention them to his guest. He knew that it was none of his business and the poor boy would find out soon enough. Anthea climbed into the back of the big black car. Then Danny got in and put his arm around her shoulders. "I wonder if they'll be sitting that close on the return journey," the manager mused to himself.

The drive out to S.W.19 took forty-five minutes. As the big car swung off Church Road and into the crowded grounds of the All England Club the spectators pushed forward to get a closer view of its occupants. A few groupies squealed in ecstasy. Others who recognised him smiled and waved. A middle-aged man in a checked jacket and string tie held up a Stars and Stripes. And the band of the Royal Marines was playing "Raindrops".

Danny smiled back. He was feeling on top of the world. Sitting in a Rolls Royce with Anthea by his side, the centre of attention — indeed adulation — of the crowd and he was about to walk on to the most famous and hallowed turf in the world to win the Wimbledon Singles title. Not just the prize money but also £50,000 from the bookmaker. And, of course, the prestige and honour which would ensure him top seedings and top appearance money at all the tournaments in the world for the next twelve months. To say nothing of the commercial sponsorships.

When the car purred to a stop in front of the Players' Entrance they were confronted by a solid wall of reporters and photographers. Some of them had copies of the tabloid which they pulled out and pushed in front of Danny's eyes.

"Do you wish to make any comment on these photos?"

"Why do you come to Wimbledon with one girlfriend and yet go to Bali with another?"

"Is Miss Férier pregnant?"

"Does your fiancée know of your other relationships?"

"What sort of example do you think you're setting to all the youngsters in the schools and tennis clubs who look up to you as a hero?"

"In the light of all this scandal are you still going to play the Final?"

They were pushing copies of the paper in front of Anthea as well. She grabbed one and looked at the photos that had been taken on Turtle Beach. They were saucy, intimate and, to her who had always trusted Danny, absolutely outrageous and unacceptable.

The inch thick headline read: "The Secret and Sordid Life of Dan Holland." On the next page was the story. "Although Danny Holland, to-day's finalist, has been seen at

Wimbledon with his long time girlfriend — and some say secret fiancée — he has a penchant for disappearing to exotic locations for raunchy holidays with half-blood Tahitian girls of dubious reputation as these exclusive photos show. Danny Holland is not the nice, smiling, clean-cut American sportsman that he and his television evangelist father would have us believe."

Anthea was the first to crack. She rolled up the paper and smashed it across Danny's cheek. "You bastard!" she cried out before bursting into tears. She went to storm away but found that she was surrounded by a solid mass of cameramen. All snapping away. For them it was a double banger and the photos that they were now getting would fill the front page and several others to-morrow. It wasn't every day that they could do a follow-up on the lead story of the day before.

The helmeted bobbies began to clear a pathway through to the doors of the Players' Entrance. Danny went to put his arm round Anthea and told her to come inside with him and sort it all out. "No, I never want to see you again," she screamed. She fought her way through the crowd to find a taxi to take her back to the Carlton Tower. She packed her things and went straight to Heathrow. By the time she heard the result of the Final she had already been in the air for an hour on her way back to America and out of Danny Holland's life forever.

As he walked out on to the Centre Court Danny glanced at the inscription above the doorway. Kipling's immortal words:

"If you can meet with Triumph and Disaster,
And treat those two imposters just the same."

"We'll see," he said to himself.

He lost the Final 1-6, 2-6, 3-6. His play was lacklustre, he missed easy shots and double faulted on vital points. He just couldn't concentrate. The same tabloid that had published the pictures accused him of "throwing" the match and not giving the spectators their money's worth.

At the end of the match he shook hands with Sven and then walked to the presentation area where the Duke of Kent handed the Cup to the smiling and triumphant Swede. Then Danny had to walk up and receive his trophy for being runner-up. He didn't even smile as the Duke shook hands with him. "Don't worry, Danny," said the beautiful, blond Duchess of Kent, "the crowd was on your side. We all feel for you very deeply." He smiled for the first time. Then he went off to the changing room and returned to his hotel, skipping the customary after-Final press conference.

For this the tabloids berated him the next day. "Surly" and "a bad loser" were some of the descriptions while the one that published the photos wrote that the real reason why Danny skipped the press conference was that he had to rush back to his hotel room to jump into bed with some other "exotic naked floozy". The tabloid readers lapped it all up as they sat in their dingy council houses reading all about it. It was the hottest item since the previous week-end when the same paper had published pictures of a baby with three heads.

Danny spent the evening alone in his hotel room while all the other competitors were dancing the night away at the Wimbledon Ball. A small group of photographers and reporters were keeping a twenty-four hour vigil outside the Carlton Tower in the hope of getting some more shots of Danny to keep the story alive for a third day. They knew that his room was seventeen floors above the main entrance and, well, wouldn't it be a scoop if he decided to commit suicide and jump out the window? They could get a shot of him as he landed and so keep the council house tenants entertained for yet another day. Almost as good as the baby with three heads! But Danny didn't oblige them. He just sat in his room, watched television and pondered his situation. "It's just not worth it," he kept saying to himself.

He had always thought that to win Wimbledon would be the greatest thing in the world. But not at the cost of losing his fiancée and having his life shattered. He couldn't understand how the press could ignore his tennis and all the free coaching that he had given over the years and yet harp on a tiny private incident that took place on an island eight thousand miles away. Almost in another world. He began to think of that other world — the waves, the palm trees, the coral, the turtles, the smiling and obliging Balinese, the warmth, the colour, the easy-going night life and all the carefree and laid back people. He stretched out on the bed and closed his eyes. And dreamt of those magic days that he had spent in Bali.

He reached across for his diary and looked at his tournament schedule. He had already agreed to play in the next three: "But I can't," he thought. "Not if I play like I did to-day. My heart's no longer in it. What's the point if they can do this to you? I'm quitting."

The next morning his 'phone rang at nine o'clock. It was Reception. "I know that you don't want any calls, Mr. Holland, but the Chairman of the All England Club is on the line."

"Put him through."

"Good morning, Danny."

"Good morning, Air Chief Marshal."

"I just want you to know that at the Ball last night several members of the Committee and some of the players and even the Duchess of Kent asked me to tell you how upset they are at what has happened."

"Thank you but it's not your fault. As you know, I've always loved Wimbledon and I love coming to England."

"Yes. I know. Those blighters are a law unto themselves."

"Well, thank you very much. I appreciate your call."

He got out of bed, had breakfast in his room and then sat down to write three brief letters to the tournament managers saying that he would be unavailable owing to personal problems. Then he rang Singapore Airways and asked for a seat on their first flight east.

"Be at Heathrow in three hours' time, sir."

He rang Reception to say that he would be checking out. A few minutes later the 'phone rang again. It was the hotel manager.

"There is a problem, Mr. Holland. The press are stationed at every exit of the hotel — even the service door that we used yesterday."

"Well, how am I going to get out?"

"May I come up and have a word with you?"

"Certainly."

When Danny opened the door five minutes later he found that the manager was accompanied by a beautifully made up young woman who gave off a powerful and fragrant scent.

"Come in," said Danny.

"This is Miss Thompson. She runs the beauty shop on the ground floor. The photographers down there are quite frantic. They are likely to do anything and I am worried that some of the elderly guests might get injured in any rush. Therefore, I suggest that Miss Thompson make you up as a woman and that way we'll get you to the airport without injury."

Danny smiled to himself. He didn't resist. He was past caring. It was all so incredible. And besides, he would do anything to get out of his prison. Miss Thompson produced a wig, a dress, high heeled shoes and a handbag and began powdering his face.

"Well, I'll do it all except the handbag. No way am I carrying that," said Danny.

"That's what they all say," said the manager.

408

"What do you mean?"

"Oh, we often do this for rock stars and others who are under siege here. They don't mind any of the rig — not even the false breasts — but they all draw the line at the handbag. It's the only part of the kit that's never been used."

"I don't blame them," said Danny.

When he had been transformed by Miss Thompson he went down to the front entrance and climbed into a taxi for Heathrow. As he did so some of the cameramen snapped him.

"Who's that?" he heard one of them ask.

"Oh," replied another, "probably the tart who's spent the night with Danny Holland."

"Good, it's worked," thought Danny as the taxi drove out and turned right into Sloane Street and the Knightsbridge traffic. On the M4 he crouched down on the wide floor of the cab, changed back into his normal clothes and instructed the driver to return the disguise to the Carlton Tower.

The hotel manager knew the time of departure of the flight. He rang Heathrow to confirm that it had left on time. Then he announced to the reporters that Danny had left the hotel some time ago for an unknown destination.

"Which door did he use?" one of them screamed.

The manager decided to have some fun. "This one," he said. "And what is more, you got a photo of him." The cameramen looked stunned. "The one you called a tart did spent the night in Danny Holland's room." The reporters pulled out their notebooks and started scribbling. "It was Danny himself!"

The dishevelled looking pressmen did not like being beaten. Their job was to ridicule and destroy others, not to be made fools of themselves. But their's was the last laugh. The next day's tabloids splashed the photo of Danny in disguise across the front pages. The headlines read: "The truth at last — Finalist is Transvestite!"

The article went on to suggest that he could just as easily have played in the Women's Singles since he seemed unsure of his sexual identity. All sorts of dark and sinister bisexual activities were implied in the article and the council house tenants were unanimous in their verdict that Danny Holland, millionaire tennis player, was definitely the most dreadful and immoral person that they had ever read about. In every chapel and pub throughout England and Wales his name was mud. And not just in Britain; letters of condemnation were written to newspapers all over the world by vicars, women's libbers, old maids and others who considered sex on the beach to be a worse crime than murder. A bishop in Perth even advised Australians against visiting Bali because of the immoral types whom they were likely to meet there. And in a particularly unchristian act his evangelist father, fearful of losing the financial contributions of his followers, publicly disowned him on his weekly television show.

On the 'plane to the East Danny found himself sitting next to a man of about thirty with black curly hair, a beard, stained jeans and a red floppy jersey with a Campaign for Nuclear Disarmament badge on one side and a Greenpeace — Save The Whales on the other. He looked distinctly out of place in the First Class Section. But he was not a tabloid reader and so did not recognise his fellow passenger.

Danny pulled out the Jeffrey Archer paperback that he had hurriedly bought at the Heathrow bookstall and began reading in an attempt to take his mind off the events of the past twenty-four hours.

When the meal was served the man with the beard embarked upon some conversation. In his thick Yorkshire accent he told Danny that he was a trained geologist who was being sent out by his company to explore for copper in the jungle of Bougainville Island off New Guinea. Danny wondered how he reconciled the anti-nuclear badge and the saving of the sea mammals with his job of ripping out the

410

virgin jungle in someone else's country in pursuit of profit. "No doubt everyone has their price," he mused. The geologist struck Danny as being a know-all.

"And where are you going?" he asked Danny.

"To Bali. In Indonesia."

"I wouldn't go there on principle," said the bearded one. "I don't agree with their form of government. It's a dictatorship, you know. I read in the Guardian that there is press censorship in Indonesia. That's what is so good about Britain. We have a free press and anyone is free to print whatever they like."

"Yes, I know," said Danny as he put his head back into his Jeffrey Archer.

He stopped over for a day and a night in Singapore and then flew on to Bali. Before boarding his aircraft at Singapore Airport he stopped at the newspaper shop to buy a Straits Times and an International Herald Tribune. As he scanned the international rack for the Herald Tribune his eyes caught sight of the London tabloid headlines and photos which alleged that he was a transvestite. He stared in disbelief at the article and stood there shaking his head. "I can't even get away from it out here," he thought. He just shrugged his shoulders and walked away. "Hell, I guess the masses have to be provided with some sort of entertainment. After all, they no longer have public hangings and ... it's not the football season."

■

There were some glassy blue barrels rolling into Legian Beach. Decent, clean five footers. Several surfers were out there and Adrian was second to last in the line-up at the Legian end. He was riding well-shaped left handers in his usual easy, fast, fluid style. Dayu was sitting on the beach watching him. So were several others including a rather jet-lagged and emotionally drained young man with fair hair, blue eyes and about four days' stubble on his face.

It was Danny Holland's second day in Bali and he was only just starting to unwind after all the trauma that surrounded his Wimbledon Final. He sat on the sand and watched the surfers — their style, their speed, their movements. He could see that the surfer who was second from the end had more skill and daring than the others and he watched him for about half an hour. He tried to guess which waves Adrian would go for and which direction he would follow. Danny was way out at first but by the end he was getting it right almost a hundred per cent of the time. He had spent the last few years trying to anticipate which way his opponent would hit the ball. "Surfing is not all that different from tennis," he thought. "That guy out there is playing the wave. And every wave is different just like every shot on the court is different. You never know where or how you are going to have to meet it. It seems you have to be waiting in the right position to catch the wave just as you have to be in the right spot to hit the ball back over the net. That's what sport is all about. Skill, speed, timing, anticipation and the right mental state to win. And not to crack under pressure. That was my mistake in the Final. But hell, I wonder if that guy out there could still keep his balance and drive his board if he had to contend with all that newspaper crap. I think not! Maybe I'll take up surfing. It might help take my mind off what's happened. And the skills don't look all that different. Balance. Movement. Even backhand and forehand."

He buried his wallet in the sand under his towel and ran in for a swim. The sea was warm and he body-surfed for nearly an hour. When he came out he was completely refreshed.

Adrian had come in when the waves started to close out. He was sitting on the sand with Dayu watching the orange sunset cast its fiery glow across the sparkling ocean. There were some Balinese families washing and bathing and laughing at the water's edge and all the usual massage ladies, food sellers, pi dogs and deeply tanned sunbathers. They watched a fair haired young man in black Hom swimming trunks come out of the sea, flick the water out of his hair and walk up to his towel which was only a few yards from where they were sitting. Dayu nudged Adrian.

"What is it?" he asked.

"That man! Wasn't he at Pascal's party? The one with that dark French girl?"

Adrian looked across. It was hard to tell since Danny had four days' growth of beard on his face.

"I wouldn't think so," said Adrian. "He was going to play Wimbledon and then there are heaps of tournaments in America. I distinctly remember him saying that there was only a week or two a year that he could have off."

"Well, I'm sure it's him. Wait! I'll pretend to walk down to the water and when I come back I'll go right past him and have a look."

Adrian watched her walk down the sand. Ever so gracefully. "She looks so terrific on the beach," he thought. "It's just a shame that she's so frightened of the sea."

Danny was watching her too. He didn't recognised her from the party because to him all the Balinese girls were alike. But he couldn't help but notice her statuesque figure as she stood by the water's edge in just the bottom half of her pink bikini, her pert little breasts — the colour of *café noir* — glistening in the orange glow of the setting sun. He watched her walk up the beach towards him and then turn away to where Adrian was lying. Their eyes had met.

"Yes, it's him," she said to Adrian. "But he's grown all that ugly hair on his face. I don't like it."

They looked across and saw a lady selling sarongs sidle up to Danny and stand in front of him. She was on her way home but decided to make one last and lucky attempt at a sale. Up went her hands to her head. She grabbed the big bundle of brightly coloured clothing and lowered it to the ground. She then started her sing song chant as she laid her goods out on the sand. Danny had nothing else to do and was pleased to make some purchases. "Saves me sweating my way round the markets," he thought. He chose a couple of sarongs and two pairs of beach shorts. The lady looked pleased.

"How long have you been in Bali?" she asked.

"This time? Only two days."

"Ah," she thought, "he won't know the proper price so I'll start very high." She looked pensive. Then she smiled. "Thirty thousand rupiah for the lot," she said.

Danny did a quick mental conversion. "Hell," he thought, "that's even dearer than if I bought them in the States." He looked across to where Adrian and Dayu were sitting and called out, "Excuse me. Do you know how much I should pay for these?"

"How much is she asking?"

"Thirty thousand."

They stood up and walked over to the place of sale. Dayu gave the cheating woman a cold stare and told her in Balinese that she should be ashamed of herself and would come back in the next life as a pi dog.

"Twenty-five thousand," the woman cried out.

Adrian winked at Danny and said, "If it was me and I was buying them all at once — as you are — I would pay ten thousand. Twelve at the most."

The woman heard the figure and looked crestfallen. "No, no," she said. "Fifteen thousand."

Adrian laughed and said, "Ten thousand." They eventually settled on twelve thousand and the lady walked away in mock annoyance, having made a clear profit of six thousand rupiah.

"Gee, thanks," said Danny. "I haven't had much experience of bargaining but I knew that her opening bid was a bit over the top."

"Hey, I think we've met before," said Adrian. "At Pascal's party."

"Of course," said Danny. "I remember you now. Both of you. That was such a super show. Is Pascal still here?"

"No, he's gone back to his office in Paris. I thought you were going back too. To Wimbledon."

"Yes, I've been."

"How did you do? I haven't read a paper for weeks."

"I lost in the Final. To Sven Magnusson."

"Oh well, there's always next year," said Adrian confidently.

"No, I won't be playing next year or any other year. I've given up tennis forever."

"Why?"

"Well, it's rather a long story." Danny looked him in the eye and then related all the terrible things that happened to him on the day of the Final and the later allegation of transvestism. "That's why I've come back here. To get away from it all and try to think things out in an atmosphere of sanity and simplicity. Away from all the ridiculous pressures that other people seem so eager to create. I'm growing a beard so that I won't be recognised. I don't mind telling you because I know that you're a top sportsman yourself. I was watching you surf out there. I really like your style. I'm sure you have some understanding of the pressures that top sportsmen can be under."

"Yes, but you don't need to worry out here. Everyone's pretty laid back in Bali."

"That's what I thought last time and look what happened! Some rotten sneak with a camera!"

"Well, do you really think that you have to grow a beard? Isn't that going a bit far? It's so hot here and anyway Dayu doesn't like it. She told me."

Dayu looked embarrassed but then she laughed. So did

Danny. "Why, what's wrong with it?" he asked.

"Better for men to have hair on their head and not on their face," she said. "Like Adrian. It's much more handsome. Balinese men don't have hair all over their face."

"It's true," laughed Adrian. "I've seen a few Balinese men with small, neat moustaches but not one with a beard."

"Well, I don't like it either," said Danny. "And I guess 'when in Rome' and all that. I'll shave it off to-morrow."

"Ah," thought Dayu, "that's much better. He'll look handsome again. And clean."

By now it was almost completely dark and the palm trees were throwing their long, sinister shadows across the sand.

"What are you doing to-night, Danny? Do you want to eat with us?" asked Adrian.

"Yeah, well I don't know anyone here. So if you don't mind that would be great."

They agreed to meet at the White Gardenia at eight. Adrian and Dayu walked back to their cottage and Danny made his way up through the sandhills and trees to the small cottage that he had taken for a month. It was in a Balinese family's compound and, at only three dollars a night, was a world away from the suite at the Bali Beach Hotel where he had stayed on his previous visit with Yvonne. But it gave him the privacy and anonymity that for the moment meant more to him than anything else.

When they met at the restaurant they ordered *gado gado* and some cans of Bintang. Dayu was pleased to see that Danny had taken her advice and shaved off his facial growth. "Much better," she said. "No Balinese girl would go out with a man with hair on his face. Ugh!"

"I don't think it would be a good idea for me to be seen with a Balinese girl," said Danny. "It would just be playing into their hands. I mean, if they were to come in here right now and see us having dinner, one of them would push

Dayu's face across to mine while another would take the photo. Then they would dream up some outrageous sexual crime and pin it on me. And they would publish it world wide and millions of people would read it. And believe it!"

Dayu thought he was joking. Surely no spirit could have those sorts of powers. She whispered to Adrian, "Would they really come in and push me into Danny's face and let all the people in England and America see it?"

"Yes," he replied, "if they knew that Danny was here." She just shrugged. She knew that she would never understand the ways of the West.

"But," said Adrian, "anyone who reads that sort of crap and believes it is not worth worrying about. I mean, their own lives must be so boring and narrow. I'm into living life and getting the most out of it — especially on the waves — and I couldn't give a damn what other people do with their time or their private lives. I'm just not interested."

"Nor me," said Danny. "I've always been too preoccupied with the task in hand — winning tournaments — to worry about the petty things of life. But it appears that we're in the minority."

"It's because we're achievers and they're not," said Adrian. "People who write and read that kind of garbage are just plain jealous. They're jealous of a good looking millionaire tennis player who can enjoy himself with a luscious lady on a warm tropical beach while they have to slave away in their dirty factories and dumb offices to grapple with the mortgage payments and their boring, ugly wives. They can't play championship tennis themselves so they spend their lives knocking those who can."

"Yes, but what I can not understand is how they got the photos. There was nobody else on the beach. Except a middle aged couple down the far end. And they were sunbathing in the raw too."

"Well, do you think it was them?"

"I don't know. We spoke to them and they seemed friendly enough. And I don't recall seeing any cameras. In fact, I distinctly remember him saying that he wished he'd brought a camera to take a shot of the turtles that we could see on the rock."

"Well then, it must be the gods," smiled Adrian. "The island is full of them, you know. And apparently they see everything."

"Yes, but surely they don't carry cameras. And besides, gods are meant to be good. Whoever set out to cause all this trouble must be really evil. Demons in fact."

Adrian turned to Dayu. "Which demon would have planned and carried out all this mischief?" he asked.

"There is only one that could have done so much damage. The most powerful of all — Siva, the god of destruction."

"Well I'd sure as hell like to meet him and smash his face in," said Danny.

"No, you mustn't do that," said Dayu. "You must make offerings to him to stop him from doing you even more harm."

"I don't see how he can hurt me any further. I've already lost my fiancée, lost the Final, lost £10,000 which I put on myself with a bookmaker and, because I can't bring myself to play any more, I've lost my career and income as well. Furthermore, my father has publicly disowned me and cut me out of his will. All that I've got left is a condominium at Palm Beach, a Porsche in the garage and a few investments. Unless he steals those off me as well I don't see how your Mr. Siva can do me much more harm. And I'm not in the habit of making offerings to my enemies."

"Then you will come back as a pi dog," said Dayu.

"Oh, this is crazy," said Danny. "I haven't even done anything wrong. If I'd robbed a bank I wouldn't be held up to such odium. All I did was allowed myself to be seduced in the

418

warm sun by a beautiful girl. Hell, I'd be abnormal if I didn't. What am I meant to do? Just because I happen to be a good tennis player am I supposed to live like a monk just to keep a whole lot of dumb readers happy? It's ridiculous! And I don't believe in all this hocus pocus reincarnation stuff that I'll come back as a dog if I don't make offerings to the spirits. The whole thing is crazy!"

"Of course it is," said Adrian. "But it's no less crazy if you try and explain it by our standards."

"What do you mean?"

"Well, if it wasn't one of the all seeing Balinese spirits that took the photos then it must have been a man. Or a woman. And it wouldn't be a Balinese since their concept of morality is not yet depraved enough to destroy and virtually blackmail a man for making love to a beautiful girl. And fortunately their so-called primitive civilisation does not yet extend to the dubious benefits of a tabloid press. So it must have been a Westerner. Either the two people to whom you spoke on the beach or someone else whom you didn't see."

"But there was no one else on the beach! And that man was complaining that he didn't have a camera."

"People tells lies. Especially for money. And the more money at stake the greater the incentive to lie. That's how most people get ahead in the world."

"Well, I'm sick of all these lies. Especially in the press. I reckon the government should make a law against publishing all these pictures and lies."

"Yes," said Adrian, "but they won't. They're too busy clobbering some poor guy for smoking a joint or squeezing the last sixpence of taxation out of a widow. They are too gutless to pick a fight with the press. Instead they reward the owners and editors with knighthoods and peerages."

"But," said Dayu, "if it was the man on the beach who caused all the trouble then he will suffer some very bad karma himself."

"Nonsense," said Danny. "I don't believe in karma. It doesn't work. Not for me anyway. I've always tried to do the right thing by everyone. I've sacrificed big money tournaments to play Davis Cup for America. For two weeks every year I give up playing and instead I coach black kids in New York. Free. I even pay for the hire of the courts. It costs me more than $100,000 in lost appearance fees and prize money. But I've never minded. I've always been polite to tournament officials and I've never lost my temper or sworn on the court like most players do. And what do I get in return? More abuse and more lies written about me than all the other players put together. That's why I don't believe in karma. And if it was that rotter on the beach then he is probably right now spending it up big and large while my career lies in ruins. He will have benefitted from his ill-gotten gains and I have lost. So, where is the karma? Or, in Western parlance, the justice of the situation?"

"Well, you're right; there is no justice in it at all," said Adrian, "but karma is a more complex thing and sometimes works in mysterious ways. For all you know the person who took the photos might now be worse off than you in some way or another."

"It's hardly possible. I don't see anyone else being accused of transvestism on the front pages of the world's newspapers."

"I agree that it's unlikely. But one thing I've learned since I've been on this island is that they don't seem to have any rational or logical explanation for anything. You really have to stretch your imagination and bend your mind. You should hear some of the reasons that they give for things! I tell you, Bali would be a nightmare for a scientist or a logician. But for a creative artist like me it's got everything — colour, mystery, beauty, warmth, contrast, sensitivity. And waves! But they don't think like us at all. It's always been that way and it always will be. You know:

420

*'East is East and West is West
And never the twain shall meet.' "*

"Yeah, I know Kipling," said Danny.

"Yes, and Kipling knew the East," replied Adrian. He sat back in his chair. "And I'm glad it's so different because therein lies its charm and appeal. Its strangeness. Its mystery. And you shouldn't discount the power of karma just because you can not at this moment see how it is working."

"Adrian is right," said Dayu. "Karma always works. But we don't always know."

"Well," said Danny, "it sure hurts to think that some son-of-a-bitch got paid a lot of money for taking those photos and now he's having a good time on it."

Smee had indeed been spending money by the bucketful. Before he left for London he bought himself some new suits at Saks Fifth Avenue and a set of oil paintings of tropical fish for the walls of his study. And Alice bought her wretched diamond at Tiffany's. While in London they received the New York papers and read that a prospective Presidential candidate was going yachting in the Bahamas for a couple of days. The Smees flew to Nassau direct from London in the hope of getting a compromising shot of the poor fellow with his arm round some good time girl. They chartered a small motor boat and tailed the yacht for two days but to no avail. On the third day Smee took his boat out to one of the reefs off Nassau and did some diving. Unfortunately he stepped on a spiky sea egg and his foot began to bleed. Quite a bit. So he called off the expedition and returned to New York.

Unbeknown to Smee the spores of the sea egg had penetrated through the wound and infected his body with tetanus. Soon the poison was flowing through the blood stream to his muscles and central nervous system. His jaw locked rigid, he could no longer swallow and his normally serious face developed a sardonic smile which made him look

421

ridiculous. The next day his cranial nerves became paralysed, he had a brain haemorrhage and died. Karma.

When Alice went to the local shopping centre to buy some food and drink for the funeral she was in a real flap. So as not to lose it, she wrapped her new diamond necklace inside a handkerchief and put it in her pocket. It was unseasonably cold in the car park and she felt a sneeze coming on. Without thinking, she pulled out her handkerchief to stifle it. She did not see the tiny necklace drop on the ground and roll into a muddy drain. Karma.

■

Adrian took Danny with him to Uluwatu. Danny winced when they passed the turn-off to Turtle Beach. From a distance the sea at Uluwatu looked so blue and calm. But when they parked the bikes they could hear the waves thundering into the cave.

While Adrian pushed his board into all sorts of extraordinary positions and generally revelled in the five foot surf Danny sat on a rock at the top of the cliff and watched. Below was a sheer drop of a hundred feet to where the waves were crashing against the rocky cliff face. As he sat there in the warm sun he began to feel more relaxed. He followed every wave and every ride and soon began to imagine that he was down there himself. "And I will be before long," he vowed. "First thing I'm going to do when I get back to Kuta is buy a surfboard."

Adrian was enjoying the fast hollow lefts of Inside Corner directly beneath where Danny was sitting. His last ride brought him right into the cave. He climbed the old bamboo ladder and one of the Balinese boys followed with his board.

Danny and Adrian sat at a table under the cool, shady thatch of the *warung* and drank some ice cold orange juice.

"Next time I'll come surfing with you," said Danny. "I'm going to buy a board as soon as we get back. Will you come with me to help me choose it?"

"Certainly, but you'd better not start surfing here. It's too wild. Ulu's not for beginners. Try the beach break at Legian. Once you've got the hang of that you can come out to the Reef with Thierry and me. The rides are so long out there because the coral underneath the sea holds the wave together and it keeps its shape until it has passed over the reef. Thierry will help you too. He was a beginner only a few weeks ago. Now he can do all sorts of manoeuvres but he still hasn't been inside a tube. That's his next goal. In fact it's his only goal."

When they got back to Legian and walked through the door of Adrian's cottage a strong smell assailed their nostrils. "What's that?" asked Danny.

"Beats me. Dayu! What's that horrible smell?"

"Not a horrible smell," she replied. "It's a durian."

"A what?"

"This," she said as she held up a large round fruit almost as big as a coconut. It had a hard shell and sharp, prickly thorns. She cut it open and scooped out its pulp and seeds. They all tasted it. "You like it?" she asked.

"No," said Danny politely.

"Yuk," said Adrian less politely.

"But durian is very special fruit in Bali," she said. "Most Balinese have it as a treat."

"Well, that's one of the island's pleasures that I can do without," said Adrian.

Dayu ate the rest of it herself. "But I don't understand you," she said. "It's truly delicious!"

They attacked a couple of paw paws instead. "Hell, I've only been here three days," said Danny, "and already I've eaten more fruit than I normally do in a week."

"It's good for you," said Adrian. "It is far more healthy to eat fruit here than in the West."

"Why is that?"

"Because here they don't poison all their fruit and vegetables with pesticides like they do in the so-called advanced countries of the West. If consumers could see the pure poison that the growers in the West spray regularly on their crops I swear they wouldn't eat them. But it's not like that in Bali. All this fruit is clean."

"And delicious," said Danny as he munched on a fresh pineapple.

After sunset Adrian and Danny went up to the surfboard shop at Kuta. Leaning against the walls were all kinds of boards — nine foot malibus, bonzas, twin fins and short single fins. All had been well used and showed the obvious scars of dings from the coral which had been repaired with various degrees of skill. Danny remarked that they were all second hand ones. "I want to buy a new one. It's like buying a tennis racquet. I wouldn't get a second hand one."

"We only have used boards," said the man who was in charge of the shop.

"That's right," said Adrian. "It's not a rich country and they don't import them. All these boards would have been sold to them by surfers. Sometimes the guys run out of money and have to hock off their boards but usually they just can't be bothered taking them back on the 'plane. Either they have too much baggage or they are going on to other non-surfing places and it's too much hassle to carry them around. Some of these boards would have been traded half a dozen times."

"Wait," said the man. "I have one that was brought in this morning by an American. It looks new. No dings. He said he'd used it only a couple of times." He removed some boards from the wall and pulled out a very new looking six and a half footer. It was white with some bold red and purple artwork on it. Adrian looked it up and down and felt it and told Danny that it was as good as he could hope to find.

"There's not a single ding in it and it's a good one for a beginner," he said.

"I'll tell you what," said the man. "You may pay for it and take it and if you don't like it you may bring it back and take another."

"Thanks," said Danny. "How much?" It was the equivalent of sixty dollars.

"You've got a bargain and I'm sure you'll like it," said Adrian as they walked out of the shop.

The next morning Adrian and Thierry took him out into the waves at Legian. He began by lying on the board but, under their expert guidance, he was soon standing up and riding the waves straight into the beach. "Incredible" he called out to Adrian who rode in alongside him. Danny was a natural and Adrian could see that, with his tennis player's understanding of balance and timing, it wouldn't be long before he would be doing bottom turns, re-entries, loops and all the other manoeuvres in the advanced surfer's armoury. But, most important of all, Danny was enjoying it. It was a whole new experience for him to stand up on a flimsy piece of fibreglass and walk all over the water like a god. As soon as they returned to the beach he wanted to go back into the surf.

"Oh, let's have something to eat first," said Adrian. "And a massage to loosen up all the muscles that you have been pushing out there in the water. Then you'll feel better and be more ready to get back into it."

Danny spent so many hours in the waves that by the evening he was exhausted. Surfing provided him with just the distraction he needed and in the warm and soothing atmosphere of Bali the nightmare of Wimbledon receded steadily into the distance. He surfed with Adrian and Thierry at Airport Reef and loved travelling in and out in the small outriggers, jumping into the warm Indian Ocean and paddling out to the reef. Some of his best moments were spent riding the long, beautifully formed surf that rolled over the reef. And they all rode the more tricky waves at Uluwatu. At least when it was under six feet. If it was anything bigger than that only Adrian would venture out and the others would watch from the cliff top. Or swim at the small, sheltered beach around the side of the cave. Or sip cool drinks in the shade of the thatched *warung*. Or engage in friendly banter with the smiling Balinese. Or lie on one of the benches and be massaged by gentle, skilful hands. And at night they all went to the Jolly Frog and danced to the funky music. As Dayu said to them one night, "You are always dancing. In the daytime you dance on your surfboards in the water and at night you dance at the disco."

■

Adrian and Dayu decided to have a late afternoon snack at the Ocean Wave. The tables were full and there were hardly any spare seats. They saw a couple of backgammon players get up from a table. There was one other patron sitting there — a lovely looking girl with long honey coloured hair who was reading a paperback.

"Mind if we sit down here?" asked Adrian.

"No, not at all," she replied with a smile. They ordered banana pancakes and ice cream and mango juice and then started talking to their table companion.

She introduced herself as "Belinda" and said that she had arrived from Perth the previous day and was spending a couple of weeks at the Kuta Beach Hotel.

"Oh that sounds nice," said Adrian.

"Your's sounds nice too," she said after Adrian told her about the cottage. "I've walked the whole length of the beach," she said, "and it's quite the craziest patch of sand I've ever seen. Everybody is doing something different — kicking footballs, building sandcastles, practising yoga, fishing, trading clothes and jewellery, throwing frisbees, flying kites, standing on their heads. You name it and I've seen it in the last couple of hours."

"Oh yes," said Adrian, "the beach is a world in itself."

"How do I get back?" asked Belinda. "I'd like to return by road and have a look at all the small shops. But I don't know how to get to the main road."

"Just go up that track over there and you'll find yourself on Rum Jungle Road and turn right at the end. Then you're on the main road back to Kuta."

"And can you recommend any places to go in the evening? I don't want to go to the Australian bar where they have the beer drinking contest."

"I don't blame you," said Adrian. "It's not really a place for nice girls to go. Only bushies. The best place to go at night is the Jolly Frog but not before about 11.30. It's dead before then. We shall be going about midnight. You're welcome to come with us."

"Midnight!" exclaimed Belinda. "But surely there's somewhere to go before that?"

"Yes, the Mango Tree. That's where everyone meets first. It's just a place to have some drinks and pass the time before dancing. It's about half way along the main road between here and Kuta. Have you got a motor bike?"

"No, not yet. But I'm going to rent one to-morrow."

"Don't worry. We'll come and call for you at the hotel." Then he remembered that the police were pulling people up for being three on a bike. "No, I'll get Danny to call for you instead. He's got his own bike and it'll be easier."

"Who's Danny?"

"One of my surfing buddies. He's up at Kuta at the moment trying to make an overseas call at the 'phone exchange. He'll probably be there all the afternoon. But he'll be able to call for you about nine o'clock."

"That's really kind. Are you sure it's no trouble?"

"No, he never has anything to do at that time of night.

He'll be only too pleased."

"What did you say his name was?"

"Danny."

"Danny who?"

Adrian hesitated. "Danny Holland."

"You mean the guy who played at Wimbledon?"

"Yes, but he doesn't like to be reminded of it. He's out here trying to relax and get away from it all."

"Poor fellow. I don't blame him," said Belinda as she thought of the photos that had been splashed across the front pages of the Australian papers a month earlier. And her mother's reaction — "Disgusting!" And the local bishop's sanctimonious call for Australians not to go to Bali to be corrupted by such low types. All of which made her more eager than ever to meet Mr. Danny Holland, tennis player and lover boy *par excellence*.

"I promise that I won't mention it," said Belinda. "At least not until I get to know him a bit better." Adrian smiled to himself. So did Dayu.

Danny rode along the sand to the Kuta Beach Hotel and parked his bike outside its pagoda like lobby. He expected Belinda to be waiting there but she wasn't. He inquired at the desk and they rang through to her room. "She is waiting for you in her room, sir." A smiling porter led Danny across an open courtyard to a cottage type bungalow. On the small verandah Danny could see a very slim girl, quite tall, and with long, fair hair that fell loosely to her shoulders. In the light of the overhead electric lamp he could see her clear, fresh complexion, blue eyes and an open expression that suggested warmth and friendliness. She was wearing a salmon pink cotton dress and a necklace of white puka shells that she had bought on her way back from Legian.

"Hi Danny," she said. "Would you like a drink before we set off?"

"Thanks. I'll just have a Bintang."

She turned to the porter. "Can you bring a couple of cans of Bintang and a vodka and orange for me?"

"Of course, madam," said the little man as he hurried away.

"What brings you to this place?" asked Danny. "It seems that just about everyone has a story to tell as to why they are here."

"Oh, nothing special. It's winter in Perth and I was bored stiff. Then it rained for a week and I thought, 'Hell it's only three hours' away so why not?' Besides, it's slow at the moment where I work and they were happy for me to take some leave before the summer when we're busier."

"What is your job?"

"I work in a florist's shop at Claremont. That's about three miles from the centre of Perth. I love working with flowers."

"And when is the busy season?"

"Oh, we have three: Christmas, Saint Valentine's Day and the Jewish New Year."

They talked on for nearly two hours. "Well," said Danny, "we'd better move on. It's too late to go to the Mango Tree so we'll ride along the beach to the disco."

"Is it as far as I walked to-day? Where I met Dayu and Adrian?"

"Further. But it's nice in the moonlight. There's hardly anyone else on the beach so you get a good feeling of space. And, of course, it's fun listening to the waves."

Adrian and Dayu got tired of waiting at the Mango Tree so they went on to the disco. "Oh look! There they are," cried Dayu as she and Adrian walked through the arched entrance to the accompaniment of David Bowie's clear and distinctive voice blaring out of the speakers.

Danny and Belinda were on the dance floor and looked as if they cared for no one but themselves. It was several numbers later before they walked off to get some drinks to cool down the insides of their hot, sweating bodies.

"Oh hi, Adrian and Dayu," said Danny when they finally met up. Belinda complimented Dayu on her dress and Adrian asked Danny about surfing plans for the next day. "Well, do you want me to call round for you or not?"

"Who knows?" replied Danny vaguely. "To-morrow's another day."

When Adrian did call round to the cottage at precisely 8 a.m. there was nobody there. The door was unlocked and he walked in. "Hey, Danny," he called.

Ketut, one of the sons of the family, appeared on the path outside. "Mister Danny not in. Not come home last night."

"Thanks, Ketut," said Adrian as he climbed on his bike and rode out to Uluwatu with Thierry.

Danny had in fact just woken up in the Kuta Beach Hotel with Belinda asleep beside him. He leant over and kissed her on the cheek. She woke up and they talked and giggled and played for a while and then went out on the verandah.

"I feel so good," said Danny. "And look at the weather. Not a cloud in the sky."

"And look how clear and blue the sky is," said Belinda. "It's probably still raining in Perth."

"You must forget about Perth while you're here," said Danny. "Just like I have to forget about Wimbledon. This is another world. A little paradise in the middle of a troubled sea. We must make the most of every minute we're here. We are the chosen few." She laughed and gave him a playful slap on the buttocks. "Anyway, what do you feel like doing to-day?" he asked. "Do you have anything planned?"

"Nothing. Except I want to hire a motor bike up in the main street."

"We can do that later. After dark. Let's spend the day in the sunshine. On the beach. You can get on the back of the bike and we'll ride right up to the end of the sand. Where it meets the rocks. But first I want to call back to my cottage."

"What for?"

"To have a shave." Belinda started laughing. "You see, Dayu says that the Balinese are disgusted by men who have hair on their face. And we wouldn't want to upset the natives, would we?"

They rode to the cottage and Belinda sat on the verandah while Danny went inside and stroked the Wilkinson blade down his face to destroy the overnight stubble. When he stepped back on the verandah there were four members of the Balinese family sitting on the ground talking to Belinda. They were saying "Bee-lin-dah" as they tried to pronounce her name. But it didn't sound right so they called her "Missus Danny" instead.

They rode up the main road towards Seminyak and then turned down the Jolly Frog road to get to the beach. As they passed the disco they could see several boys sweeping the floor and stacking the empty bottles. "It looks different in the daytime," said Danny. "No crowds, no music, no motor bikes." The boys looked up from their brooms and waved as the bike roared past.

The tide was low; they found a strip of quite firm sand and rode along the water's edge. The scattered groups of swimmers and sunbathers soon passed and they had the whole beach to themselves. They crossed a fresh water stream where some Balinese women were washing their clothes. And that was the last sign of human life they saw until they reached the rocks. Sitting on the rocks were half a dozen motionless fishermen holding their lines. They didn't acknowledge the arrival of the motor bike by so much as a turn of the head. "Better not disturb them," said Danny. "Or the fish."

They did a wide turn and rode slowly back along the beach. It was the middle of the morning and frightfully hot.

Belinda put her mouth close to Danny's ear. "What is it?" he asked.

"I have to have a swim to cool off; otherwise I'll die."

He swung the bike to the left and rode up to the nipa palms at the top of the beach. Then they ran down the hot sand and plunged into the cool ocean. "This is just so good," enthused Belinda as they splashed around in the small surf. She climbed on to Danny's strong shoulders and dived into the waves as they broke.

When they ran back up the beach Danny pushed the bike into a clearing in the trees where they lay down on their towels and gave themselves up to the sun god. Their only company was a huge butterfly that was resting on a palm frond. Belinda remarked on how its bright red wings toned in with the red flowers of the nipa palms.

"Yes," said Danny, "but at least it doesn't have a camera to take photos of us for the tabloids."

"How do you know that it's not one of Dayu's *leyaks*?"

"Oh, shut up," he said as he leaned over and kissed her on the lips.

They spent the rest of the day swimming, sunbathing and laughing. It was about three o'clock when Belinda said that she was in dire need of a drink. "My throat is completely parched," she gasped.

"Mine too," said Danny as he stood up to go for another swim. He could hardly believe his eyes. There was a lone Balinese lady in a long sarong walking along the beach with a bucket on her head. "Oh, look!" he said to Belinda. "That poor woman must have walked for miles. I wonder if she's got any drinks."

As they ran down the sand the woman turned and walked towards them. "Deee-rink, deee-rink," she called out. They sat down and drank four bottles of orange juice between them and talked and laughed with the lady.

"How much?" asked Danny. The lady smiled and

modestly asked for a thousand rupiah. "No," he said, pretending to be annoyed. The lady looked troubled. Then he smiled. "You are like an oasis in the desert," he said. "We were nearly dying of thirst. Here's five thousand." The woman was beside herself with delight as she nodded "*terima kasih*" a dozen times and made off back along the beach.

After their swim they rode along to where all the beautiful bodies were stretched out on the sand in front of the Ocean Wave. They pulled up beside Adrian and Dayu who were busy trying to shake off a persistent young beach trader who was showing them a carved wooden elephant. "Very good ele-pan," he kept saying. But it was rubbish; the tusks didn't match, the end of the trunk was chipped off and one leg was much shorter than the others.

"It's no good," said Adrian. "It's broken."

"Yes, but not broken very much," pleaded the boy.

"No, I don't want an elephant," laughed Adrian. "Or an 'ele-pan'. All I want to know is whether Danny has given up surfing or not. Has the romance of the waves given way to some other kind of romance?"

"No, it's just that I decided to sleep in. We've had such a good day up the beach."

"Oh, it's been super," said Belinda.

"How was Ulu?" asked Danny.

"Good. Five feet. Thierry and I stayed in for three hours."

"I'll come with you to-morrow."

And he did. He managed to find enough time for both Belinda and the waves which was just as well because over the next fortnight there was a veritable feast of surf. Five to six feet at Airport Reef and six to eight feet at Uluwatu. The swell was consistent and the waves clean and glassy with plenty of power. It was all that any of them could ask for.

Danny and Belinda were totally smitten with each other and every day was better than the last. "We seem to be on a steadily rising curve of happiness," laughed Danny one night when they were all having dinner together.

"That's your karma starting to work for you," said Dayu.

Two days before her scheduled departure Belinda was sitting on the beach with Danny in the pre-dawn glow after a hectic night of dancing and partying. "I'd be crazy to leave this beautiful place — and you!" she said. "I've never felt so good. I think I'll stay another week."

Later that morning the two of them rode across to Sanur. To the Qantas office in the lobby of the Bali Beach Hotel.

"I want to change my return flight to a week later," said Belinda.

"No problem," said the genial Javanese clerk who promptly reissued the ticket for the later date.

"Now all I have to do is ring home and tell my folks that I won't be coming back on Saturday as planned. I'll wait an hour or so and by then my father will be home for lunch. I'd rather tell him than my mother as I'm sure he would understand."

"Will you tell them why you're not going back for another week? And whom you've met?"

"I'll see. Probably. May as well be open and truthful at the start. After all, you're not an ogre."

"There are millions in the world who would disagree with you." They both laughed. Now that a reasonable period of time had passed Danny was beginning to see the funny side of it. Especially now that he could laugh at it all with Belinda who made a point of twisting it round to suit themselves. She would say things like, "Now just pretend that you're back on Turtle Beach. And there are no cameras this time." It certainly put the whole thing in a different — and better — perspective. But when Belinda suggested that they stop on the terrace by the pool at the Bali Beach and have a drink Danny backed off.

"No way! Some rotter might recognise me and take a photo and then it would start all over again." Instead they drove out of the shrubbed lawns of the hotel and into the native part of Sanur. They stopped for a glass of pineapple juice at a *warung* which consisted of an old canvas canopy that was held up by some rough hewn branches. But it was clean, friendly and cheap. And Danny felt safer and more relaxed than if he had been part of the international goldfish bowl at the Bali Beach Hotel.

Belinda looked at her watch. "Hey, we'd better get back to Kuta. I want to place that call from my room and it'll be lunch time in Perth by now."

They rode back with the hot sun blazing down on their backs. When they reached the hotel Belinda ordered some beer and fresh fruit to be brought to her room. Then she lay back on the bed and dialled the operator. "I wish to ring Perth please. 9 - 386-4571."

"There is a delay of two hours on all international calls. We shall call you back when we get through."

"Damn," she said.

"What's up? No one home?" asked Danny. ·

"No, no. We have to wait two hours."

They lay together on the bed while they waited for the operator with the tiny voice to ring back. Which she did. Three hours later.

"Hello. Is that you Mummy? How are things? Is Daddy there? No? Oh well, I just want you to know that I won't be coming back for another week. Same flight and time of arrival but a week later. Why? ... Well, I'm having such a good time and I need another week to sort myself out ... Well, yes. You could put it that way ... He's really lovely and I'm sure you'll like him. No, he's not Australian. Oh, don't be silly. Of course he's white. Well, not really." She looked across at Danny's naked body lying on the bed. "He's brown in fact. Rather tanned from the sun. Yes. American."

"What's his name?" asked her mother.

"Well ... "

"Surely you must know his name."

"Yes, of course. Danny ... Danny who? Oh, Danny Holland ... Yes, the tennis player." There was a scream from the other end of the line. "No, Mummy, he's *not* a transvestite. You don't want to believe all the lies that you read in the papers." There was a click. The 'phone went dead. Mrs Connie Broughton had fainted and fallen to the floor.

When she came round she immediately dialled her husband's office. He was in a board meeting and had left a message with his secretary that he was not to be disturbed under any circumstances. "Get him," ordered his distraught wife in a voice that sounded as if it was about to utter its last gasp.

The secretary tapped on the boardroom door and caught the hapless husband's eye. "What is it?" he asked.

"Telephone," she mouthed.

"Excuse me," he said to the others as he walked out to the reception area.

When he heard his wife's voice at the other end of the line he knew that something terrible had happened. "You must fly up to Bali right now — to-night — to bring your daughter home."

"Why? Has she hurt herself?"

"No, it's worse than that; she's fallen for a transvestite." She then started sobbing into the telephone.

Her husband could get no further sense out of her so he put his head through the boardroom door and said, "Gentlemen, I am sorry but I must leave you. My wife has suffered a bad turn and I have to go home immediately."

He went below to the staff car park, started his grey Rolls Royce and drove out to his fine Georgian mansion in Dalkeith which overlooked the beautiful Swan River.

Philip Broughton was one of Western Australia's leading mining magnates. A millionaire many times over he had started life as the son of a brewery worker on the other side of the river at Fremantle. He left school in the year that Germany invaded Poland and went straight into the Army. And the sands of North Africa. He had been besieged at Tobruk, had a Military Cross pinned on his jacket by Monty and even operated a small cigarette black market among the soldiers for which he was court-martialled.

After the War he had gone prospecting in the outback of Western Australia — sometimes in areas where no white man had been before — and he discovered a large copper mine. Having obtained the proper licences he then persuaded three friends to put up the money to enable him to develop it. That was in 1952. Now they were all multi-millionaires and they owned other mines all over the state — copper, gold, zinc, lead and iron ore. In short, Philip Broughton had seen all sides of life and was curious to know what had prompted his wife's outburst on the telephone.

He didn't have to wait long. As soon as he pulled up outside the front door his wife opened it to let him in. She had two glasses of brandy in her hand. "Quick, drink this. You'll need it," she said.

They went and sat down in the sunny conservatory and Philip asked her what it was all about. She uttered just two words: "Danny Holland."

"You mean the fellow who played in the Final at Wimbledon?"

"I mean the transvestite! The pornographic sex maniac who fornicates with native women in front of the cameras for all the world to see. That's who your daughter is living with up on that terrible island!"

"Well, I must say he's a damn fine tennis player. But on the day Magnusson was just too good for him."

"Is that all you can say? I'll never understand you men! You're all the same. Sport, sport, sport! Nothing else matters.

Well, have you booked your flight up to Bali and two tickets back or are you just going to sit back and let her be molested by that monster?"

"I have no intention of going to Bali. I've got important appointments all the week and anyway she's old enough to know her own mind and make her own decisions. I'm sure that he's a very nice fellow. If she's our daughter then she wouldn't have chosen anyone second rate. Of that I'm certain. And I shall reserve my opinion until I meet the man. As I always do."

"But what about the stories?" She burst into tears again.

"Very likely newspaper fabrications." Philip Broughton knew the ways of the press and their ability to create news rather than report it. He had often read untrue speculation and rumours about his own company in the financial pages of the paper and he had enough experience of the world to know the importance of making one's own judgement rather than listening to other people's stories. "Hell," he thought, "if I'd listened to what everyone else said back in '52 I would never have started that mine."

He also had a healthy respect for strong, red blooded men and he knew that, whatever else Danny might be, he certainly wasn't a wimp. Wimps don't reach the Wimbledon Final. He himself liked the occasional bit on the side. That was why he had that fictitious interest in that fictitious mine up at Kalgoorlie — three hundred and fifty miles inland from Perth. Many Perth businessmen had a phantom Kalgoorlie branch or a phantom Kalgoorlie mine. Some doctors even had phantom Kalgoorlie practices. That's what Kalgoorlie was all about. Its streets of bordellos had survived from the raucous gold rush days of last century and provided an ongoing service for Perth businessmen who tired of their wives and needed to do a little bit of business out of town. At their Kalgoorlie branch. Or mine. It was usually overnight business and a return flight to Perth the next day. And Philip

Broughton was no different from the others. And so it wasn't hard for him to give Danny at least the benefit of the doubt.

"So you're not going to do anything?" pleaded his wife.

"No, not at this stage."

"Well don't come crying to me if to-morrow's papers splash nude photos of your daughter across the front pages. With that brute doing all sorts of terrible things to her. Oh, our little Belinda!" She resumed her sobbing. A few minutes later she dried her eyes and poured herself another drink. "And I don't know what the bishop will think. After all, he's the one who advised people not to go to Bali in case they met people like Danny Holland. We should have taken his advice and not let her go. Of course, he won't let them get married in the church."

"He will if I give him another ten thousand dollars for his bloody cathedral fund."

By the end of the week Connie Broughton had calmed down a little. Every time she mentioned the matter — which was every few minutes of the day — her husband merely repeated his statement, "We shall reserve our judgement until we meet him — like all sensible people would."

However, the outward calm was broken by a telegram which they received from Belinda on the day before she was due home. "Danny's decided to come with me. We'll see you at the Airport. Love Belinda."

"Well, he's not staying in this house!" screamed Connie.

"Why not?" asked her husband.

"Because I wouldn't feel safe. I mean, he might molest me. Or even you since he's a transvestite. And none of our friends must meet him. Just think of the gossip around Dalkeith! I couldn't stand it. And of course you won't be able to take him to your club for lunch."

"Why not?"

"Because it's a 'men only' club. And therefore, as a transvestite, he wouldn't be eligible. I distinctly remember

439

the newspaper saying that he would have been able to enter the Women's Singles. And it would blow all your chances of being President next year."

Philip had had enough. "I have to go and get some things from the garage," he said.

"Well, I'm going upstairs to check the lock on our bedroom door."

Philip sauntered out to the garage. It couldn't be seen from the house. Then he walked across to the gardener's cottage. Chipper, the gardener, was repairing the lawnmower. "Good morning, boss," he said cheerily.

"No, it's not," replied Philip. "Can you give me a Kalgoorlie call in about five minutes."

"Certainly boss."

Philip had never regretted installing a separate 'phone line in the gardener's cottage. Five minutes later Chipper put down the lawnmower and went inside to ring the main house.

Philip answered. "Yes," he said. "Oh, not again. Yes, I know how to fix it. I'll bring a mechanic up with me. Bloody nuisance." He put the receiver down and turned to his wife. "The suction machine has broken down again in the mine at Kalgoorlie. If we don't go and fix it to-night the air will become poisonous and we won't be able to work it for months."

"How long will it take?" she asked.

"We'll work all night and I'll fly back to-morrow about midday."

"Well make sure you do. The 'plane gets in at 6 p.m. and I don't want to be in the house on my own with Drag Queen Danny."

"We'll wait until we meet him," said her husband for the thousandth time.

Philip spent the night with Rosie whose vocation in life was to keep mining magnates happy when they came to Kalgoorlie. The good thing about miners was that they often gave a lovely bonus in the form of an opal or two from their mines.

Danny was exactly as Philip had expected — clean cut, well-dressed, personable and polite. Even Mrs. Broughton was surprised to see that he was wearing clothes as he walked through the Arrivals Gate. She more or less expected him to walk through naked. Or in a dress.

Day One was tense. Day Two was a little better. On Day Three the ice started to melt. And Day Four was the turning point. Philip plucked up enough courage to announce at breakfast that he was taking Danny to lunch at his club.

When the guest later appeared in his three piece Boss suit, Gucci shirt and grey and pink tie of the International Lawn Tennis Club even Connie had to admit that he wasn't such a bad chap after all. At least with his clothes on.

At the club Philip introduced him to the doyens of the Western Australian business world and they sat down to lunch with Commander Townley, the Governor's Private Secretary, and Sir Leadmine Ground who was reputed to have dug up more mining dirt than any other man in the world. As they were leaving Philip turned to the commander and said, "I'll see you to-night. What time is the reception?"

"Five-thirty for six o'clock. Oh, and do bring your charming guest. I'll square it with His Excellency. I know that he likes Americans. He used to be Flag Officer on the Royal Yacht and he often speaks warmly of the occasion when the President came on board to visit the Queen when they were tied alongside at Bermuda."

"What!" exclaimed a horrified Connie when she heard the news. "But the bishop will be there. Whatever will he think?"

"Stuff the bishop!" cried her husband. "He doesn't run the state — although I know he'd like to with all his narrow-minded ideas. Danny's been invited by the Governor — or at least by the Private Secretary — and that's that!"

"But what if the bishop hears about it and gets to the

Governor first? He might rescind the invitation. If he doesn't, then the bishop might go to the newspapers and make a scandal."

"I'm sure the Governor is sensible enough not to take any notice of that narrow-minded old windbag."

And so it proved. Danny was a great hit at Government House. Everyone wanted to meet him and those who did were bowled over by his charm and good looks. "Lucky Belinda!" they all said. The bishop kept his distance and told a number of the women that Satan also appeared very attractive when he offered the apple to Eve. This only whetted their female appetites all the more and everyone to whom the bishop spoke in these terms immediately made a beeline for Danny — to meet him and hopefully to touch him. "Lucky Belinda!" they kept saying.

"Just like Eve and the apple," the purple clad cleric muttered into his glass. However, he cheered up a bit when old Sir Leadline shuffled over and pushed a cheque for $10,000 into his pocket. "For the Cathedral Fund, your lordship."

After Danny's brilliant debut at Government House Connie came to realise that, far from saddling herself with a deviant, Belinda was lucky to have chosen a man who was charming, loving, good looking and, most important of all, rich. A condominium at Palm Beach and a Porsche were not to be sniffed at. "Belinda could hardly have done better for herself," she kept saying. Soon she was asking questions about marriage plans.

"Too soon yet," said Belinda. Connie's hints and pressure soon became so great that Danny decided to go back to Bali to think things over. And of course Belinda went with him.

Her mother's last words to her at the Airport were, "Now don't you let that young man slip through your fingers. Just keep him happy. There'll be lots of other girls with their

442

eyes on him."

◼

Back in Bali Belinda moved into Danny's cottage. "It's not as luxurious as the Kuta Beach Hotel but I like it better," she said as she unpacked her clothes.

When they went down the beach the next morning they saw Nicole and Dayu lying on the sand. "Where are the guys?" asked Danny.

"Surfing. Always surfing. We are surf widows," said Nicole.

"Well, you're the most spunky widows I've ever seen," laughed Danny.

"They are out on the reef. Airport Reef. We may see them before dark if we're lucky. Yesterday they were there from eight in the morning until 2 p.m. Today — who knows? They got up in the dark and it is now eleven o'clock."

They heard a roar of motor bikes coming along the beach. "Oh look! Here they come," said Nicole. "All they'll want to do is to eat."

"Hi Belinda! Good-day Danny!" called Adrian as he stopped his engine.

"Oh, we are so hungry," said Thierry. "Let us go and eat and then we can hear all about your trip to Australia. When did you get back?"

"Yesterday."

"Good trip?"

"Oh yeah," replied Danny. "Everyone was so kind to me. It was super. But it's even better to be back here. What have the waves been like?"

"So so," said Adrian. "There have been flat spells but we've also had some classic days when there have been some nice, healthy tubes. Like to-day. Guess what, Dayu, I got six hundred yard rides."

"You surfed for six hundred yards?" she exclaimed.

"No. Six rides of about a hundred yards each. It was pure magic. Until it closed out. That's why we've come back early."

"Oh," said Nicole in mock reproach. "I thought you'd come back to see us. Because you couldn't bear to be away from us any longer."

Adrian had heard this line before. Every surfer's girlfriend had made the same point at one time or another. He gave the standard answer. "But it means that the times we do spend together are that much more precious. Besides, I'd be grumpy and unhappy if I couldn't surf. And that would be no good for anyone."

"I know," sighed Dayu as she remembered the flat patch of the previous week when there was no surf for five days. Adrian got so down in the dumps that she began placing special offerings to the gods to ask them to stir up the ocean and create some surf. They made her wait but on the sixth day they sent in some beautifully formed six foot tubes. Adrian was happy again.

"Besides," said Thierry, "if I was with Nicole all day we would get on each other's nerves. It is better for me to surf because when I am out on my surfboard I can think of her and how beautiful she is and look forward to coming back to her."

"Me too," said Adrian. "I often think of Dayu when the lip of the wave comes over me and takes me into its womb."

Dayu considered what they said and came to the conclusion that they were right. "Yes," she said, "I think it is better that way. Adrian has to surf and I can't surf so we have to be apart some of the time. The gods have planned it that way. I know that he is very happy when he can surf and I would rather have him in a good mood for half the day than have him with me all day in a bad mood."

"Well spoken," yelled Adrian. "Now we must eat. I'm starving."

The girls picked up their towels, put on their sarongs

444

and followed the others up to the cafe-bar at the top of the beach.

They sat down and ordered almost everything on the menu. The girl who took their order had to use three pages of her note-pad to write it all down. They began to laugh and the girl laughed so much that she got all the orders mixed up but it didn't matter; Adrian and Thierry ate more than half the food and the others had the rest. Dayu began to think that they must have invisible spirits inside them with infinite stomachs.

Belinda and Danny told them all about their time in Perth and asked what had been happening during the two weeks that they had been away. After about half an hour Adrian looked out through the open front of the bar and saw that there was still a good breeze blowing off the sea. "If this offshore wind holds," he said, "then Padang Padang will be working to-morrow. Let's make an early morning of it."

"Agreed," said Danny.

"Me too," put in Thierry. The three girls just sighed.

■

They set out at seven the next morning for Padang Padang. When they pulled up on their motor bikes forty-five minutes later they could hear the mighty roar of the great left handers that were crashing over the shallow reef.

"I hope they're as good as they sound," said Adrian as he flicked the strap of his surfboard cover over his shoulder and made his way down the steep rocky steps to the sand. Apart from a row of naked fishermen standing in the sea the beach was deserted. And they could see only three surfers out on the distant wave.

"Well," said Adrian, "we're off to surf one of the greatest lefts in the world."

They paddled out through the deep barrels that were thundering over the reef. Padang Padang was a unique wave and it took Adrian a while to get the feel of it. But he did and soon lost himself inside its perfectly formed tubes.

Danny's surfing had improved enormously. His natural sense of balance and timing that had taken him to the top in tennis also helped him to master the waves. Already he was a better surfer than Thierry. He was more co-ordinated and he selected his waves more wisely. The Frenchman was wild in the water. He didn't always recognise his limitations and, with more courage than judgement, went for the big ones and invariably got wiped out and thrown all over the place.

"Thierry tries to walk before he can crawl," laughed Adrian.

"Yes, but I just love those big ones," he replied.

"Well, as long as you're enjoying them, that's the main thing."

"Ooh, but I am. And I know that it won't be long before I ride inside a tube. I shall beat you, Danny. I shall ride my first tube before you do." But Adrian had his doubts.

Danny tried to get inside the deep and powerful barrels but it was not easy. He kept getting wiped out in the swirling water. He had another go when he saw a long, shapely barrel rolling towards him. He was up on his board and riding down its face when suddenly he saw a great roof of water come over his head from behind and fall in front of him like a theatre curtain. And he was inside it. On the stage. Alone. "Hell," he thought, "this is more magical than walking on to the Centre Court." He stared up in childlike amazement at the hollow tunnel of water that totally surrounded him. It was beautiful, artistic, soothing but also frightening. It was like being in another dimension. He was completely cut off from the outside world. In his own universe. The only way back was if the wave let him through. "Maybe it'll keep me!" he thought. Crash! All his dreams came to an end as the hollow wave closed over him and threw him into its swirling whitewash.

He looked up and saw Adrian who was hooting and

waving his hands above his head. "Bravo, Danny!" And Thierry had just been wiped out again.

"Oh dear! I see that you have beaten me into a tube," he said to Danny. "But I shall do it very soon. Maybe to-day." But he didn't.

When they came in Danny was in a world of his own. He had just had the greatest experience of his life. Inside that amazing wave. It was like a revelation. He had felt safe and secure in there. And so free. Safe from all the insidious pressures of professional tennis, money making and the media. He had only the wave to worry about. No secret cameras. No press reporters. No bishops. Just the beauty and simplicity of the wave. It was the perfect world. But it had lasted for only a few seconds. A fleeting, evanescent, god-like instant. But he now knew what it was like. And it put all other things into a different perspective. Like the Wimbledon Final. Could he have got so much sheer, ecstatic pleasure from holding up the great silver cup in front of the crowds? He would never know. But of one thing he was sure: it couldn't possibly be a *better* feeling than being inside a tube. "The only sad part," he thought, "is that it came to an end. Like everything." But for Danny it was an awakening; he had been elevated into an almost spiritual dimension. And the worldly things seemed less important. Less relevant. He no longer cared so much what people thought about him. All that really mattered now was getting inside another tube. And Belinda.

"What's the matter, Danny? You're very quiet," said Adrian as the three of them walked up the beach with their boards under their arms. "If it was Thierry who had just ridden his first tube we would never hear the end of it. Nor would anyone in Legian."

"That's right," said Thierry. "When I finally manage to get inside one of those magic tunnels I shall throw a big party to tell everyone what I have done."

447

"Well, you'd better hurry up," retorted Adrian. "After all, we don't want to come in our wheel-chairs. We wouldn't be able to dance!" He ducked the handful of sand that Thierry threw at his face.

"You might laugh but I know that it won't be long now," said the Frenchman. "I nearly did it to-day but they were just a little bit too big."

They walked up to the rock where they'd left their towels. The fishermen were still standing waist deep in the sea. The only others on the beach were a group of little children who came running up to them with small cowrie shells in their outstretched hands as offerings. Adrian took some and smiled. "*Terima kasih*."

"*Terima kasih*, sir," the children smiled.

"Why are they thanking you?" asked Thierry. "I mean, they gave you the shells."

"Yes, but they think we're gods. That's why they are making offerings to us. Just like they do in the temple. And because we are gods they think that we have the power to give out good things. And so they thank us for them."

"I shall try it," said Thierry. He took some of the shells from one of the children.

"*Terima kasih*," they all cried. Everybody laughed.

"Go on, Danny. Your turn." Danny knelt down on the sand to the same height as the children and took a handful of the beautiful tiny shells.

"*Terima kasih*," they all said and clapped their hands.

"Now, do you feel like a god?" asked Adrian.

"Yeah. Both out there in the tube and here on the sand," replied Danny.

"There you are," said Adrian, "you have graduated from being the media's punchbag to a god in a very short time."

"Yes," said Danny, "and I sure trust these kids more than all those flea bitten scumbags out there in their white

448

shirts and ties who have given me such hell."

They climbed up the narrow, rocky steps and jumped on their motor bikes. It was quite a struggle to force the gutless 100 cc machines up the steep trail. But they did it. In first gear.

The ride into the village of Pecatu took fifteen minutes. It was stifling hot so they stopped at the market for some coca cola. The shop girl pulled the bottles out of a tub that was filled with cold water and the remains of some slabs of the ice that had been delivered by *bemo* from Kuta earlier in the morning.

They sat on the ground outside the shop and drew thirstily on the straws. A small crowd began to gather: villagers, pi dogs and some squawking hens. "Surfing?" asked the villagers. "Good Surfing? Beach? Padang Padang? Good Surfing?"

"Yes, it was great," said Thierry. "And Danny got his first tube." They all looked at Danny simply because Thierry had pointed to him. But they didn't understand what had been said. So Thierry picked up an old piece of piping that was lying on the dirt road. It had once been an exhaust pipe on a motor bike. Then he asked for a matchstick. He pointed to the top part of the match — the striking part — and then to Danny's head. The villagers all nodded their understanding. Then he pointed to the rest of the match. And then to the trunk of Danny's body. They nodded again. He picked up an oval shaped leaf and pointed to it and the surfboard. Yes, they understood. "Danny, give me a bit of your chewing gum." Thierry then stuck the bottom of the matchstick on to the top side of the leaf. The crowd were now staring in eager anticipation of what might happen next.

"Perhaps he is a magic man," they thought. "Or a god. Whatever he is he certainly has spiritual powers."

Then he picked up the exhaust pipe and made it move like a breaking wave. "Yes," they nodded. They still understood. So he held up the matchstick-leaf figure and put it in one end of the pipe. They watched in silent wonder as he blew the flimsy object through the hole. When it came out the other end they all clapped and cheered wildly. Then they turned their attention to Danny whom they believed had godlike qualities. They laughed and touched him on the arms.

"Time we left," said Adrian. "These people will soon expect us to rise up to heaven or something. We may as well quit while we're ahead."

They walked over to their bikes. "Damn," said Danny.

"What's the matter?"

"My front tyre. Look at it. Flat as a pancake."

"It must have gone down with all that steep climbing we did at the start of the track."

They squatted down to look at the soft, black rubber. So did the villagers. "Wait!" said one of the men. He pointed to a boy who was running away up the main road. They waited and the boy returned carrying the most antiquated looking hand pump that any of them had ever seen.

The villagers made the surfers sit down and gave them some pineapples to eat while they themselves set about pumping up the tyre. It took quite a long time. Then, the task accomplished, there were smiles and "*terima kasihs*" all round as the three surfers climbed on their bikes for the ride back to Kuta.

"It just shows that I'm not a god after all," laughed Danny. "Gods don't get flat tyres. I think that my status in their eyes was deflated as much as the tyre."

They found the girls in their usual spot on the beach reading their fashion magazines. Danny kissed Belinda and whispered in her ear, "Had my first tube ride." She smiled warmly.

"And what is your excuse this time?" asked Nicole. "I suppose you got a flat tyre or something."

"As a matter of fact we did," said Adrian. "But the

villagers pumped it up for us."

"Let's go for a swim," said Thierry. "It's so hot."

"Leave us out," said Danny. "We'd rather just lie on the beach."

"They are not very active or communicative to-day, are they?" said Nicole as they walked down the sand.

"I think they are at the apex of a very great love affair," said Thierry.

"And, of course, he rode his first tube this morning," said Adrian.

"Oh well, that explains it," said Dayu.

"What do you mean?"

"Danny obviously has a very powerful spirit inside him which is giving him all this luck. He rides a tube and is happy with Belinda. I am pleased for him as he is a good man. He deserves it."

"Yes," said Adrian. "He's certainly a different creature from when he first arrived. Can you remember how scared he was when he was hiding behind his beard and didn't want anyone to see him? He really was a shattered wreck."

"I remember," said Dayu, "but we did tell him that he was due for some good karma but he didn't believe us. Maybe he will believe it now."

That night they all ate at the Coconut Grove. They had big dishes of *nasi goreng* — well stocked plates of fried rice and chicken with two fried eggs slapped on top. And side salads. And warm chupattis. And fruit salad — mango, pineapple, paw paw, bananas and mandarins with coconut and peanuts on top. And thick, black Balinese coffee. And several cans of Bintang.

"If this was last month we wouldn't be sitting here for dinner," said Thierry. "We'd be at Manoel's like we were most nights. And he would be fussing around us in his precise way. He always used to come over at least six times during the meal to ask us if our food was all right. He was the best

451

restauranteur in Bali. I do miss him even though he was very inquisitive and asked people many personal questions about themselves."

"Oh come on," said Adrian, "he didn't do it in a nasty way. He was just curious."

"True," said Nicole, "but he did like to find out everything."

"Almost like a woman," said Adrian. Smack! He got a chupatti right in the face. Amid all the laughter he called out, "What did you do that for, Dayu?"

"It wasn't her; it was me," laughed Nicole.

Adrian looked at Thierry and said, "Really, old chap, you should exercise better discipline over her." As he turned, Belinda dropped a piece of ice down his back. He jumped out of his chair as he tried to locate it. As he went to sit down again Dayu pulled his chair away. He landed on the floor. Thump! On his bottom. They all laughed hysterically. Even Adrian. Then they saw the manager coming over.

"Ooops, here's trouble," said Danny. "Oh, no it's not, he's smiling."

"Balinese smile even when they're angry," said Adrian.

They smiled back at the manager as he approached. "I am so glad to see that you are all enjoying yourselves but I think it will be better if we don't serve you any more beer. You may finish what is on the table and then you may have fruit juice or lemonade for the rest of the evening."

"But we're not drunk," protested Adrian.

"I know, sir. But I think you will feel better if you drink fruit juice. Better for you."

"Now you see what you've done," laughed Thierry.

"All I said was that Manoel was curious. Like … " They were all waiting. " … the cat."

"Anyway I don't see why we can't go back to his restaurant," said Belinda. "Someone else must be running it now and you could sit there and drink a toast to your late friend. I

452

think it would be a nice gesture."

"We can't," said Nicole.

"Why not?"

"It's closed down. The Balinese won't work there because they believe it's inhabited by demons."

Dayu shuddered. Her last image of Manoel came into her mind. "I kissed him good-night," she remembered, "and then the evil spirit must have come out of the shadows and killed him. It must have been hovering there when we said good-bye." She looked up at the others and said what she always said when Manoel's name was mentioned. "Manoel was a very good man."

"Oh yes," said Thierry. "He was always kind and polite to us. He was such a distinguished old gentleman. Why would anyone want to kill him?"

"I wish they could find the murderer," said Nicole, "and hang him. I would be willing to pull the rope myself."

"They won't find him," said Adrian.

"Why not?"

"Because he was killed by the communists and they are too clever to get caught; they are very experienced at killing people. Good people like Manoel."

"Well, where is the karma there?" asked Danny. "A good man like that is murdered and his rotten killer is walking free. Just like the swine who took those photos of me on the beach. He would have got rich by selling them."

"So you're still sceptical about the old karma, eh Danny?" asked Adrian.

"I reckon."

"But you seem pretty happy at the moment?"

"Oh yes! To-day has been the happiest day of my life. All day I've been on a high — the tube, the beach this afternoon, Belinda. Everything!"

"So you admit that some good might have come out of the Wimbledon fiasco?"

"Yes. For sure. But they didn't have to be so hard on me, did they?"

About half past eleven they moved on to the Jolly Frog. Danny and Belinda danced through most of the numbers. In a world of their own. Danny barely looked round when the contessa tapped him on the shoulder to ask him how he enjoyed his trip to Perth.

"It was great, thanks. But we're really happy to be back. There's no place quite like Bali. It's crazy but I love it."

"Oh, I know," replied the contessa. "It's full of so many interesting people from all over the world. Like the man I'm with to-night. Freddie. That's him up at the bar getting me a drink. The one with the black curly hair and the blue shirt. He is so interesting. He has his own social column in one of the London papers and once he flew from New York to London in a balloon."

"A pity it didn't pop," thought Danny.

"Freddie is going back to-morrow night," continued the contessa. "I'm going to miss him as he's such fun. You should come and have a drink with us later and meet him. I must go now. I can see him picking up my tequila from the counter." She swept off in the direction of the bar and Danny and Belinda went the other way. Straight out the gates of the disco and on to the beach.

"If he goes back to-morrow like she said then all we have to do is stay away from there to-night and keep off the beach to-morrow," said Danny. "Then we should be safe."

They rode along the wide swathe of moonlit sand towards their cottage. On one side they could see the flickering lights of the beachfront cafes; on the other the vast, forbidding sea.

"I don't want to go back yet," said Danny. "It's been such a good day that I don't want it to end. Let's go and lie in the sandhills and look up at the stars. I've got something I want to tell you."

They lay down and rested their hands on a mound of sand. He asked her if she believed in reincarnation. "You mean that when I die I shall come back as a princess if I've led a good life but as a dog or a flea if I've been a bad girl?"

"Oh nothing as specific as that. Just the general idea."

"I've never really given it much thought."

"Well, I don't believe in it as you put it but I think that within one life from birth to death you can have several lives. Maybe 'scenes' would be a better word. I know because until I came to Bali mine was a life of relentless and never-ending pressure to achieve a goal. To win Wimbledon. Always living out of a suitcase. Never staying in one place for more than a week or two. Haggling with tournament managers over appearance money. Being forced to meet a lot of social climbing plastic people and boring sports officials. Never having any life of my own and never really having any friends. And certainly no relaxation. If I ever put my feet up I used to feel guilty that I wasn't practising my serve or doing calisthenics or filling in my tennis knowledge in some way or other. It was nothing but hassles, pressures and problems. And then all those lies."

"But surely you must have had lots of friends among the players. You were all going to the same tournaments, weren't you?"

"Yes, but most of them hate each other. They're all so damned competitive. And bitchy behind your back. And friendship is always limited by the background knowledge that one day you might have to play the guy in a major final where $50,000 or $100,000 is at stake. Friendship is difficult under those circumstances. Besides, I used to keep my distance from the other players because in their off hours all they did was talk about tennis, their matches, their appearance fees, their coaching clinics, their tax dodging schemes. Nothing else. I didn't want to listen to it all night as well as all day. That's why I decided to come down here for a week with Yvonne. It was just the distraction that I needed at the time. And it relaxed me which was good for my build-up for Wimbledon. After all, I did reach the Final. And I only lost that because of extraneous factors. But the point I'm making is that, for all the so-called rewards, I was never happy. Not inside myself. The condo at Palm Beach is let for fifty weeks of the year and I only get to use it for a fortnight. Same with the car. What's the use of having a nice red Porsche if you can drive it for only two weeks of the year?

So, as I see it, one life ended for me when I arrived here after Wimbledon. I shed all my previous life. Or, to be more precise, it was shed for me. No more Anthea. No more tennis. No more globe-trotting to tournaments. No more of the back-stabbing bitchiness of the players. Instead, a new life. Different place. Different friends. Surfing and — most important of all — you. Now I want to ask you another question. Do you believe in magic?"

"You mean white rabbits popping out of black hats?"

"No. Bali magic."

"Depends what it is."

"Well, to-day I had my first tube ride. It was the most wonderful thing I've ever experienced. And it sort of set a theme for the whole day. Now that the day — or should I say the night — is ending I want to crown it with a piece of pure magic. Will you marry me?"

They both laughed. She didn't even have to answer. They immediately started talking about wedding plans.

"Maybe your father should marry us," she suggested. "After all, he's an evangelist."

"Yes, but he's not a Christian. He is just a charlatan who uses the Bible to suck huge amounts of money out of old ladies who lock themselves in their apartments every afternoon and watch his disgusting theatrical performance on their television sets. He treated my Mom something dreadful before she died. Used to beat her up. And now he tells his simple minded audience how badly he behaved and how he regrets it because my Mom is no longer around and he can't tell her how sorry he is. Then he cries on the screen and asks forgiveness from God. All the old ladies feel sorry for him and send him a whole lot of donations. That's how he earns his living. I'd be more proud of him if he kept a brothel. But I don't want to see him again. Not after he disowned me on the television when the pictures were published. He even said that I was possessed by Satan. As I said, he is not a Christian and will say anything to make money."

"And we can't get married in Perth," said Belinda, "because the newspapers would make a big and nasty issue of it … " She laughed and looked at Danny. They both said in unison: "And whatever would the bishop say?"

"It's all so ridiculous," said Danny. "Let's get married here. Right here on the beach. To-morrow."

"No, not to-morrow," she said.

"Why not?"

"Because of that newspaper creep from London. He's not going until to-morrow night."

"Oh yes, of course."

They discussed it further and decided to get married on the beach in a week's time so as to give Belinda's parents enough time to come up from Perth.

The next day they announced their plans to Adrian and Dayu and Nicole and Thierry. "Oh, I am so glad," said Nicole. "I just love weddings. I shall have a new dress made by one of those dressmakers here who are so good and so cheap. You must come with me, Dayu, and we will choose some fabric."

When the telephone exchange opened Belinda placed a call to her parents. Connie was beside herself with joy but was a little disappointed that the wedding would not be in Perth with a big reception at their home in Dalkeith. But she understood the reasons and couldn't bear the thought of another press campaign against Danny. "Good God," she thought, "next time they might even mention me!" The last thing that Connie Broughton, respectable Dalkeith matron, wanted was to be named in a scandal.

Philip Broughton took the news in his usual calm manner and booked First Class tickets to Bali for himself, his wife and their friends, Bill and Elizabeth Harker. Bill Harker was one of the three men who had backed Philip financially way back in 1952 and they had been business partners ever since. Among other things Bill was a marriage celebrant and was only too happy to conduct the service as he had always been particularly fond of Belinda.

They booked a couple of suites at the Bali Beach Hotel and arrived on the Qantas flight just as the sun was setting on the day before the wedding. Connie brought a simple white wedding dress for Belinda and, after some discussion, Danny agreed to Connie's suggestion that he deck himself out in his Boss suit, Gucci shirt and International Club tie.

They all had dinner at the Bali Beach Hotel on the night before the wedding — Belinda and Danny, Philip and Connie, the Harkers, Adrian and Dayu and Nicole and Thierry. It was the first time that Danny had been prepared to show himself there in public. As they were about to sit down Belinda whispered to him, "You don't mind any longer about coming here?"

"I no longer care," he replied. "I'm just happy to be with you and nothing else matters. They can't hurt me any more. I'm above it."

"So you believe in karma after all?" smiled Adrian. "Good things are happening to you because of all the good that you've done to others?"

"Yes, but only since I've come to Bali. *The second time*."

"And the Wimbledon trouble was all parts of karma's mysterious ways?"

"I guess so. I'm glad it's turned out this way but they

needn't have been so hard on me."

"But, if they weren't, you might have stood the heat and not come out here."

"And not met me," laughed Belinda.

"True. Yes, I must say I believe in karma."

"I knew he would," thought Dayu. "Sooner or later. You can't stay in Bali a long time without believing in it."

■

The day of the wedding was warm and sunny. Danny and Belinda had chosen the same part of the beach where they had lain together on the night that they decided to get married. In fact, the very same spot.

They arrived there at nine in the morning when there weren't many people around. Danny had insisted that, since it was a private matter, he didn't want the whole of Bali turning up. He especially didn't want people like the contessa bringing all her crowd, stealing all the attention and turning it into a circus. So the only invited guests were Belinda's parents, the Harkers and the Balinese family who owned the cottage where Danny had stayed since his arrival. The bridal party consisted of Adrian as best man and Thierry as groomsman while Dayu and Nicole were two very beautiful bridesmaids. And of course there were some uninvited guests: a couple of old wrinkled fishermen, some massage ladies with bundles on their heads, a group of wide-eyed Balinese children, a couple of German surfers who had just come out of the water and three horrible looking pi dogs. Just before the ceremony began the Balinese chased the dogs away. They didn't want the dogs' bad spirits to get inside the bride and groom and so curse their union.

Belinda looked truly beautiful and had a circlet of white flowers on her head. Gardenias and orchids. "You are like a Balinese lady," laughed Danny. "They always have something on their head. Usually a basket of clothes or a bag of ce-

459

ment."

Bill Harker applied his strong, clear voice to the words of the marriage vows and Danny sealed the ceremony with a long kiss on the bride's lips.

They adjourned to the Bali Beach Hotel where the reception was held in a private dining room that had been beautifully decorated with flowers. Long tables groaned beneath the weight of bottles of Veuve Clicquot, lobsters, prawns, roast pork, chicken, rice, mangos, strawberries, paw paws, pineapples and a huge wedding cake.

It was early in the morning so they decided to have the speeches first with some champagne. In fact, quite a bit. Bill Harker proved to be a great raconteur of all sorts of funny and unbelievable things that had happened to him in the outback. By lunch time everyone was very hungry and very merry. Most of them had made a speech. Except Philip. Never one to push himself to the forefront in social matters, he usually left those sorts of things to his wife. But at the end of the meal he called for silence. All he got were some rude and light-hearted remarks.

He asked the waiters to leave the room. They closed the door behind them. Philip then said that he had spoken to Belinda earlier in the day and asked her if all the guests were "padlock" safe. Not to reveal a secret. She had said that to her knowledge they were. He told the guests that he took her at her word and knew that they would not let him down.

He recalled how he had not been present in Perth when Belinda was born because she was three weeks premature. He had been working in the outback and wasn't due back in the city until just before the day of her expected arrival. "Two things happened to me on that magic day," he said, "and to this day I have never told the story to anyone. Not even to Connie." All eyes turned to Belinda's mother who was staring dumbly into space. "As I said, two things happened. One in the morning and one in the evening. I shall tell you about the evening event first. I was back at my camp in the Pilbara cooking dinner over the camp fire — just me and my two black fellas. I could see headlights approaching and I was a bit apprehensive that it might be robbers so I grabbed the rifle. But it wasn't. It was the postmaster from the town of Dunrobin some forty miles away. He handed me a telegram and said, 'I thought it was worth driving all the way out to give you this.' It was the announcement of Belinda's birth. The postmaster had brought with him a crate of warm beer and all four of us sat round the fire and toasted the event in appropriate fashion."

"What happened in the morning?" called Bill. "We're still waiting for that."

"I haven't forgotten," said Philip. "In the morning we were taking samples on a great stretch of barren landscape that was part of my claim. We were trying to find out if there was any copper or iron under the ground. I already had two copper mines by then and was looking around to establish a third. Well, it was the first day that we'd been able to work for a week because there had been great dust storms. Unless you've been in the outback you can't ever imagine how they blow the sand and dirt around. Well, I left the two abbos to their task and walked up to the top of a rise to see what was on the other side."

"And you saw a naked woman running towards you," called out Bill.

"No, not that time," laughed Philip. "There was a great valley that went for miles. Not a tree in sight. Just brown landscape. Like the moon. So I sat down to rest and to look at it. But I could feel a hard, jagged object under my buttock. So I moved a few inches and scraped the sand away to see what it was. It must have been uncovered by the dust storms of the week before."

"And what was it?" called out his life long friend and business partner.

"This," said Philip as he pulled out a crumpled, slightly soiled white handkerchief. "I put it in the bank vault in Perth and always intended to give it to Belinda on her wedding day. Because I found it on the morning she was born I reasoned that it was meant for her and not for me or anyone else."

"He is a sensible man," thought Dayu. "He knew that the gods put it there for Belinda."

"Well, what is it?" called Bill. "Surely you didn't find someone's white handkerchief and keep it all these years."

"Belinda and Danny, here is our wedding present. We hope that it brings you good fortune and great happiness."

They walked up to where Philip was standing. Belinda unwound the handkerchief and pulled out the largest diamond that any of them had ever seen. It was almost half an inch in diameter. They all gasped. "Oh my God!" cried Bill Harker's wife. "It's big enough to be in the Crown Jewels."

"Thank God the contessa's not here," thought Danny. "It would be in all the world's papers by to-morrow."

After everyone had touched it and held it up to the light Danny rose to thank Philip and Connie. But he was so overwhelmed that he could hardly speak. "But what are we going to do with it here? There are no banks to put it in."

"Bury it in the sand," called Bill.

"No," said Nicole, "he might forget the exact spot and not be able to find it."

"Then we could have a treasure hunt," laughed Thierry.

"Just keep it away from my cottage," called Adrian. "If that uncle of Nyoman's hears about it he will tell his jim to steal it out of your pocket. That little blighter seems to get his hands on everything."

"Silence!" called Philip. "I have anticipated the problem and will reveal the details to Danny and Belinda afterwards. In the meantime, back to the food. Call back the waiters and ask them to refill the champagne glasses."

Later that night Philip told Belinda and Danny that he

and Connie were flying to Hong Kong the next day for some shopping and he would deposit the diamond in the vaults of the Standard Chartered Bank in des Voeux Road in Danny and Belinda's names and they could uplift it at their convenience. "The important thing," he said, "was to get it out of Australia and away from our greedy tax authorities. If I'd sold it, those thieves would have taken almost all the proceeds in tax. And if the bishop heard about it he would have been at me for the rest. This way it's better for everyone all round."

The next day Belinda and Danny went to the Airport with Philip and Connie and the Harkers. Philip had the diamond in the inside pocket of his jacket. They said good-bye and watched as the four of them boarded the Cathay Pacific flight for Hong Kong. Then they went back to their cottage to load up their two motor bikes for a ride round the island. Before they left they called round to Adrian's cottage.

"It'll be a novel type of honeymoon," laughed Belinda. "We'll be roughing it a bit. Staying in native *losmens* because there aren't any hotels in the back country. We just want to get away to some place different for a few days and be on our own."

"And," said Danny, "it sure beats going to stay at some flash hotel in Singapore or Hong Kong and having to play ladies and gentlemen with all the old folks in the dining room who are spending their golden handshake money."

"Or widows spending their husband's life insurance money," laughed Adrian.

"Or divorcees spending their property settlement money," chipped in Thierry.

"Remember to take plenty of hundred rupiah notes," said Adrian. "And definitely nothing higher than five hundred."

"Why? I've just cashed some traveller's cheques and I took it all in ten thousand notes. They fit into my wallet easier. I was just going to break one down each time I needed it."

"You won't be able to," said Dayu. "When you get outside the tourist area — Kuta, Legian, Denpasar — it is almost impossible to cash a big note. Even a thousand rupiah. The people just don't have that sort of money to give you change."

"That's right," said Adrian. "Things that cost a thousand rupiah down here can be bought up there for a hundred or even fifty."

"Hell, but they're cheap enough here," said Danny in amazement.

"Yes, but you'll find that once you get out of here you'll be hard pressed to spend fifteen dollars a day. Between you. Don't worry, it's a nice feeling to enjoy yourself almost for free. And you'll have whole beaches to yourselves, and warm sea and coral and beautiful fish and lots of smiling, polite people wanting to do things for you. Yes, you're right. It's a million times better than paying big bucks to stay in a sterile concrete and glass structure in the middle of some big city." And so it proved.

The honeymoon luggage included sun lotion, mosquito coils, foam mats for lying on the sand, sarongs, candles lest the outlying villages not have electricity, water bottles and towels but no surfboard. "It's too big to carry on a long journey," said Danny, "and besides, lots of the beaches will be surrounded by reef barriers. Anyway, I've got so used to surfing with Adrian and Thierry that it would kind of feel funny to be out there without them."

Like an army on the march in India they tried to do their travelling in the early morning so as to avoid the sweltering heat of the midday sun. On the third day they were riding along the north coast of the island about 10 a.m. "Let's stop," called Belinda when they slowed down to drive through a small village that was little more than a clearing in the coconut trees. "I can't go any further without a cold drink."

All the people ran out of their houses to clap and wave as the bikes went past. In the middle of the village they saw a small stall that was set up under the shade of an umbrella like banyan tree. They stopped and asked for a cold drink. The lady did not understand so Danny ran his eye under the bench and found a box of soft drinks. He pulled out four of them — two of orange juice and two pineapple. But they were not cold. "Too bad," he said as the lady opened them and watched in amazement as they made short work of all four bottles. Danny paid her two of the hundred rupiah notes that Adrian had told him to bring and watched as she put them into a cardboard box. The only other money there was a few coins — fifty rupiah, tens and many fives.

There was a pile of pineapples stacked against one of the many trunks of the banyan tree. The lady reached over and grabbed a couple and proceeded to cut them into vertical slices. She smiled as she handed them the pieces. "*Terima kasih*," said Belinda. "And *berapa*?" The lady just smiled and shook her head to indicate that she didn't want any more money. By now almost the entire village had gathered round the newcomers; some were staring in astonishment but most were smiling and laughing.

"I wonder if there's a beach near here," said Belinda. "I feel like falling in the sea to cool off and then lying on the sand."

"Me too," said Danny as he chewed big chunks out of the sweet, yellow pineapple. When he finished he stood up and smiled at the crowd. He could remember the Indonesian word for beach. "*Pantai*?" he asked.

"Ah, *Pantai*." They all smiled and nodded knowingly to each other. All eyes turned to the village headman who stepped forward and motioned Belinda and Danny to sit down in front of him on the dusty road. The man picked up a short stick and began to draw lines in the dust. He pointed to a side track that they could see leading off to the left a few yards further on. Danny nodded. The man smiled. He drew the stick along a short distance and then put a cross over the line and shook his head. "Right. We obviously don't take that track," said Danny. Then the man drew another line and curved it to the right. Danny nodded again. Then he made a line to the left at a right angle and moved the stick a bit further.

"*Pantai*!" he said in triumph. Danny and Belinda stared at the lines and committed them to memory.

"We may as well give it a go," said Danny. "If we get lost we can always ask a farmer or someone."

They thanked the man and rode slowly towards the first turn-off. The track was not much wider than their bikes. The overhanging coconut trees gave them some respite from the hot sun and after ten minutes they took the turning to the left. The coconut palms gave way to a banana plantation and they changed to a lower gear to ride up a small rise. On the other side was the sea. And a small beach about half a mile long with rocks at each end.

"Do you get the impression that we're the only ones in the world?" asked Belinda.

"Yes," replied Danny as he stopped his bike just before the soft, white sand. "Oops, we're wrong. I can see a couple of fishermen on the rocks."

They ran into the cool sea and swam for nearly an hour. For the rest of the day they alternated between lying in the hot sun on the sand or at the top of the beach in the shade of the pandanus trees. Three native boys walked by and sat down on the sand with them. They could not speak English but, after much laughing and muttering the word "*losmen*," the kids eventually worked out that Danny was asking if there was some place where they could put their heads down for the night.

One of the boys stood up, put out his hand – palm downward – and waved his fingers in the Balinese way of beckoning. They followed him along the beach in the direction of the rocky point on the left. The nipa palms and pandanus trees came right down to the sand. The boy led them up through a small hole in the trees and they followed him through a dark passage for about twenty yards. They came to a grass clearing which looked out over a small sandy beach on the other side of the rocks. In the middle of the open space was a small grove of pandanus trees with their awkward looking tubular trunks, thorny leaves and pineapple like fruit. The boys all pointed to it and smiled.

"Yeah, nice pandanus trees," said Danny.

They kept looking at him and saying, "*Bagus, bagus!*"

"Yes," he smiled, "it's very good. *Bagus.*"

The boys couldn't make him understand so they laughed, got down on the ground and disappeared through a narrow slit between the trunks. All that Danny and Belinda could see were three pairs of dark eyes staring through the hole and beckoning them to follow. Danny went in first. "Wow, Belinda, you should see this. It's like a room inside a tree." Belinda couldn't believe her eyes. All the thin trunks were growing in a kind of circle around an empty piece of ground that was just big enough to lie on. It was a bit of a squash with five of them in there; the boys were laughing and were obviously proud to have led them to such an exotic spot. There was soft sand on the ground and a few strips of light were peeking through the small gaps in the grey branches.

"Look," said Belinda, "there's even a roof to keep us dry if it rains. We could live here for weeks!"

"Well, let's try it just for a night," said Danny. "What do you reckon?"

"Oh, for sure."

They clambered out through the narrow entrance and stood up to stretch their backs. "What about food?" asked Belinda. "If we spend the night here we'll have to ride back to the village and get some fruit or something."

"Maybe our little guides can help us," said Danny. He pointed to his mouth and pretended to eat. The eldest of the three boys smiled knowingly as if he had been waiting for Danny to make the gesture. Again he put his hand out, waved his fingers downwards and led them through some nipas and casuarinas at the landward end of the clearing. They walked up a narrow track and came to a plantation in the wild — banana trees, paw paws, mangoes, breadfruit and coconut trees. All laden with ripe fruit. Again the boys stood with a proud smile on their faces. One of them reached up and picked a delicious looking mango and handed it to Danny.

"*Terima kasih*," said Belinda. They picked what they thought would be enough for an evening meal and walked back to the pandanus grove. They crossed a small fresh water stream which they later discovered flowed into the sea and passed to within a few feet of their new home.

The boys stayed with them until the sun went down. Then they scampered off back to their family compound before the spirits of the dark emerged. Danny and Belinda went with them as far as the bikes and gave them five hundred rupiah each. "Did you see the look on their faces?" he said to Belinda. "You'd think that I'd given them half the world."

"Yes, they're so naturally friendly," she said as they got on their bikes and rode them up to the trees by the clearing. They unloaded their gear and Belinda crawled inside the tree room and lay the foam mats down on the sand. They filled the water bottle with clear, cool water from the stream and lit some candles to illuminate their "room" for the night. Belinda cut the fruit into slices and they ate it heartily before it got too dark.

As they sat and watched the moonlight dancing on the sea Belinda started humming. "What tune is that?" asked Danny.

"I don't know. It's so peaceful here and I just love it even though there's nothing to do."

"Oh, I'm sure that we'll keep ourselves occupied. And happy," laughed Danny. "We'll start with some music." He pulled a small portable stereo out of his pack and went to slip in a tape. The stereo was a wedding gift from Thierry and Nicole.

"Which one are you playing?" asked Belinda.

"It's one that Adrian gave me. It's the track of a surfing movie that was made a few years ago. He reckons it was the best film he's ever seen and some of it was shot in Bali. He gave it to me last week and it's real soul stuff."

"What's it called?"

"'Morning of the Earth.' I'm sure you'll like it. I do." They lay on the ground in each other's arms and absorbed the smooth, gentle rhythms of the tape.

"Oh, that's such nice music," murmured Belinda. "Let's play the other side."

Danny leaned across to switch over the tape. "Damn," he said. "I don't' remember which button is 'Play' and I can't see in the dark."

He tried the middle one but it was the switch for the short wave radio. "B.B.C.World Service. This is London calling. Here is the news read by … " came the clear, crisp tones of the man in London.

"Let's listen," said Belinda. "I haven't heard any news for ages."

"All right," he said lethargically.

"Black nationalist guerrillas using a heat seeking missile have shot down a Rhodesian Airways Viscount that was flying from Kariba to Salisbury. The 'plane crashed in thick jungle that is infested with wild animals and terrorists. Rhodesian security forces have reached the site and have located a group of six survivors who told how the 'plane crash landed in a jungle clearing with more than half the passengers still alive. Shortly afterwards terrorists appeared out of the trees and murdered all the survivors except for the group of half a dozen who had left the 'plane to seek help. The terrorists responsible have been identified as members of the ZIPRA faction which is funded by the Soviet Union and church groups in Britain and Scandinavia."

"Bloody bastards," said Belinda.

"In Belfast an I.R.A. bomb has exploded in a Protestant kindergarten, blowing to pieces several young children and their teacher ... In Beirut a bomb in the Muslim quarter has killed more than a dozen people ... An earthquake in Mexico has killed more than a thousand peasants and left fifty thousand homeless ... The floods in Bangladesh are continuing and airborne relief workers report thousands of corpses floating down the swollen rivers. There has also been an outbreak of cholera ... At least twenty depositors have jumped out of high rise windows in Chicago in the wake of the latest savings and loan company failure ... "

Belinda pulled her arm away from Danny's embrace and hit the switchboard with a violent blow. The stereo fell on its side. Silent. "You must promise never to turn it on to the news again. At least not until after our honeymoon," she said.

"But you're the one who wanted to listen to it."

"I know, but I never want to hear it again. Here we are in this perfect, peaceful place and we have to hear all those terrible and wicked things. It's enough to ruin the evening."

"No it's not," he said. "We're in another world here. Our own. In fact we don't even know where we are."

Belinda thought about it and started to laugh. "Well," she said, "the sun went down over there so that must be west."

"Top of the class," said Danny as he moved his hands gently over her breasts. "I wonder what's down the other end. In the east."

"Probably New Guinea," she replied.

Danny got the stereo going again and put on the other side of "Morning of the Earth". They lay on their backs in the warm night and looked up at the starry heavens. They could hear the tiny waves that were rolling up to the high tide mark only a few feet away.

When they crept into their exotic, candle lit bedroom Danny took Belinda's slim, bronzed body into his arms and they lay together talking, giggling and playing. "I couldn't think of a better place to conceive a healthy, handsome child," he laughed. Belinda mumbled her agreement as she smothered her husband with passionate kisses in preparation for a night of wild love-making.

The next morning when they climbed out into the sunlight they could see the three Balinese boys walking along the beach towards them. One of them was carrying something. When they got closer and started calling out *"Selamat pagi"* Belinda could see that it was a bowl. Their three friends had brought them fried rice, chicken and fish for breakfast. The boys stayed with them all day and caught some crabs which Danny cooked on the fire. About four o'clock they all had a big feast — roasted crabs, the rest of the rice and some mango, paw paw and bananas. As on the previous day the boys left just before dark. Danny got them to understand that he and Belinda would be leaving on the morrow and he gave them five thousand rupiah each. *"Terima kasih"* they beamed with smiles as wide as the moon.

"Well, on our own for another night," said Belinda. Which was only partly true. A couple of hours after sunset they were visited by a giant lizard that emerged from the trees. The pre-historic looking reptile appeared to be checking out its territory and then returned to the wild. At nine o'clock Danny lit a mosquito coil and they turned in.

They didn't see their three friends the next morning. After waking at five-thirty and eating some pineapple they packed their bags and rode back up the trail to the main road. In the coconut plantation they saw a group of boys at the top of the trees cutting off the nuts. They all called out and waved and vigorously shook the fronds. *"Selamat pagi, selamat pagi,"* they cried as the bikes tore past.

On the road back into Denpasar Danny and Belinda had difficulty adjusting to all the traffic and noise after the peace and quiet of the countryside. "Hell," screamed Danny as they pulled up at an intersection, "how are we going to handle Hong Kong? This is bad enough."

"What's that?" called out Belinda above the noise of the screeching, roaring and tooting traffic.

"I said 'how are we going to handle Hong Kong'?"

"I don't know but I guess we'll find out soon enough." Which was true because, away from the distractions of Kuta, they had been able to think clearly about themselves and the future. They realised that Bali was a sort of transformation process that had brought them together and given them each other but that it was now time to move on.

"Well," said Adrian after dinner on their first evening back, "you seem to have had a fantastic time."

"We couldn't have enjoyed ourselves more," replied Danny. "Everything went right. The bikes ran well. Not even a flat tyre. And you were right; it hardly cost us anything."

"Yes," thought Dayu, "the good karma is continuing. And most importantly he now believes in it."

"We should all have a few good weeks of surfing ahead of us," said Adrian cheerfully. "This off shore wind promises to hold — I'd say well into next week."

"Well ... " said Danny without smiling.

"What?"

"We've decided to leave. In three days' time. You see, now that we're married we want to set ourselves up together and we can't do that here. Bali has been so beautiful for us and so good to me that we want to leave while we're on top. Who knows, our fortunes might change. But if we go now we'll always think of it as a kind of paradise that held a special power over us. A kind of magic."

"What do you mean — your fortunes might change?"

"Well, all that trouble I had with the newspapers had its origins here in Bali. On Turtle Beach. But that was karma — or Bali, which is probably the same thing — casting its spell on me and directing my life. Because of what followed from Turtle Beach I came back here and since then everything has gone so well. The two best things in my life — riding tubes and meeting Belinda — have happened here."

"What about playing the Final on the Central Court?" chipped in Adrian.

"No, that was not a success. Or even a thrill. It was a disaster. As I was saying, Bali has given me good karma but I don't believe that such good things and happiness can last forever. As you know, there are always a few troughs between the crests of the waves. And, because Bali is so precious in our memories, we want to leave while we're on the crest."

"Come on, Danny, you're talking like you're depressed or something," said Adrian.

"No, not at all. In fact, far from it. But I remember how high I was feeling when I drove through the Wimbledon gates for the Final. The Rolls Royce, all the cheering crowds and then — kaput! Everything went sour. The wave broke and threw me. It was the deepest trough after the highest crest. Well, now that I'm on top again I don't want the same thing to happen."

"It won't."

"Probably not, but we want to get settled anyway. We're going up to Honkers to see about selling the diamond. And I'm going to sell my condo at Palm Beach too. After the simplicity of Bali I don't think we could handle the Palm Beach scene."

"So what are you going to do? Live on a desert island?"

"No, nothing as dramatic as that. We're going to buy a farm in northern California or maybe Oregon and live on the land. Near the coast of course so that I can still surf. So that's why we're keen to leave and get started with our new venture."

"I'm so looking forward to it," said Belinda. "I've always loved horses and Danny says there's lots of open country up there."

"There's also lots of forests," said Danny.

"We'll be sorry to see you go," said Nicole. "But I'm sure you're doing the right thing. You know, *mon chéri*, if we really thought about things seriously we'd probably decide that it was time to leave too."

"I'm not going until I can ride inside a tube," said Thierry. "As soon as I've done that we will then talk about leaving."

"Anyway, what are you plans, Adrian?" asked Danny.

"Dunno. Listen, Thierry and I are going to the Reef to-morrow morning. Do you want to come with us? It should be five to six feet." He changed the subject as quickly as possible. Unlike Danny and Belinda, who were so carefully planning the future together, Adrian was living only for the moment — the waves, the sunshine, Dayu. Life at present was far too laid back, too sensual and too enjoyable to face hard decisions like leaving. Bali was like a never ending party. And who wants to go home from a party? But something that Danny said troubled him. About the good times not lasting. Deep down he knew Danny was right. It had been brought home to him pretty brutally on the night that Alex was killed. "Danny seems to know what he's doing; I don't," he thought. "Oh well, I suppose it will work itself out in its own mystical, illogical Balinese way. Karma. The gods. But hopefully not the demons."

Dayu too was thinking about what Danny had said. She knew that everything in Bali was a balance between the opposing forces of good and evil. *Kaja* and *kelod*. The gods and the demons. The mountains and the sea. She too had been happy since coming down from the village to the exciting life at Legian. But, as Danny had said, maybe the good karma would not last. Not for him and Belinda. Maybe not for her and Adrian. She decided to put out more offerings to make sure that the bad spirits were appeased and would not come and cause trouble.

On the day before Danny and Belinda flew to Hong Kong the three boys went surfing at Airport Reef. The waves were only about three feet. Then the swell dropped completely and left them becalmed. They had told the boatman who brought them out not to come back for three hours.

"But he'll probably come back sooner once he sees how the surf's dropped," said Adrian. "In the meantime we may as well just lie on our boards and wait. The water's warm enough."

"Yes," replied Danny, "but I can feel the sea urchins on my hands and under my finger nails. They are bloody irritating."

"I know," said Adrian. "They live among the coral."

They could see Thierry some distance away talking in French to some other surfer. They started talking about when they might meet up again. "You must come and stay once we get our farm on the West Coast," said Danny. "We'd both like that very much. And Dayu too."

"Let's go one better," said Adrian. "Because you and Thierry and I have had so many good times together in the waves and because you are leaving to-morrow and this is our last surf together let's make a solemn pact that some time within the next two years we'll all come back here and have some more crazy times in the surf."

"Belinda and I plan to have a kid by then."

"Great. And what would you call it? Wayan — the first born?"

"No ... Adrian."

"And what if it's a girl?"

"Who knows? Maybe 'Adrienne'." They both laughed.

"Look! Here comes Thierry with some fellow."

"This is Pierre," called Thierry. "He is from Tahiti and has been here for only one day. He cannot find the boatman who brought him out. He must have gone back. So I said that he can come back with us."

"Fine," said Danny. "I can see our boatman coming now."

"It is no good talking to Pierre. He does not understand a word of English." They smiled at the fair headed Frenchman and pointed to their outrigger that had just set out from the beach.

"Hey, Thierry, come over here. We're going to make a solemn pact."

The three of them now had the noses of their surfboards touching. "Repeat after me," said Adrian. "We do solemnly swear that, although we hail from three different continents, we are linked together by the waves in bonds of true friendship and we shall return within two years to pass more happy hours together in these sacred waters." Then they all thumped their fists down on their boards, gave the surfer's handshake and burst out laughing.

"It's as solemn as the marriage ceremony," laughed Danny.

"And just as binding," retorted Adrian.

Pierre looked at them as if they were crazy. "I guess he's having second thoughts about coming back on the boat with us," laughed Adrian.

Belinda and Danny flew up to Hong Kong the next day. They stayed at a middle range hotel off Nathan Road and rang the bank on the day after their arrival.

"Yes, your father said that you'd be calling," said the manager, Robert MacAlister, a genial, sandy haired Scot of about fifty. "I'll be free to see you at two o'clock."

After lunch they made their way across the choppy waters of the harbour on the Star ferry and walked the couple of hundred years from the terminal to the bank. They smiled at the two large stone lions guarding its entrance and then walked into the cavernous banking chamber. The manager bade them sit down as he handed them a sealed letter from Belinda's father.

"Dear Danny and Belinda. I ran into Mark Grocott at the Hong Kong Club. He used to by my lawyer in Perth before he came up here and quadrupled his salary. Told him about the diamond in general terms and he said that he had a client whom he believes would be interested in buying it. If you wish to sell, ring him on 5-791341. Love, Father."

They rang Mark Grocott who invited them to dinner at his apartment overlooking Repulse Bay. After a sumptuous Chinese meal of fourteen courses that was cooked by the two *amahs* under the supervision of Mrs. Grocott, they discussed the sale of the diamond.

"It just happens that there's a big meeting taking place in Hong Kong at the moment between de Beers and the representatives of the diamond cutting factories of Antwerp, Amsterdam, Tel Aviv and Hong Kong. They've got some financial matters to sort out. We could get a small group of them to come to the bank and value it," said Mr. Grocott.

The valuations varied from US$5,000,000 to US$8,000,000. Mark Grocott's client, whose identity he refused to disclose, offered $6,000,000 and the following week Danny and Belinda met Mr. Grocott in the manager's office at the Standard Chartered Bank to finalise the deal. The diamond, which had been brought up from the vaults, was handed over to the solicitor and he passed them a cheque drawn on his trust account for $6,000,000. He placed the diamond back in the vault and Danny and Belinda handed the manager their cheque.

"You don't need to change this to Hong Kong dollars," said the manager. "We have American dollar accounts and it is better to leave the money here in Hong Kong until you need it as there will be a lot of interest and our tax rate is much lower than in the States. Since it stays in American dollars you won't lose anything through exchange rate variations when you eventually remit it. When you buy your farm we can send the amount over by telex and you'll receive it the next day."

"Thank you," said Danny, "we'll leave it here in the meantime." There were smiles and handshakes all round. Everyone was happy — especially the bank manager who finished up with both the diamond and the money.

"How shall we celebrate?" asked Belinda after they returned to their hotel.

"Well, do you want to go to dinner at the Peninsula? Or the Mandarin? I think we could afford it!"

"I don't know," she said. "It's too hot. I don't feel like dressing up."

"Nor do I. Let's just go walking up Nathan Road and we'll find somewhere quiet and exotic. As long as I'm with you I don't mind where we go."

Belinda put on a thin cotton dress and Danny donned some long cotton pants that he had bought from a beach seller at Legian for four dollars. He put on a batik shirt and they set off up Nathan Road. They passed the bustling Jordan Road intersection — the "Piccadilly of the East" as Danny called it — and continued on in the direction of the Temple Street night market. They passed dozens of shops selling the latest in electronic equipment and emporiums overflowing with rolls of brightly coloured Chinese silks. The strong smell of Cantonese food came wafting out of the crowded, noisy restaurants while from other rooms they could hear the constant click of mah jong tiles on wooden tables.

They cut through a small side road to get to Temple Street. They could scarcely believe their eyes. A bare breasted Balinese lady in a long green sarong was coming out of a greengrocer's shop with a big basket of fresh vegetables on her head. They watched her cross the road and disappear into another doorway.

"Is that for real?" exclaimed Danny. "Or am I seeing things?"

"Let's see where she went," said Belinda. They walked a few yards along the darkened street and saw the lights of a restaurant. Its name was written in small neon lights on the front. They stood there and read it. "Gado Gado Restaurant. Genuine Balinese Food."

"Well," laughed Belinda. "Looks like we've solved the problem of where to eat."

They went in and sat down. A smiling Balinese man walked over to their table. "*Selamat datang*," he said as he handed them the menu.

"We're thirsty," said Danny. "Do you have any beer?"

"Of course, sir. What would you like? Bintang or San Miguel?"

"Two ice cold Bintangs please."

The little man trotted off to fetch the beer. Danny and Belinda ran their eyes down the list of dishes: *nasi goreng, nasi campur, gado gado, satay*, prawns, turtle soup, *mie goreng, gule, opor ayam*.

"Seeing that the place is called 'Gado Gado' we'd better have some," said Danny. "Logically it must be their best dish."

"You should know by now that nothing is logical in Bali," replied Belinda.

"True. Well, we'll have it anyway and just trust in the gods."

The meal was delicious. "The spiciest I've ever tasted," pronounced Belinda. They finished off with fruit salad — Balinese style — and some thick Balinese coffee. They sat on and on until the manager went and locked the door. Danny got up to pay.

"No, no. Sit down, sir. I am about to serve some arak. Would you like a glass? And you too, madam?"

"*Terima kasih*," they replied.

The manager looked pleased. "You've been to Bali?" he asked.

"Yes, we've just come from there."

"And were our gods good to you?"

"Most definitely," they replied.

The manager came over and sat at their table. "I want to ask you something," said Danny. "How many Balinese restaurants are there in Hong Kong?"

"Our's is the only one. But there is one other restaurant that serves Indonesian food. It's over at Central. It is run by people from Java and most of their dishes are Javanese."

"You mean you're the only one that sells Balinese food?"

"Yes," was the proud reply.

Belinda and Danny smiled at each other. They were both thinking the same thing: the gods had led them there for their special celebration.

They spent a further week in the colony — going up to the Peak in the funicular railway, shopping in the Stanley market, swimming at Shek O and sampling the Chinese food in Kowloon.

On the Pan Am flight to San Francisco the stewardess came up to Danny and said, "Haven't I seen you somewhere before? Have you ever played at Wimbledon?"

"No, that was another person," he replied. After she'd gone he turned to Belinda and said, "That's true, you know. I was reincarnated in Bali. I've had two lives. Before B and after B."

"What does 'B' stand for? Bali or Belinda?"

"Both."

Chapter Fifteen

The Outrigger

As he lay on the sand in the hot sun Adrian was thinking of a conversation he had had the previous night with a couple of surfers who had just returned from a week on the nearby island of Lembongan. "No crowds at all. You have the whole beach to yourself. Not like the more popular breaks in Bali," they had said. He turned over on his side and asked Dayu if she had ever been to Lembongan.

"No, only ever been in Bali," she replied.

"Well, I've heard that there are some really good surfing spots over there and that it's well worth a trip. I'd like to go there next week for a few days. What do you think?"

For an instant she hesitated — the instinctive reluctance of a Hindu to cross the sea — but then she thought of the excitement of a foreign adventure with her white prince. "Yes, if you go, I go," she said as she contemplated the afterthought that, if she didn't go, Adrian might well fall in love with one of those dreadful Lembongan ladies. "When do we go? I must get ready," she said.

"Well, I have to renew my visa but I can do that on Monday so we should be able to find a boat to take us across on Tuesday."

Dayu thought for a moment as she calculated what day it was in the Balinese calendar. It was not an auspicious day to travel. However, she knew that if she was going to stay with Adrian and make him happy she must not let too many spiritual obstacles get in the way. Yet, no matter how much she tried to rationalise it to herself, she could still hear some powerful force inside her saying "Don't."

Adrian duly extended his visa and then rode to "Madé's" restaurant at Bemo Corner where he had arranged to meet her at midday. He found an empty place at the long table in the front which was open to the street. He wedged himself between two sets of German card players, ordered an iced orange juice and waited for Dayu.

When she arrived she squeezed into a place opposite him; it was just a few square inches between a Hamburger and a Frankfurter. "Everything okay?" she asked. "We go to Lembongan?"

"Yes, to-morrow. I have arranged for us to go on a boat — an outrigger in fact."

Her smile faded. She could hear the spirits saying "Don't." She tried to put them out of her mind. She wondered at the confidence of Westerners and the ease with which they could make decisions without any reference to the spirits. She believed that therein lay their strength which was why they were so much richer and more advanced than the Balinese. She knew that she must try to think like them and not be held back by the endless and illogical strictures of the spiritual world. But ... it was difficult.

That afternoon Adrian took his surfboard to the departure point near Sanur and left it with the boatman whose name was Ketut. "How many passengers will there be?" he asked.

"Four persons — you and girlfriend and two American surfboard men," replied the boatman.

"Good, we'll be here at eleven in the morning. *Selamat sore.*"

"*Selamat sore.*"

The next morning they packed their clothes into Adrian's blue nylon bag and tied it on the back of the motor

482

bike. They said good-bye to Thierry and Nicole who were themselves going to spend a few days up in the craft centre of Ubud. "You must tell us what Lembongan is like," said Thierry. "If it is as good as Bali then maybe Nicole and I might go there for a few days."

"It's not as good as Bali," said Dayu who was horrified to think that anyone could be so foolish as to believe that a silly little island like Lembongan could be compared with Bali which the gods had picked out as the centre of the whole universe.

When they arrived at the take-off point they found Ketut loading up the boat in a state of general bedlam. Cans of petrol, live chickens, large baskets of vegetables, a goat and several loudly chattering Balinese women were all being packed in to the thirty foot outrigger. But no lifejackets.

"Any lifejackets?" asked Adrian.

"No, not necessary for outrigger," replied Ketut. "Very safe."

Soon the Americans arrived with two surfboards each and three large bags. These too were loaded in to the boat and it sunk a bit further in the water. The Americans introduced themselves as "Scott" and "Andy". Ketut collected the fares from everyone and began to pull the rope to start the ancient looking outboard motor. As he did so five native boys emerged from the nearby undergrowth and ran down the beach. They too climbed in to the boat.

"Don't you think that we're a bit overloaded?" asked Adrian.

"No, no," replied Ketut. "Very good boat. Very safe. One day took twenty people." They took him at his word although Adrian and the Americans made a few cynical comments.

The engine fired with a whimper rather than a bang and they set off at a slow but steady speed for the other island. Adrian's feet were kept warm by the feathers of the chickens that were resting on the bottom; there was barely enough room to avoid cramp.

Bali appeared smaller and smaller as they plied their way across the glistening ocean, leaving a small backwash in their wake. After half an hour the sun was blotted out by some large black clouds that were coming across from the west. The swell of the ocean began to pick up and it wasn't long before small waves were splashing over the sides of the heavily overladen craft. The chattering women kept smiling and laughing as they watched the waves with mounting excitement. The young boys were grinning and every time that Adrian or the Americans cast an ominous glance at Ketut he too just smiled his toothless grin as if to say "Aren't you lucky that we have the bonus of exciting seas all for the normal fare?"

The boat was now bobbing up and down in the wild sea. It seemed to Dayu that *pasih* was contemplating what to do with this little group of people who had dared to sail on such an inauspicious day. She began to weep and Adrian leant over and kissed her.

Some of the native women began to vomit as the wildly lurching outrigger was being tossed in all directions. The boys now smiled only when one of the Westerners looked at them. But Ketut was no longer smiling.

Adrian was looking out to port when he saw a big mass of water approaching at a distance of about two hundred feet from the boat. His years of riding heavy surf had taught him almost all there was to know about waves and the ocean's moods and he knew that this one would swamp the boat completely. He yelled to Ketut to swing the boat ninety degrees to port so as to point the bow in the direction of the swell. Onward and relentlessly it came. Adrian stood up and screamed to the others to put their hands over their heads in case they should be thrown against some of the so-called superstructure of the flimsy outrigger. At the last moment he grabbed Dayu and told her to dive over the port side to avoid being hit by the boat. In another minute it was all over.

As Adrian floated up through the swirling water his first thought was for Dayu whom he knew was not at all accustomed to the wiles of the ocean like he was. He saw her paddling towards the boat which had not been destroyed. Instead, it was submerged about a foot below the surface of the water. She grabbed the side of the sunken outrigger and was panting as Adrian swam over to her. Her sarong had been torn off and the only garment that she had been left with was her yellow halter top. Her hair was soaking and there was a look of real fear on her face.

Adrian, relieved to see that she hadn't been hurt, grabbed her and held her close. The natives had all managed to survive and were gripping various parts of the completely submerged boat; only their bobbing heads could be seen above the surface of the water.

Scott and Andy were calmly swimming among the debris of empty cans, baskets and vegetables as they attempted to retrieve their surfboards and bags. These they tied to the boat's single bamboo mast that was protruding out of the water. The goat had drowned and the chickens were flying around and making a great commotion. Adrian looked across at the two Americans. Andy was tying the leg-rope of Adrian's surfboard to the mast.

"Thanks, mate," said Adrian.

The sea was still rough and each new wave threw them around as they tried to keep hold of the sunken boat and maintain their heads above the swirling sea. And then it began to rain.

"Have you got any radio or flares, Ketut?" asked Adrian.

"No radio, no flares," came the reply.

"My God," exclaimed Scott.

"How many boats come this way?" asked Andy.

"Sometimes many, sometimes none," replied the boatman. They were none the wiser.

"Oh hell," thought Adrian, "we could be here all night — and all to-morrow!" For the first time he realised the gravity of their plight. "Christ," he thought, "we could all die here!" He tried to banish the thought; he knew that the situation called for calm and courage and not despair.

With a carefully cultivated confidence which he didn't at all feel he called cheerfully to the Americans, "Oh, it'll be all right. We can paddle on our boards to Bali and then call up the coastguard." He didn't even know if there was a coastguard.

"Yeah, good idea," called back Andy. "It's all we can do."

"Well, I've got a wetsuit in my bag which I could wear to protect me from the cold and other things," said Adrian, deliberately suppressing the mention of sharks.

"We've got one set of rubber between us," said Andy.

"Good," replied Adrian. "One of us should paddle towards Lembongan and another back to Bali. Whoever reaches land first should alert the police to get the rescue services into operation."

"Yes, captain," laughed Andy.

"You're not going to leave me here?" whispered Dayu.

"Only for a little while, my love," he said as he pulled her closer towards him.

She began to scream hysterically. "No, no, no. Don't leave! If you leave, I never see you again. Don't go, please don't go!" She let out some long, high pitched howls. Slap! Adrian's hand came down on her cheek with a gently stinging blow. She stopped screaming and began sobbing.

"I am sorry, my darling," he whispered into her ear, "but if you become hysterical so might the others. Whatever happens we must remain calm. Otherwise there is no hope for anyone. If I don't go and get help we might all die."

"I just don't want to lose you. Maybe I come on surfboard with you?"

"No, we'd both sink to the bottom of the dark ocean."

The warmth of his face and words reassured her as she bounced up from under another wave, her face now wet with salt water rather than tears.

It was about two in the afternoon and Adrian asked Ketut how far they were from Lembongan. "About half way to Lembongan," he replied.

Adrian turned to Scott and Andy and said, "Right. I reckon that we are about ten miles from Bali and it would probably take us about three hours to paddle back there. Of course, if one was to meet a boat on the way it would make things a lot easier. According to Ketut it is about the same distance to Lembongan and so one of us should head towards Bali and the other to Lembongan. It will be dark in about three and a half hours so we really must get on our way. It might be possible to find a boat with a decent engine as soon as we land and, if the seas calm down a bit, we could perhaps get back here before dark. If not, we can spend the night getting the emergency services ready to begin searching at first light to-morrow. It sounds crazy — two surfers paddling off on their own in different directions in the middle of nowhere — but there's no alternative. Either that or we all stay here the night and probably die. There are some peanuts and biscuits in those two tins and a bit of fruit floating around from the baskets."

He turned to Dayu and told her to eat some of the contents of the tins later on and to share the rest with the others. She pressed her nose into his damp, salty face and they kissed wildly before being swamped by yet another huge wave. Her intuition both as a woman and as a Balinese well acquainted with the moods and vengeance of the spirits told her that, if Adrian paddled away into the distance, she would probably never see him again. And yet she knew that the deed

487

had to be done if there was to be any hope of rescue. She clung to him tightly — both as her lover and as a symbol of survival. With her nimble little toes she split open the velcro fly of his boardshorts and pushed them down. Their bodies moved in rhythm with the current. First gently and then more vigorously as a powerful rush of water carried them several yards. They writhed around together in the swirling sea ... closer, closer ... until a great wave came and tore them apart.

When it was over Adrian swam across to where Andy had tied his surfboard and jumped on it. He reached for his soaking bag and pulled out his wetsuit. By lying on his back on the board between swells he managed to pull the tight rubber suit up his legs, put his arms through the sleeves, and then pull it up over his chest. Andy did the same and the two of them lay on their boards and discussed strategy. The American reached into his bag and pulled out a water-proof wallet. He unzipped it and took out some money. After counting it he gave half of it to Adrian and told him to tuck it down the inside of his wetsuit.

"You never know," he said, "you might need it for something. If you don't you can give it back to me later." There was a slight trace of anxiety in his voice.

All three surfers put their heads together and said a prayer. The Balinese took their cue and invoked the good offices of their gods. Adrian then paddled across to Dayu and gave her one last kiss — just a peck on her left cheek. He turned and paddled away. She did not see him go as her tears were merging with the salty residue of the last wave.

They had decided that Andy should paddle back to Bali while Adrian would head for Lembongan. As they departed the old Balinese ladies, still clinging to the sunken boat, let out a resounding cheer and used their free hands to wave good-bye. "*Selamat jalan,*" they yelled.

The two surfers paddled vigorously with their strong arms and shoulders. Andy pushed on through the driving rain and every now and then looked sideways to see if any fishing boats were passing. There were none; indeed, any that had been out had immediately returned to Bali when they saw the storm approaching.

After a while the sea seemed to become a little calmer and Andy's anxiety began to fall by one or two degrees. The swells were still coming from the north-west and he soon grew accustomed to the noise and swirl of the ocean. Casting his eyes to starboard he thought he saw some big grey object gliding beneath the surface of the water. He kept looking; suddenly he froze as a huge tiger shark passed right under his board. Instinctively, he pulled his hands out of the water and put them behind his back. He watched as the wretched creature kept going — apparently impervious to the strange plate of fibreglass with a healthy meat meal lying on top of it. Soon his back started to ache from the paddling so he paused and took a break.

After a couple of hours he began to get scared as he had sighted neither land nor a boat. Admittedly, the visibility was very poor but the thought did cross his mind that by now he might be travelling in the wrong direction and would never be seen again. Another encounter with a shark might not pass quite so satisfactorily.

When it became dark he realised the full extent of his predicament. He doubted if he would survive the night. He hadn't even had anything to eat or drink since nine in the morning.

It must have been about four hours after dark when he saw a light in the distance ahead. "Thank-you, dear God," he yelled and then, as an afterthought, "Oh yes, and thank-you too, Huey." With renewed vigour he pulled his hands through the water — good, clean strokes — and headed towards the beacon. More lights came into view and he thought that he was almost there. However, it took a lot longer than he anticipated and the muscles in the back of his neck were aching terribly. He slowed down a bit and relaxed. He now knew that he was going to make it and that he would live to see another day and ride another wave.

As he approached the largest group of lights he could identify the high profile of the Bali Beach Hotel at Sanur where he and Scott had gone to the disco one night with a couple of girls from London. "A nice rum and coke will be the first thing that I ask for," he thought as he began to plan what he would have to do once he landed. He knew that there was no hope of finding the castaways in the dark and that all he could do would be to inform the authorities to begin their search at first light in the morning. He thought of the others fighting for their lives in the ocean and he silently cursed Ketut for not having any flares on board. "He had everything else," he thought. "Enough chickens for a banquet, enough vegetables to provide a market, goats and petrol but no bloody flares! Or lifejackets!"

As he came close to the shore he could hear music from the outdoor disco as it wafted through the warm tropical night. The rain had stopped and the sea was quite a bit calmer. He put his right hand in the water for the last time and a few seconds later his board touched the sandy bottom. He rolled off it and pulled himself up on to the narrow sandy beach. He lay there — too weak and exhausted to stand up. He crawled a little further up the sand, pulling the surfboard as he went; he hadn't even thought to untie the leg-rope. He turned over and lay on his back for some minutes. In a state of semi-consciousness.

The only person who saw Andy drag himself out of the water and flop down to rest on the sand — just like a green turtle landing to lay its eggs — was Wayan, a skinny old Balinese man who was sitting under a casuarina tree enjoying a pipe of opium. He was dreaming of times long ago and thinking of how good the gods had been to keep him safe and out of the reach of the evil spirits all these years.

He had been born in Sanur many moons ago but had no idea how old he was. Over the years he had seen many bad and mysterious things washed up by *pasih* and, as he stared at Andy's prostrate body, he decided that it was better to have nothing to do with it. He could remember as a child the Chinese steamer that was wrecked just off Sanur Beach in 1904. The villagers believed that it was a gift from the gods and so they sailed out in their *praus* and looted it. They momentarily forgot that it was lying in *pasih*. It wasn't long before their karma turned bad and the demons asserted themselves. The owners of the vessel complained to the Dutch colonial government in Java and they decided to invade the island and bring it to order.

Wayan could hear the branches of the casuarina tree rustling in the breeze. He lit another pipe as he recalled the day when he had been fishing with his father less than fifty yards from where he was now sitting. They were standing in about three feet of water holding their lines when they saw a fleet of Dutch ships appear on the horizon. Closer they came until they dropped anchor just outside the reef. Wayan and his father were excited at all these new gifts from the gods and ran to get their *prau*. This time the loot would be many times greater than the old Chinese ship. Boom! Boom! His father fell down dead as a shell from a Dutch warship landed on the beach. Then more. "*Pasih* is really angry to-day," he thought as he dashed into the coconut trees to get away from the powerful demons.

He then thought of the day when, as a young man, he was on the beach taking part in a cremation ceremony for one of the village elders. Just as he and the other villagers were about to scatter the ashes into the sea he looked up and saw a dark shadow beneath the surface of the usually clear blue water. He pointed it out to the others and they stared in wonder at the shadow which became darker as it approached the shore. Then millions of live rats with long tails were washed up on the beach and began scampering into the hinterland. There had been a tidal wave a few hours earlier and the villagers did not quite understand how to treat this new manifestation of the demons' displeasure. They came to the conclusion that the rats were lost souls who had left *pasih* and were seeking to be liberated from the sea and all its dangers. So they let them run inland and many cremation fires were lit to free the rats' spirits.

After the rats the next evil cargo to be thrown on to Sanur was the Japanese in 1942. He could remember watching their arrival and witnessing their brutality as a fat yellow-skinned officer with little round glasses on the end of his nose pulled out his sword and chopped to pieces a Chinese lady and her baby who were hiding in a beachside *warung*. He had seen that with his own eyes. It had been for real.

What was not so real were other strange and terrifying beings that he thought that he had seen rising out of the sea. Like turtles with long poisonous spikes protruding out of their shells. And sharks with as many feet as a centipede. And crabs with claws as big as the Bali Beach Hotel. No, he decided, he couldn't be sure that he had seen such strange creatures. They had appeared only in his opiated dreams.

He just sat there staring at Andy whose black wetsuit was rising and falling in rhythm with his breathing. To Wayan the boy was just the latest harbinger of evil that *pasih* had deposited on the beach and there was no way that he was going to get involved. Chinese steamer, Dutch warships, live rats, Japanese "people slicers" and now, in the middle of the night when the power of the spirits was at its strongest, this strange man dressed entirely in rubber clothes who looked like one of those American moon men. "Maybe he is from the moon," he thought. He lit another pipe and fell into a reverie about the mysteries and dangers of the deep.

Fortunately for Andy not everybody shared the old man's fears and his indifference to washed up bodies.

Colonel Beresford and his wife, Audrey, were spending a week at the Bali Beach Hotel as part of a world trip. The colonel had recently retired as manager of a big insurance company in Johannesburg and, with all their children having fled the nest, they had decided to use some of his "golden handshake" money to see the world. Not surprisingly they found Bali to be a particularly charming and romantic place and they especially liked to take a walk along the small beach in front of the hotel each evening after dinner. "Not fit for a dog to be out in this weather," said the colonel but his wife insisted, saying that they would be gone in a few days' time and so they might as well make the most of it.

They left the bright lights of the lounge bar, walked across the terrace beside the swimming pool and stepped on to the beach. They decided to walk along towards the road and then back through the hotel's main entrance. It was darker than usual and they had walked only about thirty yards when they noticed a dark object in front of them. At first they thought that it was a native lying down — just like they do in South Africa. As they moved closer they saw the surfboard and the white face of the American.

"Are you all right, old son?" asked the colonel. There was no reply. Colonel Beresford crouched down and checked that the body was still breathing. "Well, thank God it is," he said. He then tried to open Andy's eyes but they flicked shut again. "You know, Audrey, I think that a cup of hot tea will do the trick. He must have got caught round on the rocks during the storm or perhaps he has been drugged. Who knows? Why don't you go up to the bar and fetch a thermos of tea and a drop of brandy. I'll stay here in case he wakens. Get Nyoman to come back with you."

A few minutes later Andy opened his eyes and became aware of Colonel Beresford's ruddy face with its white moustache and blue eyes. "Hello, sir," he said. "We've been shipwrecked."

"How many of you?" asked the colonel.

"Too many."

"Where are the others?"

"Out there."

"Good God," exclaimed the colonel as he looked across the inky blackness of the limitless sea. "Well, we can't do anything until the morning. First, we must get you into a warm room. My wife will be down here in a minute with some hot tea and brandy to warm your innards."

"Thanks," drawled Andy as his eyes began to close again.

Mrs. Beresford arrived with Nyoman, the barman, and they administered the good liquids to the drained out surfer. He sat up and untied the leg-rope. Nyoman picked up the board and Andy was soon able to stand up and walk to the hotel — slowly at first as every step was something of an ordeal for his utterly exhausted body.

When they reached the foyer of the hotel Colonel Beresford spoke with the manager and told him as much as he knew and offered to let Andy sleep in the spare bed in their suite for the night. The manager wouldn't hear of it and said that there was a vacant room just across the corridor and that Andy could stay there as long as he liked and without charge. The manager also contacted the chief of police at Kuta to come and talk to the shipwrecked sailor to try and ascertain exactly what had happened. Andy was taken to the Beresford's suite for a shower and the colonel loaned him some clothes.

About an hour later three policemen from Kuta arrived to interview him. They had maps and asked him to point out the spot from where they had sailed as well as the approximate position of the sunken boat. Andy, whose head was now clear, obliged to the best of his ability. They asked many questions and said that all they could do was send a patrol boat out in the morning. There were no 'planes available as they were all involved in a military exercise over in Sumatra.

"Do not worry, sir," said the senior policeman. "If they are still alive the patrol boat will find them in the morning." They then shook hands with Andy and made their way to the manager's office to telephone the military command to alert the patrol boat.

Andy thanked the Beresfords for their kindness, crossed to his own room and fell into a deep sleep — the sleep of the saved and the thankful.

■

Adrian had paddled at a steady pace as he made his way in the direction of where Ketut had pointed him towards Lembongan. He looked back a few times to the human specks in the sea as they clung to the submerged wreck. "Just spots in the ocean," he thought and yet it was the centre of his own universe. Dayu — all alone in the strange sea. Helpless and frightened, her very life depended on his paddling and good luck. He wondered how Andy was going. Surely one of them would reach their destination and raise the alarm to save the others.

It began to get dark and still there was no sight of land. He knew that he mustn't panic or despair but deep down he began to have some serious doubts. "She could already have drowned," he thought, "and there is no guarantee that I am going to make it either."

After a few more hours he began to think that it must be after midnight. It seemed to his tired and confused mind that he had been in darkness for a longer time than he'd been paddling during the daylight hours. He was close to the point of exhaustion and despair when he looked to starboard and saw a line of palm trees through the dim moonlight. "Eureka!" he cried as he turned his board towards the shore. A few minutes later he was on the beach but ecstasy quickly turned to disappointment when he looked in all directions and saw nothing but darkness. Tired, hungry and thirsty, he wondered how long it would be before he could make contact with a village.

He had never been to Lembongan; it was unknown territory. He knew that there were surf breaks and reefs but of the island itself he knew absolutely nothing. He walked along the beach to look for a stream to quench his thirst. About three hundreds yards along the sand he stepped into some cool flowing water and fell down and drank from it copiously. He took off his wetsuit, threw it on the sand and lay in the gently lapping water for several minutes. Everything was silent except for the sound of the water. He thought he heard a noise over by his wetsuit. When he looked across he saw a long dark thing moving along in front of the blue rubber. The black cobra was less than six feet away from him. He froze and then slowly and with as little noisy interruption as possible to the water he crawled sideways and then stood up and walked away. He watched the cobra glide up the sand and into the undergrowth.

He picked up his wetsuit and went back to where he had left his surfboard. He could hear an occasional rustle high up in the trees and guessed that there must be monkeys in the forest. He sat on the sand for nearly an hour thinking about all kinds of things — the fate of the castaways, where he was and when he would be able to get some food and make contact with a village, whether Andy had been able to raise the alarm and when he would next have Dayu's warm body in his strong but now aching arms.

Out of the corner of his eye he could see a dark movement along the beach. It was coming towards him along the tide line. At first he thought that it might be a man who could lead him to some food and the police but as it came nearer he noticed that it was too long for a human being. A moment later he could also see that it was too jagged as the profile of a crocodile at least twelve feet long appeared through the darkness. He grabbed his wetsuit and silently but speedily backed into the bushes at the top of the beach. "My God," he thought, "how many more are there?"

The lumbering beast went past and Adrian lay down in a small clearing and rested his head on his rolled up but still damp wetsuit.

He heard something dart through the trees behind him. As the noise retreated into the distance he asked himself what it could have been. "Too big for a pi dog. Maybe a leopard or a black panther or even just a plain old wild pig." He was now having to make a big effort to stay awake as the exhaustion of the paddling was beginning to take its toll. But he knew that to fall asleep in this jungle of the unknown could be fatal. It was taking him all his time to stay alert to sounds which he knew he had to listen for if he was to survive.

He reasoned that, if he went down on to the sand, he would stand out as an object of curiosity for any of these creatures and he had no wish to put himself in their sights. On the other hand, if he were to stay in the bush, he would be less likely to see snakes but at least he wouldn't be so visible. So he opted to stay in the undergrowth a few feet up from the beach.

It became harder to stay awake and he began to hallucinate. First it was the monkeys smiling at him and adopting human forms and then others — people whom he knew — assuming the forms of monkeys. Then it was the leopards. They were all around him — grey spotted leopards whose spots became black, then purple and then crimson. Then came the tigers. Or were they zebras? Whatever they were their luminous green stripes lit up the whole night. Then the whole jungle came alight and Adrian could see right through it — all the way to the other side of the island. The trees were still there but their trunks were made of see-through glass. Ah oh, the colours — there were thousands of rainbows reaching across the sky in all directions and on the ground even more and brighter colours. There were luminous pink elephants copulating with the greatest vigour in pits. Hundreds of elephants and dozens of pits. And huge grey and green dinosaurs clambering across the earth. And the pythons. All the branches of the glass trees suddenly turned into writhing pythons. Interlocked in all sorts of weird and wonderful knots and ties. And from the direction of the sea came a huge explosion as a million tons of water burst out of the ocean. Out of the spray came all the brightly coloured coral in the strangest shapes, sizes and colours. Then the coral moved up the beach and attacked all the luminous animals and smashed the glass trees. The noise was terrifying. The jungle had become a scene of devastation. There were dead animal carcasses everywhere but they were no longer the greens of the tigers and the pinks of the elephants. Just a grey and black mess. The only colour left in the world belonged to the coral — now in all sorts of weird shapes as it danced on the remains of the dead animals to signify the ocean's supremacy over all land based creatures.

Adrian woke up with a start. At first he thought that all the deadly creatures of the jungle were watching him and would attack him if he moved any part of his body. He lay still and rigid as a corpse. Then slowly a flicker of reality began to penetrate his mind and he dared to move his little finger ever so slightly. Nothing happened so he moved his hand about an inch. The animals did not attack so he came to realise that it was all a dream. He opened his eyes and sat up. It was daylight. His rubber suit was still damp so he hung it on a branch to dry. He walked back to the stream and took a drink. There were some coconuts lying on the beach which he cracked open with a sharp rock and drank their white milk. He picked some paw paws from a tree and sat down to a tropical fruit breakfast. At least he was no longer hungry.

The thought of Dayu still out in the ocean nearly drove

him out of his mind and he determined to seek help for them as soon as possible. He grabbed his wetsuit and surfboard and began walking along the beach in what, according to the sun, was an easterly direction. After about twenty minutes he noticed a couple of black specks on the distant shoreline. He quickened his pace and soon saw that they were fishermen dragging their nets. Black, naked and shining in the early morning sun they smiled as he approached although there was a barely perceptible look of surprise beneath their smiles; the sight of a lone white man walking along the beach was not one that they came across every day.

Adrian spoke to them in stilted Indonesian and they soon understood that he wanted to go to the village. They led him up a track through the jungle. After about ten minutes they came to a clearing where there was a group of twenty grass huts on wooden stilts that stood around a village green. All the people of the compound came out to greet him — from the oldest women with their sagging, leathery breasts to the little children who kept running up to touch his legs as if he was the village god. They made him a brew of black tea and gave him a dark brown sarong to wear.

He told them that he wanted to go to a big village to see the police. At the mention of the word "Polisi" their expression turned to one of fear. To them the police meant taxes and fines and bribes. If a policeman ever came to the village he would never go away without exacting tribute in the form of cash or crops or chickens.

One of the old men of the village came to understand that the police were needed to sort out some problem of Adrian's that had nothing to do with the villagers. This man called to his son who came over and bowed to the visitor. The son, aged about twenty-five, led Adrian to an old motor bike that was resting under a straw roof. He motioned him to sit on the back and, after a few efforts, the engine fired and away they went. They rode along a track that soon widened out into a road that was the width of a single vehicle. They drove for ten minutes through jungle.

Soon they reached a larger settlement where they pulled up outside a white stucco police station that stood at the back of a small lawn. In front was a flagpole from which flew the red and white banner of the Republic of Indonesia.

The officer on duty gave Adrian a surly look. He spoke a little English and Adrian was able to make him understand what had happened. The cop was quite unmoved. He realised the helpless plight of the young man standing in front of him and said, "You want help, you must pay me for accident report. Very much trouble. You pay me one hundred thousand rupiah and I make accident report."

Adrian began to argue, claiming that he had been shipwrecked and did not have any money whereupon the sour looking man in uniform dismissed him and returned to his papers. Just about out of his mind Adrian began shouting at him and asked to see his superior.

"Not here. Now pay money to me or go away. And you must not come into police station wearing only a sarong. If you show no respect to authorities, we no can help you."

Adrian suddenly remembered the money that Andy had given him and which he had tucked into the fold of his sarong. He felt for it and pulled out what he thought were ten notes of ten thousand rupiah each. He handed them across the counter to the greedy little man whose face remained impassive. The cop counted them carefully and placed them in a drawer. Still no smile. Just as he reached for his pen the front door swung open and an older and more friendly looking officer walked in and disappeared into another room.

"Is that Mister Chief of Police?" asked Adrian. The man did not look up from the report that he was now writing. Adrian rushed over to the door of the other office, knocked loudly and walked in. The chief officer stood up and smiled.

Adrian spoke to him in a mixture of Indonesian and

English. Once again he explained his tale of woe. As it unfolded the smile on the other man's face was replaced by a look of extreme gravity. When Adrian added a bit at the end about the lack of co-operation from his colleague and the demand for the "accident report fee" the officer's look turned to one of annoyance. "My apologies, my biggest apologies," he kept saying. But he didn't bother to retrieve the money and return it. He picked up the telephone. "Sit down, sir, I shall ring the military."

It took him ten minutes to get through to the army headquarters. They told him that they had already been alerted and that a search was under way. "Thank God," thought Adrian, "at least Andy must have made it." His thoughts then turned to Dayu and the others still in the water and he wondered if they had survived the night. Under his breath he uttered a quick prayer, "Please God keep her safe and alive in the water." He hoped it wasn't too late.

■

After Andy and Adrian had disappeared from the sunken boat the others had filled in their time by dodging the waves that threatened to smother them and looking out through the dark drizzle to see if they could spot a boat. A fishing boat perhaps or even one of the small freighters that trade between the islands.

A giant turtle swam by and Scott reached for his spear gun which was in his soaking bag. By the time he got it the creature had disappeared. He kept the gun by his side and ten minutes later an even bigger one swam past and this time he managed to catch it. The old women let out a cheer. Seafood for dinner. There was little else to cheer.

They began to realise the unlikelihood of any vessel reaching them before the morning as the rain was still heavy and visibility was steadily decreasing. The young boys were kicking around in the water, splashing each other between

501

dodging the waves and looking out for more turtles. Scott envied them their naivety. By now they were the only ones who were still smiling.

Dayu began to cry and Scott swam over and put his arm round her. She smiled faintly but seemed to be troubled by some premonition of danger. He tried to boost her spirits by relaying to her some of his own false confidence but his worthy efforts failed to make much impact.

Scott and Dayu were swamped by a wild swell that flowed over them. When he opened his eyes again he could see a boat approaching from the direction of the rain. It was none too sturdy looking but at least it was big enough to take them all on board. He estimated it to be about ninety feet long and could hardly believe their luck. He started yelling and waving his arms. "We're saved, we're saved," he called to the others. The old ladies looked up but none of them were smiling. Scott wondered why. He watched the boat slow down as it approached the bobbing heads in the sea. He could see some Asian men running around on the deck and then ... And then ... No, his eyes must be deceiving him. There must be some mistake. Now that the ramshackle craft was almost right above him he could clearly see a man standing on the bow with a shotgun protruding from his hip. "Pirates," said Ketut.

The boat, which bore no markings of any kind, had pulled up so close that its wash swept over the heads of those in the water. The man on the bow called some orders to a couple of his Malay crewmen. Two skinny looking wretches came up from below and started talking to the Balinese in Malay. Since the Malay and Indonesian languages are very similar Dayu and the others could understand what was being said. The old ladies started wagging their heads in denial when one of the men asked if they had any gold or silver jewellery. Then the boatmen pointed to the American's speargun and signalled for him to bring it to them.

502

On instinct and without thinking the matter through Scott thought that, if that was all they wanted, they could willingly have it. He put the gun round his neck and swam around the boat to where the pirates were beckoning. Just as he reached the side of the vessel two of the crewmen jumped into the sea on the other side with a tremendous splash. Scott wondered what was going on as all he could hear was the swish of the water. And he could see nothing except the spray from the two men coupled with the rise of a swell rolling in from the other direction. The next thing he heard was a piercing scream from Dayu as she kicked and fought in a hopeless attempt to escape the strong, rough grip of the seamen. Yelling, screaming, almost drowning, she was dragged by the men over to the near side of the boat and pushed up a rope ladder.

Scott was at first confused by all the commotion but, as it slowly dawned on him what was happening, he screamed out, "You dogs, you filthy murdering dogs." The man on the bow yelled at him. When Scott looked up the pirate fired a shot that flew just over his head. Then another. Scott dived under the water and held his breath for as long as he could. He really believed that he was going to be shot there and then. When he emerged and opened his eyes the first thing he saw was the terrified looks on the faces of the old women. The young boys were also frightened as they ducked under the water to avoid further imaginary shots. He could hear Dayu's screams from the deck of the boat where she was being held down by several seamen. The next sound was the noise of the boat's motor as it was put on to full throttle. It sent up a wild spray and heavy wash as it headed off in a south easterly direction.

Scott and the others were stunned and some of the old women were sobbing. They, like Dayu, knew the ways of the pirates — unlike Scott from the Western world of Venice Beach, Los Angeles. When he realised the full import of what had happened he began to imagine all the terrible things that they would do to her. "Bastards, bloody bastards," he screamed.

The man who had stood on the bow and fired the shots was the skipper, Gold Bar Cham, a former Thai fisherman who had been pirating in the South China Sea for nearly ten years. He had bought his present boat in 1976 after a particularly profitable descent on a group of gold bearing, starving Vietnamese refugees who were found floating on a junk mid way between Vietnam and Borneo. The fall of Saigon to the communist guns in 1975 was a great bonanza to the pirates of the South China Sea. Hundreds of thousands of Vietnamese had put to sea in whatever craft they could find in order to escape the horrors of life under their new communist masters. Among the fleeing refugees were some of Saigon's most prosperous merchants, many of whom had converted all their assets into bars of gold for their new life in the West. And so they floated towards Malaya, Hong Kong and even Australia — half starved and unarmed but with their pockets overflowing with bullion.

After a while the trade fell off as the later refugee boats carried Vietnamese of lesser means — fishermen and farmers — who found that life under communism was just as unbearable for a poor man as it was for a rich one. Since the later boats contained only thin, bony flesh and no gold the pirates turned their attention to other sources of income like drug smuggling and luring some of Bangkok's teenage prostitutes on to their boats under false pretences and spiriting them off to mid-ocean transfers with ships that would take them on to Arabia for the sexual gratification of filthy rich oil sheikhs. But even that was becoming more difficult: the girls were getting more canny and were refusing to get on the boats. And the wretched DEA of the Americans had been beefing up their patrols in the China Sea. So Cham, priding himself on being a man of business as well as a cut-throat murderer, had extended his vision to new products and new markets which included the interception of small, unarmed coastal traders that plied between one or other of the fourteen thousand islands of Indonesia. Sometimes he took silver jewellery, watches, turquoise, pearls, tortoise shell and the valuable green snail shells that were on their way to the great shell markets of Jakarta and Madura.

On the day of the storm he had just intercepted an overloaded fishing vessel off an island about twenty nautical miles north west of Lembongan. He had taken a good haul of both tortoise shell and green snail and a small quantity of fresh fish — at least enough to feed his crew for the next few days. He had left the terrified fishermen with the rest of their catch only because he didn't have any use for it.

When the storm came up Cham sought a safe spot for his ramshackle but seaworthy boat. He looked at his charts and decided that the best course was to steer down into the strait between Bali and Lembongan and to sit out the storm on the leeward side of the latter.

It was about three in the afternoon when his watchman on the for'd deck picked up some unusual objects on the rain sodden lens of his telescope. He called out to Cham who put the ancient instrument to his good eye. He smelt the sweet aroma of loot when he saw the bobbing heads in the water.

Gold Bar Cham realised that if he was going to keep Dayu on board for the Arab slave trade he would have to pass to the east of Bali and then south into the Indian Ocean. He reasoned that there would be little chance of being intercepted before dark as, although the storm was dropping, visibility was still very limited and boats would be staying in their anchorages. He would have a clear start of nearly twenty hours. He knew from experience that naval vessels were few and far between in the vast expanses of sea which separate the thousands of islands in the great archipelago. Indonesia's naval vessels were usually sailing near its borders with other nations — the Philippines and Malaya and hardly ever in the waters around Bali.

"People go missing all the time and for all sorts of reasons," he thought. "Runaways, criminals, smugglers, prostitutes. Why should one girl — probably a village girl — bring out the Indonesian navy on an expensive and probably futile search? The odds are certainly against it."

Over the years Gold Bar Cham had sold many Thai girls to the Arab traders and he knew the market well. If a girl was really beautiful — and a bit different and exotic — she would fetch a very good price and it could well be worth the long trip to the transfer point in the Maldives to hand her over. And, of course, there were other things that he could pick up at the transfer point — pearls, drugs, weapons, gold.

He knew that the waters around the Maldives were unpatrolled as only a handful of their twelve hundred beautiful islands were even populated. That is why some of the uninhabited ones were used as transfer points for the various illicit cargoes that support a certain stratum of the shipping industry — gold to India, Lebanese hash to Australia, guns to Tamil rebels, and nubile Asian girls to Arabia.

Dayu was taken to a cabin below by her rough Malay captors. They were skinny opium addicts with a distant look in their eyes. One of them had no teeth at all and the other had only two top ones that looked like sharks' fangs. They shared a cabin with four others and in the centre was a small table on which rested some burnt down candles and opium pipes. The cabin was hot and stuffy and reeked of all sorts of unpleasant smells. They gave her a towel as her halter top had been torn off during the melee in the water and she was completely naked. She wound the towel around her dripping and trembling body.

The two men made her a pot of tea and gave her some biscuits and a dish of rice, beans and fish which they heated on an antique stove. They didn't say much and soon her screaming and sobbing ceased as she tried to come to grips with the reality of her situation. She did not think that these two would violate her; she believed — rightly — that their tastes lay in opium rather than sex. But what of the others?

After she had eaten they took her to a small cabin where there was a bunk and not much else. They gave her a saucepan of cold water and a well used cake of soap. She threw the water over her head and had a "shower" to wash the sea salt out of her pores. She lay down on the bunk and closed her eyes.

After directing his boat for about an hour and making sure that there were no patrol boats on his tail, Gold Bar Cham stepped down to the tiny cabin and stood in the doorway staring at the apparently sleeping girl. Her wet towel was thrown on the floor and she was lying under a dirty white sheet. He was struck by the classical beauty of her face — the long slender nose, the perfect little eyelids and high cheekbones.

Consumed by both his own lust and his curiosity at whether he had plucked a valuable prize for the Arabs, he bent over and lifted the sheet. Dayu screamed when she looked up and saw the scarred, broken toothed face that was now only a few inches from her own. When he reached down and fondled her breasts with his rough, dirty hand she became positively hysterical. He pulled his hand away and stepped back to the doorway. He didn't want anyone to go crazy on his boat and nor did he wish his crewmen to think that she was so repelled by him as to resort to loud screams. Cham, rough pirate though he might be, was very sensitive about the image of his masculinity.

"Perhaps she is virgin," he thought, "in which case she will bring a very high price indeed. If she is not virgin, then I can go to bed with her — later. Either way I win. Maybe I go to bed with her and still sell her as a virgin. Ha! Ha!"

He went to his own cabin and looked at the charts. He

worked out that, if he proceeded due south from Bali into the wide expanses of the Indian Ocean, he would be well clear of any pursuing vessels or even 'planes. Then, when they reached latitude nine degrees south, they would turn eighty degrees to starboard and head in a straight line for Bounty Atoll in the Maldives. Cham knew that Bounty was one of the best exchange points in the East. There was usually an Arab trading vessel there and he would be able to exchange the girl for either gold or dollars. The last cargo that he took there was a consignment of twelve Thai girls for which he was paid sixty thousand dollars.

"Sheikh man gets much money for oil. Then uses money to buy girls — good business for me and girls make sheikh man very happy. Ha! Ha!" he thought. "There is a price for everything and money can buy anything in the world. That is why it's much better for me to be pirate than fisherman. More money."

He closed his charts and sauntered into the wheelhouse to tell the helmsman to proceed south. He then sat down on a bench and rolled some buddha into a cigarette and lit it.

When the head of the Basarnas search and rescue organisation arrived at his office at seven the next morning he learned that the nearest patrol boat was sheltering on the other side of the island and that it would take about three hours to reach the search area. He gave orders for it to proceed there immediately. Looking up at the sky he thanked the gods that at least the storm had passed and there would be clear visibility. He wondered if they would find anyone alive.

It was after ten when the vessel, a sixty-two foot motor launch, reached the area which Andy had pointed out on the map the previous night. The launch did several wide swoops as it scoured the waters between Bali and Lembongan.

Several spots appeared on its radar screen — fishing vessels, submerged reefs and even a few rafts. It checked out a few of them but the object of the search remained undetected. By midday the captain was privately thinking that there was no hope of finding them and he began to pace the after deck and look out to sea for floating corpses. "We'll keep the search going until an hour before dark and, if there is no sighting by then, we shall go back to Bali," he said to the helmsman. "There won't be any point in searching to-morrow as they couldn't survive two nights in the sea."

Just after one o'clock a small uncertain mark appeared on the bottom right hand corner of the screen. It came on stronger as the boat continued on its north western course.

"What's that? We'd better check it out," said the captain. As they steered towards the spot he looked ahead and could hardly believe his eyes. Black heads bobbing out of the blue sea and a couple of waving arms. He slowed the boat and pulled alongside as gently as possible for he knew that by now they would be thoroughly exhausted and might not be able to survive the waves that would be created by the launch.

He wondered why there was some hesitation by the castaways to swim over and climb on board. It was as if they were checking him out — especially the one with the short blond hair. A couple of the sailors jumped into the sea and helped the old ladies towards the ladder which had been dropped over the side of the boat. "*Pelan, pelan*," called the captain. The gentle way that they guided the old women up the rope ladder reassured Scott that the launch was indeed a rescue vessel and not another bunch of body snatchers. The native boys climbed up and then Scott, who handed his surfboard up first. The sailors laughed when they saw the board. Their warm smiles relaxed the atmosphere.

■

One of the few services that the police chief on Lembongan provided for Adrian was a passage on a fishing boat that was due to depart for Bali at two in the afternoon.

The sea was now calm and the sky clear — a far cry from the conditions of the previous afternoon. Adrian sat on the deck and cast his eye in all directions as he searched in vain for Dayu and the others. "Or maybe their floating corpses," he thought in a black moment of despair.

It was dark by the time they reached Bali. Adrian thanked the fisherman and looked round for a *bemo*. He couldn't be bothered bargaining so he agreed to pay the full fare out of what was left over from the money that Andy had so sensibly loaned him.

The *bemo* rattled along the rough, pot-holed road and they eventually reached the main police station from where the search was being directed. Adrian rushed through the doors with his heart pounding in expectation of what he might or might not find. He could hear the sound of English voices inside. They ceased abruptly as he entered. Scott and Andy were sitting on a bench facing Colonel and Mrs. Beresford.

"Thank God you made it. Where's Dayu?" he asked with a real air of relief. He knew that, since Scott was there, they must have all been rescued. Dayu had probably gone back to the cottage to get some clothes. Or maybe she was in with the chief of police making a statement. Perhaps she was tired and was sleeping after the ordeal. All these thoughts raced through his relieved mind.

There was an embarrassed silence as the other three looked at Scott. He was the best one to speak. After all, he was the one who had seen it happen. Scott opened his mouth but the words refused to come. Some moisture appeared in his eyes.

"Did she drown?" screamed Adrian.

"No," mumbled Scott. "She didn't drown."

"Well, where is she?"

"I don't know."

"What do you mean, you 'don't know'? You were with her, weren't you?" Scott looked down at the polished floor. He was completely tongue tied.

At this point Colonel Beresford took over the conversation. With the natural command of an officer and a gentleman he took full control of the situation. "You must be Adrian," he said. "I'm Walter Beresford and this is my wife, Audrey. We picked up Andy when he landed on the beach last night. He was nearly dead from exhaustion. We informed the authorities but the earliest that they could begin the search was at first light this morning. They found your people at about two this afternoon but your girl-friend was not there. Scott said that yesterday afternoon a pirate boat approached and they took away your girl and his speargun. The pirate fired warning shots and there was nothing that Scott could do to stop them. They tricked him into leaving her before they grabbed her out of the sea."

"Oh my God!" gasped Adrian. The worst thoughts began to seize his fertile imagination. Rape, mutilation, torture, bondage. The images multiplied. "Can't we find them?" he screamed.

"I have already discussed that with the chief of police," replied the colonel. "They would have a start of two nights and a day and could be hiding off any one of a thousand or so islands that could be reached in the time available. They might already have dropped the girl off."

"Not likely," said Adrian. The thought of a gang of pirates abusing his precious and helpless Dayu filled him with horror. He stormed into the office of the chief of police and asked when the 'planes were going to begin searching.

"No 'planes. Air Forces all over in Sumatra on military exercise. No can do," said the chief in a tone of bureaucratic finality. Then he smiled and said, "I wish that I could help you, Mister, but there are no 'planes available. I shall tell the patrol boat to search all to-morrow for the pirate criminals."

"They'll never find them," retorted Adrian. He raised his voice. "You say that there are no 'planes. Then find one and start the search in the morning." He strode out of the small office. Livid and completely out of his mind.

Colonel Beresford heard the last part of the conversation through the thin wall. He walked into the chief's office and addressed him with a rare mix of command and deference. He told the chief that if he did not find a 'plane that night to commence operations at first light in the morning then he, Colonel Beresford, a man of foreign rank and distinction, would personally call on the Governor of Bali and report every detail of the unsuccessful rescue attempt. The chief secretly cowered before such a prospect and said that he would persuade the Air Force commander to provide a search 'plane the next morning.

Colonel Beresford and the police chief then looked at the charts and discussed the likely movements of the pirates. "I believe that they will be heading through all these islands towards Borneo and thence to the South China Sea," said the police chief. Colonel Beresford agreed. "There is nothing east of here that would be rewarding for pirates," continued the officer, "and south of Bali is the huge Indian Ocean. No land for thousands of miles. It is unusual for pirates to come as far east as this; their usual hunting ground is the South China Sea and around Borneo."

"Right," said the colonel. "We should draw a circle around the point of the wreck to a distance of about three hundred miles bearing in mind that they would have had a start of a couple of days."

The circle covered a remarkably large area of sea and islands. "We should leave out the south and east and concentrate on the north and west," said the police officer. "That area alone would take several days to cover."

"Quite," replied Beresford.

512

As a result of these misguided deliberations the pirates had another day and night to sail further away and well past the point of any possible interception by search 'planes.

The Air Force commander was keen to help but his hands were tied as a result of the annual war games in Sumatra. Unfortunately, one lost girl was not sufficient cause to interrupt an exercise that involved fifty-five thousand air, land and sea personnel. However, he did have in reserve a couple of Sunderland flying boats with standby crews to fly them. He briefed the crews early the next morning and they flew in great arcs over the sea in the search area. They spotted thousands of small craft — fishing boats, ferries, old wooden freighters, junks and rafts but it was like looking for a needle in a haystack.

When they returned to base they reported that they had not seen anything that matched the rough description of the unmarked pirate boat that Scott had given to the Balinese police. As it happened they were right, since Cham and his crew of cut-throats and opium smokers were now but a tiny speck in the limitless expanses of the Indian Ocean.

The crafty pirate had left Dayu alone for the first night while he sat on the deck contemplating how he could sell her for the best possible price. She stayed in the tiny cabin and divided her time between sleep and worry. The two Malays, Abdul and Mohammad, were neither kind nor beastly to her — just indifferent. On one occasion they offered her a pipe but she refused.

On the second night Cham told her that she was to come and sleep with him in his dirty, smelly cabin. She shook her head to say "No" and then put her face into her pillow and began sobbing. He lifted the sheet and touched her with his coarse hands. She tried to resist. He then told her that if she wouldn't go "jig-a-jig" with him, he would throw her overboard. Into *pasih*. She believed him. She knew that she was completely in his control and that, if she was to survive and hopefully see Adrian again, then she would just have to accept the fate that had been pre-ordained for her by the gods.

Her main fear was that she would be abused by the whole crew so she tried to strike a bargain with Cham. In a mixture of sign language and words she made it clear that under duress she would sleep with him but with no one else on the boat. She needn't have worried as that was exactly what he had in mind. Gold Bar Cham was not the type to share anything with anybody and certainly not with his crew whom he always treated like dirt, paying them poorly and frequently beating them and threatening them with one of his several guns. He let them smoke opium because it relaxed them and made them feel good and so they became more docile and less likely to have the energy to mutiny.

Cham took her to his cabin and pushed her on to the bed. She survived the night only by inventing vivid and powerful images of other things so as to blot out the reality of what was happening.

During the days Cham encouraged her to rest as he wanted her to look her best when he would offer her for sale in the Maldives. He had found out that she wasn't a virgin and this made him feel better about sleeping with her. At least he was not depreciating the sale value of the asset by his lustful conduct.

He never spoke a word about her intended fate. Whenever she asked him his answer was always the same: she would be happy and no harm would come to her. Of course, she didn't believe him.

Apart from the fact that it was a pirate boat crewed by opium addicts and skippered by a man who was about to sell an unwilling girl into slavery, the rest of the journey was quite uneventful — warm, clear weather, calm seas, a bit of fishing, rice meals and the usual chatter of the men as they went about their daily tasks.

Dayu was allowed to go up on the deck for a couple of hours each morning to have a shower with a bucket of water and to breathe some fresh air. This was done not out of kindness but to maintain her in a reasonably healthy state for the coming sale. Whenever she was taken on to the small deck a chain was tied around one of her ankles and then secured to a bulkhead amidships. This was to prevent her from ending her own life by jumping overboard and drowning. In such an event Cham stood to lose several thousand dollars. The chain was long enough for her to take a few steps and move around within a very limited circumference. It reminded her of the pet monkey at the cottage which was chained to the tree — also by the ankle — for the same purpose. Movement but no escape.

Nor could she escape from the nights. Every time that Cham climbed into the bed she could not help but compare the scarred, unshaven brute with the slim, tanned, athletic figure of Adrian, bursting with energy, riding the waves like a god and loving her with both strength and tenderness.

One night she went to sleep early. Adrian came into her dreams. He was running to her with his fair curls blowing in the breeze. And he was laughing. In the next image of the dream he was lying in bed with her. She felt him run his hand over her shoulders and massage the back of her neck. She could feel his hand. Sure and strong. As she was about to kiss him she opened her eyes and screamed as the deformed face of the pirate came into view. Cham pulled his hand away from the back of her neck. She put her head into the pillow and sobbed uncontrollably for half an hour. Then she stopped. Drained and exhausted and utterly broken. There were no more tears to cry. There was no escape. All she could do was wait for the gods to take her back to Bali.

■

Adrian too was nearly out of his mind with anguish and uncertainty. When Alex had been killed in Melbourne he at least had the consolation of knowing what had happened. He had even seen her mangled corpse being put into the ambulance. But here nothing was certain. All that was known was the fact that she had been plucked out of the sea by a gang of pirates. After that they had just vanished into the overcast weather and had not been seen again. Indeed, the chances of her ever being found seemed slighter with each passing moment. They could have thrown her overboard as fodder for the sharks. They were probably abusing her in some hideous manner. They could have landed on any one of the thousands of islands in the area and left her stranded.

He lay awake most of the night with strange hallucinatory images passing through his mind — all vivid, horrific and frightening. Occasionally he fell asleep and then invariably reached out to touch her, couldn't find her and woke up screaming. He just couldn't believe the reality of what had happened and the suddenness and uncertainty made it worse. He was in the Slough of Despond. He couldn't even share his sorrow with Thierry and Nicole; they had already gone to Ubud.

The next day at the police station he was told that the flying boats would make one more search during the morning and then return to their base in East Java for lunch. "After that there will be no point in continuing the search," said the chief of police. "The more time that passes the further they can get and so the wider the search area. We have now reached the point where it is useless to continue looking for them. However, as I said, we shall make one last attempt this morning."

Adrian waited at the police station until the early afternoon but no word came in from East Java. He went out for some lunch and returned at three o'clock. Still no word. At twenty past three Colonel Beresford arrived to get an update on the situation and finally at four o'clock came the news that the Sunderlands had returned to base at midday without any results and would not be resuming the search.

Adrian had been half expecting the bad news. Everything over the last three days had been so zany and terrible that a satisfactory or happy ending would be quite out of character. Colonel Beresford could see that he was distraught and asked him if he was spending the evening with friends. Adrian replied that he preferred to be on his own.

"Listen, my good man, my wife and I would be delighted to have you for dinner at our hotel. I think that you need to be with someone for a while."

Adrian's first instinct was to refuse as he had no wish to join the stuffed shirts in the dining room of the colonel's hotel. However, he did feel the need for company — preferably mature and supporting company. Even though he had known the colonel for only a couple of days he liked him and appreciated his experience of life and apparent command of situations. And so he compromised: dinner with the Beresfords but not at their hotel.

They ate at a small *warung* at Sanur. The colonel asked him about some of the dishes that were listed on the handwritten menu.

"Well, I'm sure we'd be doing the surfing fraternity a favour if we had some shark's fin soup," said Adrian. "It's the only creature that I really hate. The old shark is the dread of all surfers. Besides, the broth is quite tasty. The fins are dried and then boiled to extract the gel."

"We've tried it in South Africa but not in the East," said Mrs. Beresford.

"Ah, but it is better to have it in Asia," said Adrian with a mischievous grin.

"Why is that?" asked the colonel.

"Because the Asians regard it as an aphrodisiac."

"Well, in that case we'd better have a double helping,"

laughed Mrs. Beresford.

Adrian explained some of the main dishes.

"Frogs' legs!" exclaimed the colonel.

"Yes, they catch them in the rice fields at night."

"What are they served with?" asked Mrs. Beresford.

"They usually come on their own. The tiny legs of about forty frogs. Bent at the knee. But you can ask for rice or vegetables as well."

"I'll try them," she said. The colonel asked Adrian to choose for him the tastiest dish on the menu so long as it was indigenous to the island.

"Well, I guess that would have to be *gado gado*."

"Right, my boy, now tell me what it is."

"It's a vegetarian dish. Steamed bean sprouts and lots of vegetables. But the real taste is provided by the spicy peanut sauce that they throw over it."

"Sounds delicious."

"It is. I think I'll have some too."

They discussed cricket for a while and then the conversation inevitably turned to the pirates. "I suppose the most that we can do now is to ask that chief of police to put out a general alert to all police stations within a thousand miles with a description of your girl and whatever details we have of the boat," said the colonel. "But since it doesn't seem to have any markings the chances of finding it would appear well nigh impossible. Unless it is flying the skull and crossbones."

Adrian sunk his head into his arms and sat for a long time in silence. He was half expecting Dayu to walk into the *warung*. And yet deep down he had come to the conclusion that he would probably never see her again or feel the sweet warmth of her body against his. Mrs. Beresford put her arm around him and he looked up. He started to tell them about his visit to Semang and how beautiful she looked on the first night when she wore the cheong-sam. The colonel gave his opinion that some of the Balinese girls whom he had seen were absolutely stunning and if he was not happily married to such a lovely lady as Mrs. Beresford he might well have stayed on in Bali and lived with one of them.

The next day Adrian set off for Semang to break the news to Klian. The task required courage worthy of a Victoria Cross. All the way up he kept blaming himself for the whole thing. The more he thought about it the greater the guilt. It was the chain of events that linked him to Klian, to Dayu and to the village of Semang.

"They will think that both my Dad and I are bad spirits sent to bring them trouble.

First, their noble act of bravery and kindness in giving protection to my father and his mates. And for that they had their temple and house burnt down by the Japs. Then, many years later and quite unnecessarily, I turn up and take away the apple of Klian's eye and lose her forever into the hands of the worst rogues on earth. True, she wanted to come and Klian agreed − reluctantly − but, had I not intruded, she would still be in the village instead of lost in *pasih* on a pirate boat. And now I have to tell them that she is missing and I don't know where she is."

He remembered the pact that he made with Klian when the old man agreed to let her go down to Legian. And his parting words, "You will look after her just like we looked after your father and then bring her back safely."

"What if they don't believe me when I say that she is lost? I mean, the whole thing is pretty incredible. I was saved and she wasn't. They will blame me for leaving her in the sea. But what else could I do? Someone had to paddle for help. I wouldn't have been able to do any more than Scott and he was shot at by the pirates. Even if I get the police to confirm the story that won't be any good either because these people don't trust the police. That was one of the first things Klian told me.

Maybe they'll think that I'm just concocting the whole

thing so as to steal her away for my own pleasure and gratification. They know that I took her to Legian; they will probably now think that I want to take her to Australia and so I have dreamt up this ridiculous story to con them into thinking that she is dead. They'll certainly rue the day that my father arrived in their village. But for that incident they would still have their old temple and the *klian* would still have his beloved grand-daughter."

By the time he rode through the big wooden gates at the entrance to the village he was starting to wonder if they would lynch him under the banyan tree. He drove along the lanes towards Klian's house — past busy householders who were still repairing their homes after the eruption.

The old man was sitting on the verandah in the same blood red sarong that he had been wearing when Adrian first saw him. There was a troubled look on his face. "Where's Dayu?" he asked.

Adrian sat down and told him the whole story. Instead of embarking on a tirade of abuse as Adrian had half expected, the old man simply turned his face towards the mountains. He seemed to be in a state of trance. "It is the gods," he said. "Their ways are very strange."

He thought back to 1965 when he had lost all his offspring in the killings. Except Dayu. The sweet gift that the gods had left for him. Almost as if she was meant to make up for the others. And now she had been taken too. By evil spirits. *Leyaks* of the sea dressed as Thai pirates. He knew the ways of the spirits — and the pirates — and was sure that she would not return. Worse still, if her body couldn't be found and cremated, then her soul would not be released from it and she would not be reincarnated into another life. Thus, her whole life process would be terminated forever. She was in the worst situation possible.

When he had lost all his family in the 1965 killings Klian had consoled himself by keeping and looking after Dayu and watching her grow into a beautiful young woman. But now there was nothing. The main light had gone out from his life. All he could do now was prepare for his own end and wait for the gods to come and take him away. To snuff out his present life and release his soul so that he could then move into another — and better — life form. The endless process of reincarnation which provided Bali with all its living creatures from the *pedandas* to the pi-dogs.

Klian turned away from *kaja* and looked at Adrian. The trance like expression on his face began to vanish. Then it was no more. He tried to say something but couldn't. And then he cried. And cried. And cried. Uncontrollably and without pause.

Adrian knew that the *klian* wouldn't live much longer; he would die of a broken heart. So he got up and quietly walked back to where he had parked his bike. He looked back and saw the women of the house attending to the Klian. They had brought out a big bowl to gather all the tears.

The next morning Adrian ran into Scott and Andy in the main street of Kuta. "Listen you Seppos, the colonel and his wife are leaving to-morrow. I reckon that we should go and see them to-night and take them a bottle of Scotch as they have been so bloody kind," he said.

"Agreed," said Andy. "After all, they picked me up from the beach when I was half dead."

"I've got a better idea," said Scott.

"What's that?"

"If we're going to Sanur then we might as well take our boards and have an hour out on the reef. It's a right hander and we're all natural footers."

"I don't feel like surfing," said Adrian.

"Look, man, it's just what you need. Come on, we'll go and get our boards. Oh, and don't forget your wetsuit. The

521

coral is damned sharp."

"Yes, I know," replied Adrian. "I left a bit of my leg there last time."

When they arrived at the hotel the Beresfords were out so they left the whisky at the reception desk and made their way through the hotel grounds to the beach. It was late after-noon and the waves had nice, clean faces and long, peeling lines. It was low tide and they had to be very careful to avoid the sharp, exposed pieces of coral. They enjoyed some good, long rides and shared a few laughs. It was the first time that Adrian had laughed since the shipwreck. But he was also thinking of Dayu and of their brief, intense, but ever so evanescent relationship. A magic moment that had now passed. Just like riding a wave, he thought. It came like a surging swell, he was on the peak ever so briefly, and now the wave had crashed and vanished into the ocean. Waves, like women, he thought, can overwhelm with their orgiastic power. But the intensity of the pleasure can not last; only its memories.

Finally the light began to fade and they paddled back to the beach. They peeled off their wetsuits and went to lie for a few minutes in the warm, tiny waves that were lapping on to the beach. From where they were lying they could see a couple of windsurfers trying to keep their brightly coloured sails blowing in the gentle offshore breeze.

"Look at those wind wimps," said Adrian as if they were members of some sub-human species.

"Pathetic," replied Scott.

"Too gutless to have a go with a proper surfboard," said Andy. "Look at them clinging on to the sails as if it's their mother's apron strings. In the States we tried to have them banned."

"I'd support that law," said Adrian. "I reckon that I'm a pretty tolerant sort of guy but I draw the line at those creeps."

"Me too," chorused the others.

"Let's change the subject. It makes me angry just to think of them moving in on *our* ocean with all their funny paraphernalia. Always getting in the way of proper surfers."

"Ouch!" cried Scott as he jumped up in obvious pain.

"What's the matter?"

"Something bit me on the leg and it's really hurting."

When the water cleared they saw a rather beautiful looking sea snake about four feet long making its way through the water to where a family of Balinese were sitting and laughing. Adrian called out to them. The man saw the snake gliding towards them and hurried his children on to the sand. Then he did a wide turn and came up behind it. Slowly he put his hand down behind its eyes and made a sudden grab for its "throat". A look of pleasure came across his face as he pulled it out of the water and stared at its beautiful skin. "Ah," he thought, "it is a good one. I'll be able to get a good price for the skin." And he looked forward to cutting out its flesh and boiling it for dinner.

Scott was still dancing around in pain. After a while it eased but a big red bruise was left around the bite.

"You'd better put something on it. It might be poisonous," said Adrian.

"Yeah, I once got bitten by one of those things," said Andy. "I was down in Mexico and it later turned septic."

"Ask at the hotel reception desk," suggested Adrian. "They're sure to have something. After all, some of the guests must have been nipped over the years."

They slung the dripping wetsuits over their arms and headed up into the hotel grounds. Andy and Adrian stopped off in one of the poolside cabanas to change into their clothes and comb their dripping hair. Scott went straight in to the lobby and told them of his woes. They gave him a dose of anti-histamine and he soon felt better. Then all three of them, spruce and tidy, presented themselves at the Beresfords' door.

The colonel opened it and was delighted to see them. "Come in, come in. Audrey, we have some delightful company for a cocktail." They gave him the whisky and he poured them some martinis from his own stock. As he handed one to Adrian he whispered, "Any news — good or bad?"

"Nothing," he replied.

They stayed with the Beresfords for about three quarters of an hour. The colonel gave them all his card and offered them hospitality should any of them ever visit South Africa.

Scott said that he was definitely going to go and ride the great waves at the legendary Jeffrey's Bay.

"Then you must come and stay with us in Jo'burg," said Mrs. Beresford. "No surf, I'm afraid as we are six hundred kilometres inland but we could take you to the country club, the game park and some other interesting places."

"Yes, we would love to have you to stay," added the colonel. "I like you Americans. Fought with your fathers at Cassino. Great chaps! Tough in battle too. Wretched monastery. Germans everywhere ... " He drifted off into memories.

"Well, good-bye and thank you for your kind thought. Walter loves his Scotch," said Mrs. Beresford. She took Adrian aside and gave him a kiss on the cheek. "Keep your pecker up and don't despair," she whispered in his ear.

■

Nine days after the shipwreck caused him to change course towards the Maldives Cham began to spend more time looking at his charts and yelling directions to his helmsman.

It was to Bounty Atoll at a point two degrees south of the Equator and seventy-three degrees east of Greenwich that Gold Bar Cham steered his ship of crime. He had been there a couple of times before to collect gold shipments that had come from South Africa and which he delivered to the south-west coast of India. They had been extremely profitable trips. The severe restrictions imposed by the Indian government on gold imports had caused the precious metal to fetch a premium price on the black market. Provided only with an undeveloped and shaky stock market, rich Indians preferred to invest in jewels, gold and precious stones rather than stocks and shares. They preferred to see their wealth and show it off.

It was about midday when the unmarked Thai vessel dropped anchor on the leeward side of Bounty Atoll. There were three other ships at anchor but, without either pennants or markings, they were as unidentifiable as the Thai boat.

Cham drew an AK 47 and a Walther P 38 pistol and dropped a dinghy over the side. Taking three Malay crewmen as his bodyguards he attached a small outboard motor and set off for the sandy shore.

There was already a party of half a dozen Pakistani looking characters who were gathering coconuts into brown sacks. Two of them were armed but they came down to greet the Thais with their rifles hung loosely over their shoulders. They were friendly and eager to find out what cargo Cham was carrying. He didn't tell them but asked if any ships were going to the Persian Gulf. They pointed to the vessel furthest out — a small, rusty freighter. Cham thanked them and they gave him a couple of sacks of coconuts. It was all very friendly and polite.

Cham motored out and pulled up alongside the Arab boat which had sailed to the Maldives from South Yemen with a cargo of automatic rifles, rocket launchers, mortars, explosives and missiles for the Tamil insurgents in Sri Lanka. The arms had already been transferred to another unmarked vessel for onward shipment to Sri Lanka and the captain was keen to find some other cargo to take back to Arabia at a profit. He leaned over the side and spoke to Cham in English.

Cham's mastery of the English language was not good but he made the captain understand that they might be able to do business. A rope ladder was dropped down and the pirate clambered up the side. The Arab was unarmed; however, Cham did not see the two crewmen crouching behind some barrels with their Russian made semi-automatics pointing in his direction. It was only a precaution and after a few minutes Cham found himself sitting on the deck of the Arab's cabin drinking tea.

The captain introduced himself as Hussein and Cham asked him about the market for Asian girls. The Arab was keenly interested but he pretended indifference. He knew that, provided the girl was something special, he could make a profit of several thousand dollars on the transaction. "Must see, must see," he kept saying. He and Cham got into the dinghy and made their way over to the Thai boat.

When they climbed up to the deck Cham shouted some orders to a couple of his men who immediately went below. He took Hussein into the open sided wheelhouse and poured him some whisky. The Moslem downed it in no time. "After all," he thought, "when I am on a Thai boat I am out of Allah's sight."

The men who went below told Dayu to wash herself and wrap a thin cotton sarong around her body. They then took her up to the wheelhouse. She was terrified as Cham had told her the night before that they would probably be meeting an important man who would take her on his boat and return her to Bali. She didn't really believe him; nevertheless, a germ of hope did reside in the depths of her mind and therefore she could not completely discount the possibility of a safe return to her island and to Adrian. It was only this confusion that stopped her from screaming and resisting the transfer to another ship.

Hussein was most polite and gave her a friendly smile. "At least he looks cleaner than the Thais," she thought, "and

526

not so rough."

Cham pulled off her sarong so that the purchaser could inspect the goods. Dayu stood naked and glistening in the sun. "Yes," thought Hussein, "I will be able to sell her for a very high price." He then touched her to see how warm she was. Very warm. He turned to Cham and said, "Yes, we may now discuss business." Cham told Dayu to return to his cabin. Hussein noticed her naturally gracious step as she did so.

The Arab was impressed. He knew that she would bring an excellent price in the Gulf and, of course, there was the added bonus of having a warm body to sleep with on the long journey back to Arabia. Hussein had three wives back in Dubai but he had been at sea for nearly two months which made Dayu's purchase even more attractive.

Cham and Hussein talked and bargained for about twenty minutes, the Arab suggesting that the fall in oil prices had caused a drop in the value of certain commodities — including Asian girls. Cham could see that beneath the impassive exterior the Arab was genuinely keen to buy. After much play acting and bargaining they agreed on a price of twenty-five thousand dollars. Now it was Cham's turn to hide his pleasure behind a facade of seeming indifference. He told his crewmen to take the Arab back to his boat to get the money. He then went down to his cabin to enjoy one last encounter with Dayu who was by now both confused and very frightened.

On hearing the approach of the motor Cham quickly got dressed and went up to the wheelhouse. He and Hussein counted the hundred dollar notes and drank some more whisky.

When Dayu left with the Arab Cham looked at her without feeling or emotion. To him she was a mere article of trade and an object by which he could gratify his lustful desires. He would miss sleeping with her but that was all. He could always capture another girl and the twenty-five thousand dollars was a good price.

He waited off Bounty Atoll for another couple of days and observed the arrival and departure of several more boats. One from Zanibar had a cargo of gold so Cham exchanged his dollars for gold and headed for Kerala in southern India where he knew he could get seventy per cent more than he paid for it. He would go and see old Kumar in the bazaar at the port of Cochin. He had done business with him in the past and knew him to be honourable and, more importantly, well cashed up with those ubiquitous Yankee dollars.

When Dayu boarded Hussein's vessel and saw the crew she realised that she would not be going back to Indonesia. They were all Arabs and quite unlike any men whom she had ever seen around Bali. They were lighter in colour and taller than her own people but not nearly as pale or tall as Westerners. She went below and buried her head in the pillow and cried and cried and cried. For Adrian. For Bali. Even for boring old Semang.

Chapter Sixteen

The Contessa

Scott and Andy decided to go out for the evening to try and unwind after the trauma of the last few days. They went first to the night market where all the stalls were buzzing with noise, movement and laughter. Andy bought a Walkman and some tapes and batteries to replace the ones that he had lost in the shipwreck. Then they walked across to a row of smoking, smelling food stalls where satay sellers were crouched over their charcoal grills calling out for business.

They stopped to watch a girl holding a frying pan over some red hot coals. "What are they?" asked Scott. "Banana fritters?"

The girl kept her eye on the pan. "*Pisang goreng*", she said without looking up.

They heard a voice behind them. It was a Balinese tout who was a commission agent for several of the stalls. "Yes, sir. In English they are 'banana fritters' but in Bali we call them '*pisang goreng*'. This girl makes the best ones in the night market. And the cheapest."

"How much?" asked Andy.

"One hundred rupiah each. Ten American cents."

"Too much!" said Andy with a smile. He meant it as a joke but the tout thought he was being serious and reduced his commission.

"Then special price for you. Sixty rupiah each."

"You serious?"

"Of course, sir."

"Okay, I'll have four." He paid his money and the tout took a quarter for himself and handed the rest to the girl who was sweating over the fire.

They walked on past some more food stalls. "Hey, what's this? A plant shop?" laughed Andy. There were banana leaves piled as high as the canvas canopy that served as a roof. It was one of the busiest stalls in the market. Customers were buzzing around and calling out their orders.

"Ah, good evening, sir," said the smiling stallholder. "Would you like some *lontong*?"

"Why not? Let's try it," said Scott.

"No, not for me. I'm full after the fritters."

"Okay, just one please." The man wrapped some rice in a banana leaf and then steamed it. He handed it to Scott who had a quick taste before he passed over a crumpled hundred rupiah note.

"What's it like?" asked Andy.

"Dee-licious!"

At half past ten they jumped on their motor bikes and rode to the Jolly Frog. When they were at the bar buying their first drinks Andy felt a tap on his shoulder. It was Barbara, a Californian girl whom he had met just before his ill-fated trip to Lembongan. "We're sitting over by the sea-wall," she said. "Third table along. Come across and we'll have a dance later."

"Okay, we'll bring our drinks over."

On their way they passed a table of British surfers whom they knew from Uluwatu. "Where have you guys been?" asked one of the Englishmen. "You missed some great tubes at Ulu yesterday."

"To Lembongan," said Scott. "But we didn't get there. We came back."

"Why? Were there no waves?"

"Yeah, but they were all in the middle of the strait.

530

Sinking boats." They then related the gist of what had happened — the shipwreck, the seizure of Dayu, Andy's swim to shore, the rescue of the survivors and the futile search for the pirates.

"Are you guys kidding or did it all really happen?"

"Scout's honour," they replied.

The Englishmen told some others and soon the news fanned across the tables like a bushfire. At least it was different from the usual chatter about the height of the waves, who was sleeping with whom, and which restaurants served the best cocktails. By the time the contessa heard the story it had been considerably embellished. She gasped in horror, sat back in her chair and cried loudly, "Oh, and to think that she was my best friend!" This statement aroused considerable interest among the other half dozen people at her table all of whom were relatively new arrivals who did not know either Dayu or Adrian.

"What was she like?" someone asked.

"Oh, ever so nice," replied the contessa who had barely spoken more than two words to Dayu in all the times that they had met. All attention was now focussed on the contessa as she reeled off the numerous occasions that she had spent with Adrian and Dayu — Pascal's party, nights at the Jolly Frog and countless times on the beach. She soon became the object of great pity as others sympathised with her in the loss of her best friend.

"Oh, don't worry about me," she said. "I'll get over it. It's poor Adrian whom I feel for. My heart goes out to him. He was so much in love with her and now he'll never see her again. She's probably in Arabia already."

"Arabia?"

"Yes. It's obviously the slave traders who have taken her. A girl as beautiful as that would bring a very good price. Oh, what a terrible thing to happen! And there's nothing we can do about it. If only Pascal was here he'd be able to do something."

"Pascal?"

"He's a great friend of mine who is a lawyer in Paris. He is very influential and would have been able to press the authorities to make a proper search and find the pirates. Poor Dayu!"

The reactions of people were mixed. While all were horrified at what had happened most of those who knew Adrian were reluctant to go round to his cottage and express their condolences. Some didn't feel like intruding on his private grief while others momentarily resolved to visit him but the next day found that the waves and the beach had a greater priority.

Not so the contessa. She was bored with the Jolly Frog. The suave Spaniard who had brought her had drunk too much and was not paying her enough attention and so she decided to go to Adrian's cottage to comfort him. In short she wanted to get right to the heart of the drama.

"I must go and see him — now," she said as she pushed her drink aside and stood up from the table. As she went out through the entrance she heard the bells of a pony cart as it pulled up with a group of singing revellers who climbed out and staggered up to the hole in the wall to buy their entry tickets for what remained of the night.

"Good," she thought, "I'll take that instead of being cooped up inside a *bemo*. It'll take longer but I feel like a ride in the open air. It's so warm." She gave directions to the driver, negotiated the fare and then sat back sedately in the bright cotton upholstery of the seat.

The little horseman pulled the reins and the horse trotted off along the strip of metal that formed a one lane road through the rice fields. "You go to see your boyfriend?" asked the driver who was surprised to see a girl all dressed up and alone.

"No, I go to see another girl's boyfriend. A girl who has

532

been lost in the sea."

"Ah, *pasih*," said the driver. "Very bad." He didn't utter another word.

When they pulled up outside the wall of the uncle's compound the contessa asked the driver to wait. "I'll see if he's in," she said. She walked across the lawn and saw Adrian sitting on his verandah talking to Thierry and Nicole who had just returned from their trip to Ubud. She walked back to the horseman and paid him the fare. Then she returned to the cottage and regally ascended the steps in her turquoise and glitter dress.

"I have only just heard the news," she said in a voice not much louder than a whisper. "And I want you to know how upset I am. Is there anything that I can do to help? If only Pascal was here! He'd be able to find her." She sat down and Adrian asked her if she would like a drink.

"A gin and tonic would be nice. Only if you've got it. With ice."

Thierry said that he had some gin at his cottage and went to fetch it. There was no tonic so he brought back a bottle of lemonade instead. "Sorry, no ice," he said, "and will lemonade be all right?"

"Yes, thank you."

The contessa very carefully extracted most of the details of the accident without appearing to be unduly nosey. "She was so sweet," she kept saying. "I'm sure she'll be found. We must pray to the Mother of God to bring her back to us all. On the day that she returns I shall throw a big welcome home party and ask all our special friends to come and celebrate. I shall start planning it to-morrow." Even this blind optimism didn't change Adrian's opinion that he would never see his loved one again. But the contessa was bright and cheerful and did a lot to lighten and gloomy atmosphere. Adrian started yawning and the contessa said that she must go but she would call again on the morrow to see how things were.

"Thanks," said Adrian.

She then announced her intention of going to the Hamburger House for some coffee. Thierry and Nicole decided to go with her. They tried to press Adrian but he said he couldn't face the bright lights and the crowd. When they had gone he snuffed out the kerosene lamp and went inside. He couldn't bear to go up to the loft. Memories. And probably spirits. "After all," he thought, "the whole thing is pretty bizarre and I don't discount anything happening on this crazy island. Underneath its superficial serenity it is a place of extremes. Paradise one minute and hell the next. Beauty and terror. Peace and violence. But isn't that always the way of the world? Yes, but in other places there is not such a concentration of extremes. This place is different. It must be the gods." He loosened his sarong, lay on the downstairs bed and closed his eyes. He could hear the waves crashing on the beach. Somewhere out there was the pirate boat. And Dayu.

■

Travis Barclay was on his honeymoon with his fourth wife, Cherry, whom he had married at Malibu some ten days earlier. They had flown to Hong Kong for three days' shopping and then on to Bali for a week of total relaxation before returning to the crazy bustle of Los Angeles where Cherry had an interior decorating business and Travis was a movie producer.

They had begun the evening with dinner at a seafood restaurant. Then they went to a snake dance where both the snakes and the girl dancers contorted themselves into all sorts of weird and wonderful positions. "Honey, have you ever seen anything like that before?" exclaimed Cherry.

"Yes."

"Where?"

"In Beirut. The belly dancers."

"I didn't know you'd ever been to Beirut, honey. What's

534

it like?"

"It was the most beautiful city in the eastern Mediterranean. Lovely beaches, perfect climate, wonderful shops. It seemed to have everything. Now it's a whole load of trouble."

After the snake dance had finished they crossed the road to a late night bar where they spent an hour drinking and talking to another honeymoon couple. They were walking arm in arm back to their hotel when they passed the Hamburger House.

"Why don't we go in for some coffee, honey?" said Cherry. "I'm not tired and it seems to be full of gaiety."

They sat at a table about half way along the side wall and ordered a couple of cappucinos. And then two more. They were laughing and joking with the waiters and with the Brazilians at the next table. They both looked up when the contessa walked in with Thierry and Nicole. "Hey, babe, that broad's got real presence. And style," said Travis.

Cherry leaned over and kissed him on the cheek. "Now honey, you just keep those cute little eyes where they won't get into any trouble."

"Hell, I was only speaking professionally," he said. Travis began to think of all the work he would have to deal with on his return to the studio. Shooting would shortly be starting on the new version of Romeo and Juliet and they hadn't yet found anyone for the lead female role. "Oh well," he thought, "at least we've got Romeo sorted out. That limey actor is bloody good. And I guess by now they've drawn up a short list of actresses from which we can choose the leading lady."

They watched as the contessa sat down and started to relate to the eager listeners a far more detailed account of the accident than had hitherto been available.

"And the pirates jumped into the sea and pulled her on to the pirate boat. Black patches over their eyes. The poor thing was screaming in terror. And then Adrian had to paddle his surfboard through miles of rough seas that were filled with thousands of sharks. He had to fight them off with his bare hands. Then he landed on an island of cannibals. He was completely naked and was chased along the beach by a wild man-eating tiger. When he reached the village he was still naked and he was almost eaten by the cannibals. They even lit the fire to roast him. Oh, he was so lucky to get out alive." She even built herself into the story. "Of course, I was meant to go to the island with them. To catch a turtle so that I could make some tortoise shell jewellery to go with my new dress."

"And why didn't you go?" asked Flavio, one of the Brazilians.

"Because at the last minute I was invited to a party. Otherwise I would have been on the boat. And I would not be sitting here talking to you now. There would be no more contessa. No, I would be on the pirate boat with Dayu and the pirates would be raping me which is what they will be doing to Dayu right at this very minute." A look of horror appeared on some of the faces. At all the surrounding tables conversation had long since ceased. The contessa now had an audience of about fifty. All listening with great interest. "And," she continued, "it won't be long before she is in the slave market in Arabia. Being measured and priced by fat oil sheikhs for their harems. And once she gets into the harem that's the end of it. She'll never get out. They'll chain her to the room. They might let her walk round an enclosed court-yard for a few minutes each day but she won't be able to escape. They'll have armed guards and they'll shoot her dead if she tries to flee. One can only imagine the outrages that they'll commit on her! Of course, they'll whip her. And to think that, but for a party invitation, I would be there myself! And she was my best friend." The contessa began to sob. Several men pulled out their handkerchiefs and rushed over to wipe her eyes.

"Oh, the poor creature!" said Cherry. "What a terrible

536

ordeal she's been through." She looked at her husband of eight days. He was staring at the contessa. "Honey, are you listening?" she asked.

"What? Did you say something?"

"I said what a terrible time that poor woman has had. Losing her best friend."

"Eh?" He closed his eyes and tried to concentrate. The waiter who brought over their third lot of cappucino looked at him and assumed that he was in a trance.

"Probably brought on by the contessa's sobbing," he thought to himself. Then he wondered if all the European customers would go into a communal trance. "I hope not," he thought, "they might start smashing all the cups and saucers." The waiter walked over to the counter and continued to stare at Barclay who was obviously possessed by a very potent spirit to have buried his head in his hands for so long. He watched in terrified suspense. Then he saw Barclay leap in the air and scream. "Yes, it is an extremely powerful spirit," thought the waiter.

"Eureka! I've found her! I've found her!" screamed Barclay.

"Calm down," said his wife who tried to sit him back in his chair. "What is it?" she asked anxiously.

"Juliet! We've been scouring the States and Europe for months and here she is right over there. I've never seen a display like it. Can you imagine her doing the dagger scene? If we can nab her the thing will be a winner. And that means dollars. Millions of them." He blew a kiss in the air.

"I think you're right, honey. It was a great performance … " But Travis wasn't listening. He was on his way to the contessa's table where the men were still busy wiping away the last of the tears.

"Excuse me, madam, could I have a private word with you?" asked Travis in his most courtly manner. The contessa looked up through her still misty eyes. She smiled at the confident looking, forty year old American with the strong, handsome face. "Would you like to come over to where my wife and I are sitting?"

The contessa followed him to his table and sat down in the spare cane chair. Barclay introduced his wife and then pulled out his business card and pushed it across the table. The contessa read it. Barclay came straight to the point and asked her if she would like to play Juliet in the great movie where filming was due to commence in a couple of months.

"I know a born actress when I see one and I've never seen an audition as good as you did a few minutes ago," he said.

"But she was my best friend," pleaded the contessa.

"Oh, I'm sure she was and I wasn't suggesting anything to the contrary," said Barclay. "And if you take up the part and come to California it'll at least take your mind off losing her."

"I know what it's like to lose your best friend," said Cherry, "because my best friend was killed last year when a wall fell on her in the house she was decorating. She was crushed to death and it took me months to get over it."

"Would you be free to leave your present commitments and be ready for filming in L.A. in two months' time?" asked Barclay.

The contessa took her time in answering. "Well, I am very busy and it would involve breaking several international engagements and contracts but I suppose if the money was right I would be able to make the effort."

"Well then, it's settled. We'll put you up at the Beverly Hills Hotel. You only have to learn your lines. There's obviously nothing we can teach you in the way of acting. By the way, your accent is Continental, isn't it?"

"Yes," she replied.

"What is your nationality?"

"I am Italian."

538

"Perfect. Absolutely perfect. And where do you come from in Italy? Rome? Milan?"

"No, our palazzo is just out of Verona."

"I don't believe it!"

"Why not?"

"Verona. That's where Romeo and Juliet came from. Juliet was a member of the Capulet family. You're not a Capulet by any chance, are you?"

"No, I am of the d'Annunzio family."

"It's unbelievable!" exclaimed Barclay. "Such a coincidence. Maybe you are a reincarnation of her."

"Perhaps," smiled the contessa.

They discussed a few more aspects of the film and she discreetly raised the matter of the fee. "Let's not even talk about it," said Barclay. "We've budgeted half a million dollars for the part. I'm prepared to pay you a third of it as a deposit immediately upon signing the contract and the rest in regular progress payments until the end of filming."

"Half a million dollars!" thought the contessa. She was down to her last fifty dollar traveller's cheque and had been wondering how she would ever be able to pay the monthly rent which was due on her cottage at Legian. She managed to conceal her glee; it was the hardest piece of acting she'd ever done.

"Well," she said coolly, "you will have to send the contract to my lawyer in Paris. Here, I shall write it down for you." She wrote Pascal's name and address on a thin paper serviette and handed it to Barclay.

"Right," he said. "Can we meet to-morrow for lunch and you can give me more details. Then I shall telex the studio and they'll make out a contract for half a million dollars and post it to Monsieur de Ratton in Paris for perusal. Then you sign it or he may sign on your behalf. We are staying at the Lotus Land Hotel at Legian and we shall expect you for lunch to-morrow. About midday. We'll be poolside and we'll have a cool cocktail waiting for you."

The Barclays got up to leave. "Just one more thing," said Barclay. The contessa looked up in anticipation. "We're really sorry about you losing your friend. You must have been very close to her."

"Ooh, I was," cried the contessa as she burst into tears again. Tears of joy at the sudden and unexpected change in her finances.

Back at her cottage the contessa found it difficult to sleep in the midst of so much excitement. She began to worry that Barclay might change his mind. "Maybe he was drunk," she thought, "and people are always expansive when they are drunk and say silly things." She wouldn't be happy until she had the contract in her hot little hand.

She woke at six the next morning and decided to go for a swim. The sun was not yet up but the cicadas were singing in the trees. She put on her sandals and a pink sarong and set off for the beach. Her route took her to within a block of Adrian's cottage and she couldn't resist going there to tell him what had happened.

Adrian too couldn't sleep and was sitting on his verandah listening to the Beatles' ballads on his Walkman. It was the first time he'd played the tape since the afternoon of Alex's funeral when he had gone down to Torquay to try and come to terms with his grief. Now, as he contemplated the events of the last seventy-two hours, the whole thing had a sense of *déjà vu* about it.

"Oh, hi," he said when he saw the contessa walking along the path. "Have you had any sleep? I couldn't get a wink all night."

"I slept a little. I have come to tell you my good news. It seems that out of your troubles some good has come to me and I want you to be the first one to know. The accident has caused me to get half a million dollars."

"How come?" asked Adrian who was more than a little

surprised.

"Well, last night after I left you I went to the Hamburger House. I was just telling a few people about what happened to Dayu when this man — he is a Hollywood producer — came up and offered me the lead part in Romeo and Juliet. I am to be Juliet. They start filming in two months. I am to be paid half a million dollars. I am having lunch with him and his wife at twelve to-day to arrange the final details."

"That's great," said Adrian. "I'm so pleased for you. I'll make sure that I go and see it."

"Yes," continued the contessa, "and it is all because of Dayu. If she had not been captured I would not have been telling the story that caused the producer to approach me. I believe that it is her spirit that led the man over to my table. He could see that I was very fond of her."

"Yes, we've all had some good times together," said Adrian as he remembered how Dayu had loathed the contessa and regarded her as nothing more than a man-chasing exhibitionist.

"And now we must go and tell Thierry and Nicole about my good fortune."

Adrian followed her across to the other cottage. "Yoo hoo! It's me. Contessa. I have something important to tell you."

"I'll go down and see what she wants," said Thierry as he wiped the sleep out of his eyes.

"Yes, I don't think that I could take her at this hour of the morning," said Nicole who was still half asleep.

Thierry was surprised when he opened the door and saw the contessa and Adrian standing there. He was even more surprised when he heard that she was half a million dollars richer than when he last saw her a few hours ago.

"Oh, congratulations! I couldn't think of a better person for the role," he said.

"That is what Mr. Barclay said. I shall do my best."

541

"Who is playing Romeo?" asked Thierry.

"I don't know yet. Only that he is English. How I love the English! But I shall find out at lunch. Now I must go for my swim. Maybe you come with me, Adrian?"

"No, I have to go back to the police station to see if they've heard anything during the night."

"Of course. Well I shall let you know how the lunch goes."

Thierry went back upstairs and told Nicole the amazing news. "I'm not surprised," she said, "after the performance she gave last night."

"Yes," laughed Thierry. "I've never heard bullshit sound so realistic. But she shouldn't exaggerate so much."

"Oh, I don't know; she got half a million dollars out of it."

The contessa had her swim and then did some yoga on the beach. Her breakfast of fresh pineapples and mangoes was followed by a massage on the beach by a young Balinese man. Then she returned to her cottage to dress for lunch. She chose an apricot coloured Dior creation and some pearls that had been in her family for more than a hundred years. At half past eleven she set off for the Lotus Land Hotel.

The Barclays were stretched out on a couple of lounge chairs by the pool. The contessa joined them and the waiter, resplendent in white shirt and bow-tie, came over to take her order. He then walked over to the tiny thatched roof bar and mixed her a martini.

They had lunch under the shade of palm leaf umbrellas on the terrace by the pool. The Barclays ordered prawns while the contessa settled for frogs' legs and rice.

"This film is expected to break all box office records for a Shakespeare movie," said Barclay.

"And who is the man whom you have chosen to play Romeo?" she asked.

"Michael Beauchamp."

"Michael Beauchamp!" exclaimed the contessa. "Oh, he is such a darling. It should be a great success." She was already considering the likelihood and ramifications of an off-screen romance with the dashing, good-looking Englishman. The world wide publicity, the glamour, the sheer drama and excitement of it all.

"I'm sure we'll make a wonderful pair," she said.

"There's just one thing," interjected Barclay.

"What's that?" asked the slightly nervous contessa.

"There's one torrid scene where the top of Juliet's dress falls down and exposes her bare breast. You won't mind that, will you?"

"No, I would not object," said the contessa whose only attire on the beach were her earrings.

"Good," said Barclay. "I only mentioned it because there are a few actresses nowadays who have been got at by the women's movement and who like to make an issue of that sort of thing. They only do it as a ploy to force us to pay them more money. They always come round in the end. For a few more bucks."

"No, I am not that type of girl," said the contessa in a soft voice.

"Good. Well, I don't think that there's much else to discuss. I have telexed the news back to the studio. They are preparing the contract and I'll have a look at it as soon as I get back on Thursday. Then I shall send it straight to Monsieur de Ratton who can sign it for you and the deposit of $170,000 will then be paid into your account immediately. By the way, you'd better give me the number of your bank account." The contessa wrote it on a spare page of the menu and handed it to Barclay. He looked at it. "B.N.P., Rive Gauche. Shouldn't be any trouble at all. When can you reach L.A.?"

"I'll need to go straight to Paris and have a few days there and I could come to Los Angeles after that."

"Fine. Just let me know and we'll book a suite for you at

the Beverly Hills."

After she left the table the contessa went straight into the hotel lobby and booked a call to Pascal in Paris. An hour later she heard his familiar voice on the faint line.

"My financial problems are over," she declared.

"Why? Have you become engaged to a millionaire?"

"No, but I am now half a millionaire myself."

"What?"

"Yes," she said as she started to explain it all.

"Oh, that is splendid! I shall look over the contract and make sure that it's all to your advantage. *Au revoir*."

"No, not yet," she screamed into the telephone. "You must send me some money. I shall pay you back out of the movie money. I have only fifty dollars left and I have to get to Paris and I don't have any tickets."

"Don't worry. I'll go into the UTA office here and pay for an open ticket. Then all you have to do is to collect it and tell them what flight you want to go on."

"But that won't be enough. I'll need at least another two thousand dollars."

"Why?"

"Because I must throw a big party before I leave."

"Of course, I forgot. I'll send you two thousand, five hundred. Will that be enough?"

"Thank you, Pascal!" she cried as the 'phone went dead.

■

As soon as he returned to Los Angeles Barclay sent the contessa's contract to Pascal who studied it and duly signed on her behalf. Three days later the sum of $170,000 was sent by telex from the Bank of America, Beverly Hills, to the Banque Nationale de Paris, Rive Guache, and credited to the contessa's account which had been showing a debit balance of eighty francs for the past seven months.

While all this was going on in the western hemisphere

the star herself was busy organising her farewell party. She hired a place which had formerly been a disco but which had been closed down for several months. "I shall reincarnate it," she told its happy owner. She then went and invited about a hundred and fifty people. "Everyone who knows me must come to the party and share in my success," she told the crowd at the Jolly Frog the night before.

The natives of Legian were all swept up in the hysteria of the party. They liked the contessa and when she went into the shops to order large quantities of food and drink the smiling staff said to her, "Ah, you're having a party. Very good. All parties very good but contessa party number one."

Many young men spent the day itself decorating the big thatch covered square space with flowers and palm fronds. One of the shops that sold bootleg cassette tapes provided the stereo system; the proprietor considered it both a privilege and a pleasure to mount the disc jockey's chair for the night. The family who owned the contessa's cottage provided its menfolk and their friends to look after the door. During the day there were continuous comings and goings as ice trucks, beer wagons, food carts and humble peasants dragging palm fronds all converged on the scene of the party. The contessa went and bought four leather jackets from the most expensive leather shop in Kuta. As prizes.

She reckoned that she had invited about a hundred and fifty but, allowing for the inevitable extras, she catered for two hundred. The news of the party spread far and wide and the other discos decided that it wouldn't be worth opening since everyone would be at the contessa's show. They couldn't see any point in paying their staff good money and have no one turn up.

The place that the contessa had hired was situated on the main Kuta-Legian road and was only a few yards from the corner where all the *bemos* congregated. And so, with its central and public position and the closure of the other discos, the contessa's party became the sole centre of action in all of Kuta and Legian.

The arriving crowds soon grew so thick that the Balinese men had to form a human wall across the front entrance while the contessa stood there and called out which ones were her guests who could come in and which ones would have to stay outside. A traffic jam soon developed as more and more *bemos* arrived to drop off their passengers. They couldn't get away again through the milling crowds and parked motor bikes that cluttered the narrow road. Since the other discos were closed for the night the satay sellers, who usually set up their portable charcoal grills outside the Jolly Frog and the other places, all came and parked themselves outside the contessa's place and began cooking their kebabs.

After a while the police arrived to find out why the traffic on the Kuta-Legian road was not moving. They soon realised that there was nothing they could do to clear the thousands of people who had gathered there. One group of them, carrying clubs, fought their way through to the entrance where the contessa was still directing the operation of letting in her guests and keeping out the others. "It's my farewell party," she told the police. At first they were very angry with her for causing so much trouble including a complete cessation of all traffic movement between Kuta and Legian. She then told them that she was leaving the next day to go to Hollywood to play the main role in the biggest film of the year.

"Soon you will be able to go to the big picture theatre in Denpasar and see me on the screen stabbing myself with a dagger. A *kris*. Just like in the *puputan* when all the Balinese stabbed themselves outside the palace. But I won't really die."

Their attitude changed. They became more accommodating. They didn't want to offend her when she was obviously possessed by such a powerful spirit. Soon they were

546

laughing and joking with her. She sent one of the Balinese into the bar to fetch a bottle of arak and some glasses. She poured a glass for each of the cops and they all toasted her coming trip to Hollywood.

"Is there anything we can do to help you with the party?" they asked. "We want everything to go well for you."

"Yes, there is something which I would love you to do."

"What?" They were only too pleased to help someone who could go into a trance on the movie screen, stab herself with a *kris*, and not even be hurt. Besides, they were enjoying the arak and were looking forward to the 50,000 rupiah that she had promised to give them all at the end of the night.

She pointed to the row of sweating Balinese men who were standing shoulder to shoulder across the entrance to stop the crowd from breaking through. "If you could replace these poor little men with a row of policemen it would prevent the crowd from bursting through. If the line breaks everyone will rush in and there'll be a crush and hundreds of people will be pressed to their deaths. Piles of dead bodies! That would be bad, wouldn't it?"

They thought about it for a moment. Not just bad but catastrophic! A disaster of that magnitude would mean that they would all lose their jobs. And then how would they feed their families? No wages and, worse still, no bribes. So they readily agreed to the contessa's request and called up more reinforcements on their two-way radio.

Meanwhile the police outside on the street were diverting the stalled traffic on to another road which, by a circuitous route, by-passed the bottleneck outside the party. When enough police had fought their way through to the entrance they took over from the men from the contessa's cottage. They formed a solid uniformed row to prevent unwanted guests from bursting inside and causing the terrible crush that the contessa had described so vividly. She arranged with the barmen to keep the police supplied with

547

plenty of arak for the rest of the evening and then went inside to mix with her guests.

The thousands who were out on the street realised that they wouldn't be able to penetrate the police picket line so they settled down to have their own party outside. It was a warm, still night and the music could be heard loud and clear. Some started to dance in the street; others were drinking, eating from the food stalls, kissing, singing or just sitting on the roadside absorbing the atmosphere of the biggest party that Bali had ever seen.

Inside it was all flashing lights, loud music, tripping couples and wonderful costumes. The contessa had told everyone that it was a "Romeo and Juliet" party. All the men had to dress as Romeo while the ladies were asked to come as Juliet. Most of them got it right but some of the less knowledgeable confused the word "Romeo" with "Roman" and turned up in sheets and togas and with laurel wreaths on their heads. "But you are fifteen hundred years out of time," she cried when she saw the togas. "You should take them off if you don't want to destroy the theme of my party." Several did — and danced in their shorts and underpants.

The contessa glided from group to group, kissing all the Romeos and nodding graciously at all the complimentary remarks that guests were making about the party. Adrian, who had arrived with Thierry and Nicole, overheard some of the women bitching to each other about the contessa's stunning and wildly cut black satin and lace dress. He even heard one of them say that she hoped the film would be a flop while another added that it would be a good thing if the contessa broke her legs so that they would have to find someone else for the part. It made him angry. He knew from Dayu that the contessa was not well liked by other women. But this was going too far. He swung round and faced them as they were about to embark on another diatribe against their hostess.

"If you don't like her then why do you come to her

party? And I see that you don't mind drinking her liquor either," he said scathingly as he looked down at their half empty glasses. Even in the dim light he noticed that the girls were slightly overweight and not very smartly dressed. They weren't a patch on the contessa in either style or appearance. "Or in generosity of character," he thought.

He went to walk away when one of them, who had had a little too much drink, called out: "And who are you anyway? One of her gigolos?"

He didn't answer for a moment. Then he turned back and said: "The contessa is both beautiful and kind. The gods like her and they look after her. And that is why she was given the movie role. And" — he rubbed it in — "half a million dollars. The contessa gives out good karma and receives the same in return. You should try it some time."

He walked across to where Thierry and Nicole were sitting with drinks in their hands. Suddenly the music stopped and the compere held up the four leather jackets — a pink one and a white one for the girls and two black ones for the men. He called the contessa up on the stage and asked her to pull a number out of a hat. She closed her eyes and spun around so many times that she nearly lost her balance. Then she pulled out a number and looked at it. "*Octo quarto*," she called.

"What? Say it in English," the crowd called back.

"Eighty-four," she cried. Everyone pulled out the numbered tickets that they had been given when they came in the door and looked at them. The winner was one of the four girls whom Adrian had heard criticising the contessa. He shook his head in sadness as the two-faced bitch strutted up to the stage and was asked by the contessa to choose one of the jackets. She selected the pink one and was kissed by the compere as he handed it to her. Adrian watched in disgust as she returned to her friends who began admiring it and trying it on.

Another number was called out and Alban, a cheerful mountain bike rider from Innsbruck, went up and chose one of the black jackets. Everyone cheered as he tried it on and made a few smart gestures — including a long and passionate kiss with the contessa. Then the prize for the most beautiful girl was awarded to a slim, blond girl from England who smiled demurely when she was handed the white jacket. "But she is so beautiful!" exclaimed Thierry. Then the contessa clapped her hands for silence and announced the prize for "the handsomest man". Adrian blushed when she looked across at him. "Come on, Adrian," she called, "I am waiting for you. To see if it fits you."

He walked up on the stage and the contessa kissed him passionately and then made him put the jacket on over his blue and white cotton shirt. He grinned and the contessa called out to everyone: "It is a perfect fit. We have made the right choice."

The music started up again and Adrian walked back to where Thierry and Nicole were sitting. "I have known it since yesterday," said Nicole. "The contessa told me."

"What?" asked Adrian.

"That she was going to give the prize to you. To try and make you happy and take your mind off the accident."

"That doesn't surprise me," he said. "They all say that she is a drama monger — which she is. And a bit of an exhibitionist and a man chaser — which she is. But underneath it all she has a heart of gold and that is more important than anything else. It is from her heart that love springs. And she has got plenty of that. I think she'll make a wonderful Juliet. I just hope that she won't be destroyed by those bitchy gossip columnists."

"Oh, I don't think you need to worry," said Thierry. "The women journalists will write terrible and petty things about her; the men journalists will all praise her and, since there are more men writers, the contessa will come out on top."

"Good logic," laughed Adrian.

He felt himself being grabbed from behind. It was the contessa. "And now I must dance with the most handsome man on the floor."

"Hey, thank you for the leather jacket. It's absolutely super and just what I needed. I had my last one ripped off my back by a couple of knife wielding Maori thugs in Australia and I've been meaning to buy another one but never got round to it."

"Oh, its nothing. But you must think of me every time that you put it on. And you will be able to tell people that it was given to you by a famous film star."

"How do you think you'll go? Do you reckon that you'll be able to remember all the lines?"

"Yes, of course. I've already started. I found an old copy of Shakespeare in that second hand book shop at Kuta. Do you know the one?"

"Yes. I bought a book there myself when I first arrived."

"I found the Complete Works and I've been reading it on the beach between swims. I've read Romeo and Juliet eleven times and some of the others as well — MacBeth, Othello, Hamlet. What a great writer he was!"

"Yes, I know. My father is a Shakespearean scholar. He lectures on the subject."

"Then he'll have to go and see me in the film. And take all his students with him. Will you promise to tell him?"

"Yes, of course."

Suddenly the light stopped flashing for a moment and settled its bright beam on David Isaacs, the one armed Israeli whom Adrian had not seen since Pascal's party.

"Oh, look! There is David," exclaimed the contessa. "I am so glad he could come. I saw him yesterday for the first time in months. He is such a famous novelist, you know."

"Yes, I met him at Pascal's party." Adrian could well

remember how Dayu had recoiled from going near him because she believed that his stunted arm was possessed by an evil spirit.

They went over and started talking to him. He was very serious and polite as he told them how he had been staying for the past two months up at Lovina on the north coast of the island. "I found a very nice *losmen* and I was able to work on my novel day and night. If I was down here there would have been too many distractions. Like to-night. It's not that I don't like going to parties. I enjoy them when I go but I don't go all that often. But," he smiled at the contessa, "I'm really enjoying this one and am so glad that I came back just in time for it."

"But I have to go to a party every night," exclaimed the contessa. "Otherwise I would get very bored."

"I never get bored," he said, "but if I went to a party every night I probably would."

The contessa stared at him in disbelief. "He is nice," she thought, "but I do not understand his thinking."

"What's Lovina like?" asked Adrian.

"Much quieter than here. I stayed just out of Lovina and everything was so cheap. I ate fresh seafood every night and cooled off in the water every day. It was so peaceful and I just tapped away on my typewriter in my own time and now I have completed the first draft."

"What's it about?" asked a curious Adrian.

The writer was deliberately vague. He was always reluctant to talk about his books before they were published. "It's about the complexities of being an Israeli — the rewards and the problems."

"I'm sure it will be a great success," enthused the contessa. "Just like my film. Ooh, it is all so exciting."

The music stopped and the lights came on. Two of her Italian friends, Sergio and Giovanni, climbed up on the stage and announced — amid much shouting and laughter — that they were going to make a presentation of flowers to the contessa as a gesture of thanks for putting on the party. "And for my coming film," she called out as she walked up the steps on to the stage to hug and kiss her two admirers. Three Balinese men were struggling through the crowd with the biggest floral arrangement that any of them had ever seen — hibiscus, frangipani, gardenias, marigolds and many other brightly petalled specimens.

"It is so beautiful!" gasped the contessa. "When I am on the film set I shall think of you all." She started to blow kisses to the crowd.

"The la-di-da bitch thinks that she's already in Hollywood," said the girl who had won the pink leather jacket. Her friends nodded their spiteful agreement.

Suddenly a Balinese man pushed through the crowd and jumped up on the stage. It was Wayan, the head of the family who owned the cottage where the contessa stayed. He had only a limited grasp of English but he had learned his lines well during the last few days. Everyone went quiet as they wondered what he had to say.

"You have brought great pleasure to our village and we do not want to see you go," he said to the contessa. There were tears in his eyes. "We know that you are now very famous and we want to give you something very special to remind you of our island and our culture. It has been specially made for you." He pulled out from under his red cotton shirt a brand new *kris*. It had a straight blade about twelve inches long and a beautiful, carved mother-of-pearl handle. Engraved on the bottom of the shell was the word "Contessa".

The star was most moved by this spontaneous gesture which was so unexpected. She looked closely at the *kris*. It made her think of the dagger scene at the end of the movie.

"I wonder if they'll let me use this for the dagger," she thought.

She flicked it in her hand and tried to remember the lines. She knew that the eyes of at least two hundred people were upon her. She remembered that there was a tube of bright red lipstick in the tiny pocket of her dress. She whispered to the three men who were on the stage and asked them to form a ring around her. As they did so they wondered what on earth she was going to do next. She pulled out the tube of lipstick. Then she bent down and loosened her dress in the front. Wayan looked down and was surprised to see her smearing red lipstick all over her left breast. He had known the contessa all the months that she had been staying in his guest cottage. He knew better than to be surprised at anything she might do. He wasn't even surprised to see her naked breast. He had seen it many times before; at the cottage the contessa never wore anything up top. Just like the Balinese ladies.

The crowd were starting to call out things like "Boring" and "Why are we waiting?" The contessa pulled the dress back up and the men opened their circle and let her through. "Just like a genie," thought Sergio.

She stood on the edge of the stage and asked for the bright lights to be toned down. Then she started in full cry. She became Juliet acting out the dagger scene. She walked up to Giovanni and kissed him. Then she cried:

"Thy lips are warm."

Everyone was enthralled. All eyes were on the stage. No one spoke. Complete silence. Then she raised the *kris* and stared at it.

"O happy dagger,
This is thy sheath. There rust and let me die."

Then she did a mock stabbing and let her dress fall down just enough to display her bright red breast in the half light. Then, after just long enough for everyone to take in what had happened, she fell towards Giovanni's arms. But he wasn't expecting her and she slipped out of his grip and on to the floor. She hit her head as she landed and became concussed. The effect was truly dramatic. The crowd gasped. Some of the girls screamed when they saw all the red on her breast. Everyone who was more than a few feet away from her believed that it was real blood and that she had stabbed herself to death.

"Well, she won't be going to Hollywood now," said the girl with the pink leather jacket. There was a telltale smirk of satisfaction on her plump face.

On the stage Wayan knew that the contessa was only play-acting. But it didn't appear that way to one of the Balinese barmen, Nyoman, who watched the whole scene in horror. He stared fixedly as the powerful spirit inside the contessa caused her to stab herself. Then he felt the power of the same spirit move down and get inside his own body. He fell into a deep trance.

There was a large carving knife on the counter with which he had been cutting slices of meat for the sandwiches. Still in a trance he picked it up, jumped up on the counter and raised the knife in the air just like the contessa had done. Then he plunged it into his chest. The blood spurted out and sprayed over several people who were standing beneath him — including the beautiful English girl who had won the white jacket. She screamed in horror as she saw the white leather splattered with bright red bloodstains. The barman fell down to the floor with a thud. Dead.

By now many of the girls were screaming hysterically. Adrian suddenly remembered the terrible scene that he witnessed in the Monkey Forest when all the Balinese went crazy in a communal trance. He knew how much they believed in the spirits and feared that with all the screaming, the stabbing and the blood anything was likely to happen.

He rushed over to where the other barmen were standing. It was a desperate attempt to prevent them from going into a communal trance and repeating the fatal act *en masse*. On his way he brushed past a group of Americans. "Quick," he said, "help me grab the Balos and push them outside. Otherwise there'll be trouble." They followed him and then physically picked up the small Balinese men and hustled them outside to where the line of police was still standing.

The captain of the police looked concerned when he saw all the big, burly tourists manhandling the local people. He walked over a few paces with an angry glare on his face. Adrian told him what had happened. He called over another policeman and they rushed inside. People were still screaming but there were only Europeans left there. All the Balinese — except for Wayan on the stage — had been pulled outside. The two cops pushed their way through the crowd to the dead man. He was lying face down in a pool of his own blood.

When the contessa came out of her concussion she felt hot, groggy and confused. She could hear screaming and believed that it was the noise of the happy dancers squealing above the music. But she couldn't hear any music. She looked down and saw a large crowd gathered around the bar. She didn't like all the attention being directed down there and away from her. So she slowly closed her eyes and wondered what was going on. The next thing she heard was the sound of boots coming up the steps of the stage. She opened her eyes and saw an Indonesian policeman staring down at her. He looked aggressive. Slowly she stood up and looked around. She then knew that something terrible had happened to her party. But what? Giovanni rushed over in an agitated state and rapidly began to tell her what had happened. His hands were waving round in the air as he pointed to the dead body.

"Oh, how terrible!" she cried and fell down again. This time in a swoon. The policeman caught her as she dropped and they laid her out again on the floor of the stage.

It was all too much for the police captain — the thousands of half drunk people outside blocking the street, the barman who had stabbed himself to death, all these screaming people and now this crazy woman lying on the floor who says she is so famous but who has clearly been the cause of all the trouble. The poor man had had enough. "If something is not done to break up this crowd," he thought, "there will be more deaths and I will get into great trouble for not doing my job properly."

He knew how many police were on duty in the Kuta area for the night. Certainly not enough to clear the thousands from the road outside let alone break up the disorderly scene inside. So he pulled out his two-way radio and called headquarters and told them that the army would have to be called out. The police and army were under the same command. "About ten platoons should be sufficient," he said. "As well as all the police that we have on duty."

The commanding officer of the military camp situated eight miles inland from Kuta was watching a boxing match on television in the officers' mess when the call came through. He was surprised and a little alarmed at having to rouse his men from their sleep and send them off in trucks in the middle of the night. The last time he had to do that was during the coup in 1965 and he shuddered when he thought of the mass killings that followed on from the events of that fateful night. He just hoped that this would not be the same.

"It's always at night," he thought, "when the spirits are strongest. Just like when the volcano exploded. That was also at night. Oh, how I hate being called out to restore order when the demons are at large. Anything is likely to happen!"

He braced himself, swung on his belt and pistol, gave the order to draw sub-machines guns, and went out to the trucks to take charge of his men. They had often trained for this type of scenario with the result that they were all dressed and ready in exactly six minutes. Then the convoy of troop carrying trucks and jeeps rumbled into Kuta as fast as they could.

The villagers who saw them pass had the same fears as the commanding officer. Was it 1965 all over again? The street sellers and late night pedestrians rushed inside and put more offerings on their household shrines. In some villages that they drove through the trucks were seen by wise and alert elders who rushed to their signal towers and beat the *kulkul* drums to summon everyone to the temple. They knew that special prayers must be offered to the spirits to stave off whatever disaster must be brewing as a result of the dash of the army trucks. Whole villages rose out of their beds and ran to the temple to pray. Such were the ramifications of the contessa's party.

En route the commanding officer received orders to proceed to the Kuta-Legian road near the *bemo* stop and disperse the crowd. When the trucks reached their destination they drove right up to the edge of the revellers. As the troops clambered out the commanding officer stood up with a megaphone and told everyone to go home. Immediately. There was a bit of light hearted banter and then the crowd moved off in orderly fashion. The food sellers and *bemo* drivers were ordered away and they went very quickly. They greatly feared the military/police. There were no incidents and after fifteen minutes the traffic was once again flowing normally.

Inside the disco the police turned on all the lights and ordered everyone to leave and go home. After the road was cleared the dead man was taken out, put in a covered van and driven away.

As Adrian and Thierry and Nicole filed out through the doorway they looked back and saw the contessa still lying on the stage. The two Italian men were with her as well as her Balinese landlord and the policemen. "Well, at least she's got Giovanni and Sergio to look after her," said Thierry, "and so there is no need for us to stay. We had better go home like the policeman said. Her party was not really a success, was it?"

"No," replied Adrian, "it was a bloody shambles."

As they walked across the small courtyard to the street they saw the girl with the pink leather jacket leaving with her friends. When she saw Adrian she said in a catty voice, "What about your friend's karma now? She caused the barman's death. Is that good karma?"

Adrian looked away. He felt sorry for her for having such a jealous and nasty nature. "It's like being possessed by an evil spirit," he thought. "Only worse. At some time the spirit leaves you but that bitch will carry her jealousy with her for the rest of her life."

On the stage the men were waiting for the contessa to regain her senses. She was feeling groggy and disoriented with all the alcohol she had drunk, the heat of the night, the cigarette smoke and the screaming. But now all was quiet. She opened her eyes and sat up. When she became accustomed to the bright lights she looked around her. At the emptiness, the cigarette butts and empty beer cans on the floor, the drooping flowers, the palm fronds fallen down from the walls. "Oh, my party!" she cried. "Whatever has happened to my party?"

Giovanni told her more details about the barman and she burst into tears again. The police officer asked her when she was leaving the island. "To-morrow," she sobbed.

He considered arresting her and holding her at the police station until the 'plane left. To stop her causing any more trouble. Or another death. But then he thought about the bad spirit inside her that had already wrought so much havoc and decided that he could not risk letting it loose in the police station. "The spirit might depart from her and stay with us," he thought. "Then all sorts of terrible things will happen."

He asked her where she was staying and Wayan replied that she was renting a cottage in his compound. The police captain wrote down the address and asked Wayan some more questions about her. Finally Wayan promised to take her back to the cottage and not let her leave until the morning when she was due to catch the 'plane. Giovanni gave a further undertaking to remain with her and not let her out of his sight.

"Otherwise we arrest her and put her in prison," said the policeman. "Now you must all go."

The contessa could see the *kris* in his hand. She smiled sweetly and asked if she could have it back. "I need it for my film," she pleaded.

He thought about it and decided that it was too dangerous to give such a deadly weapon to someone who was so possessed. "No, I keep it for to-night," he said. "If you are good girl and stay at your cottage I shall give it to you to-morrow. On the 'plane. Not before. What time does 'plane leave?" She told him "I shall be there," he said. "Now off you go and no more trouble."

When they reached the cottage the contessa fell on her bed and started sobbing uncontrollably. "It is such a disastrous start to my international career," she cried. "If this gets into the newspapers it will be terrible. They will say that I killed the man. But I didn't."

"We know that," said Giovanni. "No one in the West would be so silly as to say a thing like that."

"Well, I hope not," she said, "because I have always tried to do good to people. It is not in my nature to hurt them. And I feel terrible that it was something that I did that caused the boy to lose his life." She began sobbing again.

Then Wayan spoke for the first time. "Do not worry," he said. "You did not cause his death. It was the spirits. I know him and he was a very bad boy. Always stealing things. And he did not respect his elders. It is a good thing that he died as he can now be reincarnated into another life. If he had kept living he would have got worse. It was time for him to go and start another life."

This explanation cast a whole new light on the affair. The contessa began to feel better about things. But not about the party. In her mind parties were everything. And this one was to launch her on the path to fame and success. She started crying again. This time she cried herself to sleep.

The next morning they found that they didn't have to hire a *bemo* for the trip to the airport. A police van arrived at nine o'clock and three uniformed men jumped out and marched on to the contessa's verandah.

"What is it now?" she cried as she looked up from packing her designer dresses into suitcases. The whole place was a shambles with clothes scattered everywhere. There were too many to fit into the cases.

"We come to drive you to airport," said the police captain. "To make sure no more trouble. When you leave?"

"I'll be ready in ten minutes," she said.

"Okay. We wait in police van. Hurry up." They went out and lounged round the van and smoked their *kretek* cigarettes.

Giovanni helped her with the last of the packing. After the three Louis Vuitton suitcases were closed there were still several dresses left over. "What are you going to do with these?" he asked.

"Oh, I don't know. I don't really need them any longer as I shall buy a whole lot more with my money when I get to Paris." At that moment Wayan walked in to say good-bye. She pointed over to the bed. There were half a dozen dresses lying there — three Diors, a couple of Yves Saint Laurent and one of embroidered Thai silk. "Would your daughter like these dresses?" she asked Wayan.

"*Terima kasih*," replied the grateful Balinese. "And I wish you much happiness in the film. I am sure that you will be very good. And all the village will go to Denpasar to see you on the screen."

"Thank you," she said. "And I have been very happy

here and I thank you for all your kindnesses. We must get going now."

Giovanni was putting the last of the suitcases into the van. He climbed in the back with the contessa. The driver turned on the ignition and they sped off to the airport. One of the policemen was holding a couple of machine guns. "What are they for?" asked the contessa.

"In case there is any more trouble," was the sour reply of the police captain. She didn't say another word.

They passed through the airport gates and the contessa saw the terminal whizz past out the back window. "There's the terminal," she cried. "You must let us out."

"We go straight to 'plane," said the captain.

"But why? Some of my friends" — she nearly said "fans" — "might have come to see me off. I want to say good-bye to them." But no amount of pleading or acting could persuade the captain to change his course. He had strict instructions from his superiors to take her straight to the 'plane. They pulled up alongside the steps that led up to the Garuda DC10 which was to take her on the short hop to Jakarta. From there she was to take the UTA flight to Paris. Her cases were loaded on to a trolley and driven away to the luggage hold. She kissed Giovanni good-bye and then turned to the captain and asked in a soft and trembling voice: "Did you bring my *kris*?"

He pulled it out from under the dashboard of the van and handed it to her. "Thank you," she said in almost a whisper and then turned to mount the steps. When she reached the top a cabin steward appeared.

"Good morning, madam," he smiled. Then he saw the *kris* in her left hand. "I am sorry but you'll have to hand the *kris* to me. It is classified as a weapon and passengers are not allowed to carry weapons on the 'plane. We shall return it to you when we land in Jakarta."

She looked at the *kris*. Then she began to count the

number of minutes that she had had it in her possession since it was presented to her the previous evening. Maybe five minutes before it was taken by the policeman on the stage. Then perhaps another minute to-day. Just the time that it took her to climb the steps of the aircraft. Then she thought of the trouble it had caused — one death, the destruction of the party and all the sobbing and heartache that followed. She concluded that it must be possessed by a terrible and powerful spirit. "Maybe it's a *leyak*," she thought, "in the shape of a *kris*!"

She looked up at the polite young cabin steward. "Here," she said. "You take it. You keep it. I don't want it back."

"No, no. We return it to you in Jakarta."

"No," she said slowly and emphatically. "I never want to see it again. You take it and keep it. Understand?"

"Yes, ma'am," said the surprised and confused cabin steward.

The contessa walked to her seat and sat down. She could smell the perfumed insect repellant that had recently been sprayed around the cabin. She pressed the button on the side of her seat. It sprang down and she leaned back. Now that she had got rid of the accursed *kris* she felt that all her troubles had ended. Soon the 'plane started up and the contessa flew off to a life of fame, glamour and excitement.

Back at the cottage Wayan was staring at the dresses that lay on the bed. Some were black, two were green and one peacock blue. Alone among the Balinese he had not believed that the contessa was possessed of a bad spirit when she did the dagger scene. He had seen her smearing on the lipstick. Wayan believed that what followed with the barman had been pre-determined by the gods. In fact he believed that the contessa was possessed by a good spirit. What else could explain the bountiful gift of beautiful dresses for his daughter? It was really a gift from the gods. They had got inside her and, although it was the contessa's hands which gave them, the dresses were really from the spirits. He was happy to think that the gods were so pleased with him and his family as to give them such a fine gift.

He went outside, put on his sandals and ran along the dusty track to the *warung* where his sixteen year old daughter worked in the kitchen preparing rice dishes. He took her home and showed her the dresses. She was delighted and tried them on. She had never worn a dress before. Only sarongs. She liked the blue one best. The one with all the glitter. It was a Dior. She tried it on again. It was a bit too full for her waif like figure and, instead of being knee length, it fell almost to the ground. She liked it and wore it back to the *warung* where she resumed boiling the rice in the steamy kitchen. Wayan watched her run along the dusty track. "Maybe the dress will bring good luck to her," he thought, "just like it did to the contessa. Maybe my girl will also get job in a film. And half a million dollars." He smiled at the thought of it.

Chapter Seventeen

The End

On the morning of the contessa's departure, Adrian went down to the beach to check the waves. "Yes," he thought, "the best spot would be the channel about two hundred yards along. Those nice, peeling tubes are just waiting to be ridden."

As he walked back to his cottage he could hear the strong voice of Demi Roussos coming from the stereo at Chez Thierry et Nicole. He looked in to ask Thierry if he wanted to join him for a surf. When he stepped through the gap in the wall which totally enclosed their garden he could see that they were otherwise engaged. He turned to go away. "*Non, non*, come on up here," called Nicole from the verandah as she went to wrap a sarong around her richly tanned body.

"Thierry is so lucky," he thought. "Gosh, how I miss Dayu!" When he stepped on the verandah Nicole touched him on the cheek and said, "I can see that you are a little sad. But come. To-day is going to be very special. I can feel it in the air. Look at the sky. So clear. We shall all have a lovely day on the beach."

"You know, in another five minutes I was going to come and see if you were awake to go for some waves," Thierry said to Adrian. "But you must have known so you came here first."

"And what am I to do?" asked Nicole. "Sit and watch the action like Madame Defarge and do my knitting?"

"Yes, just sit on the beach and wait for us and then smile and look pretty when we come out," said Thierry teasingly. "You are like the icing on the cake. A great session out there and some magic rides. Then to be rubbed down by the spunkiest girl on the beach. Just to make the man happy!" He winked at Adrian.

Thierry rubbed some wax on his board and the three of them walked down the narrow track towards the sea. It was still early and there were more dogs on the beach than people.

"I am so happy this morning; I don't know why," laughed Thierry as they were paddling out. Adrian started stroking windmill style — both hands ploughing through the water at the same time. Thierry did the same and they started laughing.

Adrian got some clean rides and Thierry, after wiping out a couple of times, managed a perfect take-off and saw the lip of the wave throw itself over his head. The next thing he found himself inside a hollow tunnel of water. He could hardly believe what was happening. With his board being driven by the power of the water he felt like a god. He put out his fingers and let them pierce the vertical wall of water. It was like gliding through the tunnel of the Metro in Paris. Only much nicer. The magic moment seemed to last an eternity as all his senses were so finely tuned to this new sensation. Then the swirling water closed in on him and he was thrown off his board. He came up to the surface and looked round for Adrian. He could see him lying on his twin-fin a long way out. Adrian waved and raised his fingers in the V for Victory sign. He knew that it was Thierry's first tube and he thought back to when, as a thirteen year old at Torquay, he had had his own first tube ride. "Like most things in life the first one is always the best," he thought.

Thierry paddled out through the white foamy water to where Adrian was lying in wait for the next set.

"Did you see my tube? I thought that I was in heaven. Now I know what surfing really means. I don't think that I will ever be the same again. I must go in and describe it to Nicole. No, I shall try and do it again." The excited words all came out at once. Adrian smiled to himself. He was truly happy to welcome his friend to the select fraternity of tube riders. He looked around him at the sparkling blue sea of the balmy morning. "Well, you couldn't have had your first tube in a more perfect setting," he said. "It's Bali at its best."

"I know. I know. I am so lucky. God is good to me to-day. Nicole felt so nice this morning and now this wonderful new experience inside the wave."

Another set was coming in. Thierry paddled like mad to take the first wave but it left him behind and he just rose and fell with the swell of the water. On the next set he was luckier. He managed to get inside a beautiful barrel of water. And then another.

When they eventually returned to the beach — drained, exhausted and euphoric — Thierry threw his dripping body on to Nicole and told her of his mighty feat.

"Now you'll have to throw the celebration party that you've been promising us all these months," laughed Adrian as they walked back to the cottage.

"Yes, I just wish that Danny was still here. I must write and tell him what I have done. I shall go out and buy some arak and, Nicole, can you prepare some food and we'll have a party here about nine o'clock to-night and then later we can all go off and dance at the Frog. It is just a shame that so many of our friends have already left but I shall invite the Brazilians and also the English surfers who always go to Uluwatu. And, of course, Scott and Andy."

"Yes, they're a good crew," said Adrian.

"Now that you have lost yourself inside a Bali barrel, *mon chéri*, can we now book our ticket back to France?" asked Nicole.

"Yes, I shall go to the Garuda office at Kuta on my way to see the Brazilians."

"I shall stay here; it is too hot to go rushing around," said Nicole as she plucked a red hibiscus from the tree and put it in her hair.

After Thierry had gone Nicole said that she wondered if it would be as difficult to make the airline bookings as it usually was to make an international telephone call.

"Yes," replied Adrian, "Bali's not exactly a high tech place, thank God. I'd rather put up with a few inconveniences and leave it the way it is."

"*Moi·aussi*," she replied. "It is its very difference that makes it so charming."

They both looked up when Madé, one of the daughters of the household, glided graciously along the path towards them.

"*Selamat sore*," they said.

"*Selamat sore*," she replied. "Must come. Must come. Uncle say."

"I wonder what it's all about," said Adrian as they walked behind the girl towards the uncle's house. "After all, he didn't even say anything when Dayu got lost."

"It must be very important," said Nicole. "Has he ever called you over before?"

"No. He's never said more than 'hello' to me since I've been here."

"Sit," said the uncle when they stepped on to his verandah. He dismissed the other Balinese and stared for a long time at Nicole. He hadn't intended her to come; just Adrian. However, he realised that it would be good for her to hear what he had to say so that she could provide a woman's perspective on the proposal. "Women dance too," he thought. "And it seems that they have more influence over their men than Balinese women do. And I have even been told that many men in the West do what their women tell them. Ugh! What a terrible place the West must be! I'm glad I live in Bali ... with my jim." He looked across at Adrian. "Business," he said without smiling. "You like going to disco?"

"Yes, I've been most nights since I've been here. Most people go."

"Which disco you go?"

"Usually the Jolly Frog."

"Why that one so good?"

"They play really good music, all our friends go there, the setting by the sea is quite unique and the atmosphere is good. It's always alive."

"And the music is good for dancing," said Nicole. "I think that we girls like dancing better than the men. Sometimes the guys just sit round and drink and talk about the surf."

"Ah," thought the uncle, "it is good that she speaks her mind. And she is not as stupid as I thought." He pulled out a notebook and wrote in Indonesian that Western women like dancing more than their boyfriends. He looked up to resume the conversation. But then he started writing again. That Western boys like to drink and talk about surfing.

"Must disco be right next to beach?" he asked.

Adrian thought for a moment. "Not necessarily but it's probably better. It means that there's plenty of space to park the motor bikes on the sand. And, of course, for surfers it is always reassuring to hear the crashing of the waves even if you can't see them in the dark. At least you know that you can look forward to some good rides in the morning."

"Are most people who go to the disco surfers?" asked the uncle.

"The guys are. But not the girls — of course not," replied Adrian.

"Which beer you like to drink at disco?"

"Well, there's only Bintang and San Mig. I always drink

Bintang."

"If there were other beers would people buy them?" He pulled out a typewritten list and handed it to Adrian. There were about a dozen brands listed: Fosters, Swan Lager, XXXX, Tooheys, Tiger, Carlsberg, Tuborg, Bass, Budweiser and Becks.

"Hmmm," said Adrian. "But you can't get these beers here. I've never seen them."

"No, not yet. But I have a very good business friend who is a four star general in Jakarta and he says that Bali will soon be one of the biggest international tourist places in the world."

"Ooh, I hope not," said Nicole.

"Can't you do something to stop it?" pleaded Adrian.

The uncle stared at him in amazement. "Why would I want to stop it? All these tourists will bring big money to Bali. That is why I am talking to you. The general and I are going to build a new disco down by the beach. We have just bought the field from the three grandmothers who own most of the land around Legian."

He pulled out some rough architectural drawings of a big oblong building with a high thatched roof. The side facing the sea was open and there was a long bar that ran along the back wall.

"Why not have several small bars?" suggested Adrian. "That way you will avoid a big crowd congregating around the drinking area. Each bar could have a particular theme. The Surfers' Bar. The Ladies' Bar. The Bintang Bar. If you named a bar after a brand of beer then the brewery might come to the party."

"What do you mean — 'come to the party'?"

"They might pay for the cost of building the particular bar that bears their name." The uncle was writing furiously.

"And you should have a pizza parlour as well," said Nicole. "People get hungry late at night. At 3 a.m. when the

Jolly Frog closes all the people get on their motor bikes and drive to the Hamburger House for something to eat. They are hungry. But if you had a small kitchen and a counter you could sell pizzas during the evening. All you need is a few tables for the diners." The uncle kept writing.

"And you need lots of flashing lights," said Adrian. "They help to loosen people up and then they enjoy themselves more."

"And it is always so hot dancing," said Nicole. "Sometimes I feel like walking straight off the dance floor and into a swimming pool. If you could have a small pool then all the dancers could cool off in it and then go back on the floor."

"Why not a small bar by the side of the pool?" added Adrian. "Then we could have a drink while cooling off in the water."

"But what if people break their glasses in the pool?" asked the uncle. "It would not be good for business to have glass floating around and people with bleeding feet."

"Plastic tumblers," replied Adrian.

The uncle picked up the list of beers and again showed it to Adrian. "Which of these beers would be the best to sell here? My friend, the four star general, will be able to help me get a licence to import them to Bali. But I only want to start with four brands. Which four should I choose?"

Adrian studied the list. "Well, I guess that a fair mix would be two Australian beers and one each from Europe and America. I would suggest Fosters and Swan and Carlsberg and Budweiser."

"You think they are the best?"

"Yes, I do."

"That is good because it is better to have much Australian beer."

"Why?"

"Because my friend, the general, he say that Australian government not like their people to come here and spend money on ganja and get stoned because they get no tax. But they would be very happy for their young people to come here and get drunk on Australian beer because Australian government get good tax on every can of Australian beer that is sold."

"That's true," said Adrian. "Money seems to be the bottom line of everything."

"Yes, I know," said the uncle.

They sat on the verandah for more than an hour and spoke exclusively about the proposed disco. Adrian applied his artistic talents to redraw the entire setting. It incorporated all the suggestions that he and Nicole had made and the uncle was delighted with the result. "They have paid their rent a thousand times over," he smiled to himself.

He then tapped their knowledge on another money-making matter that he was considering. "If Bali is to be first class international holiday place we must stop the drownings," he said. "Too many people drown here. Especially at Kuta. People won't come here if they believe that the sea will swallow them."

"True," said Adrian, "but most of them don't know how to handle the waves. That's all it is. You don't get surfers drowning."

"When Nyoman was in Australia he saw surf life-savers. You know surf life-savers?"

"Yes, I suppose they save a few lives," said Adrian churlishly, deliberately concealing the fact that not a single life had ever been lost on an Australian beach while it was patrolled by life-savers. "But life-savers are more trouble than they're worth. They think they own the beach just because they stick a few flags in the sand. You must remember that if you had life-savers then not so many surfers would come to Bali."

"Why?" asked the uncle in amazement.

"Because at the moment surfers can come here and surf

anywhere they like. That's why so many of us come. But if there were life-saving patrols they would stick up flags and say that you can't surf here and you can't surf there and surfers would soon get sick of it and go somewhere else. You're better off to have the drownings."

The uncle thought about it for a moment. It was a complication that he hadn't considered. "No," he said, "I think it would be better to have less drownings. Even if fewer surfers come to Bali there would be more tourists overall if they know they won't drown."

"But they won't come if there are fights on the beach," said Adrian.

"What do you mean?"

"Well, if the clubbies — that is the life-savers — get too bossy the surfers will punch them up. And hit them with their surfboards."

"Hell," thought the uncle, "this young man thinks of everything. Why hadn't I thought of that?"

"And who will pay for the beaches to be patrolled?" asked Adrian.

"My friend, the general, and me."

"That is very kind of you but how will you get your money back?"

"When life-saver saves man from dying the man will be so pleased that he will give us much money. Make us very rich. After all, we would have saved his life."

"Unfortunately it doesn't work that way," said Adrian. He was at last telling the truth. "In Australia when the clubbies pull people out of the water and save their lives many of them barely say 'thank-you'. And not many even send a donation to the surf life-saving club. It's sad but true."

"What funny people," thought the uncle. He now knew that he would be foolish to have anything to do with the life-saving business. Better to let them drown than to have all those sorts of problems! He decided that discos would be a far better way to cash in on the expected tourist boom.

On their way back across the lawn Nicole turned to Adrian. "Well, what do you think of it all? Good or bad?" she asked.

"I don't really know. I have mixed feelings. But I felt it was our duty to help him as much as we could because it's the only thing he's asked me for all the time I've been here."

"Yes, I agree," she said, "but didn't you exaggerate a little about the life-savers?"

"Perhaps. But not much."

"Well," she said, "I just hope that, if we come back in a few years' time, the place will still be much the same as it is now. Let us hope that it doesn't get like some tourist places — just a big concentration of development and sleaze. Yuk! That would kill all its romance and charm. I would not like to see Bali ruined in that way."

"Nor would I," said Adrian. "I guess they have to have some development but surely they won't allow it to wreck the place."

"*Mon Dieu*! I hope not," she replied.

"I feel so strongly about it," said Adrian, "that I'm going to do something to stop it."

"You can't!" said Nicole with a shrug.

"Can't I? You just watch."

He went out to the kitchen hut and picked up the sharpest knife from the bench. He walked back outside and chopped a frond off a young coconut palm. Then he sat down on the grass and started to cut the leaves into strips. He wound them into a small basket and cut off the ends. "Have we got any rice?" he asked Nicole. She found a small bag of it behind the door of the kitchen. Then he walked across to the other side of the lawn and picked a bright pink hibiscus. He plucked off its petals and arranged them artistically in the basket. Then he went and fetched a stick of incense.

Nicole was smiling to herself. "You have done it so well.

574

Just like a Balinese!"

"Hell, I watched Dayu do it often enough," he laughed.

When all was ready he lit the incense and Nicole walked with him to the shrine at the back of the cottage. There were two other offerings that had been placed there by members of the uncle's family.

"To which god are we making the offering?" asked Nicole.

"I don't know. We'll offer it to all the gods and ask them to use their spiritual powers to fight off the demon of ugly development. If that one ever gets loose in Bali it will be the nastiest and most dangerous demon of them all."

■

Thierry returned laden with bottles of arak and cans of Bintang and they set about preparing for the party. Adrian and Thierry carried several slabs of ice from the nearby *warung* and lay them in a large tub. They carefully placed the bottles between the slabs and set up a bar on the verandah while Nicole was busy in the kitchen preparing some snacks. Thierry opened a bottle of arak and poured it into three glasses. Then he rummaged through the box of cassette tapes to choose a selection for the evening. "It is so important to play the right music. It can make or break a party. Since the party is to celebrate my tube ride I want to have some happy music." He poured Adrian another arak.

All was ready by 8.30 so Adrian walked across to his own cottage, had a shower and donned a pair of white cotton trousers and a red and green shirt. Then he dabbed his face with after-shave, combed his hair and went to walk out the door. As he stepped on to the verandah he saw something move in front of the trees. In the dim light of the kerosene lamp he could see a figure. In a long white dress. "Must be someone for the party," he thought. Then he saw the long black hair. And then the face. At first he couldn't believe it and thought that it must be the effect of the arak. But when he saw the long lines of the white cheong-sam and the familiar shape inside it he knew that he was not hallucinating. "Dayu!" he screamed.

She hesitated at first, then smiled and ran into his wildly outstretched arms. They spun around, kissing madly, laughing and crying.

"*Mon Dieu!*" screamed Thierry when he came to see what all the commotion was about. "Now we can have a real celebration party."

"I knew," said Nicole when she too kissed Dayu, "that to-day was going to be something special. I could feel it in the air and I remarked on it to Adrian."

Adrian ran his fingers down the long, slender lines of the cheong-sam. It was the first time that she had worn one since the night he first met her at Semang. "That's a different cheong-sam, isn't it?" he asked.

"Yes, I bought it in the silk store in Singapore," she replied.

"Singapore!"

"Yes, I have just arrived from there on the 'plane. It landed an hour ago. Didn't you hear it fly over the cottage?"

"No, we were listening to tapes."

"Well, I caught a *bemo* from the airport and it got a flat tyre by the Jalan Padma so I walked from there. It is so good to be back in Bali."

"But … Come on, sit down and have some arak and tell us what happened. We've got about half an hour before the guests arrive for a party. To celebrate Thierry's first tube which he rode this morning. Now it seems we'll be celebrating something different."

Dayu told them all about the journey to the Maldives on the Thai boat, carefully avoiding the worst parts. "And then, after they moved me to the Arab boat, we sailed off in the morning and I was very frightened as I was sure they were taking me to some bad place. About the middle of the afternoon I heard a loud helicopter over the boat and the men started to run round in a great panic. Two of them came down and locked me in a cupboard and stuffed a salty rag in my mouth so that I couldn't call out. Then about half an hour later there was a great commotion and I heard a gun go off and then men with heavy boots began to walk noisily over the deck. Two English sailors in dark blue trousers and light blue shirts forced open the door of the cupboard and they took me up on the deck and asked me many questions about why I was there. I could see a big grey warship next to the Arab boat and there was a big flag flying from its high mast. I recognised it as the same flag as the one that hangs in the temple at Semang and which has acquired magical powers."

"The White Ensign," exclaimed Adrian. "It does not surprise me. The Royal Navy has always had the power to board vessels involved in the slave trade and there is no flag more feared by the cut-throats of the ocean than the White Ensign blowing from the mast of a British warship."

Dayu explained how they took her on board the frigate, H.M.S. Royalist, and gave her a clean cabin and plenty to eat and drink. "The Arabs were locked up in the cells at the bottom of the ship," she laughed.

"Good," said Adrian. "The best place for them. And how did you get to Singapore?"

"I stayed on the frigate for eight days and then we arrived at Singapore. They contacted the Indonesian ambassador and he came down to the ship and collected me. I stayed with him for two nights and he gave me money and I went shopping with his daughter. That is where I bought the cheong-sam. Then he put me on the 'plane this afternoon and I came back to Bali."

"Bali," thought Adrian. "It's such a powerful and mind-bending experience. The eternal theme of the mountains and the valleys. You can't climb one and appreciate it without having been down in the other. The crest and trough of the wave. *Kaja* and *kelod*. And I have had an overdose of both. It is all part of the unknowable workings of karma. Just as Matt said when I first came here. And he knew the East better than anyone else. But to-night I'm on the crest of the wave. As high as Mount Agung."

"Are we at the right place for Thierry's party?" called a voice from the far end of the dark path. It was a group of Cornish surfers and their girl-friends.

"Yes," called the excited Frenchman. "We are celebrating."

"What are we celebrating?" they asked.

"Oh, one or two things," replied Adrian as he held Dayu tightly in his arms.